*The*

# LEGEND

*of*

# FIRE

# MOUNTAIN

# *The*
# LEGEND
## *of*
# FIRE
# MOUNTAIN

## TRANSLATED BY KATE NORTHROP

Author of *The Fire Blossom* and *Fires of Change*

# SARAH LARK

Text copyright © 2015 by Sarah Lark
Translation copyright © 2021 by Kate Northrop
All rights reserved.

Previously published as *Die Legende des Feuerberges* by Luebbe in Germany in 2015. Translated from German by Kate Northrop. First published in English by Amazon Crossing in 2021.

Published by Amazon Crossing, Seattle

www.apub.com

Amazon, the Amazon logo, and Amazon Crossing are trademarks of Amazon.com, Inc., or its affiliates.

ISBN-13: 9781542092418
ISBN-10: 1542092418

Cover design by Faceout Studio, Amanda Hudson

Printed in the United States of America

*The*

# LEGEND

*of*

# FIRE
# MOUNTAIN

# *Part 1*

## THE STRING OF THE KITE

OTAKI, WAIRARAPA, GREYTOWN (NORTH ISLAND)

CHRISTCHURCH, CANTERBURY PLAINS, DUNEDIN
(SOUTH ISLAND)

AUGUST 1880–APRIL 1881

# Chapter 1

"I'm a little scared," Matiu admitted.

The tall Maori boy wore a new brown suit that was still too loose for his wiry frame. His dark curls had been cut short and were combed back stringently. Linda Lange, his foster mother, assumed that he had used pomade to tame them. Natural curls were rare among the Maori, and she believed that Matiu had inherited them from his English father.

"It doesn't make sense to be scared, Matiu, you're going to meet your family," Linda's daughter Aroha said impatiently.

The two of them were quite close, and Linda suspected that they were in love. Matiu had surely told the girl about his fears, while he'd only let Linda and her husband, Franz, see his joy about meeting his family of origin.

"That's true, but I don't even know them, and I can't speak Maori properly."

Matiu shifted nervously from one foot to the other while he kept a lookout for the train. Linda, too, was anxious for its arrival. It was drafty and cold on the station platform in the little town of Otaki. She wanted to get back home as soon as possible to the old *marae* where she and Franz lived with over a hundred Maori children. The Langes had run the home for Maori war orphans together for about fourteen years, during which time it had been transformed into a boarding school. Franz and Linda's first charges were now grown up and had either returned to their tribes or found work on farms in the area or businesses in Wellington. Linda was happy that she'd be able to see a few of them later. She had shopping to do on her way back, and three former students worked in shops in Otaki. But first, she had to reassure Matiu.

"Your Maori is excellent," she told him. "Besides, your tribe would have all the patience in the world for you even if it wasn't. You read their letters. They're thrilled that you contacted them. They remember your mother well. You have close relatives in the *iwi*, and you know they think of the tribe as one big family anyway. You won't be able to get away from all the mothers, grandmothers, brothers, and grandfathers." Linda smiled encouragingly.

Matiu was unusual among the Langes' charges in that he hadn't spent the first years of his life in a Maori village. He had come from Patea, a town in the Taranaki area, as a three-year-old. A captain of the military settlers whom Linda had known from her own time in Patea had brought the child to them, and had told a tragic story.

"One of our settlers slept with a Maori woman from one of the conquered villages, and she brought the boy into the world. The couple lived together for a while," he said. "We couldn't tell if she was with him of her own free will, or if she'd been kidnapped. She didn't speak a word of English. Then the woman died, perhaps from a fever, or maybe from a broken heart. For a while, the man kept the child. He soon found a white wife in Patea who took care of him. But when she got pregnant herself, she didn't want the boy anymore." Captain Langdon had seemed self-conscious, almost as though he were ashamed of his pity for the little one. "So I thought I'd bring him to you."

Of course Linda and Franz had accepted the child, and Linda had taken the opportunity to ask Captain Langdon for news about the settlement where she'd lived with her first husband before Aroha's birth. He reported that the area was at peace again. The settlers who'd received the land as compensation for their military service in the Taranaki Wars were farming it, and there had been no further violence.

At the orphanage, Matiu hadn't been raised as a *pakeha*, as the Maori called the white settlers. The children there did learn to speak English, but they also spoke Maori. Both Matiu and Aroha spoke the language fluently. Omaka Te Pura, the Maori priestess who had spent the last years of her life helping the children of the orphanage, had identified which tribe the boy's mother had belonged to. The woven blankets she'd left behind, which Captain Langdon had wrapped the child in, were typical of the Ngati Kahungunu.

In the aftermath of the Taranaki Wars, there hadn't been much news of the tribe. They had been driven away like many others on the North Island. But just a few weeks earlier, Franz had heard that the Ngati Kahungunu had resettled on their traditional land in Wairarapa, and encouraged Matiu to contact them.

The boy was not at ease with his mixed origins, and the fully Maori children had teased him often. So Matiu wrote a letter to the chieftain, which took him days to complete. With Aroha's help, he had labored over the tiniest details. Soon, he received an unexpectedly warm reply. Matiu learned the name of his mother, Mahuika, and found out how terribly the young woman had been missed by her family. She had in fact been kidnapped by the Englishman, together with several other young men and women. The Ngati Kahungunu hadn't ever heard from them again. The tribe had enthusiastically invited Matiu to visit, and today the young man would finally meet his family. There was no reason for him to worry, Aroha thought.

"You can speak Maori!" she said. "Besides, I'll be there to help if you get nervous. We're going to have such an adventure! I've never been in a real *marae* before. Except at Rata Station, but that doesn't really count."

Aroha had nagged her mother and stepfather to let her accompany her friend on the journey. Franz, in particular, was unhappy about it. After all, the girl was only fourteen years old—young to travel alone, especially with a young man whom she was very obviously attracted to! Young people in Maori communities often had their first sexual experiences very early, which scared Franz Lange, who had been raised as a very strict German Lutheran and had been a reverend of the Anglican Church for almost twenty years. But Linda had assured him that both Aroha and Matiu were responsible young people who'd been raised with *pakeha* values. They wouldn't be transformed by a few nights in the communal sleeping house of the Ngati Kahungunu.

In the end, it had been Aroha's academic achievements that won her the argument. Despite being two years younger, the girl had insisted on going to Wellington with Matiu to take the college matriculation exams. They had both passed the tests with flying colors. Aroha argued that she deserved a reward for that, and Linda was finally able to talk her husband into allowing the "children" to travel together.

"Why doesn't the *marae* by Rata Station count?" Linda asked.

Rata Station was a sheep farm on the South Island that belonged to Linda's family. She had grown up there with her sisters, Carol and Mara. They'd had a good relationship with their Maori neighbors, who belonged to the Ngai Tahu.

Before Aroha could answer, an earsplitting whistle sounded. Linda embraced Matiu and her daughter one more time as the train roared toward the platform.

"Up to now, you've been my family," Matiu said softly as Linda hugged him.

Linda smiled at him. "And we always will be! Even if you decide to stay there—"

"What?" Aroha said, shaking her head. "It's just a visit, Mama, nothing more. He—he wants to go to college—"

Matiu didn't reply. His gaze hung on Linda. "So you don't think it's ungrateful? You don't mind that I want to visit my people?"

Linda shook her head fervently. "There is nothing ungrateful about finding your roots, Matiu. And you will always be welcome here." She smiled. "But the next time we see one another, I want to hear your *pepeha*!"

Her last words finally brought a smile to Matiu's face. The *pepeha* was a speech of introduction used by Maori that described their origins and their ancestors. Matiu had never been able to offer his; he hadn't known it. That was about to change.

After following Aroha into a compartment, he waved to Linda from the window, his face shining with courage and relief. Aroha could hardly wait until the train to Greytown began its journey. She loved to travel. So far, she hadn't seen much of the North Island where she'd been born. But she'd visited the South Island twice to get to know her relatives at Rata Station.

"Now be honest," she told Matiu as the train left the platform. "Are you really thinking about staying with your tribe?"

At first, there wasn't much new to see through the large windows as the train glided through the fields and meadows around Otaki. Aroha and Matiu knew every stone, every tree.

Matiu reached for his girlfriend's hand. He still couldn't believe that Reverend Lange was allowing them to travel together. For him, any time he could spend with Aroha, especially alone, was a gift. Originally, the two had been raised like siblings. Linda hadn't wanted to send the abandoned three-year-old to sleep with the other orphans, but instead had let him live in the cabin she shared with her husband and daughter. Aroha had only been one at the time. For two years, she had shared a room and often a bed with Matiu. The serene, contented Aroha had calmed the little boy, who'd been plagued by fears and nightmares.

When Matiu was five, Omaka sensed that the other Maori orphans were beginning to shut him out, so she'd moved him into her own cabin and taught him the language and legends of his people. When the priestess died, Matiu moved into one of the boys' sleeping houses. Over the years, Aroha had remained his best friend and playmate. But when they'd reached adolescence, that relationship had grown deeper.

"I would never leave you," he said seriously. "Not for all the tribes, families, uncles, aunts, fathers, and mothers in the world."

"What about the sisters?" Aroha countered mischievously. "There are surely pretty girls among the Ngati Kahungunu. And, um, Revi Fransi says they aren't shy."

"Revi Fransi" was the Maori children's nickname for Reverend Franz Lange. Aroha also used this name for her mother's second husband.

Matiu watched, both amused and charmed, as she blushed at her own bold words. To see the blush, one had to look closely, for despite her light eyes and blonde hair, Aroha had darker skin than most *pakeha* girls. Visitors often assumed she was a mixed child, like Matiu. When Aroha was little, she had once asked her mother if that were true. After all, she even had a Maori name. But Linda had assured her that she had gotten her coloring from her biological father, Joe Fitzpatrick. His eyes, too, had been the color of glacier water, in contrast to his unusually dark skin. The blonde hair came from Linda's own family. And Omaka had given her her name. It meant "love."

"Aroha, I'm yours!" Matiu said earnestly. "No girl in the world is as beautiful as you are. I could never love another."

Aroha's feminine curves still needed time to develop, and her slender face seemed almost childish. But for him, she had already blossomed into a perfect beauty. For him, she was warmth, tenderness, and comfort. Omaka couldn't have given her a more fitting name.

Aroha smiled happily. After all, she really wasn't worried about losing Matiu. He too was a permanent part of her world, and it was unthinkable that he'd reject her. At the moment, at least, the view from the train window occupied her more than Matiu's declaration of love. The train had left the Otaki area and was now headed toward the Rimutaka Range, a mountain range between Hutt Valley near Wellington and the Wairarapa Plains.

"Look at those peaks!" Aroha exclaimed.

So far they had been crossing through light woodlands consisting of manuka and rimu trees, nikau palms and tree ferns. Now the tracks led over bridges under which wild rivers flowed. Soon they passed through one tunnel after another. The Rimutaka Incline was a wonder of railway construction. Legions of industrious workers, among them some of the military settlers, had made the clever dreams of daring engineers come true, rendering the landscape accessible. The tracks led along the edges of abysses and through tunnels, where Aroha reached for Matiu's hand, shocked by the sudden darkness. But the inclines were even more exciting.

"How can the train possibly get up there?" she asked. There were hardly any large trees anymore, just low ferns, rata thickets, and storm-twisted groves of low beeches. The mountains rose up before them like an unsurmountable blockade.

"The locomotives are very strong. And there's also a new kind of track. A special middle track that allows stronger drive and safe braking," Matiu said, lecturing.

"Still, it's unbelievable," Aroha said, and peered fearfully into an abyss. The hillside had been cleared of trees for the construction of the tracks, which seemed to be clinging to the mountainside. "Whoever built this certainly couldn't have been afraid of heights. I get dizzy even if I look down!"

"More than one person lost their lives here," the ticket collector said seriously as he entered their compartment. "There were terrible accidents while it was being built, and they still have to be very careful. The rain often washes stones and debris onto the tracks or floods the tunnels. You're lucky with the weather. In winter, we sometimes have to stop service for days on end. It's also very expensive to maintain this line, thus the high ticket prices." He smiled and raised his ticket punch.

Aroha and Matiu returned his smile tensely. They hadn't imagined that a trip by train could actually be dangerous.


"Hold me tight," Aroha said as the train rounded a hairpin curve.

Matiu put his arm around her, a little shyly. So far, he'd never dared such a thing.

"Nothing will happen to you," he said gently. "Not as long as I'm here."

# Chapter 2

Growing up at the orphanage, Aroha and Matiu had always imagined Maori warriors as tattooed, half-naked men with their hair tied in topknots, their eyes rolling wildly, their hands clutching spears and war clubs. After all, neither of them had ever seen a Maori in traditional garb. Omaka hadn't dressed in the European style, but her woven skirts weren't all that different from the long skirts that the *pakeha* women wore. Reverend Lange hadn't allowed her to walk around with her breasts bare, and her short tops were usually covered by a cape, to protect against the cold. They'd never seen skirts made of dried flax leaves, and Omaka hadn't been tattooed. Her high rank as a tribal elder had forbidden it. In the Ngai Tahu *marae* near Rata Station on the South Island, all the men and women dressed like *pakeha*, and very few of them were tattooed.

But Aroha and Matiu didn't know what to expect of the Ngati Kahungunu. After all, they were one of the tribes that had fought in the Maori Wars. They surely still dressed traditionally and practiced the old rites and lifestyle. With a mixture of horror and curiosity, Aroha and Matiu imagined wild war dances and ferocious singing. Had they ever cut off the heads of their enemies and shrunk them? Matiu had heard that the Hauhau movement had even practiced ritual cannibalism.

The two teens were almost disappointed when the train arrived in Greytown and they saw the people waiting for them on the platform: a man and a woman, both around thirty years old, dressed in unremarkable clothing. The man wore denim trousers and a torn shirt. The few tattoos on his face were shadowed by a broad-brimmed hat. The woman had a small tattoo around her mouth, but her hair was pinned up like a *pakeha* woman's, and she was wearing a simple cotton dress.

Matiu instantly regretted wearing his stiff Sunday suit. Aroha, who wore a tailored light-blue traveling outfit, had to bolster his courage as they left their compartment.

"Come on, they aren't going to eat you!"

Matiu grinned. The couple certainly didn't look ferocious. On the contrary—when they recognized the young man, broad smiles lit their faces.

"You must be Matiu," the woman said in strongly accented English.

"Your family greets you," the man added. "I Hakopa, brother of Mahuika. This Reka, sister."

The young man stared incredulously at his aunt and uncle, too overcome to get a word out.

Aroha stepped forward. "I'm Aroha," she said. "We can speak Maori."

*"Kia ora,"* Matiu said.

"Don't speak English?" Reka asked in surprise. "I think: you live with *pakeha*, I practice English special for you." She smiled. "Welcome! *Haere mai!*"

She placed her hands on Matiu's shoulders and offered him her face in *hongi*, the traditional greeting. Matiu felt her nose and forehead against his own, and all at once felt at ease.

"Of course I can speak English," he said in Maori. "We learned both in Otaki. I was just so surprised."

"He hadn't counted on being met by family right at the train station," Aroha added. "And we also thought there would be a kind of *powhiri*, and—"

Reka and Hakopa laughed, but it sounded more bitter than cheerful.

"Here?" Reka asked. "You thought we would sing and dance for you at the train station?"

Aroha blushed. "No, we—we just thought—because you live here now . . ."

Hakopa's face hardened. "Yes, daughter, we live in Wairarapa. But that doesn't mean that the land belongs to us. The *pakeha* tolerate us being here. They have allowed us to build a *marae* on our land again, but only if we adapt. We dress like them, we work for them, we don't make any demands when it comes to land ownership. They let us sow a few fields, but not the most fertile land. Our tribe used to be rich. Now we have to be careful so we can survive, without provoking the whites."

"Our *marae* isn't in the city, but outside, in the woods," Reka added. "We don't seek contact with the *pakeha*, and they don't seek contact with us. You never would have found us if we hadn't come to pick you up."

Aroha nodded, feeling stupid. How could she have believed that the train would take them directly into a Maori village? Or even into a world where the Maori were still in charge of Wairarapa?

"Of course, when we arrive in the *marae*, we will welcome you properly," Hakopa assured them. "We're so happy that you've come back to us, Matiu. And you've brought your *wahine*?"

"Yes!" Matiu exclaimed. "The *pakeha* say we're too young, but Aroha is going to be my wife."

Hakopa smiled. "She is welcome in our tribe. But come now, the others are waiting for us. Are you hungry? We prepared a *hangi* for you."

Aroha's eyebrows rose. She'd heard a lot about the meals cooked in traditional pit ovens, but she'd never tasted one. The Ngai Tahu at Rata Station didn't build *hangis*—there was no volcanic activity in the Canterbury Plains that could be used to heat them.

In front of the little Greytown train station, a hay wagon with two rather scrawny horses waited for the travelers.

"That belongs to us," Reka said proudly, as though it were a huge accomplishment.

Hakopa heaved Matiu and Aroha's trunks onto the wagon bed, and the visitors climbed in too. There were no benches to sit on, which Aroha liked, but Matiu seemed worried about his suit. Reka and Hakopa climbed onto the front seat, and Hakopa guided the wagon through the tidy main street of the little town.

"They named it Greytown after the governor who tricked the Ngati Kahungunu out of it for a ridiculous price," Hakopa explained bitterly. "We call this place Kuratawhiti. We didn't settle here because we didn't want to anger the spirits of the Waiohine River. That was wise. The *pakeha* are fighting floods to this day. Besides, the earth spirits started quaking as soon as the first settlers set foot here."

"Strangely enough, none of it has frightened them away," Reka remarked. "I'm starting to believe that the *pakeha* aren't scared of anything. That's what makes them so strong; they are stronger than us in that way."

The wagon was rolling out of town toward Lake Wairarapa. The *marae* was near the lake, but not close enough to see water from the houses.

"The banks are marshy," Reka said. "Good for hunting and fishing, but not to live on."

All around Greytown there was fertile farmland controlled by the *pakeha*. Finally, a path along the river led into the woods, and after another half-hour ride, the fence surrounding the Ngati Kahungunu *marae* came into view. It reminded Aroha and Matiu of the fence around their school: it was made of raupo reeds tied together with flax. It wouldn't stop attackers. The Ngati Kahungunu must not be worried about enemies—either that or they had nothing worth stealing. Aroha and Matiu had seen illustrations of the big, colorfully painted, wooden, totem-pole-like god statues that guarded the entrance to traditional North Island *marae*s. But here, there was just an undecorated gate, now standing open. A few children were playing nearby, and upon seeing the wagon ran off excitedly to announce the visitors' arrival.

Hakopa steered the horses toward the meeting ground, which was surrounded by communal cooking and sleeping houses. Aroha was disappointed by the buildings. Her stepfather had renovated the *marae* on the school's grounds with his first fosterlings, and had allowed them to decorate the houses with traditional carvings and paint them. One was more beautiful than the next. Here, there was hardly any carving at all, and the houses seemed to have been built in a hurry. This *marae* felt temporary, as though the residents weren't sure they would be able to stay.

But as far as the welcome went, Aroha and Matiu's expectations were fulfilled. The tribe had prepared a ceremony—not as formal as one to honor complete strangers would have been, but elaborate enough to welcome Matiu to his tribe. The tribe's young women danced a *haka* as Aroha and Matiu climbed down from the wagon. They sang about the ocean and the lake where they caught fish and hunted. The song described the country and the tribe's life. The chieftain and the tribal elders had gathered in front of the *wharenui*, the meeting house, while the *ariki*, a man who was still quite young and didn't have full facial tattoos, stood off to one side with his family. It was *tapu* to touch the chieftain, Te Hanui; not even his shadow was supposed to fall on one of his people. The elders, by contrast, happily exchanged *hongi* with Matiu, and a few of the women did the same with Aroha. One of the oldest women broke into tears as she rested her forehead against Matiu's.

"Your mother's mother," Reka explained to the embarrassed young man.

The woman must have had a high rank in the tribe, because she then led the whole gathering in prayer. She seemed to expect Aroha and Matiu to know the words, but Reverend Lange's tolerance hadn't stretched as far as teaching his students how to summon the spirits. Reka recognized their hesitance, and asked Matiu afterward if he would also say a prayer.

"To the *pakeha* god," she said. "Because we don't want to exclude him either. We're all baptized, after all."

That seemed strange to Aroha. She found out later that the *pakeha* had made it a requirement: in order for the tribe to resettle on their land, they'd had to accept the *pakeha* religion. Every Sunday, the chieftain sent a delegation to church, usually young people and children who hadn't had bad experiences with the *pakeha* god and his followers yet. To protect his people, Te Hanui had learned to be rather flexible. He'd only had the position for a few years, and his predecessor had been killed in the Second Taranaki War. Or had it been afterward? Aroha's head was spinning as she listened to one of the elders say the *mihi*, a speech that told of the present, the past, and the future of the Ngati Kahungunu, and introduced both the living and the dead.

"Our ancestors came to Aotearoa with the canoe Takitimu, guided by Tamatea Arikinui. His son Rongokako married Muriwuenua, and they had a son, Tamatea Ure Haea. His son Kahungunu was born in Kaitaia, and he founded our tribe. Kahungunu traveled south from Kaitaia and fathered many children. They built villages and had children of their own, and they became farmers and carvers and canoe builders. Here are three important branches of the Ngati Kahungunu. We belong to the Ki Heretaunga. We lived by the sea . . ."

The storyteller told of forts being founded, fights with other tribes, and the five Ngati Kahungunu chieftains who had once signed the Treaty of Waitangi, hoping to live in peace with the *pakeha*. The tribes had planted grain and vegetables for the white settlers who, at that time, worked mostly at the whaling stations along the coast.

"But then the sheep farmers came and let their animals graze on our land. They gave us a few trade goods, and then a little money, and said the land belonged to them!"

The storyteller sounded furious, and angry noises came from the audience. A shiver went down Aroha's back. She'd heard such stories since she was a child. From Omaka and from the children who came to the orphanage. At some point Linda had explained to her that the Maori had a completely different concept of ownership than the *pakeha* did. They'd accepted the money and allowed the farmers to settle on their land and let their sheep graze there, but it didn't occur to them that they were giving it away permanently. When the whites began to build towns and cities, and required more and more land, the Maori began to defend themselves. The fighting began, and both sides were completely convinced that they were right. Both Maori and *pakeha* insisted that the other had broken the treaties.

But, Aroha learned, this tribe's difficulties hadn't really begun until the advance of the Hauhau movement, whose prophet Te Ua Haumene had sworn to drive the *pakeha* from Aotearoa. Many, especially young chiefs, were swayed by the Hauhaus' teachings, causing skirmishes and killings. As it turned out, the *pakeha* had not been responsible for the abduction of Matiu's mother and the other people from this *iwi*. They'd been taken as prisoners of war by the Kupapa, a Maori tribe that had become dependent on the *pakeha* and fought on the side of the British. Somehow Mahuika must then have come into contact with the English military settler, who had gotten her pregnant.

"And when the war seemed to have ended and we mourned our dead, the *pakeha* turned their ire on us . . ."

The storyteller continued in a tone between grief and outrage, saying that the governor had accused his *iwi* of supporting the Hauhau during the Taranaki Wars. It was a pretext often used in the 1860s to confiscate Maori land. Matiu's tribe, which had always been peaceful, had tried to defend themselves against exile, but they had no defense against the weapons of the English. Fortunately, the Ngati Kahungunu ki Wairarapa had offered them asylum on these lands. The Ngati Kahungunu ki Wairarapa had a large, important village in Papawai, a fort to the southeast of Greytown. Matiu's *iwi* hadn't wanted to join them, but had remained independent.

"Our souls are not anchored here," Matiu's grandmother Ngaio said later. "Our *maunga* are the hills and the cliffs around the water that you call Hawke's Bay. Perhaps one day we will return."

That explained the provisory feeling of the village; the *iwi* wasn't happy there. But Aroha knew from her mother that it could have been much worse. Many of the people driven from their land had been resettled in regions where their traditional tribal enemies lived. That had caused more tragedy.

Matiu sucked up every word of the *mihi* like a sponge, desperate to understand his own history. Aroha, on the other hand, was relieved when the storyteller finally finished and was honored with applause. Afterward there were songs, dances, and prayers, and gifts were exchanged. Matiu and Aroha had brought a few carvings from Otaki, which they now handed to Matiu's relatives. Ngaio gave Aroha a piece of jade.

Finally, the young people sat around the fire with Matiu's family and enjoyed the meat and vegetables that had been prepared in the pit oven. Aroha thought the food was delicious. She was happy that Matiu finally seemed to be relaxing. After looking stiff and insecure during the greeting ceremony, he was finally chatting warmly with a few young warriors. Aroha felt at ease too, until Reka turned to her.

"What about your story, Aroha?" Matiu's aunt asked. "Everyone is curious. They're just too shy to ask you. Matiu's *wahine*—a *pakeha* with a Maori name who speaks our language. We've never met anyone like you. Where is your *maunga*, Aroha? Which canoe did your ancestors come to Aotearoa in? Which mountain or lake do you feel connected to?"

Aotearoa was the Maori word for New Zealand, and every Maori person knew the name of the canoe that had brought their ancestors to the island.

Aroha blushed. At least Reka hadn't asked for her life story in front of the entire tribe. The girl swallowed and took a deep breath.

"I am Aroha Fitzpatrick," she said, then began to improvise. "My ancestors came to Aotearoa aboard the *Sankt Pauli*."

Actually, that only applied to one of the girl's ancestors, a man whom no one in Aroha's family wanted to remember. In the same night, Ottfried Brandmann had raped and impregnated Linda's mother, Cat, and his wife, Ida, mother to Linda's half sister Carol. Cat herself had been born in Australia and brought as a baby to the South Island, where she'd spent her childhood in a brothel at a whaling station. Nor did Aroha know how her father, Joe Fitzpatrick, had come to New Zealand. He was from Ireland, but claimed to have studied in England. Linda said she'd never discovered whether that was true.

"Your father was a swindler, Aroha, a swaggerer, a storyteller. Life with him was interesting but dangerous."

Her mother spoke about Joe Fitzpatrick with reserve, but her stepfather made no secret of his disdain for the man. Revi Fransi always said that, above all, Joe had been a liar, and he always grimaced when he spoke about him.

Aroha knew that Linda had been the one to leave Fitz, as everyone called him. Somehow, another woman had been involved, and the last straw had been when he'd abandoned his wife and baby during a Maori attack in the Second Taranaki War. Linda hadn't gone into detail, and Aroha hadn't pressed. Franz Lange had always been a loving father to her. She didn't need another. In that sense, her *pepeha* was accurate. Franz had also come to New Zealand on the *Sankt Pauli*.

"My family settled on the South Island at first," Aroha said. "Only after my mother married did she go to Patea with her husband. He was supposed to be given land there."

"Stolen land?" Reka asked sternly.

Aroha bit her lip. Joe Fitzpatrick had been a member of the Taranaki regiment of the military settlers. He had been promised land that had been taken from the Maori, but lost it when he was dishonorably discharged for cowardice.

"They didn't keep the land," Aroha answered vaguely.

Matiu's grandmother had been listening with concern. "And where is your soul anchored, my child? It sounds as though you have no home."

Aroha didn't know if she should nod first or shake her head.

"Yes, I do," she said resolutely. "I grew up in Otaki, on Maori land. My parents always say we're just using the land, it doesn't belong to us." Actually, the Anglican Church had requisitioned the old Maori fort for their orphanage without asking anyone. But at least the Te Ati Awa who'd lived there had already left of their own free will. "But my *maunga* is nowhere on Aotearoa," Aroha continued. She smiled. Matiu's relatives were hanging on every word. "Omaka, a *tohunga* of the Ngati Tamakopiri who helped my mother during my birth, anchored my soul in the realm of Rangi, the god of the heavens."

A whisper ran through the crowd. All at once, it seemed as though the entire tribe was listening.

"She sent my soul toward the sky with the smoke of the fire in which she burned my afterbirth, and named Rangi as my protector."

16

"She must have been a great priestess!" Reka said, her eyes wide. "To send a soul to the sky like a kite at a New Year's festival . . ."

"She put you under the protection of powerful spirits," Ngaio said respectfully. "Omaka must have had much *mana*. But if such a *maunga* is lucky for you, child, remains to be seen. You will always be a traveler. You will never have a place where you belong."

Aroha shook her head determinedly. "No, *karani*," she said. "I like to travel very much, that's true. I would like to see the entire world. But I belong to Matiu. Here on earth, he is my *maunga*." She nestled against the young man who was sitting next to her.

Matiu smiled joyfully. "I'll hold onto her tightly, *karani*," he said, and pulled Aroha close.

The old woman didn't return his smile. "Be careful, grandson," she said softly. "It can be dangerous to be the string of a kite that the gods desire."

# Chapter 3

Aroha and Matiu spent several wonderful weeks in Wairarapa. Matiu joined the young hunters and warriors. The local *rangatira*, who was training the boys to use traditional weapons, was delighted to include him in the lessons. Aroha laughed when she saw Matiu in warrior garb for the first time, and the other boys teased him good-naturedly when he revealed his rather lanky, barely muscular chest.

"You need to eat more," Reka declared, and spoiled her nephew whenever she got a chance.

Lake Wairarapa turned out to be an ideal location for fishing and hunting. Aroha learned from the other girls how to set traps, and chatted with them about Matiu and their own love interests. At first, she blushed. Revi Fransi had been right; these girls were startlingly forward, but soon she didn't think anything of getting undressed in front of the others and comparing her small breasts with those of her friends.

"They're still growing," the somewhat older Rere assured her. She herself was well developed and had already made love twice with one of the young warriors among the reeds by the lake.

Soon Aroha allowed Matiu to convince her to go down to the lakeshore with him. It was a sunny, early spring day, and the two of them took a blanket so they could lie down and kiss and caress each other. Unfortunately, it had rained the day before, and it was too cold to get undressed. Still, Aroha allowed her friend to touch her breasts through her dress. Matiu didn't find the caresses particularly exciting. His new friends' descriptions had sounded much more promising. Nonetheless, he assured Aroha that he couldn't imagine more beautiful breasts.

With her heart pounding, Aroha's hands wandered under the waistband of Matiu's pants, and she was startled when his member stiffened in response. However, the other girls' stories had prepared her for it, and she was proud to have excited her beloved. During their stay, Aroha and Matiu didn't entirely lose sight of the strict morals they'd grown up with, but they did learn quite a bit about male and female bodies.

Matiu also learned even more about the history of his tribe. His grandmother was a *tohunga,* the herbalist and priestess of the tribe. She told him stories for hours, stories about his maternal ancestors, the warriors' heroic deeds, and the beauty of the women. She described life by the sea: fishing and the men's adventurous trips in their canoes, dangerous cliffs, white beaches, and fruitful green hills watched over by friendly spirits. Matiu listened attentively, but many of the stories were just strange to him. He had always been more interested in technology than stories. Hunting and the arts of war didn't come easily to him either.

Therefore, it was a welcome change for Matiu when the chieftain suggested that he and Aroha accompany the churchgoers to Greytown on Sunday. Aroha had been wearing the colorful skirts and bodices of woven flax fiber to see how they felt on her body, but both of them changed back into their regular clothes for the occasion. Matiu was relieved. He hadn't wanted to admit that he'd been freezing in his warrior's garb. He could scarcely believe the other young men wore it even in winter.

The two visitors caused quite a sensation in the small local church. Reka, under instructions from the chieftain, introduced them to the priest. Of course, he had heard about the school in Otaki.

"Reverend Lange is doing excellent work there," the priest said enthusiastically. "You have a high school diploma, my son? The Maori people here don't send their children to school. There is one in Papawai. It just doesn't have the best reputation . . ."

After the service, there was coffee, tea, and cake in the parish room, and the priest invited the Maori to partake. Reka's expression made it clear that he did not normally do so, and was making an exception that day for her visitors. Everyone sat at long tables, and the Ngati Kahungunu quietly ate cake while Aroha chatted animatedly. The girl described the orphanage and school at Otaki in glowing colors. Matiu soon lost interest. As luck would have it, he'd been seated with several men who were working on the railroads, or who had previously done so. He listened to their stories with intense interest, relaying them to Aroha afterward.

Aroha was unmoved by the details, but relieved by his enthusiasm. As much as she enjoyed being with the Ngati Kahungunu, she had no desire to remain for good and was glad that Matiu felt the same. The young man could hardly wait to start studying mechanical engineering.

On Monday, a surprise was waiting for Aroha. After breakfast, Reka and Hakopa came to ask her to translate for the chieftain.

"The reverend from Greytown is here," Reka said. The look on her face suggested she saw him less as a man of God and more like the devil. "He wants to speak to the *ariki*, and I'm supposed to interpret, but my English isn't that good. Will you help, Aroha?"

Aroha nodded. In front of the chieftain's house, she ran into Matiu, surprised that two interpreters were needed. They greeted the reverend, who looked quite unhappy to be standing in the drizzling rain. He seemed to be waiting to be invited inside.

"The *ariki* will receive you out here," Aroha explained. "No one is allowed to share a room with a chieftain, or to share the same air with him. The Maori call it *tapu*. His, um, his shadow could fall on you."

The reverend snorted. "I know quite well what *tapu* is, Miss Fitzpatrick. Pagan nonsense. Of course, I'm prepared to show the chieftain respect. But isn't there a way to do that without getting rained on?"

Aroha led the man under the scanty protection of a nikau palm. She didn't like being outside in this weather either, which was why she'd put on a blouse and skirt that morning, combined with a warm jacket. Matiu had used the reverend's visit as an excuse to dress more warmly too, changing quickly into denim pants and a leather jacket.

The chieftain, however, appeared in traditional garb, protected from the rain only by a valuable cloak with feathers woven into it.

"*Kia ora*, Reverend," he said in greeting, without approaching the man. "I am very pleased to be able to welcome you to our village. My people have great respect for you."

Aroha translated his words. The reverend nodded and replied with a few similar pleasantries. However, a slight reproof crept into his next words. He was pleased about the visit to his Sunday service, but would be much happier if the chieftain and tribal elders would also attend church.

The chieftain answered evasively. "I have my duties," he told the reverend. "And our elders—they can't walk very far anymore. It's a long way to Greytown. You'll have to content yourself with the young people."

"And the children like to go to Sunday school very much," Aroha added.

Actually, the kids had only had positive things to say about their classes because there was always milk and cake there. But Aroha didn't mention that part.

The clergyman's face lit up. "That's exactly what I wanted to talk to you about, *ariki*. The school. I've noticed that several of your children are clever and enthusiastic. But they hardly understand enough English to follow my lessons. And of course they can't read and write—"

"It's a long way to the school in Papawai," the chieftain interrupted. "The children would be walking for many hours every day."

"Isn't there a boarding school there?" Aroha asked.

She immediately felt the chieftain's stern gaze on her. Apparently, the distance to the school was no less of an excuse than distance for the elders to attend church. Matiu's grandmother, for one, walked the woods for hours every day to collect herbs. The walk to Greytown certainly wouldn't have been difficult for her.

"Reverend, the Ngati Kahungunu ki Wairarapa live in Papawai," the chieftain explained. "We are the Ngati Kahungunu ki Heretaunga. Of course, we're not enemies; on the contrary, we're brothers. But still, we have different roots, and many in my tribe are hoping to return to Hawke's Bay one day. Our land was confiscated unfairly. It must be possible—"

"Then it's even more important for your people to be educated!" the reverend declared. "If you had judges, surveyors, and politicians in your ranks, everything would be easier for you. You must send the children to school!"

The *ariki* shook his head. "They would be alone among strangers," he insisted.

The reverend pursed his lips. Then his expression changed; he seemed to be about to play his ace.

"It needn't be the school in Papawai," he said cautiously. "Listen, when your young visitors came to my sermon yesterday, God gave me inspiration. Reverend Lange runs a school for Maori children of different tribes in Otaki. Why don't you send a few of your youngsters there? They wouldn't be alone. They would have mentors in Matiu and Miss Fitzpatrick."

Aroha didn't know how to translate the word "mentor," but the clergyman's suggestion sounded reasonable to her. She and Matiu had thought it a pity that the tribe's children didn't attend school, since they were obviously interested in learning. The young people spoke broken English, and many had entreated Aroha and Matiu to practice with them. Several also wanted to learn to read and write.

Aroha decided to support the reverend's plan. "Revi Fransi and my mother, whom the children call *koka* Linda, are like parents to the students. And it's true, the children come from many different tribes, sometimes even from enemy tribes. At the very beginning, it was a problem. But Revi Fransi came up with a game. He rowed the children down the river to the school in a boat that he named *Linda*. That way, they could say they had all come in the same canoe to their part of Aotearoa. Everyone was satisfied with that. It was very important to Revi Fransi that the children got along."

The chieftain bit his lip thoughtfully. Aroha suspected he wasn't afraid of conflicts among the students, but worried that Reverend Lange would overdo the Christian aspect of the education. There were hardly any Maori chieftains who turned down educational opportunities for the children of their tribes, so long as they remained rooted in the traditions of their people.

"It's not even that far away," Matiu suddenly said, to everyone's surprise. "Only a few hours by train. The children won't have to stay away for years; they could come home during vacations."

The chieftain fingered the feathers on his cloak. "Reverend Lange wouldn't have anything against that?"

It was an open secret that most Christian missionaries didn't like to release students from their clutches. Many tribes had had bad experiences with this. The children, whom they had sent trustingly, had returned years later, completely changed. They hadn't received a high school diploma or even a real education. Instead, they had been trained to be submissive servants and maids, who would be given work in *pakeha* households. Such people were no longer at home in either world, Maori or *pakeha*.

Matiu and Aroha both shook their heads.

"Revi Fransi doesn't do that," Matiu said, trying to reassure the *ariki*. "The children in Otaki are happy."

# Chapter 4

"And she'll come back? You'll promise me that?"

Aputa, little Haki's mother, was asking Aroha the same question for the fifth time.

Aroha reassured her again. "We'll take good care of Haki. Won't we, children?"

Haki was the youngest of the four children that the Ngati Kahungunu were sending to Otaki with Aroha and Matiu. They had planned to take only children over the age of ten, but Haki had insisted. She was extraordinarily clever, very lively and independent. After much discussion, her parents had reluctantly agreed.

Aroha used the need to protect the youngest to bond the little group. She'd often seen her parents doing the same thing. When the children were given a challenge to work on together, especially if one appealed to their sense of responsibility, it prevented rivalry. Except that Anaru, Purahi, Koria, and Haki were quite unlikely to argue. They were far too proud that they'd been chosen to represent their tribe in Otaki.

"I'm going to be a lawyer!" twelve-year-old Anaru said confidently. "I will take our case to the *pakeha* court, and we'll get our land back!"

Of all the children, Anaru spoke the best English, but Koria wasn't far behind. Purahi was fascinated to learn more about the construction and upkeep of the railway system. He peered excitedly into the distance for the train that was about to arrive. Matiu and Aroha, the future students, and their parents were waiting on the train platform. Purahi's and Haki's mothers had broken into tears, and Koria's mother kept smoothing the skirt of her daughter's new *pakeha* dress. The church congregation in Greytown had donated hand-me-down clothes, as well as school supplies such as reading primers, notebooks, pencils, and books.

Aroha knew that Revi Fransi wouldn't expect them to arrive with any of that, but it made the children feel especially important.

"You can read me this book during the trip," Koria ordered, holding up a copy of *The Little Princess* for Aroha. "When we arrive, I'll already be able to speak English."

"It won't work quite that quickly," Aroha said with a smile, and also reassured Anaru's father again that the children would be fine at her parents' school.

"What about this monster?" Purahi's mother shouted over the whistle of the approaching train. "Won't it devour the children?"

She pointed to the engine, which Aroha had to admit did look very threatening to someone who had never seen a train before.

"That's not a monster, it's a steam engine," Purahi said with a laugh. "It's pulling the wagons that we'll ride in. Like a horse, only much stronger."

"It looks more like a dragon to me," his mother murmured. "Are the *pakeha* able even to tame dragons?"

"Matiu says the engines sometimes even push the trains," Purahi said excitedly. "And they put on the brakes while they're climbing. We're going over the mountains, and through tunnels."

"We have to get in now, *koka*," Matiu said gently to Purahi's mother. He called her "aunt" because she was also part of his large family. "You have to say goodbye to the children now."

Matiu and Aroha exchanged *hongi* with Reka, who furtively wiped the tears from her eyes.

"You must come again next year," she told her nephew. "No matter what your *karani* says."

The farewell between Matiu and his grandmother had been very emotional. The old Ngaio had given him a blessing that Matiu hadn't understood. Like all *karakia*, which were prayers, blessings, and curses, it had been said extremely fast. But it had scared Reka terribly. She hadn't explained it to Matiu and Aroha, but the old woman apparently assumed that she would never see her grandson again.

Now, Matiu smiled at his aunt. "I'll come and bring the children back to you," he promised. "First thing next summer. That's when we have vacation at the university. Then it will also be nicer here. Not as terribly cold as it is today."

It was often windy in Greytown, but that day the wind was unusually icy. The force of it took Aroha's breath away. The girl was happy when she finally sat down in their compartment. She showed the excited children to their seats and checked that they all had their tickets ready while Matiu stowed their bundles in the nets above. Then the heavy iron wheels of the engine set into motion, and the children waved cheerfully to their parents. It was quite clear that they weren't sad to be leaving, while Purahi's mother almost collapsed on the train platform. Her husband had to hold her up. Haki's mother ran a short way with the train, distraught at letting her little one go. The other parents seemed more relaxed. Koria's mother even managed to smile as she waved to the children.

"So, now the book," Koria ordered as soon as they were underway. "What kind of story is it? A princess is a chieftain's daughter, isn't she?"

"The first tunnel is at Prices Creek, right?" Purahi asked Matiu. "Or is it the Siberia? Which one is longer?" He'd tried to learn every construction miracle of the Rimutaka Incline by heart.

Aroha read and translated the story for the girls, who knew little about *pakeha* customs. The level of the language was also too difficult for them. At the same time, Matiu explained to the boys how the incline railway engine worked and the purpose of the brake car, insofar as he understood himself. They hung on his every word, and couldn't hide their enthusiasm when the train finally stopped at a switchyard at Cross Creek. There, the engine was detached and replaced with a stronger one at the back of the train. The railway employees didn't mind the children disembarking and watching from a safe distance as the heavy machine was hitched behind the two passenger cars and the freight car.

"It's going to push us up the mountain!" Matiu shouted over the wind.

Aroha and the girls had sought protection in a makeshift hut. The uncomfortable shelter was the Rimutaka Incline Railway's only concession to comfort. Here, not many passengers were expected; the line was primarily used for freight. On this clear September morning, however, there were quite a few travelers.

Aroha saw a family with children, and important-looking men who were on their way to Wellington for business. Many of them were staring at the Maori children and whispering among themselves. It was rare for Maori people to travel by train.

After the locomotive had been attached to two more freight cars and a manned brake car, a shrill whistle commanded the passengers to board the train again. Aroha followed the call gladly. The wagons weren't heated, but offered protection from the ice-cold wind.

"Are we going to Sib—Sib—what's it called again, Matiu?" Purahi asked.

"Siberia. That's right, we're going there now. The engineer who named the tunnel imagined it was as cold and barren as Siberia, in Russia. It's supposed to snow a lot there."

"But don't tickle me again in the tunnel, Anaru!" Haki said with a giggle.

While Purahi was absorbed by the technical miracles, Anaru hadn't been able to resist pestering the girls a little in the first tunnel between Greytown and Cross Creek.

"Is it just me, or is the train swaying?" Aroha asked. She looked up from her book as the wagon made serpentine turns around narrow curves, wrapping herself more tightly in her cloak. The wind roared infernally outside and found its way through the smallest cracks in the wagon walls.

"Don't be silly," Matiu said. "The train is fastened very securely to the tracks; that's why the middle track was invented."

"I think it feels kind of wobbly too," Koria said, not sounding particularly concerned. "Because of the wind. Actually, you should be able to put a sail on a train, like a canoe."

Aroha and Matiu laughed.

"The train is much too heavy for that," Matiu told the little girl. "That's why it can't tip over or be blown away. It—" Matiu went silent when it suddenly felt as though the train was actually leaning out over a curve. "Must be the Siberia Curve," he said with feigned cheerfulness.

All at once, he had a bad feeling. Aroha gazed fearfully down the steep incline they were riding along, and suddenly she felt a jerk. The wind caught their wagon, and it leaned dangerously over the abyss.

"Get down! Take cover!" someone cried.

Aroha instinctively threw herself on the floor and clung tightly to the foot of the bench. Out of the corner of her eye, she saw Koria being catapulted along the center aisle, while Haki crawled through the open door of the compartment.

"Out! I have to get out of here!" the girl screamed.

Her voice mixed with the desperate cries of the other passengers. The wagon tipped farther and farther, and it certainly wasn't on all three of the tracks anymore. The wooden walls groaned, and the coupling between the train cars creaked shrilly.

"Out!" Haki cried again. The little girl slid across the floor of the crooked wagon toward the main door.

"No, Haki! You can't get out now!" Matiu staggered after her.

The door suddenly opened as though by a ghostly hand, light flooding into the wagon. Aroha was flung across the compartment. She held on to the wall with all her strength to keep from being thrown from the train. At that moment, the wagon lost all purchase on the tracks. It derailed and tore the second passenger car after it.

The people screamed with terror. They called their families and God. Aroha was paralyzed with fear. She had just seen into the abyss. If the engine that was pushing them came loose and fell, it would be shattered at the foot of the mountain. No one would be able to survive that.

But then there was another infernal crash, and sudden braking. Aroha heard passengers crying out in pain as they smashed against windows and walls. The wagon hung crookedly for a moment, and she slid helplessly toward the open door, grabbing hold of the step to stop herself. She looked down and was confronted by the ghastly image of train cars hanging in the air below the curve. It looked as though a spoiled little boy had derailed his toy train. For now, the couplings seemed to be holding, and the heavy locomotive was working against the storm, holding the train together.

But Aroha herself couldn't withstand the wind and gravity anymore. Another strong gust rocked the cars and she lost her grip. She crashed into the hillside and rolled down. She cried out with pain and tried to grab on to something, but her right arm wouldn't respond. She tumbled helplessly down the mountainside until her head hit a boulder.

Everything went black. When Aroha came to, she felt as though it could only have been a few moments that she was lost in the merciful darkness, only to find herself in hell again.

The first thing she saw was the derailed train, which swayed above her like an absurd threat. Only then did she look at the hillside, covered with bleeding bodies. She heard screams, crying and moaning, terrible sounds that were carried away by the wind. Aroha's head hurt, but then she began to think again.

Matiu! Where were Matiu and the children? Were they still in the train? No, the last time she'd seen Matiu and Haki, they were moving toward the door—the door that had then opened. Were they safe? Had they been badly injured or killed?

"Matiu! Koria! Anaru!"

Tears filled her eyes. She tried to stand up and made it to her knees—and then she saw Matiu. The young man was lying on a rock projection. Aroha crawled toward him. It wasn't far, but it seemed to take hours. Her right arm kept giving out. Finally, she lay panting next to him and looked into his pale, lifeless face.

"Matiu, I'm here! It's Aroha! Matiu, say something!"

She tried to lift his head, and then she saw the blood. There was a wound on the back of his head. His arms and legs looked strangely twisted. For one terrible second, Aroha thought Matiu wasn't breathing anymore. His chest hardly moved. She raised herself up on her left arm, and put her face close to his, trying to feel if he was breathing. He was.

"A—Aroha . . ." His voice was hardly more than a whisper. "You—you're alive."

Aroha tried to smile. "Of course! After all, you were with me. Remember what you told me on the way to Greytown? You said that when we're together, nothing can happen to me."

She would have liked to stroke his face, but she was afraid of losing her grip and falling on him. So she laid her cheek against his. Matiu's face was cold.

"I—I can't move . . ." Matiu whispered.

Aroha pulled herself up a little more. "You're all beat up," she said. "I think my arm is broken too. But it will all be fine, Matiu . . ."

Matiu made a face. He was growing more and more pale. No, he was . . . gray.

"Aroha, could you . . . kiss me?"

Aroha felt his words more than heard them.

"I'll try," she said softly, and put her lips gently on his. She thought she felt the light pulse of his breath as she kissed him. "How's that?"

Matiu didn't answer. Aroha saw that he had closed his eyes. His face seemed to collapse. She tried to feel his breath again, and began to panic. Finally, she managed to put her ear to his chest to listen for his heartbeat. She couldn't find it, only hearing the groaning and whistling of the wind around her.

With difficulty, Aroha sat up and pulled Matiu's head into her lap. He had to breathe again! He would breathe, now! She bent over him and whispered encouraging, tender words. With horror, she realized that her skirt was soaked with blood.

Then she began to scream.

# Chapter 5

Aroha didn't know how she'd gotten to the little hut in Cross Creek. She could only remember vaguely that she'd hit a man when he'd tried to pull Matiu out of her arms. Then she'd fainted again.

Only when she heard Koria's voice and someone tried to give her a sip of hot tea did she come to her senses and understand what had happened. That is, if she would ever really understand that Matiu no longer existed, that he'd just stopped breathing as she kissed and held him.

She felt Koria's little hand in her own. The children . . . she had to take care of the children. Haki . . . oh God, where was Haki? If Matiu had been flung out of the train car, the little one must have . . .

"Haki is dead," Koria said, her voice calm. "And Purahi is dead. I found them both. I searched for them. I found them all." The little girl trembled. She was half frozen, but apparently uninjured.

"Didn't you fall out of the train?" Aroha asked with difficulty.

She felt the cold again in spite of the hot teacup that had been pressed into her left hand. Her right arm was in a sling, and her shoulder hurt terribly.

Koria shook her head. "No. I slid into a corner of the compartment and got stuck there. I only banged my knee a little. When the train stopped moving, I jumped out. I slid a little at first, but I stopped myself. Then I let go and rolled down, and—and then I found everyone." Her body began to rock slowly back and forth. "I found them all . . ."

"What about Anaru?" Aroha asked quietly.

"The other Maori boy is injured," reported a woman who'd been distributing tea to the survivors. "They're taking him to Greytown on the train right now."

"On the train?" Aroha's voice rang with pure horror.

The woman nodded. "What else are they supposed to do? There are no proper streets, at least none good enough to transport people with injuries, and even the train will take hours. Of course I understand that none of you will want to board a train again soon, but there's no other way. Don't worry, the storm has stopped now. The engine that was sent to help had to stop in a tunnel so the same kind of thing didn't happen again."

Aroha wasn't ready for the details of the terrible accident, but the woman related them meticulously. As the train had gone around the Siberia Curve, it had been caught by a gust of wind estimated at 120 miles per hour. That had caused the first two passenger cars to derail, and then the freight car too. Miraculously—the woman had not grown tired of thanking God for it—all of the couplings had held. The engine had remained on the tracks thanks to its weight, and had prevented the cars from falling.

"The people who'd been thrown out said that the cars were hanging above them, swaying as though they were going to fall. They crawled away as far as they could. Most of them were injured. Others leaped out of the cars in panic and broke bones. You were lucky, little girl."

She turned to Koria, who didn't understand a word and probably wouldn't have even if the woman had been speaking Maori. The girl rocked back and forth with a ghostly rhythm.

"I found them, I found them all . . ."

The helper regarded her skeptically. "Is something wrong with her? Did she hit her head or something?"

Aroha didn't reply. "Are—are there many dead?" she finally asked in a tired voice.

"Three," the woman said. "All children, all Maori. And one little white boy looked hurt very badly too. They're also being brought to Greytown. Everyone badly injured is going with the first train. They'll come and get you afterward. Unfortunately, they only have one wagon and a small engine available. Everything else was involved in the accident."

As Aroha discovered later, the driver of the brake car had reacted to the accident with incredible presence of mind. He had uncoupled his car immediately and rushed back to Cross Creek to arrange for a rescue train. But for Matiu, Haki, and Purahi, it had been too late.

"I'm cold," Aroha whispered.

The woman wrapped a blanket around her. "There will be more tea in a moment," she said comfortingly.

Aroha felt as though she'd never be warm again.

Aroha, Koria, and the other lightly injured survivors had to hold out for several hours in the unheated hut until the train finally returned. Aroha barely registered any of it. She found herself floundering in a sea of cold and grief, and her dislocated shoulder screamed with pain. Her head pounded. As though from a distance, she heard Koria's exhausting chant:

"I found them, I found them all . . ."

Night had already fallen when Aroha was finally brought to the parish hall in Greytown. A provisory sick bay had been set up there, and an overtired-looking doctor came to reset her shoulder.

"This is going to hurt now, little lady," he said regretfully, and it was true; it hurt terribly.

But Aroha felt too weak to scream. She only whimpered as the arm sprang back into joint. The pain slowly faded, but she was too exhausted to be relieved.

After some time, she felt a cup at her lips again, and she mechanically opened her mouth, but then she had to cough. Only the second time was she able to get the whiskey down. The third swallow sent her into a deep sleep.

When Aroha awoke the next day, her shoulder hardly hurt at all anymore. The doctor had fixed her arm across her chest with bandages. But the pounding in her head and the burning in her heart were much worse. Matiu, Haki, Purahi . . . Aroha rubbed her temples. She would have liked to believe that it was all a bad dream, but then of course she wouldn't have woken up in a parish hall full of military cots. There were so many people talking, crying, and moaning . . . Aroha's headache got worse. She would have preferred to escape into sleep again, but then she remembered Koria and Anaru. Where were the children? She should have been taking care of Anaru the day before!

Aroha sat up with difficulty and fought back the heavy pulsing in her head. She swayed a little as she stood up, but felt as though she could breathe more easily. Then Aroha looked down at herself and almost screamed again. Her skirts were covered with dried blood.

Aroha clung to the back of a chair that was next to her bed, and caught the eye of one of the caregivers.

"Wait, miss, I'll help you!" The small, plump woman rushed toward her. "You're Miss Fitzpatrick, aren't you? Sit down, I'll bring you a cup of tea. My name is Mrs. Clever."

"What about the children?" Aroha asked. She was hoarse, and her own voice sounded strange to her. "Koria and Anaru—how are they?"

"You mean the Maori children?" Mrs. Clever asked, and pushed Aroha back onto the cot. "They were picked up this morning. Very early, it wasn't quite dawn, and the doctor wasn't very pleased about letting the boy go. But the parents insisted . . . Well, I suppose the broken leg will also be able to heal in the Maori village."

Mrs. Clever sounded doubtful, but Aroha felt relieved. At least Anaru wouldn't die.

"The reverend also telegraphed your parents," Mrs. Clever said. "They will be very relieved that nothing worse happened to you." She stopped another woman who was passing with a teapot, and got Aroha a cup. "Honestly, you could go home already, the doctor said. But you were staying with the Maori, and I—um, we—didn't know if you were still welcome there." Mrs. Clever gazed at the floor as Aroha looked up in surprise. "After everything that happened . . . Oh, for goodness' sake, my dear, what happened to your skirts? We'll have to find something new for you quickly. And water to wash, as well."

She busily went on her way. Aroha leaned back, exhausted. Mrs. Clever was right, she shouldn't stand up yet. But then a spiteful voice startled her.

"Is right that *pakeha* girl covered in blood!" The voice was raised above the general murmuring, crying, and moans. It belonged to a large Maori woman who was standing between the rows of beds. In the general bustle, her entrance hadn't been noticed, since she was wearing *pakeha* clothing. Now everyone stared. Aroha hunched her shoulders uncomfortably. She recognized Haki's mother approaching her, apparently prepared to cast all her grief and anger in her direction. "Blood means death!" she shouted at Aroha. "That caused bad luck. You, girl, caused bad luck. You promised me, bring Haki back. 'Will be happy, Haki. Will learn, Haki . . .'" She repeated the words that Aroha had used to soothe her fears the day before. "And now? Now my Haki dead!" She sobbed loudly, but then stopped herself. "And Purahi dead too. Like his mama said, eaten by *pakeha* dragon. And Koria talk crazy, must drive out evil spirits. You fault, *pakeha* girl! You fault!"

The woman came closer threateningly. Mrs. Clever determinedly placed herself between the two of them. But then someone else stepped in.

"Calm down, Aputa, it's no one's fault."

Reka had entered the parish hall. Now she spoke to the woman in Maori, and tried to put a comforting arm around her shoulders. Aputa shook it off.

"It's her fault! I curse her! I curse you, *pakeha* girl. The spirits of the dead will follow you! You will never find peace!" she raged in Maori.

In the meantime, the doctor and reverend hurried to the scene. The men stepped up behind the raving woman who was now waving a stick at Aroha. Aroha realized it was a *tiki wananga*, also called a godstick. It was decorated with carved god figures and was one of the traditional tools of Maori priests and priestesses. The sight of it made her shudder. Omaka, too, had owned a *tiki wananga*, and Linda had once told her how she'd used its power to curse a young woman. Aputa seemed to want to hit Aroha with it. The men held her back, grabbing both of her arms. Reka took the stick from her.

"We understand your pain, but now you must go," the reverend told Aputa gently.

While being escorted away, Aputa broke into tears. Reka turned to Aroha, holding the *tiki wananga* carefully, as though the stick could burn her.

"She can't curse you," she explained to Aroha, who was trembling. "She doesn't have enough *mana* to do that. She's no *tohunga*, she has no power. The spirits won't listen to anyone who is raging with pain. You must forgive her, Aroha. And I hope the spirits will forgive her too. She shouldn't have taken the godstick. She must have stolen it from Ngaio. Actually, she isn't even allowed to touch it."

"Maybe Ngaio lent it to her," Aroha whispered. "As revenge for Matiu."

Reka shook her head. "Matiu's grandmother is grieving, but she doesn't blame you. It was an accident. She also foresaw that something would happen, and she knew she would never see Matiu again. But she couldn't know *when* the accident would take place."

"She said it could be dangerous for him to love me," Aroha said with a sob. Only now did the *tohunga*'s words make sense to her. "*It can be dangerous to be the string of a kite that the gods desire.* That's what she said."

"Even then it wouldn't be your fault," Reka said gently. "The most it could be is a jealous god. But I don't believe it, and you shouldn't believe in such things either. You pray to the *pakeha* god, and he's always supposed to be good, kind, and wise."

It didn't sound as though Reka really believed it herself, but she clearly wanted to comfort Aroha.

"I talked the tribe into sending the children to school," Aroha insisted. "Haki's mother is right. I promised to take care of her child, I—"

"Excuse me, but you should go now too," Mrs. Clever said gently but decisively, interrupting the conversation in Maori between Aroha and Reka. "I'm sure you mean well with the girl, but you're upsetting her. Miss Fitzpatrick has to rest, she's injured."

"She injured in soul," Reka replied in English. "She must understand, she not fault for death of children."

Mrs. Clever nodded. "When she feels better, she will understand. After all, it's nonsense. The girl had nothing to do with the train accident. I will tell the reverend to talk to Miss Fitzpatrick, after she's slept for a while." She turned to Aroha. "Come, my dear, drink this." She held up a cup of clear liquid. "The doctor says this will give you good dreams."

Aroha obediently took the laudanum and immediately felt a pleasant tiredness seeping through her. But she didn't have good dreams. Her dreams were about Matiu, Haki, Purahi, and the tribe. They all pronounced her guilty, and they didn't tire of repeating Aputa's curse.

# Chapter 6

Franz Lange took the first train to the Rimutaka Incline. When they'd first received a telegram from Greytown, Linda had wanted to go. In fact, she wouldn't even have waited for the train; she would have ridden to Wairarapa on horseback. But Franz was able to talk her out of it. For one thing, the trail that wound its way through the mountains was long and dangerous. Traveling on horseback would have taken her at least two days, and in the end, she would have arrived after the train. Besides, Reverend Lange might be able to appease the Maori, who were blaming the *pakeha* for the loss of their children—especially Aroha and the Greytown reverend.

*Now, of course, they won't be sending their children to your school or my church,* the clergyman had written in his telegram. *Another generation growing up without faith or education.*

"I wonder which part he cares about more, faith or education?" Linda remarked. "And I can understand the Maori point of view quite well. Of course they won't be trusting anyone with their children right now. You should probably wait until next year to try to talk to them about school, if at all. At least wait until they've grieved and everyone is thinking clearly again."

Franz shared her opinion for the most part, but he didn't want to disappoint the reverend.

"It says quite clearly that Aroha isn't in danger," he reassured his wife. "Of course she's sad and distraught after what happened. And aside from that, she was very fond of Matiu, as we all were. It might help his family if I tell them that again, and we should hold a prayer meeting for him as well. It might just get the Maori back into the church."

Linda had her doubts, but she decided not to contradict her husband. Sometimes Franz still clung to unrealistic notions. Back when he'd come to Rata Station from Australia, he'd been living in his own little world. The sanctimonious community he'd grown up in had shaped him, and in the beginning, he'd been an annoyance to everyone at the farm. Later, though, Franz had changed. Working with the Maori children and living with Linda had transformed the inflexible fanatic into a friendly, moderate Christian who was able to invoke a certain level of understanding for almost all kinds of human error and bedlam. In practice, he almost always did the right thing—no matter how exalted his former dreams had been.

"Fine, you go, but bring Aroha home as quickly as you can," Linda said finally. "She needs her mother now."

Franz found Aroha at the reverend's house in Greytown. Pale and distant, she was sitting in the clergyman's guest room, staring out the window at the mountains. The house was located on the top of a hill, and the view was beautiful. It had snowed the night before. Franz would never have admitted it, but it had taken all the courage his faith could give him to brave the train ride in that weather. The wooded mountain ridge looked as though it had been sprinkled with powdered sugar. Aroha, however, didn't seem to notice. Her gaze was misty, and her movements were slower than usual as she turned around in her chair to face Franz. Her arm was in a sling, fixed to her chest with bandages.

"Matiu's dead," she said quietly, as if Franz hadn't heard. "And the children. It's all my fault, I—"

"That's nonsense, Aroha! What are you talking about?" her adoptive father exclaimed.

The reverend had told him that some Maori people blamed Aroha for the accident, but it hadn't occurred to him that she might be taking their accusations seriously.

"At least she's talking now," the reverend's wife remarked from the doorway. "First words she's said since she came here. And she's barely eating. All she does is stare out the window. Poor thing, it's like she's frozen."

Franz heard her, but he only had eyes for his daughter. He approached her. "The reverend and I are planning a prayer meeting for Matiu," he said. "And for the other children. This afternoon. We'll pray for their souls, beseech the Lord for his help—"

"What help?" Aroha asked in a hollow voice. "It's too late, they're dead. God should have done something earlier, before Rangi could cut the ties . . . But God doesn't want people to love each other. Maybe all the gods want to punish us; maybe they were all against us."

Franz frowned. He was about to make a sharp retort, but then he followed the instinct of kindness that Linda had so painstakingly cultivated in him. He pulled Aroha into his arms gently.

"Child, what scattered thoughts you have," he admonished her, but in a kind tone. "Of course God has nothing against people loving each other. On the contrary, Jesus even wants us to love our enemies."

"Our enemies, but not Matiu!" Aroha sobbed suddenly. "You and the others kept saying we were too young. You said we should take it slow with love. And we waited, and we were chaste, but . . ."

She bit her lip. She and Matiu hadn't been all that chaste. Would God hold that against them? Since the accident, all Aroha could think about was blame.

"Child, none of this has anything to do with the train accident." Franz Lange was starting to realize that Linda was right. It might have been better for her to pick up this poor, miserable creature that their cheerful daughter had become. "Aroha, we should go shopping now," he said finally. "You can't attend Mass dressed as you are."

Aroha was wearing a dress that was much too big for her. Her traveling clothes had been ruined, and her luggage had been lost when the train derailed.

"I don't need anything," Aroha mumbled. "And I don't want to go to Mass, I . . ."

Franz pulled her upright, his jaw set in determination. "Of course you're going," he said sternly. "And you're coming home with me tomorrow. It's best if you forget about all of this as soon as you can."

Some time later, Aroha found herself wearing a black dress and a warm black coat as the two reverends welcomed the community in the Greytown church. The reverend's wife was seated next to her. Reka sat on Aroha's other side; she was the only Maori representative who had come.

"Ngaio wanted to come too, but she isn't feeling well. She's casting spells for Koria, because her spirit is still in the mountains where the train derailed. Ngaio and the other *tohunga* will help her find her way back to us. But it is tiring, and Ngaio is exhausted. We also had to perform cleansing ceremonies for the *tiki wananga* that Aputa desecrated. And we're saying *karakia* for Aputa herself. And for you, daughter. You're holding Matiu's spirit prisoner. You must let him go."

Aroha grimaced. "Yes, first he held me, and now I hold him," she shot back. "We'll see if the spirits can cut this string as easily!"

Her eyes flashed with genuine intensity for the first time since the accident. Reka got the message: Aroha was prepared to challenge the gods.

"No god or spirit can cut that tie," she told the girl gently. "You must do it yourself."

Reka lowered her eyes as the reverend's indignant glare came to rest on her. He was already intoning the first prayers, and the churchgoers were supposed to remain silent.

Of course, Franz Lange kept his promise of calling on the Ngati Kahungunu before going back to Otaki. He agreed with Reka, who had expressly asked Aroha to join them. The tribe was grieving, but aside from Aputa and Purahi's mother, nobody was blaming Aroha. However, Aroha declined the invitation vehemently.

Franz spoke to the chieftain and the tribal elders, but he was unable to sway the Ngati Kahungunu council. They would not be sending any children to his school. But they gladly accepted his suggestion of a memorial service for Matiu and the children. Franz gave a moving speech that was less about God and more about Matiu's happy childhood in Otaki. In the end, Matiu's relatives, at least, seemed to feel somewhat comforted. Ngaio presented him with a jade pendant in the shape of a small deity for Aroha to wear.

"I know you not want daughter to wear *hei tiki*. *Pakeha* only want cross. But is good for soul."

"It good memory of Matiu!" Reka agreed in English. She knew the old *tohunga* was trying to appease the gods that were watching over Aroha, but it wouldn't have been prudent to explain it to the reverend like that. "And gift from tribe, from grandmother. Then Aroha know we not angry."

Franz swallowed his objections and, that evening, handed the heathen fetish over to his daughter. Aroha contemplated it for a long time.

"Sky and earth . . . ," she murmured.

When Franz examined it more closely, he was able to make out two tiny figures in a tight embrace. Papa and Rangi, the earth goddess and sky god, who had to be separated to create the world of man.

Franz mumbled something about superstition while Aroha silently put the *hei tiki* around her neck. Franz didn't say anything more; he had other worries at the moment. He had been planning to travel back home the very next morning, but Aroha was absolutely refusing to take the train.

"I can't do it!" she whispered. "You have to understand, Revi Fransi, I can't! I'm never getting on a train again."

"Then you must stay here until spring," Franz declared staunchly. "Yes, I know, we could go on horseback, but it would be madness in this weather. We might be surprised by snowfall, we might get lost . . ." And besides, Franz thought, he wasn't a great rider. He knew how to drive teams of heavy work-horses, but holding himself steady on a saddle horse for hours on end was torture. And he certainly wouldn't have dared to guide a potentially unsteady horse across difficult terrain. Still, Franz wouldn't leave Aroha here with the reverend; she wouldn't have stayed anyway. He could see the wheels turning in her head as she went over her options. "Maybe the doctor can give you another sedative before the journey," he suggested half-heartedly.

Franz didn't approve of the fact that the reverend's wife gave his daughter a teaspoon of laudanum every night so the girl could sleep. But to get Aroha back home, anything would do.

Aroha finally gave in to necessity, but she refused to be sedated during the trip. She boarded the train, deathly pale but composed. This time, the day was windless and rainy. As she gave Greytown a last glance, all she saw was a sleepy town shrouded in clouds. There was little else to remind her of her last journey with Matiu. Franz placed his hand on top of Aroha's as they left the station. Her fingers clenched tightly around his. Just before the Siberia Curve, she closed her hand around her *hei tiki*. Franz wasn't about to forbid her from doing so, but he said a prayer for the victims and had her speak the Lord's Prayer with him when they reached the scene of the accident. The conductor blew the locomotive's whistle to honor the dead, and Aroha jumped at the shrill sound. She didn't look out the window—though Franz had made sure on the way there that there was nothing left to see. The carriages had been hoisted back onto the tracks, and the wounded and the dead had been recovered. Snow and rain had washed away the remaining blood. The Siberia Curve was now just a hairpin turn like many others on the route.

Aroha relaxed a little after the train left the scene of the accident behind and rattled into the Siberia Tunnel. Franz watched her slowly remove the *hei tiki* from around her neck, carefully place it in a small leather pouch, and stow it in her bag.

He never saw her wear the little pendant again.

# Chapter 7

"What if we just send her somewhere else for a while?"

As usual in the last few weeks, Linda was watching her daughter with concern. While the other children horsed around in the common rooms, played, and did their homework, Aroha only sat at the window and stared listlessly out at the meeting ground, which looked dusty in the autumn sunlight. A few of the children were playing rugby there, but Aroha didn't seem to be interested in the game. She stared into space, lost in dark thoughts.

It had been more than six months since the girl's return from Wairarapa. Aroha's injuries had long since healed, but the wound in her soul was deep. No matter how hard Linda tried to cheer up her daughter, or at least distract her, it didn't work. Aroha mechanically did the chores that Linda assigned, though she preferred working in the kitchen or doing laundry to working directly with the children. She answered questions only with yes or no, and whenever left to herself, she brooded without any sign of interest in the world outside her head.

"Send her somewhere else?" Franz repeated. He was tightening the screws on a gas lamp. Repairs, great and small, were among his favorite leisure activities. "Where could she go? She's not going to get on a train again, you know that as well as I do."

Train travel was the reason Linda's attempt to distract her daughter with a trip to see Karl and Ida Jensch that summer had failed. In the past, Aroha had been very happy to visit them in Russell. She loved the sea.

"I was thinking of Rata Station," Linda said. "She wouldn't need to travel by train. You could bring us to Wellington with the wagon, and then we could take a ship directly to Lyttelton Harbor."

Franz smiled at his wife. "And you'd also like to visit your sister and mother, I bet?" It was still difficult for Franz to think of Cat Rata as Linda's mother. For a long time he'd believed Linda was the daughter of his own sister, Ida—and therefore, his niece. Their relationship almost didn't happen; he never would have courted such a close relative. "You can go anytime you want, with or without Aroha."

Linda rolled her eyes. "This isn't about me," she said, "even though I'd be extremely happy to accompany her. You'll be fine here without me for a while. But Aroha has to start thinking about something else. She could make herself useful at Rata Station. She could help with the sheep, ride horses . . . and she'd have people her own age for company."

Franz's brow creased, and he glanced at the children in the common room.

"Is she lonely here?" he asked. "Does she have nothing to do? Linda, just half a year ago, she was busy every day doing something useful. It's only since the accident that she's been like this. Maybe we just have to try to engage her more, and be stricter with her . . ."

He sounded unconvinced of his last suggestion. After all, it wasn't as though Aroha were disobeying them in any way. There was nothing to punish her for, and the truth was, her constant grief tore at Franz's heart just as much as it did his wife's.

Linda shook her head. "Franz, of course there are plenty of children around her here. But she thinks of them as too young to be friends. After all, she was in a class with the students Matiu's age. They've all gone off to college now."

The Langes had tried to encourage Aroha to attend the University of Wellington. She was still very young, but there had been an opportunity for her to share a dormitory room with an older friend, Pai. Aroha had declined. Without Matiu, she wasn't interested in Wellington anymore. She was also afraid of bringing bad luck to Pai.

"She always used to enjoy taking care of the younger children," Franz said.

Linda sighed. "She doesn't trust herself enough anymore. You saw that yesterday. She didn't even want to go swimming with the little girls. She was afraid they would drown! She told me that in all seriousness, even though those kids swim like fish. And that pond in the woods isn't more than three feet deep. If she has to do anything with the children, she almost dies of fright."

"And that wouldn't also be the case with horses and sheep?" Franz asked, shaking his head. "It's all pure nonsense, Lindy! The death of those children from Wairarapa wasn't her fault, and Matiu's death certainly wasn't either. She's having delusions—"

"Which she obviously isn't getting over, here!" Linda exclaimed. "As long as she is surrounded by Maori children whose parents have entrusted them to us, she will keep reliving the scene before the train departed. She'll keep remembering how she reassured Haki and Purahi's parents that nothing could happen to their children. And then the accusations by Haki's mother . . . I can't even imagine how hard it would be for her after the vacation, when new children arrive."

Every year, Maori parents brought their children to the school in Otaki themselves and asked anxious questions, just as Aputa had. And every year, Linda and Franz spent hours trying to comfort them. For Aroha, it would be pure torture.

"Perhaps she'd feel less nervous with *pakeha* children," Linda said. "And sheep and horses really shouldn't be a problem. Aroha has always enjoyed working with the animals at the farm. What's more, she'd be out in the fresh air. She'd worry less, and she'd be tired in the evenings and sleep better. She's still taking so much laudanum, Franz! And she still has bad dreams almost every night. It can't go on like this. Let's just try Rata Station. If that doesn't help, then we'll have to think of something else. But it's better than doing nothing."

Aroha accepted her parents' decision without argument. She'd already spent her vacations at Rata Station twice, and had always enjoyed herself. Now she didn't feel any excitement at the prospect of going there, but at least she wasn't scared. To the contrary. At least at Rata Station, no one would ask her to take care of any Maori children. Of course, there were *pakeha* children there. Linda's half sister Carol and Carol's husband, Bill, had two boys and two girls between the ages of two and ten. March, the daughter of Aroha's aunt Mara, and Robin, Aroha's uncle, were about six months younger than she was. Robin was younger than Aroha because Linda's mother, Cat, had gotten pregnant again when she was over forty.

While Aroha spent the last few days before their departure drowning in her personal grief, Linda was anxious to go. She had high hopes for their stay at Rata Station, and Carol shared her opinion. A change of scene would do Aroha good.

*We have a very nice mare here, ready for Aroha to ride,* Carol wrote. *She's very gentle. There's nothing that helps to distract one better than a good horse!*

Linda felt that way herself. She had grown up on the farm with Carol, and the sisters had even run the business together for a while. They had always found working with the animals very satisfying, and she still kept a horse for riding— even though Franz complained that it was a luxury.

Finally, Linda helped her daughter pack. That was another thing that wouldn't have been necessary in the past. Before her trip to Wairarapa, Aroha had thought for days about what she wanted to take with her, and what gifts she should bring for Matiu's relatives. Now she watched apathetically as Linda made choices for her.

"On the farm you'll mostly need riding clothes, but you should bring one or two nice outfits anyway," she told her daughter, and put a blue tea dress decorated with lace into the suitcase. Aroha hadn't touched it since the accident.

"What I'm wearing is enough," Aroha replied.

Linda pressed her lips together. For a long time after her return, Aroha had worn nothing but the black dress Franz bought for her in Greytown. When Linda finally put her foot down, she'd slipped into a gray skirt and a white blouse without caring enough to fight. In the boring outfit Aroha was wearing that day, she looked like a middle-aged teacher.

"Those clothes aren't warm enough," Linda said. "It's cooler on the South Island than you think. Besides, you look like your own grandmother dressed like that—not to insult Mamaca, of course. She would never dress in such an old-fashioned way!"

Catherine Rata, whom everyone called Cat, wasn't particularly fashion savvy, but she certainly didn't dress like an old woman. She usually wore riding habits, but as a wealthy sheep baroness, she also owned elegant clothes for visits to the city and appearances at social events.

Aroha made no objection. When it was time to begin their journey to the South Island, she obediently put on the burgundy-colored riding habit Linda had laid out for her.

Franz gave one of his older students the job of driving the pair of horses that would bring the two women to town. The wagon wasn't terribly comfortable. Actually, it was nothing more than an old hay wagon with benches affixed to it. It could hold ten to twenty children at a time, and also transport heavy loads. Linda and Aroha were thoroughly jounced, but at least the trip wasn't long. In the years following the Taranaki Wars, the roads between Otaki and Wellington had been properly finished. Entire armies of soldiers and military settlers had passed that way. The roads were even good enough for the heavy vehicles that were used to transport supplies.

Linda spent the time telling her listless daughter and their attentive young chauffeur how it used to look there. The forests that the road passed through had been dense and dark when the land still belonged to various North Island Maori tribes. Back then, the natives had been able to hide there from the *pakeha* for months on end without their forts or villages being discovered. Nowadays, the forests surrounding the Wellington region were quite a bit thinner. Much wood had been needed for the many new *pakeha* settlements along the road. The Maori had been relocated. There were no longer any *maraes* close to the capital city.

Then the road turned and led along the coast, and Linda enjoyed the view over the cliffs and the beaches. Aroha, of course, didn't notice any of it.

Linda had planned to spend the night at a good hotel, and she was excited for the chance to amble through the streets of Wellington and enjoy the shops. Aroha's change from her usual outfit had encouraged her. Perhaps the girl would consider accepting some new clothes. But her daughter only shook her head, and Linda felt a stab of helpless anger. For a moment, she considered forcing Aroha, but then she decided not to pursue the matter, and they continued to the harbor. On the trip from Lyttelton to Rata Station, they would be going through Christchurch. Perhaps Aroha would be more open to change by that point. What was more, Linda was anxious to get the sea crossing over with as quickly as possible. After all, her experience with ships was much like Aroha's with trains.

Years ago, Linda and Carol had been aboard the brig *General Lee* when it sank. They were on the way to a wedding in Fiordland with Cat and Chris when a storm drove the ship far from its intended course and into a reef. After many days in a lifeboat, Linda and Carol were rescued. But Cat and Chris had been stranded on one of the Auckland Islands. They survived there for over two and a half years, while Carol and Linda thought they were dead and were forced to fight to keep Rata Station.

Ever since then, Linda had hardly dared to set foot on a ship. It was a great sacrifice for her to not just take the ferry to Blenheim and then the train to Christchurch, but instead for Aroha's sake to make the much longer sea voyage to Lyttelton.

As she boarded the ship with her daughter, Linda pulled herself together so she could at least stay on deck long enough to wave goodbye to their young chauffeur. Then she quickly withdrew to the cabin.

Aroha gazed flatly at the North Island. For her, there was nothing left there that was worth bidding farewell to. But then, when the land was out of sight and the ship began to dance over the waves of the Cook Strait, Aroha began to feel more at ease. She was about to retire to the cabin when the wind came up and tugged at the bands of her hat. Since the train accident, she'd hated wind and always sought shelter whenever she heard so much as a rustle in the trees. But now a light breeze was blowing, totally unlike the terrible storm that had derailed the train. Aroha realized that she was enjoying the caress of the breeze on her skin, as well as the spray that rose up when the bow of the ship plunged against the waves. She took off her hat and held her face to the sun. And then she saw a flash of silver. Dolphins! Excitedly, the girl peered into the water at the lively animals accompanying the ship with wild leaps. For the first time in many months, she wasn't thinking about Matiu.

But soon she began to feel guilty again and went to find her mother. As expected, Linda was looking rather green in their cabin. The strong waves in the Cook Strait had made her seasick, and not even Aroha's report of the dolphins could cheer her up. Aroha was forced to take care of her, and didn't have any more time for brooding.

When evening fell and her mother had finally fallen asleep, Aroha went up on deck again. Of course, it wasn't really proper for a girl to go alone, but she needed fresh air. As she kept an eye out for dolphins, Aroha thought about Linda and Carol's experience with the *General Lee*. She wondered if the sisters had ever felt guilty about that. But what could two eighteen-year-old girls have done to prevent a ship from sinking? Just as little as Aroha could have done to prevent the train accident.

The thoughts shot through Aroha's mind before she could block them, the way she usually did. Her parents had been trying for months to convince her she couldn't have done anything to save Haki, Purahi, or Matiu. Even the public authorities' official investigation of the accident had determined that no one had been at fault.

Aroha rubbed her temples. The memories of the accident were still terrible, but the weight on her heart seemed suddenly lighter.

For the first time, she was able to sleep that night without sedating herself. Linda would have had more need of the laudanum.

# Chapter 8

The next day, the sea had calmed a little. Linda was feeling better, too, although she preferred to stay holed up in her bunk.

"Nothing's going to happen, Mama," Aroha told her. She felt hungry—that was new too—and she wanted to go up to the dining hall for breakfast. Linda had booked a first-class passage, although Franz disapproved and had said it was wasteful. But Linda received a regular payment from Rata Station that allowed her to indulge occasionally. Besides, she felt that having her own cabin to retreat to during a sea voyage was no luxury but an absolute necessity. "We're sailing along the coastline; you can see the shore when you're on deck," Aroha was explaining.

"We could see the shore from the *General Lee*, too, but then we were suddenly blown miles and miles off course." Linda took a deep breath. "I'm sorry, dear, there's no way you'll be able to get me excited about sea travel again in this lifetime. I just keep getting dizzy, no matter how many times you tell me the sea's calm right now. Still, I'm glad you're developing an appetite. I'll have them bring some breakfast to the cabin."

Aroha wolfed down some eggs and toast with marmalade, and then went up on deck with her mother's blessing. Time seemed to fly by. The ship had traversed the Cook Strait during the night and was now sailing south. The South Island's coastline was stunning, rough cliffs alternating with bright and dark beaches. There were old abandoned whaling stations and tidy little settlements to see as well. These were all *pakeha* settlements, Aroha noted, torn between relief and guilt. Here, at least, no Maori had been driven out of their villages. The South Island had far fewer native settlers than the North Island. The mere two thousand Maori who had been living here during the arrivals of the English had arranged themselves quite well with the *pakeha*. There had been far fewer bloody conflicts here than in Aroha's homeland, which was, in part, surely due to the fact that there weren't as many different tribes here. The Ngai Tahu were the main tribe on the South Island. The respective *iwis* didn't fight among themselves, and they supported each other when confronted with the *pakeha*.

Sometime during the afternoon, their ship reached the quaint natural harbor of Lyttelton. It was quite a bit smaller than Aroha had expected of such an important harbor town. After all, practically all the immigrant ships that didn't come in through Dunedin docked there. Still, most of the immigrants only stayed for a night and then moved on to Christchurch, which was substantially larger. For this, they had to brave a mountain pass that had once been quite treacherous; now, there were well-established roads there as well. There was a team of horses from Rata Station waiting for Linda and Aroha at the harbor. Cat was sitting on the coach box and welcomed the new arrivals with a smile.

Aroha waved and caught herself smiling back. It was good to see her grandmother and the two sturdy bay mares again. Even they were part of the family. With a heavy heart, Linda had sent her first horse, a cob mare named Brianna, back to Rata Station when she got older, and Cat had used her for breeding on several occasions. Linda had received the first foal, and she still rode it. The other young horses lived in the stables at the farm. Brianna was still alive too; Aroha had learned to ride with her during past vacations.

As soon as Cat spotted Aroha, she hopped down. It seemed she was unsure whether she could leave the horses to their own devices while she approached her granddaughter. From afar, Catherine Rata's age was difficult to discern. She held herself upright and moved with fluid grace. The first few strands of white hair were still barely visible among the blonde. For her visit to "civilization," as she liked to say, she had pinned it up. More often than not, she simply let her hip-length hair tumble down her back, negligently tied in a ponytail with a leather band or held away from her face with a wide, Maori-style headband.

On this day, Cat was wearing an elegant, burgundy-colored riding habit that she could have worn to afternoon tea in town. She was probably planning to make a short stop in Christchurch. Rata Station was by the Waimakariri

River, quite a ways from the city. Perhaps Cat was even planning to spend the night there. Aroha was surprised to find herself intrigued by the thought. The North Island and all that had happened there was slowly fading from her mind. Of course, she still felt all the pain for Matiu and the children, but it no longer seemed to outweigh everything else.

Linda left her sanctuary in the hold as soon as the boat was securely docked. She asked a steward to bring their luggage ashore, then ran ahead, falling into her mother's arms.

"Mamaca! It's been so long!"

"Oh, much too long!"

Cat laughed and hugged Linda tighter. In fact, she'd visited her daughter just last year. Considering that they were sheep barons, Chris and Cat Fenroy were unusually fond of traveling. But of course they knew that Rata Station was in the best hands with Carol and Bill. And yet, Cat knew how much Linda must have been missing the farm and her family. Linda and Carol had been raised as twins although they only shared a father, and as a result, they were as close as sisters could be. Throughout their youth, they'd expected to stay at Rata Station together, or at least live on neighboring farms. Fate had intervened, and both women were very happy with their respective lives. But as much as Linda loved the North Island, the school, and her work with the children—she sometimes wished she could be a little closer to Rata Station.

"How's the farm doing? How's Brianna?" Her last question sounded a little anxious; the mare was almost thirty.

"She's enjoying her golden years," Cat said with a laugh. "She's got several great-grandchildren by now. And, Aroha, by the way, Carol's planning on giving Brianna's latest foal, Cressida, to you."

"Cressida?" Linda asked.

Her mare's ancestors had been Welsh Cobs from the famous stock at Kiward Station in the Canterbury Plains. Traditionally, their foals got Celtic names.

Cat shrugged. "Robin," she said. "You know how it is, whoever sees a foal first gets to name it. And Robin loves Shakespeare. If it had been a little stallion, he'd probably have named him Troilus."

"Well, lucky for Cressida!"

Linda was happy and relieved to see her mother so lively, but she was even happier to see the change in Aroha. Of course, she still wasn't quite the self-assured, lighthearted girl she'd been, but she seemed far less withdrawn than usual.

"Come now, we should leave soon," Cat was saying. "Unless you're completely famished, that is. Then I suppose we could find a pub here. But I'd prefer to go over the Bridle Path as soon as possible and then have dinner in Christchurch. Chris booked us a room at the Excelsior—it's the newest and fanciest hotel on the square. I can't wait to see it. We'll be meeting him there for dinner. He's dealing with something at the Sheep Breeders' Association."

"Jane?" Linda asked.

When there was trouble, she was quick to assume that her former neighbor Jane was responsible for it. Jane Te Rohi to Te Ingarihi, nee Beit, had come to Rata Station with Chris as his first wife. However, she'd fallen in love with Te Haitara, the local Maori tribe's chieftain, while Chris had fallen for Cat. The two of them had separated amicably. Years later, Te Haitara had believed himself to be married to Jane, whereas business-minded Jane had used her technically still-legal first marriage to claim ownership of Rata Station when Chris and Cat were shipwrecked. She'd driven Linda and Carol from the farm, and in doing so, triggered a terrible chain of events.

But that was a long time ago, and Jane happily managed business for Maori Station, a sheep farm run by Te Haitara's tribe. Another factor that ensured a good relationship with Rata Station was the marriage between Jane's son, Eru, and Carol's half sister Mara. Still, Linda hadn't managed to forgive Jane yet.

"No, not Jane," Cat replied. "It's more about various members' strange ideas about rabbit control." A few years back, the creatures had been introduced to New Zealand, and with no natural enemies, were threatening to become an actual infestation. "A few sheep barons want to introduce foxes and other predators to control the rabbits—with the hidden agenda, of course, of founding hunting societies. Chris is pretty wary of all this. But we don't have any problems with Jane. She's mellowed lately; she's becoming almost domestic and motherly . . ."

"Motherly?" Linda asked warily as she handed a tip to the steward, who was hefting their luggage onto Cat's cart.

"Almost, as I said," Cat replied. "Anyway, she's taking care of Mara's daughter now. March and Jane are inseparable. With that girl, it seems she's finally found somebody who shares her interests."

Jane Te Rohi to Te Ingarihi's loving husband had chosen her Maori name, which meant "English rose," much to Chris's amusement. Far from a delicate flower, she was a dedicated businesswoman. Adam Smith's theories of economics were her bible, and she was rather unchallenged by the task of overseeing their relatively small sheep farm. Originally, it had been her dream to expand her business under the leadership of her son, Eru, and everyone assumed that she'd also made investments in railroad construction. Theoretically, she and her descendants could have ruled over a small empire. But Eru had turned his back on his mother and on *pakeha* dealings quite dramatically. A *moko* master had turned his face into a piece of art—in the eyes of the Maori, at least. To most *pakeha*, it just looked terrifying. There was no way a man with such tattoos could assume a leading role in business.

"Well, young March seems to enjoy arithmetic," Cat continued. "And she's been doing business from a very young age. She thoroughly fleeced Robin years ago when she bargained for some of his marbles. You'd think she was Jane's granddaughter by blood."

In fact, she wasn't. Eru was raising March as his own, but she was the result of his wife having been raped by a Maori warrior. Te Ori had kidnapped Mara during the Taranaki Wars and held her as a slave for several months. Eru, who had loved Mara since they were young, had finally freed her.

"What about the boy?" Linda asked. Mara and Eru also had a son, Arapeta.

"Oh, Peta's taking after Eru," Cat said calmly, "except he isn't really a traditionalist. He's more *pakeha* than Maori. But he's practical and likes to help with the sheep. He's a very nice boy. And he doesn't seem rebellious; he tolerates Jane's attempts at raising him. She wants to hire a private teacher for him and March now, someone to teach them the essentials of economics. As if she hasn't done that herself! Besides, March has already mastered the art. She was so sweet, offering to take over the bookkeeping of Rata Station for Chris—"

Linda smiled. "Only to then relay all the numbers to her grandmother, accurate to three decimal places."

Cat nodded grimly. "We have nothing to hide," she said. "It's just the deceitfulness that bothers me. Mara should really be keeping an eye on that. Jane has far too much influence on the girl."

"Mara isn't paying attention?" Linda said, frowning.

In the past, Mara had been a lively girl with a keen eye for detail who never missed anything happening on either of the farms.

Cat shook her head. "Mara mostly plays the flute. These days, Maori all over the country see her as a *tohunga*, and sometimes people come from far away to study with her. She enjoys teaching the children of the tribe—and Robin. He's also a diligent flute player, although without any kind of talent. It drives Chris up the wall." Cat smiled. "But other than that, Mara isn't doing much. She lives in seclusion; it's almost as though she and Eru are all each other need. Eru doesn't like going out either. Jane used to pick on him at sheep breeders' conventions sometimes. And he really knows a lot about the animals. But he hates running the social gauntlet. People stare at him like . . . like . . ."

Cat sighed. There had barely been any riots on the South Island, but of course people in Christchurch knew about the havoc the tattooed warriors of the Hauhau movement had wreaked on the North Island. That was why the *pakeha* mistrusted anybody adorned with the traditional *moko*—especially on the South Island, where the Maori hardly ever had tattoos anymore. Since Eru didn't wear his *moko* with pride, as he had in the beginning, but instead was ashamed of what he'd done in his youth, he preferred to avoid encounters with white people.

"Mara's become quite reclusive too," Cat went on. "It's not that she doesn't love her children. When they were little, she was very tender with them. But now she's a little . . . well . . . withdrawn from earthly concerns."

Linda had hoped that fierce Mara had put her abduction and abuse behind her. But now she could also see in Aroha how profoundly traumatic experiences could change a person.

Aroha climbed up on the coach box.

"Why don't you drive?" Cat suggested.

She knew that Aroha was capable; the girl also drove Franz's team of draft horses. But these mares were a lot livelier. Linda's heart leaped for joy when she saw her daughter nod.

Aroha skillfully drove the team of horses across the pass, and Linda felt a warm sense of homecoming as she gazed down from the highest point at Christchurch across the broad vastness of the Canterbury Plains. Grazing land, only occasionally interrupted by rivers, streams, small forests, and rock formations, stretched from here to the Southern Alps. Linda thought of the thousands of sheep grazing on the South Island. She was looking forward to being at Rata Station soon.

First, however, came Cat's visit to "civilization," and their night at the sumptuous new Hotel Excelsior. Cat had grown up in meager circumstances—first at the whaling station, and then at a *marae*. She was able to survive under the most primitive of conditions, but deep down, she had a soft spot for luxury. Upon their arrival in Christchurch, she retreated to her room to get changed, and she recommended that Linda and Aroha take a warm bath before dinner.

"Spoil yourselves a little. We'll be back to a simpler life at the farm soon!" she told them, laughing.

Linda didn't need to be told twice. Her log cabin in Otaki offered few comforts—the community kitchen had running water now, but for her own bathing, Linda still had to carry the water herself or ask a few of the older students to fetch some for her. For that reason, she rarely took baths—in summer, she washed in a pond that was part of local Maori land in the nearby forest, as the Maori children did. Franz was always very worried that some notables from Otaki might catch his wife there while she splashed around naked.

Now, she ran a bath for herself while Aroha rooted through her suitcase in a strange mood somewhere between exhaustion and restlessness. The hotel was so elegant . . . The thought of not having anything appropriate to wear made her uncomfortable. Finally, she put on her blue tea dress and tried not to think of how much Matiu had admired her in it when she'd worn it to their graduation ceremony.

When the pair went downstairs an hour later, they found Chris Fenroy in the lobby waiting for Cat.

"Aroha, look at you; you've become such a beauty!" her step-grandfather said in greeting. "The tomboy's turned into a real young lady. Can you still ride, or will you have them row you over to the Butlers' for tea now?"

Linda laughed at his teasing words. The Butlers, who ran a farm farther up the Waimakariri, placed great importance on formality. Deborah Butler's tea parties were famous—and infamous.

Aroha gave Chris a mischievous look—Linda thought she could see a sparkle in her eye for the first time since Matiu's death.

"I prefer coffee," she retorted. "And I'm looking forward to meeting my horse, although I'm finding it hard to remember her name."

Chris grimaced. His laughter lines made the expression look a bit wrinkled—years of farm work in the sun and rain had aged him more obviously than Cat. Still, Chris Fenroy was good-looking. His thick hair, which he still wore longer than the current fashion, fell casually around his face when he moved. His hazel eyes shone as bright as ever, and his joy at seeing his stepdaughter Linda and his "granddaughter" again made him practically glow from within.

"Now, don't tell Robin," he confided, "but we've been calling her Sissy. Dorothy started it because she couldn't pronounce Cressida, and Carol thought the name was fitting."

Dorothy was the elder of Carol and Bill's two daughters, and she was four years old. Linda's sister had given birth to two boys, and then two girls.

Linda was about to ask him about the children, but then Cat appeared on the stairs. She was wearing an elegant, loose-fitting dress, and the eyes of all the hotel patrons were riveted on her. Cat didn't pay them any heed. She was used to it, although their interest wasn't focused solely on her extraordinary beauty at the moment, but on the cut of her dress, as well. Cat abhorred corsets and had taken to wearing reform dresses lately. For dinner that evening, she was wearing a gold-colored silk robe with long, wide sleeves embroidered with red blossoms.

"Rata blossoms," Chris said with a smile. "The dress is from a seamstress in Dunedin; it's beautiful . . . And just between us, it cost a fortune. But let's not think about that tonight."

He chivalrously held out his arm to her, offered the other to Linda, and led the three women toward the spacious dining room, which was decorated with golden chandeliers and velvet curtains. It took them a while to get there. Several people approached the Fenroys as they crossed the lobby. As sheep barons, they were well known among the high society of Christchurch, and some of the guests remembered Linda as well. They asked her polite questions about her life on the North Island and congratulated her on her pretty daughter. Linda could see that Aroha was a little embarrassed. She seemed lost in all the luxury.

Finally, the Fenroys were led to an elaborately set table, and they all studied their menus, which were hand printed on fine paper. Linda felt sorry for Aroha; she was the only young person among so many distinguished-looking adults.

"Didn't Robin want to come?" she asked Cat and Chris. "Aroha could have had some company."

Cat shook her head. "No. Robin doesn't care for fancy dinners. He would have accompanied us if we'd decided to attend a play afterward. And that would have been too late for me. Besides, I'm more interested in talking to my daughter than lamenting the love and loss of some Shakespeare protagonist. Not that the plays aren't . . . enjoyable."

By her pinched expression, Linda gathered that Cat wasn't very fond of Shakespeare. She didn't know much about plays herself. Neither Cat and Chris nor Ida and Karl had ever taken their daughters to the theater. During the building phase of Rata Station, they'd had other things to think about—and back then, Christchurch hadn't had much to offer in the way of culture, anyway. That had certainly changed now.

"Oh, don't pretend that you enjoy the bard of Stratford-upon-Avon," Chris teased his wife. "She'd never admit it, Lindy, but plays bore her to death. I can see it in her eyes that she's counting sheep while the main characters drool over each other on the stage . . ."

"The same is probably true for the other sheep barons too," Linda said with a laugh. "I can't imagine the Redwoods or the Deans family in tuxedos or evening gowns in a theater either. Maybe the Butlers. Although the captain—"

"Captain Butler made his money as a whaler," Chris said. "He's no aesthete. Still, when there's a famous theater company in town, they all come to Christchurch like the virtuous people they are. It's all about seeing and being seen, isn't it? We're high society in the plains." Chris puffed up his chest, and Cat and Linda laughed.

Aroha was picking at her shrimp cocktail. It tasted good, albeit unfamiliar. She didn't have much to say about Shakespeare. She'd read a few of his plays in school, and she'd been to the theater in Wellington with her class once. They'd seen *Uncle Tom's Cabin*, by Harriet Beecher Stowe.

"So Robin was upset that you didn't want to go see a play tonight?" Linda inquired cautiously.

Cat shook her head. "Not upset, exactly," she replied. "Robin has plenty of patience for the ignorant people around him." She laughed self-consciously. "And the theaters in Christchurch aren't famous enough to warrant him worrying about missing all that much. He only suggested it, and when we didn't take him up on the idea, he opted to stay home. He's making himself useful, at least."

Chris snorted. Linda's stepfather seemed to be of a different opinion regarding the work her half brother Robin did at the farm. She decided it might be prudent to change the subject. She was enjoying the ambience as well as the wine and the exquisite food. She certainly didn't want to ruin Cat and Chris's evening by pressing a difficult subject.

"Well, we'll see him tomorrow," she said.

# Chapter 9

Cat seized the opportunity to go shopping with Aroha and Linda the next morning. She knew that Franz was painfully frugal, and Linda found it difficult to spend money on nice clothes. She always said she never had a chance to wear such things in Otaki anyway. Cat almost had to force her to accept an elegant dark-blue ensemble and two white blouses to go with it, but finally Linda couldn't resist either and bought a matching hat for herself. It wasn't a boring everyday hat, but a delightful little creation with feathers and tulle.

Linda was pleased with her purchase, but it made her even happier that Aroha had tried on a few of the new reform dresses. She wasn't only paying more attention to her reflection in the mirror than she had for the past six months, but even reacting to her appearance with amazement. She finally chose an aqua-blue dress with a printed flower pattern. It was still much more reserved than the dresses she'd worn before Matiu's death, but at least it wasn't black.

Toward noon, the women met Chris again and continued to Rata Station. Linda was surprised by the good condition of the road that led along the Waimakariri River. Before, it had only been possible to reach the farm in one day from Christchurch by boat, but now there was plenty of space for the horses to trot. They decided to take a short break at the Deans farm, and were received warmly. After a snack, they continued quickly through the plains, and Linda happily lost herself in the views of her old homeland, with its gleaming river and endless sea of tussock grass. She commented knowledgeably about the condition of the sheep that grazed by the side of the road. They arrived at the farm as the sun was setting.

"Just in time for dinner!" Carol exclaimed. She had come running out of the house as soon as she heard the wagon. Her clothes smelled of freshly baked bread. She hadn't even paused to take off her apron. She was carrying her youngest daughter, two-year-old Irene. She handed the child to Aroha before warmly embracing Linda. "Here, isn't she sweet?"

Aroha, visibly shaken, accepted the child. She really was extremely sweet. Irene had blonde curls like her mother. Carol's other daughter, Dorothy, had dark hair. Carol had always said that Dorothy took after her mother, Ida, although her husband, Bill's, hair was also dark.

"You look good," Linda said with pleasure, when she got the chance to step back and take in her half sister.

Carol was still slender in spite of having given birth to four children. Her skin was slightly more weathered than Linda's, the result of long hours working under the open sky. There were also a few more crow's feet at the corners of her eyes. But otherwise, the two women could still be mistaken for twins. Carol, too, had eyes that were slightly too close together, very full lips, and blonde hair that was difficult for her to tame. She had bound it loosely in a bun at the nape of her neck, from which it was escaping. It made her seem younger than Linda. The reverend's wife preferred a tidy appearance.

"Come on in before everything gets cold," Carol said, ushering them inside after hugging Aroha, who had passed the patient toddler to Linda. "I cooked for all of you. You only have to bring the wine, Mamaca."

She winked at Linda. Cat enjoyed her wine very much, and always had a good supply. She'd surely taken the opportunity to stock up in Christchurch.

Chris passed the horses' reins to a groom who was working in the stables, and then helped Cat take her shopping into their own house, which was nearby.

Afterward, they joined Carol and her family. In the conservatory, a long table had been set. The Paxtons lived in the large stone house that Chris had once built for himself and Jane, and the big family had finally filled the structure with life. Chris and Cat preferred their simple log cabin. Chris and Jane had lived there while the stone house was being built, and later, Cat had chosen it for herself. In the first years of their relationship, she had insisted on living there alone. Chris had only been allowed to visit her. However, after a while they hadn't been able to keep away from each other, and when Carol married Bill and Cat was finally talked into marrying Chris, they had permanently moved into the smaller, cozier house together.

"The conservatory is a recent addition, isn't it?" Linda asked as Carol assigned seats at the long table to her children. The two boys, Henry and Tony, sat across from Linda and Aroha, and little Dorothy climbed onto a chair next to her mother with a serious expression on her face. Irene sat on Carol's lap.

Carol nodded cheerfully. "Yes. Bill enclosed the veranda with glass, so we could still sit 'outside' in colder weather. It's nice, isn't it? And so practical. I can see everything that's going on in the farmyard, even if I'm stuck in here with the little ones."

She frowned slightly. These days, Linda was the more domestic of the two sisters. Carol preferred to work with sheep and sheepdogs. Even now, two young border collies that she had been training were frolicking around her feet. But with four children, she had a lot of housework, and maids and nannies were difficult to find. Carol could have trained a local girl, but she lacked the motivation.

*If I have to teach a girl everything she has to know first,* she'd thought, *then I might as well do it all myself.* Instead, she was raising her sons to help her in the house.

"Are we ready?" Linda asked as she helped Carol to carry in the food. The smell of the roast lamb and sweet-potato casserole made her mouth water. Chris opened the first bottle of wine.

Carol glanced at the table. "Robin's not here yet," she said, not sounding particularly surprised. "He must have forgotten the time again." She glanced at her children, apparently considering who was least likely to get lost if sent to get Robin. Finally, she turned to her niece. "Go tell him dinner's ready, Aroha. He must be in the barn feeding his lambs."

Chris frowned. Taking care of orphaned lambs was usually the job of the farmer's wife. A fourteen-year-old boy offering to do it was unusual, to say the least.

Aroha stood up willingly. She was hungry, but also eager for another quick look at Sissy. Cat had shown her the mare for a moment on the way in, and Aroha was completely enchanted by the heart-shaped blaze on her forehead and her large eyes with long lashes. Like all of Brianna's foals, she was a bay, brown with a black mane and tail. But did she also have white socks? Aroha quickly snatched a piece of Carol's fresh bread and made her way outside.

As always, the peace in the barn did her good. The horses and cows chewed their hay, and every now and then one of the animals snorted gently. Two of them made noises of welcome as Aroha stepped inside. At first, she couldn't see Robin anywhere, but Sissy gazed at Aroha and accepted the treat from her hand with her soft lips. Aroha whispered a few endearments, and then stopped to listen. She heard a sound like someone casting spells or invoking spirits. Aroha stroked Sissy's broad forehead one more time, and then curiously crept closer to the source of the sound, only to be captivated by a soft, melodic voice that seemed to be overflowing with all the passion in the world.

*"It is my lady. Oh, it is my love. Oh, that she knew she were! She speaks, yet she says nothing. What of that? Her eye discourses. I will answer it . . ."*

Aroha peeked around the edge of the stall and saw Robin, who was standing behind a bale of hay, staring longingly at a fat, tricolored barn cat.

*"I am too bold. 'Tis not to me she speaks. Two of the fairest stars in all the heaven, having some business, do entreat her eyes to twinkle in their spheres till they return."*

The cat blinked lazily at the boy. She seemed to be listening carefully but also finding the entire thing quite dubious. Aroha was examining her young uncle more carefully now. During her last visit, Robin had still been quite childlike, but now he was much more grown-up. He was tall and very thin, almost fragile. His curly, platinum hair played around a slender, expressive face like a glowing cloud. The twilight in the barn made his paleness look ethereal.

*"What if her eyes were there, they in her head? The brightness of her cheek would shame those stars as daylight doth a lamp . . ."*

The glow in Robin's eyes bathed the cat in warmth and love. Aroha couldn't see their color in the dim light, but she thought she remembered that they were brown, like Cat's. The expression on his face was almost supernatural. She decided to let the boy know she was there.

"Good evening, Robin," she said. "I didn't know you were so fond of cats."

Robin started in shock, then smiled warmly when he recognized his niece. They'd always gotten along well.

"Good evening, Aroha, how nice that you're here. And yes, I do like cats. Don't you?"

"Yes, of course, but not like—"

Aroha stopped herself and bit her lip. When Robin saw her expression, an amused smile lit up his face.

"Ah! That must have looked strange. You must think I'm crazy, but I was just practicing. That was *Romeo and Juliet*, act two, scene two. He sees Juliet at the window and speaks a monologue. It's just easier if you look at someone." He pointed to the cat, which was stretching.

Now Aroha remembered why she knew those lines. "You mean . . . that was your Juliet?" she asked in amazement, watching the cat leaving. It seemed to have had enough of human company.

Robin nodded.

"Oh, my goodness, you were gazing at that creature as though you were actually in love with it!"

"I was trying to, at least," Robin said modestly. "That's the whole point. Romeo loves Juliet, and that's how he looks at her. But I don't have to direct it to a cat," he said. "For example, I could look at you instead." He smiled again. "That would be even better; after all, you could answer me! You could read Juliet's lines."

Aroha's heart tightened. At first, she'd been distracted by the strangeness of the moment, but now more memories were surfacing. She'd read *Romeo and Juliet* in school, and the students had laughed and insisted that Matiu and Aroha read the lovers' lines. She could almost still hear Matiu's unsure recitation. The boy had been completely embarrassed. And yet . . .

"No!" Aroha cried. "No, I can't . . ."

She felt her eyes fill with tears, and quickly rubbed them away. She didn't want Robin to see. But the boy looked at her seriously and bit his lip.

"Have I upset you? Oh, I'm so stupid, I'm sorry! It reminds you of your boyfriend, doesn't it? The boy who . . . who died in the accident?"

Robin came closer, and seemed to be considering whether he should put his arms around her. He decided against it. Aroha sighed with relief. She still couldn't stand such closeness.

"I'm sorry," Robin said again. "Really."

Aroha had heard those words often. People said them automatically after a tragedy. But Robin seemed sincere. His eyes widened as if he actually felt her pain.

"Thank you," she said woodenly.

Robin rubbed his nose. He seemed younger again.

"If there's anything I can do . . ." he murmured. "I know how it—I mean, I try to understand . . ."

And then Robin's expression changed again. Once more, the boy became Romeo, the tragic lover, who now gazed uncomprehendingly at the corpse of his beloved.

*"For here lies Juliet, and her beauty makes this vault a feasting presence full of light . . ."* The boy stopped quoting and thought for a moment. "For fear of it I will never leave thee, and never stray again from the palaces of the darkest night . . ." he improvised.

Aroha could hardly believe it. Shakespeare's words, and Robin's, expressed precisely what she had been feeling for so many months.

Robin continued. "I drink to you, wherever you are."

Aroha could no longer hold back her tears.

Robin's face fell. "I didn't mean to make it worse, Aroha, I really didn't. It's just—you woke the words in me, I—Oh, I must be crazy." He smiled. "At least my father says so. You were sent to call me for dinner, weren't you? I always forget. It's just that things are so peaceful here at this time of day. It's ideal for practicing. The farmhands are eating too now, and no one usually comes out."

"Only Juliet," Aroha said, laughing through her tears. She pointed at the cat, which was now curled up in the corner of a stall.

Robin grinned. "Sometimes I talk to horses," he admitted. "Or brooms. But I prefer living creatures."

"What about the lambs?"

Aroha saw a pen where three wooly little animals were sleeping.

A wistful expression crossed Robin's face. "I like lambs," he said, sounding slightly bitter. "But it seems that caring for little things is all it takes to ruin one's reputation. The herders keep calling me 'girly.'"

Aroha smiled at him. "They should hear you pouring your heart out to Juliet. Then the thought wouldn't even occur to them. Especially if you ever play the part with a real girl instead of a lamb."

Robin grinned at her. "A lamb really couldn't be my Juliet," he said. "Even my powers of imagination don't stretch that far. After all, the silly babies would either interrupt me with their bleating or wander away."

A little later, they were all sitting at the table. Aroha helped herself to a large portion of roast lamb, while Robin regarded the platter with distaste and only took a tiny piece when Carol insisted for the second time. It was very clear that he didn't want to eat it. Aroha almost felt guilty.

Chris, though, seemed impatient. "Eat properly, Robin! You're far too thin. What will become of you if you don't eat meat?"

Robin didn't answer, but obediently filled his mouth and chewed with obvious disgust.

"Oh, leave him alone," Cat said. "Just have more of the casserole, Robin. It's got plenty of cheese on top. That will fatten you up too." She smiled indulgently at her son, and then her gaze wandered to Linda. "Robin doesn't like meat. We have to accept that." The last words seemed to be intended for her husband rather than her daughter.

Linda nodded. She hadn't noticed what her half brother was eating, but now she began to observe Robin. She couldn't help but admire his graceful movements. Robin had excellent table manners. He was an obvious contrast to Carol's lively children, who waved their forks in the air and talked all the time with their mouths full. Robin only spoke when he was spoken to. Aroha engaged him in conversation a few times, but Linda couldn't hear what they were saying because she was sitting at the other end of the table, surrounded by the noisy children. Robin seemed to be answering politely and kindly, and kept smiling at Aroha. It was obvious he liked her. But would the grieving girl be open to a real friendship? Did the two of them have anything in common? Linda felt a vague kind of sympathy for the young man. It was very clear that he didn't fit in on the farm.

After dinner, she broached the subject of Robin. The small children had gone to bed, and Aroha, Robin, Chris, and Bill had retired to their rooms, as well. Cat opened a bottle of wine for herself, Linda, and Carol. The three of them enjoyed it together in the conservatory. It was an unusually warm autumn evening, and they had the French doors wide open. The moon was glowing in the sky over the Waimakariri, and the water shimmered silver.

Cat sighed and took a sip of wine. "Oh, Robin is a good boy, but he's definitely a different type."

"He was always very sensitive," Carol added. "With the sheep, for example. When he was little, I once found him standing next to the shed during the shearing, crying. He thought the shearers were handling the sheep too roughly, and he said they were afraid."

"I thought he'd grow out of that kind of thing," Cat said. "But it's actually getting worse. Once he watched Chris slaughter a chicken, and he didn't speak to him for three days. I don't think it was to punish him . . . I think he just couldn't get a word out because he was so shocked. Since then he's hardly eaten any meat. He wouldn't eat any at all if we left him to his own devices. Chris and Carol insist on it."

They could tell by Cat's tone that she didn't approve. She'd grown up with the Maori, and had adopted their ways of child-rearing. It went against her instincts to force a child to do something.

"You can't just let him get away with every bit of nonsense," Carol said in protest. "Mamaca, he lives in another world, and that isn't good for him."

Cat sighed again. "He's just different," she explained. "He wants to be an actor. He told me that his greatest wish is to play Hamlet someday. If I've understood correctly, Hamlet is a prince who speaks to the spirits. We saw a performance in Christchurch, but I couldn't make heads or tails of it. And Robin also told me all about *A Midsummer Night's Dream*. Playing Puck is another dream of his. And *Romeo and Juliet* . . . I think Gibson told me and Ida that story around the campfire when we were on our way from Nelson to the Plains."

The journey with Ida, her first husband, Ottfried, and his friend Joe Gibson, who'd had some higher education, was the only time Cat had encountered literature growing up.

"Robin could play Puck," Linda said. She sometimes taught at the school, and had read most of Shakespeare's best-known plays. "He's a fairy, isn't he?" She smiled. "Could it be that Robin is a changeling, Mamaca? Could he have been exchanged for a fairy child while he lay in the cradle? He doesn't look like you or me, or even like Chris."

Cat laughed somewhat bitterly. "Chris also said something of the kind once," she replied. "Except he was thinking more along the lines of me having been led astray by a selkie. You know, one of the seal people, like in that Scottish song. There were lots of seals on Rose Island."

Cat had gotten pregnant with Robin while she and Chris were castaways after the *General Lee* sank, and his parentage was completely without question. She laughed, but then her face turned unexpectedly serious. She gazed out over the farm and river with a melancholy expression before she continued. "He looks like Suzanne. I can't remember her face exactly anymore, but her platinum hair, her pale skin, her delicate bone structure . . . it's Robin."

"Suzanne?" Linda asked. The name rang a bell, but she wasn't sure in what context.

"Suzanne was my mother," Cat explained. "Have I really never told you about her?"

She refilled all three glasses.

"You've mentioned her," Carol said. "But rarely, and your descriptions were . . . well, meager, at best."

"We don't know anything about where Suzanne came from or what she was like," Linda added. The sisters gazed at Cat expectantly.

Cat shrugged. "There's not much to tell," she said. "I'm sorry to say this, but I think there wasn't much left of Suzanne's sanity or the person she originally was by the time I was born. How else could she have not even given me a name? She'd been destroyed by whiskey and men . . . She barely noticed that I was there. The other whores—" Cat stopped herself. "There were two other women at the whaling station who sold themselves. Both of them talked to me occasionally, tossed me a bit of bread or gave me a sip of milk. Just like a stray kitten. That's what they called me. Kitten. But Suzanne looked right through me. Actually, she looked right through everyone. She—she lived in another world." Cat's voice broke when she realized that Carol had just said the same thing about her son. "I only know that she was beautiful," she said finally. "She was completely disturbed, but she was still beautiful."

Linda and Carol drank their wine in silence, neither wanting to make uncomfortable comparisons between Suzanne and Robin. Cat had only known Suzanne as an empty shell, but originally, she must have been very sensitive, and susceptible to addiction. And there must have been a reason Suzanne had lost herself so completely. She needed protection, and she didn't get any.

Linda laid a hand on her mother's arm. She understood. Cat was extremely worried about her son.

# Chapter 10

"Why shouldn't Robin become an actor?" Aroha asked her grandmother in a tone of voice that bordered on scolding. That morning, Cat had asked for her impression of Robin as they'd visited Brianna in the stables together, and Aroha had told her about Robin's performance in the barn—which preyed on her conscience, since Robin's recitations were supposed to be a secret. But she'd had only nice things to say about him; surely he wouldn't blame her for mentioning it. "He sounded quite convincing to me," she continued. "It was almost a little eerie. One moment he was Robin, and the next he was Romeo. Maybe that's how it has to be for actors. I mean . . . it wasn't like that for anybody in my class when we read the play in school." She swallowed. Matiu had recited, but he had always just been Matiu.

Aroha was now working with Sissy for the first time, and her grandmother was helping her. They'd been lunging the horse in a ring. The mare was already saddled and had been very patient about it. Now, they led her back to the stables, contented.

Frowning, Cat brushed away a strand of hair that had come loose from her ponytail. "You say that as though we would be against him acting," she said. "And I'm sure Robin thinks we would be too. But that's not the case. As far as I'm concerned, he can become whatever he wants to be, and Chris isn't stopping him either. Even though Robin confuses him, he's Chris's son, and he loves him very much. We don't need an heir for the farm either," she said, smiling. "Even if you're not interested, which I doubt, seeing how skillfully you handle the animals."

Aroha gently stroked Sissy's neck and beamed at the praise.

"Carol's children are following in her footsteps marvelously," Cat continued. "The boys are already helping more than Robin probably ever will. They're working with such a passion. So if Robin decides he wants to do something other than breeding sheep, we're fine with that. We know how to support him if he wants to be a doctor or a veterinarian, or—um—a reverend . . ." Cat didn't seem quite comfortable with the latter. "But an actor? How would he begin? Robin mentioned a school in Europe once where they teach music, dancing, and acting. But even if that school were to accept him . . . he may be a talented actor, but he's not at all musical. Honestly, I just feel so reluctant, sending a boy like Robin to Europe on his own." Cat almost confessed to Aroha that she didn't think he was self-assured enough for such an undertaking, but she caught herself. That wasn't a fear to share with a fourteen-year-old girl, especially one who might convey her words to Robin later. "He's just too young," she finished.

"And besides," Cat complained to Linda later, "I have a bad feeling about that whole theater life." She obviously felt that she had to justify herself. Aroha's little reproach had bothered her, and she didn't want Linda to think poorly of her and Chris.

"I don't know any actors personally, but as I told you, we're usually invited when there's some company performing in Christchurch. We'll often go, if only because Robin urges us to. There's usually a reception for distinguished community members. We all get to shake hands with those luminous stage figures. It hits Robin so hard that he can't get out a word for days afterward. But to me, all those people . . . Well, they seem self-centered to me. Very, very conceited, and it seems that there are rivalries too. If you ask me, those companies are like a sea full of sharks. I doubt that Robin would be able to handle all that."

Linda shrugged. Inwardly, she agreed with her mother. She didn't see Robin as a fighter.

"Maybe you could prepare him for it," she said. "You could send him to high school, for example, instead of giving him a private tutor. It would get him away from home; he'd make some new friends. He might not learn how to recite Shakespeare correctly, but he'd learn how to assert himself more."

Cat was finishing up the dishes with Linda's help. Mother and daughter had had a quick cup of coffee together before getting to work on the farm. On the first morning after their arrival, Linda had appeared in her riding habit, brimming with enthusiasm to take on her old responsibilities, and she immediately and seamlessly reintegrated herself into farm life. That way, she could give both Cat and Carol some relief, which in turn would give them more time to spend with Aroha.

"Lindy, we've thought of that too, of course," Cat replied a little too forcefully. "Especially since the education he's receiving at the moment isn't to his liking at all. If he's artistically inclined, it would make sense to teach him that way. It doesn't have to be acting. He might have a talent for painting or writing, even writing plays. Unfortunately, the teachers Jane hired don't have a feeling for it. Arithmetic—or mathematics, as it's called now—bookkeeping, economics . . . even their history lessons seem to be mostly about the development of new markets. And it just keeps getting worse. Jane's expecting a young economist from Edinburgh; March is so excited. The man studied at the same university where Adam Smith used to teach, or so the two of them keep boasting."

"All the more reason Robin would benefit from a school of his own choosing," Linda said, feeling vindicated.

Cat raised her eyebrows and smiled bitterly. "But he won't go, Linda. He pretends he can't wait to study political economics—Lord knows what that's supposed to be. You see, there's another passion in Robin's life other than acting. And unlike William Shakespeare, she's mercurial, beautiful, and well on her way to becoming a little shrew, just like Jane Te Rohi to Te Ingarihi: her name is March Catherine Jensch."

Linda dropped into a chair, the dishtowel still in her hand. "Mara's daughter."

Cat nodded. "He's hopelessly in love with her."


"So why won't you come to Dunedin, then?" Robin asked, gazing desperately at March. Aroha had accompanied her young uncle down to the Maori village to visit March and her half brother Peta. She'd been watching Robin in uncomprehending fascination as the calm, friendly boy transformed into a blushing, nervous wreck. It had taken him forever to get up the nerve to invite March and Peta along. "They're performing *Hamlet*. And it's the Bandmann-Beaudet Company. We might never get a chance to see them again!"

March, who was trim and petite, rolled her eyes. Beautiful eyes, Aroha had to admit. She'd never seen anyone with such luminous, azure-blue eyes before. They were prominent in her heart-shaped face with its glowing golden-brown complexion. March was wearing traditional Maori garb—a long skirt and a revealing woven top.

"But we already saw *Hamlet*," she reminded Robin. "In Christchurch. And I thought it was pretty boring."

"Well, you were only twelve," Robin objected. "Maybe you didn't fully understand it back then. And besides, you can see *Hamlet* twice, or three times, or . . . well, every actor plays it differently."

March frowned, her smooth forehead creasing. "I don't care how it's played, it's still always the same stupid story. The main character sees ghosts and swears to avenge his father, but doesn't manage to do anything. Just one jab with a sword, and it could all be over with. But no. Once Hamlet's finally able to pull himself together, he gets the wrong man!"

March shook her head, making her thick, jet-black, hip-length hair sway back and forth. Aroha thought to herself that March might not believe in ghosts, but surely, all the fairies of the court had been present at her cradle when beauty was being distributed. Not to mention her physique . . . March already had very feminine curves, as opposed to Aroha, who was three-quarters of a year older than she was.

Robin watched the girl in agony. "It's a tragedy," he said. "A long, fateful story. Hamlet—well, he's insecure, he suffers, he's let down by his mother and his friends. He—"

"I've seen it," March repeated. "And I don't need to see it twice."

"You could go shopping in Dunedin," Peta interjected. Unlike March, who looked both *pakeha* and Maori, twelve-year-old Peta took after his Maori father and grandfather. His eyes were green like his father, Eru's. The boy was very tall for his age and quite stocky. "You keep saying you need new clothes." Peta gave her an innocent smile.

"Granny Jane's taking me to Christchurch to go shopping before Mr. Porter arrives," March told him, composed.

Aroha wondered if she was trying to torment Robin.

"Christchurch isn't the same as Dunedin," Peta said. "Aren't you always going on about how the city's so much more sophisticated?"

Originally, Dunedin had been a fairly parochial town, having been founded by strictly religious Scotsmen. But many things had changed there during the gold rush. Over the last few years, upscale stores had moved in.

March considered this. "What about you? Are you coming?" she asked Aroha. "We could go shopping together, just us girls. That'd be fun!"

"I'd love to go shopping with you too," Robin said eagerly.

March shot him a withering glance that suggested she had her reservations about his sanity. A boy who voluntarily offered to go shopping with two girls? Aroha thought he was overdoing it, no matter how keen he was on convincing March to come along. Other than that, she concluded that March wasn't tormenting Robin on purpose. She simply didn't understand the boy's feelings for her. Peta, however, hadn't missed the signs. He'd skillfully set out his bait. Now Aroha just needed to play along . . .

"I—I don't know," she replied. "I'd like to go to Dunedin, I've never been there. And I like theater." She turned to Robin. "I just don't want to go by train."

March frowned. "You don't want to go by train? I've never heard of such a thing. And it doesn't really matter if you like it or not, does it? You can get almost anywhere quickly by train, and there's no need for taking care of horses and all that."

Aroha blushed. "I . . ."

"Aroha's been through some bad experiences," Robin explained. "I can completely understand why she'd be afraid."

"Afraid?" March asked. "Oh, right, that accident. I'm so sorry, I hadn't thought about it. But not taking the train anymore? You can't be serious, Aroha! Yes, what happened was awful, but the odds of something like that happening again are virtually zero. Statistically."

"What?" Aroha gave her an uncomprehending look.

"Statistics. Calculations of probability," March repeated. "Haven't you ever heard of them? Listen, do you know how many railroad lines there are in New Zealand? There's the South Line and the North Line, North Island Main Trunk . . ." She counted them all off on her fingers. "Every day there are . . . oh, I don't know, three or four trains passing those routes. That means hundreds of passengers in a day, and thousands in a year. And how many accidents do we know of that happened in the last few years? One! Besides, it was a new and famously dangerous line, under extremely harsh conditions too.

Weren't the wind speeds over a hundred miles an hour?" Now March seemed to remember the circumstances of the accident surprisingly clearly. "Now, if you compare one fluke accident to all those trips without incident, and if you add external circumstances to the calculation, you'll get a probability of zero-point-zero-something percent that such a thing would ever happen to you again in your lifetime."

Aroha bit her lower lip. "But . . . what if I'm cursed?" she asked quietly.

March rolled her eyes and threw up her hands.

"This just keeps getting worse, Aroha," she said. "You don't really believe in curses, do you?"

"Maori people believe in them," Aroha murmured.

March nodded. "They certainly do," she said soberly. "But I know better. I did an experiment."

"You did what?" Robin and Aroha asked simultaneously.

Peta made a face like he'd just bitten into something sour. He seemed to know the story.

"Auntie Linda told Peta and me a story once," she said, "about that *tohunga* who used to live at the school with you."

"Omaka," Aroha said.

"It was about how Omaka cursed the girl who had her kauri tree destroyed. After that, I couldn't sleep because I was so afraid, but Granny Jane said that there are no ghosts, and that curses don't work. I think my mama disagrees. So, I decided to find out myself. I planted nine *kumara* plants. I cursed three of them, and sang *karakia* and prayed for another three, like you're supposed to." Cat, who had grown up with the custom, still sang *karakia* to her crops, and Linda sang them in school with the children. But ever the dutiful reverend's wife, she sang Christian songs as well. "I didn't do anything to the last three plants," March said.

"So?" Robin asked anxiously. "Which ones grew better?"

March giggled. "The cursed sweet potatoes gave the biggest harvest. And nobody got a stomachache from them. There wasn't a big difference between the others. Curses don't do any damage, and *karakia* doesn't work either."

"But you don't even know the right words!" Peta insisted. "Or did a *tohunga* teach you a *makutu*? You don't have enough *mana* for that kind of thing anyway.

You're just a simple girl. You have to be pretty powerful in order to curse somebody. In a way that works, at least."

March pursed her lips. "A curse is a curse," she contended. "But even if you're right . . . What sort of ancient *tohunga* with *mana* could Aroha have provoked so much that she'd curse her? Or her boyfriend?" She gave Aroha a provocative sidelong glance. "What did you do, Aroha? Did you burn a kauri tree in your fireplace? Did you demolish a sacred mountain?"

Aroha bit her lip again. "No, nothing like that," she said flatly.

"Of course you didn't!" March exclaimed. "And that's why nobody cursed you. You can relax about taking the train to Dunedin. There's no way it'll derail."

"And we'll be there with you too," Peta said. "Won't we, March?" He gave Aroha and his half sister an encouraging smile.

"Of course," March said.

She seemed to have completely forgotten about the fact that she'd been categorically refusing to go to Dunedin only moments ago. Normally, Aroha would have admired Peta's trick, but at the moment, she was still too busy coming to terms with her fears. It was not comforting to her that people she cared about were boarding a train with her. If anything, it made her fear worse.

Robin gently put a hand on her arm. "Nothing's going to happen," he said kindly. "Lightning doesn't strike the same tree twice."

Aroha nodded. She wanted to believe that with all her might.

# Chapter 11

The train journey was uneventful.

Not only did March and Peta come along, but Carol and Bill did also. They were happy about the chance to get away from farm work for a little while, even if they weren't very interested in attending the theater. Linda would have been very pleased to go; she had never been inside one of the famous theaters. However, she'd had to return to Otaki early. She was needed at the school. Aroha's decision to take the train to Dunedin had made her much happier than going herself ever could have.

"She's finally getting past the accident," Linda said with relief as she bid farewell to Cat and Carol. "I can't tell you how grateful I am."


Of course, Aroha was far from being able to enjoy the train ride. She sat next to Robin, pale and nervous, and didn't say a word the entire trip. She didn't need to either. Robin, reveling in anticipation of the performance, regaled her with the complete history of the Bandmann-Beaudet Shakespeare Company and the careers of its stars, Daniel E. Bandmann and Louise Beaudet.

"He's from Germany, and she's French Canadian. In that sense, it's particularly special that they're able to bring Shakespeare's English to life with such prowess. It's quite difficult, after all."

When he began to compare modern and Elizabethan English using quotes from Shakespeare, March interrupted him. She'd noticed how silent and scared Aroha looked as she cowered in the corner of their compartment. Attempting to comfort her, March brought up the subject of train accidents again. This time, her theme was the economic viability of railway companies.

"If accidents were common, no one would ever invest in the railroads," she said. "Can you imagine what an incident like the one in the Siberia Curve must have cost the owners of the Rimutaka Incline Railway? Two passenger cars, a freight car, and personal damages. Did the parents of the Maori children get a settlement? They could have sued the company—"

Carol glanced with concern at Aroha, who seemed to be shrinking, and now had tears in her eyes. She decided to step in.

"March, those people lost their children. Do you think that money could make up for the loss of human life?"

March frowned. "The parents of the *pakeha* child that died must have gotten something," she replied. "Besides, *utu* is completely normal among the tribes. Of course money won't bring the children back. But that's no reason to turn it down."

*Utu* could mean the families of victims receiving a kind of payment as compensation for their loss, but it could also take the form of revenge.

Aroha suppressed a sob. She didn't want money for Matiu, and the Ngati Kahungunu wouldn't have considered it either.

They were all very relieved when the train finally arrived in Dunedin. The large, lively city quickly got Aroha's mind on other things. She put aside what March had said and enjoyed their shopping trip. March also showed her sharp tongue in the shops, and proved to be very talented at haggling. Carol was embarrassed when the girl asked for deals in even the most exclusive boutiques.

"My cousin and I are each buying two blouses. You must be able to give us some kind of discount."

Aroha, to the contrary, had been raised by the reverend to be frugal. She admired her cousin's bargaining skills. And truthfully, most of the shopkeepers seemed to enjoy negotiating with the beautiful girl.

"Only if you wear the dress tonight to the Queen's Theater," a shopkeeper said. "It looks so beautiful on you that everyone will ask who designed it."

The performance that evening had less of an effect on Aroha than the day in the city had. The dinner in the luxurious restaurant before the show, the champagne during the intermission, and the atmosphere of the theater impressed her much more than the play itself. All the gold leaf and elaborate decoration, the gigantic chandeliers, the heavy red-velvet curtains around the opera boxes, the huge paintings in the foyer, and the brightly decorated curtain that concealed the stage before it opened to reveal a view into Shakespeare's world . . . Aroha found the Queen's Theater overwhelmingly beautiful.

Peta seemed to think so too. He too caressed the velvet-covered seats in the parterre and hardly dared to fold the program, which was printed on heavy, creamy paper, but then finally put it into the pocket of his new dinner jacket.

March, however, never let on that anything impressed her. She did look gorgeous in the new aqua silk gown, which tumbled around her body like ocean waves. But she seemed to notice the interested looks of audience members just as little as she had Robin's gleaming eyes when she walked down the stairs into the hotel lobby in full regalia. She was completely aloof. Aroha caught herself wondering if March wasn't busy calculating how much money could be made from such a performance, and how much profit would remain after one balanced it with the costs for the upkeep of the building.

Robin seemed not to notice any of the luxury surrounding the performance. Once he'd entered the theater, he didn't even have eyes for March anymore. The platinum-blond boy was now clearly anticipating the appearance of the actors, especially his idol, Bandmann. When the curtain finally rose, he hung on Hamlet's every word, totally enchanted. Aroha wondered if he knew all Hamlet's lines before they were spoken. Recently she had listened to him more and more often in the barn. Robin knew a great deal of the plays by heart.

Aroha did find the story unexpectedly exciting. The play seemed much more alive when the actors were reciting their lines on the stage than when one simply read it aloud from a book. But basically, she had to agree with March about the plot. The Danish prince might have prevented his great tragedy if he'd brooded a little less and thought more logically. Matiu had said something similar about *Romeo and Juliet* back in school: the whole thing wouldn't have ended so tragically if Romeo had just been a little more sensible. Aroha liked it better when stories had a happy ending, but of course she clapped enthusiastically with the rest of the audience during the curtain call.

Robin's eyes burned with a supernatural light. She wondered if he was imagining himself standing where Daniel Bandmann and Louise Beaudet were, as they repeatedly took bows and accepted flowers and congratulations.

"I didn't like it any more today than I did last year," March said pointedly as the curtain finally closed for the last time, and the audience began to file out of their seats.

"The sword fights were great," Peta said, probably to spare Robin's feelings. Aroha had seen him yawning several times during the show.

"What shall we do now?" Carol asked her husband cheerfully. "Shall we treat ourselves to a glass of champagne at the hotel?" She was obviously happy to have the performance behind her too. "Only for the adults, of course. You sweet young things should go to bed."

Robin stared at her. "You want to leave already?" he asked. "But I—I mean, since we're here, I'd love to get autographs from Bandmann and Beaudet."

"Get what?" Carol asked.

"Autographs," Robin repeated. "Signatures. As a memento of the evening. I want to ask Mr. Bandmann and Miss Beaudet to sign my program."

"How are you going to do that?" Bill asked. "The actors are finished, they want to go home." He, too, seemed eager to be done with the theater.

"We can wait by the stage door," Robin explained. "Until they come out. That might take a while, because they have to take off their makeup and change, and everything."

Carol furrowed her brow. "I don't know," she said. "Isn't that an imposition? Bill is right, they're done for the night. They surely have no desire—"

"But that's how it works. It's part of the whole thing," Robin insisted, sounding desperate. "Every actor gives autographs. They like to do it. Really!" His face gleamed with enthusiasm. "Please! Please, I—I have to see them close-up."

Carol sighed and wrapped her shawl more tightly around her shoulders. It had been a pleasant autumn day, but now, late in the evening, it was getting cold.

"If your happiness depends on it so much, I suppose we shall have to be patient. Hopefully Miss Beaudet is not one of those women who need three hours to change."

Robin wasn't the only one waiting at the stage door. There were actually ten or twenty, mostly younger people, crowded around the hidden door at the back of the building. They were all holding their programs, or little bound books, and had pens ready.

Daniel Bandmann and Louise Beaudet put their fans' patience to a hard test, but after a long wait, rewarded them with a generous appearance. Louise wore an elegant blue ensemble with a wide collar, combined with a fresh little hat from which her unbound red curls were escaping. Her round face was quite pale, as with most redheads. She had expressive brown eyes and a small, very clearly defined mouth. Now she was smiling graciously.

Robin had been right. Both Miss Beaudet and Mr. Bandmann were more than happy to give their fans autographs. Mr. Bandmann in particular seemed to enjoy the attention. But away from the spotlight, he was much less impressive. Aroha had wondered during the performance if he wasn't far too old to be playing young Hamlet. Now it was clear that he was. His hairline was receding, his eyes very close together, his nose sharp, and his lips oddly full. Aroha had imagined Hamlet, and especially Romeo, to look different.

The young theater enthusiasts seemed not to mind. They all gathered around and complimented the actors, and one or two of the courageous ones even exchanged a few words with them. Aroha noticed a girl, who looked only a little older than herself, blushing and speaking German to Mr. Bandmann. The actor answered in his native language, surprised, and also very kindly. Aroha saw him write a dedication on her program. *Der reizenden Miss Morris mit großem Respekt—Daniel E. Bandmann.* To the lovely Miss Morris, with great respect.

The delighted girl turned to Miss Beaudet next. To Aroha's amazement, she now spoke to her in fluent French. The result was another personal dedication, which Aroha couldn't read this time. Aside from Maori, Aroha also spoke decent German, which she'd learned from Franz, but she'd only been taught a little French in high school. Her knowledge didn't stretch beyond what she'd had to memorize for her tests. Now Aroha thought it was a pity. But at least she saw her chance to help the nervous Robin make an impression on Mr. Bandmann.

"My relative is a great admirer of Mr. Shakespeare and yourself," she said to the actor in German as Robin held out his program, dumbstruck. "He'd like to become an actor himself."

Mr. Bandmann made the effort to focus on the girl who was speaking to him, as well as the young man in question. *"Und was unternehmen Sie, mein Sohn, um diesen Traum in die Tat umzusetzen?"*

When Robin looked to Aroha for help, the actor repeated his words in English. "And what are you doing to make your dream come true, young man?"

"I'd like to attend a theater school," Robin replied quickly. "Unfortunately, there isn't one here."

Bandmann nodded. "There are very few altogether," he confirmed. "Which is a pity. But one academy is actually highly recommendable. Try the Guildhall School of Music and Drama. It was recently opened in London." Then the actor turned away; after all, many other fans were waiting.

Both Robin and Miss Morris excitedly approached the other performers who were just stepping out of the stage door. Aroha recognized the actors who'd played Laertes and Polonius. Robin got in the line before Carol and the others could stop him. His passion for the chase had been awakened. Aroha stood at his side, bored, and found herself next to the linguistically talented girl again. Miss Morris was short and a little plump. She'd eschewed a corset, and instead wore a loose reform dress. Bright blonde hair peeked out from under her fashionable little hat, and her face was dominated by alert light-blue eyes and sweet dimples. When she recognized Aroha, the girl smiled.

"You were speaking German before, weren't you?" Miss Morris said in German. "One doesn't hear it very often in this area."

"My family has German roots," Aroha explained. She wasn't a blood relative of either Franz or Ida, but it would have been much too difficult to explain the details. "I picked some of it up."

In fact, Aroha was the only family member of her generation who could speak decent German, even though the language was still spoken often at their family reunions. Franz and Linda liked to use it to discuss things that weren't intended for children's ears. Of course, that had made it attractive to Aroha.

"What other languages can you speak?" Miss Morris asked.

The autograph signing was going slowly. "Laertes" was apparently rather enamored of himself and wrote long dedications to every one of his fans.

"By the way, my name is Isabella. Isabella Morris. I'm also learning Italian and Spanish." She smiled again.

"Aroha Fitzpatrick," Aroha said, introducing herself. She was more than impressed. This girl actually spoke four foreign languages! "Other than German, I can only really speak English," she said shyly. "And Maori."

"Maori?" the girl said in a loud squeak. Isabella lowered her voice when the people around her turned to look. "That's very unusual. Miss Vandermere would be thrilled. You can speak it fluently? Not just *kia ora* and *haere mai*?" Isabella clearly knew only a few words of Maori, but she pronounced them correctly, unlike most *pakeha*.

"Just as well as I speak English," Aroha replied proudly. She described the school in Otaki.

"That's so wonderful," Isabella said excitedly. "I'm studying languages. My headmistress, Miss Vandermere, would like to offer Maori classes, but she can't find a teacher."

As Robin approached Laertes, Bill glanced pointedly at his pocket watch, Carol shivered, and March loudly announced her annoyance. But Aroha was listening to her new friend with fascination.

Apparently, Henrietta Vandermere had been running a language academy in Dunedin for some time. She came from Philadelphia in the United States of America, and had taught at the Berlitz School there.

"Mr. Berlitz developed an entirely new method of teaching languages," Isabella said. "It's not like it used to be, dry and boring with grammar and translation exercises. Instead, you start to talk right away. It's very interesting, and it goes much more quickly. Miss Vandermere learned the method from him directly, and her school teaches using the same principles. It's a small place, with less than fifteen students. That's why my parents allow me to attend. Actually, I wanted to go to the university, but my father doesn't think that's appropriate for a girl." She giggled. "If it were up to my father, I would be married soon. But I'm not even thinking about it. There are so many interesting professions that are possible when one speaks different languages. Especially here in New Zealand, where there are so many immigrants."

"I'm not getting married either," Aroha said quietly.

Isabella smiled at her conspiratorially. "Then the school would be good for you too."


The next day, when the train set off from Dunedin toward Christchurch, Aroha was too excited to be scared. She kept examining the colorful brochure she'd received that morning at Miss Vandermere's Academy on Princess Street. Carol and Bill had willingly accompanied Aroha there. They were both impressed by the kind, distinguished headmistress; the modern, comfortable classrooms; and the lively multilingual atmosphere. Of course, Linda and Franz still had to approve, but Carol was ready to advocate for Aroha. The tuition fees were high, but Aroha would pay much less because she was prepared to teach Maori while she studied herself. The next semester began in July, and Miss Vandermere said she would be pleased to reserve a place for Aroha.

Robin, too, was in a good mood, but he didn't express it this time with excited recitations. He kept reliving his short conversation with Daniel Bandmann, which had not included the word "impossible." The great actor thought it was entirely reasonable that Robin wanted to follow in his footsteps. If he could only find a way to get to London!

To the rhythm of the moving train, Robin kept murmuring the words to himself as though invoking a spirit: "Guildhall School of Music and Drama, Guildhall School of Music and Drama . . ."

# Part 2

## BLESSING OR CURSE

### Otaki (North Island)

### July 1882–December 1884

# Chapter 12

"There are two ladies outside who want to visit."

Keke, a student doing gate duty that afternoon, announced the arrival of guests just as Linda was setting the table for coffee. Linda had a little free time while Franz's older students were in class and the younger ones were doing their homework. She'd been planning to use the hour for a cozy chat with Aroha before her daughter returned to the South Island the following morning.

Aroha had spent her winter vacation in Otaki after successfully completing her first two semesters at Miss Vandermere's language school. She hadn't come home for the summer vacation, but now she seemed to have gotten over the train accident. She was dealing with the loss of Matiu much better too. She hadn't heard anything from the Ngati Kahungunu for a long time. Aroha seemed to have forgotten Haki's mother's curse, or at least she was now able to see it for what it really was: an expression of desperation from a deeply grieving woman.

Aroha had affectionately taken care of the children who couldn't go home to their villages during the vacation, and had returned to her typical style of dressing in bright colors. Her friend Isabella Morris had surely contributed to her reawakened sense of fashion. When Aroha revealed her wish to study in Dunedin, accommodation had been the only bone of contention for Linda and Franz. Miss Vandermere's Academy didn't have any student dormitories, and they didn't want such a young girl to be living alone. Isabella Morris and her parents had provided a solution.

The girls had enthusiastically exchanged letters, and finally Mr. and Mrs. Morris offered to let Aroha live with them during the semester. They didn't want any money. Mr. Morris was a successful goldsmith and jeweler, and his shop in Otago had made the family rich. "I'd rather you invested the money in your school," he'd told Franz kindly. "I've done my research; your school has an excellent reputation. So as compensation, please take in another little student in my name."

Mrs. Morris turned out to be just as lovely as her husband and daughter, and Aroha felt very comfortable in the little family's townhouse. Isabella was her first real *pakeha* friend, and the girls had quite a lot of fun together, both in and out of school.

"What should I tell the ladies?" Keke asked when Linda didn't answer immediately.

"Ladies?" Aroha asked, entering the kitchen with a coffee pot and a plateful of fresh muffins.

The girl nodded enthusiastically. "Yes, English ladies. They came in a very elegant coach. I think it's from Triangle Station."

Linda's brow creased. Triangle Station was a nearby sheep farm. She knew the owner superficially. Like most of the farmers in the area, he made contributions to the school, usually in the form of goods. But the Langes hadn't had very much to do with the Beckhams. Captain Beckham had fought in the Taranaki Wars, and still had resentments against the native people. Unlike most of the other farmers, he didn't employ any Maori, not even if they spoke perfect English and had adopted *pakeha* manners. So far, Franz hadn't managed to find a job for any of his school's graduates at Triangle Station.

"Did they say what they wanted?" Linda asked.

She wasn't particularly inclined to entertain guests at the moment, but if people from Triangle Station were actually showing interest in the school, she would give them a tour.

"They were strange," Keke said. "First they spoke far too loudly to me, as though I were hard of hearing. Then they spoke very strange English." She frowned. "Here see Maori?" she said, imitating a squawking tone.

Linda sighed. "It sounds as though we'll have to take care of them," she said to her daughter. "Will you come with me, or do you still need to pack?"

Aroha shook her head. "I'm almost done," she said. "And besides, this sounds interesting. Two women who only speak broken English? Perhaps I can make myself useful." Aroha had been learning French and Italian at Miss Vandermere's, and could already express herself quite well in both languages.

The two women were middle-aged, and they were still sitting in their carriage. A bored-looking herder from Triangle Station was sitting on the coach box. With their pale complexions and reddish-blonde hair, the women looked typically English. They were wearing practical laced-up boots and travel ensembles, topped off by elegant hats.

Linda greeted them in English. "How can I help you?" she asked them.

One of the women nodded. She must have been around fifty years old, and had alert blue eyes. Her curly hair reminded Linda of a poodle.

"My brother, Captain Beckham, tells us that you have Maori here that we can look at. Is that true?" she asked in a crisp English accent.

Linda's eyebrows shot up. "This is a boarding school, Miss . . . Beckham."

"Mrs. Toeburton, please. And this is my sister-in-law, Mrs. Richardson."

She indicated the lady sitting next to her. Mrs. Richardson was taller and thinner, and seemed more suspicious than interested.

"Yes, Maori students live here," Linda said.

Mrs. Toeburton smiled. "Well, Peter told me that he's absolutely sure they're not dangerous." She turned to her sister-in-law. "So don't fret, Serena!" Then she addressed Linda and Aroha again. "You—you will show them to us, won't you?"

Linda found the conversation rather confusing, but agreed to give the women a tour of the school. She introduced her daughter.

Mrs. Toeburton looked thrilled. "You gave her a Maori name? How original! A charming idea, isn't it, Serena? Shall we—should Jack bring in the carriage, or shall we walk?"

"The grounds are quite extensive," Linda replied, "but if you want to see the classrooms and apprentice workshops and everything else, you'd best follow me on foot. Your driver can bring the carriage in and wait for you at the meeting ground."

She explained to the coachman where he should pick up his passengers later, and invited the ladies to climb down from the vehicle.

"Is it really safe?" Mrs. Richardson asked nervously.

"It's a school," Linda repeated, annoyed. Keke was right, these two ladies were more than strange. "That means perhaps you will be stared at by curious children, or a rugby ball might come flying at your head, just like in comparable institutions in England."

"Come now, Serena," Mrs. Toeburton said impatiently, and hopped out of the carriage.

She was plump, but very agile. Serena Richardson, who was just standing up, looked stiffer. But she didn't lag behind as Linda and Aroha began to walk quickly around the grounds.

Linda explained to her visitors that the school had originally been an old *pa*, a fort, which was abandoned by the Te Ati Awa. "The tribe inherited land in Taranaki, and the people decided to live there instead. They went of their own free will, and left their land to us. No one was driven away from here or killed. That's very important; otherwise the children wouldn't be comfortable. If blood has been shed somewhere, the land becomes *tapu*. At the beginning, many children came here who had personally experienced the terrors of war and displacement. In fact, the school was originally an orphanage."

As Linda talked, she led the women to the first buildings, which had been the meeting houses in the old fort. Now apprentice workshops and kitchens, they were teeming with life. In the afternoon, the students usually had practical subjects and sports. Franz was just harnessing a pair of draft horses to the school wagon, and Linda introduced the visitors to her husband. They greeted him without interest before following Linda and Aroha into the school's kitchen, where the children were baking under the supervision of a woman from the nearby village. The next house was a workshop. Girls sat at looms, and a young Maori man was teaching other children how to carve wood.

The children hardly took any notice of the guests. Linda and Franz showed people around the school relatively often. For the most part it was funded by donations, and the patrons wanted to see how their money was being used. Linda and Aroha occasionally praised or joked with the students, and most visitors also made a few friendly remarks. Mrs. Toeburton and Mrs. Richardson, however, remained silent.

Linda was glad to leave the workshops behind and proceed to the central area of the school. The classrooms were located in the old community houses, as were the student dormitories and the lodging for teachers who lived at the school.

"All of the dormitories are named after native animals," Aroha explained cheerfully. "For example, this is Kea House, and over there is Kiwi House. The children think the names are funny, and it helps them to feel at home here. Some of them come from very distant villages, and they can't all go home during vacation."

The two women nodded, looking unsurprised. If they were indeed from England, the workings of a boarding school would doubtless be familiar to them.

"In gym class, the children play rugby, soccer, and *ki-o-rahi*, a traditional game played with a ball made of woven flax," Linda continued. "We are careful that the children don't forget the customs of their people. As long as they don't go directly against Christian values, of course. My husband is a reverend of the Anglican Church. Our students are all christened."

Linda led the women through a few classrooms that were mostly empty, and into the common room, where younger students were doing their homework under the supervision of a young Maori woman. Linda briefly introduced the teacher. Pai had been one of the first students in Otaki, and Linda was extremely proud that she'd gone to college afterward.

Then she led the strange visitors from the room. The tour was over, and the coach from Triangle Station was waiting on the meeting ground. Franz joined them there. He had asked another teacher to look after his students so he could spend a little time with the guests. He knew from previous experience that potential patrons would appreciate that.

"Did you enjoy yourselves?" he asked kindly.

Mrs. Toeburton frowned a little. "Well, yes . . . of course. You're doubtlessly doing excellent work with the children here. It's just—well, we hadn't counted on the savages being so—civilized. We rather imagined they'd be dancing and swinging spears. And weren't the Maori even headhunters?" She shuddered.

Linda raised one eyebrow. "Well, if you wanted to see a *powhiri* with singing and dancing, you should have visited a Maori village, not a school," she said tartly. "And as for spear-swinging warriors, that is not a pleasant sight. Almost as unpleasant as decapitated heads. The wars have been over for a long time, for which we all must thank the Lord. Whatever gave you the idea that you could see displays of combat here, like at a theater?"

Mrs. Richardson pouted like a disappointed child. "The travel agent who organized our trip told us there were still savages in New Zealand, and it would be possible to see them. We heard they weren't nearly so shy anymore."

"Shy?" Linda echoed. "The members of the tribes were never shy. They aren't animals! They originally welcomed European immigrants very kindly. Later, there were land disputes that finally developed into military conflicts. Now that's over, but a certain level of mistrust remains. If I were you, I certainly wouldn't barge into some unsuspecting village and expect to be received with open arms."

Franz cleared his throat uncomfortably. "What brings you to New Zealand, anyway?"

"The terraces, of course!" Mrs. Toeburton exclaimed, as though she were speaking to a mentally inferior person. "The Pink and White Terraces. One has to see them. Ever since Prince Albert gushed about them, they've been an absolute must for any trip around the world."

"You're traveling around the world?" Aroha inquired, impressed.

Mrs. Richardson nodded. "Yes, child. Such a voyage is essential for members of the upper class." She sounded blasé.

"Yes, I suppose it must take extensive means," Linda said, shooting Franz an incredulous look. She'd read that, among rich Europeans, travel had become just as much of a status symbol as elaborate houses, gardens, and racehorses. The women's magazines she enjoyed were full of articles about such things. But so far, she had never heard of New Zealand being a favored destination.

"The Pink and White Terraces actually belong to a Maori tribe," Franz lectured. "The Tuhourangi." The reverend famously never forgot anything he'd read or heard. "I don't know very much about the people, as they've never sent one of their children to our school. They don't live here either, but in the north, and that's where those wonders of nature are too. It's over two hundred miles away, if I remember correctly."

"It seems you've gone astray," Aroha joked.

Her mother cast her a stern glance. "In any case, you still have quite a long journey ahead of you to Te Wairoa," Linda said, hinting that it was time to leave. "Perhaps you'll meet Maori on the way who live more traditionally." She didn't actually believe that. Along the bigger, more traveled roads, *pakeha* had settled almost everywhere. The Maori tribes that had survived Governor Grey's "relocations" during the Hauhau movement lived either deep in the forests or had largely assimilated. "But please, be polite to them. A *marae* is not a zoo."

Mrs. Toeburton and Mrs. Richardson looked indignant and rather uncomprehending. They doubtlessly had fine manners and were very polite to their peers, and also within limits to their servants. But toward the "savages"? Linda doubted it.

"What kind of people were those?" Franz said in amazement as he sat down with Linda and Aroha for coffee.

"Very ignorant ones!" Aroha exclaimed. "And dumb to boot. Mama told them three times that this is a school, and they were still expecting to see headhunters."

"That casts a strange light on English education. Although not totally out of keeping with my own experiences," Linda joked. Her disastrous first husband had boasted about having attended the best universities in England. "With graduates of Oxford and Cambridge, you really have to be ready for anything."

# Chapter 13

Although Aroha was now able to get on a train without fearing for her life, she took the ship from Wellington to Lyttelton again. She could have traveled to Dunedin directly, but she wanted to spend a few days at Rata Station first. Her mare, Cressida—out of respect for Robin, Aroha tried her best not to think of her only as Sissy—had become a reliable saddle horse.

Upon arrival in Lyttelton, Aroha was delighted see Cressida harnessed to the waiting coach. Robin was sitting on the wagon beside Cat. Aroha greeted her family and her horse lovingly, warding off the two dogs that leaped up on her with joy.

"Really, you didn't need to bring them, Mama," Robin said when he saw the enthusiastic collies' muddy paw prints on Aroha's travel ensemble.

"Relax, Robin. I'll hand them over to their new owners before we go to meet Mr. Elliot," Cat told him. "They won't sully your dear Miss Pomeroy's dress. Remember: You're not the center of the universe. There are other things to take care of in Christchurch apart from your oh-so-important concerns!"

Aroha frowned at her grandmother's unusually sharp tone. Robin must have really been annoying Cat on the ride there for her to lose her temper like this. Besides, Aroha was surprised to see her young uncle here. He'd never come to pick her up at the harbor before.

Robin looked dashing. Over the last few months, he'd grown taller and sturdier, no longer the gangly beanpole of last summer. His nicely tailored, light-weight suit accentuated his physique, and his elfin features had become more distinctive and masculine. He was slightly tanned; Aroha assumed that Chris had insisted on Robin making himself useful around the farm. But he hadn't lost his fine features. She caught herself thinking that Robin's face might have been considered stunningly beautiful, had he been a girl.

"I'm sorry, Mama," he was saying. "I'm just a little nervous. Guess what, Aroha, I'm going to an audition! It's with Mr. Elliot, Louise Pomeroy's husband." He glanced at the girl, seeking approval.

Aroha was impressed. She'd heard about Shakespearean performer Louise Pomeroy back in Dunedin. Her theater company was in Christchurch for an extended engagement. Isabella Morris, still a theater enthusiast, was already making plans to accompany her friend to Rata Station during their next vacation, and they were going to drive out to the city to see a play.

Cat frowned. "It's not an audition, Robin," she told her son. "All Mr. Elliot agreed to do was have a quick chat with us, and listen to what we have to say. It's probably because the Sheep Breeders' Association funds a substantial part of the Theatre Royal. Robin, we pulled some strings. That's all. I don't want you getting your hopes too high."

Robin's eyes clouded over, and Aroha felt sorry for him. The boy had been working hard over the past year to attain his dream of studying at the Guildhall School in London. Chris and Cat weren't very keen on the idea, but they hadn't stopped him from ordering brochures and curricula. The result had been disillusioning. Guildhall School did teach acting, but their emphasis was on music and singing. Upon learning this, Robin had desperately tried to become better at music. But his attempts with piano confirmed what his involuntary audience had already suspected from his flute playing: Robin had no ear for music. As sensitive as he was, and as keenly as he noted every variation of tone in people's speech, he was no musician.

*He must get it from Chris,* Cat had written to Aroha and Linda in Otaki.

> *I was always a fairly good singer. Robin has a beautiful speaking voice, but he can't carry a tune to save his life. I'm not too optimistic about him studying at a conservatory—and Guildhall School of Music and Drama is certainly comparable to those.*

"Well, in any case, I'm eager to talk to them," he said stubbornly. "I know that Mr. Elliot used to teach acting in Australia. He might know about other schools."

Cat nodded patiently. "And you will, Robin. We'll meet him and Miss Pomeroy later for tea at the Excelsior. But until then, please let's talk about something else for a change. How was Otaki, Aroha? What are Franz and Linda up to?"

Despite Cat and Aroha's efforts to strike up a normal conversation, Robin's excitement and tension altered the mood as Cressida trotted along the Bridle Path. The boy didn't join their conversation, nervously toying with the chain of his watch instead. He seemed worried about arriving late for their planned meeting, and he could hardly sit still while Cat gave the young collies' new owners detailed instructions on feeding and training.

It was still much too early for tea when the sheep breeders from Otago, who had come to Christchurch specially to pick up their dogs, finally said their goodbyes. Cat and Aroha would have liked to spend the remainder of their time strolling around town, but Robin insisted on going straight to the Excelsior to freshen up before the "royal audience," as Cat called it teasingly. True to form, he'd been looking neat as a pin all morning, and his rising excitement almost made him glow from the inside out. If Arthur Elliot was easily impressed by devotion and intensity, Robin was sure to win his affection.

Unfortunately, the couple didn't look as though they intended to be impressed by much of anything. Louise Pomeroy sat in an armchair in the hotel lobby with impeccable posture but visible boredom, sipping a cup of tea. Upon their entrance, her husband gave his watch a pointed glance.

Cat took the hint, and after they'd exchanged greetings, she explained that of course, she didn't intend to detain the busy artists for long. Upon hearing this, Elliot, a tall, dark-haired man with soft features and a bushy mustache, got to his feet and bowed to Cat.

"Not at all, we'd love to make time for you, wouldn't we, Louise, my love?"

Louise Pomeroy wasn't remarkably beautiful. Her hair was an uneven dark blonde, pinned up with painstaking care at the nape of her neck. A silk flower clip gave the style an extravagant touch. The actress wore an ivory tea dress trimmed in acres of lace with a matching set of pearl jewelry and soft-looking kid gloves. She had an oval, even-shaped face dominated by large brown eyes. Aroha had thought that a renowned actress would have more presence about her, but perhaps Miss Pomeroy needed to be onstage to fully come alive.

"Would you care for some tea, Mrs. . . ." Miss Pomeroy turned to face Cat politely; she had obviously forgotten her name already.

"Fenroy," Cat repeated. "Catherine Fenroy. And this is my granddaughter, Aroha, and my son Robin." She barely waited for Aroha and Robin to introduce themselves appropriately before continuing. "To be honest, Robin's the reason I'm here. It's my son's dream to become an actor, and he's hoping—I'm not sure—for some advice, perhaps?"

"I'm a passionate admirer of your craft," Robin said, a sentence he'd evidently been rehearsing in his head for a long time. "And I enjoy studying Mr. Shakespeare's plays. The—the roles, I mean. Romeo—and Hamlet, and . . ."

He paused as Arthur Elliot gave a booming laugh and Louise Pomeroy smiled a little.

"Ah, lofty goals, my young friend!" the actor said. "So, you intend to make your debut with lead roles, do you? Do you have somebody to build a theater for you too, then?"

Robin blushed fiercely. "That's not what I meant to say . . . I—I know I still have a lot to learn—that I still have everything to learn, to be honest. I thought you might know of a school, an educational institution for actors. I've been considering Guildhall School in London. It's just"—here his voice dropped—"I'm not very musical."

"What a pleasure to see that you don't lack self-awareness," Mr. Elliot remarked.

Robin bit his lip. "But just because I can't sing," he insisted, "doesn't mean that I'm not a good actor. Take Shakespeare, for example; there's no singing there at all!"

Cat disliked the contempt with which Arthur Elliot was treating her son, and hated having to see Robin so desperate.

"It is true, Mr. Elliot, I fear that Guildhall School would reject my son—" she began.

"And rightly so," Elliot said, breaking in arrogantly. "An acting career—in such difficult times, no less—calls for versatility. I'm aware, young man, that you dream of the higher arts, and I, too, prefer to play Lear rather than prancing across the stage in a musical comedy. Thanks to my delightful wife, I have the chance to play Lear at the moment. With Louise in the lead role, the crowds love Shakespeare." He theatrically blew a kiss at his wife.

Miss Pomeroy smiled, flattered.

"But above all, what people want is entertainment," the impresario said. "Just look at Bandmann-Beaudet. Just one performance of Gilbert and Sullivan's *HMS Pinafore*, and they've got the funding for an entire Shakespeare production on their hands . . . We must all make ends meet, my young friend. If your talent is insufficient, you should forget about performing."

"But I can't!" Robin said, struggling to stay calm. "And I do think my talent's sufficient. Not for singing, but for acting. Won't you let me audition, at least, Mr. Elliot? Miss Pomeroy? If only so you can get an impression?"

Elliot was obviously about to put him off, but his wife spoke up. "We might as well listen to him try," she said kindly. Her tone of voice was understanding, but her eyes betrayed no emotion. Aroha felt suspicion stirring inside of her. Neither Cat nor Robin had signaled that the obstacles to Robin's dreams were financial. Perhaps Miss Pomeroy's indulgence had something to do with the fact that her husband used to earn money as an acting teacher, and could do so again any time he pleased? Elliot himself had just said how hard the times were for an actor. He was probably alluding to the closing of theaters after the gold rush. Was it possible that the Elliots needed money? "Why don't we let him do Romeo?" Louise Pomeroy suggested. "If nothing else, he looks the part."

Robin blushed again, but then he caught himself, determined not to give Elliot even the slightest chance to object. In that instant, the phenomenon that Aroha had witnessed back in the barn at Rata Station repeated itself: Robin Fenroy transformed into Romeo Montague. His large, soulful eyes fixed on Louise Pomeroy with a dreamy gaze, just as they'd done with the barn cat.

Aroha had been expecting Arthur Elliot to stop Robin's performance in its tracks, but to her astonishment, he not only let him perform the entire monologue, but didn't even intervene when Louise replied to young Romeo as Juliet, the two performing the young couple's first meeting. Aroha found both of them equally fascinating. Robin bestowed the same devoted gaze upon Louise that he normally reserved for March, and Louise Pomeroy seemed to become much younger. Her Juliet regarded Romeo with a certain consideration, but without the unconditional devotion he offered her from the very start. She was even teasing him a little—and on one hand, Romeo was delighted about it, but on the other, he was hurt. The performance was extraordinary.

Finally, Elliot cleared his throat. "Well . . . ah . . . not bad, young man."

Cat interrupted the man before he could launch into another monologue. "So, you don't think my son is without talent? His hopes are . . . justified?"

She didn't sound unconditionally happy about it. At the same time, Robin's audition had obviously impressed his mother too.

Elliot cleared his throat again, but Louise Pomeroy spoke first.

"Young Mr. Fenroy here is talented beyond a doubt," she said. "It was a pleasure to perform with you. However, your breathing technique and voice leading still need work, and the right posture . . ."

Aroha wondered how Robin's expression could be improved upon at all. She found his reserved demeanor much more believable than Daniel Bandmann's grand gestures had been.

"Besides," Louise continued, "a Shakespearean actor should have a certain level of experience in fencing. He needs stage presence . . . It won't do you any good, Mr. Fenroy, to simply apply at any theater company you come across. And you must prove yourself worthy in smaller roles before anyone will let you play Romeo or Hamlet."

Robin hung his head. But Cat understood what the actress was getting at.

"And where does one acquire such experience, stage presence, breathing technique, and so forth?" she asked. "You must have learned somewhere, Miss Pomeroy, just like Mr. Elliot, Mr. Bandmann, and all the others."

Louise Pomeroy raised her teacup to her lips in a dainty gesture. "Well, I, for my part, received a . . . private education."

"You learn a lot by watching, of course. With genuine talent . . ." Mr. Elliot seemed unwilling to admit that he'd started out small too.

His wife fluttered her lashes at him.

Cat sighed. "Look, Mr. Elliot, my son read somewhere that you used to teach acting. Would it be possible for Robin to take lessons from you, say, twice a week, during your sojourn in Christchurch? The town must have booked you until next year." Cat had said "the town," but everyone present, except perhaps Robin, knew that she was talking about the Sheep Breeders' Association. "We'd pay your regular rate, of course," she added. "Let us know how much you charge, and I'll write you the first check."

Louise Pomeroy and Arthur Elliot exchanged a glance, hers satisfied and his somewhat indignant. He wasn't thrilled by this new task, apparently, but he quickly allowed himself to be convinced by Cat's checkbook. Acting didn't make you rich, or at least not outside of European cities like London or Paris. Particularly when one insisted on living in hotels like the Excelsior for months on end.

"It would be my pleasure," Elliot said finally.

Cat nodded contentedly. "That's settled, then. Robin, say thank you and find a time that works with Mr. Elliot. Please keep in mind that your regular education shouldn't suffer because of this arrangement. Chris and I want you to attain the college entrance qualifications, regardless of any other plans."

Robin was beaming at his mother. It seemed that he could hardly believe his good fortune.

"Maestro . . ." he whispered adoringly as he bowed to Elliot and they said their goodbyes.

He had chosen the right thing to say, it seemed. Arthur Elliot looked flattered, and just as satisfied as his wife as the Fenroys took their leave.

# Chapter 14

Cat, Robin, and Aroha headed back toward Rata Station the same day, spending a night on the way at the Deans farm. The Deans family were all very impressed, but also somewhat astonished by Robin's plans.

"Is it possible to make a living that way?" William Deans asked Cat worriedly after Robin had retired for the evening.

The young man had excused himself early, and was probably brooding over a book of Shakespeare plays. After Mr. Elliot's advice not to reach directly for the stars, he'd announced that he would immediately begin to study the minor roles.

Cat shrugged. "The famous actors do. But I have no idea about Robin. In any case, he has nothing in common with Elliot. But he doesn't necessarily have to earn a lot of money. The farm produces enough to support him if necessary. What's important to me is that he's happy. And also that he can stay out of Chris's way for a while. Chris still thinks he can change the boy by getting him involved with the farm work. But that does more harm than good. Robin's willing enough, even though he hates it. But if a couple of stubborn rams decide to break through a fence, he jumps aside and lets them go. Then we have to do the whole roundup all over again. Of course that turns the herders against him. They make fun of him. Even Tony and Henry, Carol's boys, can get more done at ten and twelve years old than Robin can at fourteen. My hope is that he'll prove himself in his lessons, and Mr. Elliot will give him a little job when the company moves on. They're staying for a year in Christchurch, and by then Robin will have his high school diploma. He would have to leave Rata Station to go to college anyway. If he pursues theater instead, I don't mind."

Chris wasn't nearly as relaxed about the subject. He overcame his doubts enough to congratulate Robin half-heartedly, but complained to Cat later when they were alone.

"You sweetened the deal for Elliot to take Robin as a student, didn't you? Admit it! We're going to pay a fortune for the lessons."

Cat let the accusation roll off her. "So what?" she said. "What's so bad about that? Do you think the man should work for nothing? Martin Porter doesn't teach at Rata Station for the love of it either." Martin Porter was the economist Jane had recruited from Edinburgh. "I wonder what that man's doing here, anyway. If he's such a luminary as Jane says, he must be able to find something better."

Chris smiled grimly and raised an eyebrow. "I saw him with little March yesterday. He practically worships her. He looks almost as besotted as Robin. And March is using every trick in the book to flirt with him. And I found out why he's here instead of gallivanting around Europe. Our dear Jane lured him in with the promise of a professorship at a newly established business school. He was quite surprised when he was confronted with just two students, plus Robin preparing for his final high school exams. Te Haitara said that Porter almost turned around and left. The only reason he stayed was March's eyes."

The next morning, when Robin dutifully set off to attend class at Maori Station—and share the news of his audition with March and Peta—Aroha took the opportunity to check out the new tutor.

Martin Porter turned out to be a very tall, dark-haired young man, who walked slightly stooped as though he were afraid of hitting his head on the top of a door frame. But the entrances to the Maori houses were actually quite low, contributing to the young economist's discomfort in the Ngai Tahu *marae*. Otherwise, he seemed quite self-confident. Cool hazel eyes gazed out from behind his glasses. The frames had only recently become popular. Most people still preferred lorgnettes, monocles, or pince-nez. Porter's lips were thin, his hair was full, his face was oval and even, and his nose narrow and nicely shaped. He was quite a good-looking man, and his expression immediately softened when he saw March. March had become more grown-up and feminine in the last year, and seemed more mature than her fifteen years. However, her contributions to the lessons were rather cynical and precocious. Aroha often didn't like what she heard.

"Adam Smith says that an actor's work isn't very useful," March countered when Robin told her about his success with Elliot.

"He said it wasn't very *efficient*," Peta said, correcting her. He sounded a little apologetic. "And it's not, really, at least in the traditional sense of the word. After all, you aren't manufacturing anything when you play Hamlet."

"It makes people happy," Robin argued. "That's also worth something!"

Martin Porter opened a thick book and also added his two cents. "Whereby the question arises whether the appearance of an actor as Hamlet contributes to the general social happiness or to personal happiness," he lectured. "There's no question that the acting profession is recognized and legitimized by our culture. Although it's not likely to increase the wealth of society."

"But there's certainly a market for theater performances," Robin said unhappily.

Aroha assumed that he'd dutifully read the thick book as well. She'd seen the title: *The Wealth of Nations*.

"Theaters—"

"Profit from the wealth of the owners of large estates and manufacturers," March, the model student, declared. "Just as servants and day laborers do. Even though they aren't always very useful either. For example, why should an adult woman need a maid? Can't she dress herself?"

Martin Porter gave her a look that would have counted as dreamy if it hadn't been for his lack of experience with emotional expression. "That's a well-formulated thought, March. I think we will all discover that the invisible hand that guides the market will make such occupational profiles obsolete. The human energy that's set free by their elimination will flow into production through the principle of labor organization. A factory no longer needs people who are specially trained in a craft anymore. Everyone will be able to work anywhere after a short introductory period."

Porter launched into a lecture about production increase. According to Adam Smith, it would lead to general prosperity and, with it, the growth of societal and personal happiness. March was the only one who seemed interested in wage-setting strategies and pricing. Robin was clearly drifting on his own cloud somewhere. And Peta seemed not to like what he was hearing, but he wasn't old enough or experienced enough to put his doubts into words. After the lesson, he nodded enthusiastically when Aroha told March that Mrs. Morris's chambermaid seemed to enjoy her work in spite of it being old-fashioned.

"I don't believe it would make her happier to work in a factory," she said.

March shrugged. "But she'd earn more money that way."

"I wouldn't care about earning money if I could only be an actor," Robin said with a far-off look in his eyes.

"You would care if you were starving," March said mockingly. Then she frowned. "In any case, at least you can do what you want. That's wonderful! I, to the contrary, cannot. I would like to study in Europe. Political economics or commercial science. At the University of Edinburgh, where Mr. Porter comes from. That would be a dream. Or in Cambridge, or Vienna . . . There are many good schools there. But they don't accept women."

March pushed back her hair in irritation. She was wearing it loose in the Maori style, even though she always wore *pakeha* clothes for lessons. Robin wore *pakeha* clothes as well. Only Peta showed signs of rebellion and occasionally appeared with a bare chest and a skirt of dried flax, which he'd worn for the combat training he did before class. His father, Eru, and above all his grandfather, Te Haitara, preferred traditional education, while his mother, Mara, in rare agreement with his grandmother, Jane, thought it archaic and unnecessary. However, the two women had very different arguments. Jane, like Adam Smith, talked about the inefficiency of spears and war clubs in an era of pistols and rifles, whereas Mara simply never wanted to see another war again.

"Then study here in New Zealand," Robin told March. "In Dunedin, for example, like Aroha."

For women's education, New Zealand was extraordinarily progressive. Not only did private academies like Miss Vandermere's accept female students but public universities did as well.

"It's not possible to study anything useful here," March declared disdainfully. "At least nothing that has to do with economics. In that respect, we might as well be living on the dark side of the moon. It makes one wonder what that says about our country! No courses of study for politics or economics—"

"And no acting schools," Aroha added before March could work herself up. "Apparently, New Zealand isn't offering its people the education they want."

A few days later, Aroha began her third semester in Dunedin, and she was very happy to return to her language studies. She thought it much more useful to learn to communicate with people of various nationalities than to study Mr. Porter's dry lectures. She hadn't been able to form a definitive opinion about the man, or the relationship between him and March. They were doubtlessly fascinated by each other, but they weren't the type to be sidetracked by sentimental notions of romance. Martin Porter might be attracted to March, but surely he wouldn't risk his job by getting too close to the young girl. And March obviously had a crush on her teacher, but Aroha assumed it was more because he was a clever economist whose knowledge she could profit from than because he was a man of flesh and blood.

Therefore, the relationship didn't promise any exciting developments. In Miss Vandermere's Academy, where male and female students attended the same classes, there were much more interesting emotional entanglements. This semester, her friend Isabella's love for a student from Wellington kept Aroha on her toes. Isabella was trying to keep the relationship a secret.

"I want to finish my studies first. Then I can decide what to do next," Isabella said.

Only the following autumn did the young man appear politely at the Morris family's door with a bouquet of flowers and officially ask permission to court their daughter. This resulted in endless discussions and arguments about whether it would be proper for Isabella and her admirer to continue to attend classes together. Fortunately, the end of their studies was in sight. Isabella would soon be taking her final exams, and Aroha's third and probably last year was about to begin.

At the beginning of winter, she received news from Rata Station. In a letter, Carol reported that Martin Porter had left Maori Station as soon as his contract with Jane had expired. The young man had found a more appropriate position with the Canterbury Spinning and Weaving Company, which ran a factory in Kaiapoi, a small town near the mouth of the Waimakariri River. His job was to optimize the workflow.

*But it just sounds like he's trying to reduce the workers' wages as much as possible,* Carol said in a letter to her niece.

*At least that's what I understand from March, who is as enthusiastic about him as ever. She's also continuing her studies with him, twice a week. She's been accompanying Robin, who travels regularly to Christchurch. That will soon end, however. The Pomeroy Dramatic Company's residency in Christchurch is coming to an end. Of course Robin is terribly depressed about it. The only thing that cheers him up is the prospect of getting a small part in their last Shakespeare production at the Theatre Royal. Perhaps he'll do such a good job that they'll hire him and take him with them. I hope so very much, for his sake. He worked quite hard during the last year, and Mr. Elliot has spoken well of him.*

Aroha wrote back, saying that of course she would come to the performance in Christchurch, even if she had to skip a few classes. Robin was playing Lysander in *A Midsummer Night's Dream*.

"It's a real part," he'd declared proudly.

Aroha hadn't made it to the premiere, but she came to Christchurch for the closing night. Robin met her at the train station. During the run of the show, he had spent a lot of time in Christchurch. There had been performances almost every day for four weeks.

Mr. Elliot had taken on two additional acting students in Christchurch, and they, too, got their moment on the stage. However, they'd been offered unimportant walk-on parts. Lysander, on the other hand, was one of the leading roles in the play. He was a young lover who was thrown into confusion by a magic potion.

Robin played the part brilliantly, and Aroha hadn't expected anything less. She liked the play, with its romantic sets, fantastic costumes, and colorful characters, much more than *Hamlet*, which she found rather dark. She applauded enthusiastically as the curtain fell after the first act. Then the audience was released from the spell for intermission.

In the foyer of the theater, which was almost as luxurious as that of the Queen's Theater in Dunedin, champagne was being offered.

"Robin is very impressive onstage," Cat said. "I don't think he's any worse than any of the other actors. What do you think?"

Aroha agreed wholeheartedly. She thought Robin was even better than most of the others. He practically glowed on the stage, and played Lysander's young love, fervor, and innocence so convincingly that one could feel it. Louise Pomeroy doubtlessly had stage presence too. In the spotlight, she seemed far more commanding than she did in everyday life. Arthur Elliot, to the contrary, played Oberon woodenly and self-importantly.

"It's certainly pleasant to watch," Chris said. "I just wish that acting wasn't such an unprofitable art form."

"Doesn't he get any money for his performance?" asked March, who had turned up for the closing show so as not to completely disappoint Robin.

She looked breathtaking, as usual. This time she was wearing a low-cut, midnight-blue evening gown. Aroha never would have dared to show herself in something so formfitting. What's more, March had caused something of a stir by entering the theater on Martin Porter's arm. Aroha wondered if she'd gotten permission from Mara and Eru, but thought it unlikely. Jane was much more likely to have opinions about who her granddaughter went out with. Did March even care?

Aroha got the impression that March wasn't trying to keep any secrets about how intimate she was with Porter. Her former teacher seemed a little embarrassed about that in front of Cat and Chris. Luckily for him, neither of them would ever waste a word speaking to Jane about it.

"Money?" Chris said sarcastically. "You're surely joking. This is an honor for Robin, an accolade from his esteemed teacher, as it were. We're the ones who are paying. Just the costs of his accommodation in Christchurch alone—"

"Now, stop that!" Cat said. "Think of it more as a final exam. There are always fees involved, at least in private education. Isn't that true, Aroha?"

"That's right," Aroha said, although in truth Miss Vandermere compensated her quite handsomely for teaching Maori.

The headmistress of the language academy had waived almost all of her tuition fees, and had offered a paid teaching position upon finishing her studies. However, Aroha wasn't sure if she wanted to take it. She was interested in becoming an interpreter.

Cat squeezed her husband's arm. "Perhaps Elliot really will give Robin a job when they're finished here and continue their tour."

"What? When he could just as easily get him for free?" March scoffed. "Forgive me, Auntie Cat, but I don't think that's very likely. Even in theater, supply and demand rules. If there are few applicants for a job, it's paid well. If people are standing in line for it, then the employer will lower the wages. And if the candidates even pay for the chance, then Elliot will probably look for new students during his next residency and take more money for putting them onstage."

"Talent must be a factor, as well," Aroha said, though she knew March wasn't entirely wrong. "He could get much more use out of Robin than from a beginner."

March shrugged. "You'll see."

The next morning, Robin wanted to talk to Elliot and Pomeroy. On the evening before the final show, there had been a reception for the actors and their guests at the Excelsior, but of course there hadn't been time for a private conversation there. Arthur Elliot and Louise Pomeroy were constantly surrounded by a ring of admirers, and Robin, too, got plenty of compliments. The Deanses were especially enraptured. It was the first play they had ever seen, and they could hardly believe how magical it had all seemed. William Deans had congratulated Chris and Cat on their talented son.

"I didn't think it was possible that I'd stay awake through the whole thing. Shakespeare . . . That's more for professors than for the likes of us. But your boy makes it so alive! Now I understand why people pay for the privilege to see it."

The praise had given Robin courage. He was determined to broach the subject of a job. But he didn't quite dare to speak to Elliot alone. Shyly, he asked Aroha to accompany him.

"Shouldn't you bring March instead?" she teased. "Since it's a business negotiation?"

But she gave in immediately when she saw Robin's tortured face. The boy looked like he hadn't slept all night, worrying about the best way to approach Elliot.

Finally, they decided to catch the couple at breakfast in the hotel restaurant. Elliot invited the two young people to join them with uncharacteristic affability.

"Now we can bid you a more personal farewell, Robin," he said.

"And also reassure you how much your Lysander impressed us," Louise Pomeroy added. "A year ago I wouldn't have believed it. But now, I swear you will play Romeo, my boy! If you continue to work hard."

"But where should I work?" Robin burst out. He certainly hadn't imagined the interview going this way. "I thought—I thought you might offer me a job. I don't even want much money." Aroha thought of March, and had to make an effort not to roll her eyes. "Not even major roles. Just—just the possibility to keep learning and gathering experience."

Elliot shook his head. His regret and sympathy seemed almost real.

"Robin, my boy, as much as I'd like to give you the chance, at the moment we are actually reducing the size of our company, not taking on new members. Besides, we already have someone your age. I can easily fill all the parts that you could play with other members of the troupe. Times are hard for our craft, boy. Ten years ago, things would have looked different."

Elliot explained to his devastated listener what Robin had known for a long time: During the gold rush, many theaters had opened, especially in Otago. The people had had money and were willing to pay for entertainment. In the 1870s, that had changed. The gold ran out, and many companies could no longer afford to run their own theater. They toured through the country, performing in town halls, schools, and sometimes even under the open sky. They often earned only just enough to pay for their next meal. To attract visitors on a large scale nowadays, one had to offer something special, such as Pollard's Lilliputian Opera Company, which worked with ten- to thirteen-year-old children. The little ones sang and danced. It had made their director, Thomas Pollard, rich.

Robin sighed. Even if he'd been able to sing, he was already too old for Pollard.

"What should I do now?" he asked quietly.

Elliot shrugged. "You have to search. Perhaps you'll find a company that will take you on. Probably not here, but perhaps on the North Island, or in Australia. You've got the right skills, at least for supporting roles. You can project your voice, and you have talent too. You are employable, in any case."

Robin blushed at the compliment. But Elliot's voice immediately became stern. "I don't have anything else to offer you, Robin. I didn't promise anything else either. Just in case your mother has any complaints."

Robin shook his head, unable to speak. Aroha said goodbye for both of them.

# Chapter 15

"Good grief, Robin, just accept it! You don't have whatever it is they're looking for, and what you do have, nobody's looking for. Supply isn't equal to demand here—it's the simplest rule of market economy."

Robin flinched as though March had slapped him. And yet, she'd only been summarizing, in her own straightforward way, what all his friends and relatives had been telling him more kindly since he'd been rejected by Elliot.

Of course, Robin had taken Elliot's advice and gone through the ad pages of every newspaper he could get his hands on in Christchurch. Cat silently thanked the heavens that it was rare for a gazette from Australia to find its way to the local stores.

"Maybe you should consider a different job," even Aroha was saying now.

It had been several months since Robin's last performance. Another semester had passed. Aroha had been staying in Otaki with her parents since the beginning of the summer vacation, but now she was spending a few weeks at Rata Station before returning to Dunedin. On this day, she'd come along to Christchurch with Robin. Another theater company was visiting town. This time, it wasn't Shakespeare, but Edward Bulwer-Lytton's *The Lady of Lyons*. Aroha and Robin had gone to see the play with March and Martin Porter. Porter was there representing Canterbury Spinning and Weaving Company. During the reception for invited guests that followed, Robin had spoken to the theater company's director. The man had certainly appeared to be impressed by Robin's accomplishments, but he hadn't done much to raise his hopes.

"You must be pretty good if Elliot was willing to cast you as Lysander. But we're not hiring right now, and we almost never perform Shakespeare. Only comedies and operettas. And if you don't sing . . ."

Robin had returned to his relatives, crestfallen.

"You could study something in college," Aroha went on. "Literature, maybe. That's got something to do with acting."

"I don't want to read plays, I want to act!" Robin insisted. He was in low spirits, and all of his newfound confidence had evaporated again. The dark circles under his eyes made him look even more ethereal than usual. "I can do it! Even Elliot said I can do it!"

"If ye ask me, ye're even better than that Mr. Elliot," Martin Porter added, to everyone's surprise. "I don't pretend to know much about theater, but I've attended several performances in Edinburgh, and in London too. And the way ye embody a role, it's so convincing, and that's a rare thing. Elliot must have noticed too. Robin, in a few years' time, or maybe even a few months, ye'd be better than him, and Louise Pomeroy'd drop him like a hot potato. That's one reason he'd never have hired ye. A man like Arthur Elliot wouldn't make it far in Europe. He doesn't play roles, all he does is act up. But you . . ." He smiled. "I had to give ye so many bad grades in mathematics, but yer Lysander definitely deserved top marks!"

The sparkle returned to Robin's eyes for a second. "Do you think I should go to England, Mr. Porter?"

Martin Porter shrugged. "Aye, ye should at least consider it. With yer parents. Did Elliot write ye a reference? Or, even better, Louise Pomeroy? She's actually famous; even Europeans will have heard of her. Maybe ye could write to a few theater companies in England and ask if they'll give ye a chance. It doesn't have to be an engagement, but maybe a kind of—ah—apprenticeship."

March groaned. "That's just going to cost more money," she remarked.

"It could be a good investment," Porter argued. "Ye know quite well that income must be preceded by investments. My family invested in my education, too, and so does yours, March. Of course, a scientific education might be a safer investment than an arts education. But, as ye also know, oftentimes bold investments are the most profitable ones. Robin, ye won't get rich wi' a theater company, playing small theaters in New Zealand. Still, better-known actors in England aren't just revered; they actually make a fair bit of money."

It had taken Robin another sleepless night to get up the nerve to talk to his father about Porter's idea. And still, he thought it all sounded very good. An "investment" sounded businesslike and respectable; it was more likely to appeal to Chris than "art."

Robin went on a ride with his father, intending to present him with the idea when he got a chance. A few sheep had run off and had to be recovered from Maori Station, preferably before Jane could find the opportunity to get upset. Chris had gone out with two sheepdogs to herd them in, and Robin had offered to come along and help him. Aroha joined them too. She jumped at any chance to ride her beloved Cressida.

"If it were me, I'd talk to Cat instead," she told Robin, having guessed his intentions immediately. "She'll convince Chris."

But Robin was determined. He wanted his father to finally take him seriously, and he had to learn to fight his own battles. His short stint with the Pomeroy Company hadn't just given him insights into the more beautiful sides of acting, but also into the merciless competition between actors. There had been bad blood between the younger members of the company when Robin, an acting student, had snagged the coveted role of Lysander. There wouldn't always be an Arthur Elliot in his corner. The next impresario might need some convincing.

Robin decided to use this conversation with his father to practice his rhetorical skills. He seized his moment and presented the goals he was working toward pragmatically, just like Martin Porter had, not desperately or emotionally, as he would have before.

Chris gave it some thought. They had been able to find the sheep and had herded them back onto Rata Station land. Now, they were taking a break in a little copse of rata trees. The day was nippy, but the sun was out. The wind plucked blossoms from trees and bushes and blew them into a stream that the horses were drinking from. Aroha enjoyed the contrast of dark and light layered against the endless backdrop of the plains. But neither father nor son noticed the beauty of the landscape. All Robin did was gaze at his father pleadingly while Chris toyed with his riding crop, not looking his son in the eye.

"Investments," Chris finally repeated. "That word makes me think of railroad construction or factories. Although I don't like the way Mr. Porter runs that factory down in Kaiapoi . . ." Robin bit his lip. He really didn't feel like talking about working conditions at the textile mill right now. He let out a breath of relief when Chris returned immediately to the subject at hand. "Investments are a calculated risk. But your theater career, Robin . . . that can't be calculated in any sense. To me, it sounds like we'd be sending you to London for pleasure."

"It's not for pleasure!" Robin objected, insulted. "This is about my career."

"It's the career you desire," Chris said. "A desire that could end up costing us an arm and a leg. Not to mention the risk. You want us to send you to England alone? You only just turned seventeen. You've never had to take care of yourself before."

Robin's lip quivered. He'd found himself close to tears a lot lately, too often for a young man of his age. He knew Chris had no patience for it.

"You don't believe in me," he said quietly.

Chris rubbed his temples, obviously trying hard to remain calm, and sighed. "Of course I believe in you," he said, taking a deep breath. "You're doubtlessly talented, and you impressed us all during that play, as we've told you several times before. All I wonder, Robin, is whether that's a blessing or a curse. It's like you're living in the wrong place at the wrong time. Believe me, I know what that's like. I felt exactly the same when I first started my farm here. I'd never wanted anything but this farm; I was prepared to work for it like a mule. I even married Jane Beit, although—I have to admit—I was more scared of her than in love with her. And it was all for this land. The only problem was that it didn't make any profit. And I tried so desperately to cultivate it. I plowed and sowed, and yes, I even harvested a little, but sending the grain to Christchurch cost me more than it brought in. It's not that I didn't have the talent, or that I wasn't trying hard enough. It's just that it was hopeless. The farm only started generating a return once Karl came up with the idea of sheep farming. But for you, Robin, there won't be any sheep. It's unlikely that there will suddenly be theater companies popping up like mushrooms all over New Zealand, and I don't think theaters in England are just sitting there waiting for you either. Face the facts, Robin, and do something else. At least for now. Once you're a little older, and a little more assertive, boy . . . For goodness' sake, don't start crying!"

Chris leaped to his feet and walked over to his horse, shaking his head in frustration over his strange child.

Robin dabbed at his eyes. "I'll do it anyway," he whispered. "I'll show them all!"

Aroha thought it sounded like a line from a play.


But then, something happened that nobody at Rata Station could have predicted. Two days before Aroha's departure for Dunedin, Robin came running into Carol's kitchen with a newspaper in his hand. Cat, Carol, and Aroha were busy canning summer fruit. In the oven, sweet buns were baking, filling the kitchen with their fragrant aroma.

"Here!" Robin cried out triumphantly. "This is where I'm going to audition!" He held out the newspaper to Cat, then pulled it back and started to read aloud. "*The Carrigan Theater Company is hiring actors: comedians as well as thespians of the more dramatic craft, male and female.* I'm going, Mama! I'll audition! I'm sure they'll hire me. Oh, Mama, Carol, Aroha! Finally, finally a chance!" Robin seemed to be on the brink of dancing.

"Let me see that." Cat took the newspaper, looking skeptical, and sank down in a chair to read the ad for herself.

Robin was bouncing from one foot to another, clearly agitated. "The company's in Wellington," he told Aroha and Carol. "I'll have to get to the North Island as quickly as possible!"

"We should talk to Chris about this first," Cat said uncertainly as Carol reached for the paper.

Aroha glanced at it as well. The ad was rather inconspicuous. Small and concise, it was tucked away between the business openings and wedding announcements.

"What did you want to talk to me about?"

Chris was just coming inside, followed by Carol's husband, Bill, and four sopping-wet but happy sheepdogs. It was time for coffee, and the men had smelled the fresh pastries. They were both wearing oilskins; it was pouring outside. Still, they were in good spirits as they peeled off their coats—at least until Cat handed the *Wellington Times* over to her husband.

Chris skimmed the ad. "And why is this theater company looking so desperately for actors of all stripes while all the others are full up?" he asked.

Cat rubbed at her forehead. The question had occurred to her also. She would have loved to fulfill her son's wishes, but she had a bad feeling about this.

"Maybe we should write to Mr. Elliot first and ask him if he's heard of this company before," she suggested.

"Mama, no, that would take months!" Robin objected. "All the jobs will be taken in the time it'd take Mr. Elliot to answer. And maybe he's never even heard about the company because it's only just starting. New theater companies get founded all the time—"

"Only to disband again very quickly," Chris said dryly. "You heard Mr. Elliot: Only a select few actors are able to live decently from their craft."

"But it's worth a try! It's not Australia, Dad, or England. It's just the North Island."

"We could telegraph the Elliots," Cat mused, although somewhat half-heartedly. She had no idea where the Louise Pomeroy Company was at the moment.

"Why don't we just ask Mr. Foreman?" Aroha said. Mr. Foreman was the head of the company they'd just seen perform *The Lady of Lyons*. "I think his company's still in Christchurch. And I could ask around in Dunedin. There are several theaters there. I'll just go there, ask to talk to the directors, and ask them whether they know Mr. Carrigan. He must have performed somewhere before he had the resources to found his own theater company."

Robin shook his head. "All those things would take much too long," he argued. "It might already be too late." It was always a few days before the *Wellington Times* could be bought in Christchurch. "I should leave right away. Which suitcase can I take, Mama? Or perhaps just a day bag? I won't need that much, and perhaps you could send me some things later."

Cat looked around, at a loss. She hated having to stop her children from doing things, and this was Robin's lifelong dream. But still, all her warning bells were going off. She would have preferred to confirm that the Carrigan Company was respectable before letting Robin go.

Chris looked at his wife, then his son, and gritted his teeth.

"I'll drive you to Christchurch tomorrow, Robin," he said. "We'll go looking for Mr. Foreman. If he can't help us, there would still be the possibility of taking a train to Dunedin to ask around in theaters there."

"But Dunedin's in the wrong direction!" Robin cried.

"There are always ships leaving from Dunedin for the North Island," his father told him. "We'd hardly lose any time at all."

"We?" Robin asked.

Chris nodded. "Yes. I'll accompany you to Wellington, and I'll check out Mr. Carrigan myself before I let you travel around with his company, Robin. I want your mother to be able to sleep soundly."

Cat gave her husband a grateful smile while Robin went on complaining. He was sure that their trips to Christchurch and Dunedin would be a waste of time. The shortest way to the North Island was taking the train to Blenheim, and then getting on a ferry that crossed the Cook Strait.

"How is it going to look if I turn up with my father in tow?" he whined. "Mr. Carrigan's going to think I can't do anything on my own."

Chris shook his head. "Don't talk back to me. Anyway, you're still a minor," he reminded his son. "You can't even sign an employment contract yourself. So Mr. Carrigan will surely understand why I'm accompanying you. If he's even considering hiring underage actors, that is."

"I could tell him I'm older," Robin declared, making his family smile indulgently.

Chris stood up and reached for his oilskin coat. He seemed to have lost his appetite for sweet buns.

"Robin, it's a theater company, not the foreign legion. If Mr. Carrigan offers you a contract, he'll want to see your papers. So stop this nonsense. You can start packing, or you can think about what you'd like to bring to the audition, or whatever it is you need to do to prepare. We're leaving tomorrow morning. And Bill, we should be able to get in another few hours of work on the shed now. Maybe we can at least get part of the roof finished before I leave you alone with all the work tomorrow."

At five o'clock the next morning, Chris was up and ready to leave. Cat was preparing a special breakfast.

"I can't tell you how grateful I am," she said as she set down a plate of scrambled eggs and freshly baked bread. "I know you think this is all useless, but Robin—"

"Is my son too," Chris said calmly. "And I want to see him happy. Where is he, anyway? We said we'd be taking the boat as soon as the sun was up."

Robin hadn't been sleeping in his parents' tiny house for some years now. He had his own room up at the stone house, and he often ate breakfast with Carol's family.

"Perhaps he overslept," Cat said, although she found that hard to believe. Suddenly, the bad feeling she'd had while reading the ad was back. "I'll go over and check in on him."

Her premonition got stronger as she crossed the yard, seeing that no lights were on in the stone house. Nervously, she opened the unlocked door without knocking and ascended the wide stairs to Robin's room, only to find it deserted, the bed unused. There was a note on the bedside table.

*Gone to Wellington. Please don't be angry, but I have to do this alone. Wish me luck! Love you all, Robin*

Cat felt a chill of fear creeping up inside of her. She found Aroha in the hall and quickly informed her of Robin's stealthy departure.

Aroha was wide awake immediately. She regretted that she hadn't heard Robin leave. Guilt stirred in her again.

"I should have kept a closer eye on him," she said, crossing her arms and hanging her head in worry. "Good Lord, we might have guessed he'd do such a thing!"

Cat gave her a disconcerted look. Had it really been so obvious? She herself had been taken completely by surprise.

Meanwhile, Carol and Bill had heard voices in the hall and come out of their bedroom. But the Paxtons hadn't heard any more of Robin's departure than Aroha had.

Carol pulled Cat, who still seemed to be frozen in place, into her arms. "Don't worry, Mamaca," she said, trying to comfort her. "He probably hasn't gotten very far yet. Let's get dressed now, and then we can talk about what we're going to do."

Aroha threw on a bathrobe. "I'll go see if he's really gone already. And if so, whether he left by boat or by horse."

Cat shook her head. "Of course he's gone," she murmured. "He may be naive, but he wouldn't have waited until morning."

"I have to get to Wellington immediately!" she told her husband as she stepped back into their house. "Or to Blenheim, at least. If I'm very lucky, I'll catch him before he can board the next ferry. I'll find him, one way or another, I—"

Chris shook his head. He didn't seem at all surprised. "You'll do nothing of the sort, Cat," he said sternly. "Nor will I, for that matter. The boy's made his decision, and we have to let him go."

"But he's still much too young."

Cat had frantically started pinning up her hair, getting ready to rush out. Now, she lowered her comb, discouraged.

Chris poured a cup of coffee and pushed it toward her. "I'd been earning my own money for quite some time when I was seventeen," he told her, "and at that age, you were already considered a *tohunga*, and you were interpreting for a Maori chieftain. Linda and Carol weren't much older when they took over the entire farm here." Cat was about to argue, but Chris didn't give her a chance. "Yes, I know," he went on. "Robin's different. He's special. Maybe even special enough that theater companies in Europe would scramble to hire him. I don't know. Maybe we really would have ended up giving him a chance to try—in one or two years' time, if he still wanted it so badly by then. But now he's taken the decision from our hands. And I don't know about you . . . but it actually makes me respect him a little more. To be honest, I wouldn't have thought him capable of something like this." Chris took his wife's hand. "He dove in, Cat," he said seriously. "If he discovers how cold the water is, that can only help him, in the end."

# Chapter 16

Robin Fenroy disembarked from the ferry in Wellington and could hardly believe that he was really there. He was all alone, on his own terms, without his parents' permission! Until the ship had left Blenheim, he had still been afraid that Cat and Chris would turn up and drag him home. He had taken the early train from Christchurch and bought a ticket for the first ferry the next day, but he knew that his mother was capable of anything. He immediately felt guilty for thinking that. Of course Cat didn't mean him harm. To the contrary, she loved him. But no one at Rata Station, not even March or Aroha, understood how much acting really meant to him. He had to take the chance, even if there was a danger that Mr. Carrigan would send him away because he didn't have any papers. He would just have to give the impression that he was of age, and fully responsible for his own life!

For the hundredth time, Robin read the ad that he'd torn out of the *Wellington Times*. The Carrigan Company had listed a hotel as the address for auditions, which Robin thought was logical. If Mr. Carrigan was really putting together a theatrical company for the first time, of course he wouldn't have a rehearsal space at a theater yet.

Robin decided to treat himself to a meal at one of the inns by the harbor. During the crossing, he'd constantly fought seasickness, and he still wasn't particularly hungry, but he thought it was important to be calm and satisfied for the audition. Above all, Robin was thirsty. He ordered lemonade, and the girl who served it to him gave him a curious look. After he'd finished the drink and poked around unenthusiastically in a vegetable pasty, he held out the newspaper clipping to her.

"Can you tell me—how to get there?"

The girl laughed. "Are you an actor?" she asked with admiration.

Robin blushed. "I—um, I'd like to be," he admitted. "I was hoping for a job."

The girl studied the clipping more carefully. "That's not so far from here," she said. "It's a guesthouse right here in the harbor." She paused for a moment. "It doesn't have the best reputation, though."

Robin bit his lower lip. Was the girl trying to warn him?

"Perhaps—perhaps Mr. Carrigan chose it because of the central location," he said.

The girl laughed. "The Royal Albert Hotel also has a central location," she said. "Besides, it's much more comfortable. I think it's more likely that Mr. Carrigan chose the Golden Goose because it's cheap. So don't expect very much pay. Anyway, you just walk straight along the street from the pier, and then take the third right."

Robin thanked her politely and counted out the coins for his meal. He had to be careful. The hundred pounds that he'd received for his pocket watch in a Christchurch pawnshop had already shrunk significantly after the travel expenses and spending the night at a cheap guesthouse in Blenheim. He was relieved he didn't have to take a cab.

Feeling somewhat optimistic, Robin set off. It only took a few minutes for him to reach the Golden Goose, which turned out to have a pub on the first floor. The stench of stale smoke and spilled beer wafted out of the open door of the faded two-story building. A thin man was busy mopping the floor. The pub was furnished with rickety tables, wooden chairs, and a stained bar behind which was a rather meager selection of liquor. Robin almost left in disgust, but then he saw the stage at the other end of the room. It was a platform roughly nailed together out of raw boards; absolutely nothing comparable to the stage at the Queen's Theater or the Royal, but there was a curtain made of tattered red velvet. Robin's heart beat faster. The Carrigan Company was certainly not wealthy, but at least they existed.

"Can I help you?" asked the man with the mop.

Robin nodded and took the newspaper clipping out of his pocket. "I'm looking for Mr. Carrigan," he said.

The thin man cast a quick glance at the ad and shook his head. "There's no Mr. Carrigan here. Only a Miss. Miss Vera Carrigan is a guest here, with her company. They're a sorry lot, to be sure. Did you want to audition?"

Robin nodded nervously. "I—I have some training. I studied with Mr. Arthur Elliot in Christchurch, and—"

"Yes, yes, you can tell her that," the man said. "Go up to room fifteen. The lady will be delighted."

Robin quickly thanked him and felt his way up the dark stairs. The hallway didn't look any better than the rest of the place, and it smelled of urine.

It was easy to find room 15. Robin took a deep breath before knocking on the door.

"Hello?" a low-pitched female voice said.

Robin found the tone odd, but courageously turned the door handle anyway. He gazed into the semidarkness of a rather large room. Curtains on the windows dimmed the light. The room was dominated by a double bed with a tattered dark-blue bedspread. There was a stained wingchair covered in the same material, a low table, and a secretary desk with a matching chair. The armoire was half open, and clothing seemed to have been stuffed into it haphazardly. On the bed lay a heavy, dark-haired woman wearing a red dressing gown. Robin thought that was rather strange, since it was already one thirty in the afternoon.

"Who do we have here, then?" the woman asked, making a kind of cooing noise. "What a pretty boy. Come in!" A sharp smile played over her broad face. Vera Carrigan had narrow lips and large, dark eyes, which now gazed at Robin searchingly. "Well, are you coming?" she demanded. "I don't bite."

Robin wasn't convinced of this, but he stepped into the room anyway and took out the newspaper clipping again.

"Um—My name is Robin Fenroy," he said. "I'm replying to your advertisement." Then he rattled off his entire list of qualifications and experience. "If you like, you're welcome to contact Mr. Elliot. He would doubtlessly speak for me," he concluded, with unaccustomed courage.

Now Miss Carrigan showed clear interest. As she sat up, her dressing gown slipped a little. Robin blushed when he realized that she wasn't wearing anything beneath it.

The woman noticed his dismay and smiled. "Forgive my appearance," she said easily. "I only just woke up. Well, you must know that, my lovely. As actors, we are creatures of the night."

Robin stood stiffly in the middle of the room, and watched warily as Miss Carrigan stood up and approached him. She had a stocky build and was very tall, even taller than he was. There were traces of stage makeup on her face, surely from the night before. Her hair fell loose over her shoulders and back in thick waves.

"It's true, you're a very pretty boy," she repeated flatteringly. But then her voice became businesslike. "What roles do you want to play? Hamlet? Romeo?"

Robin blushed again. "That's my goal, of course—but I know—I know that one must start small. As I said, I played Lysander—"

"We cut Lysander," she informed him. "We perform Shakespeare in slightly edited form. We can't find enough actors."

Robin began to see a glimmer of hope. "How could that be?" he asked. "So many actors are out of work. No company wants to give a chance to a young actor like me."

He held his breath for a moment, afraid he sounded both insecure and insubordinate.

Vera Carrigan grinned. "Well, let's say I don't hire just anyone," she replied. "It has to . . . fit, somehow." She put a finger under Robin's chin and regarded his face more closely.

Robin forced himself not to pull away. "Shall I recite something?" he asked.

She nodded, looking bored. "Go ahead, then." A sly smile transformed her face. "A fiery lover, my dear. Yes, that's exactly what I'm looking for today. Show me your Romeo, little man."

Robin didn't know what to do. Was the actress making fun of him? Or was she trying to loosen him up? Finally, he pulled himself together and performed Romeo's monologue, the same one he had used to convince Elliot.

*"But soft, what light through yonder window breaks . . ."*

As usual when Robin was performing, after his first few words he forgot where he was and submerged himself entirely in Shakespeare's world. The filthy pension room became the Capulets' garden, and Vera Carrigan, who was surely over thirty years old, transformed into the beautiful young Juliet, to whom Romeo's entire heart belonged.

She interrupted him after the first five sentences.

"Wonderful," she said tersely. "You're very cute. Mr. Lockhart will be delighted. And if you look at little Leah that way . . ." She grinned. "Then I'll be jealous."

Robin stared at her uncomprehendingly. "Does that mean . . . you'll hire me?"

Vera Carrigan nodded. "But I don't pay dream wages, kid. Fifty shillings a week, if we have work. If I don't earn anything, you don't either. But you don't have to worry about that, I always get something. We can talk about it. Now get yourself a room here, and we'll see each other later. You can try something this evening. We'll discuss it over supper, at six downstairs in the pub."

Robin couldn't believe it. "Thank you! I'm very grateful to you. But shouldn't we discuss what parts I'll be playing?"

Vera Carrigan held up her hand defensively. "You will do whatever is required, kid. What's your name? Robin? That's how we always do it."

Robin blushed, but then out of fairness decided to confess his greatest weakness.

"I—um—I just can't sing."

Vera Carrigan gave a deep, throaty laugh. "Kid, that never stopped others from raising their voices," she said. "You'll hear Leah, later."

"But I *really* can't sing," he insisted, hoping desperately at the same time that the actress wouldn't retract her decision.

The leader of the company took him by the shoulders and shoved him gently out of her room. "Sometimes it's good when people don't sing. Even though in parts of our trade it's sometimes necessary. You will earn your keep, little Robin. Don't worry."

Robin didn't understand what she was talking about, but a chill ran down his spine.

The man in the taproom already had the key for Robin's room in his hand. He'd apparently had no doubt that the young man would get the job, which only added to Robin's confusion. His room was on the same hall as Vera Carrigan's and was similarly furnished, just not as large. The first thing he did was push the curtains aside to let light in. It wasn't much use, because the house across the street blocked the sun, but he still felt as though he could breathe more easily. He wondered if he should use the time to write a letter to his mother. The Fenroys were doubtlessly worried, and they would be happy to hear his good news. In his daydreams on the ferry, Robin had imagined writing such a letter in delightful detail, but now he felt no sense of triumph, rather fear. Vera Carrigan was completely different from Louise Pomeroy or Louise Beaudet. What awaited him in this company?

When Robin entered the taproom at six o'clock, it was still empty.

"Miss Carrigan and her crew are in the back room," Jeff, the owner of the Golden Goose said. He began to busy himself at the bar. "A meal is coming soon. The cook is a little late today, but you'll get something to sink your teeth into before the performance. Pub opens at seven."

"Performance?" Robin asked in surprise.

"At eight o'clock," the man said, and turned to his bottles.

Robin stepped into the side room, where poker players or other small groups usually sat. Vera Carrigan was enthroned at a large table. It was much too big, because across from her were only two other members of the theatrical company. She'd kept a free seat next to her for Robin. Robin's new boss smiled at him, but it didn't seem to reach her eyes. Perhaps that impression was only due to all the makeup that Vera had put on. Her eyes were surrounded by dark kohl, her tan skin had been powdered until it was pale, and her mouth was stained blood red.

"There you are, kid. And here are the others. This is our soubrette or naive, Leah . . ." She pointed to a blonde, very young woman. Leah had stringy hair, a heart-shaped face, nearly invisible eyelashes and eyebrows, and pale skin. Without heavy makeup, her expressions wouldn't be visible past a theater's first two rows. Only her violet-blue eyes showed any kind of expression. Robin noticed they now reflected a kind of surprise, and he wondered if it was him she found confusing, or everything. She was very thin, and her dress hung loosely on her almost childlike figure. Robin guessed that she was about eighteen, or at the most twenty, and could hardly believe that she would really drink the whiskey on the table in front of her. But he soon discovered that he had misjudged her.

"And this is our character actor, Bertram Lockhart," Vera continued. "Bertram, as I said, you now have someone to share your love of Shakespeare with. We will be performing many more of his works soon."

"I can't remember any Shakespeare play that only has four roles," the stocky, dark-haired man grumbled as he stood up and offered his hand.

"Robin Fenroy."

Robin shook the large paw as well as he could, and realized that, with his high cheekbones, clearly contoured lips, and Roman nose, the man might have once been called handsome. Now, however, his face looked bloated and the dark eyes were glassy. The whiskey on the table was certainly not Bertram Lockhart's first that day.

"My name will tell you nothing, my days of glory are long past. London, Sydney . . . I was once in the Royal Shakespeare Company. Hard to believe, isn't it?"

Robin believed that the man had stage experience at the very least. His voice was strong and clear.

"And now you will be our Romeo . . . but hopefully not only with Vera." The actor smiled sarcastically.

Robin blushed. Vera Carrigan must have told the man about his audition. Had she made fun of his inaptitude? But then he gathered his courage and told Lockhart about Elliot and his performance with the Pomeroy Company. Bertram listened with interest. But all of it seemed to pass Leah by. Robin wondered if she had no surname. In the meantime, the food arrived. A plump woman with a stained apron brought a platter of fatty meat swimming in brown gravy and some overcooked vegetables. Robin helped himself to the latter and tried to refuse when Bertram poured a glass of whiskey for him. However, the actor wouldn't accept his objections.

"Take a sip, boy, out of courtesy. And believe me, you'll need it. The Pomeroy Company, the Bandmann-Beaudet Shakespeare Company . . . Well! You'll find that things are a bit different here."

With that, he knocked back his own whiskey and poured more. Leah took a sip from her glass as well. Robin managed to stretch the one glass until it was time for the performance. He listened as the company planned their evening. The discussion was mainly about the order of performances. What each individual would perform seemed to be left up to the actors themselves.

"At the end we'll do *Othello*," Vera finally ordered. A large glass of beer was now in front of her.

Bertram Lockhart winced. "I can't promise," he murmured. "It depends if I'm drunk enough by then."

Shortly before eight o'clock, Leah disappeared, followed closely by Vera. Robin would have liked to talk to Bertram, but he didn't dare. The old actor seemed grim and withdrawn.

Robin was glad when the women finally returned, but was taken aback at the sight of Leah. Her makeup was grotesque, her face white with red spots on her cheeks, her eyes ringed in black kohl, her mouth far too large and bright red.

Before he could say anything, the door opened and the cook looked into the room. "You can start," she said. "Good audience tonight. Jeff says there are a lot of people. So see to it that you have something to offer the crowd."

Vera Carrigan's eyebrows shot up. She murmured something to Leah and then shoved her into the taproom. Vera and Leah climbed onto the stage accompanied by howls and applause. Robin, who followed with Bertram, couldn't see any women in the audience. Basically, it had nothing in common with a theater. The chairs were still grouped around the tables. The pub's guests could turn them to watch what was happening on the stage, but they didn't have to. Many continued their raucous conversations.

But Vera didn't let that distract her. She spread her arms wide and greeted the audience, inviting them to an "edifying, contemplative, and joyous evening of pleasure." She promised that the Carrigan Company would do their best to provide unforgettable entertainment.

As for Robin, that was already guaranteed when Leah attempted to sing a song from *HMS Pinafore*. Vera announced her as Leah Hobarth. She played the role of Josephine and sang "Sorry Her Lot Who Loves Too Well." She managed to hit even fewer notes than Robin himself could have. What was more, she woodenly stood on the stage as though it were her first performance ever. Her voice was rather thin. The audience booed, which Leah hardly seemed to notice. But Bertram Lockhart appeared to feel sorry for her. He grunted and knocked back another whiskey.

"I'll go rescue her, then," he whispered to Robin.

He had ushered the young man to a table in the corner of the room, where the actors were apparently accustomed to waiting for their next performances. A bottle stood ready.

Bertram stood up and strode with surprisingly sure steps to the stage, and put his arm around Leah. With a powerful, exceptionally beautiful voice, he began to sing a duet with her. This too was from the Gilbert and Sullivan operetta. The imposing actor guided his incumbent partner in a little dance. In spite of his age, he played the youthful lover with total believability. When he finally took "Josephine" in his arms at the end, the audience clapped enthusiastically. Then Bertram cleared the stage for Vera.

The head of the company had changed her outfit. In a short, tight-fitting white dress and fishnet stockings, with a parasol in her hand and colorful ribbons in her pinned-up hair, she played a scene from a burlesque.

Bertram told the bewildered Robin the burlesque was called *The Alabama*. "Made world famous by Lydia Thompson. They say that Miss Thompson could perform the erotic scenes without making the audience feel shame." The current audience seemed to be enjoying Vera's performance very much. A few of the men whistled, and everyone applauded as she bowed with the grace of an elephant. She bent low and offered the men a deep look into her bodice. "That goes under 'contemplative,'" Bertram quipped. "Now, would you like to deliver something edifying, or shall I?"

"Me?" Robin's voice broke in a way that it hadn't for years.

"Well, we could do a scene from *King Lear*, or something from *Romeo and Juliet*," Bertram said. "They'll hardly notice the difference. Besides, if you're so enthusiastic to get on the stage . . . I'd be happy to leave it up to you."

"I—you—you want Shakespeare now?" Robin stuttered.

"It's part of the deal," Bertram insisted. "At least once or twice an evening, she has to let me play a real part. Not that the people appreciate it. It's more because I need it."

Then he stood up and took the stage again, where he decided on *Hamlet* at the last minute.

*"To be or not to be, that is the question . . ."*

Robin realized he was holding his breath. He had never seen Hamlet played that way. Of course, Bertram Lockhart was too old for the part, but that hadn't stopped Daniel Bandmann or Arthur Elliot. Both of them had played the Danish prince when they were over forty, but they hadn't been as convincing.

The aging, apparently alcoholic actor was able to convey the desperation of the confused, overwhelmed young prince extremely well, and he made young Hamlet vital and alive. Robin applauded thunderously when Bertram had finished. But he was the only one. The men at the tables only paid attention again when Vera and Leah performed another skit. Vera played a lady who was trying to control her maid because they were both interested in the same man. Leah was slightly better as an actress than she had been as a singer. Nevertheless, Robin wondered what the girl was doing on a stage. He didn't dare to ask the same question regarding Vera Carrigan, although she practically demanded it. Vera's voice was loud and powerful, her face was expressive, and her performances left nothing to be desired in terms of directness. To Robin, however, she seemed more brazen than talented.

"And now we present something joyful, my dear friends," she announced. "The newest member of our troupe, Robin Fenroy, will seduce you as Romeo . . . even though I'm sure that you'd prefer to see Juliet!"

The people laughed, and Robin suddenly felt paralyzed. He hadn't agreed to this! Did she really want him on the stage right now?

"In the meantime, I'll change," Vera said, and raised her skirts as though she was planning to take off her clothes where she stood. "As the climax of the evening, Othello and Desdemona, at night . . ." She smiled insinuatingly.

Bertram knocked back another shot of whiskey. Judging by his expression, the glass might as well have contained poison hemlock.

"Go on, then," he said, and shoved Robin toward the stage. "And do it right, boy."

Robin dragged himself to the stage as though in a trance. It was a strange feeling to stand there and look down into the brightly lit pub. The auditoriums where he'd performed before had been darker. Here, he could see the men's faces and their disinterested expressions. Robin began to panic as he realized that all his powers of imagination weren't strong enough to picture Juliet among them. He glanced briefly at Vera Carrigan, but she was still wearing the low-cut dress, fishnet stockings, and cheap makeup. And Leah? The girl was drinking another glass of whiskey as though it were water. His old barn cat had more in common with the innocent Shakespeare heroine.

Then he spotted Bertram Lockhart again. The man's gaze was surprisingly clear in spite of all the whiskey. Robin took a deep breath and conjured the image of March Jensch.

Finally, he spoke Romeo's lines in a sure voice, and as usual, a miracle happened. The ugly pub transformed into the Capulets' garden, and Juliet's slender figure appeared before him.

Robin stood on the stage, and though he'd just been doubting if he really wanted to be part of the Carrigan Company, at that moment he could only think of Hamlet's ultimate question: To be or not to be? Robin was like Bertram. The only time he truly felt alive was when he was standing on a stage.

To his amazement, Robin even received a little applause as he finished. And it made him very happy when Bertram squeezed his shoulder in recognition as he left the stage. The old actor had painted his face black, and Vera Carrigan was walking next to him, her hair loose, dressed in a skimpy nightshirt that revealed almost more than it concealed.

The actor dragged a bed to the middle of the stage, and Vera slipped coyly under the blanket.

*"It is the cause, it is the cause, my soul . . ."*

Bertram began Othello's emotional monologue while the men watched Vera writhe under the blanket. They whistled when Othello kissed her. And then, as Desdemona awakened, Robin was witness to such an obscene parody of Shakespeare's work that he had to fight back a wave of nausea.

Vera Carrigan played a lascivious, seductive Desdemona, who obviously knew all of the sins that one could commit in a bed. She molested her "husband," grabbing his crotch, fingering herself, and trying to grab his hand and lead it to her bosom, and finally stood up and rubbed her body against him. In doing so, she spoke the immortal words of Shakespeare—not in a fearful manner, but rather alluringly, cooing and laughing all the while.

Robin was glad when they shortened the scene. Vera didn't care why Desdemona was supposed to die. The audience didn't seem to care about the affair with Cassio either. The men just whistled and howled lustily as Vera put on her show.

*"But half an hour . . ."*

Even Desdemona's last desperate plea became an order. And then, Bertram wasn't even allowed to suffocate her. After "Being done, there is no pause," Vera took the old actor by the hand and towed him into the wings.

The audience rewarded them with jubilant applause. Vera and Bertram returned and bowed, and then waved Leah and Robin back to the stage to receive their final applause.

Robin felt as though he'd been slapped. He willingly drank the whiskey that Bertram poured for him as he sat down at their table again.

Two hours later, back in his room, Robin was still wrestling with himself. Was this really what he wanted? Could he bear the mockery of an art that was practically holy to him, and probably to Bertram Lockhart too? What would he have to perform next? And with which partner? He couldn't even imagine Vera Carrigan as Ophelia or Juliet—and certainly not the sallow, apathetic Leah.

While Robin was still ruminating, he heard someone at the door. The young man started in shock as it opened quietly and a beam of light pierced the darkness. A figure in a red dressing gown appeared. Vera Carrigan was carrying a candle, and her still made-up face looked ghostly in its light.

"Did you pray already, Robin Fenroy?" she said in a seductive voice. And then she was next to him. Her lips molded onto his, and her kiss smothered any attempt to reply. Robin squirmed with shame and fear, but soon also lust. Vera Carrigan knew how to arouse a man, and Robin knew nothing. Her hands seemed to be everywhere at once, her tongue slithered its way across his body, and her mouth closed around his maleness. Her dressing gown had long since slid off her shoulders and her breasts were large and heavy. "Now touch me, boy."

Vera began to guide Robin's hands. He touched her body, smelled her perfume and the sharp scent of her sweat mixed with his own. He was torn between disgust and lust as he finally penetrated her and exploded in a surge of ecstasy that he immediately felt ashamed of.

That night, Vera Carrigan made young Robin Fenroy into a man—but not the type of man he wanted to become.

# Chapter 17

Vera left Robin's room that same night, and despite everything, the young man slept like the dead. The exhausting day and the whiskey were taking their toll.

The next morning, Robin awoke with a headache and a queasy stomach. His bedsheets stank of sweat and semen, and he felt dirty from within and without. He crawled out of bed and felt his way to the privy. He would have preferred to take a bath, or to throw himself into the clear cold waters of a lake or the ocean. There was no chance for that, of course; the Golden Goose didn't even have running water.

Robin gave himself a bird bath with the stale water from a pitcher on the table. He felt a little better, but the bitter taste in his mouth lingered, even after he'd brushed his teeth. Coffee might help, he thought, and there would surely be some down in the pub—although he'd be risking running into Vera or another member of their so-called company. Well, he'd see them later, anyway, if he decided to stay.

Robin resolved to postpone his decision until after breakfast. Upon entering the taproom, he was greeted with the same scene he'd been met with when he'd arrived. Jeff was alone, wiping down tables.

The man gave him a look of astonishment. "Ye're up early, ain't ye?" he asked. "No' too typical for your craft, eh? Want some coffee? Mary ain't here yet, so if ye wan' to have breakfast, you'll have to make it yersel'. There's the kitchen."

At least the man didn't seem to be hiding anything. Robin went into the surprisingly clean kitchen and found a pot of hot coffee on the stove. There was a started loaf of bread, butter, and some jam sitting on a table, probably left over from Jeff's breakfast. Robin sat down, cut himself a slice, buttered it, and washed it down with some coffee. He was starting to feel better. Ready to think.

This, he realized, wasn't what he'd been imagining for himself. Vera Carrigan wasn't in charge of an actual theater company, no matter how good Bertram was. After the old thespian's performance, Robin believed everything he'd told him about his past. What had gotten in the way of Bertram's career had probably been his drinking problem, not his lack of talent. Vera Carrigan, on the other hand, wasn't an actress. She was more like a . . . whore?

Robin blushed at the thought of the word, especially after reminding himself what the woman had done to him the night before. But there was no need for him to be ashamed—neither he nor Vera were married or committed in any way. Indeed, Robin could have lost his innocence in the arms of a friendly Maori girl long ago without it having bothered anybody, had he been so inclined. But he'd never given in to the girls' advances; up until now, he hadn't been able to imagine himself making love to anybody but March Jensch. Except that March obviously didn't want him—Robin tried not to think about what she was doing in Kaiapoi with Martin Porter. So he could do as he pleased, and he'd enjoyed being with Vera, in a way. He'd never felt as aroused before as he had in that moment when she'd pulled him on top of her and had reared up while he'd pushed himself into her.

And yet, Robin thought, such feelings should be a part of love, the exchange of caresses and gentle words. With Vera, he felt only disgust, and her way of taking him had nothing to do with tender feelings whatsoever. The sight of her didn't even arouse him. Something like last night, Robin was sure, wouldn't happen again. From now on, he would lock his door.

But was he even going to stay? He hadn't signed any sort of contract yet, and it wouldn't be worth anything anyway without one of his parents' signatures.

Robin thought hard about his alternatives. He had about fifty pounds left—a little less, once he paid for his stay. Vera certainly wouldn't pay his room and board if he left now. Of course, he could just walk away . . . Robin discarded the idea immediately. The mere thought of skipping out on a tab made his conscience twinge uncomfortably.

But even after paying Jeff, he'd still have enough money to sail back to the South Island, and he could telegraph Rata Station from Blenheim. His parents would send him money or come pick him up, and until then, a child of Rata Station could surely receive credit at any hotel. But then what? Was he to be trapped at Rata Station until the end of time? To do work he neither enjoyed nor was very good at? Besides, nobody back home would believe that he'd declined the possibility of an "engagement" himself. They'd all just assume that Robin Fenroy had failed once again.

Robin rubbed his forehead. So he'd stay. He'd try to use the Carrigan Company as a stepping stone to more serious engagements. Of course, working here didn't exactly do wonders for his reputation. But Vera and her company traveled. Last night, they'd talked about the fact that their booking at the Golden Goose would be ending tomorrow. Next, the actors would be moving on to Greytown. They'd stay in one city after another, and he could audition at any theater along the way. Vera didn't have to find out. Somewhere, at some point, there had to be a director who'd give a young, talented actor a chance. In the meantime, Robin could learn. Just watching Bertram Lockhart would help, and maybe the actor would even be willing to teach him.

Robin drank another cup of coffee and decided to try it out for at least another night. Surely, distancing himself from his ideals a little was better than humiliation. One small chance was better than the boring, uneventful, and hopeless existence he'd been living on the South Island.

As expected, the others roused themselves early that afternoon. Mary, the pub's cook, had a light lunch ready for them, and they ate at the same pub table from which Robin had watched their performance the night before. He painstakingly picked the chunks of meat out of his stew—an excuse not to look at Vera Carrigan. She was already fully made-up, and she seemed to be wide awake and burning for action—contrary to Bertram and Leah, who both seemed hungover. Bertram was already tackling his headache with another hair-of-the-dog whiskey. Leah, silent and pale, spooned up her soup.

"So, did you sleep well, my dearie?" Vera asked him shamelessly. Bertram glanced up from his whiskey for a second, saw Robin blushing, and gave him a sympathetic look. "Did you . . . enjoy last night?"

Robin decided to refer to their stage performance with his answer, and he gushed about Bertram's acting talent.

"You're not half bad either," the old thespian grumbled.

Robin beamed at him.

"I can also see a variety of potential uses for his talent," Vera said. "How about it, Robin? Would you rehearse a scene with Leah for tonight? Something nice. Maybe with Romeo and Juliet kissing? I have a very pretty script here, it's only slightly adapted . . ."

Leah glanced up, indifferent. Robin's repulsion was apparent in his face.

Vera's eyes hardened. "You'll have to do a little more around here than just recite a few dry monologues, boy."

Robin nodded. "So . . . shall we rehearse onstage, here?" he asked Leah. "Right now, after lunch? I'll go get my copy of the script."

As he got to his feet, Robin saw Vera give Leah a sidelong glance. Then, upon reaching his room, he was confronted with the fact that the door was unlocked yet again. While he was still going through his suitcase in search of his scripts, Leah entered, wordlessly pulled her dress over her head, and lay down on the bed. She was wearing a corset, which she started to unhook. Robin was appalled, but he couldn't suppress a certain excitement as her body was revealed, bit by bit. He stared at her in disbelief.

"Well?" Leah asked. "Are you coming? If I'm supposed to memorize anything, we should get started soon."

Robin shook his head. "Please get dressed!" he urged her. "We don't need to sleep with each other. It's enough if we act as though we're in love with each other."

Leah raised her eyebrows. "Vera says it helps," she remarked. "And Bertram liked it."

Robin could hardly believe what he was hearing. He'd been so impressed by the aging thespian. But now, he was disappointed beyond measure. How could the man take advantage of the stupidity and helplessness of such a young girl?

"But he was drunk out of his mind," Leah added, which clarified the situation for Robin, but didn't excuse it.

"Well, I don't need that," he said resolutely. "Put on your clothes. We'll go downstairs and rehearse the scene onstage."

Leah did as he told her, and when the two of them went right back downstairs, Bertram smiled. Vera, on the other hand, seemed annoyed.

By that evening, Robin had taught Leah where to stand, how to move, and which tone of voice to speak in. The latter was only partly successful. Leah didn't understand Shakespearean English, and all she did was rattle off the words in monotone. At least she was fairly quick to memorize her lines, and she didn't show any signs of nervousness before their "premiere."

But when they performed their scene, Leah deviated from their rehearsed interpretation. She didn't play Juliet as a gentle girl, but as a foul wench throwing herself at Romeo, no doubt under Vera's instructions. Had she put a little more passion into the script that somebody had rewritten for them, it would have been just as ugly as Vera and Bertram's scene from *Othello*. Again, Robin questioned his decision. Maybe he should take the ferry for Blenheim the next morning, and not the train to Greytown.

After the performance, he excused himself early, and this time, he was careful to lock his door. A moment later, he heard a knock.

"Who is it?" Robin asked nervously. "I'm—I'm in bed already."

Outside the door, he heard Vera's throaty laugh. "Oh, nonsense. You're just scared of your own courage. You didn't like last night, my little innocent, did you?"

"No—yes—" Robin was tripping over his words. He didn't know what to say.

"Just let me in now," Vera ordered him. "Don't be stupid, I won't hurt you. I only want to talk to you."

Robin walked over to the door hesitantly. He didn't really want to see her, but he didn't want her to think that he was afraid of her either. And she was his boss—he had to obey her. He took a deep breath and opened the door. Vera Carrigan stood in front of him, fully clothed. She was wearing a saucy red evening dress with a matching hat. Robin flinched when she entered the room as if she owned it.

"I'm going to need you again tonight, Robin," she told him matter-of-factly. "One performance, my dearie, or rather, a game."

"Now?" Robin asked, dumbfounded. It was ten o'clock at night. "Onstage?"

Vera shook her head. "Not onstage. Up here. You could say it's . . . well . . . a test." She pressed her lips together and looked at him sternly.

"Robin, I want to be frank with you; you didn't convince me back there. I'm sure you're talented, but your performance with Leah was a little stiff. So, if you're going to be traveling on with us tomorrow . . . Well, in short, I'd like to see a little more from you. And of course it has to be now. Don't forget that our train leaves very early tomorrow. We'll . . . improvise. You must have done that before in your lessons with Mr. Elliot."

"Of course."

Robin nodded apprehensively, although improvisation had rarely been a part of the Pomeroy Company's rehearsal schedule. Elliot had placed more emphasis on voice training and the interpretation of texts. Besides, Robin wasn't entirely sure what this was all about. Vera hadn't expressed any doubts that she'd be able to put him to good use in the company.

Vera took off her cloak and Robin withdrew a few steps. Was she going to take off her clothes after all? But the actress simply continued her explanations after taking a seat on a chair, not the bed.

"All right, this is what we'll do: you'll play my husband, my dearie. We already practiced what he's supposed to do last night, didn't we?" Vera grimaced; it looked like she was trying to give him a wicked little smile. "And you'll come home to our bedroom, and I'll be there with—"

"Mr. Lockhart?" Robin asked.

Vera laughed. "I might find another actor," she said mysteriously.

Robin thought for a moment. Was it possible that someone new had auditioned with Miss Carrigan this afternoon? That would explain her doubts about Robin.

"Anyway, you'll come inside, all indignant. You'll be terribly upset that there's a stranger in my bed, and you'll threaten him, and maybe even me, a little. Show me your temper, my dearie! Just like Othello."

Robin's mind was racing. He'd never studied *Othello*. But of course, he knew the lines, more or less, and he could look them up.

"Right now?" he asked. "I mean, are we rehearsing now?"

Vera rolled her eyes. "No. Later. I'll give you some time to think about your lines. Ah, Lord above, Robin, you'll be able to hear us in the corridor outside your room. I'll turn on the blarney, and your supposed rival might be a little drunk. Or he'll play drunk, anyway. You can just wait for a few minutes, and then come into my room. I'll leave the door open. It can't be that hard! Not for somebody who considers himself an actor."

Robin swallowed. A few moments ago, he'd been doubting whether he wanted to be a part of this company. But now that the opportunity was on the line, his ambition began to stir.

"I'll manage," he mumbled.

"I certainly hope so!" Vera said, getting to her feet. She snatched up her cloak on her way out.

Robin found the entire situation disconcerting. Vera's attire too. Her elegant silk dress wouldn't have been out of place at a nice restaurant. Miss Pomeroy and the other women of her company hadn't usually cared for such accoutrements during rehearsals. They showed up in comfortable house dresses, and almost never in makeup. Vera, on the other hand, was wearing stage makeup even now. It occurred to Robin that Miss Pomeroy had done her makeup very differently. In her company, it had been all about enhancing an actor's natural features to ensure that the expressions could be seen even from the last rows of the auditorium. Vera's excessive use of powder and lipstick, on the other hand, was grotesque.

Robin retreated to his bed and dug out the script for *Othello*. He had plenty of time to study it; it was a good two hours until Vera returned. As promised, she had a man with her. Robin could hear them talking and laughing. He cast a nervous glance at the clock, letting ten minutes pass. Then he stepped out onto the landing and knocked on her door.

"Miss—um—Vera?"

"Goodness gracious! Who might that be? Not the garçon, surely? Did you order champagne, my prince, my stallion?" Vera's voice sounded just as put-on as it had onstage. Robin's misgivings grew. He nearly turned to run away. But Vera's coaxing voice issued from her room. "Then he shall come inside with this royal drink he has for us!" Against his better judgment, the boy pushed open the door—and immediately tried to stop himself from blushing. Vera was lying on the bed, her corset untied, breasts exposed. In front of her, a man was kneeling, also in a half state of undress. Small, portly, not quite young anymore. He didn't look like an actor to Robin. His shocked expression, on the other hand, did look deceptively real. "Heavens above!" Vera cried. "My husband!"

"I—" Robin choked on Othello's monologue. It wouldn't be appropriate here, surely. "How—how could you? And—who is this?"

His words didn't land with the force Vera had probably been imagining. But now, she took the lead of this terrible play.

"Don't hurt him, my love, I beg you! Don't hurt me! Oh, I know, I am guilty, for my flesh is weak . . . Leave the knife in its sheath, my heart . . ." Vera jumped out of bed, threw herself to the ground at Robin's feet, and clutched at his legs.

The man she'd just been amusing herself with looked confused. His eyes were red-rimmed; he was obviously drunk.

Sarah Lark

"Ve . . . Ve . . . Ve . . . Vera . . . y . . . y . . . you . . . you sssaid you were free t'nigh', ann . . . ," he slurred.

"Oswald, for heavens' sake, leave before he can hurt you!" Vera was standing between the two men with an expression on her face that was probably supposed to mimic concern. In Robin's eyes, this was the most primitive kind of farce, but the half-naked man seemed to be taking her quite seriously. "He almost killed the last man I got carried away with . . . Here, quickly, your trousers, your coat! Run . . . run, Oswald, if your life is dear to you!" With that, she shoved the man's things into his hands and pushed him out of the room.

"Forgive me, please, forgive me! You're the only man I truly love!" Vera howled, loud enough to be heard through the door. But she was already letting go of Robin, inspecting the wallet that had slipped out of the man's coat pocket and under the bed as though by accident. Appalled, Robin listened for any sounds from the corridor. The man was hastily beating his retreat. Vera pulled two fifty-pound bills from the wallet. "There we are," she said contentedly. "Good pay for three minutes' worth of performance, wouldn't you say?" She gave Robin a devious glance. "Despite the fact that you didn't exactly deck yourself in glory. Bertram's better at this sort of thing. When he's sober, that is."

"You—you've done this before?" It was only just dawning on Robin what he'd been a part of. "That wasn't an actor. That was just some man who—who went out with you, and this—all this was just to rob him?"

Vera grinned. "You really are a clever boy," she said, taunting him. "Don't look at me like that! Other theaters have their patrons too. Dear Oswald just made his contribution to the arts. With this money, we'll pay for the trip to Greytown and the hotel and the community hall we'll be performing at. We'll perform *As You Like It* or *Hamlet*. You can play the Danish prince, my dearie. That's what you want, isn't it?" She pressed up against him, just like she had the night before.

Robin pushed her away. "I'm not a thief!" he gasped. "I don't want any part of such a thing! What if the man decides to go to the police, or—"

Vera laughed carelessly. "He won't be talking to an officer anytime soon," she explained. "He'd be much too embarrassed. What would he tell them? That he thought an actress had spontaneously fallen in love with him, and that she could hardly wait to get Prince Charming into her bed?"

"He might come back tomorrow and ask for his money," Robin replied.

"He'll be sleeping off his overindulgence first," Vera said. "And by nine o'clock tomorrow, we'll be on the train to Greytown. Anyway, if he did show up, I'd tell him I wasn't able to find the wallet, but that I'd look again. And then I'd have somebody deliver it to his house. His wife can receive the delivery if he's at work. If I propose that, he'll raise the white flag, believe me. We have nothing to fear from that man."

"Still, I don't want to have anything to do with this," Robin insisted. "I'm leaving. Tonight, or tomorrow morning." The thought of being on the road in the middle of the night in a strange city scared him.

Vera's amused expression transformed into a look that made Robin's blood curdle. Her dark eyes were cold. He realized with a jolt that he had underestimated her. She was an excellent actress. It was only now that she'd stopped acting. This was her true face.

"It doesn't matter anymore what you want, my dearie," she said. "You were a part of this whole thing just now. Maybe it was even your idea, who knows. Or that's what I'll tell the police, anyway. I've kept a clean slate so far. Only since you showed up here . . . Anyway, you're mine now, little Robin; get used to it. I'll be frank, your performance here was pathetic. You wouldn't have been my first choice. But you're here now, and we'll both have to make the best of it. Welcome to the Carrigan Company, Robin. I'm sure we'll have lots of fun together."

# Chapter 18

The Fenroys were very worried about Robin. There was a strained atmosphere at Rata Station. Cat could understand that Chris didn't want anyone chasing the boy, but she also couldn't come to terms with just leaving him on his own. So she suggested engaging a private detective to find out if he was traveling the North Island with the Carrigan Company. It would have been easy to hire one, but Chris refused. When Cat brought up the subject again, he argued that, on the North Island, the worst thing that could happen to him would be getting stranded somewhere without money.

"He'll just have to get over himself and telegraph us," said Chris. "Or Karl and Ida, they're closer. It wouldn't feel so much like giving up. But he has to prove himself now, Cat. If you can't listen, you have to feel. That's an ugly saying, but so far Robin doesn't seem to understand his situation. If he's running around cities with a third-rate company or unloading ships to earn a living, it can only do him good."

However, Chris had nothing against doing a little research about the Carrigan Company. But Arthur Elliot and Mr. Foreman had never heard of it.

"That doesn't necessarily mean anything," Foreman said. "There are hundreds of little comedy troupes that travel from pub to pub. They used to visit the prospectors' camps, and now they perform for the railroad workers. They usually perform a few sketches and then pass the hat around. The Carrigan Company is probably one of those. If he were a girl, I'd worry very much if I were you. Most of them supplement their earnings with extra work at night. But among the railroad workers there's no demand for boys. They wouldn't dare; they'd become laughingstocks. So don't worry."

Of course Cat worried anyway, so she requested that Aroha, who was back in Dunedin, ask in the city's theaters about Mr. Carrigan. The girl did so dutifully, but without success. She was just as worried about Robin as his parents were.

But soon something happened that forced all thoughts of her relative into the background. One rainy autumn day, Miss Vandermere had Aroha summoned from a seminar where she was working on a French translation.

"What is it?" she asked Miss Vandermere's secretary worriedly. The young man had fetched her from the classroom and was accompanying her through the corridors to the headmistress's office. "Did I do something wrong?"

The secretary smiled. "No. Miss Vandermere has three very—how shall I put it—strange visitors. It's about a job. In any case, Miss Vandermere would be very glad for your help. Go on in, you'll see."

He opened the door to the office, and Aroha gazed with amazement at three Maori, two men and a woman, who were sitting stiffly in the chairs on the far side of the desk. They were all dressed in *pakeha* clothing. One of the men and the woman were older, and had tattoos. They looked very odd in the formal clothes they had selected for the meeting. Aroha suspected that the garments were new. They wore their hair in traditional styles. The old man had his long hair in a warrior's knot, and the woman's gray locks were loose. They sat bolt upright and looked tense. Aroha guessed they probably didn't understand very much English. But the younger man was speaking to Miss Vandermere. He, too, wore a suit, but with a certain self-assurance. His face wasn't tattooed, and his hair was cut short in the *pakeha* style.

"*Kia ora,*" Aroha said in greeting, and bowed formally to the Maori elders. "*Haere mai* to the Vandermere Academy."

Miss Vandermere nodded to her. "Aroha, thank you for coming."

The older visitors reacted with looks of surprise and disdain when they heard her name. But the young man smiled and stood up politely to introduce himself.

"Miss Fitzpatrick, my name Koro Hinerangi. I happy to meet you."

Koro Hinerangi's English wasn't perfect, but it was completely understandable. Aroha accepted the hand he offered.

"And this is Moana Te Wairoa and Kereru Te Ika of the Tuhourangi tribe. I hope I pronounced that at least partly correctly," Miss Vandermere said, and smiled apologetically at the elders. "Perhaps you would like to tell Miss Fitzpatrick about your concerns yourself, Mr. Hinerangi. Have you ever heard of the Pink and White Terraces, Aroha?"

Aroha thought for a moment and then remembered the strange Englishwomen who had visited the boarding school in Otaki two years earlier. She nodded.

"That's . . . a rock formation on the North Island, isn't it?" she asked uncertainly.

One of the elders whispered something. Koro Hinerangi made a soothing gesture. "Terraces at Lake Tarawera," he said to Aroha. "They holy, treasure of our people."

Aroha furrowed her brow. "They aren't *tapu*, are they? I've heard it's possible to visit the terraces."

Koro Hinerangi shook his head. "No. Spirits there friendly. Also welcome strangers." He switched to his own language. "Of course we only allow visitors accompanied by members of our tribe. We take our responsibility to the rocks and their spirits very seriously."

"The rock formations are spectacular," Miss Vandermere said, shifting the conversation back to English. "The tribe welcomes visitors from all over the world."

The young man nodded. "Was once English prince. He like it very much. Since then, always more *pakeha* want see terraces near our village, Te Wairoa."

"And they pay for the privilege," Miss Vandermere said dryly.

"Yes, they do." This was apparently not at all embarrassing for Koro Hinerangi. He looked at the headmistress, then at Aroha, and switched back to his own language. "It also takes a certain amount of effort," he explained. "The terraces can only be approached from the lake, and they are quite far from civilization. We offer the tourists accommodation and tours. That actually makes quite a bit of money for the tribe. But our visitors aren't completely satisfied yet. There are many things that could be improved, if we set our minds to it."

He gazed doubtfully at his companions, who were staring at the wall almost drowsily. He himself seemed very eager and very kind. He was tall, and much less stocky than most Maori Aroha had met. Koro's skin was dark and his hair was straight and black. His eyes were dark as coal, round and very large. They looked as lively as the rest of his face. He had full lips, a straight nose, and strikingly white teeth. They flashed as he spoke in English again.

"Only have two guides speak English good. Others in village can only speak little—"

"Like you?" Miss Vandermere asked sternly. Apparently, she wasn't satisfied with Koro's English.

"Much more bad," Koro admitted, and turned back to Aroha. "That's why we've decided to hire someone who really understands our guests' languages," he explained in Maori. "Someone who could act as an intermediary between my tribe and the visitors from other countries. So far, most of our guests are English, but we are counting on that changing soon."

Aroha nodded. European high society was tightly interwoven. If English travelers talked about the Terraces in their homes, very soon German, French, Italian, and Russian nobility and business tycoons would come to Te Wairoa.

"That why we come here," Koro said in English. "Ask Miss Vandermere, recommend someone for job."

He smiled at the headmistress and Aroha, but the other two Maori continued to show no emotion. Aroha speculated that the village chieftain had finally agreed to support Koro's mission, but had sent these elders as a sort of chaperone. Aroha wondered if Moana Te Wairoa and Kereru Te Ika had even voted against the employment of a *pakeha* in the council meeting.

"You mean to offer me this job?" Aroha addressed the two elders in Maori. Her heart was pounding. It would be incredibly interesting to work as a guide in Te Wairoa, showing foreigners the sights and having conversations with them in their own languages! Meeting people from all over the world would be much more entertaining than teaching at the academy or helping new arrivals to New Zealand get through the immigration offices. "I feel honored. It would make me very happy to help you show your guests the wonders of your land. Of course, I would treat the spirits with respect."

This seemed to please the elders. They glanced briefly at each other and nodded.

"Thank you, *mokopuna*," the old woman said.

Aroha was happy. By calling her "granddaughter," Moana Te Wairoa was telling her she was welcome in the tribe.

"And we will pay you well," Koro continued. "The visitors even give more money when they are particularly happy with the services," he added. Aroha smiled. Koro must think the custom of tipping was strange. "We also offer a place to live in the *marae* or in one of the hotels. Of course, it might be a little lonely. Other than the guests, there are hardly any *pakeha*."

"I wouldn't mind that at all," Aroha exclaimed before translating Koro's words for Miss Vandermere. Then she continued in English. "But . . . am I the only one you want to consider for the job?" She turned to her teacher expectantly.

Miss Vandermere gazed sternly from one to the other. "Can I tell the young lady's parents that it's safe for her to accept such a position? In terms of propriety? It's absolutely unacceptable for Miss Fitzpatrick to live alone in a hotel."

The elders gazed at her uncomprehendingly, even after Aroha had translated. After a moment they replied, and Koro also added a few words.

"One of the two guides is Mr. Hinerangi's mother," Aroha told her teacher enthusiastically. "She lives with her husband and children in a large house. He says I could live with them, if I prefer that to a hotel. My parents would certainly have nothing against it. Please, Miss Vandermere, recommend me for the job!"

Moana Te Wairoa and Kereru Te Ika must have sensed the urgency in her voice. The woman spoke briefly to Koro. Miss Vandermere toyed with her fountain pen as she waited.

Koro spoke English again; it was apparently important to him that Miss Vandermere understood.

"Moana Te Wairoa is ambassador of chieftain. She says, is same if Miss Fitzpatrick is man or woman. Is same, if recommend or not recommend." He turned to Aroha. "If you want job, *wahine*, you have job."

Moana Te Wairoa stood up slowly, and respectfully exchanged *hongi* with Aroha. The women rested their foreheads and noses against each other; a contract between Aroha Fitzpatrick and the Tuhourangi had been made.


When Aroha's school day was over, Koro met her in front of the academy. He was hiding behind one of the pillars that flanked the formal entrance. Aroha smiled, greeting him in Maori.

"Were you waiting for me?"

Koro nodded. "I hope that's all right for you. I know the *pakeha* might think it's not proper for a man to talk to a girl that he doesn't really know."

Aroha shrugged. "We've been properly introduced. Besides, you aren't making declarations of love," she joked, "you just want to talk to me about the job, right?"

She would have spoken differently to a *pakeha* man, but Maori customs were much more relaxed when it came to communication between men and women.

Koro grinned. "We'll start with the job, but we can leave the other option open to discussion," he said, joking back. "But really, Aroha . . . May I call you Aroha?"

Aroha smiled. "Of course!"

"I actually wanted to talk to you again without the *pakeha* woman," Koro said, pointing at the school.

"And without the elders," Aroha added.

Koro nodded, and looked sheepish. "You're very good at dealing with them. Moana is very touched, and so is Kereru. If we have to work with the *pakeha*, then he says it's better with someone like you. You must tell me why you can speak our language so well and how you know our customs. Can we talk somewhere?"

Aroha took him to a café near the school where the staff was used to seeing young men and women sitting together discussing their studies. There was no danger to Aroha's reputation if she sat down with Koro there.

"Moana and Kereru weren't very happy about coming with you, were they?" she asked after she'd ordered coffee and scones. "Is it possible that the spirits of the Pink and White Terraces actually do care how many *pakeha* come visit them?" She smiled mischievously.

Koro winked at her. "You could put it that way," he said. "Although the spirits are the least of our problems. Besides, my mother and Kate Middlemass, the other guide, have a very good relationship with the spirits."

"Miss Middlemass is the other guide who speaks English?" Aroha asked.

"Exactly. My mother is half Scottish, and Kate is from England. The *pakeha* visitors rely on both of them. They organize canoes and oarsmen to bring them to the terraces. The spirits have never complained. Of course, it concerns the villagers. There are differing opinions among the tribe."

"Some of the people don't like *pakeha*?" Aroha asked. "Or does it bother them to accept money to take people to sacred places?"

Koro raised his eyebrows and pursed his lips. The expression looked funny, but also a little desperate.

"Almost everyone likes the money," he said. "It's only one or two priests who are warning us that wealth can corrupt us. In the village of Wharenui Hinemihi, they've given the totem poles gold sovereigns for eyes instead of paua shells." Aroha stared at him in disbelief. "But the *tohunga* generally keep out of it. Most members of the tribe like the money, but they have little respect for the *pakeha*. They think the travelers are silly, and they really are often quite naive. They make it easy for our people to trick them and take advantage of them. It's shameful, but some of our tribesmen have become racketeers. And some of them won't do anything anymore, now that the tribe is rich. They just lounge around and stare at the visitors. They drink and beg."

"What does the chieftain have to say about that?" Aroha asked.

"He views the *pakeha* as a necessary evil. He wants the money too, but he doesn't like what the influx is doing to the tribe. He can't do anything about it."

"He could close the terraces to visitors," Aroha said.

Koro laughed. "Against the will of most of his *iwi*? He would immediately be demoted, and that would be disastrous. The *ariki* is a very reasonable man and supports the few members of the tribe who are prepared to receive the *pakeha* as respected guests. They don't take advantage of them or look down on them. People like my mother and Kate are glad to accept the *pakeha*'s money, but they offer them something for it. We have reasonable, fixed prices. Our goal is to offer the people clean accommodation, good food, and friendly service. And we're also glad to give them a look at our lives. What harm is there in performing a *powhiri* every few days to welcome new *pakeha*? But if we want to organize all of it better, then we'll have to begin soon, or else we'll miss our chance. Even now, the first white people are coming and building hotels. Nearby in Rotorua, there are hot springs, and it's all in *pakeha* hands. The government is pleased to offer land to experienced hotel keepers. Our best advantage is our proximity to the terraces. One can set out directly from Te Wairoa. And there is only one hotel, which is run by a Scotsman. The next *pakeha* houses are about ten miles away. It's almost an entire day's journey on the bad roads."

"But the roads could be improved," Aroha said.

"Exactly," Koro said darkly. "If that happens, Te Wairoa could become superfluous as a destination. Unless we work to make the village more attractive, that is. Will you help us do that? If you are as good with the other elders as you are with Moana and Kereru, perhaps they'll finally understand what's at stake."

Aroha smiled. "So you don't just want me to wrap the *pakeha* around my finger, but the *ariki* and his advisors too?"

Koro nodded and winked at her again, this time conspiratorially. Aroha's heart grew warm.

"Then let's see what can be done."

# Chapter 19

Over the next few weeks, Aroha simmered with excitement. Most travelers came to New Zealand during the summer months, November through February. They normally came down the Whanganui River, visited the Rotorua hot springs, and then the Pink and White Terraces.

As expected, Linda and Franz readily agreed to allow their daughter to accept the job with the Tuhourangi. Linda was glad that Aroha would be living on the North Island again, although fairly far from Otaki. She was planning on visiting her daughter up in Te Wairoa—perhaps even with Franz in tow.

*We don't have to come right away; the terraces won't be disappearing into the lake anytime soon,* she wrote in a letter to her daughter. *Franz has been talking about sharing the school's administration with someone younger. Our dear Pai married one of the pakeha teachers recently. The two of them would be worthy successors. Who knows, maybe Franz will treat himself to a bit of traveling then.*

Aroha responded from Dunedin, saying how much she was looking forward to showing her parents the local sights. She told Linda that there were hot springs next to the famous terraces. Koro was hoping to build a hotel or guesthouse there soon.

Cat, on the other hand, was sad that Aroha was leaving the South Island.

"Everybody's leaving," she said unhappily when Aroha told her about her new job.

Aroha tried to spend her weekends at Rata Station now and then, even during the semester, if only to comfort her grandmother. The mood there was still gloomy; the Fenroys hadn't heard from Robin in months. Cat was desperately worried, while Chris and Carol thought she was overreacting. They assumed Robin had taken some odd job, too proud to simply come back home after failing to join a theater. It made sense to them that he'd be ashamed, and that he wasn't writing home because of it.

"Why, who else is leaving?" Aroha inquired in an attempt to take her grandmother's mind off Robin. Cat told her that Peta had started attending high school in Christchurch. March had also left Maori Station. She was living in Kaiapoi with Martin Porter. "Unmarried?" Aroha squealed. "And in Kaiapoi, so close to Christchurch? I can't imagine all the gossip!"

Cat shrugged. "I think Mr. Porter's reputation in Kaiapoi is ruined one way or another. Apparently, working conditions at the factory are a living hell. Since there's hardly any other employment options for the poor immigrants there, he can keep salaries criminally low. I've heard they recruit new arrivals right at the docks, before they can even come up with any other ideas. I'm not sure if that's really Mr. Porter's doing, but he oversees the factory now, and he's earned himself a reputation for being strict. Of course, March is applying herself as well. The factory owners even pay her a steady salary. Most of the factory workers are women, so it seems like she's a kind of intermediary there. But Peta says the women hate her just as much as they do Porter."

"What's Peta got to do with all this?" Aroha asked.

"He's the one who told us everything," Cat said. "This industrialization thing is a completely new world for us. Porter's factory processes wool, and probably from our sheep too. At least the men have the option of working on a farm instead, but the women are dependent on weaving at the mill. When Carol and I or the Deanses and the Redwoods visit town, we never even see any of them. And we only meet the other end of the chain, the factory owners, at social events. And then, of course, we don't talk about the working conditions. But Peta went to see for himself. Jane says he needs training outside of high school, so he works at the counting house with March and Porter during school vacations now."

"Jane again?" Aroha asked, agitated. "I mean, Peta has parents! Shouldn't they be making the decisions about his education? And anyway, what do Mara and Eru have to say about March and Porter?"

Cat shook her head. "Mara and Eru don't care. Eru's following in his father's footsteps. They'll make him chieftain one day, and he'll do well for himself. He's an intermediary between Jane and the tribe; he makes sure that everything goes smoothly with the sheep breeding, and that nobody feels exploited or cheated. All the Ngai Tahu are happy. And all Mara cares about is her music. She raised her children lovingly; she never let March suffer from the circumstances of her conception. But since neither March nor Peta have ever shown the slightest bit of enthusiasm for flute playing, she simply forgot about them at some point. Aroha, Mara lives in her own world, or she shares it with Eru, at least. She's happy with her husband, and because she's respected as a musician. Students come from all over the country to learn from her, even *pakeha* who are interested in traditional music. Some private scholar from the west coast keeps inviting her to give lectures. That's something she seems interested in; she does it very enthusiastically. But she couldn't care less whether March lives with Mr. Porter unmarried, or what Peta thinks about working conditions at the factory in Kaiapoi. As long as their children are happy, Mara and Eru keep out of it. And if they succeed in making Jane happy in the process, even better. To Jane, the two of them are the answers to all her dreams. March is turning into the businesswoman her grandmother always wanted to be, and Peta plans to study law."

"Really?" Aroha asked.

Cat smiled. "He says that working at the factory has been eye-opening for him. He's started reading books by some German authors—Marx, Engels, Bebel—and he wants to fight for workers' rights. Eru and Te Haitara think it'd be better for him to fight for Maori rights, of course, while Jane hopes he'll become a business lawyer. Peta lets them all believe what they want; he's always had a gift for diplomacy."

"How could March and Porter be such slave drivers?" Aroha marveled. "Of course, March isn't particularly empathetic. But I don't think she's a bad person."

Cat shrugged. "She says that Peta exaggerates, and that conditions in Kaiapoi are a lot better than in the big cities in England or America. My understanding is that weaving and spinning mills always come with dust and noise, and the air is bad. The expensive machines have to be used as efficiently as possible, which means running them all day and all night, so twelve-hour shifts are fairly normal. I don't know how to judge any of that. Maybe I should go and have a look for myself, but since I can't change anything, I don't see the point in burdening myself with it. Peta can go and change the world once he's grown. I have my own son, my own problems."

On her way back to Dunedin, Aroha was presented with the opportunity to visit the mill. She would be accompanying Peta on his way to Christchurch, where a new school week was beginning, and taking the train from there. Peta had his own little boat that he could row up and down the Waimakariri. This was a major undertaking for a boy of only fifteen, but Peta was burly and strong like all the men in his family. At the moment, the current was favorable, so all Peta had to do was keep the boat in the middle of the river, deftly avoiding any rapids. It meant that the boy had time to chat with Aroha, and of course, she asked him about March and the factory in Kaiapoi. Peta waxed eloquent on the subject, talking a mile a minute about low wages and bad working conditions, and how much the tranquil little town of Kaiapoi had changed since the factory was built. Finally, he cast a glance at his pocket watch. It was still early; they'd left at the crack of dawn.

"You can come and have a look if you want," he said eagerly. "Kaiapoi's right at the mouth of the river, and the factory's close to the shore. It uses a lot of water, and they run it right back into the Waimakariri, dirty and reeking as anything. And nobody says a thing about it!" Peta snorted.

Aroha thought for a moment. The Waimakariri was carrying them quickly past reed-covered banks and wide-open plains overgrown with tussock grass. The scenery was so peaceful; she could hardly believe that there was something so repulsive happening nearby.

"You'll be late for school," she pointed out.

Peta waved his hand dismissively. "I'll think of an excuse. The boat had a leak or something. Besides, you have enough time. Your train leaves at twelve, right? We'll be in Christchurch well before that."

"Can we just walk into the factory like that?" Aroha asked.

The gray swaths of morning mist that lay draped over the mountains had only just begun to dissipate, and the peaks of the Southern Alps were still obscured. Aroha would miss this beautiful landscape once she was on the North Island. But the land around Lake Tarawera must be wilder; there were even supposed to be volcanoes there.

Peta shrugged. "The early shift starts now," he told her. "And I bet March would be honored to show you around. So would Mr. Porter. They're actually proud of what they do there."

Aroha fretted for a moment over making Peta late to school. But her curiosity about the factory won out. Aroha could hardly believe that her cousin was involved in ruthlessly running a mill at only seventeen.

"All right, but not too long," she finally said. "A short visit, not a big tour of the place. Just a quick look will be enough."

Peta gave a bitter laugh. "I have no doubt that will be enough for you," he said. "Unfortunately, the workers are stuck there."

Kaiapoi, which had originally been a charming fishing town with a small shipyard, came into view shortly after they'd passed the mouth of the Waimakariri.

Canterbury Spinning and Weaving Company hadn't built their factory in the middle of town, but a short distance away on the road to Christchurch. Aroha had been imagining a gigantic, hulking mass of stone, but it seemed the architect had actually made an effort. The front of the building with its arched windows was simply designed, but not plain. Only the wall that ran around the perimeter of building had a military look to it. The steam-powered engines inside were running, and the gigantic chimneys were alive with smoke. There weren't any larger buildings around the factory premises, or any of the colorful houses typical of the area. Instead, low, primitive huts hugged the factory wall.

"The workers live there," Peta explained. "And don't think the proprietors provide them with these houses, like the mining companies in Europe do. This company doesn't care, especially not Mr. Porter. The workers have to take care of themselves, so they end up quickly knocking something together when they arrive. They've had to cut down all the trees in the vicinity—the local Ngai Tahu issued some complaints already. These people are advancing into Maori land, and there's been trouble here and there."

The workers' settlement stretched around the factory walls, just like the villages that used to spring up at the feet of castles and fortresses in the Middle Ages. Unfortunately, this place didn't look anywhere near as cozy as the European timber-framed settlements Aroha knew from books. Instead, it all looked neglected. And yet, the buildings couldn't have been that old—the factory had only been there for four years. The narrow alleyways stank of filth and human and animal excrement. Obviously, people just threw their waste out onto the street. They were doubtlessly hoping that the next rainstorm—and there were many of those in the Canterbury Plains—would wash the paths clean again. In effect, all it did was turn them into mud.

Peta tied up his boat at a jetty a short way upstream from the spinning mill, where some scruffy-looking fishing boats were bobbing on the current. To get to the factory, they had to walk through a part of the settlement. Aroha wrinkled her nose and lifted her skirts.

There was a lot of activity around the factory. Men and women, the latter sometimes tugging children along, were making their way toward the entrance. Female laborers had no reason to worry about dirtying their dresses, as they were hemmed just above the ankles. Aroha was a little surprised. People didn't take such matters too seriously on farms, when women showed their ankles while riding, for example. But in the city, it was considered indecent.

"What are they doing with their children?" Aroha asked apprehensively.

She'd heard about child labor in England, but there was no way March and Porter would tolerate that!

"I don't know," Peta said. "In any case, they don't work at the factory, which is one thing March always mentions as proof of how humanitarian the conditions are. The truth is, it's illegal in New Zealand to have the little ones slave away in factories. But nobody gives a damn what happens to them while their mothers and fathers work all day. These people have to find somebody to look after their children—for pay, of course, which diminishes their income. Or they just leave them at home to fend for themselves. It works as long as there are older siblings there to mind them. But otherwise . . . There have been several cases of children drowning in the river."

"The factory should offer a place to keep them safe," Aroha mused.

Peta gave a bitter laugh.

They had reached the factory's gates, which were now swallowing up droves of people. Cat had said that there were around two hundred people working here. That was another thing Aroha found hard to believe.

Peta greeted the doorman and asked him to notify Martin Porter of his arrival. While they waited, Aroha read the factory regulations, which had been tacked up on the wall next to the entrance.

*Every worker is personally responsible for his/her entrusted tools.*

*If the worker cannot provide them upon request, they will be replaced with new ones at the worker's own cost.*
*If an item is damaged in a workroom and the culprit cannot be found, all the workers in the room in question will be made accountable for the damage.*
*Furthermore, there will be penalization for:*
*Disrespectful behavior against supervisors*
*The disturbance of other workers*
*Tardiness and neglect*
*Eating or drinking in the workspace*
*Smoking tobacco*
*Noise on the way to and from the factory*

"My goodness, you can't do anything here!" Aroha exclaimed.

She jumped at the piercing sound of a steam whistle. Upon hearing it, the workers started crowding through the gates even faster. Aroha paid particular attention to the women and girls. She had been worried that they would be dressed in rags, but that wasn't the case. The women were wearing dark-blue cotton dresses, sometimes printed with little white ornaments, dots or stars. The top layer was a black apron. With their sturdy shoes, it almost looked as though they were wearing uniforms. The women warded off the cold with knit shawls quite similar to the ones that market vendors wore in Christchurch or Dunedin. But here, darker shades were predominant. Everything looked somber in general. This probably wasn't just due to the morning mist, but the vapors rising from the chimney and the river. The wastewater coming from the factory must still be hot, she thought. Upon contact with the river water, it turned into foul-smelling, murky swaths.

"Look, there's March!" Aroha cried. Her cousin seemed to be conducting a kind of attendance check with a few other women who were dressed similarly to the factory workers. "Come on, let's go."

Peta hesitated for a moment, but Aroha was already running through the rows of workers, calling out to March in greeting. The young woman glanced up from a list she'd just been studying. Her eyes were shining, as if she could hardly wait for the day's work to begin. Aroha noted that March looked quite a bit older than she had at Maori Station. She'd combed back her black hair severely and pinned it up in a tight bun, and she was wearing a high-necked, white lace blouse with a simple black skirt. March had draped the matching jacket across her shoulders. But the conservative look didn't distract from her beauty. As usual, Aroha noticed the fact with a slight twinge of jealousy.

"Aroha!" March beamed at her cousin. A moment later, her gaze fixed on her half brother. "Did you drag her here to show her how terrible it is?" she asked him, half joking, half reproachful. Then she turned back to Aroha. "I'm glad that you came. Martin can show you around in a moment. But you should have waited—"

March interrupted herself as a young woman came scurrying into the court-yard, breathing heavily, and joined her group.

"Mrs. Stone," March called, raising her list and pointing at the gigantic clock that was mounted in plain sight on the factory wall. "You're eleven minutes late. I'm sorry, but I'll have to deduct one hour from your pay."

The woman's features, which had lit up at the success of just barely making it in time to join her colleagues before they entered the factory, contorted in angry desperation.

"It was only nine minutes," she contended. "I came into the courtyard at precisely nine minutes past seven. Please, Miss Jensch . . ."

"I checked you off on this list at eleven minutes past seven," March told her. "And nine minutes late is still too late. We value punctuality, as you know quite well."

"I wasn't late," the woman said, wide-eyed. "I left home on time. With my husband. He can confirm that. Jim . . ." She looked around, but her husband's group had already disappeared into the factory. "All I wanted was to bring my children to the woman who minds all the others, but she wouldn't open her door, so I had to make some noise until she woke up, and . . . and I couldn't just leave the little ones out there in the street, could I?"

March scrutinized the woman, a frown creasing her forehead. "The woman wasn't awake yet?"

Mrs. Stone nodded eagerly; she seemed surprised that March was listening to her at all. "It happens now and then," she admitted. "She . . . drinks . . ."

March grimaced. "You shouldn't be leaving your children with a drunkard," she said sternly. "Goodness knows what might happen. You are aware that two children drowned in the river last year, aren't you?"

Mrs. Stone bit her lip. "I . . ."

March was visibly losing her patience. "Well, see that you get to work," she ordered the woman. "I'll overlook your tardiness for today, but see to it that it doesn't happen again."

March turned back to face Aroha with a smile as the woman scurried into the factory, thanking her profusely. "There you have it," she said. "We're no brutes. If somebody has a believable excuse for breaking the rules, by all means, we listen to them and show them our understanding." Aroha wondered whether the situation would have ended differently if March hadn't been under the eye of her cousin and her exceedingly critical brother. "Come inside with me now; I'll show you . . . Ah, there he is!" March gave her beau a radiant smile. Martin Porter was descending a flight of stairs from the administrative offices down to the courtyard. "We have visitors, Martin."

Porter nodded and greeted Aroha cordially. He didn't seem as enthusiastic about Peta's presence, but he politely held out his hand to him in greeting too.

"Should I show ye around? Or could ye do that, March?" he asked. "I'd love to show ye the steam engines, Aroha, and the turbines! Marvels of technology; never tire of looking at 'em myself. But I've a lot to do . . . I would've preferred if ye'd given us some advance notice." There was a hint of reproach to his words.

March gently laid her hand on his shoulder. "Just leave it to me," she said. "Especially since I'm sure that Aroha will be much more interested in seeing the factory halls than the steam engines and the turbines. I know you love them, but there are people to whom they're nothing but noisy, dirty monsters."

She smiled indulgently, and Aroha was suddenly reminded of the locomotive back in Greytown, and of Purahi's mother's words: *What about this monster? Won't it devour the children?*

"We don't have much time, anyway," she said quickly.

The noise coming from the gigantic engines that propelled the mechanical weaving looms and spinning machines carried all the way out into the courtyard. There was no way Aroha was ever going to get too close to those things.

"Very well, then. Let's have coffee at the countin' house later, aye?" With the invitation made, Porter took his leave with visible relief and hurried back up the steps.

Aroha and Peta followed March through the workers' entrance. First, they entered a cloakroom of sorts. Men's and women's shawls and coats were hanging on hooks here. The women had put down their baskets, and the men their iron dishes, on long benches and tables.

"It's rather warm in the actual factory halls," March explained. "They don't need their coats in there. As for the other things . . . We don't like them bringing in baskets or bags, in case something disappears into them." She gestured vaguely at the items that had been placed all around the room.

"What could there be to steal?" Aroha asked.

March pursed her lips. "Well, rolls of yarn, tools, fabric, knitting wool . . . Some people just think they need everything. And we don't make luxury goods here either, we make everyday items. Blankets, tweeds, flannels . . ." Aroha wondered how March thought the women were going to smuggle entire bales of fabric or blankets out of the factory in their small baskets. "Anyway, people are supposed to have their afternoon tea in here; we offer them two cups of coffee per person for free," March added.

"How generous of you!" Peta scoffed.

March shot him an angry glare. "Indeed," she said. "Well then, let's go inside, Aroha. Don't worry if it seems loud at first. You'll get used to it."

The noise inside the gigantic hall hit Aroha with a force like someone beating a Maori war club against her ears. There was hammering and roaring as wefts raced through warps while a part of the warps was lifted mechanically and the others were lowered. And the heat was infernal—"rather warm" didn't even begin to describe it. Even now, only a few minutes after the start of their shift, the workers' clothing was soaked with sweat. Aroha couldn't make out how many looms there were inside the hall and what exactly the workers were doing. Their movements looked simple, but they were monotonous, repeated over and over again in the exact same way. After only a few moments, Aroha felt like she couldn't think straight anymore. The noise and the heat were giving her a pounding headache.

March didn't seem to notice any of this. She led her visitors through the rows of workers, stopping here and there and giving people instructions. Here, there was a machine that wasn't running smoothly; there, someone had to sweep up some fibers that had fallen to the ground. A woman who'd hurried over with a broom gave a hacking cough, and Aroha noticed how much dust there was floating in the air. Tiny fibers kept breaking loose from the wool.

When Aroha finally approached the spinning mill with March, she felt as though she really couldn't breathe. It was even dustier there, and additionally, there was the stench of the chemicals that were used to treat the wool, not to mention the even more deafening noise. There were men working the spinning machines, for the most part. The women played supporting roles. Some prepared wool, and others cleaned the running machines, a sight that made Aroha's skin crawl. This sort of work must be extremely dangerous. A particularly delicate woman was at work underneath one of the machines as they passed.

"Threads can break now and then," March yelled into Aroha's ear in an attempt to explain. "And they have to be repaired. It's easier if you have small hands and thin fingers. In Europe, they use children."

Things seemed quieter in the dyeworks, but there, the smell was overpowering. Aroha thanked the heavens that March spared them the visit, only taking them past the open doors.

"And if you think that was loud and suffocating," Peta remarked as they stepped outside and Aroha took a deep breath of relief that made her cough, "you should see the steam engines and the turbine rooms. The heat's oppressive, and it's dangerous. People work in there too."

"Just like they do on steamboats, or as boiler men for railroad companies," March said curtly. "Steam engines are the future; we'd be nowhere without them. Besides, the men who work with them don't complain; they're very well paid."

Aroha wondered what March considered "well paid." Those men could hardly be earning oodles of money, or their wives wouldn't have to work at the factory too.


"To determine salaries, we go by families' needs," Martin Porter explained when she asked him a little while later. He welcomed his visitors into the spacious counting house on the factory's second floor, whose windows faced out to the river as well as down into the factory halls. They were soundproofed, of course; the noise from the manufacturing facilities was barely perceptible up here. A secretary brought them a tray of coffee and buttered croissants. March helped herself hungrily. But Aroha still had factory dust stuck in her throat. She would have preferred water, if anything. "If the men and women both work," Porter explained, "they can get by quite well."

"Shouldn't salaries be based on individuals' performances?" Aroha asked.

Porter looked a little irritated, and Peta laughed. "According to August Bebel, over ninety-nine percent of all female workers earn minimum wages," the boy interjected. "On average, women only earn around sixty percent of what men bring home at the end of the day. But I'm sure Mr. Porter's going to assure you that it's because women accomplish a lot less. Especially the ones with the small fingers who repair torn threads."

March glared at her brother. "The girls here earn about twenty shillings a week. That's double what maids make."

"Ye canna really compare the two," Porter said. "Men and women, that is."

"Anyway, the women enjoy working here," March declared, triumphantly pointing to a photograph on the wall. It showed a group of newly hired workers looking into the camera. The women and girls looked serious, but quite optimistic. "You should see how proud they are when they get their first salary! They can buy nice dresses for themselves."

Peta frowned. "Drawing the eye of some drunkard who'll get them with their first child," he said rudely.

Aroha cringed. Linda and Franz would have chided him for speaking that way.

But March didn't seem bothered. "The fact that they're stupid isn't our responsibility," she said coolly. "They could just as well keep to themselves, save up their money, get better qualifications, and become supervisors. But instead, they latch onto some ne'er-do-well and have one child after another. You can't seriously be blaming the factory for that!"

Peta seemed ready to object, but Aroha thought it was time for them to end their visit. Reminding him of her train, she insisted they leave, only to be startled by the factory's whistle again.

"Break time," March said. She sounded triumphant. "We have regular labor hours here. Nine hours for the women, and twelve hours for the men. Every few hours, people get to take a break, sit down, and eat."

Upon crossing the courtyard, Aroha noticed that most factory workers' meals were composed of nothing more than a bread crust that they washed down with the barley coffee the factory provided. Since the day was dry and even a little sunny, everybody was out in the courtyard. Aside from their meager meals, their baskets contained knitting or sewing projects as well. The women used their break to knit or repair clothing for their families. Meanwhile, they chatted animatedly. The younger girls flirted with the male workers, who had formed their own groups in the courtyard. They actually seemed to be enjoying themselves.

"Well? Do you agree with me now that it's living hell in there?" Peta asked Aroha later as he led her back toward the boat.

The alleyways surrounding the factory were deserted now. Only a few women were there, minding the children. Aroha noticed with horror that one of them was holding a bottle of gin.

"I don't know," she murmured. Her head still hurt after all the noise and dust. "Of course it's horrible work. I don't know if I could ever get used to it. But March has a point. The women do earn their own money. They don't have to get married or raise a family. Before factories came along, they had no choice. And I really do believe some might enjoy working. It's better than sitting around at home and taking care of your siblings until someone decides to marry you. It's just that a lot of it doesn't seem . . . fair to me."

Aroha wasn't sure how to express her feelings. She understood that time couldn't be turned back. People relied on factories to produce things faster and more cheaply. When more people could afford things, maybe that meant they could have a better life. Revi Fransi had told her about the conditions in Europe that his family fled from years ago. The farmers in their village had basically been slaves to the squire. Cities and their factories offered more choice for people. Or theoretically, at least. Then again, there was only one factory in Kaiapoi. If people weren't satisfied with the working conditions there, they could relocate to Roslyn or Oamaru. But those places were far away.

And suddenly, Aroha understood what had been giving her such a bad feeling. The factory tied the people to this place, and factory regulations were trying to impose just as many constraints on workers as the squire had done back in Germany!

It wasn't fair that a man like Martin Porter should be allowed to estimate how much money a family needed to make ends meet, and determine their salaries accordingly. It wasn't fair that a precocious girl like March should have the power to punish adult women or be lenient with them as she pleased. Aroha felt that March's behavior toward Mrs. Stone had been incredibly humiliating.

The woman needed help, not a reprimand. She was still thinking about how to put all that into words when Peta spoke up.

"Of course it's not fair! In these kinds of factories, everything's based on profit. People like March and Porter don't care about others. They don't give a damn, no matter how much they talk about pride and advancement opportunities and independence. Aroha, you don't honestly believe that any of these girls makes enough to rent a room and live there alone, do you?"

Aroha sighed. The boy was right again. But he would be furious at the thought in her mind now. It all came back to Adam Smith's doctrine: Supply and demand. If there were more jobs than workers, factory owners would be forced to start treating people better.

She looked away. "March doesn't know what she's saying."

Peta exhaled sharply. "Well, I hope that one day, she'll understand what she's doing!"

# Chapter 20

Aroha spent the train ride to Dunedin mulling over what she'd seen. She wasn't quite sure what she was going to tell Cat about the factory in her next letter. In the end, she postponed writing to her grandmother. She simply had too much on her plate with exams coming up.

Then, a few days later, Aroha had a strange encounter. It was a fine evening in June, and she was strolling along Princess Street toward the Morrises' house. Aroha was as content as could be, having just finished her last exam at the academy. It had gone very well, she thought. She exchanged a few words with the vegetable merchant she so often bought groceries from. He offered her some fresh pears.

"Here, these just came in. Deng, weigh out a small basketful for the lady, would you?"

Mr. Peabody called to his Chinese employee, who immediately gave Aroha a small bow and hastened to bag some of the fruit for her. She greeted him with a smile. She'd seen the man a few times, but they'd never had an actual conversation. Like most Chinese people in Dunedin, Deng didn't seem to speak any English. There were quite a few of them here, compared to people from other countries. A few years back, after the gold rush had died down in the area and the European prospectors moved on to the west coast, the Otago chamber of commerce started recruiting Asians. Chinese people were thought to be industrious and peaceable, and, above all, willing to work on previously exploited, deserted parcels of land.

Aroha wondered briefly whether Deng had come here during that wave of immigration. If he had, she felt sorry for him. During that time, Aroha's mother, Linda, had been living in Tuapeka—or Lawrence, as it was called today.

Joe Fitzpatrick, Aroha's biological father, was convinced he'd find gold there. According to Linda, the work there had been drudgery of the worst kind. All one did, day in and day out, was try to wrestle the last few specks of gold dust from the earth. None of the Chinese nationals who'd come after them had made their fortunes, that was for sure.

Aroha was distracted from her thoughts by the feeling of a damp nose snuffling at her hand. She forgot all about Deng for the moment and turned her attention to Tapsy, the vegetable merchant's large, sweet-tempered dog. Tapsy would often lie out in the sun in front of the store, and Aroha would always pet her when she passed by. The young woman enjoyed life in Dunedin, but she missed spending time with animals. Back at the school in Otaki, and then later at Rata Station, of course, there'd been farm animals everywhere; dogs, cats, and horses. Aroha would have liked to have a kitten here in Dunedin, at the very least. But animals made Isabella's mother sneeze and her eyes water. Whenever Aroha touched Tapsy, she had to go change her clothes so as not to risk making her host sick. She thought of Te Wairoa with a smile. There were sure to be countless animals at Koro's *marae*.

As she was paying for her pears, Aroha scratched Tapsy's ears and promised to bring her a bone from the Morris family kitchen the next day. She said goodbye to Mr. Peabody and Deng and went on her way with a contented smile. The fruit in her bag gave her an idea. To celebrate the fact that her last exams were over, she should buy a bottle of champagne and open it with the Morrises after dinner. It would be a small gesture of gratitude for all their kindness over the years.

Aroha made a little detour to a specialty store down a side street. The owner gave her some friendly yet self-serving advice, and in the end, she left the store with two bottles of outrageously expensive champagne. There was no need for her to save up her pennies, since she'd be starting a steady job next summer. And she'd be earning a bit of money over the next few months as well. Miss Vandermere had invited Aroha to keep teaching the Maori for Beginners and Intermediates courses until she moved to the North Island. That way, the headmistress would be able to offer the language at her academy for a little while longer.

Humming under her breath, Aroha reached the Morrises' house and was just ringing the doorbell when she heard shouting, angry cries, and hasty footsteps behind her. A dog was barking. She turned around, and the first thing she saw was Tapsy. The dog was bounding after a man who was running from her, mortal terror in his eyes, and weaving between pedestrians and horse-drawn carts. He bumped into people, which earned him more angry shouts. Aroha was surprised that nobody was helping him or keeping the dog in check. Tapsy was well known in the neighborhood; everyone knew she was harmless. But then she saw the man's dark, flashing eyes.

"Watch where you're going, chink!" a wagoner yelled, almost running him over in a tangle of limbs and bridles.

"Get him, Tapsy!" one of the neighbors said, laughing. "But don't ruin your digestion with the little yellow man!"

The young man stumbled on, gasping for breath, desperately looking around for refuge. At that moment, the Morrises' front door opened. The man lunged toward Aroha.

"Please! Please, help me! That creature is going to kill me!" he cried out in perfect English.

"Don't worry, that's just Tapsy," Aroha said as she stepped aside to let him in. The man slipped inside past the confused maid. Meanwhile, Aroha grabbed Tapsy's collar. "Hush now, Tapsy. You can't just chase people through town. The two of you could have gotten yourselves run over."

Tapsy looked up at her, wagging her tail and giving the man a friendly doggy grin. In doing so, she exposed her impressive canines. The man took a step back farther into the house—where he found himself faced with the next source of danger.

"How dare you come barging in here like that! If you don't leave this minute, I'll fetch the police. Mr. Stuart, please, come quickly!" The Morrises' maid brandished her broom in lieu of a weapon. At her call, the butler appeared, wearing his most stern expression. "This man is an intruder!" the girl told him, upset. "I asked him to leave, but he refused, he . . ."

The Chinese man was caught between the butler and Tapsy. He started explaining himself desperately. "Please, please, forgive my intrusion. Mr. Peabody sent this dog after me; I was in mortal danger; I—"

"Out with you! This instant," Mr. Stuart interrupted the man, forcefully pointing him toward the door.

The man sought Aroha's gaze and then looked back at the panting dog Aroha was still holding tightly by the collar. "Miss—maybe if you could help me explain . . ."

"First of all, I think we should all calm down," Aroha said firmly. "Nothing really happened, except for the fact that I almost dropped my gift." She smiled and handed the bag over to the maid. "Would you mind putting that on ice for me, Teresa? And as for this man here, it's just as he said. I let Mister . . ." She gave the man an inquiring look.

"Duong," he introduced himself. "Duong Bao."

"I let Mr. Bao inside because he was running from the dog," Aroha went on. The maid was about to object, but Aroha stopped her. "Yes, I know, Tapsy isn't dangerous. But she's enormous, and Mr. Bao had no way of knowing what she was going to do. Come now, Teresa, imagine if you had an animal that size chasing you! Anyway, I assure you that Mr. Bao entered the house at my invitation. There's no question of breaking and entering here."

Mr. Stuart grimaced in indignation. "Miss Fitzpatrick, I doubt Mr. Morris would be as willing to welcome this . . . gentleman into his home as you are."

Aroha sighed. "Of course Mr. Morris would offer shelter to someone in trouble," she argued, although she wasn't half as certain as she was pretending to be. As friendly as the Morrises were, they didn't seem to trust Asians or Black people. Indeed, they even had their misgivings about Maori; they were quite concerned about Aroha's new job at Lake Tarawera. "Besides," she said, "Mr. Bao will be leaving immediately. I'll return the dog to Mr. Peabody now so that Mr. Bao can depart safely."

She shook Tapsy's collar emphatically. Mr. Bao and then Aroha sidled past Teresa and the butler, who slammed the door shut after them.

"Thank you so much," he told Aroha sincerely. "You—you just saved my life. How can I ever thank you?"

He looked at her directly, which surprised Aroha. Deng and the other Chinese men she interacted with always averted their eyes in deference. She'd never quite gotten the chance to look at their faces. Duong Bao reminded her of her young uncle Robin a little bit. But he was short, barely taller than Aroha. She certainly wouldn't have called his skin yellow; it was more like a light shade of bronze. His eyes, framed by short lashes, were light brown, his nose small and straight, and his lips were quite shapely.

"Oh, nonsense, no need to thank me!" Aroha shook her head. "Tapsy's a doll. If you'd tripped and fallen, she'd have licked your face. You said Mr. Peabody told her to chase you? Oh, how could he! Well, let's see what he has to say when I return Tapsy to him. And then . . ." Aroha thought for a moment, her curiosity battling with her sense of propriety. She shouldn't be walking the streets alone with a young man at all, especially not a Chinese one, given the current state of things. But she was dying to learn more about Duong Bao. "Why don't you wait here for me? We—could go get some coffee."

A bright smile lit up Duong Bao's face. "It would be my pleasure to treat you," he told her politely. She could hardly detect an accent.

"Thank you. I'll be right back."

Aroha brought Tapsy back to the shop, but she only found Mrs. Peabody, who was busy with some customers. The tradeswoman thanked Aroha for returning the dog. The look in her eyes spoke volumes. Perhaps she was aware of her husband's prejudices and didn't feel the same. Aroha was hoping to learn what had happened soon.

Duong Bao was waiting for her near the Morrises' house. He politely held open the door of the nearby café for his companion, and the young waitress inside gave him a wary look. Aroha wondered if the girl would've let him in if he hadn't been with her. Aroha and the Morris family were well known in town. Undoubtedly, the waitress was curious to learn what she might be discussing with a Chinese man. She didn't protest when they took a seat in one of the booths. Aroha ordered a cup of coffee, and her companion ordered some tea for himself.

"Do you like the tea in our country?" Aroha said, trying to start a conversation. "I mean, tea's originally from China, isn't it? It must be so much better in your home country than anything you can get here."

Duong Bao took a cautious sip and smiled. "In England, at least, the tea tastes a lot better than it does here," he replied. "It's better to drink coffee in New Zealand. Well, old habits die hard."

"In England?" Aroha asked. "Aren't you from China?"

The young man shook his head. "Not for a long time," he explained. "I've been in Dunedin for two years now, but I spent ten years in England before that. At a boarding school in Sussex, to be precise. That's where my taste for tea comes from. And for Yorkshire pudding. I had to readjust to rice and bamboo sprouts when I moved to the Chinese neighborhood here. Rats, however, are not part of Chinese cuisine, as one of the notables of this town suggested recently. And neither is dog meat."

Aroha smiled. "It seems that Tapsy was told otherwise," she teased him. "Or why was she chasing you?"

"Tapsy is . . . the Rottweiler?" the man asked, frowning. "Why would anyone call such a monster Tapsy? Well, be that as it may, it's not the animal's fault. Its owner sent it after me. Both of us, actually, Deng Yong and me."

"But why did Mr. Peabody do that? Isn't Mr. Yong his employee?"

Duong Bao sighed. "Yong—which is his first name, by the way, last names come first in China—really does work for Mr. Peabody. From four o'clock in the morning to nine o'clock at night. Plus he has to do the cleaning after the shop closes. Mr. Peabody pays him one and a half shillings a day for this, which isn't enough to live on, but too much to die. And Yong still thought that was fair until last week, when he heard about New Zealand labor laws. He wanted to ask Mr. Peabody politely whether those laws don't also apply when an employee is Chinese. Unfortunately, he doesn't speak a lot of English, which is why he asked me to translate. Peabody's answer was to sic his beast on us." Duong Bao grimaced.

"Oh . . ." Aroha looked down at her coffee, ashamed of her fellow countryman's behavior. "Mr. Deng should quit that job straightaway," she said. "You can't let people get away with this sort of thing. People try to treat Maori workers exactly the same. They think that if somebody isn't white or doesn't speak perfect English, they can do whatever they want to them. My father used to start fights with merchants in Otaki about it. They kept trying to lower the wages, even though all of my father's students speak and read and write good English. There's no excuse at all to pay them less than a *pakeha*. My parents run a school for Maori children," she added by way of an explanation.

Duong Bao shrugged in resignation. "Yong can neither read nor write in English. And he doesn't have anybody like your father to speak up for him. Instead, he has a wife and two children back in China who wait for his money every month. He supports his parents as well. So he has to take whatever he can get. As we all do. Chinese people aren't paid much, generally. I don't earn more than two shillings a day either."

Aroha's jaw dropped in disbelief. "But your English is perfect. You could work as a translator."

Duong Bao nodded. "I do. On the side. But that pays even less than my job at the laundry. Often, I don't charge the poor devils anything to come along to the employment agency, or help them with conversations like Yong's today. Unlike him, at least, I don't have family in China that I have to support."

"Why did you come to New Zealand at all?" Aroha asked. She knew she shouldn't pry, but she was fascinated by the young man. "If your family was able to send you to a boarding school in England, they must be wealthy."

Duong Bao rubbed at his temples. "I wasn't sent to England by my family, actually, but by 'Our Daughter of Heaven,' 'Our Merciful Joy.'"

"Excuse me?" Aroha said.

He smiled. "I was sent by our empress. Or rather, the empress dowager and regent for our young emperor Guangzu. Cixi, that's her name, accepted that China must open itself up to the world more. That's why she occasionally sends sons of the Chinese aristocracy to European countries to have them learn languages and qualify them for diplomatic service or jobs in international commerce. I was one of them. I was sent to England when I was ten."

"And then you were sent to a laundry shop in New Zealand?" Aroha asked, confused. "As what? A spy?" She laughed.

Duong Bao looked wistful. "No," he said earnestly. "My journey to New Zealand was not at the empress dowager's command. It was . . . I don't suppose you have heard about the Taiping uprisings?"

Aroha shook her head.

"It's been almost thirty years now," Duong Bao said, excusing her ignorance. "A man called Hong Xiuquan from Canton failed his civil service examination three times in a row, and he held it against the imperial family. After he'd come into contact with a Christian missionary, he began to have religious visions. He combined Taoism and Christianity and a few other religions into one and called for a revolution. In the end, he commanded a powerful army and conquered entire parts of the country. Over the course of ten years, hundreds of thousands of people lost their lives. In the end, the English and the French joined in on the empress's side. The imperial troops won. In 1864, Hong died, and the generals and dignitaries of his empire were executed, or they fled."

"And?" Aroha asked.

She still didn't understand what all that had to do with Duong Bao's ending up in New Zealand.

"My father was one of Hong's men," the young man explained. "He was able to flee when he parted ways with the rebels back in 1860. He took a new name, passed his civil service examination in Beijing, married a noblewoman, and made himself indispensable at the empress dowager's court. Our family was rich and held in high esteem, but one of the men who envied my father ended up learning his secret. Empress Cixi . . . well, she was more than angry. My father committed suicide before he could even be tried. I don't know what became of my mother or the rest of the family. I was immediately ordered to return from England. Fortunately, I received a warning, so instead of returning to China, I bought a passage on the next ship leaving London. The fact that I ended up in New Zealand is coincidence, more than anything. I could've gone into hiding in America or Australia instead."

"But . . . you were too young to be responsible," Aroha objected. "You were born after the revolution, and your father renounced Hong before he fell, didn't he?"

Duong Bao exhaled sharply. "The empress doesn't care about such things. When someone falls from grace, their entire family falls with them. And her reach is far. I wasn't even safe in England. Which is why I do laundry for a poverty wage in Dunedin and get chased around by dogs. But as far as dogs are concerned, you've convinced me: compared to 'Our Merciful Joy,' Tapsy is no threat."

Aroha smiled. "I'm still surprised you haven't been able to find a better job," she said. "Translators for all sorts of languages are few and far between."

Duong Bao shrugged. "I don't think anybody wants to communicate with Chinese people around here," he explained. "People mistrust us because we look different, because our cooking's strange to them, and because we . . . You know, most people come here to settle. They bring their wives and children, and their highest goal is to buy a piece of land. We Chinese people do things differently. Again, this is because of our lovely empress. May the gods reward her for all the good deeds she's bestowed upon her people." He put his palms together and sarcastically rolled his eyes toward the heavens. "But she doesn't like to let families emigrate. So men come here alone with the intention of earning money quickly, so they can return soon. But that's not so easy. Again, that's thanks to the forces of government." Duong sounded bitter. "For a few years now, New Zealand has been charging all Chinese citizens an immigration tax of ten pounds. This means the men have to come up with this tax in addition to the money for ship passage, which is hard enough on its own. The consequence is that they borrow money—often from family members, but sometimes from loan sharks. The sharks even collect their installments here, while relatives pressure the poor man's wife back home. There's no way for the debtor to get out. Normally, it takes years for them to pay everything off. And of course, during that time, none of those poor devils has the time to learn English. The men keep to themselves, live off of rice and some vegetables, and work hard. That's no reason to persecute them, but what people don't understand, they reject."

Aroha pondered his words for a moment. "I'm very sorry to hear that about your countrymen, Mr. Bao."

"Duong," the Asian man corrected her. "As I mentioned, last names come first. But I'd be honored if you'd simply call me by my first name, Bao."

Aroha nodded and held out her hand. "Then you should call me Aroha. I just had an idea. Do you speak any other languages apart from Chinese and English?"

Bao told her that he could express himself reasonably well in French and Russian as well. Aroha had suspected as much. She told Bao excitedly about her future job in Te Wairoa.

"I bet we could find something for you there," she told him. "Even if it's only as a waiter, or a clerk at a hotel desk. It'd certainly pay better than the laundry."

Bao raised his eyebrows. "I doubt it," he said. "Chinese people are always exploited."

Aroha shook her head. "The Maori wouldn't do that," she told him categorically. "They won't care in the slightest what color your skin is. Except that maybe a few girls would flirt with you because you're handsome." She smiled. "But I'm serious, the Maori are not like the white people here. And the tribe that lives near the Pink and White Terraces needs staff that can speak fluent English. If you can also offer Chinese, French, and Russian, they'd be fools not to hire you!"

# Chapter 21

Aroha spent a quiet last few months in Dunedin. She didn't even need all that much time to prepare lessons anymore, as she'd been teaching Maori since the beginning of her studies at Miss Vandermere's Academy.

At the moment, the most time-consuming part of her life was helping to plan Isabella's wedding. The young woman wanted an elaborate party with all the trimmings, and Isabella's parents were willing to organize it for her. Isabella asked Aroha to come along and look at Dunedin's best hotel with her. When Aroha happened to glance over at the entrance to the kitchens, to her astonishment, she spotted Duong Bao. They managed to exchange a few words, and he told her that he'd given up his position at the laundry to work as a dishwasher. He wasn't paid much better, but at least he didn't have to breathe any noxious fumes here. Aroha asked him again about him traveling north with her in November, and this time, Bao seemed to be seriously considering it.

On the day before Isabella's wedding, Aroha was inspecting the flower arrangements at the hotel at her friend's request, and she managed to meet Bao again for a few short moments. He'd decided to come to Te Wairoa with her. There were six weeks left until their departure, which was enough time to make any necessary arrangements. Aroha was sure that Bao would find a qualified job once she introduced him to the tribe.

That almost made her happier than Isabella's good fortune. Honestly, she didn't share her friend's excitement over the groom—George Trouth was too conservative for Aroha's taste. But Isabella walked contentedly to the altar on his arm, and later, they danced the night away. She thoroughly enjoyed "the best day of her life," all the way from putting on her wedding gown to tossing the wedding bouquet.

Aroha was careful not to catch it.

The entire Morris family had insisted upon seeing off their longstanding guest at the pier, but they reacted with utter indignation when Aroha boarded the ship to Auckland in the company of a very polite young Chinese man. Both the Fenroys and her parents had invited her to stay with them for a few days before beginning her new job, but that would have meant approaching the Tarawera region by land, and she would have had to suffer through longer train rides.

Bao was taking the same ship, although he wasn't traveling second class like Aroha, trying to keep things as cheap as possible instead. He'd hardly brought any luggage with him; all his belongings fit into a small bundle.

"We probably will barely see each other at all during the passage," Bao remarked as he bid Aroha goodbye on the pier.

"And a good thing that'll be," Mr. Morris grumbled as the man walked away. "I have to say, I'm disappointed in you, Aroha. First a Maori, and now a Chinese . . . I'd never allow my own daughter to keep such company. In retrospect, we should be glad you didn't bring dishonor on our house."

Aroha didn't acknowledge this, instead deciding to thank him again for letting her stay with them. Then she gave Isabella a hug. Her friend gazed at Aroha with envy in her eyes. Isabella had begun to grasp the fact that she wouldn't be able to live the life of self-determined occupation and frequent travels and acquaintance of many different nationalities that she had been dreaming of for so long. George had accepted a position as a lecturer at a school in Queenstown. He'd agreed to allow Isabella to earn a bit of money on the side by translating popular women's novels. But work outside the house was unthinkable now.

"Will you come and visit me sometime, please?" Aroha asked her friend.

Isabella nodded half-heartedly. Both of them knew George wouldn't permit that.

The voyage passed uneventfully. Aroha used her time to learn more about New Zealand's tourism industry in general, and about the area around Ohinemutu and Lake Tarawera in particular. She also wanted to learn about their guests—*manuhiri*, as the Maori called them—before starting her new job in Te Wairoa. To that end, she read travel reports and found out which English prince Koro had been talking about. In 1870, Prince Albert had visited New Zealand and described it as a true wonderland. Since then, the island nation had become yet another stop on the minimum six-month world tour that members of the English elite felt compelled to undertake. Aroha learned that, while English tourists were mostly aristocrats, there were also rich manufacturers, merchants, or ranchers from America who paid for their trips themselves, or even more frequently, sent their children. She'd found a newly published New Zealand travel guide in a small bookshop in Dunedin, written by Thorpe Talbot, and discovered that Thorpe Talbot was the pen name of Frances Ellen Talbot, who lived in Dunedin. She could've visited the author if she'd known sooner! But now, reading the little book had to suffice, and she'd soon see for herself what the situation between the Maori and their visitors was like.

Linda had insisted on meeting her daughter in Auckland. She'd reserved a room at a fine hotel and was determined to use every minute of their precious time talking, shopping, and exploring the city together. It had been so long since they'd last seen each other.

Linda surprised Aroha at the pier, and she greeted Bao without reservation. The young man looked tired. As he'd predicted, Aroha had seen or heard nothing at all from him; the poorer steerage passengers had been strictly segregated from the first and second classes. While Aroha had enjoyed her time on deck watching dolphins and whales, reading her travel books, and chatting with other passengers, the less-affluent travelers had had to make do with onerous conditions in the ship's hold. Now, Bao was bleary-eyed and unkempt. He apologized profusely for his appearance.

"I'm afraid there was no way to wash," he said, the disgust plain on his face. "Instead, I fear, there were lice and fleas . . ."

Linda gave him a sympathetic smile. "I'm so sorry to hear it, Mr. Duong. Do you have a decent place to stay now, at least? Aroha didn't say anything, or I would've booked a room for you as well."

Bao shook his head. "You would've been hard-pressed to find a hotel that would take me in," he remarked. "Aside from the fact that I couldn't have afforded it anyway. But I'm certain I will be received in this city's Chinese neighborhood. I have no doubt there will be bathhouses there, and I hope that I'll be able to face you in a cleaner, tidier state the next time we meet."

With that, he took his leave and walked off into the city.

"What a nice man," Linda said as she walked over to one of the waiting hackney cabs with Aroha. "Although he's far too humble. We could've given him a ride in the carriage, at least."

As planned, mother and daughter spent a few lovely days in Auckland. They enjoyed shopping on Queen Street and making trips out to the surrounding area, but they also asked dutifully in all the city's theaters for news of Robin Fenroy. Unfortunately, this came to nothing. The young man had not auditioned for any of the different companies, nor had anybody heard of the Carrigan Theater Company before. Nobody knew anything about an actor named Carrigan.

Linda and Aroha were just leaving a theater when Linda suddenly hesitated.

"What is it?" Aroha asked.

"I'm sure it's a coincidence," Linda said, "but that name . . . I used to know a Vera Carrigan. Back when . . . when I was still with your father."

Aroha turned to face her mother, alarmed by her tone. "And?" she prompted.

Linda didn't answer immediately. But then, it all broke out of her with unanticipated force. "She was the most malicious creature I've ever met!"

Aroha frowned. She'd never seen Linda judge another person so harshly before. "Was there something between her and my father?" she asked bluntly.

Linda gave her a scornful smile. "Ah, and yet again, anything I say about her is going to be treated as jealousy. It was like that back then too. In reality, nobody knows if there was ever anything intimate going on between Vera and Fitz. Neither I nor anyone else ever saw them so much as touch one another inappropriately. On the other hand, there was definitely something going on between them. It was a strange, almost eerie connection; very hard to describe. Vera was so young back then, barely fifteen, and he was about double her age. They liked to make it look like a father-daughter relationship. But it was more like Fitz was under her spell. Vera couldn't do anything wrong in his book, Vera was always right, Vera always got what she wanted . . ."

"You *were* jealous!" Aroha let slip, and regretted it immediately.

"No, I wasn't. Not in that sense. I never felt as if it was about another woman who might've been more beautiful or more interesting than me. Because Vera was neither of those things. She was a sullen child, unkind, devious—no rivalry was necessary to dislike Vera Carrigan, Aroha. I wasn't so much jealous as I was worried, because she had a bad influence on Fitz, and talked him into all sorts of things that endangered our survival. We were living in Taranaki as military settlers back then, as you know, and Fitz had duties to attend to. He didn't like it; he was an adventurer who didn't like obeying rules. Vera encouraged him to rebel. In the end, it was her fault that he got kicked out of the army."

"I thought it was cowardice in the face of the enemy," Aroha said, surprised.

Linda nodded. "It was. But it was she who pulled him into a hiding place when the Hauhau warriors attacked. She did it knowing full well that she was throwing me and my newborn child to the wolves."

"He didn't have to follow her," Aroha said.

Linda sighed. "Of course he didn't. And it's not an excuse. I'm just explaining that she had such a hold on him . . . She was incredibly good at manipulating people. She lied with a self-evidence and poise that's quite unusual, even among adults. I'd never have given a fifteen-year-old credit for being that devious."

Aroha suddenly remembered another story. Old Omaka had also mentioned a young girl who'd been the spitting image of evil.

"Was she the one who had Omaka's tree cut down?" she asked.

Linda nodded. "I didn't realize she told you about that," she said quietly. Then she raised her voice again slightly. "Vera convinced an entire squad of military settlers to chop down an ancient kauri tree and burn the pieces. She only did it to hurt Omaka, to whom the tree was sacred. It was gigantic and imposing—the wood would've been worth a small fortune if it had been handled properly and sold in Wellington. But the men destroyed that tree in an orgy of violence, spurred on by a vicious young girl. They didn't bother with the money because Vera Carrigan wanted it that way." Linda's voice was starting to sound shrill.

Aroha took a moment to digest what she'd heard. Young Vera's demonization seemed exaggerated to her. On the other hand, neither Omaka nor Linda were known for irrational hatred, and the kauri tree had doubtlessly been destroyed.

"Do you think that Vera could have something to do with Robin's disappearance?" she asked.

Linda shook her head. "No. I couldn't imagine it. Although . . . it is a little strange, because the last thing I heard about her was that she wanted to become an actress. Fitz bragged about it to me when we met that one last time. He and Vera had left Taranaki together, but then Vera joined a cabaret in Auckland. She'd wrapped the theater's owner around her little finger in her usual way. According to Fitz, she had a career the likes of Sarah Bernhardt's laid out for her. I didn't believe a word of it, of course."

"But it's possible?" Aroha asked, worried. "She could be the one behind the Carrigan Company? Robin was talking about a Mr. Carrigan, but the Pomeroy Company is named after a woman too."

Linda shrugged. "Honestly, I can't really imagine it. Vera was completely uneducated; I don't even know if she was able to read or write. And she'd definitely never heard of Shakespeare. She was young and unpredictable, of course, but she didn't like to work. It's just unthinkable to me that she could've gathered enough energy and diligence to get herself through acting training like Robin did. No, but what I can imagine her doing is shaking a leg here and there for cabarets—and probably not even that. I think it's much more likely that a theater director made her into an 'actress,' just like Fitz was passing her off as our maid. Because none of them dared to call Vera Carrigan what she was: A . . . trollop." Linda only just managed to stop herself from saying the word "whore."

Aroha had a thousand questions, but they'd come to a halt in front of their hotel. She was sure that, once they were inside, Linda wouldn't want to talk about why she thought of Vera as a whore, despite the fact that her husband had seemingly never touched her.

The two women were quickly distracted when the receptionist not only handed them their keys, but a letter as well.

"A Chinese boy left this for you," the man said. "A certain Mr. Donk."

"Duong," Aroha said, correcting him. Intrigued, she opened the letter, which was a courteous invitation for mother and daughter to join him for dinner at a restaurant in the local Chinese neighborhood. He stated his wish to invite them there the following evening, on their last night in the city. *"After all, Miss Aroha has expressed her interest in our cuisine on several occasions,"* Aroha read aloud, *"whereas my own culinary skills are famously limited to Yorkshire pudding and roast beef. However, in this marvelous city, I was able to find accommodation at a guesthouse, and the landlady prepares excellent Cantonese food. I will be picking you up from your hotel, of course, and will later accompany you on your way back so that you needn't be out by yourselves in our neighborhood, which must still seem quite strange to you."* Aroha looked over at her mother. "What a nice idea!"

She was genuinely excited, and of course Linda was also intrigued about following their new acquaintance into the unfamiliar neighborhood. The two women dressed meticulously for the occasion, and Bao complimented them courteously when he met them at the hotel's reception desk—eyed warily by the entire staff. A little while later, he guided mother and daughter through narrow alleyways decorated with colorful paper lanterns and flags. In several doorways, they saw small, chubby statues of deities that were apparently being fed, as there were bowls of food in front of them.

"It's how we honor our gods and our ancestors," Bao explained to them. "Each house has its own shrine."

But the men who took such loving care of their deities here were rather skinny in comparison. And the landlady of the guesthouse that Bao finally guided the two women into seemed to be the only woman in the entire neighborhood. Despite not speaking English, she greeted her visitors deferentially and immediately set down bowls of aromatic foods in front of them. There were no plates, only bowls, and in place of forks and knives, they received chopsticks.

"There are few Chinese women in New Zealand," Bao remarked while showing Aroha how to pick up pieces of meat and vegetables with the chopsticks. "There was a census two years ago. There were nine back then."

"Nine?" Aroha could hardly believe her ears. "And who do Chinese men marry here?"

Upon hearing the mischievous question, Linda looked back and forth between the two young people. Was there something in the making between her daughter and this man? But a look at Aroha's face was enough to stop those thoughts. It was clear Aroha was just curious—and she was having the time of her life, sampling the strange, often spicy foods and trying her hand at using the chopsticks. But she wasn't quite so sure about Bao. The sparkle in his eyes and his attention to each and every one of Aroha's movements left her with no doubt that this young man was attracted to her daughter.

Linda wondered whether she should really be sending them off together, but when she accompanied Aroha to the harbor the next day, this concern proved to be unfounded. Koro had arranged for Aroha to travel with a group of English and American visitors on the trip to Ohinemutu.

*There are agencies that take care of this sort of thing in Auckland—in collaboration with agencies in England and America, of course. They'll be glad to take you along,* Koro had written to her. *All you have to do is tell us when you'd like to travel. We've told them about your position. They're delighted to have a pakeha contact in Te Wairoa now. And if you travel with the manuhiri, you'll experience the journey from their perspective. I'm sure this would be interesting for all of us.*

Aroha exchanged heartfelt goodbyes with Linda, and then boarded the steamboat to Tauranga right on time. One of the agency's employees then introduced her to fifteen excited English and American travelers. They were talking animatedly about previous stops on their travels, monuments in Paris and Rome and the scenic attractions of New Zealand's South Island. They were quick to include Aroha in their discussions. Most of the older travelers were happy to have some younger company. Two young men who were traveling alone even tried to flirt with her.

Accommodating Bao on the ship was a little more difficult. The agency's representative claimed that it wasn't his responsibility. He agreed with Aroha that a multilingual employee would certainly be an asset in Te Wairoa, but he couldn't or wouldn't offer the young Chinese man a cabin alongside the rich globetrotters. Bao ended up taking matters into his own hands by speaking to the captain himself and asking for a place to sleep above or below deck. He explained that he was willing to earn his passage by helping out on board.

During their passage, Aroha saw Bao scrubbing the deck and doing odd jobs here and there. She was a little embarrassed to be eating gourmet meals with the other guests and idly enjoying the view of the cliffs of Waiheke Island and the Coromandel Peninsula's dreamy beaches while he was working so hard. But Bao seemed in good spirits, and the crew was satisfied with him.

"I'd rather be working up here than stuck below deck," he told her as they were finally approaching the Bay of Plenty and Tauranga came into view, a small, inviting harbor town.

"Tauranga means anchorage ground or resting spot in Maori," Aroha was telling the English passengers. "The Maori used this place as a harbor, and it's kept its Maori name even though there are mostly *pakeha* settlers here now. Let's take this as a good omen for our trip into the lands of our Polynesian natives. The Maori aren't natives of Aotearoa; they came by canoe from an island called Hawaiki. But that was long before the Europeans arrived."

Bao listened with the same fascination as the English and American passengers while Aroha told them about the Polynesians' canoes and the adventures of Kupe, the first settler. He'd had to flee Hawaiki after kidnapping a woman named Kuramarotini.

"Reminds me of Zeus and Europa," a retired English professor said, chortling.

Most of the travelers in their group, Aroha noted, were Americans. They didn't know much about the culture, but they were open-minded and enjoyed listening to her stories. Aroha even managed to mollify them with some more Maori stories when it became apparent that their accommodations in Tauranga were very basic.

"That just means you'll be closer to nature," Aroha said in consolation. Then she suggested to the more adventurous travelers that they should hike up Mount Maunganui, the town's local mountain. "I'm sure we'll get a marvelous view of the town and the forests we'll be crossing tomorrow from up there."

They planned to travel by horse and carriage the next day. There were around forty miles between Tauranga and Ohinemutu, and Aroha knew from Koro's descriptions that the way was difficult. The travelers would be on the road all day.

"But they're building a road there now," a young Maori man leading Aroha's little group of hikers up Mount Maunganui told her. "By next summer, it'll be much easier to reach Ohinemutu and the springs in Rotorua."

Aroha translated this into English for the group.

"And besides, the view will more than compensate us for any difficulties we might encounter," the English professor declared and pointed south, where jagged peaks jutted toward the sky. "Those mountains are still active volcanoes, Miss Fitzpatrick, are they not?"

Aroha noted with amusement that she'd already become a guide for these *manuhiri*. Her advance reading was paying off.

"Not too active, I can assure you," she told a few women who'd followed up the professor's remark with nervous questions. "The big one is Mount Tarawera. It's near the Pink and White Terraces. That mountain is sacred to the Tuhourangi. They traditionally bury their deceased chieftains at its foot."

# Chapter 22

The next morning, two-wheeled sulky carts made for rough terrain were waiting for the travelers. Some of the guests were upset at how primitive the traveling conditions were, but most seemed determined to enjoy the adventure. Again, there was no space for Duong Bao—he hadn't even found a place to spend the night in Tauranga, but the horses' owner had invited him to sleep in the stables. The man wouldn't have had a problem with letting Bao ride along on one of the wagons, but they were already filled to capacity with the Europeans.

Bao wasn't deterred by this. "I'll just make my way there on foot; I'll be arriving a little later," he told Aroha. "As long as I don't get lost." He turned to the young Maori who was driving Aroha's wagon. "Is it hard to find?"

The man shook his head. "Not hard, easy. Just follow wide path. That *pakeha* path."

The stretch of land that the *manuhiri* had to cross to reach the natural wonders belonged to several tribes. They'd all had to give their approval before the road could be built, and it wasn't very far along yet. Only a mile or so after Tauranga, the road narrowed to a track; soon all they were left with was a muddy, rocky bridle path that had been hacked through the forest, barely wide enough for their primitive wagons. The travelers got shaken about thoroughly, and despite the beauty of the surrounding landscape with its thick fern groves, waterfalls, and strange rock formations, even Aroha had had enough by afternoon. Her back hurt, and all she wanted was a bed.

Surprisingly, some of the travelers proved much more robust than she. Two elderly English ladies, in particular, were still talking enthusiastically about the exotic plants and crystal-clear little lakes that reflected the mountain view.

"I wouldn't be surprised if we suddenly came across a fairy or a gnome!" one of them was saying.

"With some hot tea for us, perhaps," the professor grumbled. "Or how about a massage?"

Aroha made a mental note of his words. Hadn't there been talk of hot springs nearby? Perhaps they could offer the *manuhiri* a day there. They could relax with hot baths and massages before continuing their trip to the Terraces. The longer these people stayed, the more money they'd spend. According to the two English ladies, there were already similar offers at the hotels owned by *pakeha* in nearby Rotorua. The ladies were planning on enjoying the spa there for a few days after their visit to the Terraces. The hotels run by Maori in Ohinemutu, however, didn't have the best reputation—and soon, Aroha found out that this wasn't just because of travelers' prejudice, but that there were good reasons for it.

Dusk was falling as the wagons rumbled into the settlement, and the travelers would've been happy to arrive, had their first impression not been completely disappointing and disconcerting. The place was surrounded by a fence of woven raupo like most other *maraes*, although nobody had bothered to cut back the clumps of dried reeds to a consistent height. The only effort the local *tohunga* had put in had been in the design of the entryway, which was guarded by two gigantic red statues of deities.

The English ladies turned away from the grimacing tikis in disgust.

"Heavens, how hideous!" one of them said. "Trolls in fairyland! And look how obscene they are—the—nakedness, and the red paint . . ."

"Terrifying," the other lady said in agreement, gazing into the statues' flashing paua-shell eyes, which almost made them seem alive.

"The tikis are there to protect the village and drive away enemies," Aroha hastened to explain.

One of the American ladies huffed indignantly. "They're certainly doing that much," she remarked. "It makes you want to turn right back."

The local children, who'd been playing by the side of the main road and were now running toward the new arrivals, seemed friendlier. Aroha noticed that they were wearing a peculiar mix of traditional garb and *pakeha* clothing. They were barefoot and looked as though they hadn't bathed in a while. But now, they were rushing up to the wagons, some even jumping up and grabbing at the hands and clothing of the *manuhiri*.

"Mista, Mista, you pennies?"

"Money, Missis?"

"We very poor, Missis, Mista, we nothing to eat . . ."

The children held out their open hands, and the first few bewildered travelers began reaching for their purses.

"For buy bread, Missis . . ." A little boy attached himself to Aroha's wagon. "Hungry!"

Aroha didn't believe a word the child was saying. None of the boys and girls looked malnourished, and besides, she knew from Koro that the children here definitely didn't have to go hungry. All of this was merely a game to relieve the *manuhiri* of their money. Aroha felt a rush of annoyance. She wondered why the children's parents didn't put a stop to it.

"How terrible!" one of the American ladies said, a disgusted expression on her face, throwing a handful of pennies at the children.

That, at least, made the little ones let go of the wagons. They merrily started picking up the coins.

Meanwhile, the wagons had arrived in the village, which was a strange mixture of a *marae* and a small *pakeha* settlement. Between the meeting houses and farmhouses typical of a traditional Maori village, which were lovingly decorated with colorful paint and carvings, roughly hewn huts were interspersed: shops, cookhouses, and hotels. The wagons rolled on toward the meeting ground, where their journey ended. From there, they could see the meeting house, which was decorated with particularly intricate carvings—the entrance, yet again, was flanked by grimacing tikis.

"More monsters," another American lady said nervously. "How can anyone pray to such terrifying gods? Is this a temple or something?"

"Do they make sacrifices?" an English man asked warily. "I went to Mexico, which is Christian nowadays, thank God, and I saw some formidable pyramids—they were built for similarly hideous idols. They made human sacrifices there in the old days."

The visitors flocked nervously around Aroha, who explained to them that the Maori carvings might not be to the *pakeha*'s taste, but the gods certainly weren't thirsty for *manuhiri* blood.

The meeting ground was rapidly filling up. Men and women—dressed much like their children—were clustering around the visitors. Some of them offered places to spend the night, others were announcing carvings and woven products for sale, and even more were trying to coax the visitors into one of their cookshops, or sell them drinks and sandwiches from vendor's trays.

"You thirsty, Missis? Ginger ale, like England!"

"Very cheap, Mista . . . What you give for *hei tiki*? Is lucky . . ."

In their tiny forms, the *manuhiri* didn't seem to find the idols so frightening. Several of the travelers were fondling the little pendants made of jade or bone, looking intrigued.

"Very cheap, Mista, two shilling!"

Aroha gasped involuntarily. Even the sandwiches and drinks were being offered at exorbitant prices.

"I carry things to hotel!" a young warrior told her. "One shilling?"

"You see Maori dance? You see *haka* before, madam? We show tomorrow. We come get from hotel before leave for Terraces. Must see, madam, call the spirits!"

Two of the girls were quite successful at luring the two English ladies in. The ladies seemed genuinely interested, and to Aroha's confusion, they began haggling like horse dealers. It seemed that, as a globetrotter, one got used to haggling over the prices of wares and services. The Maori and the *pakeha* quickly became involved in loud, sometimes downright aggressive bargaining. Aroha felt a headache coming on.

But then, somebody called out her name over the din. "Aroha! I thought I might pick you up here. Even if it's just so you don't run back the way you came!" A beaming smile lit up Koro Hinerangi's countenance.

He elbowed his way to where she was standing and offered his face for *hongi*. Aroha touched him with her own nose and cheek and felt better immediately. Koro smelled warm and earthy, and he exuded an air of calm and contentedness.

The Maori greeting caught the attention of two of the *manuhiri*.

"How interesting," an American woman said. "You're rubbing noses, right? I thought people did that instead of kissing here . . ."

"You want do?" A Maori woman pushed herself in between the visitor and Aroha. "I do with you. I show you. One shilling!"

"What kind of circus is this?" Aroha asked, appalled, while the woman and the American began haggling.

The crowd was slowly beginning to disperse. The owners of the four colorful two-story wooden hotels around the square had coaxed the guests into their houses. Aroha didn't have the slightest clue what sort of arguments had convinced the *manuhiri* to choose one over another. At any rate, the visitors were now traipsing along with the hoteliers and suitcase carriers to finally get some rest in their rooms.

Koro led Aroha to the guesthouse farthest from the village center, and he carried her luggage himself. The baggage carriers knew him and should have realized that there was nothing to gain. But still, they implored Aroha until Koro sharply called them to order. At the hotel reception desk, she met the English ladies again.

"This house here is supposed to be quiet," one of the ladies explained.

"That true," Koro confirmed in English. "Nobody bother you in room. Room have keys."

Aroha wondered if this wasn't true in all the hotels. In any case, she accepted the key to her room with a sigh of relief. Koro carried her suitcases upstairs for her, and the English ladies haggled with the hotelier for the same service. It seemed that wasn't included in the price.

"They haggle over every little thing," Koro said with a sigh as he led Aroha along the hallway lined with paintings of the Pink and White Terraces. "And they're so annoying. You'll see once we take a walk through the village. How about it, Aroha? Would you like to freshen up first, or are you hungry?"

"Both," Aroha told him. "The journey here was dreadful. The agency should arrange for a longer break, perhaps even a picnic on the way. We were famished when we arrived. Give me half an hour, would you? Then I'll come downstairs, and you can show me around."

When Koro nodded, she stepped out of the hallway and closed the door of the simple but clean room behind her, realizing that her need for peace and quiet had disappeared in an instant. Only moments ago, she'd felt tired and overwhelmed, but meeting Koro had filled her with new energy.

She was pleased to find a basin in her room, and she rooted through her luggage for her toiletries. Aroha rinsed off the grime that had settled on her skin during the trip and freshened up a bit for a stroll through the village. A half hour later, she had washed and put on something more suitable, and brushed and pinned up her hair. Smelling of the peach-blossom perfume she'd treated herself to back in Auckland, she met Koro in the hotel lobby. Triumphantly, she noticed a flicker of admiration in his alert, dark eyes.

"You're so beautiful," he told her. "I think the *pakeha* don't say it quite so openly. But I'm telling you now."

Aroha smiled at him. "Thank you," she said just as openly, and noticed how much she'd missed this kind of relaxed conversation during her years surrounded by *pakeha* in Dunedin. "You're looking good yourself. The warrior's garb suits you."

Koro was wearing a woven, knee-length skirt, leather thongs with tikis and other ornaments on them around his neck, and a cape made of raupo fibers and feathers. The cape was likely a concession to the *manuhiri*. Traditional warrior's garb called for a bare torso. Furthermore, Koro had forgone the traditional war clubs and knives. At first glance, he looked the picture of tradition, but on closer look, everything he wore was carefully adjusted to the tastes of *pakeha*.

"It's certainly worth considering how you dress around here," he said as if in answer to Aroha's silent question, while leading her through the village. Now, during the early hours of the evening, there was a lot of hustle and bustle in the souvenir shops and restaurants. The new visitors were exploring the village, merrily striking up conversations with other guests who had visited the Terraces the day before and were spending a final night in Ohinemutu before traveling back. "My mother prefers *pakeha* clothing. She says it makes the *manuhiri* trust her more. At the same time, our guests like to see how we live, what we wear, and what we eat."

"It's a balancing act," Aroha said sympathetically, drifting toward a makeshift cookhouse that smelled enticingly of fried fish. "I suppose you'd like to show them without scaring them away, right? But *haka* dances are usually reserved for war. Or is this all they do?"

She pointed to a couple of scantily clad Maori girls who were dancing and singing in a corner of the square while their friends played the flute and drums. The two young men from Aroha's travel group were standing there, slack-jawed. The girls were wearing woven tops to go with their short dancing skirts, but the tops showed more than they hid.

Koro grimaced. "That sort of thing always sells well," he remarked. "Also, I'm afraid the girls don't have a problem with following the men back to their hotel rooms for a bit of cash, either—or they take them out to the woods, which the hotel owners prefer. There's been trouble before; sometimes the parents of some young *pakeha* find out what's going on, or somebody just shamelessly cheats on his wife. And as for the war dances, you're right, we've had *pakeha* who ran away screaming because they were afraid that somebody was about to slaughter them. On the other hand, they seem to like the thrill of it when the warriors grimace and wave their spears around. The best way to do it is to offer chaperoned dance performances, just like we do with the tours of the Terraces. Basically, somebody takes the *pakeha* by the hand and explains to them what the songs and dances mean. We hope that you'll do that in Te Wairoa soon. We call the show a *powhiri*, but it isn't actually a full-length ritual, of course. The *tohunga* would refuse, and rightfully so. Dancing a little for these people is well and good, but accepting them into our tribe . . ." *Powhiri* were meant to unify hosts and visitors in the eyes of the gods. The ritual stretched over several hours, and most *pakeha* wouldn't have had the patience for it. "In any case, the *manuhiri* like our shows, and we don't charge them all that much to see them," Koro went on. "Still, they sometimes pay a small fortune to see a bit of hopping and skipping in the streets. Only later do they realize that they were cheated, and then they get angry."

The two of them had entered the cookhouse and were now sitting at a rickety table. Koro shooed away a few children who were trying to beg Aroha for money.

"Missis, please, you eat fish and *kumara*. We hungry . . . One penny!"

"Those are the cook's children," Koro told Aroha, annoyed. "And Aku knows full well what they're doing out here. She sees it as a nice little bonus. She doesn't care that the guests can't stomach her food because they're being pestered by sup- posedly half-starved children." He sighed and curtly thanked an unkempt young girl as she brought over large plates of fish and sweet potato and placed them on the table in front of Koro and Aroha. The service certainly wasn't friendly, but the food seemed all right. "We don't get many satisfied guests around here, Aroha," Koro said before they both dug in. "If the Terraces weren't so amazingly beautiful, I don't think anybody would ever come."

# Chapter 23

The next morning, the unfortunate business practices of the Maori were the number-one subject of discussion among the English and American tourists. They'd left early for Te Wairoa, which was only ten miles away, but the roads were even worse than those from Tauranga had been. Morale was low. The two English ladies were the only ones who still seemed fairly optimistic, although they were still holding grudges against the residents of Ohinemutu.

"All I wanted was to do a quick sketch of one of the dancers," one of them complained. She'd been scribbling little drawings in her travel journal the day before. "I didn't ask them to sit for me or to go to any trouble, or anything like that. And still, they asked me for money. They wanted money for everything they did!"

"And what do they spend it on?" the other woman said, equally indignant. "On proper clothes or food for their children? No, nothing of the sort—they go out and buy alcohol! Did you see those drunkards?"

Aroha hadn't seen them. She'd been very tired, and Koro had taken her straight back to her hotel after dinner. But he'd told her about it. Alcohol abuse had been part of the community's problems since the Terraces and hot springs started bringing in extra money.

Aroha tried to mollify the furious travelers, now starting to complain to Koro, who was walking next to the cart with long, efficient strides. He cringed in shame even though the behavior had nothing to do with him.

"Ohinemutu belongs to the Ngati Whakaue," Aroha tried to explain. "But Mr. Koro Hinerangi here is a member of the Tuhourangi, the tribe I'm going to be working for soon. They're in charge of the Pink and White Terraces. Neither Koro nor his tribe are responsible for anything the people in Ohinemutu do."

But she knew it was pointless. To their guests from England and America, all Maori were the same.

"In Te Wairoa, we try be more friendly," Koro assured them. "But have patience. All new for people. Are not used to *manuhiri*."

At first sight, Te Wairoa didn't look much more inviting than Ohinemutu, but it was smaller and looked more traditional. The tourist accommodations were located outside the *marae*. There had once been a mission there, and the buildings were grouped around a small church that was kept in good condition. This inspired the guests' confidence straightaway, and they weren't harassed by anyone trying to sell them things. Sophia Hinerangi and Kate Middlemass welcomed them warmly in fluent English.

"We'll be taking care of things from here," said Koro's mother, a pretty, petite woman who looked surprisingly young. Her only tattoos were around her mouth—enough to make her look exotic, but not fearsome. Her eyes were just as jet-black and lively as her son's. "I'll be arranging your trip to the Terraces. First, we'll row you across Lake Tarawera in a large boat—an old whaling boat we bought just for this purpose. After that, you'll be taken on a short hike to Lake Rotomahana, where you'll be getting in canoes. Those will bring you straight to the Terraces."

"And we won't be asked to pay extra fees three more times, will we?" one of the Americans asked warily.

Sophia smiled. "Certainly not, sir. I pay the oarsmen; all you'll be paying is a fixed fee before the beginning of the tour. And you get to choose if you'd prefer Miss Middlemass or me as your guide. And don't try to haggle: we both ask the same amount."

During the arrangements that followed, many of the visitors chose Sophia. Kate spoke fluent English as well, but her voice was rather intimidating, unlike Sophia's, which was pleasant and singsong.

"Yes, both of us get enough work," Sophia told Aroha later. "This group here is fairly small. But yesterday morning, we had thirty guests, so it got a little tight in the canoes. I know one guide alone couldn't have managed. Kate and I work together, hence our price arrangement. You wouldn't believe how often people try to pit us against each other to save a few shillings. Visitors love to complain about the Maori in Ohinemutu, but the *manuhiri* were the ones who taught them how to haggle. But let me welcome you properly, Aroha! May I call you Aroha? Seeing as you'll be living with us. Or do you prefer Miss Fitzpatrick?"

At first, the tour guide had greeted Aroha briefly while she was taking care of her guests. Only now that all their questions had been answered and their accommodations assigned was she able to focus on the young woman, welcoming her cordially as a guest in her house. Aroha assured her that her first name would do just fine.

"I assume we'll be speaking Maori between the two of us," she added, switching to her hosts' language.

"Well, you're quite fluent," Sophia said, impressed. "Just as Koro said. I've been hearing a lot about you!" She smiled mischievously and winked at her son. "I heard you even won over Moana and Kereru. What a feat! Most of the elders here are quite wary of the influx of visitors, and they don't like what the money's doing to the younger people. I understand that, but sooner or later, they'll have to see that the *manuhiri* are our future. I grew up at a mission station in Kerikeri. I know the *pakeha*. They won't just go away again one day and return the land to the Maori. On the contrary, they'll take more and more of it, with the argument that we don't know how to use it properly. If we're to live in peace with them and survive, we have to convince them of the contrary. Parihaka was a good example."

"Parihaka?" Aroha inquired.

"It was a village in Taranaki," Sophia explained, "founded by a so-called prophet and veteran of the Maori Wars, Te Whiti. Te Whiti tried to defend the Maori land against the influx of *pakeha* settlers with peaceful methods. He failed at first; the English had the village evacuated. But his idea lives on. We're in a much better position here. There'd be a widespread uprising if people tried to take the Terraces away from us. Or there would be, at least, if we succeed in making friends with some of the *manuhiri* and they supported us."

"I'll take Aroha over to your house now," Koro said.

Sophia smiled. "Yes, you must be tired. And tomorrow, you'll come along on the tour of the Terraces with us."

Sophia reached for Aroha's luggage, but Koro took it from her. He insisted on accompanying the two women to the Hinerangis' house, although he didn't live there anymore. He'd told Aroha that he shared a sleeping house with some other young warriors.

"It's not that we're constantly prepared for war or anything," he told her. "The other young men work for the *manuhiri*, just like I do. Most of them row boats or drive wagons. Others make the *hei tikis* or war clubs that people buy as souvenirs. We rarely practice fighting. But we dance often. We want to offer the *manuhiri* something for the *powhiri*." He winked. "I perform the *wero*," he told her proudly. *Wero* was a war dance performed by the village's best fighters. It had originally been a demonstration of the tribe's preparedness for defense. "You'll be impressed with me!"

Aroha laughed. She liked Koro's open flirtation. "The question remains whether the *manuhiri* will give you a bigger or smaller tip if I tell them about traditional headhunting," she teased.

Sophia shook her head at their banter and laughed. She wondered whether there was something brewing between her son and the young *pakeha* girl. She had nothing against it. She herself had been born from a mixed marriage.

"There we are!" she said finally, pointing to a large house on a hill just outside the village. "Welcome to my home and my family, Aroha."

She offered the young woman her face for *hongi*. Aroha felt the soft, warm skin against her own face, and she felt secure right away.

Just as Koro had told her in Dunedin, Sophia Hinerangi's family was very large. It took Aroha some time to get to know all the children and young people. Some of them still lived in the house, and others were already married or living elsewhere. Now Sophia was introducing her to her husband, Hori Taiawhio, and her three youngest children, who were the spitting image of Hori, a stocky, kindly, full-blooded Maori who looked nothing like Koro.

"You've got so many siblings," Aroha said while Koro carried her suitcases up to a room on the second floor, greeting four more boys and girls on the way.

Koro laughed. "There are seventeen of us in all. I know the *pakeha* can hardly believe it, but it's true. Fourteen are from my mother's marriage with my father, Koreoneho Tehakiroe, and she has three children with Hori. She's a remarkable woman."

"Your father died?" Aroha asked sympathetically.

Koro nodded. "Yes, he died some years ago in an accident. But we all have a good relationship with Hori; he took over the father role for us. The youngest ones can't even remember Koreoneho."

"I can't remember my biological father either," Aroha confessed.

She wondered why she was mentioning Joe Fitzpatrick to Koro. But she told him what little she knew, and felt inexplicably lighter afterward.

Koro smiled at her as she told him about her *maunga* in the clouds. "Then you're the right one to be working with the *manuhiri*," he said. "You understand them better than we do, since we're bound by our *maunga*. I mean, they must be restless and without roots, or they wouldn't go searching all over the world."

"I'm not restless," Aroha said, setting him right.

Koro shook his head. "Of course you're not. To the contrary. You're at home wherever you go under Rangi's sky. But you're freer than we are. You dance like a kite in the wind."

*As long as nobody catches me,* Aroha thought suddenly. The last time she'd told anybody the story of her *maunga* had been at the Ngati Kahungunu *marae*. That was a long time ago, but she still clearly remembered Matiu's grandmother's words: *It can be dangerous to be the string of a kite that the gods desire . . .*

After Matiu's death, she'd made up her mind never to fall in love again. She wondered whether she'd be putting Koro in danger if she failed to abide by her own decision.


Sophia Hinerangi had been right. Their tour of the Pink and White Terraces was just as well-organized as she'd promised. The *manuhiri* were in a noticeably better mood than they had been the day before. That night, Koro had rounded up his friends to sing and dance for them, contented with the tips that the guests gave them of their own free will. They hadn't made much, as one of the oarsmen was telling Aroha now. Sophia was right. These globetrotters weren't the most generous of people.

Now, though, Sophia and Kate's groups were sharing the whaling boat being rowed by twelve cheerful Maori boys. They sang and chatted animatedly during their journey, and the atmosphere was relaxed, yet charged with expectation. The weather was cooperating too. Although the previous day had been overcast, the sun was shining on this calm November morning. There wasn't the slightest bit of wind, and their boat glided across the lake bordered by forests and cliffs, with Mount Tarawera looming over them.

"Is it true that the volcano could erupt at any time?" one of the American women asked fearfully, pointing at Tarawera.

Sophia gave her a reassuring smile. "That's what *pakeha* scientists say. But we Maori can't remember it ever spitting fire before, and we've been here for a long time. Still, we should all try not to anger the gods of the mountain. It watches over our tribe, you know. We bury our chieftains at its base, and its spirit combines with theirs. We feel safe in its shadow, and visitors who entrust themselves to us can too."

"We don't have to bring the spirits any sacrifices, do we?" one of the English ladies asked anxiously, turning to Kate.

Kate shook her head. "All you have to do is approach this place with true respect," she explained. "Don't break off any stones, and don't carve your names into the Terraces' rocks. You're welcome to make sketches of Otukapuarangi and Te Tarata if you wish, of course, but you shouldn't touch the stones."

Otukapuarangi, "fountain of the clouded sky," and Te Tarata, "the tattooed rock," were the Maori names for the Terraces. Sophia was the one guiding them there, and she used it as an opportunity to show them other hills, waterfalls, and streams that could be seen from the boat. She told vivid stories about the gods and spirits that lived in them, and in the process, she managed to make the Maori pantheon a little more accessible. She showed her visitors the *hei tiki* she wore around her neck next to a cross. Sophia was baptized, but like so many of her mother's people, she was able to integrate her faith in the Christian god with her belief in the numerous spirits of her homeland.

"You can take small statues like this home with you. We carve them out of jade and paua shells, and our *tohunga* sing *karakia* to them. We believe that they bring good fortune to the wearer. We have them for sale back at the village, if you're interested."

Aroha admired Sophia's skillful way of unobtrusively advertising her people's artisan craftwork. She taught them about the significance of pounamu jade and the spiritual power of the paua shell. Finally, they had reached the other side of the lake, and the oarsmen helped the *manuhiri* disembark.

"We'll be hiking over to the next lake," Sophia explained. "That's why I asked you to choose sturdy shoes yesterday. The trail isn't too difficult, but it can be rocky and damp in places."

The path turned out to be beautiful. Even here, whimsical rock formations jutted up in various places, and broad streams tumbled over rounded stones, sometimes forming basins or winding their way through jungles of ferns. Aroha thought she'd never seen as many shades of green in one place as she did now in this sunny stretch of woods between the two lakes. She gasped with surprise and enchantment just like the other travelers when Lake Rotomahana suddenly opened out in front of them after a bend in the path. It was smaller than Lake Tarawera, and it seemed even more peaceful. The canoes were ready and waiting for them on the shore.

"Look, you can see some swans over there. This lake's full of fish too," Sophia told them. "Maybe you'd like to try some trout from Lake Rotomahana tonight? All the hotels in the area and several cookhouses offer fish."

Sophia and Kate's groups split up now, getting into different canoes. Sophia told them some more about the landscape, but the guests were so excited that they were hardly listening. Very soon, the Pink and White Terraces would be coming into view.

And suddenly, after the canoes had passed a peninsula that stretched into the lake, the White Terraces appeared in front of them, shining in the sunlight. Aroha's breath caught in her chest. No description or painting could ever have prepared her for the gigantic river of snowy-white solidified rock with vapors rising from it. Here, geysers, which had originally created the Terraces, spat out hot thermal water in short intervals.

"The water contains a mineral called geyserite, and it builds up in layers. That's what created the Terraces," the English professor lectured while the visitors took in the view. "The material's better known as opal. People make it into jewelry."

"Hush, please!" an American woman told him.

Like all the others, she was staring at the miracle of nature in front of them, enraptured. The flat rocks were clustered around smaller and larger pools of water that sparkled in all the colors of the rainbow.

"You'll be able to bathe at the Pink Terraces," Sophia said. "We've created places, especially for the women, to get changed. But we don't touch the larger White Terraces."

"Yes, only the gods should bathe there," Aroha said, touched. She was speaking Maori, and Sophia smiled at her. "Will you sing *karakia*?" she asked the guide.

The Terraces were sacred to the Tuhourangi, and Aroha knew they should be greeting the spirits.

Sophia shook her head. "No. This group here may be fairly open-minded, but some of the very Christian *manuhiri* would be shocked by such a thing. The *tohunga* do, of course—and I think they pray for us too. You could come here some time with Tuhoto *ariki* if you'd like. He'd like to meet you, regardless."

"Is he the chieftain?" Aroha asked.

"No, he invokes the spirits and maintains our connections with our ancestors," Sophia explained. Those were a priest's tasks. The chieftain of a tribe normally bore the title of *ariki*, but it was also used to honor elders and priests. "And he isn't too happy about the path our tribe is on regarding the *pakeha*. Not that he's categorically opposed to bringing guests to the Terraces. He'd just prefer to . . . give them a more spiritual understanding of the place. And he never accepts money in return."

The oarsmen let their canoe slowly glide past the White Terraces. The *manuhiri* got a chance to admire the rock formations, write down their impressions in their travel journals, or make sketches. Only then did they move on to the Pink Terraces, which were narrower, but hardly less impressive. Their color was due to the sunlight falling on the rock at a different angle. Like the White Terraces, they were made of white opal.

"People say they're the same color as our rainbow trout," Sophia said. "We'll tie up at the foot of the Terraces now, and I'll take you to the bathhouses."

Aroha hadn't brought a bathing costume with her. She didn't even own one. Any time she'd gone swimming with the Maori girls in Otaki, she'd done so naked or in her undergarments. Her adoptive father, Franz, had initially been upset about the children bathing like that, but Linda had convinced him to let it be. The pond in the grove of trees near their school was very secluded. Surely, no *pakeha* from town would ever stray there. And if any Maori boys ventured over, the worst that happened was a bit of good-natured teasing. At home, the children saw their relatives' naked bodies too. The Maori weren't bothered by nudity.

In Te Wairoa, however, the Tuhourangi honored their guests' rigid moral code. There were bathhouses tucked away in the woods, and Sophia and Kate were adept at helping the ladies untie their corsets and crinolines and getting them into their high-necked bathing gowns. The more daring of them swam in one of the several natural pools out in the open. For the others, a hut had been put up over a smaller pool by the edge of the Terraces. There, the two English ladies were secretly enjoying the water, hidden from the eyes of the men who were splashing around in a different pool several paces away.

"The water's wonderfully warm, and it's good for your skin," Sophia was telling Aroha. "Sometimes, we come here by ourselves and bathe in peace without the *manuhiri*. It's a popular destination for couples. Very romantic."

Aroha wondered why she was thinking of Koro . . .

After their baths, the groups paddled back across Lake Rotomahana. Before the hike back between the two lakes, the group took a break, and Sophia and Kate handed out sandwiches.

"We could have eaten those back at the Terraces," one of the American women said. "I'm famished."

"The Terraces are sacred to the Maori, which makes them *tapu*," Aroha explained. "People generally don't eat or drink in places like those."

One of the English ladies frowned. "Do I understand correctly?" she asked. "These people cannot eat or drink before their idols, but they bathe . . . naked?"

Aroha made Koro laugh that night when she told him about the English lady's remark. While the guests had been swimming, the oarsmen had gone fishing. Sophia had bought a few trout from them, and now they were roasting the fish on an open fire in front of her house. Koro had come, and he'd brought Bao, which made Aroha happy. She'd begun to get concerned about her friend.

"Oh, no need to worry," Bao told her cheerfully.

He'd arrived in Ohinemutu two nights before, around midnight. The difficult road had only taken him a few more hours than the rest of them had needed by wagon. But he'd quickly fled Ohinemutu, appalled at the prices for rooms. Finally, he'd spent the night in the woods, and then made his way over to Te Wairoa at the crack of dawn. Upon his arrival, he'd found a job immediately at the Rotomahana Hotel.

"The owner's a white man," he said, "which surprised me. You said, Miss Aroha, that natives owned all the inns here. Still, Mr. McRae—I think he's from Scotland—turned out to be an honorable man. He offered me good pay and excellent accommodation. The rest of the employees, who are all Maori, sleep at the *marae*, so I get the hotel's entire staff area to myself. My room is huge. I can't remember ever having so much space to myself." Joseph McRae had asked around for Aroha and had given Bao the day off to visit his acquaintance. "He extends his most cordial invitation to you, Miss Aroha. He'd like to get to know you, seeing as you'll doubtlessly be working together often while you look after the *manuhiri*—did I pronounce it right, Mr. Koro? If you have the time, he'd like to have dinner with you tomorrow. Our house specialty is smoked trout. It would be a pleasure to serve you personally!"

"Well, I doubt the trout could be any better than this one here," Aroha said, beaming at Koro. The young Maori put a piece of filet on her plate. "Still, I'd love to come, of course. What about you, Koro? We'll all be working together now . . ."

Over the next few days, Aroha visited all the hotels in Te Wairoa. Indeed, apart from the Rotomahana, they were all owned by members of the Tuhourangi tribe. The Maori were trying their best to adapt to the *pakeha*'s needs. The guest-houses were clean and friendly, designwise—Sophia and Kate must have already gotten rid of the carved totem poles that were normally stationed around the entrances. But there were still communication problems, which was a reason why many visitors preferred Mr. McRae's hotel. It was the best hotel in the area, and now it was even more attractive because of Bao. The Scottish owner had him wearing a butler's uniform, and the Chinese man put his boarding school education to good use, impressing the English aristocracy with his impeccable manners. He was rewarded with plenty of tips.

Aroha immediately started teaching English to the Maori working at the other hotels—her experience with the Berlitz teaching method came in handy. Aside from that, she regularly went over the *powhiri* schedules with the singers and dancers. Visitors were to be entertained for an hour with traditional dances and singing at a fixed price. After that, the musicians would be available to show their instruments to interested *manuhiri*.

"A small *koauau* or *nguru* would be wonderful as souvenirs," Aroha was telling a group of puzzled Maori now. "You could make some flutes and sell them—they don't have to be masterpieces. The sound isn't that important; what matters is that they're nicely decorated."

"Of course the sound is important!"

Aroha started when a tall, old man interrupted her speech with his deep voice. She'd been sitting by the fire with the musicians and dancers. Now, she straightened up. The man was dressed in warrior garb and a valuable-looking chieftain's cloak that brushed the ground as he took a step toward them. His face and torso were covered in tattoos, the *moko* making his features look strict and birdlike. His sharp brown eyes scrutinized Aroha.

"The voice of the *koauau* awakens memories long since forgotten. It welcomes newborn children into this world. The *nguru* speaks with the birds, as does the *putorino*."

"None of the *pakeha* will ever master them well enough to wake the voices of the spirits," Aroha replied. "Far be it from us, *ariki*, to desecrate these instruments. The *manuhiri* will not make them sing in their homelands. They only wish to look at them . . . and perhaps to let their children try them."

"Our instruments are not children's toys," the old Maori said persistently. "They open the path to the gods."

"Tuhoto *ariki*?" she asked deferentially, as the musicians retreated.

The old priest nodded. "So, they have already told you my name," he said serenely. "Perhaps they have even warned you. I am aware that I am considered a nuisance here."

Aroha got to her feet and bowed to the priest. "They have spoken of you with the utmost respect. I wanted to visit you soon. You . . . convene with the spirits of the Terraces, do you not? I do not wish to approach them in the wrong way."

The old *tohunga's* strict face cracked into a terse smile. "What do you care about the spirits, *pakeha* girl?" he asked her scornfully. "Don't you believe in the *pakeha* god?"

Aroha rubbed at her temples. "The *pakeha* can also feel the stirring of the divine when they see the Terraces," she said. "Every man must feel small, but also blessed when he is allowed to look upon such beauty."

Tuhoto frowned. "Are the Terraces not merely an item on a list for the *pakeha* to 'check off,' as someone once told me? Something that they look at, but do not truly see? Much the same way they take part in a *powhiri* now without truly becoming one with us?"

Aroha shrugged. "I don't know, *ariki*, and I don't presume to judge. I was brought here as a mediator between you and them. Those who wish to learn should be encouraged to, in my opinion. *Ariki*, perhaps you could come along to the Terraces when Sophia and Kate are showing them to the *manuhiri*. You could help them to see them through your eyes."

The priest laughed out loud. "Oh no, *pakeha* girl! You will not seduce me to play along with your games. Dangerous games. Our people are leaving the paths of our ancestors. They offend the spirits. They banish their tikis to the inside of their meeting houses so the sight of them does not frighten the *pakeha*, and they tear out their eyes and replace them with gold coins. They sing *karakia* for strangers."

Aroha bit her lip. "What's so bad about summoning the spirits of money?" she asked. "An *ariki* of the Ngai Tahu—the *maunga* of my mother's soul lies on his tribe's land—has been doing so for many years, and his tribe is happy."

She briefly told him the story of Te Haitara, who had met Jane Fenroy many years ago when he was desperately trying to invoke the "spirits of money." His tribe had wanted blankets and cookware, fabric and tools from the *pakeha*, but Te Haitara hadn't known how to buy them all these things. Jane had helped him then. Their way together had sometimes been rough, but the tribe was content under Te Haitara's leadership.

"Te Haitara praises the spirits of wealth at the Waimakariri River. He says that they must be at home in rivers and streams—especially since one can find gold in them sometimes, which money is made of. Also because the flow of money is always moving along, money comes and goes. Te Haitara has always had the poise to let this happen, while his wife sometimes tried to stem the flow."

Tuhoto listened attentively. "You speak well, *pakeha* girl. You think, and you are much more intelligent than I thought. I assume that you and Koro—and Sophia and our chieftain—will now try to appease the spirits and guide the flow."

"That we will." Aroha nodded humbly, but inside, she was rejoicing. The priest had understood her, and although it didn't seem as though he welcomed her plans with open arms, he seemed willing enough to tolerate them.

But Tuhoto *ariki* wasn't finished. He towered over her, and all at once, Aroha was struck with a feeling of foreboding. His shadow, stretched out in the sunset, mingled with that of Mount Tarawera.

"Well then, may the spirits be merciful with you," he said quietly. "For the river of fire that once created the Terraces froze over long ago."

# Part 3

## WORLD ON FIRE

HAMILTON, TE WAIROA, ROTORUA (NORTH ISLAND)

MAY–JUNE 1886

# Chapter 24

This particular scene from *The Tempest* was especially vile. Vera Carrigan had recently added the play to their program, and this time, she'd outdone herself rewriting Shakespeare into sleazy burlesques. And yet, several times before, Robin had thought that things couldn't get any worse with the Carrigan Company. The first time had been his involvement in Vera's criminal deeds, and then came the corruptions of his favorite plays—Vera liked to turn innocent heroines into whores and heroes into laughingstocks. Robin had refused to participate at first, but in the end, there had been nothing else he could do. On that terrible night when she'd made him her partner in crime, he'd thought about making a run for it, of course. It would have been possible to sneak off in Wellington and return to the South Island; Vera would hardly have hunted him down. In fact, Robin had packed his things in a panic as soon as he'd gotten back to his room that night, only to discover that all his money was gone. He still wondered who might have taken it. Bertram, perhaps, or Leah? Maybe the young woman had even been acting on Vera's orders. He didn't think it had been some random thief. Nothing else had been stolen at the Golden Goose that night. Destitute and desperate, Robin had actually gone to the train station the next morning, but without his money, it hadn't done him any good. Ever since, he'd been dependent on the small salary Vera paid him. He was unable to save, and it would probably never be enough to make an escape back to Canterbury. Still, he'd seriously considered escaping again—it was on the day that Vera had started assigning him female roles in their plays.

"See, you're so pretty, my dearie, with your blond curls and your innocent little face. You might as well be a girl. You could do with some curves, of course. But just between you and me, Leah doesn't have that much going on under her dress either. I stuff cotton balls down her brassiere before every performance. Oh, we might as well do the same for you."

At first, Robin had given his boss a bewildered look. So he was supposed to play Juliet now, not Romeo? He'd turned to Bertram Lockhart in his desperation, but he hadn't been much help. "Makes you more au—authentic," the actor had slurred drunkenly. After just one look at their programs, which had changed after Robin was accepted into the company, Bertram hadn't been sober for days on end. "Look at it this way: Back in Sh—Shakespeare's times, women weren't even allowed onstage. It—it wasn't proper. All female roles were played by teenage boys."

Robin knew that, of course. But his voice had started to deepen a long time ago and he saw himself as a grown man, and besides, Shakespeare had asked his young thespians to perform the art of acting, not some disgusting travesty. Vera didn't expect Robin to bring Juliet, Miranda, or Titania to life onstage, only their obscene counterparts. Much like now, in *The Tempest*. Vera herself, dressed up as a female Prospero, tore open the curtains to expose the missing couple, Ferdinand and Miranda, to the audience. In the original version, the scene would have featured the two of them playing chess. The Carrigan Company, on the other hand, showed Bertram and Robin scantily clad and in a passionate embrace. Miranda's famous words, "How beauteous mankind is!" had a completely new meaning as "she" tugged open Bertram's fly.

The audience, of course, seemed to find the scene uproariously funny. The Carrigan Company still mostly performed at pubs or other doubtful establishments. Often enough, they'd perform at some drinking hole that Robin would have considered a brothel rather than an inn. The men would laugh at the travesty and shower "Juliet" or "Miranda" with ridicule. Sometimes the mood would change, and anger and frustration were expressed as hatred and aggression against the young man whom they assumed was a "shirtlifter."

In the beginning, Robin hadn't had the slightest clue how to deal with such attacks. He'd never heard of homosexuality before then. Bertram had finally explained it to him and had warned him to be careful. Ever since, he would run to his hotel room straight after his performance and lock himself inside—to escape from the audience as much as to hide from Vera. Vera rarely approached him these days, but when she did, he didn't dare to refuse her. Afterward, he didn't only hate Vera, but himself too—she always managed to get him aroused, no matter how much he resisted. The sight of her repulsed him, but when the lights were off, his body betrayed him, and he was like wax in her hands. Vera would usually have a good laugh at his expense. She used her dark power to reward him or punish him.

Occasionally, Vera was able to get them an engagement at a more serious establishment. Hoteliers or mayors were happy for any sort of diversion, especially in smaller towns, and they would allow the company to use their ballrooms or community halls. In the beginning, Robin lived for such events, because it meant that Vera would reorganize the program, and that he'd actually be allowed to perform scenes from Shakespeare. The condition, however, was that Bertram had to be sober enough and Leah had to be alert enough to perform. As a general rule, at least one of them would drop out, which meant that Robin had to fill in for character parts that he was much too young for, or he had to perform love scenes with Vera instead of Leah. In such situations, even his own vivid imagination failed him. Vera was an even worse actress than Leah, and he'd long since come to hate her. And so, as time went on, Robin even came to consider the Carrigan Company's more serious performances a disgrace. Things were worst when Vera noticed too late that they were going to be performing in front of a higher-class, sometimes female audience. There usually wouldn't be any time left to change the program, and Robin would almost die with embarrassment when he had to play the part of a lusty Juliet or Miranda.

On this pleasant evening in May, the Carrigan Company was performing for its usual audience, although on a slightly larger stage. The room was part of a pub in Hamilton, eighty miles south of Auckland, and it was probably used as the local amateur theater company's rehearsal room, normally. The men had built the stage themselves and were proud that it had dressing rooms and a back exit, just like a real theater. For Robin, this meant he didn't have to climb off the stage in smeared lipstick and women's clothing and make his way through a cackling crowd of spectators. He was so demoralized at this point that even this small bit of relief meant the world to him.

The young man forced himself to smile as the performers of *The Tempest* took a bow, and in spite of everything, he felt a sense of happiness and pride as the audience erupted into applause. He enjoyed being onstage—if only the plays weren't quite so awful, and his fellow actors not quite so pathetic. And yet, that could have easily been remedied, had Vera actually shown any sort of interest in the company's progress. Indeed, time and again, they would get young actors auditioning for them. In larger towns, Vera would always place ads in the local papers. Now and then, people would even stay for a little while, undoubtedly recruited under circumstances similar to Robin's.

A year after his own enlistment with the company, a young, dark-haired girl had performed with them for a few days, and Robin had spoken Romeo's lines with real passion for a change. A few months later, an adventurous young man had applied with whom he'd been able to perform lifelike swordfights. But like all the others, both of them seized the first chance they could to escape. As a rule, people would disappear overnight, and Vera refrained from hunting them down, no matter how big an asset they'd been to the company. She didn't care all that much about her actors' talent. Robin understood now that their performances weren't their main source of income but a front for her little deceptions and scams. One night, Vera would cheat on her so-called husband with a drunk admirer like on Robin's first night; another night, Leah would play the main role by letting herself get carried off to bed by a piss-drunk audience member, only to then "die" dramatically in his bed. Bertram as her father or Robin as her brother would come crashing into the room and demand hush money in return for not reporting the incident to the authorities and getting rid of the body discreetly. The horrified suitors always preferred paying to dealing with the possible consequences of a dead prostitute in their hotel room.

Robin loathed these "performances," and he played his parts quite half-heartedly. Consequently, Vera only forced him to take part when Bertram was too drunk. This happened relatively frequently. During the two years or so that Robin had spent with the company, he'd seen Bertram go through phases where the old thespian would drink little and surpass himself onstage, and shortly after that, he'd be too drunk to even find the stage for days on end.

Robin started removing his makeup while Bertram and Vera transformed into Othello and Desdemona, and Leah got ready to fall in love with a donkey as Titania. The lines, although lewd, were secondary to her obscene actions. Robin dreaded this part, but at least he hadn't had to play it yet. However, he occasionally had to perform as weaver Nick Bottom turned donkey. He and Bertram drew straws for that one, and he'd been lucky tonight; Bertram would have to wear the donkey's head.

While Bertram and Vera stepped onto the stage, Robin went over to the mirror next to Leah, who was weaving some flowers into her hair. As usual, an utterly vacant look clouded her pallid face.

"Why are you here?" Robin asked suddenly.

It was difficult for him to describe his relationship with Leah. He didn't trust her, and he had nothing but contempt for her acting abilities. But sometimes, he felt sorry for her. She seemed so lost. Or as if someone had put her under a spell.

The young woman turned to face him. "Huh?"

"Why are you here?" Robin repeated. "With the company. Why did you become an actress? I mean—"

"I'm no good at it, I know that." Leah spoke without a trace of resentment in her voice.

Robin hastily started to apologize.

But she just shook her head. "Don't bother. I realize what you and Bertram think of me. And you're right."

"But you could be so much better!" Robin said in an attempt at encouragement. "We could rehearse a few scenes. Really rehearse. I could show you how it's done. If you want."

Leah shrugged. "What good would it do? Do you think they'll discover us for the big theaters in London? No, forget it, dearie . . ."

"Don't call me that!" Robin said, bristling. Vera rarely called him anything else, but it was too much out of Leah's mouth. The young woman wasn't much older than he, and the top of her head barely reached his chin. Leah acknowledged his objection with a sniff. But Robin wouldn't give up yet. "If you don't think we could be discovered, and if you don't think you're a good actress, then why don't you do something else?"

Leah laughed mirthlessly. It sounded like she was trying to imitate Vera's throaty laugh. "Just do something else?" she sneered, and for the first time in ages, Robin could hear a spark of life in her voice. "Says the mama's boy from a rich family who can't do anything for himself. Look here, dearie, for a girl who was born on the goldfields and raised in the filth of Gabriel's Gully, there ain't much more to do. And believe me, this is better than everything I did before . . ."

"Better?" Robin exclaimed. "But Vera . . . she's awful. I hate her, I . . ."

"And I love her," Leah said simply. Her face, which had been eerily blank up until now, softened. "She saved my life. She found me when I hit rock bottom, and she made me into a whole new person. Vera's the first person in this world who's ever been kind to me." Leah sounded firmly convinced. But Robin was certain that if Vera had really taken in the girl and saved her from an even worse fate, then, surely, it was only to turn Leah into the thing she'd now become: her complacent puppet. "I'm never leaving her," Leah added, as if Robin had prompted her. "Leave me alone now. I need some of my medicine."

Leah reached for a bottle that she always kept with her in a satchel—Dr. Lester's Pick-Me-Up Tincture. Vera made sure to have a stash of this "medicine" sent to wherever they were performing for more than a day or two. Supposedly, the concoction was blood-building, and a remedy for Leah's pallor and frailty. But once, during an argument, Bertram had yelled at the young woman, telling her to stop taking the stuff. "Look here, girl, if you have to drive yourself over the edge, then do it with whiskey like any other sane person! Then, at least, you'd still be able to laugh and cry and bring a bit of life into your performances instead of staring at the wall like a corpse."

Later, Robin had asked the old thespian what he thought was in the bottle. Once again, Bertram stared at him as if he'd just dropped from the sky. "By God, boy, you don't know anything, do you?" he'd snarled. "Didn't your mama ever stir laudanum into her afternoon tea to relax?"

Robin bit his lip now. "Bertram says this tincture isn't good for you," he said shyly. "He says that laudanum is even worse than liquor."

Leah whirled around and glared at him angrily. Robin had never seen such intensity from her before, and it frightened him. "Yeah, you would know, wouldn't you, dearie?" she spat. "And you need neither, of course. Your life's just perfect! My God, Robin, if you don't like it here with Vera and Bertram and me, just leave! Bugger off to the next town over and send your family a dispatch. I'll wager they'd come pick you up in three days and ferry you back to your sheep farm all nice and cozy and wrapped up in cotton. But you don't have the bollocks, do you? Now fuck off. Oh, Vera won't like hearing about you talking to me like this."

Robin could hear Vera and Bertram behind the curtain now. He didn't feel like facing them again tonight. He hastily left the pub and shuffled aimlessly through the city, which lay in the middle of a fertile plain. It had been founded by military settlers after the Maori Wars, and it had an air of purity and tidiness to it, or so it seemed to him. He ambled over to the banks of the Waikato River, which flowed through the city, and followed it for a while. If you ignored the bridges connecting the two city districts, you might almost believe you were on the Waimakariri. Robin thought back to the river of his childhood, to the peace and safety of Rata Station. Back then, he'd longed for the exciting life of the big towns, and above all for the applause. He'd been prepared to give up everything for it. But where had it gotten him?

Mulling over these unhappy thoughts, Robin crossed the Waikato. From the footbridge, he was able to see the newer railway bridge. For a few years now, there had been a train line connecting Hamilton and Auckland. Vera was planning on going there with the company. First, they were going to perform in some smaller towns along the way, but then they'd surely find something in Auckland. Aside from Wellington, Auckland was the biggest city on the North Island. There was a harbor, and ships left for the South Island regularly.

Robin dodged a group of young men who were walking toward him, laughing and joking. Instinctively, he pushed his blond hair, which was considerably too long, behind his ear and rubbed at his eyes to get rid of the last traces of makeup. God forbid he might attract the attention of these men because he looked feminine.

Only after the men had passed was he able to relax and resume his train of thought. Robin unhappily went over his conversation with Leah again. All in all, he had to admit that Leah was right. Although it wasn't so much hopelessness as cowardice that kept him with the Carrigan Company. Bertram might have been staying with Vera because it was his only chance at getting to perform despite his drinking problem, and Leah stayed out of loyalty—either to Vera or Dr. Lester's Pick-Me-Up Tincture. She'd hardly have been able to afford laudanum on a factory worker's salary.

He, on the other hand, still had his life as an actor ahead of him; he could keep trying. Bertram Lockhart had confirmed that he was extraordinarily talented. And besides, he was nineteen now, which meant that he was of age. He could go to London and try his luck there. Perhaps his parents would even support him, since he'd proven by leaving Rata Station that he was able to act on his own initiative. His father couldn't accuse him of being entirely unfit for life anymore.

But then why hadn't he done as Leah said? It wasn't that he'd never considered simply having the money he needed for his escape sent by banker's order!

It was . . . well, maybe pride. Pride and shame had held him back. But both could be overcome. And besides, he didn't have to tell Chris and Cat the entire truth. He could simply claim that the Carrigan Company had disbanded, and that he'd wanted to take the chance to resettle in Europe.

Robin drew himself up. Now that he could see a way out, he felt better instantly. Surely, Hamilton would have a telegraph office, wouldn't it? Or should he wait until they got to Auckland?

Robin's euphoria disappeared as quickly as it had come. Having an idea was one thing, but putting it into action was an entirely different matter. What if Cat and Chris wanted nothing to do with him after he hadn't contacted them for over two years? And would they believe any of his excuses?

Robin rubbed his forehead. Maybe he should think this through first before sending a dispatch to Christchurch. Lost in thought, he strolled along the small town's shopping street, passing the brightly lit telegraph office. Robin didn't even notice.

To his surprise, Vera, Bertram, and Leah were still up when he entered the sleazy guesthouse an hour later. The pub they'd performed at didn't rent out any rooms. The actors were sitting around on threadbare furniture in the lobby and warming up at what was possibly the only hearth in the building. Robin shivered at the thought of the clammy bedsheets in their unheated rooms. And it was only fall; winter was still coming. He looked back and forth between the three of them. Had they been waiting for him?

"There you are." As usual, Vera's smile didn't reach her eyes. "And here we were, thinking you'd run off on us." She laughed derisively.

Bertram took a gulp of his whiskey. "Oh, go on then, tell him what you must, Vera," he grumbled. "Now that everybody's here."

"What's happening?" Robin asked.

"A change of plans," Vera announced grandly. "A chance to travel has come up, a request from some one-horse town called Te Wairoa. Yeah, it sounds Maori, and it is. But they have an interesting business there. Apparently, the area's so beautiful that they get lots of people from England and other places. They come to look at some rocks and hot springs, I hear. They take baths there. We're supposed to perform at a hotel. A pretty fancy one."

"How did you manage to book that?" Robin asked, dumbfounded.

"Luck, my dearie. One of the hoteliers, a Mr. McRae, had some business here in Hamilton, and he was at the pub for a pint after our performance. I got talking to him. He's always looking for entertainment for his guests. It doesn't seem like they get too many guests, which isn't surprising—being a *marae* at the end of the world, and all . . . You'd have to be a kooky foreigner to take the risk of traveling out there in an oxcart. But he's paying us properly. And as for our additional income," she said with a grin, "I'm sure we'll think of something special for our posh audience."

"So the hotelier . . . wasn't present at our performance?" Robin asked cautiously.

Bertram Lockhart slid a glass of whiskey over to him. "Of course he wasn't. Or he wouldn't have booked us . . . If he's of sound mind, that is."

"I'll pretend I didn't hear that," Vera said. "Anyway, I was able to convince the man that we can guarantee him high-end entertainment for his guests. We're a Shakespeare company, after all. You'll be able to shine as Romeo again, my dearie. Are you excited?"

Robin couldn't have been any less excited if he'd tried. All Vera and her company would do was make fools of themselves, he'd get involved in criminal scheming again, and besides, the booking interfered with his plans for escape. So he didn't say anything as Vera explained the new program to them, drinking his whiskey in silence instead. After that, he crept back up to his room, feeling depressed. It seemed like staying with the Carrigan Company was his fate . . . Yet it didn't even occur to him to simply get on the train to Auckland the next morning before the others woke up.

# Chapter 25

"Well? When are ye planning to steal dear Mr. Bao from me?"

Joseph McRae, the Rotomahana's owner, turned to face Aroha with a smile. The young woman had come over to book rooms for a group of visitors and have a quick chat with Bao. The young man was now serving her and McRae tea on the hotel's terrace. The location offered a stunning view of the lake and the volcano in the background, and this was promising to be one of the last warm autumn days of the year.

"At the end of next month," Aroha answered cheerfully. "We'll be opening our hotel on July first. Granted, it's not an ideal time for travelers, but we do get a few *manuhiri* in the winter here. Besides, it would probably be good to start out slowly. Especially since we have to train our staff first. We don't want to make enemies of all the hoteliers in the area by stealing their employees. It's bad enough that you're cross with us." She gave the Scotsman an apologetic smile.

"Ah, yes, training staff . . . that's something Mr. Bao will be invaluable with." McRae sighed theatrically and wagged his finger at Aroha and the young man. "No' very nice of ye, Mr. Bao, moving on like that after I taught ye everything!"

Duong Bao looked down guiltily, but Aroha smiled mischievously.

"It's just that we offer better pay," she contended. "As you've doubtless heard, my dowry's near bottomless. We're rich enough to offer our guests baths in tubs full of gold coins, they say."

Joseph McRae rolled his eyes and smiled. Of course he'd heard all the rumors about Aroha and Koro's new hotel in Rotorua. And he'd known that there was something going on between Sophia Hinerangi's son and Aroha Fitzpatrick long before the official announcement of their engagement. Even back when the two had come for dinner at his hotel, just after the young *pakeha* had arrived, it had been obvious to him that they were falling in love. Over the course of the next two years, he'd watched Koro court Aroha with every trick in both cultures' books. The young man had given her gifts, he'd rowed her over to the Terraces to go swimming in the moonlight. He'd accompanied her to parties—in traditional warrior garb when there was a Maori celebration, or in a formal tailored three-piece suit when the hosts were *pakeha*. During the weekly *powhiri* for visitors, he'd insist on dancing the lead role so he could impress Aroha.

The Scotsman had been more surprised at the fact that Aroha hadn't accepted Koro a lot sooner. It was hard to miss the twinkle in her eye whenever they looked at each other. But here, too, there was talk. It was rumored among the Maori that there was a curse on the young woman that prevented her from taking a husband. But Joseph McRae didn't take those kinds of things too seriously. There was a lot of talk about curses and maledictions around Te Wairoa and Ohinemutu at the moment, anyway. Some Maori *tohunga* were spreading one rumor of doom after another. After all this time, the traditionalists among them still didn't like how much their *maraes* were opening up to the *manuhiri*, and how much that was changing their lives. Aroha was responsible, in part, for many of these changes, which might explain the resentment toward her.

Meanwhile, the curse story had slowly been forgotten, and a few months back, Koro and Aroha had celebrated their engagement at the Rotomahana Hotel the *pakeha* way. They'd only been planning on having a party with their closest relatives over a meal of home-fried fish on the front porch of Sophia Hinerangi's house. But then, a rich English couple had taken the initiative.

The Sandhursts had traveled from Auckland to Te Wairoa with Aroha's own parents, and the ride to Ohinemutu had left them with ample time to talk. The English couple learned all about the Langes' school in Otaki and Aroha's job in Te Wairoa, and later, they were introduced to Sophia Hinerangi and her family. Mr. Sandhurst was an artist, and spent several days in Te Wairoa painting watercolors of the Terraces. Meanwhile, Mrs. Sandhurst got bored, and she was delighted when Aroha and Koro told her about their engagement. The lady was an avid wedding planner, and she insisted on inviting the young couple and the Langes and Sophia's entire family to dinner at the Rotomahana. Linda and Franz and the Hinerangis accepted after some hesitation, without suspecting the gossip they were creating. Rumor had it that somewhere between Te Wairoa and Rotorua, Koro and Aroha had suddenly become wealthy. And then there was the story of her dowry.

"Well, wouldna that be something," Joseph McRae commented dryly. "But all jokes aside, I still don' quite understand where that money came from. The Maori don' either. If ye wish to stop the talking, ye should reveal yer secret." The news that Aroha and Koro were planning on opening their own hotel in Rotorua, paid for by Aroha's dowry, had spread like wildfire. "Yer parents aren' tha' wealthy, are they?"

Aroha tried to shake and nod her head at the same time. "Not really, but it's no secret," she explained. "It's just a little complicated. My father, who's actually my adoptive father, doesn't have much money; that much is true. He's a reverend, and that obliges him to live his life at a certain level of poverty. But my grandparents have a big sheep farm out in the Canterbury Plains, and it's done quite well in recent years. They're the ones giving me the dowry to pay for our hotel."

"Which ye poached Mr. Bao for to run yer Chinese bathhouse," McRae said, returning to his jovial tone. "What's tha', anyway?"

Aroha smiled again. Indeed, she'd asked the young man to work at their new hotel as maître de maison. Bao had long since managed to obtain a leading position at the Rotomahana, where he trained staff and took care of the guests. Joseph McRae greatly appreciated his work and paid him well.

The observant hotelier believed that there were emotions at play in Bao's change of employment. Unrequited ones, unfortunately. McRae could see plain as day that Duong Bao loved Aroha Fitzpatrick; he adored her. But it seemed he'd never even considered courting her. McRae didn't know whether he was holding back because of his origins or because he was avoiding a rivalry with Koro. And yet, the hotelier felt sure that he'd have had a chance. Aroha liked Bao very much. And when one considered how long it had taken her to accept Koro's overtures . . . After all, Duong Bao was an attractive, eligible bachelor with impeccable manners, good education, and a friendly nature.

"We thought we could offer our guests something a little more exotic," Aroha was saying in response to his question. "Every hotel in Rotorua has bathhouses. But Chinese ones haven't been seen here before."

"My people have an avid bathing culture," Bao said with dignity.

"Which ye're an expert at, of course, Mr. Bao?" McRae said, teasing him. "How old were ye when ye left China? Ten?"

"I certainly took baths before that," Bao said stoically.

Aroha laughed. "Oh, stop it, Bao! Just admit that you have no idea. But then again, neither do the *manuhiri*, right? What does it matter? There aren't that many ways of using hot springs, so the differences between cultures can't be all that big. We'll hang some Chinese lanterns and pictures of dragons, put up some folding paper screens . . . We'll have fireworks now and then—that should be fun for our guests. Koro and I are quite fond of the idea."

"That hotel's going to be a gold mine," Joseph McRae confirmed. "Should've thought of it myself. But of course, there are nae any hot springs here. Why didn' ye want to settle in Te Wairoa?"

Aroha shrugged. "Honestly? After spending my childhood at a school, then three and a half years with a host family in Dunedin, and now my time at the Hinerangis' place, I need a little distance from all the hustle and bustle. And I don't want to be an outsider anymore. In Te Wairoa, I've always been the *pakeha* girl trying to mediate between the guests, the Maori, *tohunga*, the chieftain . . . I'm not complaining; it's been a wonderful job. But this is about starting my own family, and I'd rather live in a village with more *pakeha* as well as Maori." She smiled. "And a school. We want children of our own soon!"

McRae nodded. "Quite reasonable. It seems as though ye've thought it all through. And I canna stay angry at ye over Mr. Bao." He nodded at them. "On the contrary, I wish ye all the good fortune in the world. I'll be comin' to the wedding, of course. Even if ye won't be celebratin' it here." He winked at her.

Koro and Aroha couldn't have afforded to have their wedding at the hotel, nor were they keen on giving people even more reason to gossip. They'd be celebrating in Te Wairoa, and were inviting the entire Maori village.

"Oh, that's right, and there's goin' tae be a theater performance here next week," McRae added as Aroha was getting to her feet. "Would ye be so kind as tae post these flyers at the other hotels and the *marae*?" He handed her a small stack. "You and Koro are invited, of course."

Aroha smiled. "We'd love to come. What are they performing?"

McRae shrugged. "Shakespeare, I think."

Over the next few hours, Aroha didn't get a chance to take a close look at the flyers. As so often happened, she was needed at the *marae* to smooth things over between the chieftain and Tuhoto. The *tohunga* had caused a scene after catching a few young people holding a ritual for the *manuhiri* that he considered blasphemous. According to them, the English guests had asked them for a glimpse at the secrets of their people, like magic and places that were considered *tapu*. The teenagers had seen a chance to earn some money, and they'd brought their guests into the forest under the pledge of secrecy. There, the girls had performed sultry dances and the boys had made faces and waved their spears around. It would have been harmless, had they not also acted out sacred rituals. One of the young girls played the part of the priestess, invoking the gods, and one of the boys acted as the chieftain.

Aroha thought it perfectly appropriate that the teens were getting reprimanded for their deeds, but she also thought Tuhoto was overreacting. Stumbling upon this scene, the *tohunga* had planted himself firmly between the Maori and the *manuhiri* and had cried out maledictions and dark prophecies. His speech caused some of the participants to panic. They threw off their dancing costumes and dropped everything to follow the *ariki* down to the lake for a cleansing ceremony. Then they used their spears to threaten some curious *manuhiri* who'd followed them.

It had taken Aroha several hours to calm everyone down. At dusk, sitting on a bench on the broad front porch of Sophia's house, she nestled deeper into Koro's arms. She was shivering, but it was one of their few chances to be alone in Te Wairoa as a young couple. The large family had fled inside from the chill, leaving them by themselves. Koro had draped a blanket protectively around Aroha's shoulders.

"What a day!" He sighed. "I'll be so glad when we're finally alone in Rotorua. The others can take care of Tuhoto's spirits for him then."

"What about that scream?" Aroha asked.

While she'd been busy reassuring the *manuhiri* and suggesting that the villagers return to their work, Koro had pursued the matter of a phenomenon that was encouraging the old priest in his prophecies of doom. Apparently, the Wairoa River had dried out, only to return to its bed with something that sounded like a scream.

Koro shrugged. "It was strange, I'll tell you that," he remarked, absently but tenderly kissing the top of Aroha's head. "It hasn't rained in a few days, of course, but the stream's never dried out before. I'll make some inquiries in Ohinemutu in the next few days. Maybe they needed water and redirected it there."

Aside from the hot springs and the Terraces, there were other local destinations the *manuhiri* could be lured to. There were geysers, for example, and the Maori had discovered that they bubbled more spectacularly if one added some soap. The *tohunga* were upset about this, of course—natural phenomena such as geysers and hot springs were *tapu* as well. The government was also taking steps to prohibit the so-called soaping. But the *manuhiri* were enjoying themselves. They paid extra, and it wasn't beneath them to smuggle the soap in themselves.

"It doesn't really matter, now that the river's back again, does it?" Aroha said.

Koro nodded. "It's just so strange. I heard that there was a screech, and then, from one moment to the next, it went from dry to overflowing."

"Well then, perhaps it really was dammed up in Ohinemutu," Aroha surmised.

"Yes," Koro replied. "Like I said, I'll ask around. There's probably some harmless explanation for all of this. It's just unfortunate that it gives Tuhoto a reason to threaten people with the spirits' revenge for straying from the paths of our ancestors. He's very convincing. I heard his speech earlier, and to be honest, it gave me chills."

"He definitely believes what he's saying," Aroha said, snuggling closer to Koro's chest. As she drew her legs up onto the bench, there was a crinkling in her pocket.

"Oh, I forgot about these flyers," she said, finally taking a look. "Shakespeare . . . Maybe they'll do *Macbeth*. McRae would be happy, I'd wager. Do you know it? It's set in Scotland, and it's perfect for Tuhoto: witches, spirits, dark prophecies . . ."

She slid over, closer to the light filtering out through Sophia's kitchen window, and cried out in surprise.

"The Carrigan Company! That's the company my uncle was going to apply for a few years ago."

Koro stretched, disappointed that Aroha had shifted away. "That young man who disappeared without a trace?" he asked.

Aroha nodded. "We suspected that there was something strange behind that company. It's been awful not to hear from Robin, but his mother, Cat, has always convinced me not to worry, that he's well and just finding himself. She talks about *aka*, and I believe her. When Cat and Chris were lost at sea a few years ago, my mother knew that they weren't dead either."

According to Maori belief, *aka* was an invisible bond between people who were very close, such as mothers and their children. When it was severed, as happened when one of those people died, the other person was supposed to be able to feel it.

"Well, then you'll be able to ask the members of the company yourself," Koro said. "Then at least you'll know whether he really signed on with them back in Wellington. Perhaps you'll even meet him again. Maybe he's still with the company."

# Chapter 26

A few days later, McRae sent a carriage to pick up the Carrigan Company. There were about seventy-five miles between Hamilton and Te Wairoa over still-rough roads.

On the three-day journey, Vera complained constantly about the bumpy tracks and their uncomfortable wagon. Robin endured the ride as stoically as Leah, who slept for most of the journey, and Bertram, who drank to survive the ordeal. He was in a comparably good mood, though. The hotel in Te Wairoa promised a chance at more serious performances than the pubs they were used to, and the old thespian humored Robin by rehearsing a few actual scenes with him while they were on the road. After a bit of grumbling, Robin even read the female parts. He realized that the average audience wasn't interested in dialogues between Romeo and Benvolio or Hamlet and Rosencrantz. They'd prefer the balcony scene from *Romeo and Juliet*, or the famous tussles between Kate and Petruchio. Robin hadn't had the chance to study *The Taming of the Shrew* before, but now, he found himself having an unexpected amount of fun exchanging furious verbal fire with Bertram. When Bertram became too drunk to rehearse in the evenings, Robin lost himself in contemplation of the landscape, which was more and more spectacular the closer they got to the Rotorua area. Unlike Vera, Robin understood why people came out here to enjoy the nature. He hoped they'd let him do act 2, scene 2 of *Hamlet*: *What a piece of work is man! . . . The beauty of the world!*

Robin whispered the words to himself as their cart rumbled on through deep forests, and waterfalls flashed between dark pools, the mountains towering over it all.

Evening was approaching when they reached Ohinemutu. The coachman told them that they'd be continuing the next morning, since it wasn't wise to navigate the unfinished, rain-soaked track to Te Wairoa in the dark. He suggested they spend the night at one of the small local hotels.

"There's a pub here; we can perform," Vera told them as the company climbed down from the cart, aching all over. She had immediately recognized the spirit of the place when the local children launched themselves at the new arrivals. "I'll go and ask. Just a bit of extra income before we get to our luxury abode tomorrow."

She punctuated her words with a glare at Bertram and Robin. Here, her eyes said, you definitely won't be allowed to "invoke the divinity of mankind."

Robin flinched. The pub she'd picked out was little more than a greasy dive. They'd be performing burlesques and Vera's smuttiest adaptations here, no doubt.

"Th . . . that might not make a great im . . . impression on . . . on y . . . your Mr. McRae, m . . . my dear," Bertram slurred.

Robin figured the man probably just didn't feel like getting onstage that night.

"Oh, he won't find out," Vera said. "Have someone take you to our quarters and get yourselves ready. See to it that you sober up, Bertram. And Leah, wake up, girl! I'll see what I can do in the meantime."

The pub owners had never heard of Shakespeare before. They did, however, understand the words "extra money." Within minutes, they'd rounded up what looked like the entire village. The audience was almost exclusively Maori, Robin noted as he stood on the improvised stage. Now, just before the beginning of winter, there were fewer English guests in a place like this, and they were probably in bed by now.

The performance turned out lousy, of course—even worse than normal, Robin thought to himself. Bertram kept jumbling his words and staggered across the stage barely awake, and all Leah did was stand around apathetically, stripping off her clothes at more or less the right moments. Vera's usual *pakeha* audience would probably have been aroused by this, but the Maori were accustomed to nudity. All they did was stare in confusion at the pretty but obviously muddled young woman, unable to understand what was going on.

"Is she possessed by spirits?" a man asked Robin later after he'd unthinkingly revealed his Maori language skills by ordering some food. "And do you really get paid to recite such strange verses to people? It's not even real English, is it?"

Robin tried to explain how Elizabethan English was different from modern English by comparing Polynesian languages to modern Maori, which created even more confusion.

"So it's the language of the spirits?" the young man asked. "The type of Maori that people used to speak in Hawaiki? I bet we'll have to learn it again when we go back there after we die. Then . . . the girl's a kind of *tohunga*, yes? She speaks as though she's dead."

Robin didn't object. In fact, that was the most apt description of Leah's droning that he'd ever heard.


"Their performance was terrible. Just terrible!"

Koro Hinerangi had been in Ohinemutu that evening to ask around about the strange events involving the Wairoa River. He'd gone to one of the local pubs with Paora, a young member of the Ngati Whakaue tribe he'd known since they were both children. Paora had a reputation for being very talkative after a few pints, and Koro had hoped to get a confession out of him; all the other Ngati Whakaue in Ohinemutu had claimed to know nothing about a dam. The pub had been taken over by the Carrigan Company's performance, and now Koro was telling Aroha all about it.

"Is it possible, my love," Aroha teased him, "that you just don't know that much about the arts? Or Shakespeare, at any rate?"

Koro shook his head. "I recognize drunkards tottering around on a stage," he told her. "And girls who slur their words like they're not right in the head. Besides, I know enough about Mr. Shakespeare to know that he can't have written whatever that was, or his plays wouldn't be performed everywhere. The *pakeha* are prudes. The tourists' eyes pop when they see our girls wearing harmless *piupiu* skirts. I don't think they'd go see plays where the actors go at it right there onstage."

"They do what?" Aroha asked in disbelief. "They—uh—make love in front of the audience?"

"Well, I don't think they actually love each other. They yelled at each other afterward. And they don't have real intercourse onstage. That'd be even more indecent in the eyes of the *pakeha*, because if you ask me, I think Juliet and Miranda were played by a man. But they get as close to the real thing as possible without getting in trouble with the police. Aroha, that was the strangest theater performance I've ever seen in my life! I can't imagine Mr. McRae would like that."

Koro pulled his shirt off. It was late at night, and he'd secretly crept into Aroha's room at his mother's house. Aroha insisted on sneaking around like this. She was embarrassed to admit to the world that she and Koro had been sharing a bed for a long time. In summer, they'd made love in the forest or near the Terraces after a bath at the hot springs. Apart from the scheduled visits of the *manuhiri*, people rarely came there, and it was the most beautiful backdrop that Aroha could imagine. But now it was starting to get too cold outside. They could sleep together inside, or not at all. Koro played along patiently. He thought that his mother must have long since noticed his nightly comings and goings. But Sophia never brought up the subject. She might be a Christian, but she was also Maori. *Pakeha* prudishness was alien to her.

"You'll see for yourself tomorrow," he finished. "And now, I can show you that I might not know much about the arts or Shakespeare, but I definitely know enough about love."

Early the next day, there was another commotion in town. Again, the Wairoa River was beginning to run dry. This time there was no way of explaining it with the weather. Swaths of mist had been shrouding the mountaintops for days on end, and the night before, there had been heavy rainfall over Lake Tarawera. But the riverbed, which was normally full, was reduced to nothing but mud and sludge.

Tuhoto *ariki* started talking about angry spirits again, spreading unrest among the *pakeha* as well as the Maori. Koro still suspected the people in Ohinemutu. But Aroha saw it as a storm in a teacup. The villages could get their water directly from the glass-clear lakes. So if the folks in Ohinemutu really wanted to dam the stream to create more places for the *manuhiri* to take baths, or whatever else they could think of to compete with the hot springs in Rotorua, no harm would be done. Still, it wasn't traditional. The tribes usually avoided interfering with nature like that, to keep from angering the spirits. But that was for Tuhoto *ariki* to discuss with the *tohunga* of the Ngati Whakaue. The Tuhourangi and their *pakeha* guests had nothing to do with it.

"I wonder if it's really the Ngati Whakaue's fault," Sophia Hinerangi said nervously, after calming a group of guests with Aroha's help. The travelers had been afraid that the half-naked priest would curse them with his spirit staff. "Damming a stream to build bathhouses? That's pretty difficult. It takes effort, financial investment, and a certain ability to plan ahead. Which are things that the community in Ohinemutu lacks, I'm afraid. Just look at those shacks they call hotels. I don't know, Aroha. I have a bad feeling about this whole thing. Tuhoto has his quirks, but he's astute."

After leaving Sophia, Aroha escorted the travelers to their canoes and chatted with Kate Middlemass before setting off for the Rotomahana Hotel. The actors' first performance was scheduled for the following evening, but McRae would probably be able to tell her about his first impressions of the Carrigan Company. Bao welcomed her with tea and pastries as soon as she walked in the door. Then the hotel owner gave her disappointing news. The company was still traveling.

"Unsurprising, with this weather we've been having," Bao said.

It had been raining all day, and Aroha had just expressed her sympathy for the *manuhiri*. Like most English people, they weren't deterred in their plans to visit the Terraces by an odd spot of bad weather, but the place was prettier in the sunshine, of course. Not to mention the rainy canoe ride and hike. And Aroha didn't envy the actors traveling in an open wagon either.

"Drat, the track must be so muddy now!" she said.

"And yet, Miss Carrigan was already complainin' about their strenuous travels in Ohinemutu last night," McRae was saying as he walked into the lobby to join them. "Which didna stop her from forcin' her people onstage at the pub that evenin'. It looks like she's in need o' money. Though she seemed quite well-off when I met her in Hamilton."

"*Miss* Carrigan?" Aroha asked, surprised.

The Scotsman shrugged. "Ay, this company belongs t' a woman. Very self-confident . . . What was her first name? Willa? Vera? Right, tha's what it was. Vera Carrigan."

The evilest creature Aroha's kindhearted mother had ever laid eyes on. She started to feel jitters of fear running up and down her spine. "Please, let me know when they arrive," she told Mr. McRae, and after he'd taken his leave, she turned to Bao.

"Please find out if there's a young man traveling with them. His name is Robin Fenroy. Tall, blond . . . a little dreamy-eyed. Let me know when he arrives at the hotel. But don't tell him about me. I'd like to surprise him."

Robin flinched at the sound of a knock on his hotel room door. What did Vera want now? They'd only just arrived. He'd been led to his room by a friendly Chinese man who spoke fluent English and had chatted eloquently about Shakespeare, and now all Robin wanted was to get some rest. The last part of their journey had been hell—but who would've imagined hell to be so wet and cold? The beautiful landscape had been hidden behind a fine veil of drizzle all day long. The travelers' clothes were soaked within minutes, and the wagon driver made the men get off and push several times, whenever it seemed like they were about to get stuck in the mud. Robin and Bertram's shoes were ruined. Vera, of course, had spent the entire time complaining. Robin didn't think he could stand another minute of her that day. Although he was hungry, he'd already decided to pass up the Scottish hotelier's invitation for the company to have dinner at the restaurant with him. And now, it seemed as though somebody wanted something from him. Again.

"Come in," he called morosely, only to find himself confronted with familiar pale-blue eyes.

"Aroha?" he asked, confused. "What are you doing here?"

Aroha beamed at him. She could hardly believe that she'd really found Robin again. "I might ask you the same thing!" she retorted, inconspicuously sizing up her young uncle as she smiled.

At first sight, Robin had hardly changed at all. Only when Aroha looked closer could she see that the slight boy had gotten stronger, sturdier. His face still looked elfin, but it had lost its slightly foolish, innocent look, and he reminded Aroha of an enchanted knight from a Celtic fairy tale. The furrow that had once only appeared between his pale brows during times of intense focus or worry now looked like it was chiseled there by hardship. And Aroha noticed how long Robin was wearing his hair. At Rata Station, he'd never shared Chris's habit of wearing his hair long and tying it at the nape of his neck. He'd always worn his own hair as short as most other *pakeha* men did.

"I—we're performing here," Robin mumbled, still completely flummoxed.

"Oh, let me hug you!" Aroha approached and embraced him tightly. She hardly noticed that he shrank from her touch. "It's wonderful to see you again! We were all so worried. Cat and Chris still are. Why didn't you ever get in touch? Or write to us to invite us to a play? You—you are acting, right?"

Robin nodded. "Of course, I—Well, we don't perform entire plays. We're a very small company. We usually only perform scenes from Shakespeare plays."

Aroha smiled at him. "All the better for you then, isn't it? So you can play Hamlet and Romeo in one night."

Robin nodded. But he bit his lip, and his smile looked haunted.

Aroha's excitement evaporated. Something wasn't right here, that much was obvious. If Robin had really been proud of his work, he wouldn't have hidden away for two and a half years. "How remarkable," she said in a cheerful tone. "We could hardly believe that you went to Wellington by yourself, but it looks like it all worked out on the first try, didn't it? Did you really just audition, and this Carrigan person was impressed by you right away? Like I was, back in the stables? Are you happy now?"

She plopped down on Robin's bed, expecting him to take a seat next to her. Instead, she noticed a trace of panic flutter across his features. He pulled up a chair and sat down, his hands twisting together until his knuckles turned white. His movements seemed stiff, and not as graceful as Aroha remembered.

"I really do enjoy being an actor," he told her suddenly, as if Aroha had voiced any doubts. "What—what about you? What are you doing here?"

Aroha realized Robin was trying to change the subject. She told him a little bit about her work with the Maori and the *manuhiri,* and about her engagement to Koro. She also told him about the hotel.

"It's too bad you're not staying for the grand opening," she said finally. "Or you could see your parents too. Cat and Chris are coming here for the wedding. But I'm sure you have a touring schedule." Aroha chattered on, acting as though she didn't notice Robin tense at the mention of his parents. "Though I'm sure the two of them wouldn't mind following you to your next location. They'd be excited to see you perform."

Robin tensed even more. He paled, and his hands gripped the sides of his chair.

"Come on, what is it, Robin?" Aroha allowed herself to sound a little stricter now. "Don't you want to see your parents? Are you still angry at them? Is that why you never wrote home? Robin, they only meant well! Chris even offered to travel to Wellington with you."

Robin shook his head. "I'm not angry at them," he said curtly. "Aroha, I—we're—invited to dinner with Mr. McRae. Would you—would you like to come too?"

Aroha considered for a moment. She was dying to meet Vera Carrigan, but her instincts warned her to be careful. How would Vera react when she found out that Robin was related to Linda Lange, formerly Fitzpatrick? A moment later, she dismissed the thought. The woman probably wouldn't notice Aroha's last name. And even if she transferred her old grudge against Linda to her daughter, there was nothing she could do to hurt Aroha.

"Of course, I'd love to!" she told him. "I mean, I'm not dressed for dinner," Aroha said, gesturing at the simple tea dress she was wearing under her raincoat, "but I'm sure the occasion won't be too formal."

She glanced at Robin's threadbare dark-blue suit. It was part of the bundle of clothes the boy had taken when he'd left Rata Station. Apparently, the salary Vera was paying hadn't been enough for new clothes.

Robin blushed. "All—all my things are still wet and muddy . . ." he claimed. "The suitcase was left out in the rain, and—"

Aroha nodded understandingly. "You can give your things to my friend Bao; he'll have them cleaned for you," she suggested. "And Mr. McRae's very nice. He does care about maintaining a certain level of formality at his hotel—it certainly is the best one around—but things aren't as stiff here as they are in the big hotels in Wellington or Auckland." She smiled. "In fact, Bao and Mr. McRae sometimes both complain that the Maori cleaning women refuse to wear shoes and still haven't learned to starch a bonnet . . ."

Vera, Leah, and Bertram were already there when Aroha and Robin descended the steps to the lobby. Bao was serving them appetizers by the fireplace. Mr. McRae was sitting with his guests, who still looked half frozen, and having an animated discussion with Vera.

"Ye must visit the sights tha' attract all our guests here!" he was saying. "The hot springs in Rotorua, the geysers in Whakarewarewa, and the Pink and White Terraces, of course . . . Just join one of our canoe trips. Or nay, that'd limit ye; I'm sure ye have a rehearsal schedule. You should tell Bao when ye'd like to go, and he'll get you a carriage. But ye won't be able to explore the Terraces on yer own."

"I'm sure Sophia Hinerangi would be willing to adapt her plans to Miss Carrigan's needs a little," Aroha chimed in.

McRae greeted her with a beaming smile. "Miss Aroha! Did ye find yer—ah—relative?"

Aroha nodded. McRae got to his feet politely and introduced her to the actors. She eyed the group discreetly while they exchanged pleasantries. Bertram Lockhart must have been the actor Koro had seen staggering drunkenly onstage last night. He didn't look sober now, but he managed to greet Aroha in perfect form. Lockhart was wearing a brown three-piece suit that had doubtlessly seen better days—much like its wearer. Nevertheless, Bertram Lockhart's deep, carrying voice immediately captured Aroha's interest. She could easily imagine him as a king or a wizard onstage.

Leah, the young blonde woman, almost a girl still, seemed strangely muted. Aroha tried to imagine her with slightly fuller curves and an alert look in her eyes. Had her hair not been so stringy, and if there'd been any life in those lavender eyes of hers, Leah would easily have outshone the woman sitting next to her. So far, however, Vera Carrigan seemed to be the only member of the theater company who managed to bring some life to their small party. The curvy woman was wearing a red dress—tight-fitting with a plunging neckline, it toed the line of decency. Her hat, which was also red and sat jauntily on her thick, dark hair, was rather extravagant. The company's leader was undoubtedly a striking figure.

Aroha remembered how Louise Pomeroy had caught people's attention at the Excelsior. It seemed that actresses enjoyed presenting themselves to the public, even when they weren't onstage. But Vera had little in common with Miss Pomeroy. Her features were rougher, her dark eyes were lit up by a cold gleam, and the corners of her mouth drooped when she wasn't smiling her insincere smile. When speaking to McRae, Vera presented herself as friendly and officious, but as soon as he turned away, her eyes hardened, and her expression became sullen and disinterested. Then Aroha's name was mentioned. Vera's eyes focused on her immediately, and they flashed in a way that scared Aroha. Like an eagle homing in on her prey.

"Aroha Fitzpatrick?" Vera asked in her husky voice. "I knew a Joe Fitzpatrick once."

"Yes, my father," Aroha said shortly.

Robin gave her a puzzled look that flickered as it passed over Vera. He didn't know Vera and Joe's story, but Aroha wondered if he was afraid of this woman.

"Interesting," Vera said. "And what is . . . your relationship to our—uh—young hero?"

Her last words had a mocking tone, and Aroha saw Robin squirm.

"We're related through my mother," Aroha said politely, but as tersely as possible.

Vera didn't push any further, but her inquisitive gaze stayed on Aroha as Bao informed them that dinner was served. Throughout the meal, which was excellent, Vera was wholly absorbed by making a good impression on McRae. Aroha found her demeanor fairly obtrusive and exaggerated, but McRae seemed to enjoy it. He was flirting with her, unabashed, raising his glass to her health and obviously enjoying her company. Aroha remembered what her mother had said about Vera's strange effect on men.

The other members of the company weren't contributing much to the conversation. Leah ate in silence, and much less than she should have, Aroha thought. Lockhart was washing down his meal with far too much wine. Aroha tried to strike up a conversation with Robin. She asked him all about where he'd performed and traveled with the company, and she tried to find out more about how his life had been over the past two and a half years. But Robin answered her in tense monosyllables. He excused himself after he'd wolfed down his dessert.

"I'm so sorry, but I'm very tired after the long day of traveling," he explained. "And we're performing tomorrow, and we—we'd like to rehearse in the morning." Robin gave Bertram Lockhart a look that could only be considered pleading.

Aroha was surprised. As she'd understood it, these actors were onstage together every night. They'd been working together for two and a half years now. So what did they have left to rehearse?

"Well, I'll definitely see you tomorrow night, then! I'm looking forward to the show," she told him, wondering about Robin's wince when she tried to plant a kiss goodnight on his cheek.

Back at the Hinerangis' house, she sat down, lit some candles on her desk, and wrote a letter to her mother.

# Chapter 27

"Please! Just this once! I can't play Julia or Miranda with Aroha watching. I'd die of embarrassment. Please, Vera, *please*, I've never asked you for a favor like this before!"

Bertram Lockhart, who was still more or less sober on this first morning in Te Wairoa, nodded sympathetically. Robin had nudged him out of bed long before the time Vera usually got up, and the two of them had started rehearsals already. There were several scenes from *Hamlet* and *Romeo and Juliet* that the two of them could perform together and that could be made more interesting with swordfights. Robin was planning on holding two big monologues, just as long as they could get Leah to say a few words as Juliet or Ophelia in response. She knew the lines, and Robin was prepared to beg her not to take too much of her "medicine" beforehand. Vera herself wanted to portray Hamlet's mother. She lacked the depth and talent for the role, but that would just make Robin stand out even more by comparison.

"Oh, let him have his part," Bertram said, supporting the young actor with a vehemence they didn't often see. "For goodness' sake, Vera, the young woman who looks after the guests here is his relative. She'll tell his parents about it. And if you've got him playing a girl up there . . . he'll make a fool of himself in front of his family! And yes, I am aware that was normal in Shakespearean times."

"Exactly!" Vera crowed. "It *was* normal. And we planned it that way. I don't see why I should let you two dictate my show. And Leah—"

"As if Leah gives a damn!" Robin said.

Leah had been with them for about half an hour now, and she was just standing there, unmoving as a prop that someone had forgotten to put away.

Vera's face twisted into an evil smile. "Well then, why don't we let Leah decide? Leah, my dear . . . Would you like to play Juliet tonight?"

Leah didn't appear to have heard her.

"Leah!" Bertram boomed.

The young woman looked up. "Yes!" she said, her misty violet eyes fixed on Robin. "I like how—how Robin talks to me . . ." Leah started moving, sashaying across the stage. "Ooh, Romeo . . ." She was actually putting a bit of expression into her voice.

Vera was visibly confused, but then her frown turned angry. "Has she been drinking, Bertram?"

Bertram Lockhart kept a straight face. "How would I know?" he said calmly. "Am I my sister's keeper?"

Vera made a snarling sound, but then she took a deep breath and backed down.

"Fine then, Robin can play Hamlet and Romeo. Sweet little Leah here can slur her way through Juliet's part . . . if she's able, when the time comes. I'll be Ophelia."

Robin suppressed a sigh. Vera was decidedly too old and insensitive for the part; she'd simply shout him down. But in the scene they'd chosen, at least, Ophelia and Hamlet didn't get close enough for Vera to incorporate anything too ribald.

"Aaand," Vera said, giving Robin and Bertram an evil little smile, "as our grand finale, we'll be performing the scene with Titania and the donkey . . . Robin can really shine then. Seeing as he only wants to perform male parts today."

With that, she sauntered out, leaving Robin miserable.

"Heavens, Bertram," he moaned, "if Leah plays Titania as usual—"

Bertram waved him down. "She won't," he reassured Robin. "She'll probably fight with you instead. Alcohol makes her rebellious. You saw her just now. She disagreed with her beloved Vera. And that's just the beginning."

"So, is it true what Vera said?" Robin asked. "How did you get her to drink whiskey before breakfast?"

"Oooh, Romeo!" Leah approached Robin, trying to rub up against his leg. He could smell the drink on her breath.

Bertram grinned. "Well, let's say she couldn't find her tincture this morning, which upset her. So I put some of last night's good whiskey in her tea. I think she barely even noticed. But it does complicate tonight's performance, Robin. Vera's right that our dear little Leah doesn't have the stomach for alcohol. First, she gets all teary, and then she gets angry. There's a reason Vera buys all that expensive laudanum for her. So, we have to be careful with dosages. But don't you worry, Uncle Bertram's going to take care of everything."

Bertram Lockhart managed to stay more or less sober that day. He drank just enough to avoid any withdrawal. And somehow, he even managed to wrest the evening's narration from Vera's grip. Normally, she announced the scenes from various comedies and dramas herself, but this time, she greeted the guests and then left it to Bertram to tell people a little more about the plays they were going to captivate their audience with, as Bertram said with a wink.

Robin peered out through the curtains nervously—the Rotomahana Hotel's salon had a real stage with dressing rooms for the actors, sets, and everything they might need to perform smaller plays. The auditorium was fairly full. In the front row, he could see the English travelers, and he recognized Aroha with a tall, muscular Maori man at her side. That had to be Koro, her fiancé. The man looked skeptical, and Aroha seemed nervous. Farther toward the back, he could see a few Maori, and some Europeans he took to be the owners of various hotels, bathhouses, and stores in Rotorua. Tonight's audience was doubtlessly more educated than the Carrigan Company's usual crowd. Surely some of them had even seen a real *Hamlet* or *Romeo and Juliet* onstage before.

Robin felt his hands shake a little, but the anxiety left him the moment he set foot onstage. With "To be, or not to be," he declaimed, opening the best performance Vera Carrigan's sad little company had ever delivered. Robin was as absorbed by his lines as he'd been back with the Pomeroy Company, and even Bertram returned to something that must have been close to his former glory. Whenever the two of them had the stage to themselves, they were quick to entrance the audience. The two women, of course, were a different matter. Leah kept slurring her words, and her Juliet slumped against Romeo rather than leaning against him for protection, but Robin deftly offset her shortcomings, inconspicuously whispering her lines to her. Vera was just as bad as Ophelia as she'd been as Desdemona, but at least she'd understood that she'd better say the original lines in front of this audience, and keep her nightgown buttoned.

Toward the end of their performance, Robin trembled in terror at the prospect of their scene with Leah as Titania—and got a surprise when he bent over the sleeping fairy queen. There, draped over a bed of flowers, he found not Leah but Bertram. The gifted actor embodied his female role so hilariously that people in the audience were clutching their sides in breathless laughter. Nothing about the scene was lewd, and nobody would have considered Bertram effeminate because of his comedic performance. He was regaled with frenetic applause when he finally bowed alongside Robin, a crown of flowers drooping lopsidedly from his graying hair.

"Well, that might not have been the best Shakespeare performance ever given," Aroha finally told Koro, "but they certainly weren't as horrible as you said."

Koro raised his eyebrows, bemused. "They seemed much more . . . serious today," he agreed. "Almost like completely different people. Or perhaps it was just me. Apparently, I know nothing of the fine arts."

Aroha laughed and planted an affectionate kiss on his cheek. Then she went over to give Robin her most sincere congratulations and decided that, in her upcoming letter to Cat, she would downplay the flaws of their company and her misgivings about Vera Carrigan.

# Chapter 28

"Only six people today?" Aroha asked Sophia. The guide was leading that day's tour group over to their boats. "And Kate didn't get any customers at all?"

Sophia shrugged. "Kate is visiting relatives in Hamilton. And there was some sort of problem with the inbound ship from Auckland yesterday. In any case, we haven't gotten any new *manuhiri* yet. Today, I've only got the people here who stayed behind because of the heavy rains." She smiled at her customers, two English couples and a pair of young Frenchmen. "As you can see, it was the sensible thing to do. Yes, they'll enjoy their trip much more in the sunshine!"

Indeed, on this morning in May, they were greeted with brilliant fall weather. Lake Tarawera glowed a velvety blue, and it reflected the light wisps of clouds that were drifting across the sky. The Terraces shimmered with an unearthly light in such weather—and the baths were more fun, of course, if you weren't getting wet from above as well.

"Why don't you come along with us, Aroha? If you'd like to, that is," Sophia said. "You could translate for the French people. They told me they speak English, but I think they barely understand a word I'm saying. And you should bring along your young relative too. I heard his performance was beautiful last night. My daughter seems to be smitten with him already."

Aroha smiled. "She should encourage him, then; Robin's very shy with girls. But I'm afraid he won't be able to come along. He's on his way to Whakarewarewa right now with his company, to look at the geysers there. They won't be performing today. But I don't actually have any plans until tonight. Lucky for your Frenchmen."

"And for me," Sophia said cheerfully.

*"Bonjour, messieurs,"* Aroha said to the young men with a smile as she clambered into their boat with them. She was very pleased about the trip. It had been at least two months since she'd seen the Terraces.

She was soon immersed in an animated conversation with the two Frenchmen, who told her about their travels so far. The oarsmen were in good spirits too. The beautiful weather and the glassy-smooth surface of Lake Tarawera inspired them to sing for the strangers they were ferrying.

"What's the song about?" one of their guests asked.

Sophia and Aroha translated the lyrics for the *manuhiri*. "It's about the lake and the fishing here," Aroha explained. "Almost all Maori songs describe the land that their respective tribes live in. Each tribe has subtle differences in its traditions and its own songs and dances. The Maori are very devoted to their land, much more than we *pakeha* are. To us, it doesn't really matter where we settle in the end, as long as the area's nice and the neighbors are friendly. We're used to moving several times in our lives. But the Maori consider themselves a part of their mountains, rivers, and lakes. An old proverb from the people who live by the Whanganui River says, *'Ko au te awa. Ko te awa ko au,'* which means 'I am the river, the river is me.' It's true, tribes migrate occasionally. But they always return, in the end. That's why it was such a crime to displace them during the land wars. It doesn't matter how beautiful, fertile, or bountiful the new land and rivers might have been; the people simply couldn't accept it. And in truth, the land tribes were moved to was always quite a bit worse than the old land, which was redistributed to *pakeha* farmers."

Sophia and Aroha were both enjoying traveling with a small group for a change. This way, they were able to answer questions in much greater detail, and when the two Frenchmen said they'd like to try rowing one of the "war canoes," the oarsmen readily cleared their seats, laughing.

"Not easy!" one of them warned.

"And this isn't actually a war canoe," Aroha corrected them. "It's not even a canoe, as a matter of fact, but a converted whaling boat. Sure, it might make you feel like Captain Ahab, but I doubt it'll turn you into fierce warriors. We'll be getting into a real canoe once we get to Lake Rotomahana. You can row that one, too, if you want."

She followed this up by telling the story of Moby Dick to the Maori while the Frenchmen reached clumsily for two pairs of oars. They were aristocracy from Paris who'd probably never had to lift a finger in their lives, and Aroha was relieved to know the boat was quite sturdy.

Their hike over to Lake Rotomahana took longer than expected. Both of the English couples were a little older, and one of the men turned out not to be very sure on his feet, as did the wife of the other gentleman. Although Sophia supported the lady and the Frenchmen offered their assistance to the elderly gentleman, the walk took them quite some time. To the Frenchmen's excitement, there was indeed a traditional canoe waiting there, and since they now considered themselves expert oarsmen, they couldn't be deterred from "helping" again—which slowed the second boat ride considerably.

"We should sing a war *haka* too," one of them suggested, brimming with enthusiasm.

But Aroha shook her head. "We shouldn't ask the men to do that," she explained candidly. "First of all, they wouldn't just carelessly invoke the spirits of war, and second, the Pink and White Terraces are *tapu* for them. That means it's strictly forbidden to shed blood there. The spirits of the Terraces would be furious if people greeted them with war songs and dances."

The Frenchmen gazed at her, frowning.

"You—you don't really believe in spirits, do you, Mademoiselle Aroha?" one of them asked.

Aroha smiled. "It doesn't really matter what I believe," she replied evasively. "What matters is that the Terraces are sacred to the Maori. It's very generous of them to make them accessible to visitors from all over the world. The least we can do is respect their rules. And besides," she said, elegantly changing the subject, "this boat isn't a war canoe either. Those are longer, slimmer, much faster, and often decorated with carvings and feathers. Maori warfare is more about intimidating the enemy than actually fighting. War canoes are huge. A crew is sometimes made up of seventy men."

Aroha, Sophia, and Kate didn't usually discuss the subject of spirits with the *manuhiri* in much depth. Each of them had experienced firsthand that some Christian visitors took offense at the subject, while others turned out to be avid spiritualists who had nothing better to do than bother the Maori with propositions of séances. Aroha found the attitude somewhat inane, but at least they were being open-minded and tolerant. She'd rather not hear what Tuhoto *ariki* had to say about the subject, though.

As usual, the mood aboard the canoe became almost reverent when the Terraces finally came into view. It just seemed to be normal to experience a sense of divinity here, especially on a day as beautiful as this. The sun was already high in the sky when the canoe slid silently past the cascade-shaped rock formations. The shimmering white of Te Tarata was blinding, and Otukapuarangi nestled up against the lake in its glowing shades of pink. Not even the young Frenchmen were horsing around now. All of them understood why this stunning miracle of nature was sacred to the Maori.

"Let's keep the bathing short today," Sophia said to Aroha. "It'll be dusk before we get home."

Sophia and Aroha didn't take warm baths themselves, seeing as the English ladies needed help getting out of their corsets and into their bathing gowns and then back into their voluminous skirts. And indeed, the sun was already setting when the group finally returned to Lake Tarawera and climbed into the whaling boat.

Sophia eyed the rising mist with apprehension. "It's getting late," she said as they rowed along the south end of Lake Tarawera.

The oarsmen slowed down as visibility got worse by the minute. But the *manuhiri* weren't complaining, seemingly enjoying the surreal evening mood on the lake instead. Until the canoe appeared.

"*Mon Dieu,* what is that?" One of the Frenchmen saw it first.

A gigantic canoe, its high bow decorated with elaborate carvings, rose up out of the mist in front of them. It was rowed by a large number of men who were staring straight ahead. Other men were standing up in the boat, but they took no notice of the whaling boat with its passengers, although the canoe came close enough that they almost could have touched it. There was no sound in the tourist boat but the oarsmen's soft, terrified groans. They'd immediately stopped rowing at the appearance of the strange canoe. Aroha started at the strangers, frozen in uncomprehending horror. Now she was able to see some details: The men were Maori warriors, and they were wearing the traditional flax skirts and weapons of their station on their belts. Aroha recognized some of the weapons as axes and clubs. The men's faces were tattooed and looked set in stone, oddly lifeless, and their hair was tied up in warriors' knots and decorated with feathers. An icy chill ran down Aroha's spine. The plumage wasn't traditional for men going to war. The feathers of the huia and the white heron were bestowed on dead warriors for their journey to Hawaiki.

"That—that—"

Sophia was white as a sheet. Both of the English ladies made the sign of the cross with shaking hands.

"Let's go!" The head oarsman had come to his senses. "Those are spirits. That's a spirit canoe, a *waka wairua*."

Snapping out of their paralysis, the Maori pulled the oars with all the strength they could muster. After a few tense moments, the strange canoe finally passed them and disappeared into the mist.

"That—that's what you might imagine a war canoe to look like," Aroha mumbled.

"Imagine?" one of the French gentlemen said in English. "Mademoiselle, I *saw* that canoe! And the rest of you?"

The English visitors nodded, apparently at a loss for words. But the other Frenchman seemed to be regaining his composure now too.

"Is this a special attraction?" he asked nervously. "First . . . ah . . . you tell us about warriors and spirits, and then . . . we see something like that? Well, if it's organized . . . it's certainly worth an extra tip."

"Don't be ridiculous!" Sophia snapped at him. "That—that was—an actual *waka wairua*, a spirit canoe. And it's a harbinger of doom."

Aroha was alarmed. How could Sophia say such a thing? It would've been better to calm the *manuhiri* instead of encouraging them in the notion that they'd just witnessed something otherworldly.

On the other hand, they *had* just witnessed something otherworldly. Aroha tried, but she wasn't able to convince herself that they hadn't seen what they'd just seen. There were no warrior tribes along Lake Tarawera, and no such canoe had crossed the lake in generations! And yet, the warriors had been so close that they could have felt their breath, if they'd tried. If they'd been breathing, that was. And . . . they had been wearing dead men's feathers . . .

Sophia was looking strangely lifeless too, as though she were still gazing into another world. "Many people will die . . . ," she whispered.

Aroha drew herself up. This couldn't go on; Sophia, who was normally so business-minded, was going to scare the *manuhiri* if she kept on that way.

"I—um—I'm sure it'll all make sense in the end," she told the travelers with feigned cheerfulness. "Perhaps it was just someone playing a trick on us."

She could see in their faces that none of them really believed her.


Vera Carrigan was making Robin pay for his high-handedness about the previous night's program. Robin had been worried that she might do so, of course, but he couldn't come up with an excuse when McRae surprised the company with an invitation to take the carriage out to Whakarewarewa that morning.

"There willna be any new guests arriving today, so the carriage is goin' tae be free, and the weather's excellent."

Vera had accepted, although she'd acted disappointed at first when she heard that McRae wouldn't be joining them.

"I'm afraid that willna be possible. I'll be indispensable at the hotel today," the hotelier told her, genuine regret in his voice. "But say hello to the big geyser for me, will ye? And dinna let Arama pour soap in it again. I know it might look excitin', but it's pure mischief, and the government banned it."

Apart from the last half mile or so, the way to Whakarewarewa was identical to the one to Ohinemutu, but now in the sunshine, the trip was delightful. The woods looked magical to Robin. That was what the backdrop from *A Midsummer Night's Dream* should look like, he thought. He wouldn't have been surprised to see Puck and Oberon peeking out from behind some tree ferns or waterfalls. A little while later, the geothermal fields of Whakarewarewa spread out in front of them with the green forest as a backdrop. Bizarrely shaped white rocks jutted from the ground in places, and between them, Robin could make out azure-blue pools and bubbling mud pots. When boiling hot water came shooting out of the Pohutu geyser a few feet away from them at the edge of the path, even Leah cried out in surprise. The lava fields, the plumes of steam, and the spouts of hissing water erupting from the earth succeeded in breaking through her stupor.

The area's three main geysers were situated above a river. The rocks they rose from looked as though they'd been sprinkled with gold—some kind of mineral had to be settling there to create such an effect. Robin could hardly get enough of the beautiful, unique landscape.

"This would be a wonderful natural stage," he mused.

Their Maori guide, Arama, assured Robin that his tribe was of a similar opinion, and that they occasionally came there to dance and sing for the spirits. "They must be appeased," he said solemnly. "As much as these springs are a blessing, they can also turn into a curse. When the spirits are angry, they make the water boil in the pools. They create new spouts, and steam shoots out of the earth with unbelievable force. There are gigantic fires burning in the ground below our feet here; the spirits make the mountains melt as they please."

Robin translated his words for the others.

"Oh really?" Vera said, looking bored. "I heard," she said, winking at their young guide, "that one can bathe naked here." As if by accident, her hand brushed Robin's arm.

The young guide grinned. "We always bathe naked," he said in English. "Bath costume not practical. Yes, I show springs far from path. But must be careful. Sometimes water more hot than before."

Vera grinned. "Oh, it can't be too hot for us, isn't that right, Robin?" She turned back to the guide. "What was your name again? Ah, I remember . . . Arama . . . Doesn't that mean Adam, my dearie? Are you baptized?"

Vera flirted with the young man, shamelessly unbuttoning her dress as he led them to a hot pool that was rarely, or perhaps never, visited by *pakeha*. It was beautiful—almost perfectly circular, and framed in white where minerals had settled around the edges. The water itself was a milky shade of green.

"Good for skin," Arama told them.

Robin didn't like the smell rising from the pool's surface. It stank of sulfur.

"Go on then, undress," Vera demanded of her company.

Bertram demonstratively closed an open button on the vest of his three-piece suit. "I'll be burning in hell long enough," he said tersely. "I don't need to roll around in fire and brimstone now."

"Brimstone?" Arama asked, having cheerfully tugged off his linen trousers, and now carefully dipping his toes in the water. "Yes, nice warm, no hot. We swim."

"It's just a saying," Robin explained to him.

He, for his part, had no idea what to do. He didn't want to take a bath, especially not with Vera, whose pasty body was completely exposed now. She looked like a wriggling maggot to him. He was unable to comprehend the longing look in Arama's eyes. He preferred looking at Leah, who had dutifully stripped off her dress and was now sitting on a rock by the edge of the pool. She was impassive as usual, but her posture, rounded shoulders, and lowered head betrayed her shame, although her stringy hair almost completely covered her naked upper body.

Robin wished he could just run away. But if he didn't let Vera have her way now, she'd change their program for tomorrow night and force him to humiliate himself in front of Aroha and her friends. There was no way out!

Robin could have kicked himself—it would have been so easy to defect in Hamilton or somewhere else with a train connection to Auckland. But here, in Te Wairoa, he was stuck. Unhappily, he stripped off his shirt.

Vera slid into the pool, followed by the slightly confused Arama. The young man had never met a *pakeha* woman like Vera before.

"Come on in, Robin, my dearie. Don't be a prude! Shall we all play together a little? Maybe you could play with Arama. It's time that you understood what people have been calling you since you've been playing such a sweet version of Juliet."

Vera beckoned to Robin, who had finally stripped down to his underwear. He slid into the pool and suffered through her inappropriate touches, taunts, and laughter when his member refused to stir in spite of all her efforts. To his relief, Bertram refused to be a witness to his renewed submission. Leah was floating in the pool with them, lying on her back with her arms spread wide, but she didn't partake in Vera's little game. Arama was the only one who could see everything that was going on, and he obviously didn't understand it.

"Are you her slave?" he asked later when the young men were finally getting dressed again. "I thought *pakeha* didn't do that sort of thing. We don't either anymore." With the Waitangi contract, the Maori had officially become citizens of the United Kingdom and had therefore accepted British law. The tradition of keeping war prisoners as slaves had disappeared after that—also because wars between tribes had become rare.

Robin sighed. "Something like that," he mumbled. "And I'd appreciate it if you wouldn't tell anybody about what you saw."

The company reached Te Wairoa at sunset. In the *marae*, there was an animated discussion going on. Tuhoto *ariki* was the main speaker, and people were lamenting and praying.

"What's going on here?" Vera asked.

Robin, the only one of them who understood Maori, frowned. "I'm not sure," he said. "They're all talking about a canoe someone saw out on the lake. A spirit canoe. Rowed by dead people, or something like that. Sounds strange."

"Is bad omen," Arama added, frowning. "When come *waka wairua*, people die. Many. Many ill fortune."

"Nonsense." Vera shook her head. "There are no spirits. Somebody's been imagining things."

"Not just somebody," Robin said after listening more. "Twelve oarsmen, four English guests, two Frenchmen, the tour guide, and . . . Aroha . . ."

He looked around and finally spotted her on the sidelines of all the excitement. Aroha was talking to her fiancé, McRae, and the young Chinese man. Bao was his name, Robin remembered now. He jumped off the wagon without waiting for Vera's permission and joined the group.

"There has got to be some sort of natural explanation," Bao was saying. "Spirits in a canoe just doesn't sound possible."

"Aren't there any ghosts in China?" McRae asked. "Scotland's full of them, apparently. But I've never come across one myself. All jokes aside, Miss Aroha . . . Are ye sure it wasna a mirage or somethin'?"

Aroha shrugged. "I didn't touch it, Mr. McRae," she said. "So I have no way of knowing whether it was solid or not. But I know I saw a canoe, a war canoe full of men. And I've never heard of mirages in New Zealand before. Don't those only occur in the desert?"

"There have been stories about spirit canoes," Koro told them reluctantly. "My mother's right, they're portents of disaster. But I wouldn't believe it if you and my mother hadn't seen it yourselves."

"We all saw it," Aroha repeated. "Still, I'd like to try and find out if it could possibly belong to some other tribe first. Perhaps a nomadic tribe."

"Nomadic, but they take war canoes with them?" Koro asked, eyebrows raised.

Aroha bit her lip. She knew she was grasping at straws. The Tuhourangi wouldn't have missed the arrival of another tribe. Sometimes tribes came to visit them and see the Terraces. There was always a big *powhiri*, and the visitors were taken out to see the rock formations. They didn't come by war canoe, of course, and they didn't wear dead men's regalia.

"What should we do with the guests?" Aroha asked, sounding worried. "It wouldn't do for them to stick around out here and get wind of Tuhoto's gloomy prophecies."

"Tuhoto and the other *tohunga* are planning a cleansing ceremony right now," Koro told her. "The people are much too concerned to take care of their guests at the moment."

McRae nodded. "I'll invite them to dinner at the hotel, then," he said. "Seein' as there are only six travelers and the actors here at the moment. And fortunately, the actors did somethin' entirely different today." Suddenly, everyone was looking at Robin, and Aroha wondered why he was blushing. "If we can manage to get a lively dinner conversation started," McRae went on, "people might be able tae forget about the whole canoe incident for a while. Miss Aroha, go and fetch your group for me, would ye? Evenin' attire will be required. We'll do anythin' we can tae take people's mind off things."

Indeed, the guests showed up in festive attire—Robin was embarrassed to be wearing his threadbare suit again. Aroha wore an elegant, dark-blue dress that night. Vera showed up in a revealing black gown, the plunging neckline earning her scandalized looks from the two English ladies. But trying to take the *tourists'* minds off the spirit canoe proved to be futile. They went over their eerie experience in detail repeatedly, and after that, they exchanged ghost stories from their respective home countries. Aroha noted with appalled fascination how quickly the men succumbed to Vera Carrigan's charm. For Aroha's taste, the actress was talking far too loudly and dominating everyone's attention.

The English ladies seemed to feel awkward around her too, but their husbands hung on Vera's every word. It seemed she knew instinctively how to manipulate the men around her. She knew how to laugh conspiratorially and how to mix in innocent little touches like flattery and teasing.

Aroha wondered whether Vera Carrigan was to blame for her uncle's lack of appetite. The young man hardly looked at her all through dinner. When he did glance up, she caught a flash of desperation in his eyes. Robin obviously wasn't happy with his employer. Aroha made a mental note to talk to him about it. But tonight, she, too, was too agitated to think about anything other than their unearthly encounter out on the lake. She let the English guests' stories of séances and haunted houses wash over her, but she snapped to attention when Vera Carrigan chipped in with her experience of spirit invocation. With a hint of irreverent amusement, the actress told them a story that Aroha already knew: the destruction of the Ngati Tamakopiri's sacred kauri tree.

Vera was making Omaka out to be a warmonger who had betrayed the British soldiers' positions to the Hauhau and lured in the enemy with her singing and prayers. She claimed it had only been possible to cleanse the area of the Maori woman by destroying the tree she worshipped.

"The old hag raised quite a stink, of course," Vera said. "She waved around her magic wand like a madwoman. I assume she cursed us; or that's what they were saying in Taranaki later, anyway. It's said that some of the soldiers who were involved died a short while later. There was talk about it being the witch's doing."

Aroha frowned. She hadn't heard that part, but Linda and Omaka had left for Otaki right after the whole ordeal with the tree, and surely Revi Fransi wouldn't have tolerated any talk of curses and maledictions.

"But I didn't believe a word of it," Vera was saying with a smug tilt of her head. "And as you can see, I was right. I'm right here in front of you, safe and sound, aren't I?" She drew herself up and looked around, smirking.

"But you weren't the one to actually cut down the tree, Miss Carrigan," one of the English gentlemen pointed out, a little embarrassed to be contradicting her.

Vera laughed. "But I made the men do it," she said smugly. "Without me, they wouldn't even have realized that the witch was inciting the Hauhau to fight. And the old hag couldn't stand me anyway. If she cursed anybody, it would've been me first. Didn't do her much good, though!" She took a sip of wine, unruffled.

Aroha was tempted to point out that some prophecies just took longer to come true. But McRae beat her to the punch.

"Perhaps, my dear Miss Carrigan," he said with an admiring smile, "yer magic is just stronger!"

Aroha didn't hear Vera's reply. She was too busy slapping Robin on the back as he choked on his water.

# Chapter 29

Vera Carrigan wasn't the only one intent on throwing all warnings and prophecies to the wind. Even the Tuhourangi themselves were divided on the subject. The sighting of a spirit canoe had made an impression, to be sure. Most of the *marae* was related to one or another of the oarsmen, and they had credibility, as did Sophia. Still, the Ngati Whakaue in Ohinemutu and the Ngati Hinemihi, whose *marae* was in Rotorua, thought the ghost sighting was superstitious nonsense. They thought that Tuhoto *ariki* was behind all of it, staging the incident to lend credibility to his prophecies. They were glad to help Koro with his search for natural explanations for the phenomenon.

Aroha and Koro, who knew their guests, didn't share some people's concern that the *manuhiri* might be deterred by the apparition. On the contrary—for travelers who ventured out to the more remote corners of New Zealand, ghost canoes counted as an extra attraction. Aroha was even expecting there to be a sudden surge of guests that winter. She could only hope that Sophia would be ready to offer tours to the Terraces again by then. Since they'd seen the apparition, Koro's mother had been refusing to accompany their guests across Lake Tarawera, and Aroha was relieved that Kate Middlemass had returned. Kate calmly listened to Sophia's account of events, but shook her head at the woman's conviction that something terrible was about to happen.

"Lord knows what kind of canoe that was," Kate said. "But if it shows up again, I'll find out, mark my words! And as far as doom and destruction go . . . that's nonsense, Sophia. I can assure you, everything's fine. Come along with my next group."

But Sophia began devising new destinations for her guests. Instead of the Terraces, she took *manuhiri* to the geysers and other hot springs in the area. Her visits to the Ngati Hinemihi *marae* turned out to be especially popular, as they danced for guests every day, unlike the Tuhourangi, who only did so weekly.

A few days after the ghost-canoe incident, Joseph McRae joined them on one such trip—he wanted to witness the Ngati Hinemihi's latest offer firsthand before recommending it to any future guests. He also invited Vera and her company to come along. Bertram Lockhart grumbled about their repeated outing to the Rotorua area. He would have preferred to see the Terraces, as would Robin. But Vera was wholly focused on the hotel owner. Robin assumed she was hoping to get something out of McRae. He was pretty sure she wouldn't have stopped him from visiting the Terraces, but he didn't want to risk going by himself. Aroha had been trying to strike up a conversation with him for days, and she'd surely have jumped at the chance to finally get answers to all the questions she must be burning to ask.

After Robin's triumph on their first night at the Rotomahana Hotel, the Carrigan Company had gone back somewhat to their former program. They continued to omit any and all obscene storylines and satirical scenes, but Vera wouldn't forgo their signature catchpenny love scenes. Robin had to perform as Juliet and Miranda again. Of course, Aroha had heard and asked Robin about it the next time they met. The young man had turned beet red and explained that the casting had been born of necessity.

Robin claimed that the company just couldn't find any new actresses, at which Aroha had given him an incredulous look. "Strange, I thought that actors were the ones having trouble finding work," she'd remarked. "And now it's suddenly the other way around? Well, be that as it may, Robin, I'm not getting the impression that you're enjoying yourself."

Robin had beat a retreat before Aroha had been able to ask him more probing questions. Meanwhile, he had also realized that Vera Carrigan and his half sister Linda had crossed paths some years ago. He even vaguely remembered that story with the kauri tree. His mother had told him about it at some point. Anyway, Aroha was obviously dying to question him about Vera and the company, and he had no idea what he was supposed to tell her.

So, that day, he escaped to the Ngati Hinemihi *marae*, watched their dances, and listened to Sophia Hinerangi talk about the landscape and local tribal history. Robin didn't find the mood at the *marae* particularly pleasant. Everything there seemed artificial, too colorful, and too anxious to appeal to the *manuhiri*.

He stood in front of the deity statues with their eyes made of British gold sovereigns, eyeing them with disgust.

"You may think this is in bad taste," Sophia tried to explain to him, "as if people here are exhibiting their wealth. But you shouldn't look at it that way. In fact, the people are honoring the gods. They decorate their statues with the most valuable items they own. It used to be paua shells, and now it's coins. In Europe, I've been told that there are Christian churches virtually dripping with gold. But that doesn't stop people from being pious."

Still, Robin was strongly reminded of Te Haitara's gods of money, and here, he thought, they were worshipped even more fervently. After the dance performance, the chieftain himself greeted the visitors. In doing so, he broke all the most fervent customs of the Maori by personally offering his guests drinks and flatbread dipped in honey. North Island tradition would have required the *ariki* to stay away from his people's food. It was considered *tapu* for him to even touch it. Originally, the chieftain's food wasn't just prepared separately, but his people had used a feeding horn to avoid touching it themselves.

Sophia was watching Rangiheuea's affected behavior with skepticism too. But she only spoke up when the old man started advertising the treats he was handing out.

"Honey from Mount Tarawera! Have some, is delicious. How do you say? Specialty. Wild bee nectar . . ."

Sophia seemed to struggle with herself for a moment. But then she stepped in between the *pakeha* and the old man with a resolute frown creasing her forehead.

"Don't," she said. "Please, ladies and gentlemen . . . I'm sure *ariki* Rangiheuea means no harm, but please, don't touch that honey."

"Why?" Vera asked, pointedly reaching for a piece of flatbread with some of the honey on it. "Is it poisoned?" She peered suspiciously at the bread in her hand.

"No, of course not," Sophia said, unhappily watching as the young woman who was handing out the bread gave her an annoyed look and then demonstratively took a bite herself.

The chieftain took a piece from her basket as well, licking the sticky nectar from his fingers. "No poison," he said. "Very, very good. Special gift from tribe for honored *manuhiri*. Can buy. Very good!"

Sophia glared at him. "*Ariki*! Must you break every *tapu* here?" she asked him sharply in Maori. "Are you trying to defy the gods?" Barely able to keep her composure, she turned back to her group when the chieftain remained stubbornly silent. "Please, don't touch it," she told the visitors. "The food surely won't hurt your stomachs, but it may hurt your soul. It's *tapu* to collect honey from Mount Tarawera. Only very few *tohunga*, priests and elders, are even allowed to approach the spirits there to harvest the wild bees' nectar. They use it for special ceremonies. Anyone else who eats it is cursed."

Vera Carrigan laughed contemptuously and stuffed the piece of bread in her mouth. "Mmm. Delicious. Especially considering the story behind it. Sweet, aromatic. I've always wanted to taste the gods' ambrosia." She licked her lips in a provocative gesture. "And as for those strange *tohunga* and their curses—I've seen worse."

Vera grabbed another piece of honeyed bread and tried to hand it to Robin, but he refused. Over the last few days, he'd seen her with various different men from several tour groups. He wasn't sure what she was doing to them—she'd called on neither him nor Bertram as conspirators lately. But she must have found a way to relieve the rich Europeans of their money. Maybe she took it from the men's wallets while they were asleep.

He had a strange feeling as Sophia turned away silently. An unidentifiable shiver of panic ran down his spine.


That night, Aroha and Koro saw Sophia talking to Tuhoto *ariki*.

"The signs are all starting to converge," she said quietly when the two of them asked her about it later. "It's all going to come to a bad end, and soon."

# Chapter 30

"Oh, what a beautiful night!" Aroha said. She and Koro had just stepped out onto the front porch of Charles and Amelia Haszard's house. Aside from Joseph McRae, the Haszards were some of the few *pakeha* who lived near Te Wairoa. Amelia was a schoolteacher, and Charles ran a kind of pharmacy in town. But he was better known as a painter. His paintings of the Pink and White Terraces were some of the most beautiful ever made.

That evening, the Haszards had been celebrating Amelia's birthday. After a wonderful meal, interesting dinner conversation, and some singing along with Amelia's piano playing, their guests were getting ready to leave. Aroha was looking forward to the walk home under the starry sky. For the first time since her eerie encounter with the spirit canoe, she was starting to feel a little more lighthearted. She was holding Koro's hand, gazing up at a seemingly smiling full moon that cast its silvery light over Mount Tarawera. She felt more vindicated than ever in her decision to move to Rotorua after their wedding. She liked Te Wairoa, but she'd had enough of *hakas* and *tapus*.

One of Amelia's birthday guests, a geology professor visiting from Auckland, had offered them a halfway plausible explanation for the incident of the spirit canoe. Professor Bricks had said with a nod in Koro's direction that, if he recalled Koro's venerated mother correctly, Mount Tarawera had been a burial ground for Maori chieftains for centuries, and they'd often been put to rest standing upright and tied to poles in their war canoes. "And now you, Mr. Hinerangi, were just telling us about dried-out streams and the lake's varying water levels," he'd said. "Isn't it possible, then, that such a burial canoe, preserved by special mineral mud, or in whatever way, was washed back up to the surface?"

Aroha considered the possibility. True, the warriors had looked alive to her, but she hadn't seen them actually move. If the geyserite in the water had formed the otherworldly Terraces, could it be responsible for another miraculous feat? The professor's theory explained the funeral regalia as well, but could something as delicate as feathers possibly be preserved that way? And what could have propelled the canoe forward?

"I have no doubt that tomorrow will be a beautiful day," Professor Bricks was saying now, bowing over Amelia Haszard's hand with a smile. "And we still have a moonlight walk to look forward to tonight. What a beautiful conclusion to such a pleasant evening . . ."

He hadn't finished his sentence when an earsplitting explosion ripped through the night's velvety quiet. Aroha instinctively crouched low to the ground and dropped Koro's hand to cover her ears, just as the Haszards' children were doing. Then they started to weep in terror.

"Could that be somebody saluting me for my birthday?" Amelia asked with a nervous laugh.

Another explosion drowned out any answers they might have had. It sounded the way Aroha had always imagined cannon fire to sound—only much louder. It occurred to her that if those really were cannons, the sound must have burst the soldiers' eardrums. The Haszards and their guests ducked again at the next round of thunder—and cried out in terror as the earth started to tremble underfoot. The ground under the house shuddered violently, and then it seemed to rear up and fall back into place again.

Aroha grabbed the porch railing, and Koro wrapped his arms around her tightly. The earth groaned as one quake followed the next. Several more explosions followed in short sequence, and suddenly, the night sky around Mount Tarawera was aglow with fire. Then the earth stopped shaking.

"Fascinating," Professor Bricks remarked. "I believe . . . Ladies and gentlemen, it looks as though we're about to witness a volcanic eruption!" He squinted toward Mount Tarawera.

The scientist seemed excited, but Aroha felt paralyzed. Gigantic fireballs came billowing up from the opening where the volcano's peak had cracked open, and joined together in what looked like some kind of demonic dance. The sky, which had been clear only moments before, seemed determined now to accompany the dance with its own apocalyptic music. The air crackled, lightning flashed, and again, thunder rolled through the night. Now the fireballs turned into roaring columns of flame. Four tremendous torches rose from the mountainside, snaking their way up through clouds of vapor and smoke.

"What a magnificent sight! Even if we were to live another hundred years, we'd never see anything like this again, I assure you," Charles Haszard said enthusiastically.

Meanwhile, Amelia was reassuring the children. She took them by the hand and went inside to sit at her piano. Ponderous, solemn melodies started mingling with the sounds of Mount Tarawera erupting—and slowly, the songs became wilder and more joyous. Aroha could hear Amelia's children singing along, and some of the adults joined in as well. No one but she seemed to be scared in the least! Or were they? She glanced over at Koro and saw her own fear reflected in his eyes.

"Do you want to stay?" he asked.

Aroha shook her head, her eyes back on the exploding mountain. The eruptions weren't confined to the volcano at this point. To the right of the mountain, somewhere near the Pink and White Terraces, a column of vapor was rising.

"The water out there must be boiling," Professor Bricks remarked, still more excited than worried. "Is there any kind of hill nearby? Or at least some sort of ridge from which one could get a better view?"

Koro and Aroha gave him directions to an observation point just above the village.

"We'll come with you," Aroha said. "Or we'll walk with you to the village, at least. What—what do you think they'll be doing there now, Koro?" she asked him, switching to Maori.

Koro shrugged. "Probably watching it all and invoking the spirits. If Tuhoto's there, he'll say it's completely the fault of the *manuhiri*. Maybe we should go to McRae's hotel instead. We could reassure the guests and protect them if Tuhoto has the bright idea of leading a mob of warriors to expel the intruders in the name of the gods . . ."

Aroha couldn't imagine such a thing. The old man might have been difficult, but he'd never called for violence. Still, the thought of McRae's hotel was appealing. It was higher up, and farther away from the lake. Something told her she'd be safer there over the next few hours than at the *marae*.

Just as they were about to leave, a hot wind started to rise, and it seemed to be coming from every direction at once. Aroha almost died of fright when a gray chunk of cinder came crashing down on the Haszards' roof. She'd known these weren't just pretty fireworks to be watched with excitement.

"Come on, Koro," she said nervously to her fiancé. "Let's go!"

The pelting rain of rocks served to sober up the remaining guests as well. The gathering dissolved quickly; some people were making their way home, and some were joining Bricks as he went up the hill. Some were even going to the church. The last few songs people had been singing in the house were psalms. The Maori weren't the only ones trying to appease their gods on this night, it seemed.

The church was right next to McRae's hotel, and the reverend had already started leading the congregation in prayer when Aroha and Koro hurried by. Hot rain was falling along with the rocks now, and the volcano was hurling more and more chunks of cinder and rock into the night sky. They'd doubtlessly be falling on Ohinemutu and other villages now too. But Joseph McRae didn't seem very worried about any of it. He was standing out on the front porch of his hotel with some of his foreign guests and the theater company. It was a strange scene; some guests had raced outside in their undergarments. Vera Carrigan was wearing a red bathrobe, and Leah was only wearing a scarf over her nightgown, which displayed her emaciated body in painful detail. But nobody seemed to care much about propriety right now. The Rotomahana's inhabitants were gazing at the columns of fire over Mount Tarawera with the same horrified exuberance as the Haszards' guests had. Some were holding champagne flutes and wine glasses and were toasting each other now and then. McRae held out a bottle of champagne to Aroha and Koro.

"I'm so glad ye came," he said, greeting them euphorically. "The view from here's unique, isn' it? Ladies and gentlemen, I think the Rotomahana Hotel can provide ye with the best view around of this spectacle of nature!"

His guests nodded eagerly. The only ones who didn't seem to share McRae's enthusiasm were Robin, Leah, and Bao. Robin looked stunned, and Leah gazed up at the burning sky fearfully, uncomprehendingly. Aroha noticed that she'd put her pale little hand in Robin's. Was there something going on between him and this strange young woman?

But she immediately forgot about the potential romance when she noticed Bao's furious expression. The man took McRae aside, speaking with nervous insistence. Aroha heard snatches of their conversation. ". . . There's still time to escape unharmed!" But the hotelier waved him off, looking exasperated. Aroha led Bao over to a quieter corner of the porch.

"What's wrong, Bao? You look like you just saw a ghost."

Bao snorted, but there was naked fear on his face now. "Just one, Miss Aroha? Aren't there millions of fire spirits dancing up there right now? We have to leave. These people act as though they're watching a performance on a stage. But this is a volcanic eruption. And it won't stop at some pretty fireworks. What you see running down the side of the mountain there is lava, molten rock. It's running into the lake, making the water boil. Can you imagine the sheer amount of vapor rising from there right now? White-hot vapor? Heavens, hasn't anybody here read Edward Bulwer? *The Last Days of Pompeii*?"

Aroha tried to remember the novel he was talking about. "Umm, wasn't Pompeii buried under a layer of lava . . ."

"And Herculaneum under ash. Or maybe it was the other way around," Bao said. "Anyway, there's probably going to be ash rain here soon too. We must get the horses ready, Miss Aroha, and get out. Quickly, now!"

"And it's not just a story?" Koro asked when Aroha told him about Bao's concerns.

Aroha shook her head. "The novel's plot is, but Herculaneum and Pompeii did actually exist. The two cities have been excavated. Those people over there," she said, gesturing toward the *manuhiri*, who could obviously hardly believe their luck, "should know. In Europe, Naples and Mount Vesuvius are right at the top of most travelers' lists."

Koro bit his lip. "In that case, we should do as Bao says."

"It's just unbelievable!" Joseph McRae's voice was partially drowned out as another tremendous explosion shook the night. This time, it didn't only hurl more lava out into the air, but it actually blew the volcano's entire peak off. It shattered into billions of tiny pieces that seemed to hang in the air for a moment.

Koro grabbed Aroha's arm. "Let's *go*!" he cried. "Quickly! We'll take the horse and wagon—we can return them to McRae tomorrow."

"The wagon?" Aroha asked, confused.

Koro nodded. "If Bao's right, we'll have to get to Rotorua. Or even farther away. And the wagon has room for more people. But I can't just leave. First I have to tell people at the village that there might be more in store for them than a bit of warm rain and falling rock."

Aroha, Koro, and Bao left the gaggle of people staring raptly at the inferno across the lake, and hurried down to the stables. Guests were usually transferred to Te Wairoa by an entrepreneur from Rotorua, and there were livery stables for his horses at the *marae*. But McRae owned a sturdy horse and an all-purpose wagon for matters concerning his own hotel. There was space for up to fourteen people on the benches set along the sides. Aroha guessed that in an emergency, up to twenty-four people might be able to crowd together.

"I'll get the horse ready, and you two can go get the wagon," she told Bao and Koro.

Neither of them were particularly experienced with horses, and Bao was a little afraid of them. Now, the men were racing toward the carriage house, and Aroha grabbed the bridles and a stable lantern from a hook next to the door. She could hear McRae's skewbald gelding tossing around and whinnying nervously in his stall. The horse was normally a mellow animal. Aroha spoke to him gently as she went inside. All at once, she realized that she hadn't seen a single dog or cat in Te Wairoa all day. Sophia had been looking for her cat since that morning, and the Haszards' little daughter had been searching everywhere for her lapdog.

Aroha's measured concern turned into terror. The animals must have known that great danger was coming. They'd probably run as far as Rotorua by now.

It took the young woman longer than usual to get the snaffle bit on the twitchy horse and put him in his harness. When she led him outside a few moments later, she needed Koro's help to stop him from fleeing. Aroha, on the other hand, would have loved to escape to the relative protection of a nearby roof. The rain was starting to come down harder, and mud seemed to be falling from the sky along with the water now. Bits of cinder were mixed in with it too. A falling stone nicked Aroha's temple, sending a sharp jab of pain down the side of her head.

"Ow! Um, don't you think we should take cover?" she asked, trying her best to harness the fretful horse to the wagon.

Koro and Bao had dragged the wagon out of the carriage house and left it in the driveway for their departure. No matter what they did, the skewbald wouldn't stand still for them to attach the straps.

"No, that's what people in Pompeii thought too!" Bao shouted over the gusts of wind that were blowing stronger and stronger from all sides. "Before the lava came."

The two men were soaked to the skin and coated in mud from head to toe. In the night's surreal, reddish glow, they looked like monsters that had come crawling out of the pits of hell.

They could hear more explosions from the direction of the lake, and as if to prove to Aroha that escaping into the carriage house had been a bad idea, a chunk of rock came crashing down on the roof of the stables now, sending the skewbald into a complete frenzy. Koro needed all his strength to keep a grip on the animal. The hotel's roof wasn't safe either, it turned out. Aroha and the two men ducked as they heard the noise of splintering wood. Bao tugged a tarpaulin out from underneath the coachbox. It wouldn't do much to protect them from the rain, and even less from the falling cinders, but at least it gave an illusion of relative safety.

Just as Aroha was hitching the last of the draw ropes to the cart, McRae came lumbering toward them, his guests in tow. People were all talking at once in a panic. One of the ladies was holding a blood-soaked rag to her forehead, and the men were having an intense discussion about whether they should flee or take shelter inside.

"It's raining *rocks!*" an Englishman called out to Aroha, Bao, and Koro excitedly, as if they hadn't noticed. "Rocks! One of them went straight through the porch. Just like that . . ."

Aroha guessed that was how the woman had gotten injured. She whimpered as the muddy rain washed blood into her eyes.

"Bao, God bless ye for yer vigilance!" With a hasty wave, McRae ushered his guests onto the wagon. "Imagine if we'd had to harness the horse now . . ."

Aroha jumped up onto the coachbox and beckoned Robin to her side with an impatient gesture. "I'll drive; you can help," she told the young man. Neither she nor Robin were as strong as Koro, but they both knew how to drive a wagon and calm a fretting horse. "Where to?" she shouted.

There was no answer at first. Only the skewbald seemed to have a clear opinion. He was straining against the reins in the direction of Rotorua, away from the fire-breathing volcano.

"To the *marae*," Koro said. "I have to warn the people there; they can't just hide in the meeting house. And someone has to go get the Christians from the church."

That turned out to be unnecessary. The churchgoers were already trudging toward them, determined to flee the scene of the ongoing catastrophe. Koro and Bao helped them clamber up onto the cart.

"Let me out at the *marae*," Koro repeated.

The muddy rain was starting to flood the streets, and the skewbald reluctantly fought his way through the thick sludge. Another guest was hit by a falling cinder, and he cried out in pain, clutching his shoulder. The air was thick with vapor now, and breathing was getting more difficult by the minute. A hissing noise filled the air. The closer they got to the lake, the brighter the air became, a ghostly, orange-red light.

"We'll never get to Rotorua like this," Bao said, shouting to make himself heard over the other people's cries and the storm. "We have to find shelter somewhere . . ."

"My mother's house," Koro said, pointing.

"Yes, to the Hinerangis' house!" McRae agreed.

"We could be halfway to Rotorua right now," Vera Carrigan complained, "if we'd left at the start."

Neither Aroha nor any of the others bothered to contradict her.

"Sophia's house is sturdy, and it's protected by hills on all sides," McRae told his terrified guests. "If there's a single house in Te Wairoa that can withstand the forces of nature, it's that one."

"We'll try!" Koro shouted over the din. "Stop the wagon, Aroha." The wagon had just reached the Tuhourangi *marae*. "I'll be with you later."

"I'm coming with you!" Aroha handed the reins to Robin, who gaped at her, flabbergasted. It was no longer as difficult to control the skewbald. The horse reluctantly moved toward the lake, hardly able to make headway through all the mud anyway. He probably couldn't see much; ash and rain had long since caked his forelock together, which drooped down heavily over his eyes, obscuring his sight. "I want to stay with you," Aroha insisted when Koro objected, his voice fierce. "There's no way I can just go and save myself while you . . ."

"Well, go on, then!" Vera Carrigan hissed at her.

Aroha slid down from the coachbox and immediately lost her footing in the slippery mud. Bao caught her as she fell. The young man had climbed down from the wagon as well. Aroha had no energy left in her to ask him why he'd done it. He had nothing to do at the *marae*. He didn't even speak Maori. Still, he followed Koro and Aroha to the meeting house. People were running in all directions, debating whether to flee or stay. Aroha glanced over at the lake in horror, noting that it was rising quickly. Water mixed with mud and ash was already starting to flood the buildings closest to the lake's edge. The meeting house doors were open, and the muddy mixture was just washing over the doorstep.

"Everyone out of here!" Koro shouted at the village elders who stood in the entryway, frozen, staring in disbelief at the inferno that threatened to swallow their village. "Get out, it won't get better, it's getting worse! Save yourselves . . . Marama, give me the child . . . Bao, take the baby . . . Aroha . . ."

Koro ushered people outside. He was holding a little girl tight against his chest, and her mother was clinging to him too. Aroha tugged a whimpering boy outside by the arm, and Bao was right there next to her, a baby in his arms. Aroha felt as though she were walking into a solid wall of sludge. At least the rain of ash and cinders was letting up. Aroha tried to get her bearings.

"To Sophia's house!" she heard Koro shout.

Others took up his cry, which was drowned out by another earsplitting explosion. The little boy clinging to Aroha's hand dropped to the ground in terror. She pulled him to his feet, but he slid from her grip, sobbing. A cloud of vapor swept in, robbing them of what little visibility had been left. She dropped to her knees and tried to feel a sleeve of the child's jacket or whatever she could in the sludge, but then she heard the scream.

"Mama, *Mama!*"

It was heart-wrenching. Someone dragged Aroha forcefully back to her feet.

"No, Miss Aroha! You can't help him now . . ."

It was Bao, and he still had the baby with him. He held on to Aroha's arm tightly now, forcing her onward. Aroha's tears mingled with the mud and rain, and she tasted ash when she opened her mouth to take a gasping breath. The ashy volcanic sludge was up to their thighs now. Aroha's dress was soaked, and every step had become a superhuman effort. Gusts of wind chased rain and ash in front of them as well as entire boards and bricks from destroyed buildings. The sludge undermined the remaining foundations, and the first few houses had already collapsed with a crash. Aroha could only see the outlines of Koro with a child in his arms and the little one's mother now. The three of them had taken shelter on the lee side of a cookhouse. In her panic, the woman tried to wrest her child from Koro's arms, and then reached out for the railing surrounding the shack, looking for support.

"Koro!" Aroha screamed as the wind ripped the roof up and away from the building where he was standing. Koro ducked . . . and was submerged in the mud. "Koro!" Aroha tried to run to her fiancé, but she was jerked back again.

"Miss Aroha!" Bao held on with all his strength although she was kicking and punching at him. "Koro can do it, he's strong! He'll get out of there on his own. We'd just be a burden to him. Come now, we'll see him again in a moment."

Aroha sobbed, swallowing dirt and ash. She let herself be pulled along, fell down with Bao, and felt like giving up and letting herself be swallowed by the warm mass surrounding her . . . But Bao pulled her to her feet again. He was still holding the baby, hardly recognizable as such at this point. The blankets the child was wrapped in had soaked up the sludge; it was unlikely that she was still alive.

Half pulled and half carried by Bao, Aroha fought her way up a hillside— and suddenly, the going became easier. Ash was still raining thickly from the sky, but the mud here was only ankle-deep.

"Miss Aroha, there's the house!" Bao cried. "Hold on, little baby, I can see it . . ."

Clouds of ash had swallowed up the raging mountain and everything in its vicinity. Bao followed other mud-coated shadows as they ran, limped, and crawled toward the safety of the building. The Hinerangis' house barely seemed to have been damaged. All Aroha could hear when Bao pulled her inside was Sophia's terrified voice.

"Aroha . . . Where's Koro?"

Aroha fainted.

# Chapter 31

Aroha was woken by the sensation of someone gently wiping her brow with a wet cloth, blotting the mud from the corners of her eyes. Her eyes and throat felt like they were on fire.

"Koro?" she asked, but then she recognized Robin.

"Koro isn't here yet," the young man told her. "The Chinese gentleman said he ran into some trouble down near the village. Maybe he managed to find shelter there for a while. There are already a few search parties out."

"Is it still night?" Aroha asked, dazed.

She recognized the place she was lying—it was the woven rug in Sophia's living room, but the room resembled a field camp more than anything right now. People were sitting or standing all over the place, some of them naked or half naked, draped in blankets and sheets. It looked as though Sophia had dug out all the linens, bedding, and clothes she'd been able to find. The entire scene was lit dimly by a gas lamp. Although the room was usually bright with its large windows that looked out at the surrounding hills, Aroha noticed in the hazy light that the windows were caked with mud. She couldn't make out any daylight behind them either.

"It's nine o'clock in the morning," Robin told her. "But it doesn't look like it's going to get much lighter. There's still too much ash in the air. It's hard to breathe outside. Still, many of the people here want to go straight to Rotorua as soon as they can. They're worried that the volcano might erupt again." He put the damp cloth aside. "Can you get up?"

Aroha shrugged and started to sit up very slowly. "The mountain's calmed down now?"

Physically, she felt all right, aside from the fact that every muscle in her body was sore. But she was anxious to get changed; her clothes were still wet, and the mud was starting to form a stiff crust.

"Things have been quiet for a few hours now," Robin replied. "But the entire landscape has changed. Everything's destroyed, and . . . it looks like snow . . . like everything's frozen over. Come on, I'll help you stand . . ."

A little while later, Aroha stood on Sophia's porch, looking out at the surreal landscape. Trees and bushes had been uprooted, and those left standing were choked with mud and whitish-gray ash. The air was heavy and humid, and the light was hazy.

One after another, the people who'd sought shelter at Sophia Hinerangi's house came outside and stared out at the changed world in front of them, aghast. Vera Carrigan and a few other visitors seemed to have gotten over their initial shock. They were sipping coffee and commending Joseph McRae, calling him a hero. Apparently, they'd forgotten all about Bao's role in the escape.

"Well, I could tell my roof wasna goin' tae withstand the mud and fallin' rocks," the Scotsman was telling another white survivor. "So, we took the wagon, and off we were."

"The papers will be wanting to write about you, my dear!" Vera said, batting her eyelashes at him. "Ah, how quickly and prudently you saved us all."

Of all the people at Sophia's house, the theater company and the European travelers from McRae's hotel seemed to be the least shaken by the horrible night they'd all been through. It was no wonder, Robin told Aroha.

"After we left you at the *marae*, Mr. McRae showed me the way, and I drove the wagon here. It wasn't far, and it took us barely ten minutes. The horse was really working hard at that point. But we realized that things were getting worse. I suggested we go back; I could've picked up some more people. But McRae wasn't having it. So I took the horse over to the Hinerangis' tool shed. The poor creature was terribly agitated, but he's actually fine now. And the wagon probably hasn't suffered too much damage either. It's covered in ash and mud, of course. But if we wash it, we could take people up to Rotorua in it fairly quickly. I think that's what they're planning to do after breakfast." Robin gestured vaguely at Vera and McRae, his lips pressed together into a thin line.

The wagon sat behind Sophia's house like an ugly, dirt-encrusted sculpture. Aroha heard Vera telling McRae that they should take it and flee immediately. The old Scotsman seemed uncertain.

"Where's Bao?" she asked Robin.

Her uncle shrugged. "No idea. He slept next to you. Some of the English folks were actually upset about it. Can you believe that? As if anybody could've had dirty thoughts last night . . . But no, I haven't seen him this morning."

"He left with the first search party," Sophia told them. She was sitting on a bench in the corner of the kitchen, looking pale and shaken and holding a baby in her arms. "Right after making sure that you were all right. He said he wanted to go find Koro for you." She looked up at her. "Aroha, do you think he'll find him?"

Aroha's lip trembled. She thought of the last glimpse she'd gotten of Koro, of the roof coming down, and of him, Marama, and the child disappearing under it. "Yes," she whispered. "He'll—he'll know where to look. Is this—is this the baby Bao had?" She sat down next to Sophia in her dirty clothes.

Sophia bravely attempted a smile. "Yes, it's the child he brought with him. I'm surprised she's still alive. I think it's Lani, Makere and Henare's little daughter. Any news from her parents yet?"

A woman nearby shook her head.

"I'm going down to the *marae* too," Aroha said quietly.

But out front, the men who were handing tools to volunteers stopped her.

"We can't take you along, Miss Aroha," one of them said. "It'd be too dangerous. We're only taking strong young men. The first group sent back messengers. The road's barely passable, everything's covered in mud and ash, and visibility's poor. Te Wairoa's completely destroyed, and the lake—I can hardly believe it, but they say the lake isn't there anymore. Apparently, all the water just evaporated . . ."

"Did they find any bodies?" Aroha asked.

The man's brow creased. "There must be some. But we'll have to dig, Miss Aroha. That could take days."

"What—what about survivors? Did people take shelter anywhere?" Aroha wasn't ready to give up hope yet.

"We don't know that yet either. It's still early, Miss Aroha, and the sun isn't coming up. Please, just let us do our job. If you want to help . . . I'm sure there's lots for you to do around here."

There wasn't, as it turned out. With sixty-two refugees, Sophia's house was overflowing, but there was hardly anything that Aroha, Sophia, or her daughters could do for them at this point. The women had distributed all the food they had last night, and there weren't many clothes left either. Fortunately, Sophia did manage to find some dry dresses, and gave one to Aroha. After she was done washing and changing, Aroha started passing out clothes to the Maori women, some of whom had fled Te Wairoa naked. The idea wasn't half bad; they'd probably been able to move much more quickly than Aroha had in her soaked clothes. With a pang, the young woman remembered that she wouldn't have survived the escape without Bao.

She handed another dress to Leah. The girl seemed more alert than usual, but also irritable and restless. The same thing was true for the other member of Vera Carrigan's theater company. Bertram was anxious to leave for Rotorua as soon as possible after having repeatedly confirmed that Hori and Sophia's limited supply of whiskey had all been handed out the previous night.

Joseph McRae, Aroha was pleased to see, had decided to stay in Te Wairoa in spite of Vera's enticements, and he and his wagon turned out to be invaluable for their supply situation. He'd sent somebody to pick up food from his hotel and was now distributing it. The hotel's ground-floor pantries were intact—mud had seeped in, but it had only reached the lowest shelves. Damages on the second floor had been a lot worse. The roof had caved in, they heard, and there wasn't much left of the second floor's walls either.

Robin left for the *marae* with the second search party, proud to have been chosen for the job. Vera wasn't pleased about this in the slightest. She also fretted loudly about the possible damage to her clothes and props.

"If they're gone, we'll have to perform again as soon as possible to make up for our losses," Vera said.

As conditions improved, many of the survivors began to make their way toward Rotorua or Ohinemutu. The ones who stayed behind were those still missing relatives. They began to receive messages from other villages in the affected areas, several of which had undergone terrible damage. The news that shocked Aroha most of all was that the Haszards' house had been completely flooded with mud. Charles and the three children had died. Amelia was the only one who could be dug out alive. She was being taken to the hospital in Rotorua.

In the Ngati Hinemihi *marae*, the meeting house had managed to defy the elements. Every single member of the tribe had survived—except for the chieftain. *Ariki* Rangiheuea had been hit by a huge chunk of cinder. Sophia took a steadying breath and made the sign of the cross when she heard. "The honey," she said quietly. "The curse of the honey from Mount Tarawera . . ."

Her words hit Aroha hard, although she didn't really believe that eating forbidden food could have such consequences. But she was reminded of another curse. She'd held the thought at bay as long as possible, but now she was thinking of Matiu. With every passing hour, her hopes that Koro might return to her dwindled. Of course, it was possible that he'd stayed in Te Wairoa and was helping with the cleanup. But he would have sent a message by now.

The first search party came back just as the sky over Te Wairoa was fading back into complete darkness, the night approaching fast. Aroha saw them coming up the hill, and it sparked the last vestiges of her hope when she saw that the men were carrying a stretcher. But then she caught sight of Bao's serious expression and the shroud over the body they were carrying. Behind her, Sophia stepped outside.

"Koro?" she asked.

Bao nodded. "I thought we should bring him home to you. We . . . laid out the others on the ground floor of McRae's hotel."

Aroha kneeled next to the stretcher as the men put it down. She gently pulled away the blanket covering the dead man's face, which had been haphazardly wiped clean of mud to identify him. Aroha gently touched his face with shaking fingers, bending down over his nose and mouth to listen for his breath, and then finally pulled him into her numb arms. Suddenly, she was back in the Siberia Curve, holding Matiu in her arms.

"But—but you can't be dead," she whispered, grief-stricken. "That—that was so long ago . . . You're not Matiu . . . This can't be happening again . . ."

She started rocking Koro back and forth in her arms as she'd done with Matiu all those years ago. It couldn't be, it couldn't be, lightning didn't strike in the same place twice . . .

"Let him go, Aroha." It was Sophia's breaking voice, finally, that jarred her out of her stupor. "His body's dead. You know he has to leave now."

According to Maori belief, shortly after the body died, the soul of the dead departed.

"How can he leave without me?" Aroha asked quietly, letting go of Koro's body with one hand and digging her nails into her palm until it hurt.

Sophia, tears streaming down her face, gently turned her away from Koro's body and pulled her into her arms. "Believe me, dear, his soul doesn't want to leave either one of us," she said shakily. "But it's been severed from his body; there's nothing we can do about that. Would you trap it here? My son's soul must leave now, child. Let him go!"

Sophia released Aroha and told the men to bring her son inside. The Maori believed that if the dead weren't buried quickly, their souls would walk the *marae* as ghosts instead of leaving for Hawaiki, the legendary, dreamlike island from which their ancestors had come.

Aroha could have helped wash Koro, dressing him in warrior garb and adorning him with the same burial feathers she'd seen on the ghost canoe's crew. But it was like the young woman was frozen in place. In her head, the terrible images from the night before were becoming muddled with memories of the train accident. She saw Koro being buried alive, and she saw Matiu die, and again and again, she heard Haki's mother's words: *I curse you, pakeha girl!* And Matiu's grandmother's warning: *It can be dangerous to be the string of a kite that the gods desire . . .* Now, another man had tried to hold onto the girl whose *maunga* was in the sky. And he'd paid dearly for it.

Koro was laid to rest the next morning—and with him, over a hundred other Maori. Aroha cradled little Lani, the baby that Bao had rescued. Lani's parents were among the victims of the eruption. Seven *pakeha* had also died. Aside from the Haszards, there had been three more *manuhiri* who hadn't been staying at the Rotomahana, but in hotels right by the lake. Sophia paled when she heard their names and realized that all of them had eaten the Mount Tarawera honey during their visit to the Ngati Hinemihi *marae*. The only one who'd defied the *tapu* and survived was Vera Carrigan.

The Carrigan Company had reached Rotorua safe and sound. Robin was the only one refusing to comply with Vera's wishes. He'd stayed behind, helping with the rescue work in Te Wairoa. They were still hoping to find survivors. The night before, a rescue group had unearthed Tuhoto *ariki* from the wreck of his house. Some of the Tuhourangi had started to blame him for the catastrophe. They thought that he'd cursed the mountain to get rid of the *manuhiri*.

The rumor was fueled even further after a reckless young warrior made his way through the destroyed landscape to see what had become of the Pink and White Terraces. He'd returned, aghast, bringing unbelievable news: The famous rock formations had disappeared, swallowed by Lake Rotomahana, whose shape had changed entirely. The entire mountain vista, slowly emerging from the clouds of ash, had changed as well. Tarawera would never be the same again.

"What will become of the child?" Bao asked Aroha once the funeral ceremonies were over.

Aroha stood listlessly next to Koro's grave. She'd been quiet for hours, staring straight ahead. The only actions she seemed capable of were those required for taking care of little Lani. During the ceremony—the Maori *tohunga* and the Christian priest had held a joint service—Robin and Sophia had stood next to her, and Bao had kept a tactful distance. Now, he delicately approached Aroha with his question.

Robin answered for her. "It's Maori custom for children to belong to the entire tribe," he explained to Bao. "Traditionally, they call all the women 'mother' or 'grandmother,' and all the men 'father' or 'grandfather.' I don't doubt they'll find someone to look after little Lani. And perhaps her actual grandparents are still alive."

"No." To everyone's surprise, Aroha spoke. "I talked to the chieftain while they were laying out the dead, and to the grandparents and the tribe's elders. They agreed to let Lani stay with me."

"With you?" Robin asked, perplexed. "Would you take her in as your own? Aren't you still too young for that? I mean—you might—uh . . ."

He fumbled. It was impossible to say aloud while Aroha was still grieving for Koro, but one day, she'd surely find another man to marry and with whom she could have children of her own.

"The *tohunga* didn't think I was too young," Aroha said calmly. "They understand that she brings me comfort, as I will for her someday. It's . . . *utu*. A kind of compensation."

"But what if you . . . want to have a family of your own someday?" Robin said, choosing his words carefully.

Aroha shook her head. "I'm never going to marry, Robin. I'll never have children of my own."

# Chapter 32

A few days later, Sophia and her family encouraged Aroha to travel to Rotorua with Robin.

"You should go and see what's happened to your hotel," Hori said. "Have you given any thought to what you're going to do with it yet? Now that the Terraces are gone . . ."

Aroha rubbed her forehead. So far, her mind had been occupied with Koro's death, leaving no room for the Terraces or the future of tourism in the area. But Sophia's husband was right. She had to make a decision about her hotel. She couldn't keep doing her former job in Te Wairoa anymore either. Indeed, her only options were to run the hotel on her own, or leave Rotorua for one of the big cities. It wouldn't be hard to find work as a translator that would leave her with enough time to raise Lani, she thought. The idea did have a certain appeal to it. Everything about the place she'd lived in with Koro now raised a dull, aching pain in her chest. Still, she'd be alienating Lani from her own tribe if she left, taking the little girl away from her grandparents. Mount Tarawera was Lani's *maunga*. Or it had been, anyway. Darkly, Aroha wondered whether the volcano had hurled the souls of its entrusted children up into Rangi's arms in fire and smoke, meaning that Lani's soul would now be anchored in the sky, much like that of her adoptive mother.

She looked to Bao for help. The young man hadn't left her side since Koro's funeral.

"I'm sure the destruction of the Terraces will leave its mark on tourism in Rotorua," Bao said calmly. It sounded like he'd already analyzed the situation thoroughly. "But maybe not the way you'd expect. You saw how fascinated the English guests were by the eruption. It's likely that more of them will start showing up to see the extent of the catastrophe with their own eyes. The Rotorua tourism industry ought to prepare itself. But in the long run, advertising the hot springs should be a priority, I suppose. Then, more people will be coming here from Auckland and Wellington rather than England, but it doesn't really matter." He shrugged. "Your hotel's perfectly suited for such developments. Hosting spa visitors was the intention, wasn't it? So, if you'd like . . . If you can stand the thought," he said, giving Aroha a sympathetic look, "there's nothing stopping you from opening the hotel as planned."

Aroha rubbed her forehead again. "Well, then," she said quietly, "I suppose that's what we'll do."

"You're going to manage the hotel all by yourself?" Hori asked, puzzled.

Aroha shook her head. "No. I couldn't do it on my own. But with Bao here, it would be possible. Would you help me, Bao? Like we originally planned?"

She smiled timidly at the young man. It was her first smile since Koro's death.

Bao returned it. "Of course! Of course I'll help. We'll make your hotel the best in all of Rotorua!"

Aroha managed another sad smile. "*Our* hotel, Bao."


The next day, Aroha, Bao, and Robin got a ride to Rotorua, passing sleeping Lani between them. Aroha was only now starting to get an idea of the extent of the destruction. Over the last year, she'd traveled to Rotorua dozens of times—but now, she scarcely recognized it. The landscape, with its waterfalls, fern groves, and silent ponds that visitors had so often called enchanted, was now interred under a frosty-looking sheet of ashes. Many of the trees had been uprooted, lakes were choked with mud, and waterfalls had run dry. Where there had previously been endless shades of green, there was now only gray, with a gray sky hanging over the entire scene.

"It feels like a nightmare," Aroha said, shivering. "I keep thinking that all I have to do is wake up, and everything will be back to normal."

"Things will turn green again eventually," Bao reassured her. "The rain's going to wash the ashes off the plants and into the soil. It'll make the soil more fertile than it's ever been. New ferns will grow, and new trees will take root."

"Still, they won't be the same trees and ferns as before," Aroha said, bitterness in her voice. "The dead stay dead."

Bao nodded. "It's the law of *I Ching*. Everything's in constant transformation."

Aroha didn't feel like discussing philosophy. "How far does the destruction go?" she asked. "All the way to Rotorua? Do you think our hotel's been damaged? It'd mean we wouldn't be able to open yet; we'd have to do some renovation work first. And who knows if we have the money to do that."

Although that was the least of her worries. Cat and Chris would neither ask for the dowry back, nor would they mind if she needed more money to open the hotel. Cat, in particular, cared passionately about women keeping their independence.

"I heard there hasn't been much damage there," Robin offered. Over the last few days, several rescue volunteers from Rotorua had arrived in Te Wairoa, and they'd exchanged news. "Of course there was ash rain and some mud, but yesterday's rain washed some of that away."

During the last few miles of their drive into town, they were able to make out more and more of the original landscape, and in the end, they even got a little bit of sunshine. Aroha could feel her body relax. It was incredibly comforting to see that there were still parts of the world that hadn't been buried in rubble and ash.

At first sight, nothing seemed to have changed at all in Rotorua. Only after talking to some of the residents did they realize how deep-seated the shock was. The explosions had shaken the ground there just as ruthlessly as they had in Te Wairoa. People had seen the glowing sky over Mount Tarawera, and the columns of flame. The day after, they'd had to take in hundreds of refugees.

Robin had them drop him off at one of the more upscale hotels in the area, for which McRae provided Vera a written recommendation. The poster for their next performance was already hanging up on the wall by the reception desk. Among other things, they'd be performing scenes from *Hamlet* and *The Tempest*.

"Well, it's fitting, isn't it?" Vera said when Robin told her how disrespectful he found it for them to go back to acting while people were still burying their dead. "Ghosts, shipwrecks . . ." She laughed. "Don't be so sensitive, my dearie, it'll take people's minds off things. They don't want to be sad right now; they'd rather celebrate the fact that they're still alive!"

Vera had been in high spirits ever since she'd heard about the deaths of the other people who'd tasted the honey. Once more she'd defied a curse, and once more, she was encouraged in her conviction that the rules didn't apply to her.

"Well, go on, get ready!" she said. "We're performing tonight."

Robin took comfort from the fact that Aroha wouldn't be seeing the performance, and neither would any of the other people from Te Wairoa who'd worked side by side with him over the last few days, digging up dead bodies and looking for survivors. He would've died of embarrassment if he'd had to face the men after his performance—less because he played female characters than because of the way he was forced to portray them. His time away from the company had given him some perspective and strengthened his resolve. He didn't have to stay with Vera Carrigan. He could make himself useful and find appreciation for his work elsewhere.

Aroha and Bao found their hotel mostly undamaged. The formerly pristine white plaster front had been tarnished by the ash, and some of the pipes had burst during the earthquakes. All of those things could easily be repaired, but the place didn't exactly exude an air of comfort yet.

"We won't be sleeping here," Aroha told Bao, shifting Lani to her other arm. "I don't know about you, but I need a warm bath and a soft bed right now."

The young man agreed shyly. The last days at Sophia's place had been hard. The Hinerangis' house had never offered much in the way of creature comforts, with dim gas lamps and no running water. Compared to the current situation, however, that had been pure luxury. Since the catastrophe, the river had been choked with mud, meaning that people couldn't use it to wash. The air inside the house had not only been tainted by the smell of ripe bodies, but also of dirty clothes drying painfully slowly in front of the small fireplace. The lamps had been burning day and night, and the gas supplies had started to dwindle.

Bao was just as glad as Aroha to be out of there—but he didn't believe that any of the nice hotels in Rotorua would accept him. There was no Chinese neighborhood there.

"I know there's no water, but I could sleep here," he was saying now.

"Oh, nonsense, Bao!" Aroha said. "We'll go to the Rotorua Lodge. If there's any trouble, we can use McRae's name; he recommended the hotel to me in the first place. The hotelier's going to have to accept you as a peer soon enough anyway. He can get started now by calling you 'Mr. Duong.'"

267

Thankfully, they had no trouble at the lodge. The owner was *pakeha*—a Scotsman like McRae—but he was married to a lovely Maori woman. Waimarama McDougal welcomed Aroha and Bao with equal kindness and offered her condolences. People had heard about Koro's death, and Mrs. McDougal expressed her support for Aroha's decision to run the hotel without him.

"The *manuhiri* are looking forward to your Chinese bathhouse," she told them with a friendly smile. Rotorua Lodge didn't have any spa facilities itself. "No one's quite sure what that's supposed to be, but our guests love exotic things. We should bear that in mind too. If there won't be any *haka* performances in Te Wairoa or at the Ngati Hinemihi's *marae* for a while, perhaps we can bring the dancers here. Hot springs are good for your health, it's true, but people tend to get bored of them after three days or so. Evening entertainment is always booked out around here."

Aroha forced herself to smile back. "Well then, we'll send you an audience for your performances, and you can send us your spa visitors," she said, glancing at the lodge's notice board. She hesitated in surprise when she saw a familiar name on the list. "The Carrigan Company's performing here? Tonight?" Aroha asked, dumbfounded. "So soon after everything that happened? Are you all right with that, Mrs. McDougal?"

The young woman looked at her gravely. "Life goes on," she said quietly. "And as for the spa visitors . . . Well, the eruption was an upsetting thing for them. But you know the *manuhiri*, Miss Aroha . . . They haven't personally lost anything, and they're not grieving. But they are angry that we've had to shut down the hot springs. Temperatures have been out of control recently. Those geologists who came in from Auckland certainly raised the alarm. The mineral content of the water must've changed too. There has to be some extensive testing before we can let people back in there. The *manuhiri* don't accept that, of course. You can imagine their mood right now. My husband and I could do with any kind of distraction right now. Though the company's choice of plays does seem a little odd to me. Isn't *Hamlet* about, um, spirits? And we don't really need a storm onstage right now either."

Frowning, Aroha reached for one of the improvised flyers lying on the reception desk. *Hamlet* and *The Tempest*. What was Vera thinking?

"Please reserve two tickets for us, would you, Mrs. McDougal?" she asked. "Maybe I can find a girl to take care of my little one here for the evening. Or

I can bring her with me, at the risk of her fussing. I'd definitely like to see the performance."

The Rotorua Lodge was equipped with a large stage with all sorts of added comforts for their actors and dancers, and there wasn't just a real curtain, but also lighting and means to dim the auditorium. On that night, Robin was particularly grateful he wouldn't be able to see the audience.

As for the program, Vera hadn't chosen the worst adaptations from the company's repertoire, but as usual, they performed parodies and burlesques. Robin cringed when a piss-drunk Bertram hugged him as Miranda in *The Tempest*, and Vera couldn't resist adding in a bit of *Othello* so she could do her lusty Desdemona.

Their performance was not received well. The guests of the Rotorua Lodge were generally wealthy and well educated. Vera's obscenities were met with disdain; all the scenes got was a bit of polite applause, if even that. Once or twice, the actors were met with an embarrassed silence. Robin could hardly wait to escape to his room. Horror-stricken, he imagined having to face the hotels' other guests the next day.

After their performance, Bertram Lockhart argued with Vera in the dressing rooms. Finally, after this disaster of a night, the actor had the upper hand for a change. With relish, he accused her of not being able to read an audience.

Robin barely even took the time to wipe off his stage makeup. Surely, guests would be sitting around the bar or the restaurant now, talking about the show, and perhaps he could reach his room without having to talk to anybody. But there, waiting outside his room, was Aroha.

The young man tried to give her an affable smile. But Aroha wouldn't even let him start.

"Robin, I saw that performance," she said, visibly upset. "I suppose the version I saw at the Rotomahana Hotel wasn't your—usual thing?" Aroha was losing her composure bit by bit. "Robin, how could you *do* this? How could you perform in something like . . . whatever that just was? Here and now, after a catastrophe where over a hundred people lost their lives? What were you thinking? Was that supposed to cheer people up? And don't get me started on piousness . . . I can't imagine your program was approved by the McDougals.

Robin, how can you stoop to something like that? To such a travesty of your art? Honestly, I never cared for Shakespeare all that much, but he didn't deserve that! It's just obscene . . . ugly . . . disgusting . . ." Robin hung his head. "Well then, you agree with me," she said, somewhat mollified. "So why do you do it, Robin? Why do you go along with this?"

Robin bit his lip. "There wasn't really anything else I *could* do, and I—I had to—"

"You 'had to'?" Aroha asked, scoffing, but she stopped herself when she saw the pain in the young man's pale, miserable features. "Robin, I don't understand what's keeping you here. I can only assume that the Carrigan woman is blackmailing you in some way. But whatever she may have against you, it can't be bad enough for you to offer yourself up for such . . . abominations. Either you talk to me right now, or I'll have a word with Vera tomorrow. I'll figure out what's going on, Robin, mark my words! In any case, your engagement with this company ends today." She gazed searchingly at her uncle. "Unless you actually want to stay with her."

Robin shook his head. "It's a long story," he said.

Aroha sighed. She was completely exhausted and would have preferred to wallow in her own grief for a while. But she knew Robin needed help.

"I've got time," she told him. "Bao's taking care of Lani. Let's go inside, and you can tell me what happened."

An hour later, Robin had poured out his heart to her, and he felt unspeakably relieved. Aroha had listened to his tale of Vera's scams and Robin's role in them with surprising composure. But she didn't believe Vera really had anything on Robin.

"Nobody's pressed charges yet, have they? Well, if there's no plaintiff, there can't be a judge. And even if there were charges . . . Vera was personally involved in all those charades. She'd have to implicate herself if she were going for your demise. She'd never do that; what would she gain from it? Whether you run away or get arrested, Robin Fenroy won't be performing for her any longer."

Robin thought of the other young actors who had run from Vera. Indeed, she hadn't pursued any of them.

"Should—should I go to Auckland tomorrow, then?" he asked sheepishly.

Aroha shook her head. "No, there's no need for that. You don't have to run away; you have friends here. And I know the local police chief. He won't so much as listen to Vera, even if she threatens to press charges. I'll pay your hotel bill if you don't have the money, and starting tomorrow, you can come live with me and put some thought into what your next steps are going to be."

"I want to be an actor!" Robin exclaimed defiantly.

Aroha rolled her eyes. "Then you will be. I'm well aware of how talented you are. You'll find something else, something far better than this. Just talk to Vera Carrigan and resign. If there's a contract that has to be voided, you can tell her your lawyer will be in touch. I can come along, if you want . . . or we'll ask Bao or one of the other men to come along. Are you worried about violence?"

After what Robin had told her, Aroha wouldn't have put it past Vera to drug her star performer and abduct him. But Robin shook his head. He dreaded this conversation with Vera, but he didn't want Aroha to think of him as a coward. Though she probably already did, anyway. It was starting to dawn on him that he'd been behaving like a petulant child. He'd been cowardly and naive, but he was going to put an end to it! Vera and her company would be moving on soon—maybe even tomorrow. After that performance, surely no one in Rotorua would want to hire them.

But Robin was staying. He was free at last.

# Chapter 33

Robin would've preferred to get his conversation with Vera over with the first thing the next morning. But the actress was sleeping in as usual, and he had no intention of annoying her even more by waking her early.

So, he met Aroha and Bao for breakfast first, and he played with Lani to avoid looking at any of the other guests in the breakfast room. At least Mrs. McDougal was kind to him; Aroha had probably talked to her already. She came over and leaned on the empty chair at the head of their table.

"Will you be going back to your hotel now? Or are you going to attend the funeral service first?" she asked Aroha. "You're invited, of course, Mr. Fenroy, and you, Mr. Duong. The reverend will be hosting a service for the people who died—the *pakeha*, mostly, it would seem. They'll be buried here at our graveyard after the service. There's no use trying to send them to their respective homes, they're from so far away. But of course we will also be paying our respects to the Maori victims. Please come, Miss Aroha."

Aroha didn't have to think long before accepting. She'd been doing her best to focus on Lani, the hotel, and Robin, but she remembered what had happened after Matiu's death, the depths of that depression. She couldn't keep locking away all her grief over Koro, and perhaps the service and her future neighbors' and friends' condolences would bring her some peace. When Robin decided to join her, Bao said he was going to go back to the hotel to supervise the first few repairs himself. He'd already called in a few men for the heavier manual work. Bao put on a brave face, but Aroha could tell he was nervous about the fact that the men were white.

"Well, if they give you any trouble, they'll be hearing a thing or two from me," she said menacingly. "Bao, they'll *have* to get used to the fact that you're in charge. And you should get used to it too. If they're disrespectful, fire them, even if it means not getting the pipes fixed today. We can spend another night at the lodge if need be."

Robin gave Aroha a look of astonishment. With her commanding tone of voice, she reminded him of March a little. The thought warmed his heart. When he finally left Vera, he'd be able to visit Rata Station. He wouldn't return in triumph, as he'd dreamed, and maybe March would make fun of him. Still, the thought of seeing her again filled him with joy.


Robin followed Aroha through the church, eyes lowered. The pews were filled with people, and surely, some of them had seen the performance last night. Fortunately, the members of the rescue team he'd worked with in Te Wairoa greeted him warmly. Again, he felt at ease with them right away. There, at least, he'd held his own.

The service turned out to be quite a festive occasion, all in all. The reverend held a moving sermon, and the choir sang funeral songs, called *waiata tangi*. A large part of the parish was Maori, and among them were talented singers and musicians. Tears ran freely down Aroha's cheeks as the traditional instruments invoked memories of all the *powhiri* in which Koro had danced for her. She rocked Lani back and forth to the rhythm of the music and the silent sobs that racked her body, and all of a sudden, she knew with absolute certainty that staying in the Rotorua district was the right thing for her to do. Lani's mother had had a beautiful voice—Lani should learn to sing her songs one day.

After the service, she accepted condolences from Rotorua's residents, some of whom had known Koro. Robin stood next to her, trying not to draw any attention to himself. But then, a vaguely familiar-looking young woman approached. At the thought that she might've seen one of his performances, he blushed furiously.

"Mr.—Mr. Fenroy?" she said quietly. She was pretty and well-dressed, around twenty years old, with a wispy mane of pale blonde hair barely kept in check by a tortoiseshell clip. For the occasion, she was wearing a high-necked dark-blue travel costume with a matching hat, a simple creation of extraordinary elegance. "Excuse me . . . I asked for your name up at the hotel." She blushed faintly. "My name's Helena Lacrosse. And . . . well, I've been trying to decide for some time now if I should approach you with my concern . . ." Helena Lacrosse nervously toyed with her matching silk purse. "Because—well, I've seen you twice now in those—those plays . . ." She blushed even more deeply.

"Twice?" Robin asked in consternation.

A young woman of such obvious fine upbringing should have turned away in horror after witnessing the Carrigan Company. Robin thought he even remembered a gentleman escorting the young woman out in the middle of one of Vera's adaptations of *Othello*. He noticed now that that same man was standing behind Miss Lacrosse. He gave Robin and his companion a disapproving frown.

"Yes," Miss Lacrosse told him. "Because—well, not because I liked them, although your acting was excellent, but . . ."

Robin stopped her. "Our performances are terrible," he assured her. "I got into the group by accident, one might say, and I intend to part ways with Miss Carrigan soon."

Miss Lacrosse beamed at him in relief. "Oh, I'm so glad to hear it! But now, well, regarding my concern . . . You played Juliet recently, and Miranda last night."

Robin wished the ground would swallow him up. "I'm so sorry—" He started to offer an explanation, but Miss Lacrosse wouldn't let him finish.

"Well, I noticed . . . How do I put this? You resemble someone, Mr. Fenroy. So closely that it can't really be a coincidence. Although my fiancé disagrees. Well, never mind, I just wanted to ask you. Because . . . it's possible that we're related."

Robin frowned. "How could that be?" he asked. "I mean, I don't know where you're from, but I'm from the South Island. And my parents never mentioned any relatives anywhere else. Of course the Fenroys are, um, a family of means, one might say, in England. So if you're from there—"

Helena shook her head. "No, most definitely not. We know our lineage quite well, and there are no Fenroys involved. A British noble family, isn't it? Well, be that as it may, it's not your name that made me think so, it's the way you look. Your—your portrait's in my father's entrance hall."

"My portrait?" Robin asked, raising his eyebrows incredulously. "Miss Lacrosse, perhaps church isn't the place to discuss such matters. There's a café right across the street."

Helena nodded, relieved. "An excellent idea, Mr. Fenroy. Harold . . . ," she said, turning to face the man behind her. "This is my fiancé, Harold Wentworth," she explained. "He came here with me to meet you. We're part of a travel group from Otago." She smiled nervously. "A few young people and an entire flock of chaperones."

Robin shook Mr. Wentworth's hand with a nervous smile, excused himself briefly to Aroha, and led the two of them out of the church and over to the café across the street. The entire situation troubled him. These people weren't related to his father. Could it be Cat?

"It's not really your portrait, of course," Helena said after the men had ordered coffee for themselves and tea for her, "but my great-aunt's. It might as well be yours, though, if you had a portrait done of yourself in one of those female roles. The resemblance is uncanny. Your features, your—well, not your physique, of course, but my aunt must've been as slim as you. That fine, pale-blond hair . . . Oh, I'm aware this must all sound so silly."

Robin shook his head. "Not at all," he said kindly. "It's just that I can't imagine how some ancestor of mine could be connected to your great-aunt. Whatever happened to her? Seeing as you know your family history so well . . ."

"But that's it exactly; I don't know that part," Helena told him excitedly. "My great-aunt . . . disappeared. I don't know the details of what happened back then, exactly. It's been sixty years or more now, and that was back in Australia. But my grandfather took her painting with him when he moved to New Zealand. He remembers her well; she was his sister. And as I said, she disappeared suddenly and without a trace. I assume it was a love story of some kind. Why else would she have run away? And my grandfather's very strict, so I expect his parents were too. Maybe Suzanne fell in love with the wrong man and they forbid her to marry him, or something like that. Something tragic, in any case. My grandfather said his mother never quite got over it, and neither did he. She was so beautiful . . . so delicate . . ."

Robin looked at Helena's translucent skin, her wispy ash-blonde locks—she must resemble her great-aunt as well. And him! Now that she mentioned it, it was obvious. He hadn't only recognized her from the audience, but from his own face in the mirror. She could've been "Miranda" or "Juliet's" sister.

Robin cleared his throat. "I—well, I don't know anything about her, but my grandmother's name was Suzanne. She was my mother's mother."

Helena jumped up in excitement, but quickly sat back down again. "Suzanne, yes, that was her name! This can't be a coincidence," she cried. "Isn't that right, Harold? Coincidences like that just don't exist! Oh, I'm so glad I asked. Mr. Fenroy—or Robin, pardon me. If we really are related, I should call you Robin! Do you think I could talk to your mother? Where does she live? Does she work in the theater business too?"

Her last words sounded hesitant. Helena might have been excited to meet this new relative of hers, but his occupation wasn't any cause for celebration. Harold Wentworth, her tall, dark-haired fiancé, was scowling.

Robin hastened to reassure Helena. "My mother owns a sheep farm in the Canterbury Plains," he explained.

Helena's face lit up. "How exciting! Maybe our factories are the ones processing her wool. Funny how it all comes together. Our family owns woolen mills and tailors' workshops in Dunedin."

Aroha's entrance cut her explanation short. She'd been worried when Robin quickly whispered to her that he was going over to the café across the street with some "acquaintances." Was this Vera Carrigan's doing? She was relieved when Robin introduced Helena Lacrosse and her fiancé.

"Miss Lacrosse suspects that she's a relative of ours," he added. "Aroha's mother is my half sister. Aroha would be, um, Suzanne's great-granddaughter."

"What's all this, now?" Aroha asked, pulling up a chair. She was immediately monopolized by Helena. Before the waitress could even come to their table to take her order, Aroha knew the full story. "I can't really add anything to that," she said finally. "If I'm honest, I don't think I'd ever heard the name of Cat's mother. But she did mention Australia once. I think she was born there."

"More evidence!" Helena crowed. "Oh, you must come to Dunedin to meet my grandfather, Robin. You must! You too, of course . . . What was your name? Aroha? What a curious name. Well, he might not believe you; you don't look much like my great-aunt. But Robin . . ."

Aroha made a calming gesture. "Let's take things slow, Miss Lacrosse," she said kindly but firmly. "Perhaps you should talk to my grandmother first." As Aroha spoke the words, she suddenly remembered that her grandparents would be there next week. Her wedding with Koro would have been soon. Tears sprang to Aroha's eyes. She certainly didn't feel like talking to this effusive woman about her ancestry. "How long will you be staying?" she asked, clearing her throat.

"We, uh—I'm—expecting my grandparents' arrival in a few days' time. They're coming for . . . the opening of my hotel."

Helena clapped her hands in excitement. "How wonderful! We were going to leave soon, but we'll be staying, then, of course. I must speak to your grandmother. What's her maiden name? If it's Lacrosse . . ."

"That would mean Suzanne had a child out of wedlock," Harold Wentworth interjected. He sounded disgusted.

Aroha narrowed her eyes slightly at the man. "Rata," she said shortly. "Catherine Rata. But will you excuse us now, please? There's a lot of work at the hotel, and Robin has something important to do today." She gave Robin a sharp look. "The lady must have gotten up by now, Robin."

Robin leaped to his feet. Personally, he'd found the conversation with Helena inspiring. The young woman was right—the family resemblance and the matching names, and then Australia too . . . It couldn't be a coincidence. And even if the Lacrosse family didn't have anything to do with theater, a new relationship might yield new possibilities.

Filled with hope and energy, Robin felt strong enough to face Vera now.

# Chapter 34

Vera Carrigan had just come sweeping out of the hotel owner's office when Robin stepped into the lodge. The second she saw him, she stormed over.

"Pack your things, Robin, we're leaving today. I'm not yet sure how or where to, but I'll figure something out. This place is too snobby for us, apparently! Or at least the people here consider themselves too noble to appreciate our performances. I think we should go to Auckland."

Robin shook his head. This was his cue. "No, Vera. I won't be coming with you. I—I resign. I'm staying here."

Vera, who had already stomped over to the staircase, stopped in her tracks. "You're doing *what*?" She sounded threatening. But then she caught herself, smiling her shark's smile. "Oh, that's right, I forgot you have relatives here, my dearie. Your . . . niece, isn't it? That pretty blonde thing who was going to marry the dead Maori. I remember. And you're going to stay with her? Comfort her while she's grieving? Oh, Robin, how kind of you." She sounded as though she were talking to a child, trying to appease but not taking him seriously in the slightest.

"I've been meaning to resign for quite a while now," Robin told her. "You—you know I don't like what we do."

"So you'd rather not be a performer anymore?" Vera asked him with mock pity. "So you'd rather . . . oh, what does your niece do, again? Work at a hotel? I could picture you as a bellhop, my dearie."

"I'm an actor, and I always will be!" Robin lost control of his voice. He was almost shouting now.

The actress laughed out loud. "Not much longer, though. But listen here, Robin . . . We shouldn't be talking about this here, the walls have ears."

She glanced over at the reception desk where Mrs. McDougal was shuffling around some papers. The woman gave her a savage look.

"I'm not coming up to your room with you," Robin declared.

Vera shook her head. "Of course not, my dearie! How could I take you to my room in broad daylight? Think of my poor reputation! It'd be ruined for the rest of my days. And people might say you only get the good parts because you . . . well, you know, with your boss." She made an obscene gesture. "Let's go for a walk instead. A bit of fresh air might be good for both of us."

"The air isn't particularly fresh," Robin said evasively.

Vera tossed on the coat that she'd been carrying over one arm. Mr. McDougal must have summoned her to his office just as she'd been about to go out.

"Get on with it," she ordered Robin.

The young man jumped at her words. Then he followed her outside.

Rotorua Lodge was situated at the edge of town, near footpaths leading to the local hot springs. The hotel's proximity to these natural bathing pools was the main reason why the McDougals didn't operate their own bathhouse. A signpost pointed them to the best-known pools, but Vera took one of the other paths. Robin sighed with relief. For a moment, he'd been worried Vera was going to try to coax him into one of the pools to try out her seduction games again. But he'd heard that the springs were closed for safety reasons, anyway.

Vera wandered deeper and deeper into the geothermal area, Robin tagging along reluctantly. After some time, he recognized parts of the landscape. Arama had brought them to a hidden pool out this way. Was that where Vera was going? The actress had started to prattle on again. She was assuring him how important he was to her, and how much the company relied on him.

"You must at least give me time to find a replacement for you, Robin. And that won't be easy, let me tell you. An immensely talented young man such as yourself . . ." Vera had never talked to him like that before. In spite of all his misgivings, Robin felt a slight swell of pride. "At least come along to Auckland with us. We could change our program a little. What you and Bertram pulled together back there in Te Wairoa wasn't half bad. We'll put up a new ad in Auckland—let's see what kinds of actors drop by. Maybe we can find a talented young girl and one or two boys. Then we could perform an entire play for a change instead of just scenes. You'd like that, wouldn't you, Robin?"

Vera's voice sounded honey-sweet, and Robin tried hard not to be seduced by the idea. Of course it would be wonderful to perform full plays with a bigger company. But that was never going to happen.

Robin tried not to listen to her lies, focusing instead on the landscape. The eruption hadn't left any visible effects on Whakarewarewa, aside from a light dusting on the vegetation. If it hadn't been for the cloud of ash hanging over the area, immersing the entire world in a murky, yellowish light, it would've been hard to believe what had happened only miles from here such a short time ago.

Indeed, Vera led him to the same natural pool that Arama had shown them the previous week. It lay invitingly in a peaceful, slightly rocky clearing between tufts of raupo and tussock grass. Here and there, manuka trees grew tall between the rocks.

"Our spring," Vera purred. "Come on, Robin, it's not all bad with our company. The two of us have always had a special connection." She walked over to the spring, crouched down, and stuck her hand in the water. "It's nice and warm, just like last week. Nothing's destroyed here, Robin. Do you know why? It's because this is my spring . . . *our* spring." She splashed a little water at him in an imitation of a playful gesture. "What's mine can't be destroyed," she said. Her voice was fervent, and her eyes had a maniacal glint to them. "I take care of what's mine. Strong magic. Didn't you hear them talking? McRae sensed it. And as you can see, I can't be harmed. No crazy curses, no *tapu* . . . Only you could destroy me now, little Robin. My company can't go on without you. We need you. And you need us, you need the stage. You need my protection. We've got so much, Robin." Vera let the coat slide off her shoulders. She looked back at Robin over her shoulder and started to unbutton her blouse. "Come here and take a bath with me, Robin. Let's have one more bath together."

Robin shook his head. "No. It's—dangerous . . ."

He wasn't sure whether he meant the water or Vera, who dropped her skirt with a throaty laugh. She stood before him in her corset.

"It's warm," she cooed. "It's good. It's healing, and it can make you forget. Come, Robin, come to me. You don't really want to leave. We're one, you and I and the others. We're family. Or maybe just you and me?" She licked her lips, shaking her thick, dark hair free with one fluid motion, letting it tumble over her naked shoulders. "Come and help me, Robin," she said, pointing at the laces of her corset. "Help me open these!"

Reluctantly, Robin obliged, but then he took a step back again. This time, he was determined not to give in to her coaxing.

"I don't care what you do or say, Vera. I'm not coming with you," he said resolutely. "We're not a family. Aroha's my family. You're just . . . All you did was lie to me and deceive me. You put me down. You're like a swamp, Vera, a swamp that swallows people . . . Or like an evil spirit that can possess souls. I see you for what you are. I'm a free man, Vera, I—"

Vera's raucous laughter drowned out his words. "Oh . . . poor little Robin was possessed! But let me guess, your cousin or your niece or whatever she is found a Maori priest who sang a *karakia* for you. To free you from big, bad Vera." She let the corset drop to the ground, turned to face him, naked, and then slowly slid into the pool's warm waters. Vapor rose from the surface around her. "A *tohunga* tried that once before," she said. "That old hag. She was trying to tear Joe Fitzpatrick from me. Howled like the dog of that stupid wife of his every time she saw me. Fitz and I laughed at her . . . And in the end, I won. And then she cursed me." She laughed.

"People seem to curse you rather often," Robin remarked, gritting his teeth.

"And unsuccessfully, I might add!" Vera was floating in the middle of the pool now, her hair haloing her face like a dark aura. "It's because I'm stronger, Robin . . . I told you, McRae noticed, too . . . I've got magic. I'm stronger than those spirits . . . I spit on all the *tohunga* . . . and their spirits!" She sucked in a mouthful of water and spat it out.

Robin was reminded of one of those gargoyle rainspouts on European cathedrals that he'd seen in books. Then he felt something like a lingering, growing coldness, a shiver. Was he shaking, or was the sensation coming from underfoot?

"That's why you'll stay, Robin; because you're safe with me. Nothing can happen to you as long as you're by my side." Vera's soft, purring voice was still rising from the mist that had suddenly started to thicken.

Robin heard a deep rumble, and then the earth shook in earnest.

With a terrified expression, Vera let out a gut-wrenching shriek of pain.

Helplessly, he watched her struggle in the water. She tried to reach the edge, but at that very moment, the pool cracked open beneath her. Vera was sucked down into its depths, only to be spat out a second later by a steaming, hissing geyser, several feet high into the darkening sky. Robin, nauseous with horror, could still hear Vera's screams as the pool swallowed her up again. He'd backed away as the earth began to shake, and now suppressed the urge to attempt a rescue. The water inside the pool was bubbling; it had to be white-hot. Finally, Vera's shrieks stopped. Robin couldn't see her anymore. Steam shrouded everything around the spring as the geyser slowed.

The ground rumbled again, and Robin understood that it was time to flee. There was nothing more he could do there. All he could hope was that the spirits would show him some mercy. Feeling dogged by the curses that had finally claimed Vera, he crossed the clearing at a flat-out run, only feeling a little safer once he'd passed the first few houses of Rotorua.

# Chapter 35

"Where is he?"

Aroha was inspecting the repaired water pipes at her hotel when the front door flew open and two women came bursting in. With astonishment, Aroha realized it was her mother and her grandmother. Linda and Cat were wearing riding clothes, and looked as though they'd ridden nonstop for days.

"What are you doing here?" Aroha said, taken by surprise. "How did you find me?"

Linda pulled her daughter into her arms. "Oh, Aroha, my dear, we heard about Koro. I'm so sorry," she said gently.

Tears filled Aroha's eyes, but she was still confused. "How could you have heard already?" she asked. "How did you get here so fast?"

"We asked about you at Rotorua Lodge," Cat told her. "We heard about Koro's death there. And we heard about the eruption back in Hamilton when we were already on our way here. But you could feel the earthquakes all the way over in Wellington. It was obvious something terrible was happening on the North Island, but it wasn't possible to know exactly where it was, then. I'm so, so sorry, Aroha. You must have been through horrors. But please, tell me first, where's Robin? Is he all right?"

Aroha's eyes widened. Cat was gazing at her with frightening desperation. The only thing she'd said in her letter to her grandmother was that Robin had shown up in Te Wairoa with the Carrigan Company, and that he was fine.

Aroha glanced at the pretty carved clock that sat on her future reception desk. "Well, I last saw him three hours ago. He was in a good mood then, and he was about to finally resign from his job with that horrible woman. He must've done so by now. He's probably back at the hotel."

"Thank God and all the spirits!" Cat murmured. "I haven't slept since Linda wrote me."

As Aroha then learned, her mother had panicked upon receiving her letter with the news about Robin. Aroha's insinuations that her young half brother might be under Vera Carrigan's influence had scared Linda witless. She'd immediately sent a telegram to Rata Station: *Robin in danger. Come immediately! Linda.*

"I left right away, of course," Cat told them. "Although Chris said I was acting crazy. Quite sensibly, he pointed out that Robin had probably been with the company for two and a half years. So why would Carrigan pose a threat now?"

"Maybe because he'd run into Aroha?" Linda suggested, nervously brushing some hair out of her eyes. She didn't seem as reassured as her mother. "Or because she learned that Robin's related to me? She—she was ready to kill Aroha back then." Instinctively, she wrapped an arm around her daughter.

"That was twenty years ago," Cat said, comforting her. "Chris thought we should keep things in perspective, and he hired a private investigation agency to collect information about the Carrigan Company. The investigators in Christchurch said their branch in Auckland or Wellington would be able to send us a dossier in a few days' time. They said the head of a theater company shouldn't be hard to trace. Chris thought we should wait, if only to avoid scaring off Robin again. He might've been happy, for all we knew. And Vera . . . I'm sure she's not the most pleasant kind of woman, but we have to consider that she was only fifteen when she knew Linda. She might've changed."

"Never," Linda said, looking even more worried when Aroha shook her head.

"I don't really believe it either," Cat admitted. "Which is why I'm here now. I took the next ship from Wellington to Christchurch, bought a horse there, and then I rode to Otaki to join Linda, and we came here. We tried to send you advance notice, Aroha, but all the lines were dead. Understandable, after the catastrophe. Are you going to tell us what happened?"

But before Aroha could reply, Linda interrupted.

"I think we should find Robin before we talk," she urged. "If that woman finds out I'm here—Mamaca, Aroha—she's capable of anything. Where's the company staying?"

People at Rotorua Lodge had felt the earthquakes too. Geologists were trying to reassure everyone, but of course, there was still a general sense of unease in the air. Some of the guests had just come down to the lobby to talk to the hotel owner and his wife when Robin Fenroy burst in, pale as a sheet, shaking from head to toe and rambling incoherently. But he spoke directly to Waimarama McDougal, who listened to him kindly with a look of mild confusion on her face.

"The—the—the water, it was boiling. And the geyser—exploded. She screamed—she screamed so loud . . ." Robin tore at his hair. There was naked horror in his eyes.

"Easy now, lad, easy," Brett McDougal said. "Ye look like ye've seen a ghost."

"Yes—they took their vengeance," he blurted. "The spirits took their vengeance—the curse . . ."

"Well now, come with me, lad! Waimarama, please take care of our *manuhiri* here, will ye?"

McDougal gently pushed the young man into his office.

"You have to send someone to—to get her. I'm—I'm sure she's dead, the spirits, she—Oh my *God*, those screams . . ."

Robin buried his head in his hands. McDougal poured a tumbler of whiskey and placed it in the young man's shaking hands.

"Have a drink, lad. No, no sippin', down with it. All right, and now tell me slowly, from the beginnin', what happened."

A little while later, the hotelier returned to the lobby, looking serious, and had a whispered conversation with his wife. Then he looked around, searching for someone discreet who might be able to help him retrieve the corpse. It didn't bear contemplating what would happen if word got out that one of their guests had been boiled alive. Finally, he caught sight of Bao. He knew that the man had been the maître de maison for McRae and would be Aroha's new manager soon—the gentleman seemed like his best bet.

Indeed, Bao understood right away how delicately such matters had to be treated. A few minutes later, he headed out with McDougal while Waimarama took care of Robin. The woman breathed a sigh of relief when Aroha showed up a little later with Cat and Linda in tow.

Waimarama quickly informed the women of the situation. "It seems that Miss Carrigan is dead," she told them in a whisper. "Mr. Fenroy's fine, physically, but he's distraught. You should probably take him up to his room now. Or no, wait, I'll let you all have the honeymoon suite. There's plenty of space there, and I could have your meals brought up. But I think you should take Mr. Fenroy home with you as soon as possible."

Cat and Linda thanked her for the generosity, and Aroha nodded understandingly. It was certainly in the McDougals' and all other Rotorua hoteliers' best interest for Robin to be kept well out of sight.

But they couldn't keep the day's events from Bertram, who was starting to ask questions about Vera and Robin's absence. Upon his insistent inquiries, Waimarama sent him up to the wedding suite. She trusted Aroha would be able to deal with the actor; and in the end, it was she who told him about Vera's death.

Bertram returned to the company's rooms before going to question Robin, and wrestled Leah's "medicine" from her hands.

"Leah, my sweet," he said, "prepare yourself, because it looks like this'll be the last bottle of the stuff you're ever going to lay eyes on. If we give some to Robin, he might tell us what happened."

And so he did. With his voice heavy with laudanum and Cat squeezing his hand, Robin told the small group what he'd witnessed. As soon as the tale was complete, he fell asleep on the suite's luxurious, velvet-draped bed.

While the others digested what they'd been told, there was a knock on the door, and Bao stepped inside with a large bottle of scotch and some glasses. "Mr. McDougal asked me to bring you these," he said, filling the glasses. "We weren't able to find Vera Carrigan's body. But the new geyser's still coughing up boiling water. It's impossible for anyone to survive that."

"The devil got her," Bertram said. "Not that I'm surprised."

He clinked glasses with Bao and took a large gulp.

Linda knocked hers back in one gulp and coughed. "I know it's terrible, and no one deserves to die like that. But I think old Omaka's spirit can make its way to Hawaiki now. She'll finally be able to find peace. Her curse has been fulfilled."

"Well, she'll have company on the way there," Bao said. "The old Maori priest, Tuhoto, also died today."

After the old man had been rescued, he'd been taken to Rotorua Hospital. Sophia Hinerangi would have preferred for his own tribe's healers to look after him, but the healers were convinced that the eruption had been Tuhoto *ariki*'s fault. The doctors and nurses at the hospital had taken care of the old man in the gentlest way possible, but they weren't able to save him.

Aroha thought of the priest with grief and respect. He'd never done anything but serve his people. He hadn't deserved to die without his friends and family around him.

"Well then, let's drink to Omaka and Tuhoto . . ." Bertram said gamely. "And to the spirits, and to God and the devil. I never really believed in them, but . . . I think I'll have to reconsider my lifestyle now."

Leah, the only one who'd ever harbored friendly feelings toward Vera Carrigan, stayed silent, as did Aroha. She thought of her own curse. If she fell in love, it was going to follow her again . . .

# Chapter 36

They never did find Vera's body. That certainly made things easier for the hoteliers of Rotorua. The McDougals and Aroha agreed to simply report the actress as missing. Miss Carrigan, they told anyone who asked, had run off in a huff after Brett McDougal canceled any further performances at the hotel. No one made any more inquiries—apart from Joseph McRae, and in the end, they decided to let him in on what had happened under the pledge of absolute secrecy.

Waimarama McDougal was a little worried about the salvation of Vera's soul, but Robin and Bertram assured her that Vera hadn't been religious at all.

"And they're still reading requiems in mass," Aroha told her. "For all the people who died in the catastrophe. Miss Carrigan counts as one of them, of course."

The morning after her death, Leah and Bertram met in Vera's room to have a good look around. Bertram found a large stash of money—and Leah found two more bottles of her precious tincture. She would have been able to buy herself even more of it, had Bertram been willing to share the cash. That was his exact argument for not sharing, in the end. Leah, he reasoned, had to be protected from herself. At least he still ended up giving her and Robin the fees they were owed. It would probably be enough for a ride to Tauranga and a fare to Auckland by boat, especially since Bertram had given Leah the dead woman's clothes and the jewelry that had been in the room. Leah could pawn those things in Auckland, and then, at least, she'd have a bit of capital for something new. That afternoon, the young woman disappeared without even saying goodbye or letting anyone know where she was going.

Bertram Lockhart caught the next ride out of town as well, but he stopped to see Robin first. He told the younger actor he was going to Auckland to audition at some theaters.

"Well then," Bertram said amicably, "I'm sure, considering the business we're in, our paths shall cross again."

Robin wasn't sure he wanted that, truth be told.

The next morning, Waimarama found the rest of Vera's jewelry in the hotel's safe, and Brett McDougal decided to sell it. He used some of the proceeds to pay for the company's rooms and donated the rest to the surviving dependents of those who had died in the catastrophe. That was probably the first time Vera Carrigan had donated to a good cause, albeit involuntarily.

Sometime during the afternoon, a letter arrived for Cat from the Wellington detective agency Chris had hired. McDougal delivered it to the honeymoon suite himself.

"Must be something important," McDougal said inquisitively as he handed the letter over to Cat.

She was in the suite with Lani and Robin, who was still hungover and frazzled from the previous day's events. Linda had gone to help Aroha and Bao get the hotel in order. Bao had been right: throngs of people were flocking into Rotorua, all of them in need of accommodation. There were geologists from the universities in Wellington and Auckland, disaster crews, journalists, and curious onlookers. All the hotels in the area were booked solid, so Aroha and Bao had agreed to open the Chinese Garden Lodge the next day, which was earlier than planned. After all, apart from a few details in the bathing area, everything was ready, and these guests weren't there for cozy spa vacations, anyway.

Cat glanced at the sender's address, feigning indifference. She wasn't about to open the letter with the hotelier still standing there. Only after he'd taken his leave, visibly disappointed, did she tear open the envelope.

Aroha and Linda returned later that evening, tired and hungry. Aroha was feeling depressed too. After all, she and Koro had planned to enjoy the grand opening of their hotel together. She'd spent the day holding back tears, with Linda and Bao keeping a respectful distance. Night still fell much too early in Rotorua; the lingering clouds of ash hadn't cleared yet.

But a surprise was waiting for the two women as they entered the suite. Cat had had the table set with candles and fine china.

"I asked them to cook us something nice," she said, pouring some wine for her daughter and her granddaughter. "This isn't really a celebration, I promise. You're grieving, Aroha, and I know Robin doesn't feel much like celebrating either. But you all have to eat something, and we should drink to your hotel's opening, Aroha—in memory of Koro. I never met him, but I think . . . no, I know he'd be proud of you. And he wouldn't blame us for being proud either!"

A knot rose in Aroha's throat, but she accepted her glass and drank to the Chinese Garden Lodge—feeling slightly guilty that Bao wasn't there. He was spending the night at the new hotel, making a few last preparations.

Still, dinner was quiet. Aroha was lost in thought, all Robin did was pick at his food, and Linda only had eyes for Lani. Although she shook her head about Aroha's decision to never get married or have children, she'd fallen in love with the little girl right away. Linda had cared for many children in her life, but she'd had a baby of her own just one time. Now, she was determined to catch up as much as she could with her adopted granddaughter. That meant that she didn't exactly contribute to the dinner conversation either.

Cat was the only one who managed to liven things up. She waited until dessert had been served, and then she pulled out the letter from an inside pocket of her dress.

"*To whom it may concern: The Life of Vera Carrigan,*" she announced. "*As recorded by Mr. Lovelace's detective agency.*"

Robin almost choked on a spoonful of mousse au chocolat. He could sense the blood draining from his face, and he felt light-headed.

"That was fast," Aroha said, surprised.

"I suppose it wasn't very hard to figure out," Cat explained. "Miss Carrigan was a well-known . . . well, I wouldn't say a friend of Auckland's theater scene, but she certainly managed to get people talking about her."

"She really did end up acting in Auckland?" Linda asked. "Fitz said something like that the last time I saw him. He said she'd met an impresario who wanted to turn her into a star. I assumed he was exaggerating, of course."

"It seems that, after the entire military settlers ordeal, she went to Auckland with Joe Fitzpatrick, and Fitz, as you know well, my dear, was a jack of all trades. He worked as a custodian at the King's Theater for a time. It was managed by John Hollander back then, a well-known and utterly reputable Shakespeare performer, with whom Vera came into contact, of course. Mr. Hollander's dead now, but the detective agency talked to his widow and his children. They report that the widow still gets mad as a hornet whenever anybody mentions Vera's name."

"Now, that sounds familiar," Linda interjected.

Cat smiled. "Yes, Hollander succumbed to young Vera's charm, hook, line, and sinker. He insisted that Vera was a kind of diamond in the rough when it came to acting. She was highly talented, but had never been encouraged."

"Well, he wasn't wrong, really," Linda remarked. "She was a natural at the art of deception."

"Except that has nothing to do with acting," Robin said, sounding agonized.

Cat shrugged. "It seems that again, she was trying to feign a father-daughter relationship. Like with Fitzpatrick. This time, the girl had even more to gain from it. Hollander paid for an apartment and an alleged chaperone for her—an actress whose career at Hollander's theater was on the rise. He hired private tutors in literature and French—the classic upbringing of an aristocrat's daughter. And acting lessons, of course. The detectives couldn't reconstruct whether Vera had really wanted lessons or whether Hollander had insisted on them to compensate for his guilt for, ah, loving a girl so young. But the widow told the investigators that, after two or three years, Vera started to become a nuisance to him. Perhaps she asked him to leave his wife, or maybe she extorted money. Be that as it may, she managed to talk her way into more than a few roles at Hollander's theater. The actors gossiped viciously about that. It seems her performances weren't even close to the company's level."

Robin nodded. "She was just so bad at it!" he exclaimed. "She couldn't get her head around the parts."

"Omaka once said that people like Vera don't feel in the same way as we do," Linda added thoughtfully. "She said they're . . . different to their very core. I'm not sure what she meant, exactly."

"Anyway, there was bound to be a scandal," Cat went on. "According to the widow and the remaining actors who are still with the company, Hollander and Vera's relationship would have been exposed to the public very soon. The widow says she was worried she'd be humiliated in front of Auckland's entire high society."

"And then what happened?" Aroha asked, lifting Lani off Linda's lap.

The little girl had begun to fuss. She needed her bottle, but Aroha wanted to hear the end of Cat's story first.

"Then he died," Cat said dryly. "Hollander, I mean. It almost happened right there onstage. He was making his exit to prepare for the final curtain—and he keeled over dead."

"Did Vera have anything to do with it?" Linda asked, wide-eyed.

"The detective agency doesn't think so," Cat replied. "And why should she? His death didn't benefit her in any way. She disappeared the same night he died with a week's worth of the entire theater's earnings—a considerable sum. The investigators aren't sure where she went next, but the Carrigan Company made its debut fairly soon after that. They were able to learn quite a bit from hoteliers and pub owners. They even got ahold of one or two former members. But not the man whose name had been on the playbills in the beginning. Seeing as, initially, there were two people behind the company . . ." She looked warily at Linda.

Linda froze. "It can't be . . .?"

Cat nodded. "It was. Joe Fitzpatrick. He wrote the scripts—burlesques based on Shakespeare plays."

"That makes sense," Linda said with a sigh. "Fitz was always eloquent. And educated. And I can't imagine Vera with a pen in her hand, even with all the support she got from that Hollander chap."

"It sounds like she didn't exactly see herself as an actress first and foremost either. They say she used the company as a front for all sorts of trickery. There was prostitution, of course—but always under cover. I assume Fitzpatrick didn't like it much either when she . . . played such physical parts."

"You're suggesting that was the reason he left her?" Linda asked. "I don't think so. He must have noticed her messing around with those other men back in Patea too."

"No, Fitz was arrested." Cat looked down at the letter. "That was around six years ago. They were caught trying to steal the till at a pub. Fitzpatrick was the only one tried in court—it's not clear from the report whether he took the fall of his own accord, or whether Vera exonerated herself at his expense. Anyway, he was convicted, and she left with her 'company' by herself. As for the members, their experiences were very much like Robin's. They came in response to an ad, were happy to be accepted right away, and then got dragged into her criminal scams. But most of them realized fairly soon that Vera's threats were idle. They'd stay with the company for a few weeks and then run off. Eventually, she found a few who stayed: Bertram Lockhart, a once-celebrated performer who couldn't get bookings anymore because of his drinking problem, and Leah Hobarth, a child prostitute from the goldfields who'd probably been abused. Vera Carrigan 'saved' her from that predicament and subdued her with drugs. And then you came along, Robin. You were still too young and too stage-struck to see through Vera's scheming."

"You could say 'stupid' too," Robin replied angrily.

Cat shrugged. "I prefer 'naive,'" she said. "But if that's what you want to call it . . . You really got hoodwinked by her, didn't you?" She laid a soothing hand on her son's arm. "Well, nothing too terrible happened. Don't feel so bad about it, and take this as an opportunity to learn."

Robin bit his lip, and Aroha doubted he'd be able to get over the entire affair as easily as Cat was suggesting. From the agency's report, Cat knew about the charades Vera and her male actors had pulled off with her drunken suitors. But there seemed to be no mention of the obscene skits Robin had performed onstage. Aroha was sure that neither her mother nor her grandmother realized the extent of Robin's degradation. She, for her part, was convinced that Robin couldn't be the same person after all the indignities he'd suffered. They'd have to wait and find out whether his experiences had helped him grow, or whether the benefits were outweighed by the damage that had been done.

# Chapter 37

Aroha and Koro had been planning a party for the grand opening, but now, the young woman simply opened the hotel doors and Linda posted herself at the reception desk. During the course of that morning, a few people came by briefly to congratulate her. The other hoteliers, bathhouse owners, and souvenir shop clerks were curious, but didn't seem to have any ulterior motives. During bathing season in Rotorua, all the hotels were usually fully booked. The Chinese Garden Lodge was considered an asset rather than competition.

Aroha led her visitors around the premises, trying not to think about how proud Koro would have been, and Cat helped by serving them tea. Bao was busy training the three Maori girls he'd hired for room service and as waitresses for the breakfast room. Guests weren't expected until that afternoon—most would be coming through Tauranga, and the trip would still take several hours, considering the current situation.

Around eleven o'clock, somebody who had nothing to do with tourism showed up. Helena Lacrosse entered the lobby, dressed in an elegant beige wool dress with a contrasting short peplum jacket over it. A little hat sat jauntily on her wispy blonde hair. She'd brought along a gigantic black umbrella to protect herself from the pouring rain outside. She was handing the umbrella to her fiancé now, who followed her inside reluctantly.

Aroha, who had just come into the lobby with Cat, sighed.

"That girl again," she whispered. "I'd completely forgotten about her, with all the worry over Robin."

Helena recognized Aroha immediately and rushed over, beaming. "Aroha! Congratulations. What a beautiful hotel! If we ever come again, we'll be staying here, won't we, Harold?" Harold Wentworth offered no comment. Aroha recognized the

Grand Hotel's small, subtle crest on their umbrella. It seemed that the Lacrosses and Wentworths were used to much more luxury than the Chinese Garden Lodge had to offer. "Well, have you had time to consider coming to Dunedin to meet my grandfather?" Helena asked cheerfully. "And where's Robin? He hasn't left with the theater company, has he? Wasn't there an accident of some kind?"

Aroha confirmed that Vera Carrigan had died and that Robin was still in Rotorua. To be precise, he was at the bathhouse in the gardens at that very moment, helping Bao paint the walls and put up decorations.

"No, I haven't had the time to think about visiting you or anybody else," Aroha explained bluntly. "As you can see, I'm quite busy, and I'll be working around the clock for the next few months, I assume. Nonetheless, you're in luck. My grandmother, Robin's mother, arrived here the day before yesterday." She turned toward Cat. "This is Catherine Rata Fenroy. Mamaca, this is Helena Lacrosse, and her fiancé, Harold Wentworth. They're from Dunedin, but Helena's family is from Australia. She believes she may be a relative of yours."

Aroha ushered Helena, Cat, and a visibly listless Harold into the breakfast room—the other visitors in the small lobby didn't have to hear their family history. Then Aroha went back out to the reception desk to discreetly tell Linda what was going on.

In the breakfast room, Cat listened to Helena's story, fascinated. "It's a possibility," she said calmly after the young woman had finished. "In fact, I've noticed Robin's resemblance to my mother as well. But I'm afraid I can't help you, Miss Lacrosse. My mother was . . . mentally unsound when I knew her. She must have passed by now."

Indeed, Cat couldn't recall ever having seen Suzanne in any state other than complete inebriation. She probably hadn't even been in her right mind when her daughter was born, or she would have given her a name, at least. But Cat's common sense told her that Helena Lacrosse shouldn't be confronted with all the tragic facts of her great-aunt's life.

"And you're sure?" the young woman asked eagerly. "Couldn't she still be alive? My grandfather's still alive, and he was older than Suzanne."

Cat shook her head. Given her mother's circumstances, it had been a wonder that she'd made it to thirty. Suzanne would have had to be in her late seventies now, which struck Cat as impossible.

"As I said, she was already ailing when I was young," she said to Helena. "And she never told me anything about her family. I know that I was born in Sydney, but I don't remember the city at all. I remember the voyage to New Zealand, vaguely. I must have been three or four. Where did your family settle, Miss Lacrosse? Perhaps I'll remember something if you can tell me more."

"Those kinds of memories are hardly proof," Harold Wentworth interjected.

Cat gave him an irritated look. "Is this a hearing, Mr. Wentworth?" she asked him sharply.

"Of course not, Mrs. Fenroy," Helena declared. "For heaven's sake, Harold, you're being impossible! Mrs. Fenroy's just trying to help us, and you——"

"I'm just stating the facts here," Wentworth said sullenly. "And now it's all going to turn into a full-blown investigation. This is the Lacrosse family, Helena. Not some Smiths or Millers who have no inheritance to offer."

Cat laughed out loud. "And what sort of fabulous inheritance is your young fiancé so worried about, Miss Helena?" she asked scornfully. "To be honest, I've never heard of a Lacrosse family before. But I don't do a lot of business in Dunedin."

"My grandfather leads a fairly secluded life," Helena said. "But if you'd been attending balls in Dunedin, you might know me or my sister, Julia." She smiled. "I had my debut this fall, and Julia's was last year. She's married and lives in Australia now." Helena frowned a little. "Her husband, Paul Penn, runs our businesses over there."

It occurred to Cat that Harold Wentworth was probably striving for a similar position.

"We work with the wool processing industry," Helena went on. "My great-grandfather started it; he founded the first factory—in Botany Bay, as Sydney used to be called. He worked with convicts back then. Women, mostly. My grandfather, your uncle—"

"We don't know about that for sure yet," Wentworth interjected.

Helena rolled her eyes. "Anyway, the Lacrosses' children were called Walter and Suzanne. Suzanne disappeared when she was seventeen, and Walter, my grandfather, married a girl from Otago in New Zealand. A sheep baroness." Helena was smiling again. "She didn't want to move to Australia, so Walter followed her to New Zealand and extended the family business to Dunedin. We have woolen mills and tailor shops there now. They're all doing quite well—but my grandfather's disappointed that he doesn't have a male heir. My parents died in an accident at sea when Julia and I were still little."

"Which means there's probably quite a bit to inherit," Cat told Aroha and Linda in a worried tone after Helena and Harold finally left. "And it looks like Harold Wentworth will do anything he can to stop us from seeing even a penny of that money."

"Us?" Linda asked naively.

Cat sighed in exasperation. "Linda, one would think you'd know your way around that subject after everything you went through when Chris and I were presumed dead. If my mother really was Suzanne Lacrosse, then Robin, you, and I would be prospective heirs. But that would certainly be difficult to enforce, unless Walter Lacrosse acknowledged us as such. I'd wager that's exactly what Helena's aiming for. It's why she's so intent on getting Robin to Dunedin."

Aroha frowned. "So Robin can contest her own claim to the inheritance?"

Cat smiled. "So she doesn't have to marry Harold Wentworth! The young man doesn't seem to be the love of her life, if you ask me. If my suspicions are true, the two sisters' husbands were chosen specifically to oversee the family factories. Paul in Australia, and Harold in New Zealand. Julia played along like a good girl, and Helena doesn't dare to object either. But if her inheritance vanishes into thin air, young Harold might seek a wife elsewhere of his own accord."

"Mamaca, what a cunning mind you have!" Linda remarked, shaking her head and smiling. "What do you propose to do, then?"

Cat shrugged. "Well, Helena would've liked to cart us off on the next ship to Dunedin. But I said no. The clothes I threw in a bag when I got Linda's alarm are barely good enough for Rotorua. I'd look like Cinderella if I visited a factory magnate's home in Dunedin now. Not to mention Robin, with his threadbare suits. If we showed up like that, we'd look like poor, desperate fortune hunters." She smiled. "But I couldn't exactly explain that to Helena, now, could I? She and I agreed that Robin would come to Rata Station with me first, and that Helena and Harold would go home to gently break the news to their patriarch. Or that's what Harold believes they're going to do. If you ask me, Helena's already written to her grandfather. If Walter invites us to visit, Robin can accept. I'm sure he'd like to go to Dunedin. There are more theaters there than in Christchurch." She sighed. "I'd love to see him onstage again."

# *Part 4*

## RESPONSIBILITY

### Canterbury Plains, Dunedin (South Island)

### July 1886–August 1887

# Chapter 38

Robin tried not to feel like a failure as he boarded the boat to Rata Station with his mother. He was a little nervous about seeing everyone he'd known before his sudden disappearance. The first of them was the riverboat guide. Old Georgie was a nice fellow, but he was a gossip, and everything he heard would be common knowledge in the whole region within a few days. So they kept the account vague.

"The company my son acted with broke up," Cat explained when Georgie asked what had brought the successful young man back to the area. "A tragic death. Their director passed away in the eruption of Mount Tarawera."

Fortunately, the mention of the volcanic eruption brought Georgie to other subjects. He asked about Aroha, and showed genuine sympathy when he heard of the loss of her fiancé.

"Poor Miss Aroha has had a rough go of it," he said. "There was that railway accident as well, wasn't there? Didn't she lose a friend there too? Some people just seem to attract misfortune . . ."

"Just don't tell her that if she happens to come back here," Cat said with a sigh. She had spoken to Linda about that before the departure from Rotorua. "Aroha's afraid there's a curse on her, which is nonsense, of course. She's terribly afraid to get attached again. And there's a very nice young man, a Chinese fellow, who is mad about her . . ."

Both Cat and Linda had noticed how Duong Bao looked at Aroha. Linda was relieved that Aroha didn't return his affection. She was worried about the cultural gulf between Bao and the family. Cat didn't have any prejudice on that score, unlike Georgie, who didn't hesitate to repeat all the nonsense about Asians that he'd heard.

"Oh no, Miss Cat. The slant-eyes are sneaky, malicious, and stupid. They live on rice and rats!" he claimed.

Cat waved off his objections. "Slander and nonsense. Besides, Bao is the very image of the English public-school boy and more British than all of us put together. He could probably even beat you in rowing, Georgie. What do you bet he was the coxswain of his rowing team at Oxford?"

Georgie grumbled, while Robin brooded, staring out at the yellowish grass that covered the endless flat expanse of his homeland. There were farms here and there, with the occasional sheep nibbling listlessly at the winter grass. Robin felt none of the joy of homecoming.

Most of his trepidation concerned his father, although Chris would certainly not be hearing about his appearances as lewd women in primitive adaptations of Shakespeare. Aroha had been very discreet with his mother and Linda, and Cat would probably gloss over what little she knew. That's what she'd done with her acquaintances in Christchurch.

They'd spent a few days in the city to have a new wardrobe made for Robin. Naturally, they'd stayed at the Excelsior and had run into every sheep baron who happened to have business in town. Cat told them all about Robin's first successes as a Shakespearean actor and had left no doubt that his stay at the farm was only a sort of vacation before future theatrical engagements. Whether anyone believed her was another matter. Robin hadn't appeared terribly impressive in his worn-out suits. He was quite glad to be able to throw them away in the morning. The Christchurch tailor and his assistants had worked quickly, and he now had lovely new clothing in his luggage. On the trip to Rata Station, he wore denim trousers, a warm sweater, and a leather jacket. At least as far as appearance went, Robin knew he'd made a decent impression on Georgie, who'd surely assume Robin paid for the clothes himself. But Chris would learn that Cat had paid, and obviously he was aware of what the detective agency had uncovered about the Carrigan Company.

Robin sighed and prepared himself for an unpleasant meeting.

However, Chris Fenroy greeted his long-lost son with genuine pleasure. He was relieved to find Robin healthy, and even expressed admiration that the young man had stuck it out in the theater world for so long.

"You have no idea what a fright you gave us, leaving so suddenly like that!" he chided Robin. "You could have at least let us know that you had a job."

Robin seemed flustered, so Chris wisely dropped the subject. Instead, he asked about the eruption of Tarawera and the situation in the affected region. For Robin, the Rotorua catastrophe was almost a blessing. Whenever someone started asking embarrassing questions, Robin could always change the subject by explaining that his return to Rata Station was the result of Carrigan's death.

After a few days on the farm, Robin already felt restless. Everything was exactly as it had been before he left: the work with the sheep, cattle, and horses; even the fat barn cat who had once been his "Juliet" wound herself around his legs, meowing. It being winter, there was a lot of work to be done in the barn, and Chris, Cat, Carol, and Bill naturally expected Robin to do his part. But he had never been very skillful and now he was out of practice as well. It wasn't long until the farmhands started to make fun of him.

Once again, Robin wished that he could get away, but nothing had changed in Canterbury either. The few theaters didn't have regular ensembles but brought in well-known companies from Christchurch instead. In any case, they didn't need extra actors. Robin began to think again about going to England. Maybe his father would be prepared to send him now that he was older and had succeeded on his own for more than two years. Without Robin's knowledge, Cat actually broached the subject with Chris.

"Cat, the boy didn't succeed, he barely survived!" Chris countered. "Two weeks ago you had to rush off to bring him back unscathed, and you want to send him off to London on his own? To a big foreign city, with characters like this Carrigan lurking on every corner? I don't know, Cat. I just don't know."

Cat let the subject drop for the time being and waited for Robin to bring it up with his father himself. But before that could happen, an unexpected visitor arrived at Rata Station.

Now, in winter, the mail boat arrived at the farm around noon. After the morning's work in the barn and before the task of cooking for the family and workers, Cat and Carol used "waiting for the mail" as an excuse to sit in Carol's winter garden and chat while drinking coffee.

When Georgie's boat came into view, they put on their jackets and strolled, unhurried, to the pier. To their surprise, on this cool but dry July day, Georgie didn't just toss the mail out of the boat as usual, but moored it to let a passenger get off.

"A visitor for you!" he announced cheerfully and turned to a dignified old gentleman in a three-piece suit who was laboriously clambering out of the boat. "I'll pick you up later, Mister. Or tomorrow, whichever, depending on how things go for you here."

He tipped his hat and with strong strokes of the oar, guided the dinghy into the middle of the river.

Carol and Cat looked warily at each other. But the old gentleman didn't seem the least bit self-conscious. He pressed the pile of letters Georgie had given him into Carol's hand.

"Here," he noted. "Your mail. Reminds me of my childhood. Seventy years ago, I started out as an errand boy in my father's office."

Cat wondered if the comment was meant as a joke. The man didn't smile, though, as he scrutinized both the women and the property.

"Catherine . . . Cat Fenroy," she said shortly. "And this is my daughter Carol. How can we help you?"

The man wrinkled his brow at Carol, but held out his hand. "Walter Lacrosse," he said. "From Dunedin. My granddaughter Helena told me that you might be able to give me information about the whereabouts of my sister, Suzanne."

Carol stared at him in surprise, although of course Cat had told her about Helena Lacrosse. This changed some of the assumptions she'd held about the Lacrosses. It didn't matter what motive Helena might have had in bringing the family together: her claim that Suzanne's disappearance still pained her grand-father seemed to be proven true. Apparently, Walter Lacrosse had set out imme-diately after receiving Helena's letter.

Cat gazed searchingly at him, but could discern no family resemblance.

Lacrosse was already very old, his skin leathery and lined and his hair snow white; there was no way to know what the original color might have been. But his build was like Robin's. And his eyes were the same light blue as Suzanne's, except that Walter gazed into the world sharp as a tack, while Suzanne's gaze had always drifted about. Cat couldn't ever remember her mother looking directly into her eyes. Walter Lacrosse took in Cat's appearance without flinching. She shook his hand and returned his steady gaze.

"Your granddaughter Helena thinks that your lost sister was my mother," she said, correcting him. "If that is the case, I can only tell you that I left Suzanne when I was thirteen. At that time she worked at a whaling station in Piraki Bay. What happened to her after that, I don't know."

"What kind of work does a woman do at a whaling station?" Lacrosse asked abruptly, then caught himself, and returned to the distinctly formal tone he'd begun with. "But can it be true?" he asked. "Are you Suzanne's daughter?" He stepped closer to Cat and pulled a lorgnette out of his pocket. "Do you mind if I look at you more closely?"

Cat stood still and had to stop herself from smiling. Helena had struck her as unusually direct. Her grandfather had even fewer inhibitions.

"The chin could be right," he said. "Maybe the mouth. Your eyes and hair are different . . ." Cat was impressed by how sharp the old man's memory was. It was as if he had Suzanne's living face right before his eyes. "But you don't look anything like her," he said to Carol.

Carol smiled. "Mamaca isn't my birth mother," she explained.

"There's supposed to be a son . . ." Lacrosse said.

Cat nodded. "Your granddaughter noticed an unusual similarity between my son, Robin, and the portrait of your sister. But we really shouldn't discuss this out here on the pier. Please come in, Mr. Lacrosse, and have a cup of tea or coffee with us. You're also most welcome to stay for lunch. That way you'll surely meet Robin."

Walter Lacrosse pursed his lips. "I'd prefer to see the young man right away, if I might," he said. "I have no time to waste. If this all turns out to be nothing more than a fancy of my granddaughter's, then I'd like to catch the next boat back to Christchurch."

Cat nodded. "I understand. Georgie won't be back until afternoon, but we can find Robin. He must be with the horses."

As Cat and Carol arrived with Walter Lacrosse, Robin was sitting on the stallion, an impressive black animal with a strong neck, sweeping movements, and a decidedly rebellious spirit. Robin rode in wide circles and figure eights on the pasture to limber up the horse and get it comfortable with the reins. When he rode clockwise, all was well, but counterclockwise was another story. The young stallion tried every trick to get his rider to change direction, even feints and outright refusal.

So when Robin looked up briefly to greet the women and their visitor, the horse saw his chance. Instead of continuing to walk around the circuit to the left, at the open side of the ring, the horse abruptly switched direction. Robin stayed calm, rode one circuit to the right, and then made a figure eight and pressed hard with his calf to swing the horse back around to the left. He made his intentions even clearer with a flick of the riding crop. When the animal reacted angrily, Robin repeated the flick and let the horse speed to a gallop, but after a few ill-mannered leaps, he accepted his fate and galloped around the circuit. Robin slowed to a trot, repeated the exercise, then allowed the animal to chew the reins out of his hand to end the training.

"Were you looking for me?" he asked, stopping the horse in front of Cat and Carol.

Walter Lacrosse raised his lorgnette again. This time, when he let the glass fall, his eyes were shining.

"It's—it's amazing! The resemblance—my God, the boy is the spitting image of Suzanne! Not to say that you're feminine, lad." He turned to Robin, who grimaced. "For heaven's sake, no. Such a spirited rider! But the shape of the face, the hair, the eyes, the whole expression . . . and when you tell me that your mother's name really was Suzanne and that she brought you here from Australia . . ." These last words were directed to Cat.

"Mr. Lacrosse," she replied, "I've already told your future son-in-law. I can't offer you legal assurance, and I don't see myself in any way obligated to prove my relationship to your sister. Your granddaughter approached my son, not the other way around. If you still harbor any doubts about the relationship, you can take the next boat back to Christchurch and not bother us any longer."

"No, no," Walter Lacrosse softened. "I just thought that you could—that you might tell me more about Suzanne. Where she went after she left Sydney, what happened to her. She must have said something—about her family, and why she ran away. Was she—Is it possible she was pregnant?"

Cat shrugged. "You could do the math based on what year she left," she said. "Otherwise . . ." She wondered how to explain to the old man why she didn't know more.

"Why don't we all go back to the house," Carol said, coming to the rescue. "Robin, why don't you come along, too, when you're done with the horse. There's no reason to talk about all this out here in the cold."

Walter Lacrosse seemed reluctant to let Robin out of his sight. But he acquiesced, and while Carol went into the kitchen, he followed Cat into the sitting room of the stone house, the most presentable room that Rata Station had to offer.

"You don't have any servants?" he asked hesitantly, as Cat got him a cup of tea herself.

Cat shook her head. "No. Carol and I both prefer to care for our families ourselves. We're not used to household help, and our houses aren't so big that we can't manage on our own. We only bring in help when the sheep shearers come because then we have to cook for half an army."

While she spoke, Lacrosse looked around the house critically. "I'd imagined the houses of sheep barons would be more stately," he commented.

Cat laughed. "It depends," she said. "There are people like the Wardens and the Barringtons who've practically built themselves castles. But the sheep-breeding pioneers—the Deans, the Redwoods, and we, too, of course—started modestly and haven't seen any reason to change. We like it like this. We'll show you the farm later, so you don't think we're starving to death. We're not interested in your family's money, Mr. Lacrosse."

The old man nodded. "I didn't mean to insinuate that," he replied. "It's just that—well, Helena is very impulsive. She seemed so thrilled by her new cousin or second cousin. Harold, her fiancé, advised me to be cautious. Apparently, the two of them met your son under rather questionable circumstances. He . . . was traveling around with a group of actors?"

Cat suppressed a grimace. "Robin is a Shakespearean actor. According to popular opinion, a rather talented one."

Lacrosse smiled, suddenly almost tender. "Suzanne also had an artistic streak. Of course, she played piano, and she sang beautifully. And painted. She painted enchanting watercolors. My father threw them all out when she ran away. He was deeply offended. He almost destroyed her portrait as well, even though it was by a very well-known painter and was worth quite a bit. In the end, he hid it away and then took it with him to New Zealand."

Cat wondered if Suzanne really had been more musical than her grandson or whether Lacrosse was romanticizing things. Before she could inquire further, the house came to life. Robin had tended to his horse and managed to change his clothes. Chris and Bill arrived for the midday meal in their work clothes, and Carol's girls, both of whom attended high school in Christchurch, were bustling about noisily. Cat introduced their guest and directed him to a seat at the long table.

"Unfortunately, we only have mutton stew," Carol apologized, while not actually sounding at all contrite. "I hope you like it. If you'd let us know you were coming, we could have made something nicer . . ."

"What brings you here, Mr. Lacrosse?" Bill asked.

While Lacrosse, assisted by Robin, told the story once again for Carol's husband and children, Cat had time to get her memories of Suzanne in order and tidy them up for the ears of her loving brother. When she sat with her uncle over coffee, Cat explained that she only vaguely recalled her time in Australia.

"And you have no memories of your father at all?" Walter asked.

Cat shook her head. "I have nothing more than . . . the silhouette of a man . . ." It would have been more accurate to say "of men," since the comings and goings of Suzanne's suitors were among Cat's earliest memories. "And I think my mother was running away from something when we left Sydney . . ." There was no question that Barker, Suzanne's pimp, was running away from something, and Cat had vague memories of a bar brawl. "Suzanne came to Piraki Bay with me and two girlfriends. One of them, Priscilla, was traveling with her husband, who was a kind of . . . protector to us."

"How endearing," Walter remarked.

Chris, who was sitting across from Cat, could barely suppress a grin. Suzanne's "girlfriends" were two other prostitutes, one of whom had something approaching a relationship with her pimp. In Piraki, Barker had protected the three "fillies" because they were his source of income. He'd set them up in an improvised pub and was just waiting until Cat could also be put "into service." It was only when he'd set a date to auction her virginity to the highest bidder that she'd fled.

"Unfortunately, my mother was not well, and she wasn't able to look after me. At first, I was employed as a . . . companion to an elderly lady." In fact, Cat had done a little housework for the wife of a whaler who was kind to her. "But unfortunately, she died, and the . . . restaurant where Suzanne worked didn't need any more waitresses. So I went with a—a traveling salesman to Nelson to take a position there."

Chris wondered how she was going to work her years with the Maori into the story and decided to save her by inviting Lacrosse to take a walk around the farm.

"Have a little look around Rata Station before it gets dark," he prompted the old man. "At least the area right around the house. We actually have over a hundred acres of pasture. Oh, and by the way, Cat didn't come to the farm as my wife, but as a partner with her own stock of first-class sheep. We'll have to tell you more about that later."

He stood up, and Lacrosse followed. "Impressive!" he said, praising Cat. "Everything you've told me. You really pulled yourself up by your bootstraps. I'm sorry Suzanne wasn't any great help to you."

Cat shrugged. "She gave me the gift of life," she said. "My foster mother, Te Ronga, taught me that that was the greatest gift she could have given me, no matter what happened later. I learned to respect her for that. And there wasn't anything she could do about it," she added quickly. "As I told you . . . she was ill."

Walter Lacrosse put his hand on her shoulder before he went out with Chris. A comforting gesture.


"My conscience is bothering me," Cat admitted to Carol, who was doing the dishes in the kitchen. "I made Suzanne sound like a saint. But she was a shell of a human who didn't even say a word when they wanted to sell her own child." She reached for the dish towel. "And in a minute, I'll be saying she died of a broken heart . . ."

"Didn't she?" Carol asked softly. "There must have been a reason she was so far gone. Maybe Helena is right. Maybe it was a love story. Suzanne ran away with her beau, and then he left or betrayed her."

"Or sold her to a pimp," Cat said. "And she didn't have the strength to resist. It's true, I shouldn't be angry with her. Maybe she was just too . . . fragile." She rubbed her forehead. Then she reluctantly added: "Like Robin."


Chris and Bill enjoyed making such an impression on Walter Lacrosse. They led him through the stalls where well-tended horses and splendid stud bulls stood. The cattle lived in large, open stalls and sheds. The sheep crowded into broad pens.

"There are more than eight thousand of them," Chris explained proudly.

Bill enthusiastically showed off the new farm machines and the three shearing pens.

"This is where we shear the wool off the sheep for you to spin later," he explained. "Or do you mostly process cotton? You'd have to import that, right? Our wool meets the strictest guidelines. And we offer fleeces of very consistent quality."

Bill seemed genuinely unhappy when one of the herdsmen called him away, and Chris had to end the tour. They looked out over a couple of large fields where several hundred sheep stood, ready for sale—last year's lambs. Chris frowned as he noticed a few animals on a pasture that was still quite green, right next to the winter stalls.

"They don't belong there," he muttered and called to a farmhand who was working on a fence. "Potter? What are the little rams doing in the south pasture? I wanted to keep it for the ewes that'll lamb first in the spring."

The man sauntered over to his boss and, noticing Lacrosse, greeted him with a hasty tip of his cap. "Oh, didn't know that, boss," he said. "I thought the ram lambs looked a bit puny. I don't much like the look of their wool either. A little green can work wonders. That's why I drove them out there."

Chris nodded. "All right, then," he said calmly. "Let the critters eat the grass. We'll save the north pasture for the ewes. But you'll need to put some manure there."

"Sure thing, boss." Potter headed back to his fence.

Lacrosse walked silently next to Chris for a few steps, until the worker was out of earshot. "Brazen fellow," he growled. "Takes advantage, doesn't apologize, and can't even say a proper hello. I'd have given him a piece of my mind, Fenroy! I'd like to see someone try that in one of my businesses."

Chris smiled. "Maybe our herdsmen are made of different stuff than your factory workers. We depend on their loyalty and ability to work independently. There's nothing to be gained by lording it over them. Potter is a reliable worker, and he knows his way around sheep. Driving the rams out to pasture wasn't a bad idea; he just should have run it by me and Bill first. Getting annoyed over it won't make the grass grow back any faster."

Lacrosse didn't answer, and the atmosphere between the two men remained tense.

"A hard man, if you ask me," Chris told Cat. "I feel bad for the people in his factories. It must be no laughing matter for them."

Not for his children and grandchildren either, thought Cat. And he must have been put through the school of hard knocks by his own father. The same school that might very well have broken Suzanne.

Walter Lacrosse took the boat late that afternoon, but not without inviting Robin to Dunedin.

"I'm already looking forward to showing you the businesses, lad!" he said cheerfully. "Excited to hear what you have to say about it. I really like you, Robin. And your mother. I have to respect how far she's come, given how little Suzanne did for her. Suzanne was . . . wonderful, but a little too . . . well, indulgent, like your father, Chris." The old man smiled conspiratorially at Robin. Robin returned the smile with irritation. "Luckily, you're of a different stamp altogether," Lacrosse added. "Impressed me tremendously, the way you put that horse in its place."

"What?" asked Robin. He had long since forgotten the little skirmish with the stallion.

Lacrosse nodded. "Modest too. A very noble trait—although not always helpful in the business world. You mustn't hide your light under a bushel, lad. Ah well, we'll get there. But come to your great-uncle. Can I give you a hug?"

Robin was mortified when Walter Lacrosse drew him into a bear hug that smelled of tobacco.

"Are you really happy here?" the old man asked, before finally turning away.

Robin shook his head. "No," he said honestly, "I . . ."

Lacrosse didn't let him finish. "Thought not," he interrupted. "But don't worry, lad. We'll find something for you!"

# Chapter 39

"Call me Margery, please," March told Georgie. He had just greeted her as she boarded his boat. "I've changed my name. March sounds so odd. Nobody would hire a woman with a name like that."

"Who's going to be hiring you, March?" Georgie asked. "Oh, right . . . Margery. Or should I say 'Miss Jensch'?"

Her slim-fitted, elegant suit was as suitable for a trip as for a day at the office, and combined with a small, practical hat in dark blue, it made March look distinguished enough to be spoken to like a proper grown-up. The young lady had obviously taken pains to look older.

"It doesn't matter, really," she replied.

Georgie held his peace while March nursed her thoughts. She watched as the winter plains along the bank slid by, trying not to feel like a failure. Martin Porter had left her. True, it hadn't come as a real surprise, and if she was honest, her ardor for the former teacher had long since cooled. She knew that he was seeing Hillary Magiel, the daughter of a manufacturer from Otago. She knew he wasn't particularly enamored of the girl, a fact that had become apparent when he informed her of his engagement. "Maximum profit, my dear," he'd said. "You must see that! You're a dream, March, but I have to think of my future. Hillary comes with a house in the city and several manufacturing concerns, capable of development if you've got the know-how. You, on the other hand, would bring a few hundred sheep to the marriage. And the farm doesn't even really belong to your parents, does it? Isn't it a sort of . . . cooperative? And then there are all the Maori. No, my dear, it was a wonderful time, but nothing lasts forever . . ."

March had seen the whole thing just as soberly as Martin, and would have sincerely wished him well if he hadn't also betrayed her in business.

March wiped her eyes and told herself it was just the wind making them water. Girls cried, not businesswomen. If she gave in now, she'd only be proving that the mill owners in Kaiapoi who'd fired her the day before were right. Their smiles weren't even cold; no, they'd laughed as they'd done it.

Martin had promised to talk to the owners. The manager position was finally vacant, now that the old manager had moved up to take Martin's vacated director position. And no one would be able to fill the manager role better than Martin's assistant of many years. "You're still very young, of course," Martin admitted. "It's entirely possible they'll pick a male figurehead over you. There are always family members without a lick of business sense that need a job with a respectable-sounding title. You should be prepared for that. Otherwise, let me handle them. I'll take care of it for you."

After this promise, Martin Porter had gone away, and March hadn't harbored any suspicions but had taken over the de facto management of the factory as a matter of course. She'd set up the work plans, scheduled shifts, optimized procedures, negotiated with suppliers and buyers, maintained the earnings books, and reprimanded the workers when they produced too much waste. With the help of new machines and skillful organization, production had increased one hundred and fifty percent. The company owed all of the recent innovations to the tireless efforts of Margery Jensch.

So March was in a good mood when, not long after Martin's departure, she was called to a meeting. The representative of the Woolen Manufacturing Company had ensconced himself in Martin's old office. And apparently the factory's shareholders knew nothing at all about the true role March had played over the years. In truth, her salary as assistant to the company's director wasn't any higher than that of a clerk. Martin had always explained that such a position hadn't really been accounted for, and she'd resigned herself to it, since she was there to learn something. Today she could have slapped herself for that! She should have insisted on a proper title and on being paid what she was worth.

March let her thoughts drift back to the terrible conversation that had plunged her from one horror into the next.

"To be honest, I thought March was a nickname for Marshall," admitted a shareholder who'd never actually been there before.

Other shareholders had assumed that their director merely employed her as a secretary.

"And such a pretty one, at that!" one of them commented, winking. March's beauty had become a hindrance to her. Even shareholders who'd deigned to appear in the factory hadn't noticed her work but only her pretty face. "You can't blame Mr. Porter," continued the man jovially. "He let himself get distracted. His work was outstanding, so we can overlook his little indiscretion."

March, who by this time was realizing where the conversation was headed, glared at the man furiously.

"Are you implying that I was his lover? That he only hired me because—because we were involved?"

The answer came with a smirk. "So, you didn't have anything going on with him, girl?"

March blushed furiously. Of course, she had never exchanged so much as an endearment with Martin in the factory. But they had smiled at each other and called each other by their Christian names—another mistake.

"Let's set aside the gossip," the chairman of the small gathering said, "and get to the point: You wish to remain employed here, Miss Jensch. What can you do? I mean, do you just take dictation, or can you perhaps also write a letter on your own? Maybe even a little bookkeeping? I suppose you're overqualified to work in production?"

March stared at the man, speechless. She couldn't believe that he was actually considering demoting her to a factory worker. She gathered her wits and began to list her qualifications. She explained her business studies and the fact that, were she in Edinburgh, she would have long since had her degree—something Mr. Porter had assured her of many times.

"Unfortunately, they don't accept women at the university there," she explained, and described in great detail what her work at the factory had consisted of over the previous years.

The men listened, first politely, then with obvious boredom, until one finally interrupted her. "It sounds as though you want to run the factory yourself, young lady."

March assured them that that was indeed what she envisioned. The laughter that followed this declaration still haunted her. In the debate that followed, it became clear that Martin had not lifted a finger to recommend March for any sort of leadership position in the mill.

At some point, March had understood that there was nothing she could say in her defense that would sway them. She could not prove that her understanding of business was in no way inferior to Martin Porter's, and she knew that, even if she were able to find someone to verify her managerial accomplishments, the men would downplay her role. In any case, not a single one of the male office workers or supervisors would be willing to admit that, for the last three years, they'd taken orders from a teenage girl.

In the end, the shareholders condescended to offer her a position as a clerk. "But don't you try to convince the new director of your qualities," the chairman added, waggling his finger at March. "He's a family man with three children. I don't want to hear anything about an office affair!"

Fuming, March had resigned on the spot, and now she was on her way to Maori Station. She was richer in experience and knowledge—but without a husband and without a job.

She was relieved that, when the boat stopped at Rata Station, none of the Fenroys or Paxtons were around, nor was there any mail for the farm. That way, March didn't have to answer questions about Porter and the factory before she went home. There, of course, she wouldn't be able to creep away unseen.

And in fact, as soon as she set foot in the Ngai Tahu *marae*, people crowded around her—but without asking uncomfortable questions. No one here cared about March's work in Kaiapoi or whether or not she was married. The people were just happy to welcome her back. Usually, March found all the *hongi* and hugs irritating, but today she took a certain comfort in them. Her girlfriends chatted with her eagerly, showing genuine pleasure in seeing her again, rather than the feigned solicitousness that her acquaintances in Kaiapoi had shown her.

Of course Jane and Te Haitara were there, and no doubt Jane suspected that there was more to her granddaughter's unexpected homecoming than a visit, but for now, she simply embraced the girl.

Mara, March's mother, greeted her daughter lovingly. At the festive welcome meal that evening, she sat March next to her so they could chat. But the conversation was stiff; mother and daughter had never had much to say to one another. Mara merely listened politely to March's summary of events.

"I never felt that Martin Porter was right for you," she noted, without commenting further on the offensive treatment March had suffered from her former employer—something March herself saw as a much bigger problem.

Then Mara launched into an account of her own activities, as if it would comfort her daughter to know what fulfillment she found in playing the flute, in instrument building, and in working with researchers and musicians on the subject of Maori music. But Mara's successes held no interest at all for March. So she also just listened, and was glad when the musicians called Mara over to play.

"We're playing for you! A special *haka!*" Mara explained warmly.

March recognized the melody, and her adoptive father, Eru, smiled. For many years, it had been Mara and Eru's secret code, before anyone could know of their love. They had always managed to trick Jane with it. She'd thought the melody was a bird call . . .

It probably would have been the same for March.

Only after the party was over did the young woman pour out her heart. Jane invited her to sleep in the house she shared with the chieftain.

"All right, tell me what's wrong," she said grimly. "Let me guess. Without Mr. Porter's protection, they immediately demoted you."

March could do nothing but break into tears. Jane, who wasn't very good at comforting people, remained sitting next to her and waited until she had calmed down. She remembered similar situations from her own youth only too well. Her father had started out by allowing her to help with his correspondence. It was a matter of pure convenience for him to ignore the fact that she was taking on more and more tasks and managing them to everyone's satisfaction. But when she had become too independent, and let him know that she knew more about immigration policies than he and the whole New Zealand Company together, he'd relieved her of her position just as quickly, with words as harsh as March had just experienced. So she was outraged but not surprised when March tearfully recounted her "job interview."

"It's still a curse to be a woman," Jane said sympathetically. "It may be decades until men really acknowledge our equality—not to mention that we can't vote, so we can't have any say in the laws that affect us."

"What should I do?" sobbed March. "Should I apply to other companies?"

Jane sighed. "Child, you don't even have any references to show. Even if Porter were to write you one, and even if a company bothered to interview you, they'd conclude quickly enough that he'd done it for . . . reasons that had little to do with business."

"Is it such a sin to be good-looking?" March asked, with more than a hint of resentment.

Jane shrugged, and looked away.

"Just stay here for a while and help me with managing the farm," she said finally. "We can review the investments I've made over the years. Maybe I have enough influence with one of these companies to strengthen your application. Otherwise you'll have to think about studying something other than business. Did I tell you that Peta has settled on law? A good choice, in my opinion. If he specializes in all the subtleties of land seizure, he'll earn a fortune."

More and more Maori tribes were starting to grasp the extent to which the whites had cheated them. They'd surely rather entrust their cases to an attorney who was at least part Maori.

March nodded, even though she didn't believe for a second that her brother would specialize in land-seizure law. Peta surely envisioned himself as a lawyer for labor rights, fighting for better wages or shorter hours for factory workers. March found such justice seekers more than irritating, and Jane would be horrified if she knew. But there was no reason to trouble her grandmother with that now. It would be many years before Peta could make himself a proper thorn in the sides of New Zealand's businessmen.

March calmed herself with the thought that, in the worst-case scenario, she could start studying law herself. She didn't see herself as an attorney, but people would have to take her seriously if she specialized in business law. She didn't know of any other jurists who'd done that so far. Martin had always been annoyed when he'd had to brief company lawyers on the facts of some case. Maybe the businesses would work with a woman if no man was properly qualified to do the job.

However, it was winter and the semester had already begun, so there was nothing left for March to do but help Jane run the sheep farm. The young woman quickly determined that nothing had changed at Maori Station. It was the same animals, the same work, the same problems. With her newly won organizational knowledge, March threw herself into analyzing production conditions, but she soon realized that "optimizing labor processes" and "employing Maori livestock herders" were not mutually compatible. Jane listened to her remarks, but she often just brushed them aside.

"I know, Margery." Jane was the only person who readily accepted March's name change. "We don't need three people to round up the sheep. One and a herd dog would be enough. But the problem is that those collies don't pay attention. No one bothers to train them like Carol does at Rata Station. They rely on their natural herding instinct, but that means that the dogs mostly just run around barking. And then someone has to be there to appease the gods, because when the sheep want to eat grass in the new field, there might be a couple of spirits sitting on the roots . . . and the third goes along because he hasn't got anything better to do. He can always muck out the stalls tomorrow. It's really nonsense to let the pasture be grazed now; we should be saving it for the ewes that lamb early in the spring. But we can't do that because the fences in the lamb's corral haven't been repaired yet, and if we don't put them in that pasture, they'll break out of the pen. Which doesn't bother anyone because, 'well, they'll come back in the evening, won't they?' And if I point out that they'll trample the pastureland all day and the people at Rata Station will complain because the sheep are wandering onto their land, they say, 'well, we'll just cross that bridge when we come to it.'"

"Why haven't the fences been repaired?" March asked. "Maybe we could start there?"

Jane rolled her eyes. "I sent two men to Christchurch to buy the materials. But Cotton's warehouse had just gotten in new angling gear and hunting rifles. The men bought themselves one each and two for their friends."

"What?" March had grown up at Maori Station, but Jane had never explained the day-to-day running of the place in such detail. "They spent the fence money on rifles? What did Te Haitara have to say about that?"

Jane shrugged. "Nothing. He got one himself and thought it was a very good investment. The plague of rabbits, you know . . ." Rabbits were proliferating uncontrollably on South Island. "Other than me, everyone was excited. The men got their new toys, and the women got rabbits for the stew pot," Jane said with a sigh. "No one gave a second thought to the fences."

March shook her head. "But surely Te Haitara must understand that—"

"Te Haitara sees it as his sacred duty to make his people happy," Jane said. "The people get what they want, and very few want money. Bookkeeping at Maori Station is hellishly complicated because we don't pay actual salaries. Whatever they need, we pay for or provide for them. Most of them don't want to drive or walk to Christchurch to go shopping. They prefer to buy from the traveling salesmen or mail-order catalogs. And they're not greedy. The bottom line is that we have considerably lower payroll costs than, say, Rata Station. If the young men want new guns, well, then, they should get them. It's just frustrating that they don't think things through. Cotton's would have given us credit, no question, and then the men could have bought the building materials as well. Instead, they're making a second trip to buy wire, and we can only pray, or beseech the spirits or what have you, that this time there aren't any newfangled tents or fishing gear that they think are more pressing . . ."

Jane had long since come to terms with the labor situation at Maori Station. Years ago, her ambition had almost destroyed her marriage, and had almost cost her son, Eru, his life and freedom as well. Since then, she'd known her limits.

But March couldn't accept that. She tried to interfere everywhere, and ended up offending people. Finally, both Te Haitara and her mother, Mara, had to have serious talks with her.

"It's all about *tikanga*," March complained later to Robin. "Customs and traditions and spirituality and God knows what else. But they finally got to the point and told me, politely, to stay out of the running of the farm. I was allowed to do the bookkeeping; they didn't want to deal with all the paperwork, anyway."

"What are you going to do now?" Robin asked.

March shrugged. "Shoot rabbits," she said resentfully. "Te Haitara has a marvelous new hunting rifle. I've finally made myself really useful. A tribal elder praised me yesterday for delivering a roast to her."

Robin sighed. "I can't even shoot," he admitted. "I'd never bag them, probably because I feel bad for the rabbits. I'm not cut out for anything at all on a farm. I belong in a theater."

"And I belong in an office," March muttered. "Maybe I should just ask around in Dunedin. Grandma Jane still has two inquiries outstanding . . ."

Unfortunately, Jane didn't own enough stock in any given company that she could have an influence on personnel decisions. Most of the companies had made themselves very clear: If Jane recommended a young man, they would certainly consider it. But a woman in management was an impossibility.

*Maybe now I actually know someone with influence*, Robin thought. *After all, Mr. Lacrosse said he'd find something for me, and there are a few theaters in*

*Dunedin.* Then he told March the strange story of his supposed great-uncle who'd visited a few days earlier at Rata Station.

"Honestly, I thought Helena might be a little confused," he admitted. "Long-lost relatives, family secrets—that's something out of a novel or a play. But Mr. Lacrosse said there could be no doubt about it. He said I looked just like Suzanne. And the pieces do fit together."

March laughed. "Is he at least rich, this Uncle Walter of yours?" she asked. "What does he do?"

Robin shrugged. "I think he has a woolen mill or something in Dunedin."

March screwed up her pretty face with envy. "An uncle with a woolen mill— that's what I need! Maybe he has a job for me."

Robin smiled. "He'd probably just want to marry you. You—you do look especially nice today. The next time a theater company comes to Christchurch, would you—like to go see a show with me?"

Since seeing her again, Robin's infatuation with March had flamed up once more. Even so, he didn't harbor any hopes that she'd bestow her favors on him. Surely there was another Martin Porter waiting in the wings—this time perhaps with his own factory. Robin was just happy that she'd let him sit with her. She wasn't really interested in his tales of the theater and the strange story of his family. Maybe it was just that there was no one else to talk to. Or be silent with.

March didn't respond to his halfhearted request for a date. Like him, she stared at the river, wallowing in gloomy thoughts. The two of them sat on a boulder in the rata thicket along the Waimakariri. The river boat passed their hiding place. It wasn't on its normal schedule, and that usually meant a telegram for someone who lived upstream.

*Hopefully, it's good news,* Robin thought, without really believing it. When did telegrams ever bring good fortune?

# Chapter 40

"Robin, where on earth were you?" Cat asked her son when he came home a good hour later. Both she and Carol were buzzing with excitement. Cat had already cleaned out a suitcase. "I almost sent someone over to Maori Station," she continued. "But then I thought, not everyone needs to know about this yet. And there's no need to start before tomorrow morning if we take the afternoon train. That's why I sent Georgie off."

"Train?" Robin asked, confused. "Are you going away? Am I?" The darker of his two new suits was hanging on the wardrobe, ready to be packed. Suddenly he was seized by joyful excitement. "An engagement?" he asked excitedly. "Did a theater company write? Did Mr. Lacrosse manage something? It all happened so—so quickly!"

"Things can always happen quickly in life," Cat said seriously, setting down the black dress she had decided to take along. "And in death. Robin, we received a telegram. You and I. Walter Lacrosse, who apparently really was our relative, has died suddenly."

"What?" Robin sank into a chair. "That can't be! He was so animated. He didn't even look ill."

"It was a stroke," Cat said. "Or so they think. In any case, it was completely unexpected. He's the only one who seems to have been prepared for the possibility."

Robin frowned. "What do you mean? Did he . . . leave behind a letter?"

Cat shook her head. "He must have changed his will after he was here. That's what the telegram was about. We are supposed to go to the funeral and to the reading of his will. The funeral is the day after tomorrow, so we have to hurry.

Someone will row us down to Christchurch first thing in the morning, and we'll take the next train to Dunedin."

Robin's head spun. Mr. Lacrosse had been nice to him, and he was sorry about his death, but he didn't know the man. Maybe if he had actually visited him in Dunedin, he would have felt something, but as it was, it seemed unjust that he might profit from the old man's death.

"I feel the same way," Cat said as he confessed his feelings the next day. Robin sat in the boat with his parents. His father rowed them both to Christchurch himself.

"Just wait until you actually know what you've inherited," Chris said calmly. "It might be nothing more than Grandma Suzanne's portrait. You can start thinking about where to hang it."

Cat had telegrammed Helena Lacrosse about their arrival, and the family sent a coach to the train station. To Robin's surprise, it was a cream-colored covered landau, although hung with black cloths. The coachman wore black livery, and the horses, a gorgeous team of grays, were also arrayed in black trappings.

"Mr. and Mrs. Fenroy?" The coachman bowed, and a servant whisked away Cat's and Robin's bags. He then opened the coach door for them. The seats were covered in dark-red velvet.

"My goodness," murmured Cat. "I've never ridden in such a magnificent coach."

"Mister . . . I mean, Uncle Walter must have been rich," Robin observed.

Cat smiled. "Well, he didn't make any bones about that. But such finery! I'm excited to see what the house is like."

The Lacrosse house was in Mornington, one of the finest quarters of Dunedin, a good mile from the city center. All of the homes on Glenpark Avenue were large and imposing, but Cat and Robin still gasped when the coach finally stopped. In the wan winter sun stood a three-story building with little towers and bay windows, surrounded by a small park. It had an impressive drive and steps leading to the entrance.

The entrance was well attended. As Cat and Robin stepped out of the coach, a butler opened the door, which was hung with black ribbons. The man greeted them stiffly and led them through a small parlor into a huge foyer dominated by a grand staircase. The curved railings were ornamented with carvings, as were the massive furnishings. Someone must have spent hours hanging black mourning ribbons on the cabinets and sideboards.

Before Cat could look around more carefully, she saw Helena Lacrosse coming down the stairs. The young woman was wearing a voluminous black dress and a black bonnet. She stumbled toward Cat and Robin and flung her arms around their necks.

They returned her embrace awkwardly. Cat found the scene uncalled for, but Helena seemed determined to leave no doubt in anyone's mind just how much she mourned her grandfather. Harold Wentworth stood on the first-floor landing and looked down on the new arrivals with an inscrutable expression. Then, very slowly, he followed his fiancée.

"He passed so suddenly, we—we were completely shocked," Helena spluttered, "but he—that is, Harold said that he'd just spoken with him and then . . ."

"He had just spoken with one of the foremen," Harold explained. "In fact, he'd given him a dressing-down. I've let the man go, of course. If he hadn't forgotten to oil that machine, Mr. Lacrosse . . ."

"Mr. Lacrosse would have had the same thing happen after the next little upset," Cat said. "I don't see how the foreman should be blamed . . ."

Disinterested in this exchange, Helena pulled Robin and Cat into a wing of the entrance hall.

"Here, here. You see?"

Confused and slightly embarrassed, Robin gazed at the portrait that hung over a massive sideboard.

Cat gasped when she saw it. There was no doubt: it was her mother, Suzanne. She clearly remembered the unusually fine, silky hair that curled like an angel's. Noni, one of the other prostitutes, had often tried to untangle it when Barker decided "his" women should clean themselves up a bit. Cat's own hair was darker, but Robin had inherited Suzanne's coloring and hair. Fascinated, she gazed at her mother's tender fairy face. It was clearer than she remembered, not yet bloated with too much drink. But what made the greatest impression were the pale-blue eyes. They didn't stare dully into nothingness, as if dead, but shone warm and kind. Her expression reminded Cat of Robin too. She herself had never looked out into the world with such a soft and trusting look. In the picture, Suzanne wore a light-blue lace dress, and her tender white hands toyed with a book.

"Do you recognize her?" Helena asked excitedly.

Robin frowned. "I never met her. But . . ."

What Helena had said in Te Wairoa was right. When he played Juliet or Miranda, he looked just like the woman in the picture.

"Yes," Cat answered quietly. "That's her. That is definitely my mother. I—well, until now, I didn't really believe it, but this picture removes any doubts. I even recognize the dress she's wearing there." She vaguely recalled the lace and flounces, long since faded and stiff with dirt. Every once in a while, Noni had made Suzanne change and wash her clothes, and only then would she put it on. It had been her favorite dress. All those years. "She took it along with her, didn't she?"

Helena nodded devoutly. "It's so wonderful that we've found each other!" she said. "And that grandfather lived long enough to see it."

"Yes, one could say you've had two strokes of luck," Wentworth said archly. "Not only did the old man swallow your tales, but he changed his will on top of it. Walter Lacrosse was always quick on the draw; he did that at least three times a year. If he had got to know you better, he might have changed his mind again. So three strokes of luck, you might say."

Cat started to object, but Helena cut her fiancé off. "Be quiet, Harold! What kind of behavior is that! You know that Aunt Catherine and Cousin Robin didn't tell any tales at all. I'm the one who recognized Robin. If you don't like the fact that they're here, then you should scold me, not them." Helena's attitude toward Harold Wentworth seemed changed, and she certainly didn't seem to begrudge Robin and Cat their part of the inheritance. After she had put Harold in his place, she recalled her responsibilities as a hostess. "You must be tired after your journey," she said. "Grandpa said you live in quite an out-of-the-way place, so you must have had to get up early to take the train today. That was kind of you. My sister and her husband can't come, as it would take more than a week to travel here from Sydney. So I would have been all alone at the funeral . . ."

Harold Wentworth apparently didn't count. Cat felt confirmed in her suspicion that Helena was eager to be rid of the young man. Now, after the death of her grandfather, she saw a realistic chance of that.

"I'll see to it that you're taken to your rooms so you can rest. Dinner is at eight, informal, no evening dress required. It's just a snack, really. Although you're probably hungry now . . ." Helena seemed rather overwhelmed by the notion of managing the household. She turned uncertainly toward the butler, who was standing by the door, as motionless as a piece of furniture. "Could we . . . have something sent up for the both of them, Mr. Simmons?"

Cat quickly assured her that they could certainly hold out until dinner.

The butler bowed, his face perfectly expressionless. "A fruit basket and a bite to eat will be sent up immediately, Miss Helena. Mrs. Livingston will attend to the dinner. You needn't worry yourself about anything."

Mrs. Livingston proved to be the housekeeper, commanding a horde of housemaids, kitchen maids, and a cook, just as the butler did with a similar army of footmen, valets, and workers.

Now, a housemaid led them upstairs. Robin was bewildered to find himself in a whole suite of rooms. Cat's rooms were somewhat smaller, but even so, offered more space than her entire house at Rata Station. A tray of cold meats and cheeses with fresh-baked bread arrived promptly.

"My bed is heavenly," Robin said, impressed, as they prepared to go down to dinner together shortly before eight.

Cat hoped that her brown tea gown would be sufficient. Other than her traveling outfit, her only other clothing was the black funeral dress. Robin wore his new gray three-piece suit.

"I thought I should dress formally, even if they said it didn't matter," he explained. "The servant thought so too. Mamaca, they actually sent someone to help me dress!"

Cat smiled. "A lady's maid came to me as well, but I sent her away." She looked quite indignant. "I've probably broken the rules of etiquette already."

Robin had made the correct choice. Harold Wentworth also wore a suit to dinner. Besides him, there were two older married couples in attendance, and the men even wore tailcoats. Apparently, no one had told them this was only supposed to be a simple family supper. Helena introduced them as friends of the family, and Cat wondered frantically how she could spruce up Robin's wardrobe for the next day. A tailcoat, or at the very least a deep-black suit, would be expected at the funeral. While she was wondering when exactly the funeral would take place, she noticed one of the men was sizing up her son and herself as well. It turned out that he was the solicitor who would be reading Lacrosse's will.

The "snack" was actually a four-course meal. Robin had to pay close attention so as not to mix up the various forks and knives. Helena carried the dinner conversation herself by recounting her wondrous meeting with him. The whole thing was embarrassing to Robin, as it came out that he'd belonged to a certain company of actors. Harold Wentworth even mentioned his female roles. At least neither he nor Helena offered their opinions on Vera's questionable interpretations of Shakespeare.

Of course, Walter Lacrosse's sudden death was the other main topic of conversation.

"At least Walter had his affairs in order," the solicitor said. "Others who pass away so suddenly . . ."

Cat was tempted to remind him that the old gentleman had been almost ninety, but restrained herself and instead apologetically excused herself from the table.

"We have had a tiring journey, and tomorrow we have sad duties to fulfill," she said formally. "I'm afraid I shall have to retire now."

Robin joined her with noticeable relief.

The next morning, Cat was awakened by a young woman who brought her tea and a light breakfast in bed, while a shy and very young girl in a dirty frock laid the fire. The uniformed maid asked politely when the lady wished to get up and if she might help her to dress.

"I'm a trained lady's maid, ma'am," she added, as if Cat had suggested that the woman might put her dress on backward.

. At that moment, it occurred to Cat that the young woman would know what kind of attire and behavior were expected at the funeral, and also perhaps how to get hold of suitable clothing, so she tried to be diplomatic. She wasn't used to servants, but farmhands sometimes needed to be handled with kid gloves so as not to offend their pride. Carefully she asked the maid's name and explained her problem.

"I live in the country, Jean, and we don't even wear corsets most of the time. No, don't look so shocked! Of course I brought one with me, and a black dress as well. I don't need any help putting it on, but that's exactly what's given me pause. Would it be too plain for the occasion? When I think about what Miss Helena was wearing yesterday . . ." Helena's mourning dress had fewer frills and flounces than her usual wardrobe, but her hoop skirt had still barely fit through the door. "And my son really has nothing at all suitable to wear."

Luckily, Jean wasn't at all slow on the uptake, and she immediately began working out a solution to the problem.

"The funeral is at eleven o'clock, madam," the maid informed her. "It wouldn't really be possible to arrange something before then. At least, you wouldn't be able to have new clothes tailored. However, Miss Helena bought herself a number of nice mourning dresses when her grandmother passed. That was perfectly appropriate, of course. She was in mourning for a long time." The last sentence came out in a rush. Perhaps there was talk among the servants about Helena's extravagant ways. "And you're very slender. If we lace your corset a bit tighter, one of her dresses might just fit. They're very plain things . . . ," she added before Cat could remark that a sixty-one-year-old woman would certainly need a different style of mourning clothes than a girl of twenty. "I'll speak to Miss Helena's lady's maid about it. And I'll ask Mr. Simmons about something for Mr. Robin."

The butler. Cat sighed. Robin would undoubtedly find it mortifying to have the male staff fussing over his wardrobe. But there was nothing else to do. Better to embarrass oneself with the staff than with Dunedin's high society.

When the carriage bearing Walter Lacrosse drove up to the church at a little before ten thirty, Cat knew she had done the right thing. Helena certainly would not have been alone at the funeral; at least two hundred people were in attendance. Whispering, they all sized up the Lacrosses' new family members as Cat and Robin followed Helena and Harold up to the front pew. Cat was wearing one of Helena's dresses and a black bonnet with a veil that would have been a credit to Queen Victoria herself. Mrs. Livingston had added a black ribbon from Helena's collection to make the effect even more elegant. Cat's appearance was entirely fitting, although the dress was indeed snug. Jean and Mrs. Livingston had laced her so tightly that she could barely breathe. Eating was out of the question, and she hoped that the funeral wouldn't be followed by a formal luncheon. Finding a suitable outfit for Robin had been more difficult, but the employees of the Lacrosse house knew their business. The young man who had offered his services to Robin as a valet the day before altered one of Walter Lacrosse's own suits at lightning speed and with all the skill of a professional tailor.

"It's the latest fashion," explained the butler. "It was bought for the funeral of a business friend of Mr. Lacrosse's only two months ago. He didn't give it away afterward, as is the custom. A bit improper, of course, but in this case, it's good luck."

So Walter Lacrosse was a miser, Cat thought, whereas those he left behind spared no trouble or expense to make his funeral as pompous as possible. A choir sang; the bishop preached; the congregation pronounced copious prayers. Cat mentally thanked Mrs. Livingston for the veil that hid the fact that she knew none of the prayers or hymns. Robin could only hide under his bangs. Wentworth didn't sing either. Helena was sobbing the whole time, along with the female members of the household staff, who were seated in a side wing of the church. While offering their condolences, all of the women made an effort to sob loudly. It seemed to be expected. The only dry eyes belonged to a few simply dressed people in the back.

"Workers from the factories," Wentworth explained when Cat asked about them. "The management was instructed to send a small delegation to express the workers' grief."

That explained their apathetic expressions. These people weren't here of their own free will. Cat was more moved by their enforced sadness than by the feigned tears of the high-society ladies. Did they care at all about the death of an old factory owner? Were they worried about what would happen to them after his death?

"We're driving to the cemetery now," Helena said, her face streaked with tears.

Six pallbearers carried the dead man outside, where a black coach with four black horses awaited the elaborate oak coffin. Behind it, another coach stood ready for the family. Behind that was a seemingly endless funeral procession. Bedecked with black ribbons, the coaches of every good family in Dunedin were lined up.

"Is it normal that no one's getting in?" Robin asked his mother.

Coachmen were steering empty landaus into the line, while the owners went home on foot or were picked up by other coaches.

"That is the custom," Wentworth explained, in a condescending tone. "The burial is only attended by the closest family. The other mourners show their respect for the deceased by participating in the procession with a cavalcade of empty coaches."

Cat found that odd but could only think about her corset. "Closest family" sounded good. That meant that there would be no formal luncheon after the burial.

And in fact, the actual burial proved rather prosaic. Cat didn't know Dunedin well, but she suspected that the coachman deliberately went the long way around so that the entire population of the city could witness the funeral procession. It did cause a sensation. Passersby paused, men took off their hats, and women bowed their heads. At the cemetery, the family circle consisted of Helena and Wentworth, the solicitor and his wife, Cat and Robin, and some of the household staff, who stood tactfully to the side.

Cat sighed as she finally returned to her room in the Lacrosse house. Helena had instructed them to mourn in silence until the evening's reception. She wasn't hungry, she'd said. Cat assumed that the others would find the same delicious snack in their rooms that she discovered in hers. Naturally, the room had been tidied and the bed made, as if by magic.

Cat wished that Jean would come to loosen her corset, but right after Cat rang for her, the maid announced the arrival of a saleswoman and salesman from the most famous—and, undoubtedly, the most expensive—shop in the city. The shop had a special department for mourning clothes, and Mr. Simmons had contacted them immediately after Cat's cry for help. Now the extremely tactful pair, themselves dressed in appropriately dark clothing, held an entire collection of men's and women's fashions in readiness for Cat and Robin. They introduced themselves in one of Robin's rooms, and within an hour Cat had purchased an evening dress and a black three-piece suit for her son. The prices were horrendous, but she consoled herself with the thought that Robin would have occasion to wear the suit again later. On the other hand, she couldn't imagine wearing the unbelievably expensive dress back in Canterbury Plains.

"And don't you dare bury me in it!" she threatened Robin after the salespeople had left. "I don't want to spend all of eternity wearing a corset!"

The evening reception was a stiff affair. Dozens of strangers expressed their sympathy to Cat and Robin, speeches were given, and a chamber ensemble played sad tunes.

Helena, still weeping, stood next to Wentworth.

Since she had nothing better to do, Cat listened, especially to what the guests had to say to Wentworth. As she had hoped, she gained insight into the role that Helena's intended had played—and continued to play—in the Lacrosse family's business concerns. It appeared that Wentworth already occupied an important position in the management, which he'd taken over entirely after Walter's death.

"We'll still be able to do business with you, I assume?" asked a distinguished gentleman, presumably a supplier.

Wentworth nodded confidently. "I certainly assume so, Mr. Bench. Of course we must wait for the reading of the will, but it was promised that I would take over the running of the company, in Helena's name. The marriage will take place in six months . . ."

"We'll have to delay it, of course," Helena interjected, almost forgetting to cry. "For at least a year."

That didn't seem to be to Wentworth's liking, but of course he couldn't contradict her.

"You're not expecting any surprises with the . . . new relations?" asked Mr. Bench, with a discreet glance at Robin, who was standing shyly to the side.

Wentworth shrugged. "I think not," he said. "The acquaintance was rather new. My . . . grandfather-in-law-to-be did mention that he was thinking about leaving the portrait of her mother to Mrs. Fenroy."

# Chapter 41

The day after the funeral was dedicated to rest, but it made Cat impatient. She was used to being busy around the clock, and just sitting around and being waited on got on her nerves. Robin managed it better. He had discovered his great-uncle's extensive library and immersed himself in a marvelous edition of Shakespeare's complete works.

"If Uncle Walter had left it to me . . . ," he murmured with feeling, upon which Helena promised to give him the volume as a gift, even if her grandfather hadn't thought of it.

"Do you expect to inherit the house and all the businesses and everything?" Cat asked the young woman, as Robin withdrew happily.

Helena nodded, but with little enthusiasm. "I will inherit everything that belongs to us in New Zealand," she specified. "Julia will get the Australian holdings. They should be about equal in terms of worth, but neither of us cares about that. The factories earn more money than we could ever spend."

Cat frowned. "Are you sure about that?" she asked. "To me, it looks like this all costs an awful lot. All the servants . . . I still haven't figured out how many there are."

Helena smiled. "I've never counted," she admitted. "But I know them all by name, so if you want, I can . . ."

"No, never mind." Cat waved the question aside. "No need to make a list of everyone on the payroll. I'm just worried you might not realize that those are tremendous costs, Helena, that have to be accounted for."

"Harold takes care of that," Helena said calmly.

"And is he actually qualified to do so?" Cat asked sternly. "You don't want to be standing there empty-handed someday!"

Cat knew it was none of her concern, but she had taken a liking to her carefree young niece. Wentworth, on the other hand, she didn't care for at all.

Helena smiled. "Well, that's what he was hired to do. And he had to prove himself for several years before Grandpa would allow him to ask for my hand in marriage. It was just the same with Paul . . ." She sighed. "Julia kept hoping he'd make a critical error . . ."

Here, Cat bit her tongue, knowing she might say more about Helena's marriage arrangements than she should.

The next day was the reading of the will, and Cat planned to leave right after, although Helena begged her to stay and keep her company for a while longer. It was obvious that the young woman was bored to death, all alone in the huge house. Cat gathered it had been that way since Julia left for Australia.

"I have things to do," she said, when Cat asked. "I pay visits. Of course, not during my mourning. And I—we collect donations for the church's relief efforts for the poor. We often go to charity concerts or dinners. And of course I go shopping, and I consult with Mrs. Livingston about the food and the flower arrangements when there's a reception . . ."

It had never occurred to her to pursue a career or to make herself useful in her grandfather's factories. However, she did admit that her sister had wished she could do so.

"Julia would have liked to direct the factory herself," she said with an indulgent smile. "Grandpa always teased her about that."

Cat didn't say anything, but she felt deep sympathy for young Julia. She was again wearing her new black dress and Robin his three-piece suit. The young man also had a top hat, which he nervously turned this way and that in his hands. He tried to avoid actually wearing it as much as possible. He didn't want to think about what the farmhands at Rata Station would say about such a dandyish getup.

"We can take you to the station right afterward," Wentworth suggested, as he helped Cat into the landau on the way to the appointment with the solicitor. "You can still catch the afternoon train."

During dinner the previous evening, Cat had mentioned her young relation March, who was excited about studying business and had worked in factory management in Kaiapoi. That had made Wentworth all the more eager to be rid of the Fenroys as soon as possible. He was even downright rude when Robin naively asked if there might be a position open for March in one of the Lacrosse factories. Women, according to Wentworth, couldn't handle the pressure that businessmen routinely endured, nor could they muster enough entrepreneurial vision to lead a company. Robin and Cat had stared at the man, leaving Helena scrambling to change the subject.

From her seat in the coach, Cat nodded calmly in reply. "Yes, the afternoon train will be best. I have a great deal to do at Rata Station. There's a lot of work with the sheep in the winter."

"With the sheep?" Helena asked as she arranged her ample black skirt on the seat cushions. "Do you really work with the sheep? As a woman?"

Cat tried to remain calm. She thought that Helena would have figured that out already.

"Sheep," she said, "can't tell the difference between men and women. They go where they're led. They don't care who's whistling at the dog."

Harold Wentworth offered her an indulgent smile. "But someone has to make it clear to the dogs what they're to do. And surely that calls for a strong masculine hand."

Cat returned his smile, but hers was sardonic.

"Our dogs," she replied, "are trained by my daughter, Carol. Even as a girl she won one contest after another with them. We sell the animals too. They are in great demand. And for what it's worth, a 'strong hand' doesn't work with herding dogs. It's better to respect their intelligence. There's a reason people say that dogs are smarter than most men . . ."

Robin tried to suppress a smile, and even Helena caught the subtle rebuke and bit back a giggle. The atmosphere in the coach grew icy, and Wentworth didn't say another word until the vehicle came to a halt at the solicitor's office.

The office was luxuriously decorated with soft carpets and heavy furnishings. A secretary asked them to be seated while they waited for Mr. Fortescue. In addition to the family, Mr. Simmons and Mrs. Livingston were present. The servants remained standing.

*My last will and testament . . .*

With a solemn voice, Mr. Fortescue read out what gratuities Walter Lacrosse had set aside for his domestic servants. Among other things, Mr. Simmons received the man's gold watch, and Mrs. Livingston a piece of jewelry that had belonged to his late wife. Both seemed disappointed. They had probably expected money.

Wentworth followed the provisions for the staff with little interest. He only began to pay attention when Cat's name was mentioned.

*"To my niece, Catherine Rata Fenroy, I leave the portrait of her mother, Suzanne Lacrosse, currently located in the entryway to my house in Dunedin. I assure Catherine of my highest esteem and regret greatly that I only met her late in life and so was unable to be of help to her during her often difficult life."*

Wentworth grinned nastily.

*"To my great-nieces, Julia Penn and Helena Lacrosse, I entrust the houses and companies belonging to our family in Australia."* Here the solicitor paused for a moment, but neither Helena nor Wentworth seemed to register the shift. *"Due to the current situation, I suggest that Mr. Paul Penn pay my great-niece Helena half the value of the house in which he and Julia live, as well as the proportional income of the factories listed below. If Helena should be married at the time of my demise, Mr. Penn and Mr. Wentworth will have to agree to a future division of the factories and real estate."*

Harold Wentworth's jaw dropped in confusion and his eyes widened. Helena looked around in surprise but did not appear disturbed. Robin waited calmly. He didn't seem to think anything of it at all.

*"My city house in Dunedin, along with all of the other real estate in Dunedin and the business concerns in New Zealand listed below, I leave to my only male descendant, my great-nephew, Robin Fenroy. To my great joy, in my old age I have met the grandson of my beloved sister, Suzanne, and although to date I have not been able to spend much time with him, I am sure that he will show himself worthy of the confidence I have placed in him."*

The solicitor looked up. "I can only ask: Young man, do you accept the inheritance?"

"I—I've inherited the house?" Robin asked, confused.

The solicitor nodded. "As well as a dressmakers' shop, a woolen mill . . . all told, four or five concerns over which you would preside. A great responsibility. Walter Lacrosse evidently thought highly of you."

"What about me?" interrupted Harold Wentworth. "I mean—and Helena? And—Julia? The relationship between their grandfather and Mr. Fenroy is by no means assured. Naturally, the old gentleman wished with all his heart to find out what had happened to his sister. And then, when a possible descendant popped up, he was literally out of his mind with happiness. That's what must have led to this. He was not in full possession of his faculties. The Lacrosse sisters will contest the will!"

"Nonsense!" Helena Lacrosse said, rising. "Of course my grandfather was in his right mind. Right up to the end—I'm sure of it—and I will tell my sister so myself. Robin is without a doubt Suzanne's grandson, and if my grandfather wanted him to inherit the factories in New Zealand, then he shall." She smiled at Robin. "Congratulations, Robin!" she said kindly. "You see, my grandfather did think of you. *The Complete Works of Shakespeare* belongs to you now."

Robin returned her smile. "That—that is very kind, Helena. I don't know what to say. I . . ."

He held out his hands to her. Moved, Helena clasped them.

"First of all, I need a yes or no," the solicitor pressed. "You accept the inheritance?"

"Of course he does," said Cat.

Robin nodded.


Cat and Robin did not take the afternoon train. They drove back to Mornington with Helena—Wentworth had disappeared without a word, even before the solicitor finished reading the will. Cat was the only one who listened carefully to the details, and consequently only she understood the real extent of her son's inheritance. It appeared to consist of a woolen mill, a textile factory, and two dressmakers' workshops. On the way back, she requested a detour to the telegraph office and informed Chris of the news.

*Robin inherited. Must examine the books. You'd better come*, she wrote.

Harold Wentworth would have smirked, since after all her fine words about feminine intelligence, she had had to call a man in. But Cat only learned to handle numbers late in life. Suzanne had never had a cent, and Linda Hempleman, the wife of the whaling-station operator, had only taught her to read the Bible. Then, growing up in a *marae*, there was little reason to add or multiply. Only when Cat came to Nelson and was earning her own money did she have to pay attention to income and expenses. Of course she'd mastered basic arithmetic, but the bookkeeping at Rata Station was Chris's responsibility. And that was surely child's play compared with the factory's books.

Before anything else happened, she'd have to take a look at the businesses.

Cat briefly entertained the thought of driving over to the mill with Robin that very afternoon, but she decided to wait until Harold Wentworth ate humble pie—and that happened soon enough. The young man paid a visit to Robin in the early evening.

"I don't know what came over me before," he said, apologizing sheepishly. "Of course I never would have actually advised Helena to contest the will. It is perfectly legal for you to inherit everything. Still . . . until you have gotten used to it all, you'll need a business manager. Since I'm engaged as such already and entrusted with all the procedures, I can be of help to you. That is, if you can forgive me my childish outburst this morning."

"You can at least show us around tomorrow," Cat suggested, before Robin could make any hasty promises.

She had caught sight of the dangerous gleam in Robin's eyes. He was ready to hand over the entire running of the businesses to Wentworth so he could retreat into the library. Lacrosse's collection even held the collected works of Molière, he'd told Cat enthusiastically.

"I'd be delighted to, Mrs. Fenroy!" Wentworth replied fawningly. "Shall I pick you and Mr. Robin up just before nine?"

Lacrosse's factories lay not far from the family home. Cat could hardly believe that fine Mornington and the dirty, overcrowded industrial area, popularly known as the Devil's Half Acre, belonged to the same parish. Helena, who had joined the outing out of sheer boredom, wrinkled her nose as the coach left the wide streets and turned down dark, narrow alleyways, hemmed in with ramshackle hovels and houses patched together from tin cans, scrap wood, and corrugated steel. The few larger streets led to the various factories whose chimneys fouled the air with stinking smoke.

"This quarter was originally a tent camp built by the Chinese," Wentworth explained, scowling at a row of bars, gambling dens, and even more infamous establishments. "They came through here on the way from the goldfields, and if they found work in the city, they stayed on."

"And now they work in your factories?" Cat asked, thinking of Duong Bao.

Wentworth shook his head. "Hardly. They're too lazy and too stupid. Most of them don't speak a word of English, and the other workers don't want to have a thing to do with them. If you ask me, most of the ones that are left are working in the red-light district. Forgive me, Helena, for mentioning such things in the presence of a young lady. Otherwise, they work in small laundries where the owners can't afford better help. They've long since become a minority in this neighborhood. These houses are occupied—and by the way, the official name of the area is St. Andrew's, like the church—by Irish, Scots, Scandinavians, Germans. They didn't amount to much in their home countries, and they haven't done any better in New Zealand. They're failures, in other words . . ." Robin winced. "You'll see, Mr. Robin," Wentworth said, turning to his new employer. "You have to keep an eye on them constantly, and explain the simplest procedures ten times over. They're thick-witted and indifferent. Completely incapable of independent work."

Cat bit her tongue. Robin might have to work with this man. It was useless to antagonize him further.

"Why are they called 'mills,' exactly?" Robin asked. "These woolen factories, I mean. Nothing is being ground, is it?"

Wentworth smiled. "Good question, Mr. Robin," he said in a flattering tone. "They're called that because the machines were originally powered by huge waterwheels, so the factories had to be built on rivers. Then they switched over to pumping water from a reservoir into steam engines, and we don't need the mill wheels anymore. But the name has stuck, and most of the factories are still on the water. It's quite useful, actually; we need a lot of water for production, especially if you consider the dye works . . ."

The Lacrosses' woolen mill was a low, gray building dominated by a gigantic smokestack. At nine o'clock in the morning, work was already long underway. In the courtyard, surrounded by a high stone wall, all was still, except for a horse-drawn carriage that stood by one of the loading ramps. Wentworth scowled at it.

"The first delivery should have been long gone!" he groused. "But that's the way it is: if you're not around for a few days, people start letting things slide. I'll be right back . . ."

"Won't you show us the factory first?" Cat asked.

She was startled when Wentworth opened the door to the shop floor. The noise was hellish and the air was stale and hot. The workers stood at their machines.

"They're all women!" Robin exclaimed. He had to shout for Wentworth to hear him.

"We prefer to work with women," Wentworth confirmed. "The work isn't hard."

"Not hard?" Cat asked.

She couldn't see exactly what the women and girls were doing at their machines, but they all appeared sweaty and weary. Some of them were crawling around underneath, which looked dangerous to boot.

"Follow me," Wentworth shouted, after the noise prevented him from answering their questions a third time.

"Physically, it's not hard," he explained, as he led Cat and a shocked Robin along a quiet corridor. "In the dressmakers' shops and at the sewing machines, we employ women exclusively. Most of them only stay from the time they finish school until they get married, then they're done." He laughed. "A manufacturer from Lyon supposedly said that he only employs girls between sixteen and eighteen. At twenty, they're ready for the hospice." He stopped when he saw Cat's and Robin's horrified expressions. "Of course that doesn't apply to us here!" he hastened to assure them. "In New Zealand there are clear laws that protect the female workers. The girls only work nine hours a day, six days a week."

"Only?" Cat asked.

"In England they're at the machines twelve to sixteen hours at a time," Wentworth explained. "And there they're allowed to hire younger workers."

"You mean children," Cat said, her voice rising.

"Well, now"—Wentworth turned a bit—"at least our factories are modern and pro-labor. Ask the people. They're all happy here."

Cat remembered the workers at the funeral, but said nothing. Both Robin and Helena seemed despondent after viewing the shop floor and had accepted Wentworth's invitation to visit the office with visible relief. Cat, however, insisted on a complete tour of the damp, steam-filled, foul-smelling workshops. In the meantime, Helena said she needed to freshen up, so Cat, without further question, escorted her to the nearest privy. Immediately after she and Helena left it, Cat dressed Wentworth down for the inhumane conditions. The toilets were small and filthy, and there wasn't even a sink.

"How many women share this washroom? Fifty? It needs to be cleaned at least a couple of times a day. And you do have running water here, don't you? Why is there no sink?"

Wentworth hemmed and hawed. "The women are responsible for cleaning the washrooms themselves."

Cat frowned. "What about mops, brushes, buckets, lye? Are they supposed to supply those? This must be improved. Robin, go take a look at the men's washrooms."

Reluctantly, Robin inspected the facilities. "Just as bad," he murmured.

"So," his mother encouraged him, "it's time to give your first order as a factory owner. The washrooms must be enlarged, sinks installed, and a regular cleaning schedule established. On the clock, Mr. Wentworth. I'm assuming the girls have been expected to clean the washrooms before or after their shifts."

Wentworth looked ready to scream, but promised renovations soon. Helena seemed pained by the unappetizing conversation. She disappeared into the management's private washroom as Wentworth led his guests to the first floor. Here he introduced the staff to Cat and Robin. The various bookkeepers, clerks, and secretaries hurried to offer their condolences and make the new owner as welcome as possible.

"We've already prepared Mr. Lacrosse's private office for you, Mr. Robin," the office manager said eagerly. "Here, you see, the inner window overlooks the main room of the textile mill. And through the outer window you can see the whole courtyard. You won't miss anything. Mr. Lacrosse loved this office."

Robin looked at the man in shock, then thanked him politely. The expansive office featured a large desk and a small seating area with armchairs and a table for meetings. There were, however, no visitors' chairs by the desk. Walter Lacrosse had preferred to keep people standing.

"Would you like to see the books right away, Mr. Fenroy?" a young clerk asked. "Or will you start tomorrow? Or later, perhaps? I mean, this must all have come as a great surprise . . ."

Robin didn't know what to say, and would gladly have absolved himself of the responsibility, when the office manager turned to him and Wentworth.

"A few pressing decisions need to be made. Would you prefer that I direct inquiries to you or to Mr. Wentworth?"

"What is so pressing?" growled Wentworth, whereupon the man launched into a detailed explanation.

One of the dressmakers' workshops had complained about a new vendor, which had supplied substandard needles.

"They break in no time, and the women can't maintain production speed because they have to waste time changing needles. Do you want to complain and give them a chance to replace them, or do you want to send someone to Brunswick right away to get a few packets of the reliable ones?"

Wentworth made the decision—an intelligent one, in Cat's opinion—to do both. The factory needed proper tools as soon as possible.

"Oh yes," the office manager continued, "and the women are asking most politely not to be charged for the loss of the needles. It's really not their fault that the things keep breaking, and they've already had their wages docked because they've wasted so much time changing them."

Wentworth shook his head. "Denied," he said curtly. "The ladies should note that their contracts clearly state that they will be charged for any materials that they damage. If we start making exceptions to that, they'll find some good excuse every week for why their needles are breaking when the ones from the other dressmakers' shop aren't."

"The other workshop has been using needles from Brunswick all along . . . ," the office manager tried to object.

Wentworth glared at him. "I said, denied. What else?"

Cat rubbed her forehead. She may not have studied business, but there were many things that didn't sit well with her, both in the factory and in Wentworth's strict direction. Why, for example, was there no break room for the workers? At the moment they were streaming into the yard to eat the lunches they'd brought with them from home. Surely they were grateful for the fresh air, but what happened when it rained? What did the women with children do with them while they were at work?

Lacrosse had doubtless been a hard man, a patriarch of the old school. Cat thought about the haggard workers at the church, forced into mourning, the broken needles, and the completely innocent girls whose wages were docked; and then the obscene luxury in which the Lacrosse family lived. There were so many things here crying out for change.

But was her son the right man to take care of it?

# Chapter 42

Chris Fenroy made his opinions known in an even more drastic fashion. He arrived the next day and was just as astonished as his wife and son by the lavishness of the Lacrosse estate. The following morning, he returned from his thorough inspection of the factory in a state of indignation.

"The people work in the most wretched conditions!" he raged. "I don't even want to think about how they must live. Did you see the shacks in that neighborhood? The wages are scandalously low, although Mr. Wentworth claims they pay better than the competition. Which, by the way, is now headed up by March's young man, Martin Porter. He married the heiress of the Magiel Corporation. You'll have to take care of all that," he said, turning to his son resolutely. "You need to take a good look at the organization of the factory and listen to some representatives of the workers. If you announce you're easing a few of the rules, you'll make yourself well-liked from the start."

"Me?" Robin asked haltingly.

At his father's insistence, he'd accompanied him and Cat back to the factory and had inspected both the woolen mill and the dressmakers' workshops. Robin didn't know which was worse: the constant clatter of the sewing machines or the screech of the spinning mules, the machines in the textile mill. He hadn't felt much better in the office either. Mr. Wentworth and the office manager hadn't hesitated to show Chris the books, and Chris had checked them—or, at least, had pretended to do so. The office manager, a kind older man, saw through him in an instant but didn't call Chris's bluff. Instead, he gave his new employer's father a clear explanation, then left them alone in the office. Robin was able to understand it even better than his father, thanks to Jane's influence on his education. None of it had interested Robin, however. He just breathed a sigh of relief and nodded when his father conceded that the Lacrosse Company's books were in good order.

"I thought that Mr. Wentworth would take care of that," Robin said. "He wants to help me."

Chris glared at him. "Robin, you can't be serious!" he ranted. "First the chap was after Helena's money, and now he's after yours. He only wants to help himself. And his attitude toward his workers! You heard it yourself: he doesn't think any more of the seamstresses than he does of the machines they work on. 'I see it as my duty to get the last shilling out of both.'" Chris shook his head as he quoted Harold. The two had clashed violently during the inspection of the spinning mill. "The man is an oppressor, Robin. Throw him out."

"Or at least try to learn the ropes quickly enough that you can replace him," Cat said diplomatically. "You can't toss him out just like that, Chris. First of all, he has a contract. You can't fire him without cause. And second, he's the one who understands all the procedures and holds all the reins. If he leaves now, everything will fall apart. You have to learn fast, Robin. Listen to everything Wentworth tells you, but pay attention to the office manager as well, Mister . . . what was his name?"

She looked at Robin, but he returned her gaze helplessly.

"Todd," Chris said. "Is it really possible, Robin, that we spent the entire day with the man and you don't even recall his name?"

Robin blushed. "Dad . . . I can't do any of this. I'm not a businessman. I don't want to do it. I'm an actor . . ."

Chris shook his head. "You have no say in the matter, Robin," he said. "Your great-uncle left these factories to you, and that means both great wealth and great responsibility. You have to make a profit. A couple hundred people work for the Lacrosse Company. They're counting on the fact that their jobs are secure. And beyond that, they want to live a decent life—so you need to introduce reforms and make the factory into a place that you won't have to be ashamed of. You didn't need to take responsibility for Rata Station—there are other heirs who are glad to take over. You could do whatever you wanted. But here everything rests on you. I'm sorry, Robin Fenroy, but it's time for you to grow up."

Robin was determined to take his responsibility seriously. After his parents returned home, he dutifully appeared in the office of the woolen mill every day and tried to fill Walter Lacrosse's office with files. It was clear to him that the workers in his facilities needed an advocate. He bravely challenged Harold Wentworth—as Mr. Todd suggested—to make some changes in the running of the factory. Wentworth was sure that loosening the rules would run the company into the ground, but the workers were thrilled with the break rooms and longer breaks. Reverend Waddell, the pastor of St. Andrew's parish, visited the factory and praised the reforms Robin had initiated. The young heir contributed a large sum for the children's day nursery that Waddell had founded with the help of his industrious parishioner Rachel Reynolds. Despite all this progress, Robin struggled to get a handle on managing the business. As Wentworth nastily observed, Robin was very good at spending money, but unfortunately not so good at earning it.

Robin didn't reprimand the man because, truth be told, Wentworth was right. In dealing with suppliers, negotiating prices with customers, and working out warehousing strategies, Robin was hopelessly unskilled. He was too credulous and easily influenced. Managing finances on such a large scale was not his strong suit. Robin thought nothing of it when one salesman offered needles at a rate of a penny more than the next. What did a single penny matter? The fact that an order of a thousand packages quickly turned pennies into pounds didn't occur to him. He let himself be talked into buying new machines that the company didn't need and didn't even have room for. As his long-suffering manager explained to him with a sigh, they could contract out the sewing of buttonholes to homeworkers. The machines for that were good in theory, but the results weren't yet up to par, resulting in a lot of waste. "Did you even do any research before signing the contract, Mr. Robin?" he had asked.

Soon Robin didn't trust himself to sign anything, and left it all to Harold Wentworth to handle. Even after Wentworth went so far as to make fun of him in front of the office staff, Robin didn't dare to contradict him. Of course Robin knew that he shouldn't put up with insubordination. All it would take for Wentworth to return to his previous groveling behavior was for Robin to threaten him with dismissal. But the young man didn't want to hurt anyone, and on top of that, he was still terrified by the prospect of being in charge of the whole business by himself.

There was no one he could talk to about his problems either. He was very busy—Helena, whom he'd insisted should continue living in the Lacrosse house as long as she wished—dragged him to receptions and dinners and charity events. His presence made a convenient excuse for her not to have to be escorted by Wentworth. Robin understood this and went along without complaint, although the events were like running the gauntlet for him. For one thing, he could barely have a conversation without people trying to sound him out. How had he come into the inheritance, again? How was Robin related to the Lacrosses? Robin didn't know how to handle such questions, but Helena triumphantly recounted the story for the hundredth time. He knew well enough how tongues would wag over the shy young man who was running the company into the ground. The Lacrosses socialized primarily with other industrialists and merchants. No one in that circle had any understanding for Robin's social reforms. They considered the changes dangerous and offered him the "friendly advice" that workers who were given an inch would surely take a mile.

Although Robin had never socialized so much before in his life, he grew increasingly lonely. He avoided writing to his parents; he didn't want to complain and was even less inclined to ask for their help. Yet again he was plagued by the thought that his family would think him a failure. But Robin didn't give up. He didn't run away from running a business any more than he had run away from the Carrigan Company. Once again, Robin subsisted from one day to the next. The only difference was that he'd genuinely enjoyed acting, and every now and then he'd been able to bask in honest applause. In Dunedin he hated every day he spent in the office—and no one was applauding him there.

While Robin tried desperately to do his work justice, winter and spring passed, and the first flowers bloomed in the Lacrosses' garden and in the neighboring park. Robin enjoyed the morning, at least. He had taken up the habit of beginning the day with a ride—even though this, too, carried a sense of duty. Soon after he'd moved to Dunedin, he had a horse sent from Rata Station so he wouldn't have to bother a coachman every time he wanted to go somewhere. Chris and Cat had willingly sent him his favorite of the young horses, a sturdy brown gelding. The stable master's face had shown obvious disapproval, and Helena was beside herself when he met her for a Sunday ride.

"You can't trundle along beside me on a little pony like that!" she exclaimed, and fiddled with her riding crop in annoyance. Her thoroughbred mare—which was indeed more than a hand taller than Robin's Bingo—eyed the crop and pranced about nervously. "You see? Princess thinks it's beneath her dignity too."

Two days later, his second cousin gave him an elegant, shiny black thoroughbred gelding as a gift.

"Now, that's an impressive animal!" the stable master said approvingly.

Robin found the horse demanding. Chevalier had a lot of spirit and needed long daily rides to keep him even remotely satisfied. So Robin got up early and rode, even when it was pouring rain. His tutelage with a strict German riding teacher wouldn't allow him to leave the horse to the stable hands and only take him out when he felt like it. For the ride to and from the factory, he still took solid little Bingo, for he, too, needed exercise. As a result, Robin arrived at the factory late more often than not, and he hated himself for it. Arthur Elliot had impressed upon him that discipline was the be-all and end-all for an actor, and it never would have occurred to Robin to show up late to a rehearsal. In the Lacrosse Company offices, however, no one missed him. On the contrary, Robin often felt like he was intruding. Harold Wentworth and Mr. Todd went about their business quietly until his arrival, at which point they jumped up, led him into his office, and tried to prevent as many of his poor decisions as possible.

On this sunny November day, when Robin had let his thoroughbred gallop almost to Waikouaiti, the office was anything but quiet. Even from the hallway, Robin heard talking and laughing and, finally, Mr. Todd's voice.

"As I said, miss, if you would like to apply at our dressmakers' workshop, you can go there directly."

Then the door flew open, and Robin found himself standing in front of an elegantly, though very tastefully dressed young woman. March Jensch wore a brown suit, the neckline and hem decorated with iridescent gold cords. Her small hat, a confection of ribbons and golden-brown tulle, perched on her thick, dark hair, which she had combed back severely and fastened in a bun at the nape of her neck.

"Robin!" she cried, her tone expressing something between relief and reprimand. "Where have you been? It's ten o'clock! I was sure I'd find you in the office by now."

"And so you have!" Robin said, beaming at her. He had never been so happy to see someone. "Perhaps I am a bit late . . ."

"A bit late?" March asked sternly. "Robin, the workers start at seven! If you want to be a good role model . . ."

"I don't think I qualify as a role model," Robin murmured. "But you . . . Heavens, March! I had completely forgotten about you . . ." Realizing how this sounded, he changed tacks. "I should have written to you long ago!"

March beamed at him. "I could have written too," she admitted. "I didn't have the nerve."

"You didn't have . . . the nerve?"

Robin couldn't believe it. It had been a very long time since he'd known March to fear anything at all.

March sighed. "I thought I'd give it one last try before enrolling in the university," she explained. "At first, I hoped that something would come of Grandma Jane's contacts, but nothing did. And then I kept hoping you'd get in touch. I honestly couldn't believe that you were running a factory. I was just sure you needed help—or at least that you would call on me to be kind. You knew that I was looking for a position, and I . . ." The young woman appeared unusually self-conscious. She wasn't used to playing the role of the suppliant.

Robin, though, felt relief rising in him and renewed annoyance at his own lack of competence. Why hadn't he thought of this sooner? March was the answer to all his prayers!

"I mean . . . I understand it wasn't easy for you," she continued. "Of course you didn't want to come in with a female assistant. The gentlemen"—and here she indicated Todd, Wentworth, and the other office workers who were peeping at them through the door—"made it abundantly clear to me what the late Mr. Lacrosse thought of women in management."

Robin winked at her. "Ah, poor ghost!" he declaimed, quoting *Hamlet*. March grinned. "So you want to apply for a job here?" he asked hopefully.

March nodded. "First, I wanted to see how you were getting on," she explained. "And then, when you weren't here . . . I couldn't resist. I had to at least try."

"The young lady wishes to be employed as a bookkeeper," Mr. Todd interrupted, opening the office door. "Naturally, that's entirely out of the question. But since you appear to know her, perhaps we can find her a position as supervisor at the dressmakers' shop."

"Although I would advise against it," Harold Wentworth added, showing once again how little tact he possessed. "The young lady was very brusque with us. I'll wager she'd have problems taking orders in any position."

Robin grinned. "He's right about that," he noted, turning to March. She glared at both him and Wentworth. Before she could object to the insult, Robin continued. "My cousin, Margery, had best decide for herself. I should have offered her the position long ago, given how well suited she is to it. Gentleman, I present to you the factory's new director, Miss Margery Jensch. You do think you're up to it, March?"

Robin took in March's unbelieving look and then the glow in her azure-blue eyes. "Of course!" she said triumphantly and raised her head so quickly and eagerly that a lock of hair escaped from her bun and played around her face as she turned and confidently faced the office manager. "Would you please show me to a private office . . . Mr. Todd, isn't it? Temporarily for now. I'll choose one of my own later. Then please show me the books. I'd like to get an overview." And with that, she walked into the office.

"And . . . what about me?" Harold Wentworth was red with rage, but couldn't manage anything more.

Robin smiled again. This was good; he felt like he was standing on the stage once again. For the first time since coming to this office, he knew exactly what he had to say. No playwright could have imaged the scene more perfectly.

"You, Mr. Wentworth," he said, in a clear voice, "are fired, effective immediately."

Robin invited March into his office, which she immediately took a liking to. "It's perfect! You can see the production floors from the inner window, and from the outer one, you have a view of the whole courtyard."

"I can think of nicer views," Robin said. He finally felt up to joking again. "A view of the sea, for example."

March looked at him, confused. "You want an office with a view of the sea? Oh, well. To each his own!" She picked up some papers that had been left on the desk for Robin to sign. "Orders for machine oil? From Reynolds? That's too expensive. In Kaiapoi we worked with Keys; they deliver faster and for a better price. Get a quote, Mr. Todd, before I sign this. Is that the general ledger? Do you keep the books for the three businesses together or separately?"

Once again, Robin sat there, not knowing exactly what he was needed for. He felt it his duty to assist March. If she needed any sort of explanation . . .

But March needed no such thing. On the contrary, it wasn't long until she was pointing out a mistake to Mr. Todd.

"Here's something that's been entered in the wrong column, hasn't it, Mr. Todd? The journal doesn't match the general ledger. To which account has this transaction been registered?"

It took Robin less than an hour to realize that he not only *felt* superfluous, but he truly was. March wasn't even aware of his presence anymore, and Todd was too busy explaining and correcting the errors that March pointed out to him with relish. She took thorough revenge for the morning's slights and put the man firmly in his place. Robin could only admire her for it, although he did worry that Todd might give notice in short order.

"So what if he does?" March said over lunch. When the factory's siren called for a break at one o'clock, Todd had set aside his pen with relief. March had briefly considered forcing him to continue working, but Robin convinced her to take a break herself. He took her to a restaurant with a view of the sea, making her laugh. "Even Mr. Todd isn't irreplaceable. And besides, I don't think he'd leave us of his own free will. How many years has he been with the company? Thirty? You don't think he'd want to start over at this stage. No other company would hire him. You shouldn't let yourself be bossed around by your employees, Robin. They have to do what you want, not the other way around!"

"But what if I don't know what I want?" Robin confessed. "I'm no business-man, March. I don't know the first thing about it, and I don't enjoy it at all."

"Then why do it?" March asked matter-of-factly. "As far as I'm concerned, you can stay home tomorrow. I'll do just fine as long as you give me free rein. Do you really mean it, Robin? I can manage the factory? Did you really mean it when you fired Wentworth?"

Robin nodded uncertainly. "Yes, but he supposedly has a contract . . ."

"We'll give him severance pay," March said and made a short note on the pad of paper she'd placed by her plate. "Or we'll accuse him of some wrongdo-ing. I'll take care of it. If he doesn't show up to the office tomorrow, without calling in sick . . . Or has he perhaps been insubordinate to you recently?"

While March took ladylike bites of plaice grilled in butter, new potatoes, and asparagus, she planned Wentworth's dismissal with the brutal efficiency of a shark.

"He's Helena's fiancé," Robin pointed out.

March dismissed his concern with a wave of her hand. "The girl will be glad to be rid of him," she judged as she paged through the dessert menu. "Two birds with one stone. What is she like, by the way? Pleasant? Oh, and I wanted to ask you. I'm assuming that you'll be paying me a tidy salary so I can rent an apartment. It may be difficult to find something, though. Usually people will only rent a room to a single woman."

"You'll live with me, of course!" Robin offered with a smile. "That is, if you want to. It wouldn't be unseemly. We have so many servants, the housekeeper is quite competent, and the butler as well. I've been living there alone with Helena, and no one's gotten upset about that."

March nodded. She seemed to have checked off the next item on her list. "That's very generous of you. We can deduct the rent from my pay."

"I won't hear of it!" Robin responded indignantly.

"You really aren't a businessman, are you?" March continued, disapprovingly. "But it's fine with me. I hope Miss Helena doesn't mind. Anyway, she'll hardly ever see me. I'll be in the office by eight in the morning at the latest, and I won't come out again until the last worker has gone." She looked at the finely turned grandfather clock that stood against the wall of the restaurant. "The food was really outstanding, Robin, but we have to go now. We've overstayed our lunch hour, and that doesn't make a good impression." Robin, who routinely overstayed his lunch hour, shrugged. "I mean that *I* have to go," March corrected herself. "You can do what you want. You can sign the power of attorney over to me tomorrow. There aren't any more important decisions to be made today."

Robin stood up and helped her into the light coat she wore over her suit. He felt free, but also rather guilty. He was sure that March could fulfill his duties far better than he could, but what was he supposed to do now?

"And . . . what about me?" he asked, unconsciously using the same words as Wentworth. "What should I do? Not just today, I mean, but in general? How should I spend my time?"

March smiled. "Well, first of all, you can represent the company," she suggested. "You show yourself in public, display your wealth. Don't worry, people admire that. Many industrialists, especially the second generation, spend more time hunting or at balls or the opera than in the office. The more dazzling you appear, the better the company looks. Maybe you should become a patron of the arts as well. You like theater; do the city some good and bring in famous acting companies to put on plays. Or sponsor artists. Charity work would also be fine. Although that's more of a thing for the ladies and even more for the middle class. I can't imagine Miss Helena at a church bazaar. Just do what you want, or ask Helena. She'll be able to come up with something."

After the uproar with Robin, Wentworth had stormed out of the office and gone to the Lacrosse house to take his anger out on his fiancée. He rudely accused her of ruining the business by dragging a perfect stranger into the picture and passing him off to her grandfather as an heir. He raged against Robin, March, and even against Suzanne—at which point Mr. Simmons spoke up and forbade such insults. The butler wasn't much younger than Walter had been, and he had known Suzanne and clearly worshipped the ground she walked on. In the end, Helena banished Wentworth from the house, at least until he could calm himself down. When Robin brought March home that evening, Helena didn't know if her engagement was still on, but didn't seem too broken up over it.

The sight of March seemed to astound her; apparently she hadn't expected such a beautiful young woman. Any mistrust vanished quickly, however, when March changed for dinner without prompting, displayed excellent manners, and showed herself capable of charming conversation. March had moved in the best circles in Christchurch with Martin Porter, and neither the etiquette of great houses nor the vast number of servants frightened her.

"First of all, I think I'll take Robin shopping tomorrow," Helena said with excitement as March turned the conversation to his future life as a private gentleman and asked Helena for her recommendations. "If he wants to show himself off more, he'll need a proper summer wardrobe. On Saturday he can accompany me to an art opening. Do you know anything about art, Robin? It's a very interesting gallery, run by two women. And then on Sunday there's the garden party at the Stilltons' . . ."

Harold Wentworth didn't appear again at the Lacrosse house. His engagement to Helena was quietly called off a few months later. March, however, heard from him again soon enough. Martin Porter, who had taken over his father-in-law's firm, hired him as the director of his textile factory. March took that as a clear act of aggression. Magiel and Lacrosse had always been competitors, and Porter doubtless hoped his new employee could provide him with insider knowledge of her business. The men were probably laughing at Robin's decision to give Wentworth's job to March—although Porter surely knew what his former pupil was capable of.

Whether he feared or underestimated her, March would soon pay back her erstwhile teacher for the way he'd treated her in Kaiapoi. She couldn't tolerate any weaknesses, of course; production would have to be optimized. After a week, March called in the workers' representatives and let them know that, while they could keep the longer breaks, the workers would need to make up the time at the end of the workday. She didn't eliminate the pay increases, but she did charge the workers a few pence for the afternoon coffee that had previously been given out for free.

Within two weeks of her hiring, March had effectively reversed all of Robin's reforms. She did, however, retain the machines for sewing buttonholes. She tried them out personally and determined that, with some practice and careful observation of the very complicated instructions, the machines worked well. Since this proved to be incompatible with both quick training and higher production goals, for a while there was a constant turnover of the women assigned to the machine. If they didn't meet March's expectations, she switched them out—but not without docking their pay for any waste. The assembly-line problem was also quickly solved; March placed the machine in the workers' new break room.

# Chapter 43

"I don't know. A Maori boy? Isn't that a bit . . . exotic? I mean, shouldn't we be worried?"

Helena gazed with concern at the letter from Mara Te Eriatara. Robin had opened it over supper and begun to read it aloud. Mara explained to him and March that her son, Arapeta, had just graduated from high school in Christchurch with honors and wanted to study law in Dunedin, beginning the coming semester. Eru and she were concerned about his lodging.

"*Of course Peta can get a place in the student dormitory,*" Robin read. "*Jane doesn't see a problem with that either. However, Peta is only eighteen, and Maori, besides. Of course, he is mature for his age, but Eru and I are afraid that he'll feel lonely among a bunch of older pakeha boys. So this is why I'm turning to you, Robin. Cat says that you have a very large house now and that March is living happily there. Mightn't there be a room there for Peta as well? Eru and I would rest easier knowing he was with family.*"

March had grimaced only slightly after the reading of the letter. She didn't look forward to the prospect of living under the same roof as her brother, nor did she think Peta was particularly prone to loneliness. Mara and Eru were overreacting again. Because of their own bad experiences outside the safety of Maori Station, they'd practically become hermits.

But when Helena voiced her misgivings, March's hackles rose. "There is nothing to be afraid of. Arapeta is my brother," she said. "He's no more dangerous than I am, and no more Maori." In fact, Peta had more *pakeha* heritage than she, but March didn't think it necessary to go into detail.

Robin smiled. "And that from the woman who's been teaching our competition the meaning of fear for weeks!" he joked.

Profits at the Lacrosse factories had been growing by leaps and bounds in the six months since the young woman took over. March accepted the compliment with a satisfied look.

"You? Maori?" Helena reacted with a surprised squeal. "But you're not—I mean, you don't look like—and you're educated and civilized and . . ."

The revelation was clearly too much for Helena, who already found it difficult to define March's social status. It was the same for her social circle. For several months, the upper class of Dunedin had questioned whether it was proper to include Margery Jensch in their invitations to the Lacrosses. The young woman appeared to be related to Robin in some way, which suggested they should. On the other hand, she was an employee of the factory, which should naturally exclude her. In the end, it was March's unexpected success in the business world that made her interesting. Word had it that she came from a very wealthy sheep farm in the Canterbury Plains. So March was invited after all. Her beauty and ease in conversation quickly catapulted her into the center of the few events she deigned to attend, and soon she was downright idolized. But now it turned out she was Maori?

"I am half Maori," March explained calmly. "I know I don't look it; I take strongly after my mother. And since Mara kindly declined to give me a Maori name—although I suppose that means I have her to thank for the name 'March'—I pass as white."

"There's no shame in being Maori," Robin objected.

March raised her eyebrows. "True, but it's hardly a benefit when it comes to one's business career. In any case, my brother has a traditional name, and it hasn't occurred to him to change it to 'Peter.' He does bathe regularly, he can speak English, and he doesn't bite. You couldn't call him dangerous or uncivilized."

Helena turned red. Now and again March made it a little too obvious that she thought Robin's second cousin was rather silly.

"Peta is a lovely young man," Robin confirmed. "I'm sure you'll like him, Helena."

"So you'll let him come?" March asked.

Robin nodded. "Why not? Of course, we're a bit far from the university . . ."

March laughed. "It's only two miles," she said. "A Maori warrior could walk that in barely half an hour."

Helena blanched. "Is he . . . tattooed?" she asked.

March shook her head in dismay. "On the South Island, Helena," she said, "hardly any young Maori are tattooed anymore. My brother certainly isn't. And if we ask him nicely, he'll even leave his spear and war club at home." She turned to Robin. "Are you sure it's a good idea, though, to have Peta here? Did you know that my brother considers factory owners to be the quintessence of evil? He's constantly blathering on about unions and can rattle off *The Communist Manifesto*. There's a book by a German called Engels, *The Condition of the Working Class in England*, that's his bible. He quotes it all the time. It's a wonder he'd even condescend to live under the same roof as people like us. When he sees the servants, he'll probably die of shame. At any rate, he'll count every penny that our dear Helena spends on clothes, and every bite of food that isn't dry bread."

Robin smiled. "You exaggerate, March!"

"He sounds a bit like Reverend Waddell," Helena added.

March gave a little snort. "Except that the reverend just quotes harmlessly from the Sermon on the Mount. Engels talks about open social warfare and calls for sabotage and the destruction of factory machines. And strikes! Just imagine!" Outraged, she let her napkin fall. "Living in the same house with Peta won't be easy, in any case," she prophesied. "I'd rather send him to the dorm. Let him incite the other students to revolution!"

Helena feared the worst when, a week later, she and Robin rode to the train station in the coach to pick up Arapeta. A Maori and a rabble rouser? Despite all of Robin and March's reassurances, she imagined him sitting at the breakfast table in a grass skirt, his hair tied up in a warrior's knot, and his face covered in frightful tattoos.

However, when she saw the young man who got off the train and embraced Robin, her worries receded. Peta was tall and much more heavily built than March—who was busy at the factory and hadn't come to welcome her brother. The lines of his face showed his father's heritage more as well. At first glance, however, he didn't look Maori, especially with his green eyes. His thick, black hair was cut short but tended to stick up in all directions. Peta's expression was kind, and his smile was soft. At first glance, Helena found him more likable than March. Of course he wasn't wearing native dress but instead a good-quality suit. Helena remembered that March and Peta's parents were not poor. She didn't understand all the details, but she did know that the Te Eriataras, like the Fenroys, ran a sheep farm.

Peta made a deep bow when Robin introduced Helena to him. His response—"Delighted, Miss Lacrosse"—betrayed no accent. Helena breathed a sigh of relief. She could be seen with the young man at parties and in church without causing a stir.

"So you've taken up with capitalists," Peta said, teasing Robin when he saw the splendid coach. He wouldn't let the footman take his luggage. "I can manage the bag myself."

"Haven't we always?" Robin asked. After March's grim intimations, he'd picked up copies of the works of Marx and Engels and read them carefully. He'd found the depictions of the English laborers' circumstances and work conditions shocking. The situation there was doubtless untenable, and he was very much in favor of improving it—although he would avail himself of different means from those that Engels suggested. "I mean, my parents and your tribe have sheep farms. That means they, too, own the means of production. So they're capitalists as well, aren't they?"

Peta grinned. "I see you've informed yourself well on the subject. But that only applies to your parents, not Maori Station. We are more like a collective. However, I've never seen any indication of the exploitation of farmhands at Rata Station, so you can rest easy there."

The two young men laughed. The workers on the sheep farms, especially the shearers who made the rounds of the farms in the spring, possessed self-confidence bordering on arrogance. Both Robin and Peta had been on the receiving end of their jeers when they'd shown themselves less than skilled at shearing.

"But you actually own a factory . . . or is it two? That's a different matter than a herd of sheep," Peta said, and shook his head in dismay at the footman holding the door of the coach open for the "masters." Helena stepped in gracefully. "Seriously, Robin, you let March run the factory? I saw how she did things in Kaiapoi. Any prospect of earning money brings out the wolf in her."

Robin nodded. "She's giving the competition a run for their money all right. It's also personal for her. Did you know that Martin Porter is now working for Magiel, our competition? He always was a rather arrogant fellow, and then he hired Wentworth, whom I threw out. To be honest, I don't feel the least bit bad about beating either of them."

Peta frowned. "I don't either," he said. "Certainly not Porter. He's the one who encouraged my sister's monstrosity. But the battle the two or three of them are waging is being fought on the backs of the workers. Don't you see that, Robin? Don't you even go and talk to the people?"

"I gave them a longer break and raised their wages!" Robin cried. "They've got a break room now, and there's childcare and a nursing room. The women can bring their babies. That was March's idea. So you see . . ."

"She probably hoped it would make the women return to the factory sooner after giving birth," Peta conjectured. "Besides, that way they won't get pregnant again as quickly. The longer they nurse . . ." Helena blushed and cleared her throat. Peta apologized immediately. "Forgive me, Miss Lacrosse. That's not something to speak of in the presence of a lady. However, I have a hard time believing that my sister's decisions were genuinely altruistic. If I were in your shoes, Robin, I'd double-check on the wage increase. How long has March been running these factories? Six months or more? She's probably already changed everything back to the way it was."

Of course Robin didn't check on anything; he trusted March. He did resolve, however, to drop a larger offering than usual into the collection plate at church the following Sunday. Reverend Waddell had been most insistent in his calls for more charitable giving and social engagement of late.

"Since when do you go to church?" Peta asked his sister when she came downstairs in an elegant burgundy dress, complete with crinolines, mantilla, and a cloche hat covered in tulle. She had a prayer book tucked under her arm.

Peta had been looking forward to a relaxing breakfast. Now he saw that Helena was in a similar outfit, and Robin was wearing a dark suit of the finest cloth.

"Since I've been living in the same parish as the workers in my factories," March replied blandly. Like her brother, she had never quite settled on a clear concept of God, what with Maori spirituality, the state Christianity of the government, and Jane's intense pragmatism. "We have to set a good example. So go get dressed, brother mine!"

"How exactly am I supposed to set an example for anyone in the church?" Peta countered. "It certainly wouldn't be a good one. Religion tends to cement hierarchical relationships . . ."

"Render unto Caesar the things that are Caesar's, and unto God the things that are God's," quoted March. "It says so right in the Bible. The reverend should pay attention to that as well. Come on now, Peta, you can't get out of it."

"For the sake of the household staff too," Helena added. "In my opinion, setting a good example for them is considerably more important than setting one for the people of St. Andrew's."

Robin said nothing to that. He stared wearily through the foyer's gigantic windows at the pouring rain that made the world look as grim as his mood. While dressing, he'd found a theater program: it was four years ago already that he'd played Lysander in Christchurch. And now? This coming week he'd escort Helena to the theater once again. A troupe from Australia was performing *As You Like It*. The Lacrosse Company was underwriting half the cost, while the city and other concerns made up the rest. Robin had decided—albeit sullenly—that he at least wanted to contribute to the support of other actors. He had had letters sent in his name to companies all over the country, inviting them to come to Dunedin. This was the second time someone had responded. Robin enjoyed the performance, drank champagne he himself had paid for at the reception, and longed to stand on the other side of the curtain again.

As St. Andrew's Church was not far away, the Lacrosses usually walked, but today Mr. Simmons had seen to it that the coach was prepared. The women's elegant clothes should not be allowed to get wet and dirty. Robin felt guilty, and Peta frowned in disapproval as they drove past the servants, who were of course left to walk in the rain.

Helena wrinkled her nose as they entered the building. The crowded room smelled of damp clothing and insufficiently washed bodies. She headed confidently toward the front pew, where the other members of high society obligingly made room for her. The well-dressed women required at least three seats each in order to drape their voluminous crinolines about them. The women of the merchant class who were seated behind them were more simply dressed. And the women of the working class, many of whom were left standing in the very back, wore shabby, dark Sunday dresses that had surely seen years of wear. A couple of young girls had on pretty muslin dresses in colorful prints.

"We should really check to see where they got the fabric," March murmured disapprovingly. "Those are all seamstresses from the factories. You have to watch them like a hawk to make sure they don't filch anything."

Because of the rain, people hadn't been able to meet and exchange news as usual in front of the church, and as a result, there was a general murmur and confusion of voices inside the house of worship. There was even occasional laughter to be heard. However, as soon as the organ rang out and Reverend Waddell mounted the pulpit at exactly ten, the congregation fell silent. The people hung on the minister's every word, although at first glance he didn't make much of an impression. Waddell was a rather short man with a delicate silhouette. The narrowness of his face was emphasized by his goatee. His hairline was receding, but one could still see that he'd had brown curls when he was young. Now his hair had begun to turn gray. His black suit had seen better days; he was certainly not vain.

Reverend Waddell looked out at the members of his congregation with lively, kind eyes, as he greeted them and intoned the first prayers. He seemed to radiate care for each and every person who had come to his church.

"I see some new faces among us today," he began. "Perhaps newly arrived residents, whose acquaintance I look forward to making after the service, or perhaps visitors upon whom Dunedin and St. Andrew's may not have made the best impression, especially with today's weather. That brings us to the topic of today's sermon: Imagine that our Lord Jesus were to come to our fair city as a visitor. Surely he would not mind the weather; I think Peter would take care of that for him straightaway . . ." He smiled impishly, and the congregation laughed quietly.

"But otherwise, what sort of impression would our divine guest take away from St. Andrew's? Quite a good one, so the fine citizens in the first row must be thinking. Surely Jesus would take pleasure in their lovely houses and colorful gardens. As long as he didn't act too outlandish, and if he left a gold-edged calling card in their parlor, they might even take him along for a ride in their fine coaches or invite him to a reception or soiree with their honorable guests." Restrained laughter was heard from the back rows. "Doubtless Jesus would also enjoy walking along the high street and seeing the wares that our good citizens offer for sale without charging exorbitant prices . . ." The reverend winked, and there was whispering in the middle rows. "And wouldn't the Lord be taken with the industrious young dressmakers, who, after their day's work, still ply their needles, bringing us joy at the sight of their tidy new dresses!" Waddell smiled at the giggling girls. "For surely they dress so nicely in church to please the Lord and not to impress their beaus before or after the service." He wagged his finger at them playfully. "Sadly, however, there are also things in our community that would anger the Lord or make him sad. The sordid establishments on Walker Street, for example.

"Would he not desire to overturn the tables and throw the sinful money onto the street, as he did in Jerusalem when he banished the moneychangers from the temple? He would be shocked that part of our parish is called 'the Devil's Half Acre,' since the fiend is lurking around every corner here. The drafty houses with their thin walls—why, if the Lord were a guest of some of our poorer parishioners, he would first have to help them mop up the rainwater that is pouring through their leaky roofs while I stand here preaching. Afterward, they'd place before him a cup of thin chicory coffee and a heel of bread because, for many of us, there will be nothing more than that on the table today.

"Jesus would undoubtedly ask why that is so, since he can read the very souls of men and see how diligent and God-fearing they are. And then he would follow them into the factories and would surely be astonished at how things are made there. Clothing, blankets, cloths—many things that once were only available to the wealthiest of people and that everyone can now afford because they can be produced by machines quickly and in great quantities. Everyone, that is, except the workers who make them! 'Love thy neighbor as thyself,' says the Lord." The pastor raised his voice. "And that doesn't just mean that we should not speak or think badly of others. It also means don't do to another what you yourself would not want to endure. Don't expect something of another person that you wouldn't expect of yourself!"

March glanced irritably at Peta, whose eyes were shining.

"Let each of us here today ask ourselves how our daily life would strike Jesus were he to visit. Would it bring him joy or disappointment? Would you factory owners like to toil away at your machines for the wages you pay? Would you landlords like to live in the holes that you take money for? Would you men, who are already thinking about spending your pay in a pub or a gaming hall, like to sit home and anxiously await your return, as your wives do? Would you like to starve like your children because the money has been gambled away or drunk up? Would you good shopkeepers like to take the place of the woman who begs you to give her the wares she so desperately needs on credit just one more time? Think on this, my friends!

"However, I don't just want to exhort and reproach you. I would like to speak of the work that would surely coax an appreciative smile from Jesus's lips. Thanks, for example, to the ladies who run our soup kitchen and who cook as well for the needy as for their own families. To the people who donate clothing, so the poor can be clothed as warmly and well as they themselves. To Rachel Reynolds and the women from the children's nursery, who care for the children of working mothers as lovingly as they do for their own.

"In that regard, I would also like to mention that we are hoping for donations of books for our library. And I would like to see even more involvement in St. Andrew's Young Men. I know that the men of our parish are very busy"—and here Robin and several other gentlemen of means cowered under the clergyman's gaze—"but still, it would be nice if some might find the time to take an active role in the character development of the young boys and youths of the parish. No, no, you don't have to offer Bible studies!"—more laughter—"But perhaps you could organize ball games or singing, or maybe the craftsmen among us could teach the boys some simple skills. You might even find a willing apprentice that way." This last sentence came across as resigned.

"They don't want to learn anything," March whispered. "They'd rather go earn money in the factory."

"The Association for Youth Advancement of St. Andrew's is grateful for any suggestions," the pastor continued. "Every boy, every youth that we can rescue from the street and lead to productive employment is a win for St. Andrew's, for Dunedin, and for our Lord Jesus Christ. And now, my dear friends, I wish you a good Sunday. Tea will be served in the rectory, and it's good and hot for those who might want to warm up before they head home."

"Well, he needled our consciences well enough," March scoffed as she left the church and looked around for the coach. "But the old fellow does speak well. How much did you donate this time, Robin? And where are you off to now, Peta?"

Peta had caught a glimpse of the reverend at the entrance to the parsonage and set off in his direction. Hadn't he asked the new residents of the parish to introduce themselves?

Without a thought for March and Robin, Peta crowded with the rest of the congregation onto the parsonage's porch. None of the well-to-do citizens from the first pews were there. These parishioners were dressed in threadbare clothes, haggard and thin. The tea might well be the only warm thing these people would get in their stomachs all day. Peta was happy for them when he saw sandwiches and cookies on the tables as well.

"Greetings to you, young friend!" Reverend Waddell said to him kindly. "Would you like to drink some tea with us?" A searching look. "Didn't I just see you with the better-off families? You must understand . . ."

Peta shook his head. "I certainly won't take anyone's tea away from them," he reassured the pastor. "I only wanted to introduce myself and ask if I might be able to help. My name is Arapeta Te Eriatara. I'm a guest at the Lacrosse residence . . . or, rather, at the Fenroys'. . ."

The pastor's eyebrows shot up. True, during the service, the young man had sat next to Robin Fenroy, the heir to whom Waddell had given advice when he'd met him for the first time a year earlier. Everything had seemed so promising then. It seemed like God had finally sent a compassionate soul into old Lacrosse's office. But then just as quickly, everything changed. Robin Fenroy retreated from all of the businesses, and obviously didn't want to talk about the fact that the pressure on his workers was growing every month. That pressure seemed to be the doing of the girl who was apparently the directress of the Lacrosse Company.

Waddell's face settled into an inviting smile. "Then perhaps we will drink a cup of tea together," he said. "In my office. Robin Fenroy is, hmm, one of the most generous supporters of the parish. His offerings make a great portion of our charity work possible."

"Which wouldn't be necessary if he paid his workers better," Peta remarked.

Waddell's eyebrows rose. "So you say," he replied cautiously.

Peta laughed. "Reverend, I'm hardly suited to help in the nursery, but what can I do for the youth of St. Andrew's?"


"You could get involved too, Robin," Peta said with excitement. He was sitting with the rest of the family at the luncheon table a short time later. "They're arranging educational opportunities for young factory workers. The reverend wants them to learn to read or busy themselves with useful crafts so they don't spend all of their weekends in the pub. Mostly, they need people to teach them. Schooling for the workers is in a very poor state; as soon as they reach the minimum age, they leave to work in the factory. You could read Shakespeare with them, Robin! Or direct plays and put them on. They'd have great fun with that. The pastor says that the men's choir has usually been the most popular choice."

"They're probably rehearsing in the pub," March said. "Peta, Reverend Waddell means well, and it's certainly worthwhile to support anything that keeps the fellows from gambling away their pay. But Shakespeare? Isn't that aiming rather too high?"

At the mention of Shakespeare, workers, and pubs, Robin was reminded of the Carrigan Company's dreadful performances.

"I'll donate something for the library," he decided, hoping that Peta would drop the subject.

Peta glared at him. "I already have!" he said boldly. "*The Communist Manifesto*. I happened to have a copy with me."

"Well, then there's nothing stopping the revolution," March said sarcastically and stood up. "I'll have myself driven over to the factory; I have work to finish. While my workers have the day off. The little injustices of life . . ." She swept out of the room.

Helena seized the opportunity to follow her. "Don't forget about the invitation to the McLaughleys tonight," she reminded Robin. "A chamber concert. I'm sure it will be rather dull, but we should put in an appearance."

"It would be better for you to see how your workers live," Peta continued, trying to convince Robin. "Don't let March whitewash things; she's only telling you half the story. Why don't you ever go into the office anymore? The pastor said he used to visit you there at first, but then you disappeared. What exactly do you do all day?"

Robin would have gladly imitated March and simply fled from Peta. On the other hand, his conscience was bothering him. Thanks to Helena, he had become a fixture of Dunedin society. He was appointed with the most absurd ensembles for every possible occasion, and now owned afternoon and evening suits, tailcoats and smoking jackets, single- and double-breasted jackets, various shirts, bow ties, cummerbunds, vests, pocket squares, top hats, bowlers and other hats that he couldn't even name, as well as the most varied types of leisurewear. In these, he attended garden parties, balls, concerts, and art openings; he played cricket, croquet, tennis, and golf. He had learned how to carry on frivolous conversations with other dignitaries and their wives, and he knew how to retreat politely when someone wanted to introduce their daughter. Here, too, Helena was an invaluable help. She jealously strove to keep every other woman far away. Sometimes he even suspected that his second cousin might be in love with him.

It wasn't that Robin was terribly interested in these activities. Rather, he treated them like theatrical improvisations. The ballrooms, tennis courts, and galleries were his stages, and he played the elegant young man-about-town like a role. When March was around, at least, he was able to enjoy the amusements a bit, even though his crush on her had faded once more. Truthfully, Robin's feelings had been under a sort of bell jar for months. He wouldn't have described himself as either happy or unhappy. Only very rarely, like this morning when he had come upon the theater program, did he feel emptiness and pain.

"I give a great deal to the church," he said to Peta. "And besides, I have to show myself in society. I represent the company publicly. You don't understand. And now, you must excuse me. I have to—I have to get changed . . ."

# Chapter 44

Peta didn't let up, even when he began his studies. Naturally, he refused to take the coach to the university.

"I can walk perfectly well," he told Helena brusquely. "What would my fellow students think if I drove up every day like a prince? It's bad enough that I have to be waited on hand and foot in the house."

Resigned, Helena said nothing. She had long since lost any enjoyment in her houseguest, especially since the staff came to her every day with new complaints. Mr. Peta insisted on lighting his own fireplace; he forbade the chamber maid to make his bed and clean his room. He didn't want to take tea in his room in the morning, and he forbade Mr. Simmons, in all seriousness, from calling him "Mr. Peta."

"'Just Peta,' he said," the butler reported indignantly. "He wants me to call him Peta! And he's demanding it not only of me, but of the maids as well. They are completely unsettled by it. Miss Helena, if I allow that liberty . . . how is the young gentleman supposed to address me? By my Christian name?"

Helena couldn't imagine anyone calling Mr. Simmons by his Christian name; she'd known the butler her entire life and didn't even know what his Christian name *was*. In any case, she promised to talk with Peta, or Robin, or both. In the end, she turned to Robin, and he took it upon himself to set some boundaries with Peta.

"All right, then," the young man replied, "I will behave like one of the bourgeoisie in this house, but in exchange, I want you to visit Reverend Waddell. At least listen to what he has to say. Look at the houses that the factory workers live in. You don't have to read Karl Marx; it's right there in the Bible: Isaiah 1:17. 'Learn to do well; seek judgment; relieve the oppressed . . .'"

Since Peta had been helping out in Reverend Waddell's organization, he'd been reading the Bible frequently. Waddell was a proponent of Christian Socialism. In his view, the works of Marx and Engels were unnecessary, as was a class conflict. It was enough for the factory owners to keep their Christian values in mind, he said. Waddell and those who shared his ideas knew countless Bible verses on which they based their convictions. Ecclesiasticus, chapter 31: *He that loveth gold shall not be justified, and he that followeth corruption shall have enough thereof.* Or Amos, chapter 5: *Forasmuch therefore as your treading is upon the poor, and ye take from him burdens of wheat: ye have built houses of hewn stone, but ye shall not dwell in them.*

Robin rubbed his forehead. He had neither the energy nor the biblical knowledge to turn Peta's own weapons against him the way March did. In the Bible, the young woman maintained, it was possible to find arguments for and against practically any ideology. She made Peta furious by quoting the rules for the treatment of slaves from Exodus: *And if a man smite his servant, or his maid, with a rod, and he die under his hand; he shall be surely punished. Notwithstanding, if he continue a day or two, he shall not be punished: for he is his money.* Or on the punishment for thieves: *For he should make full restitution; if he have nothing, then he shall be sold for his theft.* Their workers merely had the cost of wasted thread deducted from their wages. She didn't know what more he wanted.

Their verbal sparring always left Robin with a bad feeling. Did March browbeat the workers in the office and on the factory floor the way she did Peta, and no one dared to tell Robin? Was he indeed shirking his responsibility by letting March do as she pleased?

"Tomorrow," he said, finally giving in. The next day was a Saturday. "You're going to the St. Andrew's Young Men's meeting tomorrow, right? I can go along. Helena will be at a tea party with her friends, and March will be at the factory as usual."

Peta grinned. "Very suspicious that you have to sneak out of the house when the ladies won't notice. But it's all the same to me. Just try not to dress like such a dandy." He cast a glance at Robin's elegant suit and bow tie. The young man was on his way to a polo match in Dunedin with Helena.

Robin blushed. His valet would ask questions. He now considered it completely normal for a servant to help him dress. He doubted he even still owned the sort of denim trousers and linen shirt that Peta usually wore to meetings of the church group.

Peta grinned again. "I'd give you something of mine, but I doubt it would fit. Oh, well, we'll see. If I can manage, I'll stop by Waddell's house after school. Maybe I can find you something in the clothing donations . . ."

And Peta, with a smirk, did in fact bring him something to wear. In the simple cloth trousers, worn leather jacket, and dark shirt, Robin felt just as much in costume as he did in the fine apparel of a private gentleman. As he quickly changed his clothes in the privy of the parish hall, he almost felt as if he were back in a pub with the Carrigan Company, preparing to take the stage. The parish hall even had a room where they could put on plays; it was here that the men's choir gave their performances and the church choir rehearsed. There were no dressing rooms, but at once he felt what he secretly called his "magic" take over. As he put on his costume, he slipped into the role he wanted to play. Peta was amazed to see how differently the young man moved in the new outfit.

"You look almost like a human being," he teased when Robin joined him. His hair was a little tousled, and his jacket was thrown casually over his shoulder. "Waddell is in his office. I told him you were coming. Let's see what he has planned for us."

Robin worried what the pastor might say about his sudden change in appearance, but Reverend Waddell made no comment about it at all. He simply welcomed his guests warmly to his plain workroom. The pulpit and chancel of St. Andrew's Church were richly decorated with carved wood, but the parish hall was kept plain. In the reverend's office stood only a desk and a couple of chairs, and on the wall a simple wooden cross.

"Please have a seat," he said kindly. He then turned to Robin. "It's been such a long time since we spoke, Mr. Fenroy. I remember our last meeting in your office well. You had initiated so many changes then."

Robin swallowed hard. "I hope that they have . . . had the desired effect."

The pastor seemed surprised. Peta had indicated that Robin had no idea what actually went on in the factories, but apparently, Waddell hadn't believed it.

"I'm afraid not, Mr. Fenroy," he explained bluntly. "The living conditions of the men and women who work in your factories are . . . how shall I say?"

"Inhumane!" Peta broke in. "Scandalous!"

The reverend shot him a stern look. "For a person whose heart is in the right place, like your young relation here, the circumstances are unbearable," he admitted. "Your workers, Mr. Fenroy, simply do not earn enough to adequately feed themselves and their children. On top of that, they live in miserable holes that they pay too much for because their landlords exploit them mercilessly."

"Do you mean to say that the Lacrosse Company exploits them?" Robin asked, more shocked than outraged. "But we pay enough. Wages are determined according to each family's needs and how many pieces each worker can complete."

"Even if the wages were enough," the reverend said, as Peta began another sharp response, "calculating them that way deprives the people of their right to self-determination. Do strangers decide for you what you do and do not need, Mr. Fenroy?"

Robin blushed. Not because he was ashamed but because he almost could have answered in the affirmative. Helena determined what clothing and personal effects he needed. His valet determined what he put on. The cook determined what he ate.

"For that matter, the calculations you use are a scandal. Women earn less than men, even when they do the same work and produce the same amount."

"We pay by the piece," Robin explained. He thought that was what March had told him. "The more a person works, the more they earn."

"But the prescribed work speed is so merciless that hardly anyone can produce more than the norm." The clergyman sighed. "So it's rare that anyone earns more than the usual wage. And even then, if they don't produce the expected quantities, their wages are docked. Mr. Fenroy, your workers are perpetually under pressure, and they can't improve themselves no matter how hard they work. The wages are simply too low."

"But if more members of a family work—and that's usually the case—then it adds up . . ." Robin felt as though he were skating on very thin ice. All he could do was repeat March's arguments and hope that the right one would occur to him.

At this point, Peta began pacing in anger. The pastor pulled him aside a moment to confer quietly, and then the young man left the room. Reverend Waddell returned to his desk and looked at Robin.

The reverend was clearly trying hard to be patient, even understanding. He pushed the objects on his desk back and forth like chess pieces as he spoke. "Mr. Fenroy, if a man and wife both work in your factory, together they earn just enough to feed one or two children. And most of them have more than one or two. So the funds must be stretched. They skimp on everything. Despite that, some families manage to keep their heads above water until the oldest child can go to work and add their bit to the family's coffers. That's why it would be such an improvement for the children to learn a trade. That way, they'll be able to feed their own families better in the future. Right now, that can't happen, because the two pennies a master might pay his second-year apprentice aren't enough to help support the family." With that, the pastor returned the inkwell and pen to their places and stood up. "Let me take you into the parish. That's why you came, after all."

Robin followed him with hesitation. "I thought . . . I would be doing something with the young men," he objected. "That's what Peta said. I don't honestly know what, but . . . perhaps I could read something with them."

The pastor shook his head sadly. "Mr. Fenroy, do look at the time." He pointed to a plain grandfather clock made of beechwood. "Does anything occur to you?"

Irritated, Robin did as he was told. It was twenty past eleven in the morning. What should occur to him about that?

"The young people that you came here to help are in your factory right now," explained the pastor. "They won't be let out until six at the earliest, and more likely closer to seven. Perhaps they'll come here afterward—that's our hope, at any rate, as we've arranged a dance tonight. Peta and a few other volunteers have offered to decorate the parish hall, which is why he's here so early. Normally, volunteers don't come until evening. At this time of day, the only people at home in the Devil's Half Acre are sick people and children—at least as far as the laboring class is concerned. The swindlers are only now waking up and bracing themselves for their work."

Robin flushed with shame. "I'd be glad to help decorate the hall," he offered.

The reverend shook his head. "No, Mr. Fenroy, let's go on a sick call instead. Don't worry; you can't catch anything, and your sensibilities won't be offended either. In Angus Smith's family there's just been what in other places is commonly considered a joyous event. Their eighth child has been born. And we will visit the mother to see if"—he coughed—"there's anything she needs."

For the first time, Robin crossed the Devil's Half Acre on foot. He had to be careful where he stepped, what with all the puddles and refuse in the narrow alleys. It was revolting—and the smells! At best, it reeked of coal, but more often of vomit, excrement, and urine. Apparently, there weren't many privies. Children and old people crouched in the entrances of the cheaply constructed houses. The children wore gray smocks, boys indistinguishable from girls. Some smocks were completely threadbare, probably handed down from one child to the next. Robin was shaken to see that most of the children were pattering about in the refuse barefoot.

"Don't you receive any shoes in the clothing donations?" he asked the pastor.

Waddell nodded. "Certainly. But parishioners don't often donate children's shoes—or children's clothing in general. Most people have several children and keep things to hand down to the younger ones. But didn't you say just now, Mr. Fenroy, that your businesses pay the families enough to provide for their children? Shouldn't dressing them adequately be part of that?"

Robin bit his lip. Now he also saw that the old people were hardly any better dressed than the children. A woman recognized the pastor and greeted him with a toothless smile. Waddell stroked the children's hair and spoke a few kind words to the old lady.

"Do come by the parish hall, Miss Janey, and bring your charges. Their mothers can never find time for that. We'll look through the donations for the children together. The little ones need warm things. Winter isn't over yet."

"Charges?" Robin asked. "She isn't their grandmother?"

The pastor shook his head. "No, Miss Janey earns her keep by watching the children of the women who work in the factory. She's one of the better caregivers—I've never seen her drunk. She used to work in a weaving mill, but she had an accident. She can hardly walk anymore. That's why I worry she won't come to us. In fact, she mostly sits in her doorway and lets the children play in the street."

"I thought there was a nursery for the children," Robin murmured.

The pastor nodded. "Yes, but it's completely over capacity. Our ladies do what they can, but they care for fifty children over the age of four. That's the best we can do. The little ones here"—he pointed at Miss Janey's barefoot sprogs—"are only two or three years old. They're too old for the nursing rooms in your factory!" he added, although Robin hadn't wanted to say anything. He was embarrassed at the very thought of nursing babies in public. "Of course, the women can't leave their children there. The tiny ones, perhaps. When the women don't have any other choice, some take their chances and leave their little baskets right there and hope that the infants won't wake up during their shift. Older ones would crawl and run around and get into trouble. They need a caregiver, Mr. Fenroy, but of course your factory doesn't want to pay for that."

Moved, Robin wondered how much it would cost to hire Miss Janey. Certainly not so much that it would decrease March's profit margin noticeably. He decided that he would talk to her about it that very evening.

The Smith family lived in a somewhat larger stone house, closer to the factory than to the church. Six renting households shared two floors. The landlord, a Scotsman, lived in the basement. The pastor led Robin along a narrow hallway. The stairways and corridors looked as though no one had mopped them in years. Waddell knocked at one of the doors, and a girl of twelve or thirteen opened it. The pastor greeted her with a smile.

"Hello, Emily! How are your mother and your new little sibling?"

The girl, a delicate, dark-haired creature, frowned. She would have been extraordinarily pretty if someone had braided her hair properly and given her a dress that didn't hang on her like a sack.

"It's a boy," she told them. "Harry. He cries all day. Mama doesn't have a lot of milk."

"But the child has strong lungs," the pastor said, trying to offer some small consolation. "May we come in, Emily? This is Mr. Fenroy. He is accompanying me on my calls today. To get to know St. Andrew's a bit better."

"Then I'd recommend some other locations," a voice came from inside.

The pastor smiled. "Mrs. Smith loves to joke," he said and entered the apartment.

Robin followed. Confused, he gazed at the jumble of beds, clothing, and household items that lay in the corners; there were no cupboards. The small room contained three mattresses—a double and two singles—in addition to a table and chair. Along one wall stood a primitive cooking area. The tiny oven clearly doubled as heating in the wintertime. On it stood a pot, with another beside it. One of the children was scraping it with a tin spoon, as if there might be some remains from the last meal. The room and a tiny adjoining chamber, in which another bed stood, were full of children. In addition to Emily, Robin counted six altogether, of all ages. The woman lying in the largest bed was holding a newborn in her arms.

"Come here, Reverend, and bless our little Harry!" she said to Waddell.

Mrs. Smith was a big-boned woman with dark hair and a red face. She was thin and wore a threadbare nightgown that barely covered her swollen breasts. She didn't appear to be ashamed, though. With her large, calloused hands, she pushed aside the cloth in which the child was wrapped and revealed his red, wrinkled face.

"He's going to start screaming again," Emily said, resigned, as little Harry screwed up his tiny mouth.

The pastor quickly blessed him.

"A handsome boy," he praised, as Mrs. Smith unabashedly pulled the child to her breast to stop him from crying. "My wife sent this for you so you can regain your strength quickly." From his pocket Waddell pulled a packet with a loaf of bread, a piece of butter wrapped in waxed paper, and a jar of marmalade. The children crowded forward like a pack of wolves.

"Hands off, that's for Mama!" Emily ordered.

She shooed her siblings away and tucked the precious food on a shelf—pieced together from discarded wood—high enough that the other children couldn't reach it.

"I'll share some with you soon enough," Mrs. Smith reassured the little ones, who had already begun to wail. "We'll have a princely dinner! Many thanks, Reverend, and God bless your wife too!"

Robin turned to Emily. "Where . . . do they all sleep?" he inquired, gesturing to the children.

Emily looked at him as if he were out of his mind. "Here," she answered simply. "The two smallest in Mama and Papa's bed; two here"—she gestured to the narrower of the two single beds—"and three here." She indicated the wider bed. "It's all right," she assured him when she saw his disbelieving look. "Two next to each other, and Johnny at the foot. I sleep there." She pointed to the little side room.

Robin wondered how she had earned the privilege of having her own room. The pastor, on the other hand, frowned.

"Don't you have any boys boarding with you anymore?" he asked Mrs. Smith with concern. "Are you managing without the extra income? You've always had two."

Mrs. Smith nodded. "We can't manage two extra anymore," she said sadly. "Johnny is taller now, and Billy can't sleep at the foot of the bed anymore." She smiled faintly. "No, don't look so upset, Reverend. We have a girl boarder! A kind young thing who works next to me at the factory. Well, we had to get rid of the boy because he was making eyes at Emily, so I thought, why not take the girl in? Of course, it's a risk for me. Angus might bed her . . ." When she mentioned the possible infidelity, she lowered her voice, but the children clearly heard her. "But better Angus's indiscretions than Emily being taken advantage of. Better that a boarding girl is running around with a big belly than my own daughter. Anyway, I can't complain so far. Neither about Angus nor the girl. No, she's a good one, is Leah. Doesn't drink, doesn't go whoring. In fact, she should be here soon. As long as I'm in my confinement, she offered to race over during the lunch break to shop and cook, although I didn't want to accept. I know how tiring it is, running back and forth in such a short time, and Emily can start the stove and go to the grocer's. Leah's a good girl, I reckon."

As she was calling down all the favors of heaven upon her boarder, the door opened. All of the children rushed to the young woman standing in the doorway with a basket on her arm.

"Sweet rolls, children!" the girl sang. "The baker gave them to me cheap; they're from the day before yesterday. It doesn't matter, we'll soften them in water and make porridge. And then we'll celebrate little Harry's birthday! And I have soup too."

Leah wore a simple blue calico dress with a white pinafore. To keep off the cold, she'd wrapped a knitted shawl around her narrow shoulders. Her fine blonde hair had been braided and pinned up around her head. It was a style that March more or less demanded of the women to keep their long hair from getting caught in the machinery. Leah was very slender, delicate, and pretty. She gazed at the children lovingly, awake and alert.

Robin stared at the young woman. Her violet eyes were no longer shaded and sunken deep into their sockets.

"Leah?" he asked. "Leah Hobarth?"

Vera Carrigan's former charge raised her gaze from the horde of children who looked ready to tear the hard rolls from her hands and swallow them dry.

"Robin?"

# Chapter 45

"You know each other?" The pastor looked in amazement from Leah to Robin.

Robin nodded and managed not to blush. Still, he didn't know how to explain. Leah composed herself more quickly.

"Mr. Fen—Robin and I met in Rotorua," she explained. "I worked there. And so did he."

"When the volcano erupted," Robin added.

"Yes. After that, I moved away." As she spoke, Leah curtsied gracefully to the pastor.

Robin didn't add anything. In telling their story, Helena didn't let on that she had met her second cousin in a traveling theater troupe; she told people that they'd chanced to stay in the same hotel and that she'd noticed him at a theater performance. He certainly didn't want to disclose to the pastor any further details about his acquaintance with Leah—and certainly not in the presence of the Smith family.

"It's a small world," Mrs. Smith said.

"Don't tell me you're *the* Mr. Fenroy," Leah whispered to Robin.

She had turned back to the children and was spooning out a thin soup from the pot she had taken from her basket. He pretended to help her.

"The soup is from Mrs. Deaver next door," Leah announced. "For you, Mrs. Smith, so you can regain your strength. It's chicken."

Robin wouldn't have been able to tell. The soup appeared to have no meat in it, only a few pieces of carrot swimming in the broth.

"We need to talk," Robin whispered below the noise of Mrs. Smith's thanks and the shrill voices of the children clamoring for soup. He wanted to suggest a café on the border between Mornington and the worker's quarter, but then it occurred to him that Leah was an honest girl now—or at least she wanted to appear so. It would be impossible for her to go out for coffee alone with a young man, entirely aside from the scandal that would ensue if Mr. Fenroy were to be seen with a factory girl.

"So, are you getting ready for the dance at the parsonage?" Leah asked, turning to Emily while casting a meaningful glance at Robin. "I promised to go with her, Mrs. Smith. Yes, I know, she's still too young, but she does so want to go . . ."

"And she'll be under our watchful eye," the pastor added in support. "I'll ask one of the volunteers to escort the girls home afterward. That's assuming you're not looking for a beau at the dance, Leah." His last words sounded stern.

Leah laughed her short, joyless laugh. That hadn't changed, at least.

"I'm not running after men, Reverend," she assured him. "I had a few princes, you know"—and the taunting look she gave Robin was so brief that no one but him noticed it—"and I'm not going to pick one up at the factory."

"A praiseworthy attitude, although it will surely damn you to solitude!" Mrs. Smith said with a laugh. "I don't rightly recall a prince ever coming around *this* neighborhood!"

"Here, let me comb your hair, Emily," Leah said. "And then we'll see if I don't have a dress you can borrow." She and Emily ducked into the little room where they slept. Only Robin heard the word she whispered to him as she passed: "graveyard."

"So? Do you like the way your workers live?" the pastor asked Robin on their way back to the church. There was more commotion on the streets now. It consisted mostly of poorly dressed women with big baskets who were rushing back and forth, trying to get their shopping done and their children fed during the short midday break from the factories. "With the wages you pay them, the Smiths can just afford this hole—but only if they take on one or even two boarders. The boarders are usually young men from the factory who don't yet have their own families. In theory, they share a bed with one or two of the sons, but in practice, they often land in bed with one of the girls. And when that happens, not all of the fathers throw them out right away like Angus Smith did when he noticed that his boarding boy was chasing after little Emily. Often people turn a blind eye to the situation if the boy pays a bit more for the privilege. Sometimes it's the wife's bed he's sharing. I've heard stories that would make a Christian's hair stand on end! But the people aren't bad, Mr. Fenroy. This is all happening because of poverty."

"I understand . . ."

Robin nodded and silently swore to put things right. It wouldn't be easy to talk with March about it; undoubtedly she would object that the other factories didn't pay any better. But at least in *his* factory, he resolved, people would earn enough to live decently.

But more than with the Smith family's poverty, his mind was occupied with the reappearance of Leah—and what consequences that might have for him. Should he even meet her in the cemetery? The "old" Leah wouldn't have had any hesitations about using her knowledge of his past life to blackmail him. Would she come up with such an idea on her own, though? Robin doubted it. As long as he'd known Leah, he'd never seen her have a single independent thought; she had only carried out Vera's perfidious orchestrations. Of course she had also never been sober. Who knew what kind of person had actually been hiding behind the veil of intoxication?

Robin decided to satisfy his curiosity. He was burning to know how Leah had ended up in Dunedin. He would have to see what happened next. Robin didn't think the girl had any evidence of his participation in the Carrigan Company, and in the worst case, he could always deny it. March probably wouldn't shrink from having Leah sent to prison for defamation of character.

"I hope you had an informative day," the pastor said when they arrived back at the church and he took leave of his young visitor. "Perhaps you will get more involved in your factory again, Mr. Fenroy . . . Robin. Even if business doesn't really appeal to you, as long as the concerns belong to you, you are responsible for them."

Robin nodded again, his mind still on his meeting with Leah. He was supposed to go to a soiree with Helena that night, but he begged off with a headache and the beginnings of a cold, and, feeling guilty, he spooned up the rich chicken soup that the cook had sent to his room.

"It's the best thing for a flu! You'll be right as rain in no time," she said.

Helena had a girlfriend accompany her in his place and disappeared with the coach around seven. March was still at the factory. It was payday, and she didn't leave her post until the last of the workers had been paid. Peta was already at the parish hall, serving the dancers punch and snacks. Robin had asked the cook to prepare a big platter of sandwiches, and the result was a collection of delicious treats, the likes of which the workers had probably never tasted before. Peta had left with it, delighted—and convinced that he had won Robin over to his cause.

So no one noticed when, dressed again in the second-hand trousers and jacket, Robin slipped out of the house. The parish hall was brightly lit, and Irish dance music rang out, along with laughter and song.

Robin withstood the crowd just long enough to cast a quick glance inside before retiring to the neighboring churchyard. There he sat on a gravestone and silently repeated Hamlet's monologue to himself while he waited.

Leah appeared half an hour later, happy to see him. "I'm glad you're already here. I can't stay long. Not that anyone's going to get too close to my little Emily. The reverend will surely keep an eye on her, and on me as well. If I'm gone too long, he'll ask questions."

Leah looked warm; perhaps she had been dancing. She also looked a bit more like her former self than she had at noon. Her hair hung loose. She had braided a few strands to the right and left of her face and pinned them around the back of her head. That kept the hair out of her face and showed off her pretty features. She wore a very simple but becoming muslin dress, adorned with small flowers. It was fitted so that the skirt spread wide over a stiff crinoline.

"Tell me!" she urged Robin. "I almost fell over when I saw you earlier. Our little Robin is 'Mr. Fenroy,' the mysterious factory owner who is never seen on the job. I expected it to be some old geezer who didn't have the strength to come into the factory, so he must have used it up on the charming Miss Margery Jensch. There has to be a reason why she orders the whole staff around."

"March is . . . a relative," Robin explained. "And she understands business."

Leah laughed. "No one can deny that. I only wonder why Mr. Lacrosse didn't leave the factory to her. Now talk. Don't make me drag it out of you!"

Robin described, in broad strokes, how he'd inherited the factory, how he hated the office work there, and how March had been his saving angel. Leah listened closely and watched him with bright, intelligent eyes.

"'Angel' is just about the last thing I'd call such a monster," she said when he was finished. "But for you, the calculations do seem to work out. She does the work, and you get to enjoy your fine life. Now, don't look so pained, I probably would have done the same thing in your place. Only I would have spent the money on Dr. Lester's Pick-Me-Up Tincture rather than on clothes and horses. That's much worse. So enjoy your life!"

"And you?" Robin asked. "I was also . . . quite surprised to see you here. What are you doing in Dunedin? Didn't you want to go to Auckland? To look for new theatrical jobs?"

Leah rolled her eyes. "Don't bother with the niceties. You know perfectly well that I didn't have the slightest chance of being hired by a theater company. I could only do what I was doing when Vera took me out of there."

"Are you still grateful to her?" Robin asked, astounded.

Leah shrugged. "I don't know. To be honest, my whole time with the Carrigan Company is a blur. But I didn't have to go to bed with some fellow or another every day of the week—only now and again. Of course now I know that 'picking someone up out of the gutter' means something different from what Vera did to me." Bashfully, she tucked a stray lock of hair behind her ear. "Whatever, she's dead, and I was pretty banged up. When I wasn't able to get any more laudanum, it was pretty rough for me. Everything hurt, I was afraid, I was sick . . . so I drank up all the money I had left. I don't hold my liquor very well. I lose my temper."

Robin smirked. "I know," he confessed. "I saw Bertram sic you on Vera that way."

Leah didn't return his smile, but continued quickly. "It got me into trouble. I bad-mouthed punters until no one wanted me anymore. I also started fights with other whores. One time there was even a real knock-down, drag-out fight in a bordello; I don't even remember what it was about anymore. After that I was in jail. Supposedly I had injured a woman and stolen a fellow's wallet. I have no idea if any of that was true or if the other women just used the chance to blame me for all the crooked things they got up to that night. In jail there wasn't any booze. For the first time in years, I could think clearly." She looked at Robin with a wry grin. "It's not like I found religion or anything like that. No enlightenment or any kind of spiritual visions. I just decided I'd had enough."

"Enough of what?" Robin asked.

"Enough of dirty pubs and dirtier men who treated me as if I were even worse scum than they were. Enough of cheap hooch and headaches the next morning and of always being angry. Compared with that, jail wasn't so bad." She smiled weakly. "Your factory sometimes seems much worse, though, Robin. In the clink we had to work, but at least we got enough to eat and everyone had a cot of her own. I just dreaded what might happen next. What if the fellow who had taken me under his wing was still waiting for me out there? Those fellows make sure that the punters don't slit your throat, but they take half your earnings for the privilege and do it to you themselves for free. So when I was released, I made a beeline for the harbor, smuggled myself onto the next ship, and was just lucky that it was going to Dunedin and not China, or I would have starved to death in the cargo hold. They locked it up after I'd hidden away in there. There wasn't anything to eat, just wool for the factories. Anyway, I survived the trip and got off board again without being seen. And then, for the first time in my life, I looked for honest work. In your factory." She laughed. "Mrs. Smith is right. It's a small world."

"And what . . . is it like?" Robin wanted to know.

"What is what like? Honesty?" Leah asked. "Nice. Really, I never would have thought so, but I like being honest as much as being sober. I'd rather have my own bed, but I like it at the Smiths'. I like the children; Emily is so sweet. I really do have to get back inside and look after her."

"I meant the factory," Robin clarified.

Leah shrugged. "Don't tell me you've never been inside. Go. You don't even have to stand at a machine, the noise alone is hell. The dust and the heat are unbearable. The work itself isn't hard, just tedious. You make the same movements over and over, and by evening everything hurts. During the break they send you outside—after the drudgery in the heat, you get rain in the yard. Most people come down with bronchitis. Every night poor Mr. Smith practically coughs up a lung. The wages are enough for me; I have food to eat and once in a while I can buy myself a dress like this one here. But that's only because I have a place to sleep as a boarder. I couldn't afford an apartment of my own. And that's not even considering what would happen if I got pregnant. That's why I'm staying away from the men. The reverend doesn't need to worry about me."

"And . . . in the future?" Robin asked. "What do you want to do with your life?"

Leah shrugged. "If a prince doesn't arrive . . . no, seriously, I'm not going to grow old in the woolen mill. I'm looking for a job in the dressmakers' shop, as soon as one becomes available. Right now they're all taken. It's more pleasant and cleaner working at a sewing machine, and you can learn how to make a dress for yourself. The seamstresses also earn better money. Later, we'll have to see. I don't plan that far in advance. And you? Won't you ever work again, Robin? Honestly, that's enviable. But I always thought you liked acting."

Robin sighed. "They don't hire princes," he muttered. "Privately I can always act a scene once in a while. At soirees. Or people gather around the piano to sing a little bit . . ."

"You can't sing," Leah reminded him.

"That's true, but I can recite poems or monologues. My Hamlet is always a big hit."

Robin's voice resonated with the bitterness that gripped him every time he wasted his talent on the socialites around him. Helena and the others didn't really listen, they just pretended to be feverish with stage fright at the prospect of their own performances. Leah might understand that, but she seemed very far from pitying him.

Still, her voice was completely calm as she replied, "If that's enough for you . . ."

# Chapter 46

Robin spent half the night thinking about reforms for the factory and how he could convey the necessity of the increased costs to March. He was determined to prevail, but feared her sharp tongue and endless discussions. He might even have to bring himself to make regular inspections of the factories to ensure that she didn't just quietly reverse his decisions again to maintain the bottom line. Up until now he'd always believed that she respected his wishes.

He appeared at breakfast early but in a bad mood, half hoping that March had already left for the office. That was unlikely on a Sunday, but it had happened. In those cases, she'd hurried from the office to the church so she could make a dutiful appearance, but then disappeared again behind her mountain of files. Robin didn't understand how she could find it enjoyable, but the young woman apparently did.

This morning, however, he found her alone at the breakfast table. She had been served poached eggs and buttered toast, and she was drinking coffee and reading the Sunday paper. She was already dressed for church; it was clear she wasn't planning to go to the office. When Robin appeared, she was delighted.

"How nice to have you all to myself, Robin!" she said in greeting. "I really must speak with you." She smiled. "I wanted to ask you for a formal meeting."

"I'm not so hard to talk to," grumbled Robin.

"No, but Helena is always hanging on your coattails," March explained. "You have to watch out; people are already talking about an engagement. And maybe that's all right with you . . ."

March took a bite of her egg. Robin's relationship with Helena was surely not the reason she wanted to talk to him, but he practically dropped his coffee cup when she mentioned it. *Engagement?* Marrying Helena was the last thing on his mind.

"But we're—we're related," he stammered.

"Second cousins," March clarified. "You could even marry a first cousin. Just keep your distance if you don't want to. But enough about that; you can think it over later. I need to speak to you about the factory. The woolen mill, specifically."

Robin tensed. She was right. His private life didn't matter right now. And she had given him the perfect opening.

"So do I," he said firmly. "I need to talk to you too. You're not going to like it, March, but we're going to have to change some things. I was out with the pastor yesterday . . ." Robin had had the whole night to rehearse his speech, and now he delivered it with a resolute voice. It helped that March made no move to interrupt. She listened, without contradicting him, as he suggested higher wages, longer breaks, and more light and fresh air on the factory floors. "We also need some kind of nursery where the women can leave their infants while they work. There's this old lady in the city who could watch them, and that probably wouldn't be too expensive. And perhaps you're going to laugh, but don't we need properly trained people in the factory? Couldn't we offer the youngest workers some kind of training so that they can get on later? And still pay them? Like an apprenticeship?"

At that point, March did roll her eyes. "Robin, apprentices aren't paid. To the contrary, many masters expect payment from their trainees in the first year. A woolen mill needs, at most, three qualified mechanics. Should we train thirty young men for that?"

Robin rubbed his forehead and sighed. "It was just an idea. But everything else we *will* change. The reverend is right: I own the factory now, and I am responsible for it."

March smiled. "That's exactly what I wanted to talk to you about, Robin. This woolen mill—it's becoming unprofitable. It'll happen whether or not we pay the workers a few pence more or less. The fact is that our entire facility is outdated. We still have machines that were invented almost a hundred years ago. There are much better and faster ones now. We could double our production, but to do so, we'd have to make some costly investments. We need to update all of the machinery. I've tallied it up, and upon careful reflection, I've come to the conclusion that it's simply not worth it. We'd need to increase production for export, and at a much lower cost than the mills in England. And we'd also have to figure in the cost of transport. We wouldn't be able to earn back the costs of modernization for years.

"Our dressmakers' shops, on the other hand, are doing fantastically. The sewing machines are relatively new, and they're easier to replace than the gigantic looms and spinning machines. We can make better use of the seamstresses' labor than the weavers'. The girls like to take work home with them, which works out for both parties: They earn more, and we increase production. So this is what I've come up with—with your approval, of course. I'd like to sell the woolen mill. I already have an interested party. It's a Scottish consortium that wants to modernize completely and secure the entire New Zealand market in the process. They'll do it, too, and they'll oust any competition." Just thinking about Porter and Wentworth being trounced brought a shark-like smile to March's face. "I'd invest the proceeds in another dressmakers' shop," she continued. "I think I've already found the right buildings—right by the harbor, an old granary. I'm thinking about marketing our products directly. So we sew clothes and then sell them in our own shops or, at most, with one middleman. And that would put us ahead of the competition, meaning Magiel. So, what do you say?" She looked at him, waiting for approval.

Robin needed a moment to be sure he even understood March's explanation, but soon he began to feel the first hint of relief. The woolen mill wouldn't belong to him anymore; he would be rid of the responsibility! It would have to close while undergoing modernization, and that would give the workers a chance to reorient themselves. Maybe they would find work under better conditions. And then the consortium would come in with brand-new machines, which would undoubtedly be easier to operate and make less of a din. With his whole heart, Robin hoped for better conditions for the men and women working in the factory. But however it turned out, he wouldn't have to worry about it anymore. He would only be responsible for the dressmakers' shops, and on that score, it seemed, Leah and March agreed: The seamstresses had it much better than the weavers. Robin thought of the young girls in the church in their homemade dresses. They always looked much livelier and happier than the ladies from the factory.

"I think," Robin said slowly, "that would be a very good idea. You have my full approval. By the way, I know . . . a young woman who works in the factory now but would very much like to change over to a dressmakers' shop. Could you perhaps do something about that?"

March seemed at least as relieved as Robin felt.

"Of course!" she replied. "Have her come by my office tomorrow, and she'll have her job. I'm really happy, Robin, that we were able to agree so quickly. It's such a pleasure to work with you!"

# Part 5

## CHEAP SINS

ROTORUA (NORTH ISLAND)

DUNEDIN (SOUTH ISLAND)

OCTOBER 1888

# Chapter 47

"You are coming to the meeting, aren't you?" Brett McDougal asked. He had run into Aroha in the city's little print shop. Both were waiting for the newest brochures for their hotels. The high season, New Zealand's summer, was right around the corner, and Rotorua was decking itself out in every imaginable way. Aroha was already worried that all of the construction presently underway wouldn't be finished by the beginning of November. "Of course," the man added awkwardly, "you should bring Mr. Bao."

Aroha shot him an indignant look. "Are you in charge of who's allowed to bring whom to the meeting?" she asked sharply. "Mr. Bao is my business director; of course he's coming. Though I don't really see any sense in discussing the government's plan again. It's a matter for the Maori. They simply must be more careful about leasing their land."

"And that's exactly why we need you, Miss Aroha. Please forgive my faux pas about Mr. Bao . . ."

Aroha frowned. Until a few months ago, no one would have thought twice about Bao attending such a meeting. He had been working in the hotel business for four years, and was well known to all in the community. But lately all of New Zealand was in an uproar over Chinese immigrants. The government had tightened immigration policies on them even further; the immigration tax had gone up. But young Chinese men—burdened with famine, floods, and political unrest in their homeland—kept coming anyway. They threw themselves with even greater zeal at the dirtiest and worst-paid jobs in New Zealand.

"It's no wonder. Now the amount they have to borrow to enter New Zealand is even higher, and they have to pay it back," Bao had explained to her. "They're under tremendous pressure, and the result is exactly what the government wants to avoid: driving wages down for New Zealanders."

It was true: there were more and more Chinese workers in Rotorua, and the white people and the Maori were equally upset about it. Previously *they* would have had those jobs—and at much higher wages.

"Come now," McDougal said. "Someone has to back up the Maori, even if it's just a gesture of solidarity. Waimarama will be there and can translate. Besides, you're *pakeha,* so the government commissioners might actually listen to you. You can't hide, Miss Aroha. Koro would have wanted it!"

Aroha sighed. McDougal was right. Ever since the Pink and White Terraces disappeared to the bottom of the lake, Te Wairoa was buried, and Ohinemutu lost all of its attraction, Maori participation in the tourism business had decreased massively. Previously, no one really noticed that the government had controlled this young industry from the start. The Thermal Springs Districts Act of 1881 had determined that the government could develop and make use of land in Rotorua. They had leased the land from the Maori and then rented it out to *pakeha,* who were willing to invest. The hotels in Rotorua had been built on this basis, while the Maori had concentrated on commercializing the terraces.

Everyone had been happy with the arrangement, but now the only attractions left for the *manuhiri* were the hot springs and geysers. *Pakeha* and Maori had to split the profits, and the government favored the white settlers. In Rotorua a constant stream of new spas appeared. Promenades were built, as well as a small zoo and an eight-hundred-acre park. The hoteliers organized concerts at the spas. Fine restaurants and teahouses opened, of which the Chinese Garden Lodge had the most successful. It combined English and Chinese tea traditions and fulfilled travelers' desires for exotic-seeming experiences. On the other hand, the government barely tolerated the offerings of the Maori—dance exhibitions and spirit invocations and the sale of handcrafts along the hotel promenades. If the tribes applied to become hotel owners or planned to open arts-and-crafts shops, however, the government made things difficult with the concession and land provision.

The next evening, a government representative was coming to Rotorua to inform local business owners of some new plans. The meeting would take place at the Rotorua Lodge, and Aroha assumed that the tribes hadn't even been invited. Undoubtedly McDougal had alerted them and sought support for his wife's people.

"All right, then, we'll come," Aroha replied, giving in.

Not that she really wanted to. Even before and after the high season, the hotel, spa, and teahouse were almost always booked solid, and neither she nor Bao had enough time for each other or for Lani, who was two-and-a-half years old and always needed attention. She was doted on by many of the guests, who assumed she was Aroha and Bao's own child. Aroha always wondered how they arrived at that conclusion, since the little one didn't look like her or Bao at all. Lani's Maori parentage was obvious, but the foreign guests had never really looked carefully at the native New Zealanders. As a result, they attributed Lani's looks to her being a mixture of white and Chinese—a combination that some frowned upon. Time and again, guests would leave under false pretenses after Aroha introduced Lani as her daughter, and they saw the little girl laughing with Bao.

Fortunately, the business was doing well enough that Aroha could afford to simply let those people leave. She didn't want to have anything to do with racists, she'd explained to Waimarama. At that, Waimarama had winked and asked if Lani might not have a little brother or sister soon.

Aroha had shaken her head fiercely. "Bao is my esteemed colleague, and he cares very much for Lani. That is all. I would be very grateful, Wai, if you wouldn't spread rumors!"

In truth, the rumors about Aroha and Bao had been circulating for a long time. After all, the two were always together, and when Lani was with them, they looked like a harmonious little family. Of course no one had ever seen them exchange intimacies; Bao's behavior was irreproachable, and Aroha still mourned for Koro. She wasn't looking for a new partner. Of course, if a young man did come courting her, he'd soon have to deal with Bao. The young man got rid of the suitor and did so with an air of possessiveness—or at least that's how the men of Rotorua interpreted it. The women only needed to look Bao in the eye to recognize how he felt about Aroha. They wondered if Aroha returned his affections, and, of course, whether a possible relationship would affect the business. "Miss Aroha does have—how shall I put it?—a taste for the *exotic*," Mrs. Roberts once observed. She ran the spa and was privy to every bit of gossip. "After all, she almost married a Maori. But a Chinaman! That's really a completely different thing . . ."

As for Aroha, she didn't spend any time contemplating her feelings for Bao. It was simply a matter of course to be with him. When Bao started a sentence, Aroha often finished it. When she went to give a member of the hotel staff an assignment, she often discovered that they had already gotten it from Bao and had completed the task. Bao and Aroha thought and behaved in such harmony that Aroha would often look up from her work, unexpectedly meet his gaze, and smile. They went on outings together, attended concerts or plays. They laughed a great deal, thought up plans and little surprises for the guests, and Aroha was delighted that Bao was teaching Lani Chinese. Through all of this, Aroha didn't think about love. In fact, she outright forbade herself from even considering a new relationship. She didn't speak about the curse; it hurt her that no one took her fears seriously. Cat, Linda, and Carol considered the fact that Aroha had lost first Matiu and then Koro to accidents as nothing more than bad luck.

"Sadly, such things do happen, child," Linda said again on her last visit. She had made the time to spend four weeks at the spa, and Carol had come with her. The half sisters had taken the opportunity to try to talk some sense into Aroha. "Listen, our Pai—you know, the teacher at our school—just lost her third baby. She could talk about a curse too." Carol added that their postmistress had just been widowed for the second time. Sometimes people just had bad luck.

Aroha had responded defiantly that she was happy with her hotel and with Lani. Of course, Linda and Carol had noticed that Bao did everything for Aroha. He was always ready to relieve her of unpleasant tasks, to protect her from demanding guests, or simply to spoil her. Aroha wasn't even aware of how often a cup of hot tea with plenty of sugar and cream appeared before her while she occupied herself with the accounts or brooded over room occupancies. She only vaguely noticed how often her horse awaited her in the stall, already saddled and bridled, whenever she wanted to go somewhere—despite the fact that Bao was afraid of horses. He had really outdone himself with his last gift: when a little stray dog had crossed his path in Ohinemutu, he'd brought it back to the hotel for Aroha and Lani. "We can call him Tapsy," he'd said with a wink.

Tapsy, a reddish-brown collie mix, jumped up on Aroha excitedly as she came back into the hotel with her stack of freshly printed brochures. Bao was busy at the front desk. Lani was standing on a chair next to him, her expression serious as she handed out brochures for a Maori dance performance to a small group of *manuhiri*. She was careful to press one into the hand of each guest, plus Aroha.

"Thank you! You are such a great help!" she praised, and gave the child a quick kiss. As always, her heart leaped in her breast whenever she saw the little girl. She couldn't imagine life without her. "What are you advertising there?" She unfolded the brochure.

"The Tuhourangi are starting their *powhiri* again tomorrow night," Bao explained cheerfully. "After the winter break. Shall we attend? Almost all the guests are going, so we won't have very many people here for dinner, and there won't be much to do in the kitchen."

Aroha frowned. "We can't, I'm afraid; we have a meeting to attend. The government is unveiling their newest plans to increase tourism. Mr. Randolph, who sold us this wonderful boardwalk last year—the one they'll still be working on well into the high season—is bringing an engineer along this time. They have some kind of plans for the geysers. And McDougal wants to get the Maori more closely involved. He's going to raise hell with Randolph so, in the future, he doesn't always keep giving all the concessions to the *pakeha*. We have to go. Koro would have wanted me to support him, McDougal said. And he's right."

"But Koro would have dealt with the government himself," Bao objected. "The Tuhourangi haven't done anything since the loss of the terraces. Since Sophia and Kate have been gone, they've left everything to the *pakeha*."

Sophia Hinerangi and Kate Middlemass had left the region after the volcanic eruption. They might have managed to get by; there were still the hot springs and geysers, and lately there had been some interest in viewing the Buried Village, as people called Te Wairoa. Resourceful *pakeha* guides even offered boat tours of the area where the terraces used to be. But the women had been too shaken by their experience, and they mourned for everyone they'd lost. They both just wanted to get away.

Aroha nodded sadly. "I hope the local tribes send representatives to this meeting and offer some new ideas so there's something for McDougal and me to support," she finally said. "But regardless of what happens, we need to be there."

Aroha and Bao arrived rather late to the meeting, and they brought Lani along. The chambermaid who was supposed to take care of the child had come down with a nasty stomach flu, so Aroha sent her to bed with a hot-water bottle and a cup of chamomile tea. The child rode in on Bao's shoulders, and Aroha hoped that the little one would fall asleep and not disturb the meeting.

Mr. Randolph, the government's authorized agent for the promotion of tourism, was just introducing Mr. Camille Malfroy. Randolph, who was known for liking the sound of his own voice, cast a withering glance at Aroha, Bao, and Lani. Their late entrance drew everyone's attention, along with murmurs and a general scraping of chairs. Randolph cleared his throat in an attempt to restore the quiet.

"As you all know, losing the Pink and White Terraces has decreased the attractiveness of the region to foreign guests. All that's left are the hot springs and the geysers . . ."

"And that's enough," noted McDougal. The Scotsman was seated in the front row.

"It is in no way enough, Mr. McDougal, not if we want to keep Rotorua on the list of the most sought-after destinations worldwide," Randolph countered. "There are geysers all over the world that erupt more spectacularly, and higher at that. Why shouldn't our guests travel to Iceland, for example?"

"Because it's rather cold this time of year," Aroha interjected.

She couldn't restrain herself. She really didn't like Mr. Randolph, a rigid little man in a three-piece suit whose face always reminded her a bit of a turkey pecking for grain. She had already bickered with him back when she worked for the Tuhourangi.

"Now, let's stick to the matter at hand, Miss Fitzpatrick!" Randolph scolded. The other participants laughed. "The fact of the matter is, world travelers don't usually let little troubles and inconvenient weather get in their way. Especially not when they're visiting locations that offer something truly spectacular. And this is where we can start. I am happy to be able to share with you today that Mr. Malfroy has developed a system that will allow us to have a direct influence on the geyser activity in our region."

Randolph seemed to expect cheers, but the murmurs of the hotel owners and businesspeople sounded skeptical.

"Does that mean you're going to make the volcano erupt again?" McDougal demanded. "I remember certain new geyser activity very well. It was hard enough to keep the deaths out of the headlines . . ."

"Of course not!" Malfroy cried. He was a tall, thin man with an astoundingly high voice. "We're talking about a sort of pipework. During the winter, I experimented with the Pohutu geyser, and it now erupts to a height of eighteen to twenty-four meters, twice a day!"

Waimarama McDougal rose, outraged. Seated at the back of the room, some representatives of the Tuhourangi and the Ngati Whakaue didn't even wait to be called on, but began to lament at full volume in Maori. They knew enough English to follow the proceedings, but not to respond in the language. Aroha started to translate, but Waimarama had already launched an outraged attack on the government agent and his engineer.

"You experimented? Messed about with the hot springs and geysers? In the name of the local Maori tribes, who own these thermal fields, I must strenuously object! The people you hear objecting back there are representatives of the tribes. The Pohutu geyser is sacred to them."

Randolph huffed. "Oh, enough of this 'sacred' business!" he said angrily. "As long as our Maori friends have no objections to putting soap in the hot springs to make them bubble more impressively, I don't want anyone giving me grief about piping the geysers. It doesn't look like the spirits care about either intervention. If you would please continue, Mr. Malfroy . . ."

Although the room was still seething like the aforementioned hot springs, Camille Malfroy now laid out the construction plans. He clearly demonstrated, with the help of diagrams, how it was possible to manipulate a geyser so as to make it spray higher. While there didn't seem to be any obvious dangers in the system, Aroha found it outrageous—and deceitful. After all, guests came to Rotorua to see the wonders of nature. Besides, Waimarama was right: the geysers were on Maori land.

When the engineer finished, an older chieftain rose and began a speech that Waimarama translated. In the name of the Ngati Whakaue, he registered an objection to the manipulation of the geysers.

"It is true that my people profit from the foreigners who come here to see our land, and our income has sharply decreased since the spirits tore the terraces from this world. And yes, a couple of young people were misled into provoking the spirits of the hot springs by putting soap in their holes. This is utter nonsense, and we condemn it. But even more so do we condemn the idea of forcing the spirits of the geysers into the ways of the *pakeha*. Nothing good can come of it, and we will protest against it. And there is much more in Rotorua that we do not like. This was once a place shared by *pakeha* and Maori alike. Together we welcomed the *manuhiri* to the city and to our *marae*. We could do business with them . . ."

"And bamboozle them!" yelled someone from the rows of *pakeha*. Aroha looked, but couldn't figure out who it was.

"We welcomed them," the Maori said, with dignity. "But now the *pakeha* are building bigger and bigger hotels, and no one wants to stay in our simple accommodations anymore. The water from the hot springs is diverted into the spas, far from Nature and from her healing spirits. You only bring the *manuhiri* to our *marae* the way cattle drivers herd cattle. *Pakeha* guides lead them, seat them on *pakeha* chairs, and from there they watch us dance. One day they go to see animals in what you call a zoo, and the next day, they visit our tribes. No one explains the meaning of our songs or dances to them . . ."

"When I ask permission to open souvenir shop in Rotorua, government not give it to me!" interrupted an impatient young Maori man in English.

Now the room was full of whispering. Mr. Randolph had to rap on the table to be heard.

"You're seeing things entirely wrong," he declared to the Maori. "Fine, about the geysers. We need to talk about that, and we will. But with regard to natives owning hotels and shops—and I want to be very clear about this—I do not at all agree that the Maori should be displayed to visitors like animals. That goes entirely against the spirit of our age, at least in the more enlightened classes of society from which our visitors predominantly come. They are interested in the culture of the natives of the lands they visit. However"—Randolph paused emphatically—"they also want to see that culture maintained! It annoys them to see a Maori in the uniform of a hotel employee. They want to see him in his warrior's garb. They want to participate in rituals where spirits are conjured. They're looking for, shall we say, the 'noble savage' in Rousseau's sense of the term, if you understand me."

"No, he doesn't understand that," said Aroha, while Waimarama translated for the Maori as best she could. "No right-thinking person understands that. We are living at the end of the nineteenth century, and that means all of us, including our Maori neighbors. We share a country and a currency, and many share the same faith. The land is full of paved streets and railways, there are factories, and the goods produced in them are things that many Maori would also gladly buy. The time of savages is long gone, if it ever was there to begin with—and I find the word entirely inappropriate for people of any sort. And there certainly has never been any such thing as a noble savage. Perhaps you recall the Hauhau Wars. A misguided prophet decided to reinstate old Polynesian customs, so his followers cut off their enemies' heads and smoked them over the fire to keep as mementos. You don't want to go back to that, do you? So you must come to terms with the fact that some Maori people want to provide services just like the rest of us. They modify their customs so they can be displayed to the *manuhiri* without shocking them; likewise the *manuhiri* need to accept that the lad who dances the *haka* for them at night will be waiting for them at the reception desk in the morning. And he'll be wearing livery as required by the hotel owner—who may also be a Maori and wear a suit instead of warrior's garb."

"Rousseau was a Swiss philosopher," Bao added, in a measured tone, "who lived over a hundred years ago and wrote in French. He certainly had a great mind, but he never traveled outside of France. Whatever he may have said about noble savages—or, rather, humans in their natural state—was speculation at best, and perhaps even fantasy."

Bao spoke matter-of-factly; it wasn't his intention to shame the government agent, but to clarify for those in the room unfamiliar with Rousseau. But the man didn't take it that way.

Red with anger, Randolph turned his turkey face toward Bao.

"Our visitors probably wouldn't wonder at Maori hotel owners when we already have a Chinaman among us. How do you claim the right to speak at this meeting?"

Bao bowed. "I was not aware," he said in a politely icy tone, "that the right to speak here depended on one's background. If I have broken a rule—"

"Oh, nonsense!" Aroha cut him off. "Anyone can speak here. Not to mention that Mr. Duong is the business manager of the Chinese Garden Lodge, Mr. Randolph, as you surely must know . . ."

"Business manager?" Randolph let his gaze slide insinuatingly over Aroha's well-proportioned figure and then over Bao. "Aha."

"What do you mean by that?" Aroha asked, her eyes flashing.

"Careful," Bao said softly. "You'll wake Lani." The child had fallen asleep on his lap.

"How touching. The perfect husband and father," Randolph said mockingly. "Don't act that way, Miss Fitzpatrick. We can all imagine how a slant-eye weaseled his way into running your hotel."

"That's quite enough!" McDougal stood up. "In the name of all the dignitaries of Rotorua, I will not tolerate such accusations against one of our own. Miss Aroha's conduct with regard to her employee is above all reproach."

"And on behalf of Mr. Duong, I will not tolerate any denigration of his qualifications," Aroha exclaimed. "Mr. Duong owes his position at my hotel solely to his education, his outstanding manners, and his managerial abilities."

"And not a little to his boss's exotic tastes, then?" Randolph would not be intimidated.

But with this affront, he had gone too far. Koro Hinerangi's services to the tourism industry in the Rotorua region were still a living memory. The crowd objected vociferously, and Randolph was forced to retreat.

"All right, all right." He began to pack his papers away in his briefcase. "It only occurs to me that Miss Fitzpatrick always seems to choose partners who might not seem entirely appropriate . . . to outsiders."

Aroha's look could only be called scornful. "I do not divide human beings into 'appropriate' and 'inappropriate.' Which is, by the way, a requirement of our shared profession, Mr. Randolph. We in the tourism industry must know how to make everyone welcome, no matter their nationality or skin color. That's what's important to people—far more important than how high the water in the geyser shoots. And kindly do not portray me as some sort of hussy who flits from one man to the next. I was as good as married to Koro Hinerangi. He died a week before our wedding, as you may remember. I am still in mourning. Should I ever decide to approach the altar, with Mr. Duong or a man of any race, the only factor in my decision would be love." She stood up. "Shall we go, Bao? Excuse us, Mr. Randolph, we have a hotel to run."

The other hotel and business owners didn't wait for Randolph to end the meeting formally. Talking excitedly with each other, they pulled on their jackets and coats. McDougal helped Aroha into her mantilla.

"You didn't mean that seriously, did you?" he asked. "You and Mr. Duong? I mean, he is charming. But would you marry a Chinaman?"

Aroha scowled. "I can only repeat what I said. When the wedding announcement is published, you'll hear about it." And with that, she left the room.

Bao, carrying Lani in his arms, followed her out. Before leaving, he said goodbye, with his usual warmth, to his acquaintances and asked the gentlemen to convey his greetings to their wives. As soon as they were in the empty streets, approaching the lodge, Aroha resumed venting her indignation. She ranted about the manipulated geysers, Randolph's racism, and the fact that her neighbors were so upset about her possible relationship with Bao.

"Even McDougal, and he's married to a Maori woman! Does he think that what's all right for a man is somehow unthinkable for a woman?" Furious, she stumbled over the half-built boardwalk between Rotorua Lodge and the spa. "We need a streetlight here, at least! Much more than a piped-up geyser!"

Bao didn't speak until they had almost reached the lodge.

"Were you serious about what you said?" he asked.

Aroha stopped. In the moonlight, he saw how she frowned. "Serious about what?" she asked.

"That you could love me, even though I'm Chinese." Bao looked into her eyes.

Aroha laughed. "Bao, you being Chinese doesn't affect my feelings in the least. After Lani, you are the most important person in my life."

She hadn't really meant to say that, and until this moment, she hadn't been entirely aware of it herself. But now, as he stood before her, Aroha suddenly realized what Bao meant to her. She blushed and turned away. They walked the rest of the way in silence.

Soon, they reached the entrance to the hotel and saw the brightly lit foyer. A girl at the reception desk let them in.

"Two new guests," Kiri reported. "From Auckland. Otherwise, all was quiet. The *powhiri* must have been nice. Mrs. Bean asked if we offer private spirit invocations and what the *tohunga* cost per hour. I told her to ask you about it. The same with Miss Peters and Miss Howe. They want to take flute lessons, and they have already bought the instruments. Three guests complained about the noise after they tried the things out in their rooms."

"Then they must have some talent. I've never been able to coax much sound out of a *putorino*," Aroha joked. "What did they buy? Conch shells?"

Kiri laughed. "Do you want to take over the front desk, Mr. Bao?" she asked. "Or should I stay? I'm afraid Timoti won't be coming tonight. He caught the same stomach flu as the nursery maid."

"Kindly stay here, Kiri." Bao insisted on speaking formally to the Maori employees, while Aroha was more casual. She had been part of Koro's tribe for too long to suddenly stand on ceremony. "I'll accompany Miss Aroha upstairs and put Lani to bed."

Lani was asleep. Bao carried her up to Aroha's private rooms.

"May I come in as well?" he asked.

Aroha nodded, but she felt rather shy. Bao had never asked before. Lani didn't wake up when he tucked her in gently. Over her bed, Aroha and Bao's eyes met.

"You are also the most important person in my life," Bao said. "And . . . if you would allow me . . . to court you . . ."

Aroha tried to smile. "Bao, you don't need to court me. I already know what I have with you . . . or might have . . ."

When he reached for her hand, she did not pull away.

"The most important person in life is the one someone loves the most," Bao said somberly. "That's how I feel about you. Is it . . . different for you?"

Aroha thought for a moment, and then finally admitted the feelings that she had denied to herself for so long. Yes: what she felt for Bao was love. It was lovely to feel her hand in his. When he felt the tension leave her body, he began to stroke her fingers softly. She got goose bumps and felt desire—after such a long time. After Koro, she hadn't been able to feel a thing for any man. Aroha did not resist as Bao gently led her away from the cradle and placed her hand on his heart.

"Is it different for you?" he repeated, but it did not sound pressing. Rather, it sounded as if he knew the answer. His other hand moved to Aroha's cheek. He stroked it gently, as if he were afraid she would shy away. "You are so very beautiful, Aroha," he whispered. "I think I loved you from the first moment I saw you. Tell me, is it different for you?" He pulled her gingerly to him.

It was different, she thought, in some ways. Aroha hadn't loved Bao at first sight, but she treasured him from that day onward. She liked his straight black hair, his soft eyes, and the crinkly laugh lines around them.

Aroha still didn't answer. But she offered him her mouth for a kiss.

# Chapter 48

"We shouldn't have done that . . ."

Lani was stirring in her little bed, and Aroha got up to check on her. She was a little shaky. The night in Bao's arms had been wilder and more passionate than any she had ever before experienced.

He stretched, turned over, and gazed at her questioningly. "Why not? All right, the honorable Aroha Fitzpatrick slept with her employee without benefit of marriage. Doubtless that's a great disappointment to the whole respectable neighborhood. But we don't have to tell them. If there happens to be some consequence—if we order the marriage license right now, nothing will be noticeable before the wedding."

Aroha shook her head, pulled on a dressing robe, and lifted the child out of her bed. "We shouldn't have done it at all," she said, waking the sleepy Lani with a kiss on the forehead. "Not now, and not later. Bao, I can't marry you. It wouldn't work; I'd be too afraid for you."

Bao stood up and pulled her and Lani into an embrace. "What is there to be afraid of?" he asked. "Do you sleepwalk and go after your lover with a knife?"

Aroha pushed him away. "That is not funny!" she exclaimed. "Bao, you know full well what happened to Koro . . ."

Bao furrowed his brow. "Koro died in a volcanic eruption. You can't possibly feel guilty about that, can you? Nothing and no one could have saved him. Had we tried, we would both be dead too."

Aroha shook her head. "That's not what I meant. I know there was nothing we could do. But there was also Matiu . . ."

As she dressed Lani, she briefly told Bao about Omaka and her *maunga*.

"And the old *tohunga* Ngaio, Matiu's grandmother, knew it: if a man wanted to bind his soul to mine, he would die. That's why I never wanted to fall in love again. It was a mistake for us to make love last night. If we were to marry . . ." Aroha's face showed pure terror.

Bao rubbed his forehead. "All right, once again, Aroha, so I understand correctly. You, one of the smartest and most sensible women I know, really believe that you are being observed by some spirits or other, who watch over your soul and keep tabs on whether you fall in love, share your bed with someone, or consider marrying in the Anglican Church? Because that was the plan, right? If I remember correctly, the Hinerangis are Christians."

Aroha nodded.

"And that had some meaning for the spirits?" Bao asked. "And what's more, stopping this marriage was so important to them that they made a volcano erupt, deprived an entire Maori tribe of their livelihood, destroyed the landscape . . ."

Aroha bit her lip. "Please don't you make fun of me too. My mother and my aunt have already lectured me like this. But I saw the spirit canoe . . ."

"And so did plenty of other people," Bao reminded her. "Are they all suffering under a curse? That's nonsense, Aroha, and you know it."

Aroha pressed Lani to her. "Shall we go have breakfast now, Lani, my sweet?" she asked the child. "Mama and Bao just have to get dressed."

"Babby, Babby!" Lani cried and stretched her arms out toward Bao.

"At least one of the Fitzpatrick ladies is glad to have me here," Bao joked, and took Lani in his arms. "Would Miss Lani like a ride to the breakfast room?"

Aroha and Bao tried not to let on that anything was different as they entered the foyer of the hotel and listened as the receptionist reported a relatively quiet night. Bao checked over the room assignments, and with Lani in tow, Aroha popped into the breakfast room and the kitchen. The cook, a jovial woman, already had a cup of milk with honey ready for Lani, and chattered away to the child in Maori as she buttered toast, fried eggs, and put jam in little jars. Aroha gratefully left her daughter with the cook and the scullery maids and took care of a few more morning duties before meeting Bao for breakfast. The two had become accustomed to drinking their coffee together. They used the time to discuss the day's plans and look through the mail. The kitchen staff set a table for them in an out-of-the-way corner of the restaurant.

"Something else occurred to me," Bao began today. He came over to the table where Aroha sat, the newspaper and a pile of mail in his hand. "About your *maunga* . . ."

Aroha tried to brush him off. "Please, Bao, I don't want to talk about it. It's hard enough, and I . . ."

"Aroha, at least listen to me for a minute. I want to take you seriously. That's why I was thinking about my own *maunga*. If my umbilical cord was buried—I don't really know much about those customs; maybe in China they burn them or keep them in jars . . . like the best part of eunuchs—then my *maunga* is somewhere in Canton. In any case, my connection to it doesn't seem to be important to the spirits. I don't feel any trace of homesickness and no bond to Canton. It was different for Matiu, wasn't it?"

Aroha nodded. "He always felt uprooted. He was so happy when he came to Wairarapa."

"There you have it," Bao said contentedly. "He felt settled in a place, and he wanted the same for you. That turned the spirits against him. I personally doubt that's enough to cause them to make a train derail, but if you want to believe that, so be it. It's just the same with Koro. He wanted to settle you in Rotorua; Mount Tarawera was his *maunga*. Again, the spirits reacted—a little overdramatically, if you ask me, but as I said, believe what you will. But then take me. My *maunga* lies far outside the sphere of influence of the spirits of New Zealand, and I have absolutely no obligation to settle in the shadow of some Cantonese mountain. I am exactly as rootless as you are, Aroha! I barely know my ancestors, and I have no house gods. I couldn't recite any acceptable *pepeha*, as the Maori call it. So why should the spirits care about me? Forget this whole thing, Aroha. I love you, you love me, and tomorrow we'll order the marriage license. It's that simple. Here's the mail."

He set a packet of letters on the table. Aroha noticed an envelope with Chinese characters.

"Who is writing to you from China?" she asked, happy to change the subject.

Bao turned the envelope over. Someone had written the address neatly in English.

"It's from Dunedin," he explained, and pointed to the postmark. "My friend Deng Yong, whom you know from the market. We shared a rather rundown bedsit. Funny, I didn't know he could write." Bao opened the letter, scanned the

401

plain piece of paper covered with Chinese characters, and smiled sadly. "That's moving. The letter is from all the men that I knew from that boardinghouse, if not from the whole Chinese community of Dunedin. Apparently, they got together a couple of people who knew some characters. There are even a few words of English in there."

"What was so important that they wanted to write to you?" asked Aroha, pouring the coffee. "Do you want a croissant? The cook has outdone herself today." She took a pastry and put another on a plate for Bao.

Bao was still deciphering the letter. "They're asking for my help," he said finally. "The situation in Dunedin is getting more and more difficult. The men live in the most primitive conditions because no one will rent them a proper room. The employers pay less and less, so there are constant hostilities. And now the local dignitaries are planning a meeting at the Princess Theater to protest against the Chinese 'infiltration' of the colony, whatever that means. Deng Yong copied the words from the newspaper. In any case, my countrymen are afraid, and they want to send a representative to this meeting to explain their position. Unfortunately, none of them speaks good enough English. Then they remembered me. They write that they will collect money and send it to me to pay for the trip; that means they must be in really dire straits. None of them has any money to spare, so they'd be putting themselves further into debt to pay for my trip."

"Then you must go," Aroha decided. "And you must pay for the trip yourself."

"And leave you here alone?" Bao asked. "Especially now?" His look conveyed the unspoken fear that, after his trip, everything would go back to the way it was before their enchanted night together.

Aroha thought it over. Despite all of her muddled apprehensions, she also didn't want to be apart from Bao. It was too exciting to have finally found each other, and what he had said about his *maunga* and all her fears sounded so logical, so comforting. She so much wanted to be able to see the catastrophes in her life the way others did. Matiu and Koro had been in the wrong place at the wrong time. Their deaths were tragic, but they had as little to do with Aputa's curse after Haki's death as they did with the anchoring of Aroha's soul in the clouds.

"I could come with you," she said. "The high season doesn't start until November. We still have two weeks. And even if we stay a few days longer, we have an experienced team here. Maybe we can get McRae to keep an eye on things."

The Scotsman had not rebuilt his hotel in Te Wairoa, and he now lived with his wife in Rotorua.

"You want to come? Really?" Bao looked as if he were about to dance for joy. "Despite—despite the spirits?"

"We'll leave the spirits here," Aroha said with a smile. "And I look forward to visiting Dunedin. I can visit old friends, and maybe Miss Vandermere's school."

"It could be dangerous, though," Bao reminded her, with reluctance. "My friends write of very real threats. You should consider carefully whether you want to travel to Dunedin with a Chinese man. Even the question of lodgings; surely no one would rent the two of us a hotel room together. It's entirely possible that I might not be able to get one at all."

Aroha waved his objection aside. "We don't need a hotel; we can stay with Robin. He lives in Dunedin now."

"That's right. He came by an inheritance, didn't he?"

"Exactly. Supposedly he lives in a palace in Mornington. He could have some influence. Perhaps he can even support you at this meeting. Oh, I'm so looking forward to the trip. I've always liked Dunedin!"

Bao wavered between overflowing joy and the knowledge that this wouldn't be the lovely vacation Aroha hoped for. He had no illusions that they would be able to enjoy a casual visit to the theater or the opera together. Aroha would have to go out alone with her relatives. But Bao put his doubts aside. He would be safe in Robin's house, and he would fight a hundred dragons to be with Aroha.

"Ask Robin first if it's all right with him, and his cousin too," he said finally. "I know Robin and I got on well in Te Wairoa, but if they don't want to have me in their fine house, we don't want to find out when we're standing on the doorstep."

Robin Fenroy was of course delighted to welcome Aroha and Bao. His reaction to her wire was practically euphoric. The wordy telegraphed invitation must have cost a fortune.

The preparations went off without a hitch. McRae was happy to take over for Aroha for a few days; he looked forward to having a hotel under his care once again. After careful consideration, Aroha and Bao decided to leave Lani in Rotorua.

"It's such a grand house," Aroha reasoned, "and no one in the family has children. No doubt they'd be put out if she made noise or left stains on the expensive furniture."

Bao, who was familiar with the running of English houses from his time in boarding school, was less worried. If Robin Fenroy really lived in the splendor that Aroha described, they would immediately find a nanny to watch the child around the clock. But he agreed with Aroha for other reasons: there were few Maori in Dunedin, and if townspeople took the little one to be their biological child, they might get aggressive.

Lani's accommodation posed no problem either. Her grandparents, who were now living in the *marae* of the Ngati Hinemihi, were happy to take her. Aroha visited the *marae* with her often, and Lani adored her Maori family.

# Chapter 49

"Is that the house?"

Aroha could hardly believe her eyes when the carriage stopped in front of the Lacrosse estate. Robin had offered to send his coach to the harbor to fetch them, but Aroha had refused. Ships weren't as punctual as railroads, and she didn't want the driver to have to wait for what might be hours. Robin had suggested that, in that case, she take a hired carriage. *Have them wait outside the house, and the butler will come out and pay them,* he had written.

"At your service, ma'am," the driver said now. At first, when Aroha had stopped his carriage, he wasn't sure he wanted to take a Chinese man, but when he heard the grand address, he changed his mind. "Formerly Lacrosse, now Fenroy. That'll be one shilling sixpence, ma'am."

Shocked by the price, Aroha opened her purse and counted out the money; she couldn't take Robin's instructions about the butler seriously. In the meantime, Bao fetched their luggage and carried it to the door. The butler, who opened the door shortly after Bao rang the bell, relieved him of the bags.

"Just leave the cases here; the boy will bring them up," he said stiffly. "Madam, sir, Mr. Robin is waiting for you in the library, unless you wish to freshen up first. If so, Jean can take you to your room."

The housemaid curtsied.

Aroha smiled at the two servants. "I would like to greet my uncle first!" she declared. "I haven't seen him for such a long time. Where is the library?"

She was surprised that Robin hadn't received them at the door himself. Perhaps that wasn't considered proper here.

The butler was about to lead the way, but Aroha couldn't wait. Instinctively, she ran in the right direction. She had to cross a large, elegantly furnished salon, a dining room, and a study to reach the gigantic room filled with books. Aroha found the house's size shocking. According to Cat, only Robin, his second cousin Helena, Peta, and March lived there. Four young people in such a castle?

Robin was sitting casually on a leather sofa. He let his book fall as soon as he heard Aroha enter. Aroha thought he looked extraordinarily well. Not as pale as before, and stronger. There were muscles under his polo shirt and white cashmere pullover. Really too warm for this time of year, Aroha thought. But it was cold in the house, with its high ceilings. They must have to heat in the evenings.

"Aroha!" Robin cried, leaping to his feet. "You have no idea how happy I am that you're here."

Aroha embraced him warmly and was happy that he no longer shrank back as he had after his experience with Vera Carrigan.

"You look wonderfully well," Robin said as he inspected her new hairstyle.

She'd braided her hair and pinned the plaits up into coils. The style made her face appear fuller and made a pretty contrast with the golden-brown hat she was wearing that day. Aroha had treated herself to some new clothes before leaving Auckland. She didn't want to stand out among all the rich people Robin surely knew in Dunedin.

"Welcome, Mr. Bao!" Robin said, turning now to the Chinese man and holding out his hand. "I'm delighted to welcome you to our home. I often remember our rescue mission on that terrible night in Te Wairoa."

Bao bowed in perfect form but wondered if Robin would welcome him as warmly as Aroha's betrothed. Their host made no mention of the fact that they'd asked for one bedroom.

Robin offered them a seat and nonchalantly rang for a girl who immediately served tea, coffee, and exquisite little cakes. He asked casually about the trip and the hotel in Rotorua. Aroha got the feeling that it didn't actually interest him.

"And how are you?" she asked, finally. "I mean, this marvelous house, the library . . . A bookworm like you must feel like you're in heaven."

Robin seemed to have been expecting the question. "It does look that way," he said. "But to be honest, being rich isn't that great."

Aroha had to laugh. "I think you must be quite alone in that opinion," she said, teasing. "I'd be happy not to have to count my pennies quite so much. Not that I can complain; we're getting on well enough."

"I'm not," Robin said, and Aroha saw his sad eyes. "I do everything wrong. Not even Leah speaks to me. And the pastor . . . he's polite enough, but you can see that he thinks I'm a bad person."

Robin ran his hand through his pale-blond, perfectly trimmed hair. On the outside, he looked like nothing less than the perfect young gentleman. He looked as though he had just come from playing tennis or golf. But the self-assurance that men of this type usually possessed—and Aroha had plenty of experience with such young parvenus in her hotel—Robin lacked. He seemed tortured.

*Hamlet,* thought Aroha. *This is exactly how the tattered, naive Danish prince should be played.* Except Robin wasn't acting now. He seemed to be living his own personal tragedy.

"Slow down," Aroha said. "Who is Leah? Not that strange little thing who acted with you? You didn't actually bring her here, did you? Were you in love with her? And the very idea that a clergyman would think you are a bad person—why, Robin, I can't even imagine that! You've never knowingly done something wrong in your entire life! Well, at least not of your own free will. That Carrigan . . . But that's long past. You didn't confess to all that, did you? Are the Lacrosses Catholic or something?"

Robin chewed nervously at his knuckle. Aroha revised her first impression that he was more grown-up. On the contrary, the young man was exactly as naive and vulnerable as ever.

"No, Presbyterian," he said. He told her about Peta and his activities in the church, and Reverend Waddell, to whom he'd promised he would take his responsibility toward the factory workers more seriously. He also told her about Leah, the new Leah, whom he'd met again at the Smiths'. "I didn't like her much before, but I came to care for her here. I had the impression that she understood me. And she has changed! She's so lively and smart and funny. She really has a good head on her shoulders. No wonder Peta has fallen in love with her."

Robin rubbed his eyes and peered unhappily into his teacup, apparently unsure if he wanted to take a sip from it or not.

"The tea is absolutely delicious," Bao said politely.

Aroha tried to follow Robin's stories. "It sounds like you were a little bit in love with Leah, but then Peta Te Eriatara stole her away from you," she concluded. "That happens, Robin. Not all love is requited. In this case, it's a point in the girl's favor. To choose a student over a wealthy factory owner? You have to respect that in such a poor girl."

"It wasn't like that at all," Robin insisted. "It hadn't even gotten as far as falling in love. She met Peta when they were out in the streets protesting against me, with all of the other workers."

"They demonstrated against you? What did you do?" Bao asked with interest. "I've heard about weavers' protests in England. But the work conditions in New Zealand are supposed to be much better."

"I sold the factory," Robin admitted, with an expression of aggrieved innocence. "Or rather, March sold it. I just signed the papers. I thought it would fix everything. The workers had been so upset about the bad conditions and the low pay."

"And you tried to help them by taking away their jobs altogether?" Aroha asked. "Robin, you can't be serious."

"I thought the Scottish consortium would pay better. And the new machines were supposed to mean better conditions. It wasn't my fault that the factory had to be closed for a few months for renovations."

"And at the risk of invoking stereotype, the Scots are not exactly known for their generosity," Bao interjected. "How did you come by the idea that they would raise wages?"

Aroha frowned. "March talked him into it," she surmised. "Am I right, Robin? She told you that the deal was totally harmless and that it would be beneficial for all concerned. She's good at that; I saw her in action in Kaiapoi. My God, Robin, did it never occur to you to keep an eye on her?"

"I never meant to do anyone harm," Robin said in protest. "The only thing people can rightly accuse me of is that I was glad to be free of the responsibility. And I still am. I'm not good at keeping tabs on March or anyone else. Or running a business. In the meantime, it's all better now. The workers have their jobs and their bread again."

"All of them?" Bao asked in alarm. "Isn't it true that your factory is now employing Chinese workers, who are paid lower wages? That will turn people against the poor Chinese. There was a passage about that in my friend's letter. I didn't understand entirely, but now it makes sense."

"What did the workers live off of while the factory was closed?" Aroha asked.

Robin shrugged. "Some found other work. Leah did. I don't know why she was so angry with me. She'd said she wanted to work in a dressmakers' shop, and March offered her a job as soon as I asked her to. Leah could have been happy there."

"Maybe she's not so selfish. Maybe she had some sympathy for that family you said she lodged with," Aroha said sourly. "My goodness, Robin, sometimes one would think you live in another world. What about the others? The ones who didn't find work?"

"I think the parish supported them," Robin said. "I made some donations. I always donate a lot. But this time, Peta got terribly upset because he said I was trying to buy my way out of responsibility. He didn't want to accept the money. The pastor did, and thanked me. He always used to be so friendly, but now I get the sense that he holds me in contempt."

"He probably does," Aroha sighed. "You really got yourself dragged into something again. What is March doing now?"

"We still have the dressmakers' workshops," Robin explained, "and shops where the garments are sold. Cheaply enough that everyone can afford them, March says. That's good, isn't it?" He gazed at Aroha imploringly.

She looked helplessly at Bao. "I don't know," she said. "Honestly, I don't understand market forces or how that all works. But yes, in general, people are happy when things are cheap."

Robin beamed. "That's what March says too. She says we can sell a lot and produce a lot and earn good money that way. I just don't know why Peta and the pastor still look at me like I'm the devil himself."

Aroha didn't know either, but she decided to investigate. Maybe she could take a look at one of the dressmakers' shops, and certainly the shops where March sold her products.

# Chapter 50

That evening, Bao and Aroha ate alone. Robin and Helena had been invited to a dinner that they supposedly couldn't decline. "The mayor is giving the soirée, dear," Helena had announced coyly. "In theory, you could come along with us, it's just . . ." She'd cast a half-disapproving, half-apologetic look at Bao, and then turned to Aroha. "I hope you understand," she'd added timidly. Aroha claimed to be tired from the journey, anyway. After Helena and Robin came down in their evening clothes, she'd congratulated herself on her decision to stay in. The outfits she'd purchased in Auckland didn't include such a lavish gown, and while Bao did own a tailcoat—after all, he always greeted their hotel guests in elegant evening dress—it was nowhere near as stylish as what Robin wore.

"We would have looked like poor relatives," Aroha said now. "I can do without this whole society scene in any case. It's enough to have to serve those kinds of people in the hotel. Although the women there don't wear anything that extravagant."

"Probably because all the crinolines wouldn't fit in their luggage," Bao speculated with a grin. "Although I would have liked to go with them. The mayor is the one who arranged the meeting at the Princess Theatre. It would have been nice to meet him ahead of time in a relaxed atmosphere."

In the end, the two of them had a good meal and enjoyed their evening alone. Neither had ever slept in a canopy bed before, and they found it stirred their imaginations most delightfully.

The next morning, Bao met with his Chinese friends while Aroha went for a stroll around town. Robin had set off for his morning ride, and Helena offered to accompany her. Aroha hadn't yet laid eyes on March or Peta, but that didn't surprise Helena one bit.

"March stays late at work every night and is gone again in the morning by seven," she explained as they climbed into the coach to be driven to the Octagon, an octagonal neighborhood where the most interesting shops were. Aroha would have actually preferred to take Dunedin's famous cable car. The nearest station was quite close to the Lacrosse house, but Helena considered the brightly painted wagons, drawn up the hills on steel cables, to be beneath her. "And I think Peta spends most of his nights with his girlfriend," she continued. "It's an absolutely unsuitable match! A factory girl! Can you believe it? Once he even dared to bring her into our house! Robin is far too indulgent. I wouldn't have allowed it, and it was terribly unpleasant for March as well. Naturally, the whole thing turned out dreadfully; the poor little thing barely knew how to eat with a knife and fork."

Aroha couldn't imagine that was true. While she had only formed a vague impression of Leah in Te Wairoa, the young woman had stayed in McRae's hotel without drawing attention to herself.

"What's more, the girl didn't say a word the whole time. It was so embarrassing for everyone. Yes, I'm of the opinion that people should stay where they belong . . ." Helena paused when she realized that Aroha wasn't answering. "Oh . . . I didn't mean that personally, of course. Your, um, Bao certainly has exceptional manners."

"He comes from the imperial bloodline," Aroha fibbed. "Tell me, where are the shops that March runs for the Lacrosse Company? Could we perhaps see one?"

Just then, the coach passed a billboard that advertised "Men's and Women's Clothing—At Even Lower Prices!" Aroha didn't recognize the name of the shop, though.

"You don't really want to buy such plebeian clothes, do you?" Helena said in protest. "I thought I would show you the really nice shops. Lady's Gold Mine, for example. It's an elegant shop that—"

"I don't want to buy anything there, I just want to look," Aroha said, interrupting her. "If March is running shops in Robin's name—"

"She isn't," Helena replied curtly. "She doesn't have any shops of her own. She just has labels with the name 'Cross' sewn into things and sells them to a few discount suppliers. She tried running her own shops for six months but gave up. She said it wasn't possible to supervise the personnel from a central office, so it was better that the shops be run by their owners."

"Does Peterman's sell her things?" Aroha asked.

The name "Peterman's Warehouse" had leaped out at her from the next billboard, advertising ladies' and men's clothing for every budget.

"Possibly," Helena replied. "I've never been there. It's not in this neigh-borhood . . . Oh, it's in St. Andrew's," she noted after glancing at the address. "Somewhere in Devil's Half Acre. The other shops are usually in the work-ing-class neighborhoods as well. We can go by later, if you really want to."

The city center of Dunedin was dominated by elegant dress shops and tailors, gourmet grocers, jewelers, and banks, but Aroha didn't find any clothing there that came from Robin's factories. Here everything was hand-sewn, exquisite, and digni-fied. Aroha had to admit she found the selection at Lady's Gold Mine enchanting, especially because the two women who ran the shop offered dresses that could be worn without a corset. Aroha thought that would be very practical for her work at the hotel, but she couldn't afford any of the shimmering ensembles.

"Put it on Robin's account," Helena suggested when, with regret, Aroha tried to walk away from a beautiful silk dress in the Empire style. "He expressly told me so this morning. Buy whatever you want." She herself tried on a conservative tea dress with a wasp waist and hoop skirt. "This one's pretty, isn't it? If only the skirt were a bit wider. It seems a bit . . . plain. Is that on purpose, Mrs. Dunloe?"

The very polite owner of the shop explained that Kathleen Burton, who designed the dresses for Lady's Gold Mine, always emphasized the practicality of a garment. "This way at least there's room for a young gentleman to sit on a park bench next to you, Miss Lacrosse, if you need to take a rest while on a walk. The skirt you're wearing now . . . It's lovely, of course, but you just jostled half of our dress stands." And, in fact, the young Maori girl who helped out in the shop did nothing but make sure that the stands weren't knocked over by the customers' hoop skirts.

Aroha cast an amused glance at the shopkeeper. She herself had wondered how Helena managed to navigate through homes less spacious than the Lacrosse mansion.

"Well, yes," Helena conceded, "if you put it that way. I'll take it. And Miss Aroha will take the Empire dress. No objections, Aroha, your wardrobe is far too modest."

Embarrassed, Aroha thanked her while Mrs. Dunloe wrote the prices for both dresses on a bill and gave it to Helena to initial. The bank listed on the account was under the name "Robin Fenroy."

"Robin has an account here?" she asked. "Do you also carry men's clothing?"

Amused, Mrs. Dunloe said, "No, but Miss Helena is one of our best and most prized customers."

"And Miss Margery?" Aroha asked suspiciously. She was startled by the way Helena had helped herself to Robin's money as a matter of course.

"Margery Jensch?" Mrs. Dunloe inquired. "Oh, yes, we furnish Miss Jensch's wardrobe as well. And we do so with great pleasure, as she appreciates the combination of elegance and practicality that distinguishes Mrs. Burton's collection." Mrs. Dunloe, a delicate older lady whose well-groomed dark hair was shot with streaks of gray, gazed at Aroha searchingly. She seemed to understand that the young woman's interest had less to do with her client's taste than with her payment history. "Miss Jensch has her own account, however," she added unprompted, before she most politely bade Aroha and Helena a good day.

Aroha was ashamed of her suspicion. As a businesswoman, March undoubtedly prized her independence.

"Robin pays all your bills?" she asked Helena casually.

Helena nodded calmly. "Yes. Everything is paid from one account. Robin doesn't pay in the literal sense at all. I don't think he ever has any money in his pocket—except for the collection on Sundays."

"Still, it's Robin's money," Aroha objected. "Don't you have your own income?"

Helena nodded indifferently. "Certainly. But that will all come together eventually, anyway. When we get married . . ."

"When you *what*?" Aroha almost dropped the package with her expensive new dress. "You want to marry Robin? Does he know?"

Helena laughed and turned toward a shop that carried extraordinarily pretty parasols and umbrellas. "Everyone in Dunedin knows," she said. "Well, Robin is still having a little trouble. He's a bit younger than I am, and people do gossip. So on that score, it's prudent to let a few more years go by. But otherwise it's an ideal match, as long as he doesn't make off with Magiel's younger daughter. But he wouldn't dare. March would stone him!" She laughed. "Besides, Rose Magiel is only half as tall as he is and twice as wide. He couldn't possibly like that." She toyed idly with a small parasol. The color perfectly matched the dress she'd just bought, and with a wave of her hand, Helena had it put on "her" account.

For the first time, Aroha had some idea what Robin was going through. It couldn't be easy to hold one's ground against both March and Helena. As a younger man, Robin had been enamored of March. Had his passion for her cooled?

"Could we go to one of the stores that carries Robin's products now?" she asked, when Helena announced that the shopping trip was over. The coach stood waiting for them at the agreed-upon meeting place. "I'd really like to see how he earns all that money."

Helena nodded stoically and gave the driver an address. He frowned when he heard it. "I don't like to drive unaccompanied ladies into that area. You don't intend to get out, do you?"

Helena grimaced. "Miss Aroha would like to have a look at the selection at the shop there," she said. "It won't take long. You can stop right out front. I'd be grateful if you'd keep an eye on us."

It occurred to Aroha that the presence of the splendid coach at a store for workers might well draw the attention of the neighborhood's less savory elements. However, she didn't say anything, but just looked out the window attentively as the coach left the city center behind and rolled through Mornington. Parks and overhanging trees lined the wide streets. Ladies on their way home from morning visits and nannies with baby carriages or older charges strolled along the sidewalks. Aroha thought about Lani; she already missed the child. Just then, the coach passed a well-tended little church with a parish hall alongside.

"This is St. Andrew's," Helena said. "Our parish. To which, unfortunately, a few of the less-decent neighborhoods also belong."

Aroha wondered exactly how one defined the decency or indecency of a neighborhood as the coach turned into the area in question. During her studies in Dunedin, Aroha had heard tell of the ill-famed quarter but had never been. Now she gazed, repelled and sympathetic in turn, at the garishly painted façades of the bars and gaming halls, and the dilapidated houses in front of which children played in filth. Between these lay the occasional pawnshop or bakery, along with stores that carried cheap clothing and housewares. Helena finally asked the driver to stop in front of one of the shops.

"Let's go in, then," she said unhappily.

The shop was dark and untidy. The owner greeted them politely enough, but watched the two ladies with suspicion as they concentrated on a pile of dirt-cheap shirts. They were nicely sewn.

"It would take me hours to sew a piece like this," Aroha said, thinking that she would certainly not do such work for two shillings a day.

"It's lightning fast with a sewing machine," Helena assured her.

The tag on the shirts read "Mags."

"So this isn't by Fenroy," Aroha determined.

"No, those are from Magiel," the owner replied. "Lacrosse wanted two pence more, and Magiel underbid them. The aprons over here are from Lacrosse, though. If you need one . . ." He sounded skeptical.

Aroha, who in fact did wear an apron at the hotel on occasion, examined the wares. Here, too, there could be no complaints about the quality of the work. It was plain fabric, but the seams ran straight.

"I assume Magiel also produces aprons but offered them at a higher price," she said.

The owner nodded. "They outbid each other constantly. The shirts from Lacrosse will be cheaper again next week, I'm sure. All the better for me—"

"And for your customers!" Helena said.

The man shrugged. "That's debatable. My customers are practically all factory workers. They have to be frugal, and naturally they prefer to get a bargain. But I expect they'd rather earn a bit more so they'd have more to spend. And the price of food can only go so low. Wheat doesn't grow any faster if you stand over it with a whip, and the baker doesn't cut people any slack either." He gestured to his stock. "People can do without the things I sell here. There are whole families that only have one pot to cook their supper in and a single cup for their coffee. They share it around. Clothes are passed from one child to the next until they're in tatters. But they have to buy bread no matter what it costs. No, ladies, I don't believe that Lacrosse and Magiel are doing any good deeds with their price wars."

Helena was sobered and Aroha angry as they left the shop and climbed into the coach.

"Why do they do that?" she asked Helena. "Lacrosse and Magiel, I mean. What do they get out of competing so aggressively?"

Helena frowned. "There was something between Mr. Porter and March . . ."

It was then that Aroha learned of Martin Porter's marriage to the Magiel heiress. And a few things suddenly made more sense.

"I will have to talk with March," she said to Bao, after she told him all she'd learned. "It would be even better if Robin did. Otherwise his reputation in the community will get even worse. Best of all would be if Robin could come to a fair pricing agreement with Magiel, or with Porter. And how was your morning?"

Bao seemed even more depressed than Aroha after her outing into the world of the factory workers. In fact, he had gone much farther into the depths of Devil's Half Acre than she had.

"Originally, the whole quarter was a Chinese neighborhood," he explained. "Until the factories came, and white people with them. The shacks were rented to them then, in some cases by the Chinese themselves. The few of my country-men who have money earn it there—with gaming halls, bars, opium, and money lending. Because of those few men, the whites are convinced that all Chinese people are crooks. These are the circumstances that I have to make clear to the mayor at the meeting next week. We'll see if he listens. My friends are at the end of their rope. They live in absolute hellholes. Seriously, Aroha, twenty men share a drafty room with the rain coming in! They earn barely enough to survive, and from that they have to pay off their ship passage and send money home. And then there are the hostilities against them. The men barely dare to set foot in the street, especially since more of them are working in the factories. When I was here before, the factory owners wouldn't accept them because they didn't speak enough English. But that's changed now. The factory owners don't care who runs their looms. The overseers keep order inside the factories, but before work and afterward, the men have to run the gauntlet."

"So yet another mark on Robin's tally of sins?" Aroha asked.

Bao shook his head. "No, it's not that. Lacrosse is certainly one of the worst oppressors, but their factory employs women exclusively. And mostly very young girls. They only have the dressmakers' shops, now."

"It's supposed to be more tolerable there than in the mills," Aroha said.

Bao shrugged. "Chinese girls stay in China. But Lacrosse's reputation is nonetheless abysmal. Perhaps you should see this 'workers' paradise' for your-self and give young Robin a piece of your mind. Your uncle is a decent fellow, but"—he grinned—"his *maunga* is drifting aimlessly somewhere in the clouds. The spirits should do something about that for once. Where can we find the nearest competent *tohunga*?"

# Chapter 51

It was actually a clergyman who brought the Lacrosse and Magiel price war to the attention of the general public. Before it came to that, however, Aroha and Bao met with one of the two other residents of the Lacrosse household. Peta showed up for breakfast the next morning and was pleased to see Aroha again.

Aroha was impressed. She hadn't seen the young man since they'd toured the factory in Kaiapoi. The angry lad had matured into a wise, level-headed law student who eagerly shared his knowledge with Reverend Waddell's congregation. Peta looked very good, strong, and excited. His suit was made of good fabric, although certainly not made by one of the finer tailors in the city. Peta was actually dressed too formally for a Saturday morning, but that was soon explained.

"A few other students and I are offering free legal advice at the parish hall. Professor Lucius is helping us."

"You'll only stir up the workers that way," Helena said, objecting.

So far, both she and Robin had been listening to the lively discussion between Aroha and Peta silently. Peta himself barely acknowledged his hosts. Without Aroha and Bao's presence, the atmosphere would have been ice-cold.

Peta gave Helena a look that was somewhere between boredom and contempt. "You're welcome to come along sometime and listen to the people's troubles yourself. You'd realize very quickly that no one even thinks about suing their employers. It would often be the right thing to do, but it's hopeless. Even if it were possible to win, it would be impossible ever to get another job anywhere. The factory owners stick together in that respect—even March and Porter. If anyone ever gets on their blacklist, they have to go hungry. No, we'll be helping people deal with rent disputes, betting fraud, or the question of whether a girl who has been raped is allowed to report her tormentor."

"Please, don't bring up such unappetizing subjects at the breakfast table," Helena said, reaching pointedly for her teacup.

"You asked," Peta said, rolling his eyes. "In any case, we're helping people and getting practical legal experience at the same time."

"We have to go now," Robin said to Helena. Apparently, he was afraid that the conversation would escalate. "Let's not keep the others waiting." Robin was already dressed for sport; apparently a golf match was planned.

Helena laid her napkin aside. "Do you golf, Aroha?"

"No," Aroha said with a laugh. "So far there's no golf course in Rotorua. Although it's surely only a matter of time. Maybe we should look into that, Bao! It would be an interesting offering for the *manuhiri*. I personally don't get very much out of the game. I find it dull."

"It's an attempt to raise a mundane stroll to an art form," Peta remarked.

He wasn't in a hurry, and enjoyed another cup of coffee with Bao and Aroha after Helena and Robin left. The atmosphere was more relaxed without them. Aroha wondered what would happen if March were at the table as well. The young woman must have her reasons for rarely making an appearance. Aroha felt conflicted about all of it. She thought Peta was reasonable and kind, while Helena was vacuous and affected. She felt slightly sorry for Robin. Peta disdained him, March didn't take him seriously, and Helena led him around like a dog on a leash.

"Do you have a little time to talk?" Aroha asked Peta.

Peta nodded and buttered another roll. "My first clients won't be coming until eleven. If they don't have to work on Saturday morning, it usually means they've been on the night shift. Then they sleep an hour or two and slip out secretly, so their landlords or loan sharks or whoever won't see them."

Aroha asked her questions about the conditions in the Lacrosse dressmakers' shops, and raised her suspicions about the competition between Lacrosse and Magiel.

"Good guess," Peta said, laughing when she brought up the subject of his sister and Porter. "Those two keep trying to outdo each other, and the two companies have never seen such profits."

"In spite of the low prices?" Aroha asked in surprise.

"Yes, because of the mass quantities they sell," Peta said. "And you can't forget that they also buy their materials very cheaply. The two companies own all the dressmakers' workshops in the area, and that means they can dictate prices to the woolen mills. The mills have to sell their materials more and more cheaply, which can only work by cutting the employees' pay. So not only do the seamstresses in March and Porter's own workshops suffer, but also the workers in the weaving mills and dye works. The factories can manage it by hiring Chinese workers and paying less. Otherwise it would be impossible to cut wages any further." He turned to Bao. "That causes even more resentment."

"I can't imagine that Robin cares very much about the extra profits," Aroha said thoughtfully. "Do you think he even knows how much money he has?"

Peta dropped the roll he was just about to bite into back onto his plate. So far his words had been tinged with sarcasm, but they were reasonable and soberly presented. Now he seemed prepared to vent his rage.

"Am I supposed to feel sorry for poor Robin now? I'm sure he complained to you about how misunderstood he is, and what a terrible sacrifice it is for him to have to go to the golf course to represent the Lacrosse Company, and dance the night away with shallow Helena. Oh, those endless wasted hours with the tailor and shoemaker . . ." Peta said, imitating Robin. Apparently, he complained regularly about his fate. "He tried doing that with me when I first came here too. So I pointed out how he could make himself useful. And what did he do? He dumped the responsibility as fast as he could, as soon as he understood how much depended on him. He could have changed everything here—"

"He's just not made for that," Aroha said, defending her uncle. "His talents lie elsewhere."

"Don't bother, Aroha," Peta replied fervently. "I could never commiserate with Robin nor admire him, no matter how touchingly he played Romeo. He's a coward and a weakling! And his grandmother, who was so worshipped by Walter Lacrosse, was as well. I heard Cat talking about Suzanne last time I was home. If one pays a little attention, it's possible to piece the story together. Apparently, little Suzanne had some bad luck. She got pregnant, but her daddy didn't approve of the man. And it seems his judgment was right, seeing as the brute left her as soon as she came running to him without her family's money. Helena thought it was romantic. What do you think?"

"I think it was stupid," Aroha replied reluctantly.

"Exactly! And your darling Robin is just like her. At least he isn't a drinker. Suzanne turned to alcohol rather than crawling back to her family. I understand her father wouldn't have been happy about the baby, but at least the child would have been given a name and something to eat. Suzanne almost let Cat starve to death. She only survived because the other whores took care of her. The woman was totally irresponsible; selfishness personified. Just like Robin Fenroy! So don't try to defend him."

Peta pushed back his chair and stood up.

"You're living off his money too," Bao pointed out. "Or do you pay for your room and board here?"

Peta laughed. It was an ugly sound. It reminded Aroha of March. For the first time, he sounded unkind.

"I don't," he admitted. "And dear cousin Helena would have thrown me out a long time ago. Robin is just too much of a coward to do it. Either that or he needs me. After all, I'm his conscience."

"He's just as much a freeloader as the others," Bao said after Peta left the room. "They complain about Robin, but they're all using him. It's not even necessary, is it? Didn't you say March and Peta's parents own a farm?"

Aroha explained the situations at Rata Station and Maori Station.

"Basically, they're all spoiled children," she concluded. "And that's exactly how they're behaving. But now, what should we do with the rest of the day? Shall we try to get a tour of a workshop with the fourth member of the rich kids' club?"

March Jensch met them in the office of the newest dressmakers' workshop. It was near the harbor in an old warehouse, a gigantic redbrick building. March had had it completely remodeled to serve her purposes. Aroha noticed that the corridors were wider and brighter than they'd been in the factory in Kaiapoi.

"The renovation cost a fortune," March said. "The stairwells in particular were extremely expensive. The architect said I was crazy, and that I could have left everything as it was. But I'm actually a little scared. We once had a bad experience in Kaiapoi. A bale of fabric caught fire and the workers rushed to escape. Not a single one of them thought of simply trying to stamp out the flames. In the end, Martin put out the fire by himself, and nothing happened.

But there were a few minor injuries because of the narrow doors and corridors. The workers came close to trampling each other to death. If the fire had spread, it would have been a catastrophe. I can still see it."

Aroha tried to take comfort in this flicker of decency.

"We work in two large halls, each with fifty machines. There are two women at each station, a seamstress and a preparer," March explained.

She proudly accompanied her guests through the workshop. She had to shout almost as loudly as she'd had to back in Kaiapoi, because here, too, the rattling machines made an infernal amount of noise. The air in the room was stuffy, which had less to do with chemicals and loose fibers, and more because the windows were too small and set too high to be easily opened. Just enough light got in to make artificial lighting unnecessary.

"There isn't much air in here," Aroha remarked.

"I don't like it either," March admitted. "But that's how the building was designed. It was a warehouse. If I'd wanted to change that, too, I might as well have had the entire thing torn down and another one built. But it has its advantages. The girls can't look outside and get distracted."

None of the women even looked up from their work as March walked past with the visitors. The women seemed only to be interested in their machines, treadling the peddles without pause. They sat on low stools, their backs hunched. The pattern-cutters had it a little better. They cut the material to fit and handed the parts to the seamstresses as quickly as they could. It didn't look particularly difficult. Each pair of women always repeated the same work. The first pair sewed sleeves together, the next attached them, the next stitched the body of the shirt. It also seemed to be true that mostly young, unmarried women were employed here. Aroha thought most of them were between the ages of fourteen and eighteen. They were all wearing cotton dresses and white aprons. It wasn't a uniform, but they were all similarly cut. The girls probably got too little sun, because they were all pale and there were dark circles under their eyes. But none of them looked like they were going hungry.

"They're paid by the piece," March explained. "The more they do, the more money they make. It's all fair here. The two women who work together share the money. The seamstresses get a little more than the preparers, because their work is more difficult."

"How long do they work every day?" Aroha asked. She thought the sewing machines were very interesting technically, and would have liked to try one out herself.

"Nine hours, strictly by the law. Everything is done by the rules here, Aroha, no matter what Peta says. And yes, we have break rooms and nursing rooms. Watch the stairs . . ."

March stepped out of the factory hall and triumphantly led the two of them to the workers' break rooms. There wasn't a yard like there had been in Kaiapoi.

"It's cold in here," Aroha said as she entered the utilitarian break room, furnished only with tables and chairs.

"Well, the girls just have to put on their coats during the break," March said impatiently. "They don't mind at all. I don't want to know how much thread and material they tuck away under their scarves and in their baskets. Of course we always check, very carefully. Would you like a cup of coffee? I can take fifteen minutes off. You should have let me know you were coming; another day would have been better. Today is payday, and I have to check the tallies."

Aroha and Bao got the hint and turned down the coffee. They breathed sighs of relief as they left the factory. It was nice to be back out in the fresh air and see the view into the green hills that surrounded the bay of Dunedin. The Otago peninsula had exquisite beaches, and the water was full of fish. After the noise of the factory, the cries of the seagulls and the soft splashing of the waves were very pleasant.

"Kaiapoi was worse," Aroha said as she headed toward a café near the factory. It wasn't much more than a shack where coffee and snacks were offered very cheaply. The well-dressed strangers were eyed skeptically. "The women here surely earn little, but at least none of them looked starved, and they were all reasonably dressed."

"But they were tired," Bao said quietly. "Terribly tired."


In the Lacrosse household, it was assumed that Aroha and Bao would accompany their hosts to church on Sunday.

"But only if it isn't too—I mean, have you ever been in a Christian church?" Helena shot Bao a disparaging look, even though he'd dressed properly for church and didn't look uncomfortable in any way.

"I attended Anglican services every morning in boarding school," he assured her crisply.

Since the weather was nice, they walked to church. March chatted along the way. It didn't seem as though she and Helena were particularly good friends, but they were polite to one another. Aroha noticed that Helena was very pains-takingly dressed. She linked her arm with Robin's and interrupted whenever he and March spoke to each other. Was she jealous? Was that why Robin, who was terrified of any form of confrontation, never asked about what was going on in the factory? Did Helena seek to prevent any contact between him and March?

As far as the congregation was concerned, it didn't look to Aroha as though they thought of Robin as an outsider. At least not until the dignitaries of Mornington realized that Bao and the Lacrosse heir had appeared together. There was much murmuring and many horrified looks, but they managed to feign politeness when Helena introduced her guests with a nervous laugh.

"This is our relative, Aroha Fitzpatrick, and Mr. Duong. Mr. Duong works in Miss Fitzpatrick's hotel in Rotorua."

"She makes it sound like you're a dishwasher," Aroha whispered to him in annoyance, but for Robin's sake, she refrained from correcting Helena.

The couple followed Robin, March, and Helena into the front pew. Peta sat at the back with the factory workers. He whispered excitedly with a pretty girl that Aroha recognized as Leah Hobarth. Peta and the girl seemed to be expectant and happy, and Aroha wondered why.

The riddle was solved when Reverend Waddell stepped up to the pulpit.

# Chapter 52

The reverend's gaze swept over his congregation. He paused for a heartbeat when he saw Bao, then seemed to forget immediately. He also kept his salutation brief. Aroha almost got the impression that the clergyman was a little nervous. Finally, Reverend Waddell laid his right hand on the pulpit as though he needed support, and then stepped to the side so he was entirely visible for his whole congregation to see.

"Could it be a sin to offer goods for sale cheaply?" Even the beginning of his sermon commanded the attention of his listeners. "At first, one would say no. And this is also because the word 'cheap' is so often used in positive contexts. 'Fair and cheap,' in the sense of 'appropriate.' Cheapness seems to be equivocated with good, at the moment, and the word 'expensive' seems to have a negative impact. However, my friends, there is something in this city that I think is decidedly too expensive. And not in the sense that I just disapprove of what is happening here, but I find it sinful." The reverend stepped back behind the pulpit and unfolded an advertising flyer. *"Special offer! Cheaper prices than ever before!"* he read aloud. "Wherever we go in this beautiful city, these flyers flutter toward us. We find the same words on billboards and in the display windows of the stores. *Cheap prices! Two for the price of one! Almost free!* My friends, I see confusion on your faces. Especially in the back rows. I know very well how the women sitting there have to save money to feed and dress their families properly. Why shouldn't they be happy when things are offered cheaply?

"But let's take a look behind these prices that we are so happy about at first glance. How are they achieved? Is the wool or cotton the cheap clothes are made of donated? No. It has to be bought, and the farmer who produced it wants a reasonable price. Does wool or cotton suddenly grow faster on the sheep or the bushes? No, the sheep can still only be shorn once a year, and additionally, the wool must be spun and woven. Cotton, too, grows slowly, and can only be harvested once a year and then processed. And does the material make itself into shirts and trousers and dresses? Of course not; the hardworking hands of seamstresses are needed for that." The reverend raised his voice. "So how is it possible to produce all these wonderful, cheaply priced things? Do the factory owners forgo their profits? Hardly. As far as I can see, they still come to church in their fancy coaches and maintain their mansions and gardens. Instead, the wages of the workers are being reduced.

"My friends, I watch with dismay as the greed for cheaper and cheaper goods is causing the factories to cut wages further and further! The women and girls in particular are being cheated. What they earn isn't even close to the value of what they produce." He waved the flyers in the air. "These goods aren't cheap. They were paid for with the lives, good health, and happiness of thousands of employees! These advertisements are anything but harmless. To the contrary, they are encouraging you all to be thieves. You are taking part in stealing people's work! Everyone here, from the housewife who buys a simple child's dress to the factory owner who has the dress sewn and takes his profit from it, is guilty of this sin. Of course, not all to the same degree. The working woman is stealing from herself, after all. The shop owner who passes around such flyers is encouraging the greed, which is worse, and the factory owner is doing the stealing personally.

"No doubt now someone will give me a lecture on market economy. Tomorrow at the latest I will find the arguments of the exploiters in the newspaper. They will write that the prices are market driven. But do we as human beings have an obligation to follow the laws of the market? Should we not follow the laws of God instead? Thou shalt not steal! Thou shalt not covet! This does not apply, gentle businessmen, only to the workers who perhaps envy your house and your carriage. It is also especially true for you, in your greed to get even more out of a young woman's labor.

"My friends, when the laws of the free-market economy are contrary to those of the Bible, then Christian values must be given priority. Christianity must not only be practiced on Sundays in the church and among your own families, but also in daily life, at your place of work and in your business practices. So renounce the sin of cheapness. Find your way back to the laws of God, which are also the laws of love. Remember that the workers in your factories are also our neighbors."

The people sat in moved silence as the reverend finished his sermon and left the pulpit. When the service was over, most of the congregation hurried quickly past Reverend Waddell. Shop owners bowed their heads just as penitently as thrifty housewives. Only March felt no compunction to hide. Standing tall, a cool, stern beauty in her black-and-white Sunday ensemble, she strode toward the reverend with self-assurance and offered him her hand in farewell.

"A very moving sermon," she said curtly. "Of course, we must discuss this matter further. Perhaps you will bring up the subject again. If you do, please be aware that not all businesspeople in this city are men."

# Chapter 53

As the reverend had predicted, the local papers reported his sermon the following Monday. In the meantime, the chastised industrialists had recovered from their shock and were defending themselves. No one was being forced to work in the factories, Martin Porter told a reporter from the *Otago Daily Times*. For example, the seamstresses were free to look for employment in households in the countryside instead. Except they might be paid even less, and of course there wasn't any interesting nightlife on the farms.

"We must see these things clearly," Porter declared. "The girls prefer working in the factory for two shillings and then enjoying everything the city has to offer, instead of dutifully serving individual families and watching the sheep graze. Can we hold that against them?"

A representative from the small-scale local trade union reacted by writing letters to the editor, one of which caused an uproar in the Lacrosse household.

"Is it true?" Robin demanded. Since the sermon, he had gotten up early every morning so he could be the first to read the paper, and now he was having a word with March before she set off. "Is it true that the women have to take work home?"

The writer of the letter explained that a dressmaker did not have much free time left if she wanted to live from the proceeds of her work and keep her job. It was common practice in dressmakers' workshops to circumvent labor laws by giving the girls homework. It was mostly detail work for items of clothing that still had to be finished by hand. The women worked at home for a small additional salary until eleven or twelve o'clock at night, and the factory owners often made the willingness to perform such additional tasks a condition of employment.

March glanced at the paper. "Of course it's true," she said coldly. "But we aren't pressuring anyone. The girls do it of their own free will. And as you can see in church and in town, they still have enough free time to sew pretty dresses and go out to enjoy themselves. It's all a massive exaggeration, Robin."

"What about this?" he said, pointing to another letter to the editor. "This woman who has to work at home. Tell me she doesn't work for Lacrosse!"

The letter was about a woman who had two toddlers and a sick husband to take care of, and therefore couldn't go to the workshop. In such cases, the factory "helped out" by giving her homework instead.

"She finishes shirts. Seven buttonholes, seven buttons, and a few hand stitches at the end of the sleeves and the side seams," Robin said. "She gets eight pence for a dozen shirts, March! And she does four dozen a day. More isn't possible, not with all the goodwill in the world. That means she earns thirty-two pence a day! And the costs for the needles and thread that aren't provided to her have to be subtracted from that. The writer wonders if it's really wage labor or just slavery. Is this Lacrosse, March?"

March shrugged. "Since the woman doesn't give her name, it's impossible to answer that. The conditions are the same everywhere. We pay just as much—or just as little, if that's what you want to hear—as Magiel. And to that I can only say, the woman has a choice. Heavens, Robin, every day we get at least ten women who would work for less!"

"And then you put pressure on your current workers so they agree to wage cuts, even though you know very well that they are much more qualified and efficient than the women who are on the edge of desperation. It's all here, March!" He waved the newspaper under her nose. "I am ashamed to death of these practices. I don't know if I can ever look the reverend or the workers in the eyes again!"

"Perhaps you'll be able to after you relieve March of her sole power and announce legal wages, fair work hours, and break times in your factory," Aroha suggested an hour later. "You can do that anytime you want, Robin. You can also challenge Magiel to do the same. If he doesn't, all of the aggravation will be taken out on him and Porter. Believe me, they'll follow suit within three days. You just have to do something, Robin. Take the wind out of their sails! Besides, the papers will be writing about something else soon, anyway. Tomorrow is the municipal assembly about Chinese immigrants."

Robin, looking exhausted, nodded distractedly and wandered out of the room.

Bao snorted. "It's not something else at all. In fact, all this anger is just going to end up being directed at the Chinese community. The mayor will probably jump on the argument that it's all our fault for taking away locals' jobs. He hasn't figured out that the industrialists are playing groups of desperate workers against each other. Do you think Robin will pull himself together enough to make those changes?"

Aroha gave him a tired smile. "This afternoon I'll sit down with Robin, as well as Helena, who wants to put in her two cents for unfathomable reasons. Robin just has to do something now, instead of sticking his head back in the sand."

Bao skimmed the other articles in the newspaper. "He should do it today," he said seriously. "So far, almost every major employer has weighed in publicly. Lacrosse is the only one that hasn't."

Aroha shrugged. "They only talk to the men. No journalist has interviewed March."

"But they might want to talk to Robin," Bao said. "And they might get angry if March won't let them."

As it turned out, it was primarily Helena keeping the press away from Robin. She'd given the household staff strict rules not to allow reporters anywhere near their employers, as Aroha learned that afternoon.

Helena did join them, but only listened half-heartedly to Aroha's conversation with Robin. Her intermittent contributions were aggressive. She complained about the workers, the reverend, and above all, about Peta.

"Throw him out, Robin! It's high time," she said in annoyance.

Robin toyed with his fountain pen and dithered between plans for completely disproportionate wage increases and the idea of just waiting out the storm. He didn't seem very focused on the subject. That evening he was invited to a soiree at the home of one of the board members who had acquired the woolen mill. Helena wanted to accompany him, as did March, for a change. It was clear to Aroha that March only wanted to find out what the businessmen in the city were saying about Waddell's sermon. As the three of them headed off to dress for the evening, Aroha was completely exhausted.

"It's like dealing with children," she said to Bao. "I felt as though I were trying to plan a business strategy with Lani. But now we have a proper list of reforms that seem realistic for both the workers and Lacrosse. The reverend should be satisfied."

"As long as Robin follows through," Bao said. "Tonight, they'll be talking up a storm. The factory owners will surely be encouraging each other not to react to the accusations. Do you think Robin will emerge from this ready to speak out against them tomorrow? If only he had the backbone for that!"

But the next day, it was already too late. Aroha, who had hoped to meet Robin at breakfast, found only an open newspaper lying on the table.

"Mr. Fenroy read the headlines and left immediately," a servant told her. "He was, um, rather upset."

"Did you read the paper already, then?" Aroha asked, reaching worriedly for the *Otago Daily Times*.

"I, um, with all due respect, miss, I ironed it," the young man said. "And, well . . . I couldn't help catching a few phrases."

"You . . . ironed it?" Aroha asked, furrowing her brow in disbelief.

She quickly lost interest in the young man's enthusiastic explanations about how ironing fixed the ink so it wouldn't come off on the tablecloth or his employer's hands during breakfast. The latest articles about the "exploitation scandal" were shocking. But the main article didn't take sides. It reported the reactions of the church committee to Waddell's sermon. They were for the most part dismissive of the reverend, saying that the church shouldn't interfere with the wage structure. The Creator, they said, had meant for there to be an upper and a lower class. A committee member even dared to assert that the laws of the economy were natural laws, and therefore comparable to the laws of God. March had probably been pleased by the idea.

On page two, Aroha found what had disturbed Robin so much. There were not only articles, but drawings. One was a caricature of Robin. He held a golf club in one hand, and in the next frame a girl treadled a sewing machine. Below that was another pair of drawings: on one side, Robin in a tuxedo, champagne glass in hand, on the other, a woman in a dimly lit room hunched over a sewing machine. *A day in the life of Robin Fenroy, A day in the life of his workers*, read the captions. Aroha read with dismay that the homeworker mentioned in the last issue had identified herself as an employee of the Lacrosse Company. Then came a report about the conditions in the factory.

> *While Robin Fenroy, independent gentleman and owner of the Lacrosse business concerns indulges in his pleasures, his home-workers are sewing trousers made of heavy cotton fabric and being paid by the piece only. The women and girls work from eight o'clock in the morning until eleven at night, and earn two shillings a day. "It's not enough to survive on," says Reverend Waddell, who made the suffering of the factory and homeworkers the subject of his sermon in St. Andrew's Presbyterian Church last Sunday. The audience included young Mr. Fenroy . . .*

The rest of the article reported in minute detail how surprisingly Robin had come to his inheritance, and that he had shown no interest in overseeing his factories, but instead spent the money copiously. Robin had been called out in front of the entire city.

*It's very telling that Robin Fenroy wasn't available for comment yesterday,* the reporter wrote in closing. *Our attempt to ask him about the conditions in his workshops was rebuffed by his household staff.*

Aroha closed the paper. She understood why Robin was hiding.


"What's that slant-eye doing in here?"

The Princess Theater on the street of the same name was almost completely full when Bao entered the municipal meeting, and the anger of the crowd immediately turned to focus on him. Bao was shaken, but judged that the people gathered would not pose a physical threat. The dignitaries actually made way for him as he walked toward the front of the room, politely whispering apologies, to reach Mayor Dawson. The local politician stood defensively, and eyed Bao with a dark expression.

"What you do here?" Dawson shouted. "If you provoke, I warn you, Chinaman, police throw you out!"

"I can understand you perfectly, Mr. Dawson," Bao said politely. "And I have no wish to provoke you." The mayor regarded him more curiously then, and noticed the elegant gray three-piece suit, the pressed white shirt. "It's just that my countrymen who have settled in Dunedin asked me to represent them at this meeting."

"Did someone invite you to attend?" the mayor snapped.

"Not directly," Bao admitted. "However, since my presence and that of my countrymen is the central subject of this meeting, we thought that perhaps I could clarify a few matters. We don't want to be presumptuous, but we believe that much of the dissonance between the citizens of this town and the Chinese workers is based on misunderstandings."

"Your English is very good," Dawson replied. "But then, why are you working for two shillings a day in a factory?"

Bao smiled. "I had the pleasure of receiving an excellent education in the beautiful country of England," he said with a bow. "By the way, my name is Mr. Duong, and I don't work in a factory. I am the manager of a hotel in Rotorua."

"I've never heard a chink with such a hoity-toity accent," said another man who was standing near the podium, preparing to give a speech.

On the inside, Bao seethed with fury. But knowing he was surrounded by abject hostility, he bit his tongue and smiled as though it were a compliment. He was well versed in diplomacy after spending so many years in England. "May I stand here with you?" he asked politely.

"You can stand over there!" another speaker said, pointing at the wall. "As long as you don't interrupt. Shall we begin, Dawson? Before more 'excellently educated' rice-eaters show up?"

Bao took his place by the wall while the mayor walked to the podium and officially opened the meeting. Dawson explained how seriously the city council was taking the citizens' worries about infiltration by Chinese immigrants. Right before the meeting, he had received news of a ship currently en route to Dunedin harbor. Apparently, the *Te Anau* was stuffed from stern to bow with Chinese immigrants. Bao hadn't heard about it yet, but he couldn't really imagine that Dunedin would be faced with a massive influx of Chinese men. The immigration taxes were already enough of a deterrent.

"Why, my esteemed fellow citizens, are we so opposed to this invasion?" asked the mayor. "Especially we who are generally friendly and open to new-comers? To answer this question, I give the floor to the esteemed Mr. Fish, a respected businessman from our beautiful city."

Mr. Fish turned out to be the man who had mocked Bao's "hoity-toity accent." He explained that New Zealand was very proud of its basically hand-cho-sen population. Thanks to the various New Zealand companies that had organized immigration, the country was largely free of the kind of "doubtful characters" that could be found in other colonies. No prisoners had been exported to New Zealand like they had to Australia, nor the poorest of the poor, as had been sent to America.

"We have seen how splendidly the descendants of the Scottish immigrants mix with those of the hardworking German and English families who live in the Otago region. So it's up to us now to maintain that standard and not endanger the excellent constellation of our population. We must not let masses of Chinese men into our country. And when I say 'men,' that's exactly what I mean! Because they are not coming with their families looking for land to work and leave to their children, but instead, only young, strong lads come, ready to snatch the wages and the bread out of our sons' mouths!"

Loud applause thundered through the room, which increased when Mr. Fish then enumerated the danger that the daughters of Dunedin faced from the "Chinamen." After all, he claimed, after the men had finished their daily work, all they wanted to do was to steal and rape, and perhaps even worse, to marry into white families and pollute the blood of the citizens of New Zealand.

The next speaker, a lawyer named Mr. Allan, received no less applause even though he contradicted the man who spoke before him. He complained that the Chinese in fact weren't planning to intermarry with the whites, and made fun of their eating habits, their frugalness, and their religion. Apparently, he was afraid that the Church of Scotland could be overrun by practitioners of Chinese ancestor worship.

"Gentlemen, it is well known that business only works if people buy things. But what will the Chinese buy in Dunedin? Rice. Rice, and nothing else. No one knows what they do with the rest of the money that they scrape together."

Bao decided it was time to speak. He raised his hand and was almost sur-prised when the mayor actually called on him.

"This is Mister . . . Duong," he said in introduction. "He is the . . . representative for the Chinese residents of Dunedin."

Bao was booed as he took the podium; however, the men went silent when he began to speak. He introduced himself again and politely thanked the mayor for allowing him to speak. Then he proceeded to correct Mr. Allan's statements. In composed words, he explained that among the Chinese in Dunedin, there were many more fathers of existing families than young people. He talked about the importance of ancestors to Chinese families, and the duties of the women to remain at home and care for older relatives. The workers had to support all of that as well as pay off the debt from their sea voyage and immigration taxes from their abysmal wages. That explained the frugality and meager eating habits of the men. He also explained that these men weren't really immigrants.

"Dunedin doesn't have to be afraid of a Chinese invasion. Nearly all of my countrymen are eager to go home again as soon as possible. However, this is made more difficult by all of the measures you are taking to get rid of them." He focused on some of the slightly more open faces a few rows back. "This is a paradox, gentlemen. You want my countrymen to leave, but with your low wages and immigration taxes, you are forcing them to stay longer than they had planned. Before you organize a resistance, consider that it is pointless anyway. My countrymen will always come to New Zealand—not to bother you, to convert you, or to infiltrate your society, but instead out of pure desperation to support their beloved families back home."

Bao thanked the audience for their attention and left the podium. The men remained silent for a moment, and then the mayor called for a vote. One hundred percent of the participants voted for a dispatch to be sent to the prime minister in Wellington:

*In a large gathering today, the citizens of Dunedin expressed their worry about the infiltration of Otago society by Chinese immigrants. We expressly advocate stopping the further arrival of any Chinese. We call upon you to forbid the entry of the Te Anau.*

The men celebrated this decision with cheers. Bao left the room without looking at them.

# Chapter 54

Representative of Chinese Immigrants in Dunedin Admits
Unwillingness for Integration

Recently, Mr. Dung, a delegate of the local Chinese community,
confirmed the suspicions of the previous speaker at a municipal
meeting in Dunedin. His countrymen find neither the time to
learn our language, nor are prepared to adapt to our customs or
manner of eating. Mr. Dung stated that the reason for this was
the basic intention of the Chinese to return to their country;
an intention, however, which they usually end up distancing
themselves from for various reasons.

"The reporter twisted my words completely," Bao said as he lowered the
paper. That morning, it was he who lost his appetite for breakfast while reading
the morning news. "It's awful. My people must think that I—I betrayed them! I
must go there immediately and speak to them. They will be waiting for a report
about the meeting, and if they read that . . ." Bao quickly got to his feet.

"But they can't even read English," Aroha said, trying to comfort him. The
two of them had the dining room to themselves that morning. Peta had disappeared, and March was already at work, as usual. Both Robin and Helena also
seemed to be keeping to themselves. "Besides, they'll surely believe that you did
your best for them. At least eat something. Yesterday, you hardly got anything
down. Oh, yes, and pack a few things to take, so the men can get their teeth
into something other than rice. It's such a pity about all the delicious food we
have here that no one eats."

Aroha scanned the paper while Bao quickly ate some bread and washed it down with coffee, and then asked the maid to pack some baked goods for the poor. Aroha had actually hoped the municipal meeting would dominate the headlines so Robin Fenroy would no longer be their focus, but it wasn't the case. It was getting even worse, because now the other factory owners were trying to shift all the blame to the Lacrosse Company. The people that Robin had dined and played golf with over the last months didn't hesitate to make themselves look innocent at his expense. Magiel, for example, claimed that he would pay his seamstresses much better if Lacrosse hadn't forced him into a price battle. The buyers of the woolen mill blamed the starvation wages of their workers on the supposedly ridiculous price that Lacrosse had demanded for the antiquated factory. All of them blamed Robin more or less directly for leaving his business decisions up to a certain "temperamental young lady." Of course they also made insinuations about Robin's relationship with March, which were made to sound even worse because he was "as good as engaged" to his second cousin, Helena Lacrosse.

Feeling depressed, Duong Bao hurried toward one of the shabbiest parts of St. Andrew's, a block full of ramshackle houses where most of Dunedin's Chinese community were squeezed in together. If the *Te Anau* actually docked, the crowding would surely get even worse.

Bao thought sadly about how hopeful the mood on board the ship must be now, and how disappointed the men would be when they were confronted with dirty accommodations and exploitation, not to mention the ire of the white population.

It was still very early in the morning. Out on the street, working women were bringing their children to babysitters. They wore threadbare jackets and shawls to keep out the damp cold. Everyone hurried toward their destination with heads bowed, apprehensive of the threatening rainclouds. Therefore, Bao heard none of the insults he would usually have to reckon with in the Devil's Half Acre. But then Bao heard heavy footsteps on the cobblestones, and men talking excitedly. Instinctively, he ducked behind a corner and peered around. Now the horde came into view. More than two dozen young men armed with clubs and improvised slingshots were headed toward the harbor. They were talking loudly all at once.

"Are we going to let the chinks in?" one of them demanded.

"No!" the others shouted together.

"Are we going to turn back the *Te Anau*?"

"Yes!" the men replied.

Bao immediately looked for an escape route. But it was hopeless.

"There!" one of the men cried as Bao tried to conceal himself in a doorway. "Hey, fellows, there's a chink! Come on, let's show him what we do to rat eaters!"

Bao ran before the others could react. He rushed around a corner, shot between coaches and handcarts, and almost tripped over a small child that was holding its mother's hand. The complaining woman got in the pursuers' way, but that only made them angrier. Bao had no illusions that he could escape. Most of the men were younger and taller than he was, and now they were also starting to throw stones at him. But to give himself up would have been insanity. The men from the Chinese neighborhood would soon be on their way to work. If he could reach their lodgings, perhaps they would help him. So Bao was sprinting as fast as he could when a stone hit his upper arm. Another hit him on the back of his head. He felt blood running down his neck.

In the meantime, there were more people in the street. The factory claxons would soon be ringing for the beginning of the shift. Bao zigzagged between men and women, hoping his pursuers wouldn't throw stones if it put white people in danger. On the other hand, it could be that the workers were in league with the attackers and would grab him. But at least he was getting closer to the Chinese neighborhood. Bao began to shout at the top of his lungs in hopes that his friends would hear him. But then a stone hit the back of his knees. Bao staggered and tripped. He tried to protect his head as the men fell on him with clubs.

Aroha spent a grueling day with Robin and Helena. Robin was completely destroyed, and Helena, weeping, also blamed him for the disaster.

"I always told you that Margery Jensch was unsuitable as a manager. Couldn't you just hire some man like anyone else would? And now they're saying you're having an affair with her! Are you, Robin? Tell me the truth, are you?" Her tearful face was full of hatred.

Robin shook his head. "I—I didn't mean for all this to happen," he stammered.

"Then you shouldn't have done it!" Helena shot back at him furiously. "Above all, you should have kept your hands off of March. Besides, she's part Maori. If that ever gets out—"

Aroha couldn't listen to another word.

"Please, Helena, jealousy won't help the matter," Aroha said. "And Robin wasn't having an affair with March, that's ridiculous. Instead, you should both be thinking about what you can do now to save your reputations, instead of wallowing in self-pity. Robin, what about the reforms we discussed the day before yesterday?"

"Oh, forget the reforms!" Helena cried. "All that ado! When Grandfather was in charge of the company, there was no need. Everyone was happy."

Aroha doubted that, but also realized it was pointless to try to get through to the two of them.

"Perhaps we should just take a trip somewhere," Helena said finally. "Disappear for a few months, until things have quieted down."

"And just leave everything the way it is?" Aroha asked, appalled. "Robin!"

Robin didn't answer. He just stared into the empty space in front of him, as though paralyzed. Mr. Simmons, his face stony, kept announcing that various reporters wished to speak to Mr. Fenroy. Helena declined hysterically, and Robin just shook his head. Aroha, however, felt they should at least address the accusations.

"You may not have any good excuses, Robin, but the others don't either. Every factory owner in this city is taking advantage of their workers, but you're the only one who's being put through the wringer. Get out there, Robin. Tell them that you see what you've done wrong, announce a juicy wage increase for your employees, and shorter shifts. Say that you see the expected losses as a fine. If you want, donate a few thousand pounds to the church. You can afford it, Robin! Of course, they'll still make fun of you and be malicious, but at least the other factory owners will be the ones in the doghouse. Go, Robin! Talk to the reporters."

"No, Robin, don't do it!" Helena wailed. "Don't lower yourself to their level."

Robin stared silently at the wall and didn't respond.

Finally, March came home at lunchtime. Furious, she called Robin and Helena to a meeting.

"I'm not going to talk to the reporters," Robin said, his voice hollow. "I don't know what to say. I didn't mean for any of this to happen, I—"

"Of course you're not going to talk to the reporters," March snapped. As opposed to Helena and Robin, who were still drifting through the house in their nightclothes and robes, she was perfectly styled. She wore the suit that she'd put on that morning for work. No stray strands had dared to escape from her tidily pinned hair, and she was poised and calm. "You would only whine to them, and that's the last thing we need. We will not hide or make excuses for ourselves, Robin. We haven't done anything wrong—"

"What about the homework?" Aroha said.

March waved a hand dismissively. "Show me any dressmakers' workshop that doesn't do exactly the same thing. You can be sure I won't let them get away with their hypocrisy. No, we don't need self-flagellation now. All we can do is push forward. Now, I want to stay in the headlines, but this time I want us to look better. And it has to be interesting for the readers."

"You mean we need to do something good that they can report about?" Helena asked, suddenly hopeful. She smiled at Robin through her tears. "Perhaps—I mean, if Robin and I officially announce our engagement—"

March glared at Helena. "Then they'll tear you to shreds! I can already see the headlines. 'Endless Parties: Robin Fenroy Marries More Money.' They would count every penny that belongs to the future Fenroys, and compare that to the wages of the poor seamstresses. Goodness, Helena, do you have any brains at all? And Robin, stop looking at me that way! Fortunately, I have a plan."

Aroha hadn't doubted it for a moment.

Before March could begin to explain, the butler opened the library door again.

"Excuse me, Mr. Robin, Miss Helena. Mr. Peta is outside . . ."

"Throw him out!" Helena and March were of the same opinion for once.

But Peta stormed into the room behind the butler and turned directly to Aroha. "Something's going on in the Devil's Half Acre! There are riots in the Chinese neighborhood."

Aroha forgot about Robin and everything around her. "What—what kind of riots?" She went pale. "Oh God, Bao is there now!"

Peta nodded. "That's what I was afraid of. I heard that a group of workers were going to the harbor this morning to stop the *Te Anau* from docking, using violence if necessary. But the ship didn't dock. It continued on to Bluff, because the seas were too rough. And the workers didn't even make it to the harbor. They got into a fight in the Chinese neighborhood, and now the Chinese men have barricaded themselves into a tenement building, and the white mob is sieging them."

"What about the police?" Aroha asked.

A chill suddenly ran through her. It was the same feeling she'd had when she'd lost Matiu, and Koro.

Peta shrugged. "They haven't even turned up, as far as I know. Stopping brawls in the Half Acre isn't exactly their priority. I don't even know for sure what's happening, I just heard it at the parish hall. The reverend is on his way there now. He wants to mediate. I thought you'd want to know, Aroha."

Aroha nodded. "What should we do now?" she asked, feeling just as helpless as she had in Wairarapa and Te Wairoa. She never should have fallen in love with Bao. The curse . . .

"We'll go there, of course," March said determinedly, in a voice that allowed no resistance. Aroha turned around in surprise. The young woman was already on her feet and headed toward a locked cabinet. "The key, please, Robin," March demanded.

Robin shrugged. "Mr. Simmons?"

Without hesitation, the butler opened a drinks cabinet and removed a key from behind a dusty bottle of whiskey. Since Walter Lacrosse's death, no one had filled a glass here.

March waited until the butler had unlocked the second cabinet, and then quickly chose several weapons. As she had expected, they were of the best quality.

"Here!" she said, holding out pistols for Peta and Robin. They both stared as though they had no idea what the weapons were. "Hurry up," she barked. "How will we look if the fellows skip work and attack innocent people? If we let them get away with that, they'll soon be making insane demands!"

Robin shook his head. He had no experience with guns. Peta, to the contrary, was a good shot. But he too refused to accept the weapon.

"March, the workers are scared of losing their jobs. Of course they shouldn't be threatening the Chinese, but I won't point a gun at them."

March looked at her brother disdainfully, then turned to Aroha. "Then you have to do it," she said. "You've handled guns before, haven't you?"

Aroha nodded. Her mother, Linda, had been an excellent shot when she was younger, and still took her gun into the woods when she wanted to cook rabbit stew at the school. She'd never taught Aroha the art, however. She'd only practiced a little at Rata Station with Carol. On the farm, everyone was expected to help fight the plague of rabbits, and Aroha had often shot at the creatures. But she'd never hit her target.

"So, are we going to get Bao out of there now?" March said impatiently. "Come on, Aroha! I can't do this by myself."

Aroha took the weapon, and suddenly felt ready to defy the spirits.

"If he's still alive," she said, her voice steady, "we're going to get him out of there."

# Chapter 55

March asked the butler to saddle two horses as she rushed up to her room to change. Aroha could ride in her wide tea gown, but March's work skirt was too tight. When she returned, she was dressed in an elegant riding habit.

"You look like you're going on a fox hunt," Aroha said, annoyed. "What are you expecting?"

"A battle," March said curtly. "But since we don't have the right uniforms and are also planning to negotiate on both sides, I chose a dress, as befits a lady. Let's go, Aroha. You don't need to change." Then she gave Robin and Peta another disdainful glance. "You should at least try to notify the police. You can send one of the servants, if you're afraid to go out, Robin. For goodness' sake, what a sorry lot you are."

The butler had the horses ready out front. When she had the time, March preferred to ride the small, light-footed horse Robin had brought from Rata Station. She didn't care if Helena turned up her nose. Robin's thoroughbred had been prepared for Aroha, and both horses wore sidesaddles.

"These things aren't appropriate for a battle at all," Aroha said nervously. At Rata Station, she'd always ridden astride. "Are you sure—"

"You don't want to waste time resaddling them, do you?" March had already swung up without help, and a stable boy gave Aroha a hand. With a slightly queasy feeling, she let him push her up onto the very tall horse. If she had to dismount, she'd never manage to get back into the saddle without help, and she didn't even want to think about what would happen if she fell off.

March set a brisk pace immediately. In spite of the cobblestones, she urged her horse into a trot, and then a canter. Aroha could only hope that her huge horse wouldn't slip. After they'd left the grand streets of Mornington behind them, however, they were forced to slow down. Carriages were barely moving in the narrow alleyways of St. Andrews, and of course there were many people on foot. March shouted impatiently at the coachmen and pedestrians and demanded that they make way.

They heard the commotion before they reached the block where the mob had gathered. The siege was focused on a building decorated with Chinese lanterns and paper dragons, where one young man had opened a cookshop on the ground floor. He made simple, very affordable meals and earned a few pennies when the men were too tired after long days at their various jobs to cook rice for themselves. It was also where Bao had met with his countrymen.

"Chinks go home!" cried a group of young white men.

They were pounding on the doors and had already torn down many decorations. Aroha hoped that none of them would think to set a fire. The house was made of raw wood, and it would certainly burst into flames very easily.

Nearby, Reverend Waddell was standing on a crate and preaching peace from his improvised pulpit. But his words were barely audible in the general uproar; no one wanted to hear about Christ and brotherly love.

March guided her horse into the middle of the crowd. "Make way!" she ordered. "You're blocking the street. Let us through, or I'll fetch the police."

The men laughed. "The police are just as keen to see the chinks burn as we are," one of them said, and to Aroha's horror began playing with a pack of matches.

"Do you think I look Chinese?" March asked sharply. "The police will certainly be very interested if you're rioting here and harassing two ladies."

She urged her horse forward again, but it was impossible to get through. Aroha's thoroughbred pranced nervously.

"And where are the ladies going, here in the darkest corner of Devil's Half Acre?" One of the ringleaders pushed through the crowd. He looked quite rakish with his dark-blond hair and piercing blue eyes. He leered at them.

"I want—my hus—" Aroha was about to explain, but March interrupted her.

"You don't have to tell this mob anything," she said haughtily, and then turned to the young rake. "It's none of your business where we're going."

The man laughed. "No? What if the ladies look like they want to have some fun? What if they're so wanton that they'd even kiss a Chinese arse? Then we could take care of them."

He reached for the bridle of Aroha's horse, and the horse reared in objection. The man backed away, but showed no fear. He murmured a few calming words to the horse, and reached out to pat its flank.

March raised her gun and flipped the safety catch. "You should be careful how you speak to ladies," she said coldly. "Especially ladies who could be helpful to you. In removing these horrible decorations, for instance."

She quickly aimed at a red lantern that was hanging above the entry to the cookshop, and shot over the men's heads. The crowd went silent as the lantern exploded. Then March nonchalantly shot a paper dragon for good measure. That earned her cries of shock. The men ducked, a few ran away, and several threw themselves on the ground in panic.

"Don't—don't shoot!" the ringleader begged as March swung her pistol to aim at him.

"Miss Jensch!" It was the reverend. "How dare you shoot a gun here? Drop the weapon immediately. You might injure someone."

"I might," March remarked. "However, I think I've taught these fellows some respect. They will clear out of the streets and go back to their jobs now."

"If they even still *have* jobs," the ringleader countered in his thick brogue. "The factories prefer to hire the chinks, who—"

"Who are less inclined to talk back, rebel, or incite violence?" March asked. "You're right about that, mister. People who do such things aren't exactly in demand. And let me guess . . . you lost your job because you couldn't keep your big mouth shut. Was it here, or back in Ireland?"

"That's—that's none of your business . . ."

March smiled. She'd hit the mark.

"Very good, Paddy," she said condescendingly. "If you call off your dogs, I'll give you a chance. Apply to the main office of the Lacrosse workshop. We're looking for a driver, and you seem to have a feel for horses."

The man stopped, his mouth hanging open. "You—you're really Margery Jensch?"

"Exactly. And now you have a chance to make up your mind while I count to three. One . . ."

March leaned back in the saddle and gazed over the anxious crowd. The young Irishman was leading a mob of at least thirty men. He seemed undecided.

On one hand, he wanted the job she'd offered, but he didn't want to lose face in front of his men.

Aroha was nervous. What if he didn't back down? What if he decided to capitalize on the hatred that the workers surely had for Margery Jensch?

As March reached three, the man made his decision.

"Let's get out of here!" he shouted to his men. "The reverend is right, Christ wouldn't have set the fuckers on fire. And we already showed one of them. Now they all know what they can expect."

The young man tipped his hat sardonically to March and Aroha in farewell.

March smiled at him. "Very reasonable, Paddy. What was your name, again?"

Aroha was desperate to get into the house to find out what had happened to Bao. But she waited with March, who calmly watched the rioters leave, until only the reverend was left standing outside.

"That's how to do it, Reverend," March said. "With a little honey and a whip. That's the language those fellows understand."

The clergyman had gone completely white. "How could you shoot into a crowd like that? If there had been a panic—"

"Then they would have run away," March said, unimpressed. "The effect would have been the same."

"What if you had hit someone?" the reverend said, stepping down from his box.

March sighed. "Where I come from, people value one's ability to shoot rabbits more highly than one's knowledge of economics. Until now, I hadn't appreciated that aspect of my education. But as you see, I was rather successful. If I do anything, I do it right, Reverend. I didn't hit anyone because I didn't aim at anyone. And now please excuse us, we have to look for Aroha's friend."

Reverend Waddell just stared at her. "The devil herself," he murmured.

March guided her horse to the entrance of the cookshop, where a terrified-looking young man appeared.

"Where's Bao?" Aroha asked.

The man didn't reply. He stared at March as though she were a creature from another world.

March pointed at the decorations she'd destroyed. "I'm sorry that I had to shoot your lantern," she said, "and the dragon. Of course I will replace them."

The man said something they didn't understand, but then bowed in front of March with such seriousness that his meaning became clear. He and his countrymen must have been watching from inside and they knew only too well that they had her to thank for their deliverance.

"Bao?" Aroha asked again desperately. If only she could remember the words that Bao had practiced with Lani: *Where is Tapsy?*

"*Zaina . . . Zaina* Bao?" She carefully slid down from the horse.

The young man nodded then, his eyes wide. "Aroha?"

"Yes," she said. "Please, where is Bao?"

The man beckoned her and March into a sparsely furnished parlor. It smelled of spices and the sweat of fear. Most residents of the house were huddled together there, armed with knives and clubs, preparing to defend themselves from the mob.

The cookshop owner said a few words, of which Aroha only understood her own name and Bao's. The men silently made way for her. A doorway shielded with only a curtain led to a tiny space where the young man clearly cooked and slept. Now Bao lay motionless on a mat there, his face so swollen that Aroha hardly recognized him. His hair was sticky with blood, and his arm rested at an unnatural angle.

Aroha let out a gasp and sank to the floor next to him. Once more, she felt everything freeze inside of her. The third. She'd lost her third partner. Aroha wished that she could cry, but she knew it would take time for the tears to come. She silently whispered his name, touched his forehead and his lips. His face was still warm.

"Is he dead?" March asked, distraught.

The young cookshop owner said something.

Aroha looked up. "Of course he's dead," she whispered. "That's—that's what happens when I love someone. It's the curse, March. I never—I never should have given in. It's all my fault . . ."

"Not dead," she heard a voice say behind her. "They beat. We come, all scream. We save."

Aroha started in surprise and looked around. One of the other men had stepped into the room. He gave her a look of pity.

Bao was alive? Aroha's mind raced. She had to do something. Clean Bao's injuries, bandage them . . . She looked helplessly around the badly equipped little kitchen. Then she listened to Bao's breathing and put her hand on his chest.

He was having difficulty getting air; the attackers had surely broken his nose. But his heart was beating strongly and regularly. Bao moaned.

"He's alive—he's really alive . . ."

Aroha had to say the words to convince herself.

"But he seems to be very badly injured," March said. "We need a doctor. Or no, it would be better to bring him to Robin's house. Who knows if a doctor would even come here. Listen, Aroha, you stay; I'll ride back and send the coach. Poor Helena, I'm afraid we're going to get blood on her fine upholstery."

The Chinese men were anxious to help Bao and Aroha. The cookshop owner fetched water and cloths. One of the men attempted a temporary splint for Bao's arm. Another got smelling salts and held them under the injured man's nose. Bao coughed and began to come to his senses. He could hardly see Aroha because of the swelling around his eyes, but he recognized her voice.

"You're here?" he whispered. "I heard the others say you saved us."

"It was March," Aroha replied. "March saved you. She was unbelievable. If I ever make a deal with gods and spirits again, I want her by my side!"

March rode back to the Lacrosse residence as though spurred by the devil, and immediately ordered a servant to take the carriage to the Chinese neighborhood. Then she sent another servant to fetch a doctor.

Bao groaned as his friends carefully lifted him into the coach. The men had beaten him terribly, but his injuries weren't life-threatening.

The doctor, who had arrived at the Lacrosse house shortly after the carriage, made the same diagnosis. He set Bao's broken nose, splinted the arm, and bandaged the wounds. He had to stitch two of them.

"Two or three ribs are broken too," he said. "You'll have to stay in bed for a few days, and you shouldn't travel for two or three weeks. But everything will heal, don't worry. And you, Miss Fitzpatrick, should have a drink. Tea is certainly refreshing, but I would also like to prescribe a large brandy. You look paler than my patient."

Aroha tried to smile, even though she felt too weak. Only now did she dare to believe that she was holding Bao in her arms, alive. The curse, if it had ever existed, was broken.

# Part 6

## AS YOU WISH

### Dunedin (South Island)

### Rotorua (North Island)

### November 1888–April 1889

# Chapter 56

After her triumph against the mob, March was in the best of spirits, but Helena was scared it would bring more bad publicity. She, too, thought that March shouldn't have fired the gun, and parroted Reverend Waddell's reasoning. Robin was simply relieved that Bao was back and Aroha had freed herself from the curse she'd believed in. He could imagine even better than the others how much she'd suffered under it, and was prepared to accept any judgment that came from the press.

"They blame me for everything, anyway," he said fatalistically. "It doesn't matter if my business manager fired a few bullets at some lanterns."

March only shook her head about Robin, and prepared herself for another attack. After she'd made sure that Bao would survive his injuries, she changed her clothes, had the carriage prepared again, and appeared at the office of the *Otago Daily Times* early that evening.

"My name is Margery Jensch. I'd like to speak to Silas Spragg."

Silas Spragg was the reporter who'd written the article about the badly paid seamstresses. However, he hadn't personally taken part in the witch hunt against Robin Fenroy. March chose him for that reason. The young reporter, a tall, slender man with dark hair and bright, clever eyes, received her in a conference room.

"Margery Jensch of the Lacrosse Company? What brings you here?" he asked. "I hope you're not planning to shoot me. There are rumors going around . . ."

March smiled. She had dressed very carefully and knew that she looked good in her burgundy ensemble with decorative trim on the jacket sleeves and the hem. Underneath, she wore a corset that enhanced her figure, and she'd styled her hair so that it framed her face in soft waves, and accented her attractive features. March's complexion was perfect, and her eyes were shining. The reporter was no match.

"I've never shot at a human being, and I certainly won't be starting with you," March said, trying to put him at ease.

"Would you like to talk about the attack on the Chinese community this morning?" Spragg said. "You played a role in it. A few of my colleagues have been talking to witnesses, but with little success so far. Aside from the fact that our honored Reverend Waddell thinks you're the spawn of hell, and a horde of Chinese workers thinks you were sent by heaven."

March shrugged. "I'll leave that decision up to the gods. Although it would certainly be interesting if one could choose between afterlives. I'm not sure if I would prefer Hawaiki or the Presbyterian or Chinese versions of heaven."

Spragg laughed. "You forgot about hell," he reminded her.

March nodded. "I was just there. At least what Otago's newspapers portray as 'Hell on Earth.' And in answer to your original question, no, I don't want to talk about the fact that a mob of white rowdies was roaming the streets this morning, threatening innocent people and beating them up just because they're Chinese. I want to talk about something completely different. As you know, I manage the Lacrosse Company—"

"Which no one can quite believe," Spragg remarked. "Such a young thing as you . . . so pretty, so pleasant to talk to."

"Thank you," March said. "But good looks and a leading position in the industry aren't mutually exclusive. Be assured that I never had any intimate relationship with my relative, Robin Fenroy. I would never abuse a man's affections in order to take out childish whims on factory workers, as your colleagues insinuate. In fact, I protected Mr. Fenroy from the jackals who were after the job of managing his factories, especially Harold Wentworth. You may know that Wentworth now runs one of the Magiel factories and pays exactly the same wages as I do. I am more successful, however. My businesses are the most productive in the area. The profits are excellent."

Spragg was about to speak, but March silenced him with a gesture. "It's no wonder, because my teacher in the disciplines of economics and business management was none other than the esteemed Martin Porter, who is currently the managing director of the Magiel Company. I worked for several years as his assistant at the Kaiapoi Woolen Mill. It's very humble of him to claim now that he has adopted his methods of management from me. It seems the teacher has profited from the student."

Spragg grinned. Up until now, he'd had no idea that there was a connection between the respective managing directors. "Does that mean one could say that the price war between Lacrosse and Magiel was based on . . . shall we say . . . a personal rivalry?"

March shrugged again. "Martin must doubtlessly prove to his father-in-law that he can make more profit than his little assistant from days gone by. But that's not what I wanted to talk to you about either. This is about the accusations you are making about businesspeople in general and the doubtlessly somewhat naive, but completely innocent Robin Fenroy, in particular. You say we are exploiting our workers, and that our workplaces are pure hell. I wish to object, because that point of view is completely exaggerated, and I would be happy to prove it. I understand quite a lot about business, Mr. Spragg, but hardly anything about sewing. At least in the latter respect, I am on a par with the girls who seek work in my dressmakers' workshops. I'm of the same age, and have a similar amount of resilience. Therefore, I would like to propose that I, Margery Jensch, lead the life of a seamstress for one month. And if you like, I will also work at a loom."

"You want to work in a factory?" Silas Spragg could imagine the headlines. It would be a sensation.

March nodded. "Under the observation of your newspaper. I can report about my experiences every day or week, as you wish."

"And . . . will you also be living like one of your seamstresses? You wouldn't be returning to Fenroy's luxurious estate after a day's work?" Spragg was excitedly taking notes.

"I would like to live with a seamstress. I already have my eye on one whom I think you know. I assume that, aside from Peta Te Eriatara, it's also Leah Hobarth who's providing insider information?" March narrowed her eyes at him searchingly.

"I won't reveal our sources," Spragg said curtly. "So you mean you would take this other girl by the hand and share her life, day and night, in every way?"

"I certainly won't be after the young lady's beau," she remarked coolly.

Spragg laughed. "That's worth a headline, at least. 'Lacrosse Manager Joins the Tedious World of Factory Workers.' And where are you planning to do this? In one of your own workshops?"

March shook her head. "No. Then I'd be accused of cheating, and of getting preferential treatment. It will have to be with the competition." She smiled sardonically. "Mr. Porter and I also worked very well together in the past."

Spragg spontaneously offered March his hand. "I like you, Miss Jensch," he said. "Wait a moment while I speak to the editor. If he thinks the project is as sensational as I do, we're in business."


Leah Hobarth agreed to help March with her experiment, but vehemently denied being involved in Spragg's previous reporting.

"I don't even work for Lacrosse anymore," she said when March asked her about it during their first meeting. It was true. When Robin sold the woolen mill, Leah had quickly gotten a job in one of Wentworth's workshops. "Of course I was angry at Robin when he let the workers down. I told him about the conditions in the mill, and he was so shocked that he immediately wanted to change everything. He really gave me hope. Humph. Instead, he ended up selling out to that Scottish syndicate that took even more advantage of the workers."

"And now it's forgive and forget, Miss Hobarth?" March said skeptically.

Leah shook her head. "Not really, but I care about Robin very much. I know him well from our . . . past acquaintance, and he will always need someone to hold his hand. When I spoke with him after he visited the Smiths, I thought, now the time has come that I can help guide him. But in the end, I left it all up to him to enact the changes we talked about. So perhaps it's my fault a little too. Still, I didn't betray Robin to the press, Miss Jensch. I quit at Lacrosse because Peta kept trying to use me as a spy."

"Please, call me Margery," she replied. "After all, we'll be sharing a bed tomorrow."

Silas Spragg cleared his throat. The conversation between March and Leah was taking place in the offices of his newspaper, and March was sure that he'd made a deal with Leah to compensate her for her participation. It was probably far too little. March would have liked to have been involved in the bargaining. Of course she wasn't getting any money for the experiment, aside from the salary that she would earn as a seamstress. The Magiel Company had agreed to hire her "on trial" for a month. "Perhaps Miss Jensch will like working for us so much that she'll want to stay," Martin Porter had told the *Otago Daily Times* with a smirk.

Spragg fiddled with his notebook. "Shall we plan the specifics now, Miss Jensch, Miss Hobarth? What about your clothes? Most of the seamstresses sew their own dresses, don't they?"

Leah nodded. "But March can also take a dress from the stock," she said. "The cut is basically the same, anyway. At least for those of us who aren't passionate tailors. We just copy the garments from the workshop."

"Does that mean every now and then you take precut pieces of material and then just sew a dress together at home?" March asked.

Leah didn't confirm her suspicion, but didn't directly deny it either. "We aren't thieves," she said.

"So, Miss Jensch will need a dress," Spragg said, beginning a list.

"Two," March said. "One for the factory, and one for Sundays. And underwear to change."

"Don't forget a shawl," Leah added. "You'll need that more than the underwear. Just wait and see, you'll be freezing early in the morning when there's no coach to take you from door to door."

"I thought I'd wear a woolen cape," March said, but immediately realized her mistake when Leah laughed.

"You'll never find a factory girl who can afford such a thing," she told the young woman. "You'll need a knit shawl. But I can't knit. Mrs. Smith made mine." March couldn't knit either, but there were cheap enough shawls to buy. "And a pair of shoes," Leah said, and pointed to her worn lace-ups. She glanced dubiously at March's suede shoes. "Ones you can walk far in, that won't immediately soak through in the rain."

Helena threw up her hands in dismay as March was leaving the Lacrosse house in her "disguise."

"Isn't that dress scratchy? For goodness' sake, I can't understand how you can lower yourself to such a level. Isn't Robin the actor in the family?"

March gave her an icy glance. "This doesn't have anything to do with act-ing, Helena, it's about practical life skills. I'm going to prove to the reverend and those reporters and all the fools who are so bothered by the misery of the workers that it's possible to live on the wages we pay. As long as one is able to stick to a budget. That requires basic mathematics and the ability to be frugal. It has nothing to do with acting."

"In that case, I wish you luck," Robin said tiredly. "And success. Although I don't really believe you'll be able to do it. I'm more inclined to believe the reverend, after everything I've seen."

Aroha embraced March and bid her farewell. "I believe you can do any-thing," she said warmly. "But if you don't succeed, you know you'll be in even more hot water."

"I *will* succeed," March said confidently. "Have a safe trip to Rotorua, Aroha, if I don't see you before you go. Though I know poor Bao is stuck on bedrest a while longer. Please give him my best."

Leah was waiting at St. Andrew's to accompany her new coworker to the Smith family home, where she still lived as a boarder.

"We moved recently," she said, "when the ninth child was born. The old apartment was too small. And now Emily also earns some money. The new place is cold and drafty, but it's bigger, and it has access to a courtyard. It's got high walls around it, so the children can be left there on their own to play."

"Nine children?" March tried to fathom how a family could get so large.

The Smiths' new home was barely more than a shack built onto the side of a two-story tenement building. March rumpled her nose as Leah led her through a corridor. It was dark and stank of cabbage and urine.

"Let me guess, the outhouse is in the courtyard, as well," she remarked.

Leah nodded. "Yes, that's one of the downsides," she admitted. "If you need to go out at night, you have to be careful. Not all the men in the house are, um, nice. A girl from the second floor was raped last month."

"And that's where the children play?" March asked, horrified.

Leah shrugged. "During the day the men are all at the factory."

A door from the corridor led directly to a shed. Another offered a view into the tiny courtyard where a few forgotten plants were moldering.

"Wouldn't it be possible to plant a proper garden here?" March asked. In her mind's eye, a vegetable patch appeared, providing additional food for the family.

"It would be if the space belonged to us alone," Leah said. "And if anyone had time to take care of it. Besides, seeds aren't free, and water from the well would have to be carried in. Although, as often as the men pee in front of the outhouse, watering wouldn't be that much extra work . . . But there isn't any proper soil; the yard is paved. I don't think very much would grow here."

March had a different opinion. She believed the old cliché: where there's a will, there's a way. She made a mental note for the *Otago Daily Times*.

Leah unlocked the door to the Smiths' shack.

"Welcome to the palace," she said ironically, and ushered March inside.

"Leah! Leah! Leah!"

March started in surprise as an entire horde of children rushed toward them. Laughing, Leah hugged the little ones and lined them up in a row. "Johnny, Billy, Rosie, Willie, Katie, Sally, Harry," she said, introducing them. Aside from the oldest girls, they all wore baggy clothes made of cheap material, and their dirty, uncombed hair hung in their faces. "Petey isn't out of diapers yet, and Emily is at the factory. This is our new boarder, children. Her name is March. Is everything all right, Sally?"

She turned to the oldest girl, a haggard, thin creature of about twelve. Sally had stringy, dark-blonde hair and an unhealthily pale, angular face.

It stank terribly in the shack. Diapers, March guessed, and old cooking smells. Then she saw the primitive coal brazier on a table within reach of the children—far too dangerous! But she couldn't see anywhere else it could be safely put. The little room was completely full with three beds, the table, and two chairs. Clothing was lying on the beds, with socks and shoes on the floor between them.

"I couldn't finish everything," Sally admitted fearfully. "Papa will be mad, and Mama, too, since I didn't clean up. The kids just throw everything around again. The boys do it on purpose to make me mad! And I still haven't fetched any water, but I was supposed to wash the diapers. Mr. Tenth is in the house, and I didn't want to walk past him. Oh, and I couldn't buy any bread either. They raised the price and I was missing a penny. Mr. Burke refused to give me credit because I'm a kid. He didn't know if Mother would approve. That would be a fine thing, he said, if every waif came to get sweet cakes and the mothers wouldn't pay for anything."

"Didn't you buy anything to eat, Sally?" Leah asked gently.

Sally nodded. "Yes, sweet potatoes. They were cheap. I just don't know what to do with them. They don't taste good when they're raw. I think they give you a stomachache." She pointed to a heap of roots that were sitting on the cluttered table between clothes and other household objects. One of them had a bite taken out of it.

March took the initiative. "I'll cook the sweet potatoes. I'm not the best cook in the world, but anyone can do it. In the meantime, you can get the water, Leah. And go to the bakery for the bread."

Leah shook her head. "I can't, March," she said quietly. "There's no money for it. I would have had the extra penny, but Sally spent her mother's money on sweet potatoes. We'll just have to make do with them until tomorrow evening."

Sally sniffed. Tears were running down her cheeks.

"It's not that bad," March said, trying to comfort her. "*Kumara* are delicious. I'll show you how to peel them."

Sally reached half-heartedly for a knife and swatted her younger siblings away when they tried to "help" as well.

"Sally is completely exhausted," Leah said as the girl leaped to her feet because a baby was crying in the next room. "Her sister Emily started working in the factory a month ago, and since then she's had to do everything alone here. She watches the children, changes the babies' diapers, and she's supposed to cook and shop and fetch water too. But she's afraid to walk past Mr. Tenth. He's a nasty old man who gropes and harasses the girls every chance he gets."

That caught March's attention. "Can't her father do something about the man?"

Leah shook her head. "Unfortunately not. Mr. Tenth is the landlord."

When she saw the shocked expression on March's face, Leah smiled dubiously. "Welcome to the Devil's Half Acre, Miss Jensch."

# Chapter 57

March Jensch wasn't easy to discourage. By the time the Smiths returned from their day's work, she had cooked the *kumara* to make a stew. A few of the struggling plants in the courtyard turned out to be herbs, and she found some scraps of wood to make a small fire. In its coals, she roasted a few of the *kumara* as lunch for the following day.

"They won't fill us up, but it's better than nothing," she said to Leah and little Sally, who was still scared of her parents' wrath because there was no bread in the house.

"We usually aren't filled up by the heels of bread we bring with us either," Leah said.

Meanwhile, March lectured the older children about how to make a fire without expensive matches, and how to cook a tasty meal without having to buy spices.

"On Sunday, I'll take you all to the woods and show you how to find edible plants. For example, there are raupo roots in every stream. You know, cattails," she added when she saw their blank looks. "I can show you how to fish too. The Maori who used to live here didn't go hungry, even though they didn't have any money."

"But they didn't have to work nine hours a day at a factory either," Leah added. "At least today we have plenty of time." At the request of the *Otago Daily Times*, Magiel had given Leah the afternoon off, and March didn't have to start at the dressmakers' workshop until the next day. "After tomorrow, I guarantee you won't have the energy to dig up roots."

March countered that she'd have left that up to the children, anyway. Sally didn't have to babysit in the shack, she could take them outside.

"What about the two littlest ones?" Leah asked.

March sighed. "I wouldn't have had them in the first place!" she said. "Nine children! How well does a factory have to pay to keep them all fed?"

Leah grimaced. "Are the women here supposed to fiddle with vinegar rinses as well?" Aside from the kitchen, there was only one other room in the Smiths' shack. The twelve people who usually lived there shared five beds. "Where would she even go? Aside from the fact that people are simply too tired after work to wash."

"Amazing that they aren't too tired to be intimate," March retorted. "Besides, I've never used a vinegar rinse. You can also just count the days and abstain on the dangerous ones."

Leah smiled flatly. "You can, March, if the man doesn't mind. Here, no one talks about such things. No one asks the woman if she's too tired or if it's a dangerous day. But you'll see for yourself. Just do me a favor and don't talk like that to Mrs. Smith. Otherwise, she might wring your neck."

That evening, at least, Mrs. Smith was delighted with her new boarder. March and Leah had used the time until her return to tidy up, fetch water, and mop the shack. The babies' diapers were soaking and all the children had at least washed their faces and hands.

"You won't get anything to eat until you do it," March told one of the little boys, who believed her, and immediately got in line with the others. March washed them off, and ascertained that they were all basically undernourished and too small for their ages. They were in no way comparable to the sturdy, independent Maori children she'd grown up with.

Mrs. Smith and Emily returned from work at seven o'clock, and Mr. Smith was expected only two hours later. Mother and daughter didn't speak very much to each other, they just devoured the stew. Leah explained Sally's problem with the bread, and the mother refrained from punishing the girl.

"You should hide a penny somewhere for emergencies," March suggested. "Sally is a reasonable child, she wouldn't spend the money on sweets."

"But the boys would steal it from her," Emily said. "They don't listen to Sally very much. They don't take her seriously."

The girl was on the edge of tears again. To March, she looked even more exhausted than the workers. Sally herself seemed to see it the same way.

"I wish I was old enough to go to work too," she complained.

"You can help me sew buttonholes, right now," Leah said. "Did you bring my work, Mrs. Smith?"

March realized then that Leah hadn't been excused from the daily homework she had to complete in addition to all her hours in the workshop. Right after dinner, the younger children were put to bed. Then the table was cleared and wiped clean enough that the flannel shirts Mrs. Smith was unpacking wouldn't get dirty. Sally, too, was given several shirts from the stack, even though the girl's eyes would barely stay open.

"You can do at least one," Mrs. Smith said sternly. "You start at the workshop or the mill in less than two years, Sally. You might as well get used to it."

March took the shirt out of the little girl's hands. "If you show me what to do, Mrs. Smith, I'll help."

Mrs. Smith snorted. "You'll have your own work tomorrow."

The homework that Magiel assigned was the same as March gave to her workers. Shirts, trousers, and dresses were sewn together in the factory, but the last few details had to be completed by hand. The machines couldn't sew on buttons, for instance. Additionally, all the shirts had to be checked for loose seams, and those had to be resewn. Mrs. Smith and Leah worked fast. In two hours, they finished the dozen shirts they had each been given. It was more difficult for Emily. She was tired and wept bitterly when she stabbed her finger with a needle while working on her second shirt, staining the fabric with blood.

"If that doesn't come out, she'll have to pay the cost of the shirt from her wages," Mrs. Smith said with a sigh, stopping her work to wash the spot with cold water. "Now, be careful!" she scolded. "And you stay awake, Sally."

Mr. Smith returned home around nine, grumbled a greeting, and ate the rest of the stew before getting into bed. The women wouldn't be finished for a long time. By the time the last shirt had been tidily folded in Emily's basket, it was eleven o'clock. In the meantime, March was almost as tired as the other women, and didn't have the energy to be bothered that she had to share a bed with not only Leah but Emily as well.

"I'll sleep at the foot," the girl offered. She pulled her dress off and curled up under the blanket. She didn't bother about changing her undergarments or washing. It was almost the same for Leah; she only quickly wiped her face and armpits with a damp cloth.

"If you want to wash properly tomorrow, you'll have to fetch water yourself," she told March. "It's too late now, the streets aren't safe. By the way, there's a chamber pot here, in case you have to go and don't want to risk the courtyard."

The courtyard wasn't entirely dark, though, thanks to March's fire still smoldering. Several women and girls who'd gone to use the outhouse over the course of the evening had expressed their thanks. "If everyone can bring back some brush, dried plants, or wood scraps whenever they go out, we could always make a fire when it gets dark," March told them. She decided to send out the little boys the next day to look for burnable material. Instead of making trouble for Sally, they should be making themselves useful. And why didn't they go to school, anyway?

March thought about everything she'd seen as she attempted to fall asleep in the narrow bed next to Leah. It would only work if she could hold still. Every movement on the old beds woke the next sleeper. But it wasn't just that keeping March awake. As a girl, she had often slept in the common sleeping house at Maori Station; the night sounds of other people didn't bother her. But here, everything was so cramped. The unwashed bodies offended her sense of smell, and the odor of the babies' diapers and the chamber pot filled the air.

And then Mr. Smith stirred too. March heard Mrs. Smith groan as he woke her. She murmured something and shoved the baby that was still sleeping in its parents' bed out of the way so it would be safe, then lay still as her husband claimed his marital rights. March could hear him panting and moaning.

"Hush!" Mrs. Smith whispered.

Then the sound of deep, satisfied breathing as he rolled off of her. The tenth child had probably just been conceived . . .

March tried not to think too much about it. At some point, she drifted off.

In the Smiths' house, it wasn't possible to oversleep. The children stirred before the crack of dawn, and then the factory claxon sounded. March was accustomed to getting up early to be in the dressmakers' workshop before her seamstresses, and she surprised her host family by not needing to be shaken like Emily and Sally. Emily had slept like the dead for the entire night at the foot of Leah and March's bed, and was now difficult to awaken. Still half asleep, she pulled her dress on before going into the next room. Mrs. Smith had coffee ready. Apparently, it was the only source of sustenance available in abundance in the Smith household. Leah and Emily had prepared some the previous evening, too, while they had done their homework.

"We need coffee," Leah explained as she quickly drained her cup. "Otherwise, we won't survive the day."

March watched in dismay as even the small children drank the dark brew. It couldn't be healthy.

Mrs. Smith finally pressed a few pennies into Sally's hand, and warned her daughter not to come home without bread this time. Then they all made their way to the factories. Mr. and Mrs. Smith worked at the Scottish consortium's woolen mill, and Leah, Emily, and now March at one of Magiel's workshops. It was in a building originally designed as a woolen mill, next to a small river. March noticed that no one had bothered with major renovations there. The old production halls were still in use, and between them were narrow corridors and stairways that had been built quickly and cheaply out of wood. In each of the factory halls, around fifty sewing machines were set up in rows. Magiel had apparently done away with the concept of teamwork between pattern-cutters and seamstresses. The cutting was done in separate rooms by the youngest and surely worst-paid girls, and two older women supervised them. The seamstresses worked independently.

March had assumed she would be received by the factory management, but Porter and Wentworth did not appear. Few of the workers read newspapers, and the *Otago Daily Times* had not revealed in which factory March's experiment was to take place. So there was a high probability that she could work there anonymously and undetected, at least at the beginning.

"Any experience?" the supervisor asked as she greeted the newcomer.

"I know how to operate a buttonhole machine," March said proudly.

The woman waved a hand dismissively. "We don't have those. The machines are too touchy. We give buttonholes as part of the homework. Have you ever operated a sewing machine?"

March could confirm that. She made a point to try every new model that she obtained for her workshops, and proved herself to be quite skilled as she threaded the machine and sewed together the leg for a pair of child's trousers at the woman's instruction. The supervisor was pleased that only one explanation was necessary.

"But it has to go faster," she said curtly. "And please be careful. The finished parts will be controlled. If a seam is crooked, we will take it out of your wages. The same with broken needles."

"They break often with the thicker materials," whispered Leah, who'd taken a seat at the machine next to March, and was hemming the trouser leg.

March figured that out very quickly. Her first needle lasted only an hour, and then she had to ask the supervisor to show her how to change it. That took time. When the claxon announced the morning break, she was nowhere near reaching her quota, let alone a bonus. Dazed, she sat up and listened to the sudden silence. Of course, the room was still full of sounds—conversation and shoes tapping on the wooden floor. But the ear-numbing noise of the sewing machines had dampened March's hearing. In addition, her back hurt from bending over the machine.

"You'll feel your legs soon too," Leah told her. "And tomorrow you'll hardly be able to move."

The sewing machines used in the factory were extremely efficient. Instead of fifty to sixty stitches per minute as could be done by hand by a skilled seamstress, they could do a thousand. They were driven by pedals, so the seamstress had to constantly move her feet up and down.

"You might get a stomachache," Leah continued. "The pedaling goes right into your lower belly. The older women all have complaints."

March remembered how Robin had once quoted Wentworth saying something that had outraged her: *A factory owner from Lyon had supposedly said that he would only employ girls between sixteen and eighteen. By age twenty, they were ready for the hospice.*

It dawned on her that the labor laws in New Zealand that limited women to nine hours of work a day had a purpose.

Both Leah and March were hungry, but they saved their sweet potatoes for lunch and limited themselves to coffee. The company provided one cup per worker, which March considered very generous. Now her mouth was dry and her throat irritated from the dust in the air of the factory floor. She would have gladly taken another cup, even though the bitter brew, served without sugar or cream, didn't taste very good. But before she had time to think any more about it, the claxon called her back to the machines. There was just enough time to use the toilet. March rushed back, feeling nauseated. The stink was unbearable, and the facilities were caked with filth.

"It's much better at our place," she told Leah, who was already treadling her machine again. "At Lacrosse, the toilets are blindingly clean."

"Do you clean them yourself?" Leah asked mockingly. "Or do the women do it for free before and after their shifts?"

"On the clock," March announced. But then she realized, to her shame, that her women were also paid by the piece. They couldn't sew shirts while they were cleaning the toilets.

Leah and March met Emily during the midday break. The girl complained of hunger; she had already eaten her *kumara* during the first break.

"It went down so easily, though," she said. "The bread is always so hard that you have to dunk it in coffee to be able to chew it."

"On the second day?" March asked with surprise and earned herself more laughter.

"We buy stale bread," Leah informed her. "Fresh bread for twelve people would be far too expensive."

March watched the other workers. Almost all of them soaked their dry bread in coffee before they put it into their mouths. That made mealtime longer, and the bread was probably more filling than the *kumara*. March wasn't very hungry herself. She was feeling too sore and too bewildered to think about food. She did feel bad for Emily, though, and gave her half of her *kumara*. The girl thanked her profusely and wolfed it down.

"We'll stop by the bakery on the way back," Leah said, comforting her. "Maybe he'll have some old sweet buns. I still have a penny. Then we'll have a party!"

"The baker is sweet on me," she confessed to March later. "He saves things for me sometimes. I could get even more if—if I were a little bit nicer to him—but I'm not doing that anymore."

March would have liked to know what she meant by that. Had Leah worked as a prostitute? March knew little about Robin's time with the Carrigan Company, and nothing at all about the others who had been there with him. She decided to ask Leah about her life at some point. Sometime when there were no clattering sewing machines, when her back didn't hurt, and when her fingertips weren't raw from the constant contact with rough fabric. After the last break in the afternoon, she was completely exhausted and couldn't have said which part of her body hurt more: her head, from the constant din; her shoulders, from the tense posture and the repeated motions of guiding the fabric; her back; her legs; or her fingers. Treadling a sewing machine for nine hours straight was completely different than operating one for just a few minutes.

March thanked all the gods when the claxon finally announced the end of the workday. She was as hungry as a wolf, but she didn't have the slightest desire to cook anything. Whatever Sally put on the table, March would gobble it up the way Mrs. Smith and Emily had the previous night.

Before the women could leave, the homework was passed out. Leah, March, and Emily received a dozen shirts each to finish; Mrs. Smith, who stopped by on her way home from her work in the sewing room, took fifteen. As a matter of course, she fully expected Sally to take over at least three of them.

Lost in thought, March staggered home behind Leah, who didn't even have the energy to drape her shawl jauntily around her shoulders or playfully pull a few strands of hair from under her tidy little hat before she entered the bakery. The baker, an overweight man with a red face and hard blue eyes, grinned at her.

"Ah, little Leah is once more honoring me with her presence! What can I do for you, my pretty? Or . . . what will you do for me?"

"I'll give you a penny, sir," Leah said flatteringly, as if she planned to give him the crown jewels. "For a couple of dry rolls. The children are hungry, after you let our Sally go without any bread yesterday. Not very nice of you, Mr. Burke. Surely you knew we'd bring you the missing penny later. And why has the bread gotten more expensive?"

The baker reacted angrily. "It hasn't. There just wasn't any day-old bread left. Your Sally has to come earlier if she wants to get any. And maybe be a little nicer too. She won't open her mouth, the stupid brat. Not to speak, and not for nothin' else neither." He made his mouth into a kissing shape.

Before Leah had a chance to reply, March came back to life. Outraged, she pushed forward.

"Just a minute, here! Surely you don't mean that you expect . . . affections from a twelve-year-old girl before you'll serve her? And that you'll charge more for your bread if she's not willing?"

The baker laughed. "I didn't mean nothin' by it, love. And 'specially not in front of a girl like you. I guess I'll talk plain with you. You new here? Another boarder with the Smiths? Soon they'll be able to afford fresh bread. So, how much do you want for a little roll in the hay, huh? A bag full of sweet buns? Fresh?"

"A day-old bun is fine," Leah said shortly. "For a penny. And keep your hands off Sally. Mr. Smith is a patient man, but the boarder boy who put his hands on her lived to regret it. We're respectable girls, Mr. Burke, and we'd rather go hungry than get mixed up in the kind of business you're suggesting."

"It's an outrage even to be asked something like that!" March said angrily. "I could call the police . . . and Sally is . . ."

"That's enough, March!" Leah snapped. "So, Mr. Burke. Do you have any buns left? For a penny?"

The baker frowned. "Nah. Not for you all, dearie. And for sure not for that 'n." He pointed at March. "There'll be others along who know how to play nice."

Incensed, Leah and March left the shop, but while March's anger was directed at the baker, Leah was worked up because March's outburst had endangered the family's food. In the past, Burke had seemed relatively harmless. But now both of them were frightened.

"I always kissed him," Emily admitted. "It was no big deal. Just a peck on the cheek. That's enough for him. And I always got a little more bread for it. Hadn't you noticed that we have less, now that Sally's taking care of the children? Sally can't bring herself to kiss the old fellow. I told her she should imagine he's a prince, but she said she can't."

"Unbelievable!" March murmured.

Leah looked at her seriously. "This is our life," she said. "If you don't have money, March, you have nothing to protect you."

# Chapter 58

"I'm off to meet Waddell," Helena said. "March is right, we have nothing to apologize for. How does one dress for this sort of visit, Aroha?"

Aroha tried not to roll her eyes. She was just glad that both Robin and Helena were prepared to take some advice about repairing the family's reputation. It was Bao's idea that the Lacrosse heirs might be able to improve it if they showed some social engagement in public.

"Robin donates a lot of money, but he never volunteers in person," he said. "The mothers of my school friends in England always helped out at church bazaars or served soup to the poor, even though they were swimming in enough money that they could have financed an entire soup kitchen, complete with staff. The Lacrosse heirs have been acting like snobs."

"The newspapers will just make fun of us," Robin said nervously. "Or they won't even bother to report on it."

"Maybe, but after a while, word will get around," Aroha said. "You have to think in the long term, Robin. Right now you're not seeing any results, but if you'd spend more time at charitable events and less on the golf course, and if March follows through with reforms at the factories—and hopefully she will, now that she's getting a taste of the life these people live—then your reputation will improve by and by."

In the end, Robin gave in as he always did. However, he was too embarrassed to offer his help to Reverend Waddell straightaway. Helena didn't have any such reservations. She was bored. Since the newspapers had made Robin their scapegoat, the usual invitations from her friends and acquaintances had stopped. Helping out at the parish nursery would be a welcome diversion. She was happy to pose for the press, surrounded by sweet little children.

"Put on an old dress that you don't mind getting dirty," Aroha advised, and earned herself a reproving glance. Naturally, Helena didn't own any old dresses, and she had no intention of getting dirty. "And as for you, Robin, St. Andrew's is surely not the only parish looking for volunteers." As she spoke, she leafed through the newspaper, looking for reports about charity events. "Here, for example, St. Peter's Church in Caversham, a Reverend Burton. The needy of his parish can get a hot meal every day at the parsonage. That's a good mile from here, also a suburb. It's an Anglican church."

"And what should I say to the reverend when he asks why I'm not helping out in my own parish?" Robin asked reluctantly.

"You were baptized Anglican," Aroha reminded him. "Tell him that you want to get back to your roots, that you don't feel comfortable with the Presbyterians."

Reverend Peter Burton received Robin in the parish hall, which was much smaller than the one at St. Andrew's. It was a tidy building alongside its own cottage, surrounded by a lovingly planted garden, and the rector swept it out himself before the soup kitchen opened at twelve. The room was already filled with the scent of cooking food, wafting over from the kitchen next door.

Burton listened kindly as Robin introduced himself and haltingly explained the reason for his change of parish. His face was covered with laugh lines, and when he smiled a dimple appeared, reminiscent of a young boy's. Otherwise, though, he seemed serious. He was a tall, slim man with brown eyes and straight, light-brown hair.

"So the sermon that my honored colleague Waddell delivered a few days ago had nothing to do with your decision?" he asked, his voice pleasantly deep. "What was it called again? 'Cheap Sins'? You are the Lacrosse heir, are you not?"

Robin blushed and lowered his gaze. "If—if you don't want me . . ."

Burton shook his head. "Mr. Fenroy, there's no such thing as 'not wanting' someone here. Everyone is welcome: everyone who needs help and everyone who wants to help. Both may be the case with you. I'm not here to judge. But please don't lie to me."

"You aren't judging me?" Robin exclaimed. "Even though I . . ." He tried to think what exactly he had to be ashamed of.

Burton regarded him mildly. "I am certainly not in favor of what has been done to the workers in the course of industrialization, in your factories as well as all the others," he explained. "However, I cannot judge to what extent you are personally responsible for that. You aren't even one of the directors of the company, if I understand correctly."

Robin nodded unhappily. "I should have been directing the company, but I did everything wrong. If I only knew how to make it right . . ."

Reverend Burton smiled again. "You are very young," he said kindly. "You have time enough to do many things right in life. Now, you can begin by getting the soup bowls and spoons from the cupboard and laying them out. That way our guests can pick them up and line up here. The ladies must be just about ready with the soup. Do help them carry the pot in, and when the guests arrive, you'll get other instructions. Ah, look, the bakery is just delivering the bread. Take it from them and cut it up . . ."

With a sigh of relief, Robin got to work and decided, to his surprise, that he enjoyed serving soup and cutting bread. The women of the reverend's parish were neither as affected as the ladies and gentlemen of St. Andrew's nor as cowed as the factory workers. The "guests," as the rector called them, didn't come from the factories, but were mostly older people or invalids.

"Veterans of the goldfields," explained one of the women helping, and told him about the gold rush twenty years earlier. "Overnight, thousands of prospectors came from Europe. The hills of the city were white with their tents, and the people who sold spades and gold pans made a fortune. The prospectors, for the most part, did not. Many looked for other jobs later; the rector often helped them with that. But many were stranded and went from bad to worse. Now that they're old, they don't have enough even to live on."

The old prospectors still had some life in them, though. They enjoyed the company of the young man in their midst, laughing with him and teasing him. Burton introduced him as "Mr. Robin," and one of the cooks immediately made the connection to Robin Hood.

"He used to invite people to dinner, too, before he robbed them," she exclaimed, laughing, as she turned to the guests. "So watch out, people!"

Robin smiled and revealed that he had been named after Robinson Crusoe. Interested, the women asked for the story. Not once during the whole afternoon did the words "factory" or "Lacrosse" come up. If anyone recognized Robin, they didn't let on.

"May I come again?" Robin asked the rector as they bade each other a fond farewell.

Burton nodded. "Of course. As I said, anyone who is looking for help or wants to give it is welcome. I just hope that no reporters show up tomorrow on your account." With that, he picked up the afternoon paper, and Robin turned beet red when he saw a picture of Helena surrounded by a few children. "Lacrosse Heiress Visits St. Andrew's Nursery," the headline proclaimed. "I love children! When I'm married, I want a whole horde of them!" the caption under the picture said. "Apparently, you also love children, Mr. Fenroy," the rector observed dryly, after he had skimmed the short article. "At least that's what Miss Lacrosse thinks. The young lady seems to want to bear a rugby team with you."

Robin rubbed his forehead. "May I come back every day?" he asked.

A week later, Robin was almost ready to tell the friendly rector about his experiences and ambitions as an actor. Peter Burton was open to everything that could bring life to his parish, and Robin no longer considered it beneath his station to consider performing in an amateur theater troupe. As he greeted the needy members of the parish and generously spooned soup into their bowls, he wondered how best to broach the subject and how much he should say about the Carrigan Company—so he almost thought it was a hallucination when he suddenly found Bertram Lockhart standing before him.

Robin had just lifted the ladle and let the soup run back into the pot. He stared at the old man, who was just as dumbfounded.

"Robin?" he said. "By the devil, boy, what are you doing here? I thought you had come by an inheritance and were sitting in some castle somewhere in, hmm, where do you go if you're a Shakespeare lover? Stratford? Inverness?" He grinned.

Robin raised a finger to his lips. "Hush. Not everyone needs to know about that, I . . ."

"You're doing good works and aren't talking about the rest? You always did have a hard time coping with real life." The old thespian laughed. "Well, then, do your duty. I'm dying of hunger!"

Robin filled his bowl. "You used to be dying of thirst," he said.

Bertram made a face. "Go on, remind me of my old sins," he said bitterly. "You're not the only one. Just today I auditioned at two theaters. They remember Bertram Lockhart all right. Unfortunately, they also remember his excesses."

Robin noticed the line that had formed behind Bertram.

"I have to keep working," he said. "Can we meet up somewhere later? In, um, a pub, maybe?"

Lockhart grinned. "Why not? I'll just wait till you're done here."

Robin ended his shift a bit early that day. No one asked any questions when he mentioned that he'd met an old friend.

"Have you seen that man here before?" he asked the reverend, glancing at Lockhart.

"Never," Burton said. "He must be new to the city. You can tell me tomorrow how you know him."

Neither Robin nor Bertram knew a pub in the area, but they quickly found an inn. Robin ordered a beer, and Bertram, a coffee.

"I gave it up," he said as Robin looked on in wonder. "Really and truly. I don't drink anymore. It wasn't easy, but some things happened, and . . ."

"You weren't able to find any engagements after Vera's death?" Robin asked.

Bertram shook his head. "Of course not. Constantly drunk and with no other experience in years but the Carrigan Company? Finally, I ended up doing monologues in pubs until someone would buy me a beer. And I slept in the gutter. I tried to drink myself to death, but then I got my act together. And you? The jackpot, eh? I could hardly believe it when I read about it."

Robin made a face and took a sip of his beer. "I can imagine better." He sighed. "Oh, Bertram, I'll never play Hamlet again. At least not on a proper stage. I'm allowed to recite a bit at social gatherings once in a while." He sighed again. "For a beer . . ."

The young man took a deep breath and unfolded the whole story: Walter Lacrosse's visit to Rata Station, Wentworth's shock at the reading of the will, his own early flailing, March's appearance, Helena's possessiveness, Peta's righteous fury, Waddell's condemnation and the consequent public disgrace.

Bertram grinned. "Sorry you've had such a rough go. But it's good to know that money really doesn't buy happiness."

Robin sighed. "Go ahead and make fun of me. You should understand best of all. Or would you prefer to do something other than stand on a stage?"

"I like boozing and whoring too," Bertram admitted. "You don't really expect me to pity you, Robin?"

Robin shrugged. "I know. It's just . . . it's not nice when everything you do wrong ends up in the papers."

Bertram laughed. "But that's part of the job, boy! When you're on the big stage, the papers talk about you. Today they praise you to the heavens, and tomorrow they tear you to shreds. You just can't pay them any mind or you'll go mad."

"I wouldn't mind theater critics," Robin said. "They could pan me every day if only I had a chance to act. But then it would be about my work. Not about whether—whether I'm a good person . . ."

Bertram stirred his coffee. "Why," he asked, "don't you just sell the company and found a theater company?"

Robin knocked over his beer glass in shock. "You—you're not serious!"

Bertram shrugged. "Why not? You're no businessman, and you don't want to become one."

"But I'm not allowed to," Robin said unhappily. "I—I have responsibilities—to people . . ."

Bertram brushed him off. "You don't have any idea how to run a business, which doesn't make me very optimistic about a theater company either, but at least you're interested in it. And as far as responsibility goes, I guarantee old Lacrosse didn't leave you his factories so you could make the workers happy! Quite the opposite. He'd probably be perfectly satisfied with what your Miss Jensch has put together there. If you change everything, the company will likely go bankrupt. And no one will like that. Pay no attention to what people say. Sell the factories or give them away. That's not a bad idea, in fact. Keep the property that you have for your company, and give the rest to your impertinent little relation. What's his name again? Peter? Or to that Reverend Waddell chap. Let them bear the burden." The actor laughed. "You do have wealth other than the factories, don't you?"

Robin bit his lip. "Far too much," he complained. "And there's always more being added . . ."

Bertram laughed. "You should make a real effort to spend it," he said. "And believe me, if you want a way to burn through money, a theater production is it. You can put together a troupe and hire good people that you can learn from yourself. Put *Hamlet* on the stage, or *As You Like It*. Then go on tour or rent a theater. If you really have as much money as you say, well then, buy a theater."

Robin reflected. The thought was enticing. But on the other hand . . . what would happen if he made a laughingstock of himself? What if he ended up with a pathetic touring company like Vera's, or if no one took him seriously?

"I can't do any of that," he muttered. "Hiring people, assigning roles, directing, constructing sets . . . I'd make a hash of it, I . . ."

"Then get some help," Bertram countered. "Find someone who's good with money. And as far as the casting goes, and the directing, I've been in this business for thirty years, boy. And I was good, as long as I stayed away from the whiskey. If you could trust me to do that from here on out . . ."

"Why did you quit drinking?" Robin asked, changing the subject. This idea was too grand for him—at least for the moment. He'd have to think it over later.

Bertram rubbed his chin. "My, eh, wife died," he said finally.

Robin frowned. "Your wife? You were married? You never said a word about that!"

"She left me," Bertram admitted. "Or perhaps I left her too. She was part of what I gave up for whiskey. I met her in the theater in Sydney and brought her along to Wellington. She wasn't a particularly inspired actress. She loved the theater, but she lacked stage presence. She couldn't bring a role to life. Still, they gave her a few supporting roles, and well . . . I fell in love. She was beautiful, she was smart, and she didn't deserve someone like me. And now I need something to drink. Order me a lemonade, boy, as hard as it is for me to say it." He sighed.

Robin ordered two lemonades. "And now she's gone," he said, prompting Bertram to continue. "How did you find out?"

"It was chance or fate . . . whatever you want to call it. I was giving it one more try at Queen's Theater, where I used to perform. And I found out that Joana had been there the whole time. Not on the stage, but behind the scenes, as a prompter, a costumer, as a girl Friday. Everyone loved her. And Lucille, our daughter, practically grew up in the theater. The child knows half of Shakespeare by heart. At the theater, I heard that Joana had been sick for weeks, so one morning I tried to stay sober and I went to see her. She was living in the most primitive accommodation, but it was clean and tidy. What Joana could no longer do, Lucille took care of—she cared for her mother right to the end. I couldn't leave my child in the lurch like that." Bertram ran a hand through his graying hair. "Dammit, all I could see was Vera's mocking look. Still, I promised Joana on her deathbed that I would look after Lucille. And since then, I haven't touched a single drop." Bertram looked sadly at his lemonade.

"And where is she now?" Robin asked. "Little Lucille, I mean. How old is she?"

"She's not little anymore; she's sixteen," Bertram said, and his eyes lit up. "A real beauty . . . a Juliet, a Miranda. The public would be mad about her. But you know how hard it is when you're gifted. I've auditioned at every theater on this island, and I've recommended Lucille to them when they didn't want me. But they won't even give her a chance to read."

"It was the same with me," Robin replied. "If you're young, and don't have experience . . ."

Bertram nodded knowingly. "We gave up," he said unhappily. "Lucille found a job at a dressmakers' workshop. I'm going to try my luck tomorrow at the woolen mill. I don't know if they'll take me at my age. If not, I'll try the harbor. They always need help unloading ships, at least by the hour. And maybe you'll give some thought to a theater. We could do it, Robin. We could do it!"

# Chapter 59

The thought of having his own theater wouldn't leave Robin in peace. Not while he sat across from Helena at a joyless dinner that Aroha ducked out of to eat with Bao in his room, and not afterward, when he retreated to the library with a book. He would have loved to discuss the idea with someone. He considered Aroha, but would she understand? Would she trust him and Bertram to pull it off? She had only ever seen the old actor when he was flat-out drunk, and she'd probably worry about what the newspapers would have to say on the matter. "A New Whim of the Lacrosse Heir."

Robin spent a sleepless night, but at dawn he finally lit upon an answer: the rector! He would ask Reverend Burton for a meeting and request his advice. With a fresh surge of courage, he set out around noon, hoping that Bertram wouldn't show up at the soup kitchen again. And apparently he was making good on his intention to look for work that day, because he was nowhere to be seen in Caversham.


The rector finally arrived when the helpers were already cleaning up the parish hall. He nodded when Robin asked for an hour of his time.

"Is it about this?" he asked, holding up the newspaper he was carrying.

"What? No . . ."

Robin looked with irritation at the paper. He hadn't even cast a glance at the morning papers that day. His mind was elsewhere.

"Whatever it's about, let's go sit together somewhere quiet," Burton said. "Come in here; our kitchen is much cozier than my office."

Robin sat down in the kitchen of the rectory, where it smelled of herbs and fresh-baked bread. Kathleen Burton greeted their guest and, smiling, set a pot of tea and a plate full of scones in front of her husband and his visitor. Robin noticed how unusually beautiful she was, although she was already in her middle years. She also seemed vaguely familiar to him; he had probably seen her at one of the receptions or concerts he'd attended with Helena.

"I know your cousin," she said, solving the riddle. "She's a customer at Lady's Gold Mine."

Robin frowned, puzzled.

"A lady's boutique downtown," the rector added. "My wife runs it with her friend."

"I just design the clothes. Claire is the one who's usually in the shop," Mrs. Burton continued. "But I've seen Miss Helena many times. She's often there." Mrs. Burton smiled. "And I think I know you as well, Mr. Fenroy. We do withdraw the money from your account, after all. You are unusually generous."

Robin nodded, irritated. He had no idea about any payments from his accounts to a lady's dress shop. The reverend regarded him quizzically.

"What can I help you with today, Robin?" he asked softly. "Is it all right if I use your first name?"

Anything was all right with Robin as long as he could pour his heart out. It didn't even bother him that Kathleen Burton stayed in the kitchen, busying herself at the stove, while he talked. He described his lifelong desire to be an actor, his studies with Mr. Elliot, and his first triumph as Lysander in *A Midsummer Night's Dream*. He spoke briefly about his years with the Carrigan Company, told of Vera's dreadful end, and finally, about the inheritance. At the end, he mentioned his meeting with Bertram and the actor's spectacular suggestion.

There was a long silence, and then the rector began, "Well, I think . . ."

"You should do it." That was Mrs. Burton, her eyes shining. "You must follow your dreams! I'm already looking forward to seeing you on the stage."

Reverend Burton cast a loving glance her way. "There you have it! You haven't even performed anything yet, and you already have an admirer."

"You—you really think—" Robin stammered. "You think I should—I could—"

"Robin, what my beloved wife and I think doesn't matter that much," the rector said thoughtfully. "What's important is that you get used to the idea that

477

you can do whatever you want. You are rich, Robin, and completely independent. You don't have to ask anyone for permission to fulfill your desires."

"If only," Robin said bitterly. "I can't do anything at all! When I sold the factory, they were all over me. Now they're all over me because I'm keeping the other businesses but haven't gotten involved with them enough. I'm supposed to enact reforms; some say they are urgently needed, and others say they'll bring everyone to ruin. I—"

The rector raised a hand, bringing Robin's monologue to a halt.

"Robin, whatever decisions we make, there will always be people who support us and others who hate us for them. The more sweeping the decisions, the more extreme the positions people take. Don't try to please everyone. You'll just drive yourself mad."

Robin rubbed his forehead. "But shouldn't I try, um, to please God? Or the spirits?"

Burton smiled. "I'm not responsible for the spirits; you'll have to ask a *tohunga* about them. As far as God goes, I'm of the opinion that he wants to see all his creatures happy."

"Exactly," Robin said with irritation. "And no one is happy in St. Andrew's, which I could change, according to Reverend Waddell . . ."

Burton shook his head. "Reverend Waddell knows that you can't turn back time. Industrialization is here, and its repercussions are even worse in Europe. A single company owner can lessen them, but only the lawmakers can really bring about reform. The workers also have to fight for change themselves. In Europe they are forming labor unions. The same will happen here soon enough. In the beginning, Reverend Waddell must have had hopes that you would improve relations, Robin, precisely because you want to please everyone. He either overestimated or misjudged you, which is understandable, since he barely knows you. He likely assumed that your great-uncle had named an ambitious young businessman as his heir. He didn't know the first thing about your real life. So please don't judge him, but also don't let yourself be too influenced by him. If you want to sell these factories, then just do it."

"Is it absolutely necessary for you to part ways with the businesses just because you want to found a theater?" Mrs. Burton asked. "Couldn't you just hire a capable director, give him clear directives about the treatment of the workers, and then just check, or have someone check, to make sure he follows your orders?"

Robin shrugged. "I'd have to ask March about that," he replied. "She knows all about such things. I'm just afraid that she wouldn't let herself be checked up on. She has her own ideas about how to handle the workers."

"Miss . . . Jensch?" the rector asked. Robin began to feel uneasy as a look passed between the Burtons. Finally, the rector opened the newspaper and laid it on the table. "I thought it was this you'd wanted to talk to me about . . ."

Robin read the headline. "Lacrosse Director Calls for Reinstatement of Child Labor."

"What? March would never have said that!" Robin declared. "She has her ways, but she would never send children to work in a factory."

"They do seem to have twisted her words," Mrs. Burton agreed. "The whole thing is a summary of her experience as a factory worker; this experiment that she's undertaken with the *Times*. She talks about a twelve-year-old girl who takes care of her seven younger siblings while her parents and older sister are at the factory. The girl is also supposed to keep the apartment clean, cook and wash for the family of eleven plus two boarders, and in the evening her mother expects her to help with the piecework. The little one is completely overwhelmed. Miss Jensch's suggestion for dealing with the problem is to let girls and boys do easy work at the factories starting at the age of twelve. The wages they earn would be invested in childcare, run by the company, where the younger ones would get one hot meal a day. She's convinced that this would mean a decided improvement in the little girl's circumstances, and she might be right about that."

"Not that anyone would take it that way," the rector said. "They'll tear Miss Jensch to pieces, and you with her, Robin. Miss Jensch has become entirely unsuitable for your business. You must strongly distance yourself from her comments and fire her."

Robin bit his lip. He was still thinking about the little girl.

"A twelve-year-old shouldn't be working in a factory and taking care of children," he murmured. "She should be in school."

"Then send the children to school!" Mrs. Burton left her housework and sat down at the table with the two men. She gazed at Robin intently. "Found a school for the children of your factory's workers, or, better yet, pay for one in Waddell's parish."

"But I . . ." Robin's head was spinning. "I can't . . ."

The rector closed the paper. "You can," he said. "That's the difference between you and Miss Jensch. If she, as business director, wants to found a nursery, she has to figure out how to pay for it. You, on the other hand, have the money. And if your assets aren't liquid, then just sell that gigantic house over in Mornington. How many servants take care of you and Miss Lacrosse alone? Do you need all that? Robin, first of all, find out how much money you actually have. I would wager it's more than you think. And then make a list. Write down what would make you happy, and then what you'd like to do for people like that child. Then get help to make those plans a reality. That can't possibly be so hard if you bring a couple of clever people on board."

"But if I fire March, I'll make her unhappy too," Robin said softly.

The rector shrugged. "That's true."

"That doesn't have to be the case," Kathleen Burton said. "Find something else for Miss Jensch to do. Put her in charge of the business side of your theater, for example. I know the young lady, Robin. She's also a customer at Lady's Gold Mine, and Claire and I are quite taken with her. Miss Jensch is extremely capable and intelligent—but she's in over her head."

"Since she took over, profits have risen by God-knows-how-many percent," Robin countered. "March is the most accomplished businessperson in town!"

"It's true; she understands her business like no one else," Kathleen agreed. "But she's entirely lacking in . . . tact. She says everything that comes into her head, and her thoughts are rather . . . unusual. And she is surely lacking in empathy. I understand that the young lady comes from a well-to-do home and has enjoyed a unique education. Who hires an economist to train her twelve-year-old granddaughter? And who is proud when, a few years later, she moves in with this man and learns how to terrorize the staff of a woolen mill?"

Robin wondered how Mrs. Burton knew all that. Some of it had been in the newspaper, of course, and perhaps March had shared some of it publicly herself. It was true that she'd always spoken openly and without shame about her studies and her time with Martin Porter.

"Now she can learn everything she missed before," Kathleen Burton continued, "about the human parts of business, and life, young and intelligent as she is. But she'll never do it as long as she has absolute control and can fire anyone who dares to disagree with her. Let me guess, Robin, the staff at your office changes all the time, doesn't it?" Robin bit his lip. "There you go. With a theater ensemble, she couldn't bounce around like that. There would be an artistic director or whatever you call it, and you, Robin, would be there with your opinion. Think it all over; you don't have to rush into things." Mrs. Burton stood up.

"Except for the business with the child labor," the rector said firmly. "That, you must set to rights."

Robin nodded. "I will," he said. "I'll start a school. I don't have to think that over. I'll go to March and talk to her. About everything. The money, the theater, the businesses . . . and I'll do it right away. I'll go pick her up from the workshop now!"

Mrs. Burton smiled. "Then I wish you good luck." She took a paper bag out of the cupboard and filled it with the baked goods that Robin and the rector hadn't touched. "Here, take these scones along for that hungry child and her siblings, and for March." She thought for a moment, and then took a loaf of bread out of the basket. "And this too, I just baked it today."

Robin could barely imagine a half-starved March, but thanked her politely and went on his way. It would still be a couple of hours before March's workshop closed, but then he could take her to a nearby café and tell her everything that needed to be done. He didn't want to be a private gentleman anymore. If he really had more money than he needed, then he'd rather be a philanthropist. And soon, if all went well, he'd finally be an actor again!

# *Chapter 60*

"It's so cold . . ."

The new girl didn't usually complain; she always kept quiet, even when Emily and her friends whispered and giggled together during the break. But today everyone was suffering, because a biting wind was blowing in from the sea and they weren't prepared for it. The last few days had brought a hint of summer to the air, and the girls had left their shawls at home. Some of them were coming down with colds. Without enough to eat, their bodies didn't have the strength to defend themselves. The number of workers staying home sick was increasing. One of the supervisors in the hall for the young pattern-cutters hadn't shown up that morning either, and Mr. Wentworth had switched the second to a sewing machine to help out. The girls would have to manage by themselves, he had said in a threatening tone. The new girl could ask the others if she didn't understand how something was done. The twenty pattern-cutters could easily imagine what might happen if they didn't manage to work at the same speed as usual.

For Wentworth, there was no risk. If the new girl made mistakes, he'd dock her pay for the ruined fabric. But so far, young Lucille hadn't made any mistakes; once one had grasped what was going on with the thread, cutting the patterns wasn't hard. However, the physical strain was another matter. The fabric used to make trousers was hard and stiff. The girls worked with large shears that hardly fit into their hands. There were already blisters forming on Lucille's fingers where the other girls had calluses. But the worst part was the cold. The factory hall was damp and the wind blew through the cracks in the windows and doors. Emily's fingers were also stiff with cold. The new girl only said out loud what they were all thinking.

"How long is it until closing time?"

Lucille had a soft, melodic voice and pronounced each syllable distinctly as though she were trying to trace the language back to its origins, as though she mourned each word that stole from her lips.

"It's hours yet . . . ," a blonde girl named Annabell said with a sigh. "You'd think they could at least put a heater in here for us. Tomorrow you should wear gloves, Lucille. Otherwise, when your blisters burst, you'll get the fabric dirty. Oh, dammit, I wish it were summer . . ."

"I can make a fire," Emily said suddenly.

All eyes turned to her.

"But it's against the rules to bring matches in here," Annabell said.

She wasn't actually sure about that. Like most of the girls here, she couldn't read and therefore had only a vague notion of the rules. But just about everything was forbidden, especially lighting an open fire in the workrooms.

"I don't need any matches," Emily said proudly. "Our boarder March is half Maori, and she showed us how to do it without matches."

"Without matches?"

The girls' interest was piqued, since matches were costly and every family tried to be thrifty with them.

"Yes. Look, I'll show you." Emily was enjoying being the center of attention for once. "If we make a fire there in the corner, it won't bother anyone. We'll use the leftover fabric scraps. No one can fault us for that; they'll just get thrown away anyhow. And the floor here can't burn."

The pattern-cutters worked on the ground level, and no one had bothered to put down a proper floor. Instead, there was just the poured cement that served as a foundation for the building. It made the room even colder.

"If Mr. Wentworth catches us, he'll be furious," one girl objected.

"But since our hands are so cold, we can't work very fast," Annabell argued. "Come on, Emily, just a little fire! Show us how it's done. Then we can warm up a bit . . ."

Emily didn't hesitate. She eagerly collected a few scraps of cloth and two of the yardsticks that the girls used to measure fabric. One was made of softer wood, the other of harder.

"So it's best if you have a stick of softer wood to rub against the piece of hardwood. This is how you do it . . ."

She made a little heap of fabric scraps, then took the harder yardstick and began to work at it as if she were trying to saw it through. She worked quickly and eagerly; she didn't want to fail in front of the others. Just as the spectators began to grumble impatiently, one of the splinters of wood that had rubbed off the yardstick began to glow. Emily tried to catch the spark with the kindling and blew on it gently. As the others held their breath, smoke began to rise—and a little flame blazed up.

"It's burning! It's really burning!"

The girls rejoiced. Then they all brought over their scraps. From the tiny flame a powerful fire grew, and Lucille warmed her hands by it thankfully. The other girls did the same.

"That is fantastic!" Annabell exclaimed.

Emily basked in the general acclaim but reminded the girls that they should get back to work. They had already lost a lot of time.

Together they dragged a new heavy bolt of cloth into the room, unrolled it, and shared out a big piece to each girl to cut. Then they got back to work. The bolt stood between the door and the fire, and the wind blew through the cracks. It made the fire flare up, playing with the scraps as it neared them . . .


"Fire!"

By the time the warning reached the third floor, where March, Leah, and fifty other young women were working, part of the ground floor was already in flames. The other workers on the ground floor, mostly packers and ironers, heard the girls' screams, and their workrooms were also piled with flammable materials. The doors and a few partitions, and of course the stairs, were made of wood. The women shouted to warn their coworkers in the upper stories, then fled outside as well.

"Go!" Leah shouted. "We have to get out before the stairs catch fire!"

The women and girls left their machines and hurried to the exits, but March stood frozen on the spot. She heard the screams from below, the creaking and banging, and she instantly remembered the panic in Kaiapoi.

"No!" she shouted to Leah and the others, placing herself in their way. "Not that way! Not the stairwell! It's surely already blocked with a hundred other people all trying to get out at once. As soon as it catches fire, it'll go up like a powder keg. Whoever gets stuck there will die!"

The others were about to object, but then they saw women from the second story fleeing upward to the third, and they heard the crackling of the flames.

"Through the window! That's the only way out!" March cried. The windows were set high but big enough that a person could climb through. March climbed onto a chair and tried to open one of them. It wouldn't budge. "We have to break it!"

March took a second chair and hammered it against the glass. A couple of women did the same to other windows—success! The thin glass quickly shattered, for Magiel had economized on the building in that aspect, as well. But once they looked through the openings in the windows, the women lost courage. The street lay far below, and flames were already shooting out of the windows on the ground floor.

"We'll all burn up!"

The women screamed and cried, while March fought to keep her head.

"Rope!" she cried to Leah. "The only chance is to climb down!"

"Do we have a rope?" Leah asked. Her face was as white as chalk, but she remained calm. "There's none here . . ."

"We have heaps of denim! Sew them together, Leah, fast! We may still have a little time." March pushed her friend to the sewing machine while she herself began to gather up the cut-out trouser legs. "If one more person helps, it'll go faster!"

March hollered at the women. A few had tried fleeing downstairs, while others were considering jumping out the windows. But then an older woman comprehended the situation and seated herself next to Leah at the machine. In the rush the needle broke, but she had enough wits about her to switch to the next machine. March ran to shut the door at the top of the stairs. Smoke was already invading the room, and the steps down to the second story were ablaze. They heard screams, even from outside. Many women and girls who had managed to escape to the street now stood there, frightened for their friends and coworkers. March looked for more trouser legs, but there were none to be found. It would have been time for one of the young pattern-cutters to bring a fresh batch.

"I've sewn them all," Leah reported. "Give me yours, Gina!"

The other woman passed her a long ribbon of sewn denim trouser legs, and Leah joined it to hers.

In the meantime, more dense smoke was coming through the cracks in the door to the staircase. The screams and howls of the women became louder. March had to bellow to be heard.

"Quiet now! We have an improvised rope. I'll throw it out the window, and then we'll let ourselves down, one after the other, without panicking. Line up!"

Leah tied one end of the fabric to the sewing machine nearest the window. The machines were heavy and anchored tight to the floor. They should easily bear the weight of a woman, and that should also hold true for the denim. Once more, March climbed onto the chair by the broken window and threw the ribbon of fabric out. She watched hopefully as it unfolded down the length of the building's façade. But then she heard the cries of the others before she grasped the situation herself.

It wasn't long enough. The rope would barely bring them to the edge of the second story, and it was at least thirty more feet to the ground.

Robin was waiting in a coffeehouse a block away. The menu there was mostly meant to appeal to the workers in the surrounding factories. During the breaks, they served drinks and small, simple meals. Now, during work hours, Robin was the only customer. He drank a cup of tea and gazed idly out onto the street. There were no people on the sidewalks; no one was out and about here in the afternoon, but wagons passed by frequently. Many were likely headed to the dressmakers' workshops. Robin watched the heavily laden wagon on its way to deliver new fabric. The great bolts were piled high on the open cargo bed. He wondered what the deliveryman did when it rained. Did he pull tarpaulins over the back? March would probably know. What would she say about his new plans? Then Robin realized with amazement that it really didn't matter to him anymore. With a little smile, he thought of the words Reverend Burton had said to him in parting: "The commandment is 'Love thy neighbor as thyself.' It doesn't say 'try to fix everything at the cost of your own happiness.'"

Lost in thought, Robin began to sketch plans for his theater in the margins of a newspaper he found in the coffeehouse. That was a thousand times better than frantically paging through it to see what people were writing about him.

He started in surprise when he heard shouts. Frightened, the servers hurried to the door.

"It's coming from the Magiel factory," one of them cried and ran into the street.

Alarmed, Robin followed him and saw the first people running out of the building.

"Fire! Fire!" a woman shouted.

Robin reached the factory in a few strides. His first impulse was to run inside—March and Leah must be in there! But more and more women and girls came running out of the building, and now smoke was billowing from the windows. The women who'd escaped reported with horror that the ground floor was in flames. Among them stood Harold Wentworth, staring, stunned, at the building. Through the window, Robin could now see the fire raging on the ground floor. Just then the windowpanes shattered and flames shot out.

"What are you doing here?" Robin asked the young factory director. "Shouldn't you be inside? There are dozens of women still in there! The factory has several stories—" He dimly remembered March telling him about the panic in Kaiapoi when she'd wanted to invest more money in renovations to the old warehouse than the architect had suggested.

"Are you insane?" Wentworth shook his head. "I was in the office on the second floor, and I was barely able to fight my way out! I'm not about to run back in there and try to keep these frightened hens in check. The women are out of their minds; they're trampling each other to death on the staircase . . ."

Exactly why Wentworth should have led an evacuation, Robin thought. But even he could see that it was too late. The last women stumbling out of the building were coughing, and their clothing and hair were stained with soot.

"They can't get down anymore, the stairs are burning," screamed a girl as she scrambled out. The hem of her dress was on fire, and Robin, along with others, quickly beat out the flames as she wailed. Someone wrapped a blanket around her and led her away, and just then the fire department bell rang out. The firemen arrived with three wagons, but the fire was already engulfing the two upper stories.

The women trapped on the second floor now smashed the windows. Their screams and cries for help rang out, and those on the ground could see hands, arms, and terrified faces.

"The windows are set too high," one of the women explained to the fire chief. "They can't just jump out."

"They'd fall to their deaths anyway," the man murmured. "Do we have jumping sheets, people?"

The men had gotten the hoses from the fire trucks and were pointing them at the windows of the burning building. Others unfolded a jumping sheet made of canvas. A girl sat, paralyzed by fear, in one of the windows. Robin understood her panic. It was too high and the cloth was too small for her to be sure she'd land on it.

A cry went up among the bystanders as someone let down a rope of fabric from the third story. Robin caught sight of March's determined face. Of course—she would always take action. But relief changed to disappointment when the rope ended just below the second story.

March appeared to be talking to girls, and then she shouted something. Thick clouds of smoke were now bellowing out of the second-story windows. It was only a matter of time before the fire spread to the workroom above.

Robin thought he could make out March debating with a very young girl, urging her to attempt to climb down. Perhaps she had concluded she might survive a leap from the second floor, but certainly not a conflagration on the third.

Then Robin had an idea. Denim—March had improvised a rope from it. But the material could also be used as padding.

"Where is your warehouse?" Robin rushed over to Wentworth, who was speaking with the fire chief. "Those wagons, the ones that deliver the fabric and take away the finished goods—where do they go?"

"The ramp is back there," Wentworth said. "The chief just sent a fire wagon over. The driver should get himself and the horses to safety. The fire could easily spread to the warehouse buildings."

"You must have the driver bring those wagons here!" Robin cried. "Quickly. If you don't, I'll do it myself!"

"March!" he bellowed to the women above. "Wait, March! I'll help you!"

He left the confused Wentworth and the uncomprehending fire chief and ran around to the back of the burning building. *Please, God,* he pleaded, *let the men not have unloaded the wagon yet.*

Robin breathed a sigh of relief. The fully loaded wagon with both draft horses stood in front of the loading ramp. The driver had surely heard the shouts and was now helping the firemen. Luckily the cargo had not caught fire, otherwise they would have had to deal with two runaway horses pulling a blazing wagon through the streets. Half the city could have burned down! Thankfully the animals were still relatively calm.

"Now we'll see just how even-tempered you really are," Robin said, untying the horses and taking the reins. He was almost frightened to death when he saw something move. He peered underneath the wagon and saw a girl cowering there. "What are you doing? Come out!" he yelled.

The girl turned her pale face, surrounded by a confusion of golden-brown curls, toward him. "It's all my fault!" she wailed. "I . . ."

"Come out from under the wagon or you'll get run over. Now!"

The girl looked shocked at his shouting, but then crept out past the big wagon wheels into the open. With a glance, Robin assured himself that she was safe, and quickly swung up onto the wagon seat. He would have to look for her later, or better yet, send the firemen for her. For now, he needed all his concentration to turn the heavy team in the narrow yard and guide the reluctant horses around the burning building. Robin saw that the firemen had managed to extinguish the fire in the entryway of the factory. A stroke of luck! Smoke was still pouring from the windows of the ground floor, but flames no longer shot out. The fire was spreading on the second floor, though. The women and girls there screamed and coughed, crowding at the windows. Some would surely jump.

"Hey, what are you doing there?" one of the men shouted.

"Make way!" Robin called to a couple of firemen, who looked paralyzed at the sight of the draft team. He made no effort to keep the horses away from them, nor from the many gawkers who were obstructing the work of extinguishing the fire. To the best of his ability, he maneuvered the wagon under the third-story window. Then he jumped out and, with the help of a few firemen who'd caught on, unwound some of the bolts to make them softer. "Jump!"

A woman on the second floor didn't hesitate. She landed safely.

"One after the other," the fire chief bellowed, and called three men over to lift the woman out of the wagon right away. "Not all at once! Otherwise you'll fall on each other!"

In fact, two or three women at a time did jump from the windows onto the wagon, or it wouldn't have been possible to save them all. As the last ones jumped down from the second story, the flames blazed up high after them and reached the window. In a panic, March pulled the denim rope in. Luckily, the chief had thought ahead, and his men stood ready to train their hoses on the second-story windows.

"Water on!"

For a short time, the smoke from the extinguished flames hid the sight of the women in the third story, slowing the effort to save them. But then March threw the rope down again and they continued, as the girls began to trust her improvised rope. With March's encouragement, two or three made their way down at a time. March and Leah were the last to save themselves. Their faces and clothing were black with soot, and they left behind black streaks as they landed on the heap of denim.

"Mr. Magiel will undoubtedly dock us for the dirty fabric," March remarked as Robin hugged her. "But I'm glad you haven't entirely forgotten how to think."

Robin smiled at her. "I've just started, March. And I'm not sure you're going to like everything I've come up with . . ."

He hadn't finished speaking when a distraught older man broke away from the crowd. Bertram Lockhart looked years older; his face was white and drawn, a mask of horror.

"Were you the last?" he asked, turning to March. "Are you sure? Because . . . I can't find my little girl. Lucille. No one knows where she is!"

"There was no Lucille on the third floor," one of the workers said. "I know all the women. Are you sure she works here?"

The actor nodded. He was about to burst into tears. "Of course. She's only been here three days. I brought her here this morning—I—if she's dead . . ."

"Does she have wispy brown hair?" Robin asked. "Like—like an angel?"

March frowned. "An angel?"

"She has little curls," Bertram said, full of hope. "Yes, fine little ringlets, like . . ."

"Come!" Robin ordered. "I think I know where she is. Oh, no, there's that Spragg fellow from the *Times* . . ." The reporter had just broken away from the crowd of gawkers and was coming toward Robin and March. "You will not speak to him under any circumstances, March! What you did to yourself there yesterday . . ."

"So what if I do talk to him!" March straightened up. "Today he can't twist my words. This is going to make positive headlines!"

She smiled at the reporter as Robin ran to the back courtyard. Bertram sprinted after him.

"She has brown eyes, and her face is still a little childlike," he said, "but she'll be a real beauty. She really isn't small, just very delicate, like an elf. I'd cast her as Peaseblossom in *A Midsummer Night's Dream*."

Bertram continued to describe his daughter, and the more Robin nodded, the stronger his voice sounded.

The girl wasn't in the courtyard anymore. "Lucille?" Robin called into the dark warehouse.

After the second call, he heard a choked sob.

"Lucille!"

Now Bertram called her name, and then a shadow separated itself from the piles of fabric and finished clothing.

The child threw herself into Bertram's arms. "It's all my fault, Daddy!"

# Chapter 61

"You won't believe what just happened to me." Smiling, Aroha entered the rooms that she shared with Bao in the Lacrosse house. With his good hand, the young Chinese man was busy packing his suitcase. His right arm was still in a cast, but otherwise he was doing much better. The couple were planning to return to Rotorua the next day, and Aroha had taken care of a few last-minute purchases. "I think the spiritualists call it déjà vu. Seriously, I feel as though I'm right back at Rata Station."

"What?" Bao stopped what he was doing. "You don't mean to say you saw a sheep in the city?" He smiled tenderly, drew Aroha toward him, and kissed her.

Aroha returned his kiss. "It has nothing to do with sheep but with love scenes." She laughed and began to tell the story. "I was walking into the stable. Since Robin let his stable hands go, we've had to bring the horses in ourselves. I never would have thought that would seem unusual to me. So anyway, little Lucille was there."

"And you realized she looks just like your long-lost sister?" Bao asked.

"Stop!" Aroha was obviously in a very good mood. "Lucille was standing on a box and looking all starry-eyed into Robin's horse's stall. She was gazing at the nag with such an expression . . . I don't know how to describe it. Maybe the best word would be rapture."

Bao laughed. "Horses can have that effect on some young girls," he said, wrapping his arms around her.

Aroha giggled. "Don't make fun of me! She wasn't just looking at it. She was quoting Shakespeare. The balcony scene from *Romeo and Juliet*. When I came in, she was at the line *My ears have not yet drunk a hundred words/Of that tongue's utterance, yet I know the sound:/Art thou not Romeo and a Montague?*"

Bao furrowed his brow. "And? What did the horse say?"

"The horse was quiet, just like the cat that Robin was swooning over that first time I caught him rehearsing lines at Rata Station. It was the same scene, the same starry-eyed expression. Back then, Juliet was missing, and this time Romeo. Seriously, Bao, if you put the two of them on the same stage, the audience would go wild. I know I've been skeptical about Robin's plan to start his own theater, but with this young couple in the lead roles and March's marketing skills, they'd surely be a hit! Anyway, the girl turned just as red as Robin had when she realized I'd caught her. I had to promise I wouldn't say anything to her father about it. He doesn't think she should be studying the lead roles yet. He wants her to build up to them slowly."

"Sounds sensible," Bao said.

Aroha nodded. "Very. But Lucille says that Juliet is her dream role, and Bao, I think she already has her eye on one particular Romeo. And not just on the stage! Something is brewing between her and Robin. It's no coincidence that she was acting with his horse and not Helena's."

Bao laughed. "Isn't Helena's horse a mare?" he said, continuing to kiss her. "As for Robin . . . there's definitely something there. He turns red every time he looks into Lucille's eyes by mistake."

"Oh, I'm so happy for Robin," Aroha said with a laugh. "The theater, the girl—and finally good press!"

After the fire in the dressmakers' workshop, the newspapers had done nothing but sing hymns of praise in honor of Robin and March. Thanks to their courage and resourcefulness, there had been no deaths and only a few injuries, although the interior of the building was entirely destroyed by the fire. The women and girls from the third story called March their guardian angel, and finally the various papers confirmed her leadership qualities. The *Otago Daily Times* was almost overcome with enthusiasm:

> In certain circles, the word is that Miss Jensch will be leaving the directorship of the Lacrosse Company in the near future. But we can assure our well-disposed readers of one thing: This won't be the last we hear of this young lady!

Nor did March let any opportunity slip by to speak with reporters. Triumphantly, she led one after the other through the Lacrosse workshops and explained the fire-safety regulations. Robin's announcement that, in addition to new management of the company, there would be a new school and nursery for the workers' children, contributed further to the general shift in public opinion. And to Robin's great relief, March didn't object to his suggestion that she give up managing the workshops and take on the position of business manager in the theater he planned to start. The new assignment delighted her, all the more since she had achieved the secret goal that had driven her in the first place: she had won the battle against Martin Porter and Magiel. Her factories stood, safe and sound, while one of his lay in ruins. He couldn't claim damages with anyone. The ground floor was totally destroyed, and the cause of the fire could not be determined. Wentworth declined a thorough investigation of the workers. The press were already tearing him to shreds since a couple of women had told the *Otago Daily Times* how he pushed them out of the way to save himself. The lack of fire-prevention measures and emergency-exit plans had all been hashed out in the papers. Magiel would have to have his other factories entirely renovated.

On top of that, the reforms that Robin now insisted upon would soon become obligations for all factory owners. After the various reports about the poor treatment of the workers, the government was organizing a commission to investigate the situation. The costs of the resulting reforms would undoubtedly further weaken the competitiveness of Porter's factories. March just needed to sit back and watch, but that didn't come naturally to her. Managing a theater was a delightful new challenge.

As the Burtons had predicted, Robin's accounts were full enough that he didn't need to sell any of the dressmakers' workshops to fulfill his dream. However, he decided to let go of the house in Mornington as soon as possible. The proceeds from the sale would go toward the school and childcare at the factory, and the parish would receive generous support as well. Robin had made his peace with Reverend Waddell and Peta. The clergyman was newly engaged in efforts to establish a labor union for seamstresses, and Robin had offered Peta a managerial position in the Lacrosse Company after he completed his studies. That way he could combine profits and social responsibility toward the workers. To Robin's astonishment, Peta didn't enthusiastically accept the offer right away, but pointed out with unaccustomed modesty that it was still quite a while until his final exams.

Bertram Lockhart smirked when Robin told him about that. He was of the opinion that Peta preferred muckraking to actually getting something up and running himself. He'd probably spend his whole life fighting hopeless battles so he could feel like a tragic hero, the old actor said dismissively.

By Robin's invitation, Bertram and his daughter had moved into the house. Their cheap lodgings in the Devil's Half Acre were unacceptable for the future artistic director of the Dunedin Globe Theatre. The new business already bore this name even before suitable buildings had been found. Lucille had suggested it, and Robin happily accepted. The young man was completely enchanted by Lockhart's daughter. He couldn't get enough of her hip-length hair that danced around her face in countless golden-brown curls—a lively face that instantly mirrored the young woman's every emotion, every movement, and every thought. Lucille was more expressive than any other actress Robin had ever seen. When Bertram had her audition, Robin was quickly beside himself. Her face was heart-shaped, her lashes long, and her brows thick like her father's. Her complexion was clear, her nose sporting a few freckles. Her lips were red with a brownish tinge that suited her brown, wide-set eyes.

Neither father nor daughter stood out in the Lacrosse house. From his days as a well-paid actor, Bertram knew how to behave in good society, and Lucille, although intimidated by the grandeur of the house, charmed everyone, even the stern Mr. Simmons.

The only person who couldn't make peace with the Lockharts' presence, nor with the developments regarding the Lacrosse Company and its heir, was Helena. Robin's sudden transformation from an indifferent private gentleman to the busy owner of a theater took her by surprise. She had never known him to be so passionate and determined.

At first, Helena was merely irritated by all this, but she became enraged when Robin disclosed his plans to sell the house. Partly out of lack of diplomacy and partly out of fear of her reaction, he did so during a dinner at which everyone was present: March, Aroha, Bao, Bertram, and Lucille.

"Where am I supposed to go?" Helena asked shrilly.

"You'll have to decide that for yourself," March shot back. "It's not as though Robin would leave you penniless on the street."

"You can live in my house, of course," Robin hastened to add. He intended to buy a much smaller house near the future theater and to staff it with perhaps two or three servants. "The last thing I want to do is throw you out."

"So I'm supposed to live on alms in some kind of hut?" Helena asked dramatically. "Without enough staff, without my lady's maid?"

"You can keep your lady's maid," Aroha said calmly. "Just pay her from your own income. You inherited quite a lot yourself, you know."

Helena bit her lip. In fact, she hadn't seen a cent of her own inheritance, which consisted of half of the family's holdings in Australia. Paul Penn, her brother-in-law, was anything but excited about having to split the inheritance with her, and he guarded the money jealously. Whenever Helena had asked him for a wire transfer to pay for one of her own purchases, like the hunting horse for Robin, he insisted he was saving her inheritance as her dowry. He assured her that, when she married, her future husband would be welcome to handle the money. At some point, Helena had given up asking. It was so much more comfortable to make use of Robin's money. He never complained about it.

Now he rubbed his forehead and brought up another subject that had been occupying his mind since his conversation with Reverend Burton.

"I, uh, don't want to be stingy, Helena. But I just discovered by accident that not only your maid, but also all of your shopping and other purchases are at my expense."

"At the expense of the Lacrosse family!" Helena cried. "My grandfather earned that money."

"And Robin inherited it," March said. "At least the New Zealand half. With your quarter, you possess more money than you could spend in a lifetime. I looked into the Australian holdings, and they are much more diversified than our concerns here, and extremely profitable. If I were you, Helena, I'd go there and take a good look—and maybe you'll find a suitable husband as well. Or do you already have your eye on someone?"

March feigned innocence, but her eyes blazed with mockery.

Helena responded with a look full of rage. "I was expecting Robin to pop the question by now," she said sharply and turned to Robin, who looked away in discomfort, while Lucille blushed. "You've been stuck to me like a burr for two years, Robin! How could I pursue any other acquaintances? In the society columns we're always mentioned together, and we've gone to every dinner, sporting event, and theater performance together. Every last person in Dunedin would have thought we were a couple!"

Robin bit his lip. "But I wouldn't have," he murmured.

Helena stood up. Where her face had been red with rage, it was now pale. "Then I beg your pardon," she said frostily, "that I've been misunderstanding you for more than two years. I will prepare for my journey to Sydney!"

And with that, she swept out of the room and left the company sitting in awkward silence. At least March and Bertram still seemed to be able to enjoy their food.

Robin hadn't sold the coach yet, so for one last time, Aroha and Bao were able to enjoy the privilege of being driven into the city in the splendid Lacrosse family vehicle. Their ship would take them directly to Auckland. Aroha noticed that the coachman not only seemed indignant as he held the door for Bao but also didn't dignify Robin with a friendly look. Ever since the staff had been reduced, the man had had to saddle the horses and care for them afterward.

"When he interviews with a new employer," Bao whispered to the others, "and is asked why he's leaving his old job, he'll say that Robin forced him into tasks beneath his dignity, and what's more, made him transport Chinese people."

"Which will finally ruin the reputation of the Lacrosse heirs in Dunedin society!" Aroha added, laughing.

That didn't bother Robin; he'd broken off with Dunedin society. They only interested him as an audience for his future theater, which he was now announcing openly in the papers. Lucille, on the other hand, gazed at Robin with concern.

That morning, Helena had made her apologies, saying she had a migraine. Robin's second cousin had obviously had enough of her "long-lost" family. Aroha imagined that she deeply regretted having approached Robin in Te Wairoa, setting all the gears in motion.

While Bao and Robin busied themselves with the luggage, Lucille took Aroha aside. A cool wind was blowing and the girl was chilled, despite her shawl. Soon she would need a new wardrobe. Aroha wondered if Robin would remember his account at Lady's Gold Mine, or whether Bertram's daughter would have to wait until the theater turned a profit and her father got his share.

"What's wrong, Lucille?" Aroha smiled at the girl encouragingly.

Lucille hesitated before she could put into words the question that weighed on her heart. "Is it true?" she finally said. "Will people really snub Robin because he doesn't have a coach anymore and because he's acting in the theater instead of representing the business?"

Aroha shook her head. "Nonsense! That was just a joke. And even if it weren't, Robin doesn't want to have anything more to do with such people. None of them stood by him when the press dragged his name through the mud. Quite the opposite; they turned against him so that no one would mention how they themselves lived lives of luxury at the expense of their employees. Robin has other priorities now."

"I knew that about Robin," Lucille said, blushing, as she so often did when she spoke of the young man. The wind plucked curls from her hair, which was loosely braided and pinned up around her face. The whole effect made her look especially bewitching. "But Miss Helena . . . Is it true . . . that Robin wanted to marry her? And that now he's—because of—" She stopped, and Aroha smiled. So Lucille hadn't missed the fact that Robin was in love with her. "It would be terrible for me if . . . he turned out to be unfaithful," the girl added.

So the girl doubted Robin's sincerity. Aroha put an arm around her. "You really mustn't worry about that, Lucille. Robin never knowingly gave Helena hope in that respect. It was all in her imagination. Robin should have clarified things earlier, but I don't think he even noticed that Helena was in love with him."

A hint of a smile stole over Lucille's face. "He doesn't notice things like that so easily," she murmured.

Aroha hugged her. "It must run in our family," she joked. "At least, that's what Bao would say. He waited quite a long time for me."

Lucille smiled faintly. Then her face clouded over again. "It's just . . . Miss Helena . . . she frightens me a little," she admitted.

Aroha paused. "Did she say anything to you? Has she threatened you in any way?"

Lucille shook her head. "No. I just don't think she likes me much."


"That may just be an occupational hazard," Aroha said later, after she'd told Bao about her conversation with the girl. The two stood at the railing and watched as Dunedin's green hills and the snow-covered South Alps slowly receded into the distance. "Those actors can't stand not being loved."

Bao smiled, but concern played across his face. "Still, Lucille and Robin should be careful. Helena is a spoiled child. She may not be able to stand not getting what she wants."

# Chapter 62

Little had changed in Rotorua during Aroha and Bao's absence. The promenade still wasn't safe to walk on, although the season was long since underway. Camille Malfroy had arrived to install his mechanical system to manipulate the geyser. McDougal and the other hotel owners were fighting with the government over who should pay for it.

Bao and Aroha found that Lani had grown, and her grandparents said she'd missed them.

"She spoke Chinese every day!" her grandfather said. "A very bright child!"

Based on the country's current attitudes, Aroha doubted that Lani's language abilities would be useful, but Bao was happy and began to teach his adopted daughter once more. He even seemed happy when an excited Tapsy jumped up on him, yipping.

"Watch out," Aroha teased him. "She's attacking you as mercilessly as her namesake."

The Chinese Garden Lodge was almost fully booked. McRae had stood Aroha in good stead. However, he was glad to give the position up.

"Perhaps I'll write a few letters to the government about the geyser pipes," he said calmly. "The Maori are divided on the question. Since the tips the *manuhiri* leave are proportional to how high the geyser shoots, some of them are happy for every additional foot, but the others are worried about upsetting the spirits. Still, it doesn't hurt anything to protest. At least that way no one will think to send the bill to the tribes."

Aroha and Bao happily took up their work at the hotel again, although Bao was still hindered by the cast on his right arm, so he spent most of his days working at the reception desk.

One rainy day at the beginning of December, he was working on the reservation list when a man entered. He was oddly dressed for a spa guest. His denim trousers and boots, the waxed barn coat and dripping wet sou'wester that he took off as he entered the lobby made him look more like a cowhand or a scout.

"What can I do for you, sir?"

Bao glanced up and looked with amazement into light-blue eyes as clear as a mountain lake. There was only one person he'd ever seen with eyes like that—Aroha!

"I'm looking for Miss Fitzpatrick," the man said, his voice powerful but pleasant. "Aroha Fitzpatrick."

Bao took a better look at the stranger, who was of rather short stature. He looked to be around fifty years old, and his face was angular and deeply lined. His skin was rather dark, as was the abundant thick hair streaked with gray. The man wore it quite long, and unruly.

"Is she here?" he said impatiently. "You do understand me, don't you?"

Bao nodded. "Of course, sir. I don't know exactly where Aroha is, but I think she's inspecting the bathhouse. Why don't you wait in the teahouse a moment, Mister . . ."

The staff would keep an eye on him in the teahouse. Bao preferred not to leave this odd person alone in the lobby with the till.

"Fitz," the man said shortly. "Joe Fitzpatrick. Now go get my daughter."

At first, Aroha thought it was a joke. Bao had found her in the bathhouse, folding hand towels, and naturally his news threw her into a dither. If it really was her father, how did he look? Would he like her? A glance in the bathhouse mirror assured her that, while she wasn't elegantly dressed, she was at least tidy. She wore a light-blue afternoon dress with an apron over it, which she quickly took off as she followed Bao into the lobby. He had left the strange visitor alone there after all. Lani padded along after the couple, and Tapsy, too, who surprised Aroha by greeting Joe Fitzpatrick like an old acquaintance. Didn't dogs have a sense for who was a good person? The thought took away some of her anxiety.

"Sir?"

Aroha addressed the man formally, since it was entirely possible that he was an imposter. She froze when she saw her own eyes in his face.

Joe Fitzpatrick grinned at her. "You have my eyes!" he exclaimed. "Although you take more after Linda. Hmm . . . maybe the shape of your face . . . and

Linda's skin was a lot lighter. But you're still pretty, Aroha! A beautiful woman, just like your mother. Is she still living with that reverend down in Otaki?"

"Franz Lange was a very good father to me," Aroha said stiffly.

At first glance, Joe Fitzpatrick struck her as likable. A smile played around his sharply drawn lips. Was it appreciative? Or a little mocking? In any case, he was a person who took life easy. Aroha remembered how her mother had described him: *"Your father is a charming swindler,"* she had said. Aroha wouldn't let the man speak ill of her adoptive father.

"And I was a bad one," Fitzpatrick said easily. "I admit it. Things didn't turn out right. But so much the better that we can get to know each other now. You're doing well, aren't you? Your own hotel! But you got that from me as well. Try something out, make something happen, get something up and running . . ." Fitzpatrick's eyes twinkled.

Aroha reminded herself that, in contrast to Franz and Linda Lange, Fitz had never managed to get anything up and running. In the detective's report about Vera Carrigan, there had even been talk of jail time.

"Where have you been all these years?" she asked, her voice rather forced. "What—what did you do?"

Joe Fitzpatrick pursed his lips. "Here and there, this and that . . . you get by the best you can. You make a good profit here with the hotel, right? It's a nice town . . . once you get used to it smelling like sulfur everywhere. And what's this? Do I have a grandchild?" He deftly changed the subject by leaning down to Lani, who approached him as trustingly as her dog had. "You're a little sweetie. Let me guess: your daddy is Maori. Well, Linda did always have a weak spot for the natives. Although not in this context, or she would have chosen a warrior over me rather than that soft sheep of a reverend. I would have understood that better . . ."

Aroha was relieved to have the opportunity to tell her father Lani's history. Finally, she revealed to him that she and Bao were getting married soon. She was pleasantly surprised by his reaction.

"Hey, then you can have a Chinese wedding!" he suggested, grinning. "Here at the hotel. That'd be good. I'll bet your guests like exotic stuff. Burn a couple of sticks of incense, invoke some spirits . . . the people would be all over it. Tremendous idea to call the place Chinese Garden Lodge. That sets you apart from the other hotels."

Fitzpatrick didn't seem to harbor any prejudices against Bao's race. Nor against the Maori. Aroha began to doubt her mother's stories. Could this man really have behaved so cruelly toward Linda and Omaka?

"So . . . what brings you here?" she finally asked. "We should sit down; we can go into the tearoom. Will you come along, Bao? Kiri can take over for you here."

Bao turned to the young woman who was just heading toward the tearoom with a tray in her hand. Aroha took the tray and brought it into the kitchen while Kiri took her place at the reception desk. She kept Lani with her, as the child enjoyed keeping her company. Bao guided his future father-in-law toward a table off to the side.

"Tea, sir?" he asked politely. "Or coffee? Perhaps you're also hungry . . ."

Joe Fitzpatrick shook his head. "Maybe a whiskey, my friend," he said. "To counter the shock of suddenly having a grown daughter! No, that's actually something to celebrate. Champagne! You do have that, right?"

Bao's face hardened. It was early afternoon. At the Chinese Garden Lodge, they rarely served alcohol at this hour. At most, a guest might want a bit of rum or brandy in their tea on a cold day.

"Of course, sir," he said stiffly.

Joe Fitzpatrick laughed. "You don't have to call me 'sir.' I'm 'Fitz.' And you're Duong? No, Bao; you Chinese put your surname first, right? So Bao. To friendship!"

He lifted an imaginary glass, so there was nothing for Bao to do but go over to the restaurant, get a bottle of champagne, and uncork it. Aroha, who had just come back, shot him a questioning look. With his chin, he indicated her father, who, unruffled, drank to her health as soon as Bao had filled the glasses.

"To my lovely daughter! And such a surprise!"

"So you weren't looking for me?" Aroha asked, taking a small sip of her drink. She liked champagne, but she still had a half day of work ahead of her.

"Not directly," Fitzpatrick said and took a long pull from his glass. "I was . . . looking for an old friend. I heard that she'd passed away here, but I couldn't quite believe it."

"Vera Carrigan?" Aroha asked, her lips pressed tight.

Fitz smiled. "I see from your face that your mother must have told you about her. Of course it wasn't like that. By which I don't mean to say that Linda was lying. Just that she had a somewhat distorted view of things."

"I met Miss Carrigan myself," Aroha said, trying not to imply anything with her words. Vera Carrigan was in the past; she didn't have to contribute to a quarrel between father and daughter.

"Exactly," Fitz said. "Your name came up when I asked about her in the village. Also a certain Mr. McRae and Robin Fenroy. Hey, would that be one of the Rata Station Fenroys? Connection hadn't occurred to me. Fenroys are a dime a dozen, and Fitzpatrick isn't that unusual either. 'Aroha,' on the other hand, is. Maybe Linda's idea of giving you such an unusual name was a good one after all. Another toast to finding you! Aroha, Bao . . ." He took another drink.

"So you learned of Miss Carrigan's death?" Bao asked. "A tragic case. They must have told you about the volcanic eruption."

"Nothing specific," Fitz said. "Only that it had something to do with the geyser. And her body was never found. That made me hope . . ."

"You can bury that hope; she's dead," Aroha said curtly. "Robin was there. There's no question."

"So this Robin had something to do with it. Interesting . . . Vera found him fascinating, did you know that? She thought highly of him, a great talent." His expression, which had been alternately calm and amused, became wary.

"Too great for a company like Miss Carrigan's," Aroha told him. "Robin was just about to leave it."

Fitz pressed his lips together. An eyebrow rose. "And then she died. Interesting . . ." His voice grew husky. He seemed to be talking only to himself. After a moment, though, he noticed how his darkened visage alarmed Aroha and Bao. He pulled out another smile. "Well, anyway. We don't have to talk about Vera's little plaything. Your hotel . . . does it do well for you?"

Aroha didn't answer right away. She was too confused, and struck by her father's choice of words. Of course she knew that Robin had been a plaything to Vera. But Fitz spoke like a father who thought it was funny when his child tormented a dog, only to shoot the animal as soon as it turned and snapped.

"All the hotels in Rotorua do quite well," Bao answered for her. "This is an up-and-coming health resort, despite or perhaps because of the loss of the Pink and White Terraces. At that time there were more short-term visitors, and business was divided between Rotorua, Ohinemutu, and Te Wairoa. The people took a look at the terraces and the geysers and then went on their way. Today we don't get as many visitors, but they stay longer and spend more money. And they want more comforts. If you're only staying one night, you can make do with primitive lodgings, but if you're spending three weeks, you want more cultivated surroundings. We're satisfied with that."

Fitz grinned. "That's nice. So I don't need to worry about my daughter's livelihood."

"No." It was Bao who answered once again. "Can we offer you something else, Mr. Fitz? We would be happy if you stayed for dinner. Until then, however, we do still have some work to do. Did you finish up in the bathhouse, Aroha?"

"Not entirely," Aroha answered, relieved.

She was also ready to end the conversation at this point, and she would really have preferred for her father to disappear as suddenly as he'd shown up. Somehow Joe Fitzpatrick didn't fit in her bright, friendly hotel. As nice as he was, it would have seemed more natural to meet him in some smoky pub.

Fitz grinned again, although he didn't seem quite as confident as he had before. "Well, since you ask, Bao—or you, Aroha, since it's your hotel, after all—you could offer me a job."

That came as a surprise. Aroha and Bao remained silent, while Fitzpatrick continued with enthusiasm. "Yes, I know, it sounds funny for a daughter to provide for her father instead of the other way 'round. But I'm kind of at loose ends at the moment, and I could use some work. Why not here?"

"Uh . . . what can you do?" Aroha asked. "I mean, what would you want to do here?"

Fitz grinned. "It'd be better for you to ask what I can't do, rather than what I can. I've done a little bit of everything in my life, Aroha. Yup, what you need here is a jack of all trades." He let his gaze fall on Bao's cast. "Someone who can do small repairs, keep the house in order. I've also worked as a waiter." He stood up and, hanging his napkin over his arm, stood as stiff and formal as an English butler. "What might I bring you, madam? Oh, an excellent choice! Perhaps a glass of champagne as an aperitif?" Fitz grabbed the champagne bottle and filled Aroha's barely touched glass with the greatest grace. "I'm a good cook, I can drive a carriage, I can clean, carry luggage. I'm just what you need, Aroha." Fitz laughed again and looked at Aroha expectantly, as he sat down again. "Let me work for a few days as a trial, and you'll see what I mean."

Aroha bit her lip and caught Bao's eye. She was hoping for some support, perhaps a tiny shake of the head, but the young man only shrugged lightly.

"All right," Aroha said reluctantly. "There really are a lot of things that need doing right now. You'd have to wear a uniform while you were working in the hotel."

It was perfectly impossible for a member of the staff to run around looking like a trapper. The guests arriving for their tea were already casting irritated glances at his shabby appearance. Fitz's face darkened again. Bao wasn't wearing a uniform.

"You could also wear a suit," Bao said, coming to his defense. "Assuming you have one. Otherwise . . . we can front you the money for one. And I'll find you a suitable room. Perhaps you can talk to Aroha about the wages in the meantime. Then we'll see to the bathhouse, Aroha."

Aroha remained behind, baffled, as he stood up. She had often negotiated wages, and surprisingly, she found it easier to talk to her father about hourly pay than about what exactly he would be doing in her hotel, what he would wear, and where he would live. Perhaps it was because his position at the Chinese Garden Lodge might well lead to gossip, at least among the staff. What would his place be? A man Friday or the boss's father?

Bao appeared to have already partly decided the answer. He suggested that they put Fitz up, not in one of the usual staff rooms, but in the area he himself had occupied before moving in with Aroha. Now Bao brought the rest of his things to their private rooms.

Aroha was unenthusiastic. "I had actually thought to offer those rooms to Kiri or Timoti." Both employees had taken excellent care in running the hotel during Aroha and Bao's absence. "And do you really think it was right to give him a job? I'm not so sure myself . . ."

Bao put his arm around her. "You can't ask a Chinese person that question. Our culture values the care of older relatives above everything else. In China it's normal for a daughter to support her father. She has to honor him and give him whatever he needs. It doesn't matter how he's treated her in the past."

"But aren't you as suspicious of him as I am?" Aroha asked. "I mean, he was in prison. Do you think it's possible that he was just released? And he's only at loose ends, as he put it, because he can't hide out with Vera Carrigan anymore?"

Bao shook his head. "I'd rather not speculate about people whom I'm obligated to honor," he said. "I don't want my ancestors to turn against us, now that we have yours to deal with. Our first assignment for Fitz should be to build them a shrine."

Of course Joe Fitzpatrick didn't build shrines for either Chinese or Maori spirits, but he did construct two new tubs in the shape of reclining dragons for the bathhouse. He thought the baths looked more Chinese that way, and although Bao couldn't confirm that, the guests loved it. Aroha's father managed to surprise his daughter and Bao in other ways as well. Fitz hadn't overpromised. He proved himself more than equal to every task and didn't appear to be expecting to sponge off his daughter. At first, he did jobs that didn't bring him into contact with the guests—various repairs needed around the hotel, restaurant, and park—and then he bought himself a suit with his own money. He also didn't hesitate to slip into livery or a waiter's uniform, especially since Bao placed him in positions that preserved his dignity. Fitz greeted the guests at the reception desk and played the role of sommelier, showing an outstanding knowledge of fine wines, both domestic and foreign. Bao only frowned occasionally when he heard him extol the "earthy sweetness" or "aroma of cocoa and pears" that supposedly set this or that wine apart.

"Where did he learn all that?" he asked Aroha, taking a sip of wine and swishing it slowly back and forth in his mouth. That evening he had brought a bottle along to their apartment in an attempt to taste its "chocolate accents."

Aroha took a sip as well, but tasted nothing but wine. "I think he's making it up," she said. "But most people know even less than he does, and they enjoy listening to him."

That proved true when Fitz tried his hand at being a tour guide. He took one tour of the geyser area, which was normally offered by the Maori, and then started offering tours exclusively for the guests of the Chinese Garden Lodge. His tours proved overwhelmingly successful.

"What the devil is better about him than all the other guides?" McDougal wondered. He'd overheard some *manuhiri* raving about Fitz's tour and thought it odd enough that he'd come to tell Aroha.

"I'll go along tomorrow," she promised.

The next day, Aroha alternated between horror and amusement as she witnessed the melodramas that her father dished up.

"You know those pools where the water looks green at certain times?" she asked Bao that evening. "Apparently, a Maori princess sank her people's jade treasure there after her tribe was annihilated by an enemy. She was the only survivor, but the chieftain's son followed her, and somehow they declared their love on the edge of the water, so the spirits turned the water green. Of course that's complete nonsense, but he has a story like that for every puddle. Some of them are quite ghastly. Chills ran down my spine at how close one or two of them came to Vera Carrigan's death. Do you think he's capitalizing on the tragedy?"

Fitz had never mentioned the subject again, nor had he inquired any further about Robin Fenroy. Of course he often saw Aroha and Bao at breakfast and observed them opening letters, from which Bao read aloud the news from Dunedin. March had found a building in Rattrey Street that would make an outstanding theater. The magnificent structure had been built during the gold rush and had housed a bank at that time. Its location was convenient to the city center, a quarter mile from the Octagon, and a cable-car line passed right by it. The renovations were in full swing, and Robin and Bertram were auditioning young actors for their ensemble. They planned to debut that coming autumn with *A Midsummer Night's Dream*. The house in Mornington still hadn't been sold. Such a large and expensive property wouldn't find a buyer so quickly. Helena was still living there and didn't seem to be in any hurry to move to Australia.

"And aside from hideous stories," Aroha continued, "Fitz has every possible attraction on the program. He drops eggs in sieves into the hot springs and cooks them. The results are supposed to taste like Chinese thousand-year eggs. Can that be true?"

Bao shook his head. "No. *Pidan* don't taste like sulfur. I was only ten years old when I left China, but they're put in a mixture of anise, pepper, and fennel, and they don't rot, they ferment."

"Well, the *manuhiri* are thrilled and fight to get a taste of the eggs. I hope they're not harmful. Fitz has figured out the trick with the soap bubbles, of course, and he and Camille Malfroy get along famously. He makes the geyser spray a little bit higher for Fitz; don't ask me how. In any case, Fitz is collecting huge tips. We're going to have problems with the Maori guides over it soon. He's ruining their business and angering their spirits as well."

But here Aroha underestimated her father again. Instead of arguing, Fitz and the Maori guides came to a mutual understanding. The tour guides—young fellows who were more interested in tips than spirits—borrowed his stories, while he got involved in the souvenir business that they ran on the side. Fitz sold *hei tiki* as amulets against rheumatism, and war cudgels as paperweights. He'd heard about the mysterious "spirit voices" of the *putorino*, and informed the people that they could call up their protective spirit by playing a certain note on the flute.

"If you can't manage to blow it, you can also drum on the table with it," Aroha said, repeating one of his claims. "It's a mystery how the man hasn't become a millionaire. He's such a gifted salesman."

"You could also say 'liar,' if we weren't talking about someone we are obligated to honor," Bao said.

Truth be told, Bao was also pleasantly surprised by Fitz, especially his ability to get people excited and encourage them. When he organized a Sunday work party, calling for the promenade to finally be brought into passable condition, not only did all of the hotel owners and shopkeepers show up, despite having argued about the costs for months on end, but also workers sent by the Maori tribes.

"It's too good to be true," Aroha remarked. She was pleased when Fitz invited the ladies from the area to a festive inspection of the finished walkway. On the walk, he carried Lani on his shoulders, and a delighted Tapsy skipped along beside him. When they reached his hotel, McDougal treated everyone to champagne. Fitz drank with him and managed, incidentally, to make his daughter's relationship more palatable to the Scotsman.

"A Chinese wedding! That'd be a thrill for the guests, all right. If I were in their shoes, I'd have the party here at your place, McDougal. The Rotorua Lodge is much bigger than our Chinese Garden. Arrange a grand evening with traditional food . . . doesn't matter if your cook knows how to make it. I bet the guests have never had Chinese food before anyway."

"If it's a success, we should let Fitz and McDougal throw weddings every week," Aroha laughed, as she and Bao lay in bed enjoying a last glass of wine—one supposedly resplendent for its aroma of lemon and fennel. "I never would have believed it, but Fitz is a gift from heaven."

The letter Aroha sent her mother two weeks after Joe Fitzpatrick's arrival was just as euphoric. She had put off writing for a while, since she knew perfectly well what Linda and Franz Lange thought of her father. However, she couldn't keep quiet about his return forever, and she was even happier that there was nothing negative to report.

"Can he really have changed so much?" Franz Lange asked.

By that time it was high summer, and the Langes were enjoying the cool of the evening on their terrace at the end of a long, hot day. The sun, setting over the nearby sea, painted the few scattered clouds golden. It offered Linda just enough light to read her daughter's letter aloud to her husband.

Linda shook her head. "No. It's always been like that. When Fitz starts something new, he throws himself into his work. And he can get things done; he's intelligent, skilled, and has good ideas. He works hard. I know you don't believe it. I've told you often enough how he lazed about in Taranaki. Vera was already in the picture by then. But when I think of Otago and the cliff where some fool thought he'd found gold . . . Fitz slaved away like a farm horse to blow the thing up! And when Vera wanted a house, he built her one in a jiffy. Or how he threw himself into the farm work at Rata Station . . ." She smiled. "That impressed me enough to make me fall in love with him. So I'm not surprised one bit by Aroha's enthusiasm. But Fitz will get bored. Fun becomes work, and work becomes routine. Then suddenly he's cranky, he slacks off, and eventually he jumps ship. That's just what will happen here. You mark my words. It's only a question of whether I should warn Aroha about it ahead of time or whether I should just wait until she falls flat on her face."

Franz sipped thoughtfully at the whiskey he'd allowed himself that evening. "What do you mean 'falls flat on her face'? Shouldn't we be looking out for her?"

Linda shook her head. "No. He'll disappoint her, and probably leave her in the lurch, if she depends on him. If the volcano should erupt again, for example, the first person he'd save would be himself. Of course that's highly unlikely, and it's not as though she's surrounded by Hauhau warriors either. Joe Fitzpatrick was never dangerous or violent. He's just a charming swindler, nothing more."

Franz frowned. "Until he met Vera Carrigan."

The sun disappeared below the horizon.

# Chapter 63

"It's none of my business, Miss Aroha . . ." Joseph McRae was visiting the Chinese Garden Lodge in the afternoon, when he knew that Joe Fitzpatrick was away with a tour group at the geysers. "And I know how indiscreet the question is. But with regard to your father . . . Is he any kind of partner in the ownership of your hotel?"

Aroha shook her head in amazement and poured him some tea. She had taken a little time off of work to chat with her old friend, especially since it was unusual for him to appear at this time and then to ask so formally for a meeting. Now, in the early autumn, there wasn't much going on at the hotel. The high season had just ended. More guests were departing than arriving.

"Of course not," Aroha answered. "The Chinese Garden Lodge belongs to me alone. When we marry, then of course Bao will be an owner as well. How did you come to the conclusion that my father would have any stake in it? Oh, of course, he always calls it 'our' hotel. But the staff do too. It shows that they feel a sense of responsibility for it."

McRae bit his lip. "I don't get a sense of responsibility from Mr. Fitzpatrick," he said. "He—well, I won't beat around the bush anymore. He's gambling, Miss Aroha. And he's using your hotel as a forfeit, so to speak."

"He's doing what?" Aroha exclaimed. "How do you know about this?"

"I often go to McDougal's in the evening for a little drink," McRae confessed. "Sometimes I miss seeing guests from all over the world. I always liked to chat with well-traveled gentlemen, and the smoking room at the Rotorua Lodge gives me the best opportunity for that."

Unlike the Chinese Garden Lodge, which only offered its guests a parlor as a place to gather, at the McDougals' there were tearooms for the ladies and smoking rooms where the gentlemen retreated after dinner to smoke, drink whiskey, and gamble.

"You know what kinds of games are played there. Well, as McDougal assured me, that's been happening a lot more frequently since your father's been in town. The stakes have also gone up. Brett and Waimarama aren't happy about it, and they've also thought about speaking to you. Well, just yesterday I was there when Fitz wanted in on a game but didn't have the stakes. He wrote an IOU . . . with your hotel as the security."

"My father is gambling for the price of an entire hotel?" Aroha asked in horror.

McRae shook his head. "Not yet. It was maybe a thousand pounds. He won, by the way, but then lost the money in the next round. That's how it always goes."

"A thousand pounds is a fortune!" Aroha said. "Why doesn't he just keep the money when he wins? I would never . . ."

"That's the crucial difference," McRae said. "You and I would never bet that kind of money on cards, and for that reason we'd never win, Aroha. Your father bets like that again and again. He is a gambler."

Aroha rubbed her forehead. Joe Fitzpatrick had been with them for four months, and the early enthusiasm that she and Bao had felt for his work was steadily waning. At first, Fitz had only forgotten a task rarely, such as leaving the reception desk unattended although it was his shift, or not showing up for tours. But recently these incidents had become more frequent, and while initially he had apologized for his lapses, now whenever Bao or Aroha spoke with him, his reactions were increasingly aggressive. Aroha thought that money had disappeared from the till when Fitz was working at the reception desk. Bao agreed, but thought they shouldn't mention it to Fitz out of respect.

"In China, we're taught to give freely to our parents. A child's money is theirs as well."

So Aroha had gritted her teeth and kept quiet, which didn't make living with Fitz any easier. Their meals together became increasingly tense, as he was no longer cheerful and brimming with ideas, making her, Bao, and Lani laugh. He had become restless and didn't want to talk about everyday things that might lead to criticism. When the conversation turned to his past, at first he had made charming excuses and joked his way out of many questions, but now he quickly grew abusive. Aroha and Bao didn't speak freely anymore, but were careful about every word they said to him. Beyond that, they had to make excuses to keep Fitz away from the till without making any direct accusations. Up to that point only small sums had disappeared, but Aroha had no illusions about the matter. If she let Fitz get away with it, there would be more. And now there was this much more serious business.

Aroha played nervously with her napkin. "What—what could have happened?" she asked McRae. "That is, if Fitz hadn't won the bet?"

"Nothing really," McRae said soothingly. "Gambling debts can't be brought to court, and if someone bets another person's money and property, it doesn't mean a thing—as long as Mr. Fitzpatrick is dealing with gentlemen at the Rotorua Lodge. Rich men, mostly older, and not prone to violence. It would just be extremely embarrassing. You understand what I mean. If someone showed up with an IOU and word got around . . . You have your reputation to think of."

"But beyond that, it's not at all guaranteed that Mr. Fitzpatrick is only playing with gentlemen," Aroha said. "What if he can't find anyone at the Rotorua Lodge who wants to play? Would he go to another good hotel? Or to a pub?"

McRae raised his hand hopelessly. "You'll have to ask him that. I can only pass along what I've seen myself. I've known you and Bao for such a long time, Miss Aroha; I feel a sense of responsibility toward you. So I hope you'll forgive me for asking such indiscreet questions."

Aroha thanked Joseph McRae gratefully and drank another cup of tea with him. But she felt as if she were walking on hot coals. Respect for ancestors aside, she had to speak to her father. And it would do no good to delay. To the contrary, every passing day increased the risk that he would fall into misfortune, and Aroha with him.

So that evening, Aroha stopped her father as he came through the lobby and cheerfully greeted her. He was wearing his good suit, so he was probably on his way to the Rotorua Lodge. Aroha was working at the reception desk, but no one else was in the lobby at the moment. She hoped it would stay that way for a while. She spoke to Fitz directly about his passion for gambling.

He didn't deny it but grinned broadly. "Sweetheart, I'm sure your mother told you that I like a little game now and again. But she probably didn't tell you how many times I saved our skins with it. There were times when money was tight in the Fitzpatrick house." He rubbed his forehead in a way that was more dramatic than embarrassed. "Oh, yes. I still remember how I came home one time and poured my winnings all over her bed, and how happy she was about it."

"But you're earning plenty here," Aroha reminded him. "You don't need to take such risks to survive."

Fitz laughed. "Oh, honey. If you don't take risks, life's no fun!"

Aroha took a sharp breath in and stood up straight. Now she had to be the boss.

"But I don't want that kind of thing going on," she said quietly. "It puts the hotel in a bad light when the employees gamble."

Fitz's face darkened. "Am I just your employee, then?" he asked sharply.

Aroha forced herself to remain calm. "You've been my employee for the last four months," she said firmly. "You came here and asked me for a job. And you got one, one that you're paid for. So you are my employee and must behave according to certain rules."

"You sound like your mother!" Fitz laughed scornfully.

Aroha nodded. "I sound like a sensible person who stands to lose her reputation or, in the case of my mother, the last of her money. And while we're on the subject, I've heard that you're not only gambling but wagering things that don't belong to you. What do you expect me to do if someone shows up with an IOU with the name of my hotel on it?"

"Sweetheart, it's just like I told your mother," Fitz boasted. "I don't lose. At least not as often as I win!"

Aroha raised her eyebrows. "That means that you cheat," she said coldly. "Which is even worse if you were caught and it got around that my father is cheating my friends' guests at poker. That would be the end of it for me in Rotorua. You must stop it, Fitz! This instant!"

"And if I don't?" Fitz's expression was threatening. "Are you going to throw me out, sweetheart? Your long-lost father? After everything I've done for you?"

Aroha's fury grew. "You've done nothing for me, Fitz. You betrayed my mother and put me at the mercy of Vera Carrigan when I was a tiny infant. If Omaka hadn't stepped in, she would have killed me. When the Hauhau broke into our house, you chose your own safety and Vera's over my mother's."

"I wanted to keep you safe!" Fitz said.

Aroha shook her head. "The judges didn't believe your claims back then, and I don't believe them now. And you've been paid for what you've done for the hotel in the last few months."

"I've increased business," Fitz said.

Aroha almost laughed. "You've contributed to the fact that we've had a good season, just as Kiri and Timoti and all the other employees have, from the gardener to the chamber maid. What's more, there's been money missing from the till, Fitz. By rights you should either return it or work it off."

"That's just rich!" Fitz exploded. "First I'm a cheater, and now I'm a thief too? Who do you think you are? I came here looking for a friend, I found you, and I stayed to help my daughter . . ."

Aroha didn't know what else to say. Fitz would just twist her words around. She wondered if he believed what he was saying or whether it was just an act. She suddenly understood how helpless her mother must have felt when Fitz used the same blustering tone to claim he'd never been in a relationship with Vera Carrigan. She was ashamed that she'd ever doubted Linda.

"I don't want to talk about this anymore," she said finally. "Bao and I have been glad to have you work here, and you've done a good job. I'll consider the money from the till a bonus. But do not talk about 'our hotel' or lead people to believe that it belongs to you. And stop gambling. I wouldn't even allow Bao to do that, so long as he's my employee, and I won't allow you to either."

"You've got him wrapped around your finger, your Bao," Fitz said scornfully. "I thought there was some of me in you, Aroha! How could I have deceived myself? You're just like your mother! She took up with that castrated monk, and you go after a fellow from the dregs of society. Real men wouldn't let themselves be bossed around. They might just decide to do what they want! I never let Linda tell me what to do, and I'm sure not going to let you." He snorted. "I quit, Aroha!"

Aroha remained calm. She'd deal with her feelings later; perhaps she might even cry. But right now she wouldn't show any weakness. Insulting Bao and her stepfather was the last straw. She had believed Fitz to be accepting of other people; it had never occurred to her that his tolerance was just another act.

"Then," she said coldly, "I can only accept your resignation and wish you good luck in your future endeavors, Mr. Fitzpatrick."

As her father left the lobby, she turned away.

# Chapter 64

Joe Fitzpatrick hadn't forgotten Robin Fenroy. His unexpected meeting with Aroha, the initial amusement of working in a hotel, and above all, the incomparable opportunity to gamble in civilized surroundings and line his pockets with winnings from wealthy and naive gentlemen . . . with all this, his thoughts of Vera had receded into the background. He had originally hoped to find her here, since her last letter had been postmarked in Rotorua. Vera had seemed to have her company well in hand, even if there really were too few actors. Unlike Fitz, Vera found it hard to keep people around. She had an insufficient grasp of the complicated interplay of flattery and threats that one needed to keep sensitive characters like actors in line. Instead, she had set her sights on addicts like Bertram and Leah—they were recruited after Fitz's departure from the troupe. To this day, Fitz didn't understand how she'd hung on to Fenroy for so long. When she wrote about the extraordinary talent that had breezed into her house, he'd assumed the boy would be on his way quickly. And now he had learned that Vera died the day that Robin announced his departure from the company! Fitz hadn't been able to find out much about the exact circumstances; it seemed the people of Rotorua were covering it up deliberately. But it was certain that Vera had come to a violent end. A death of which Robin Fenroy was perhaps not entirely innocent.

After the dispute with Aroha, Fitz had set out for Auckland straightaway. Now, on the ride from Rotorua to Tauranga, he thought it over once again. As he left behind the sulfurous vapors and a landscape still marked by the eruption of Mount Tarawera, it occurred to him that Bertram and Robin might have conspired to get Vera out of the way. There might even have been money involved. Could it be that they had participated in her fleecing of some businessmen, then plotted to use her earnings to found their own company? Just as they were now doing with Robin's inheritance, although on a much grander scale?

Fitz rented himself a room in a simple boardinghouse by the harbor in the shadow of Mount Maunganui, drank a couple of glasses of whiskey, and idly paged through a copy of the *New Zealand Herald*. He scanned the want ads and could hardly believe his eyes when they lit upon an ad from the Dunedin Globe Theatre: Robin Fenroy and Bertram Lockhart invited actors from all over New Zealand to audition for a permanent engagement as members of a Shakespeare company. In addition, they were seeking set designers and stagehands with carpentry skills.

Fitz tore the ad out of the paper. The perfect job for him! He grinned and was almost inclined to believe in fate. With another glass of whiskey in hand, he toasted the spirit of Vera Carrigan. He would try his luck on the South Island, take up the theatrical life once again, and check out Robin Fenroy in the bargain.

A few days later, he reached Auckland and spent the rest of his money on a ship's passage to Dunedin.

The address listed in the ad was in Mornington, and Fitz ascertained that this was not the theater itself, but the magnificent house that Aroha and Bao had spoken about. He would have appeared at the theater in denim trousers and a leather jacket, since he was presenting himself as a worker, but his instincts told him an elegant outfit could be useful, so he put on his best three-piece suit. As it turned out, the butler who opened the door instantly treated him with respect. Fitz returned his polite greeting with cool reserve. He didn't really know why he was playing the gentleman. When Robin Fenroy received him, it would become clear what societal role he really occupied. Still, it was fun. Fitz had never dealt with butlers before.

"How may I help you, sir?" the man asked.

Fitz would gladly have pressed his hat into the man's hand, but unfortunately, he didn't own one.

"I should like to speak with Mr. Fenroy, Mr. Robin Fenroy." Fitz could also have asked for Margery Jensch, who was listed as the contact person for stagehands. But here, too, he relied on his instincts. For some reason, he didn't want to let the butler know that his visit had to do with the theater.

"Unfortunately, Mr. Fenroy is not here, sir," the butler said. "Miss Lacrosse is, however. If you would like to speak with her . . ."

Fitz nodded casually. "Oh, yes, please. If you would announce me . . . Patrick Fitz."

Fitz pretended to search for his visiting card, but then gave up with an apologetic smile. The butler would assume he had forgotten them. At that, he wondered if he had gone too far. Of course, it was an interesting game to pretend to be a gentleman with Fenroy's staff. But how would he explain his desire to speak with Helena Lacrosse, who had nothing to do with the theater? Perhaps he could claim that he'd misunderstood the butler, and had intended to speak with Miss Jensch.

"Right this way," said the butler. "Miss Lacrosse is in the garden."

Fitz crossed the foyer and had to hold back an astounded whistle. They went on through various grand drawing and dining rooms until they reached tall French doors that opened into the park. Noble old trees lined neatly laid pathways, while flower beds, fountains, and hedges softened the arrangement. Helena Lacrosse was busy with the rose bushes. She gracefully snipped off the blown blossoms and laid them in a basket. The fragrance of autumn roses filled the garden.

As the butler announced the guest, she looked up, surprised.

"Do we know each other?" she asked, her tone reserved.

Fitz bowed with the utmost politeness. "What wonderful roses," he said, instead of answering her question. "And what an idyllic picture! A beautiful woman, surrounded by fragrant blossoms. The epitome of perfection: a garden like a fairy tale and a gardener like a dream."

Helena blushed. "You flatter me, Mister . . . Fitz?"

"Patrick Fitz, yes, Miss Lacrosse. Although I'm not one to flatter. I'm rather more inclined to speak my mind." He smiled and gave her the same look that had, years before, brought Linda to his bed. Fitz understood how to make a woman feel like she was the complete center of his attention—and not just as a matter of courtesy, but because he considered her the most interesting creature in the world.

"Have we met somewhere before?" Helena asked again. "I don't believe I remember your name."

"That doesn't surprise me," Fitz said, smiling to himself. He'd taken the precaution of using a different name in case she recognized his real one. Even Robin and March might not have recognized "Joe Fitzpatrick," though; he and

Linda had divorced before either of them was born. On the other hand, it was possible that Aroha had mentioned him in her letters or that his name had come up in the family at some point. Vera might even have mentioned him to Robin. In any case, it was better to remain anonymous. "Of course, it's possible that we may have run into each other at some point," he said. "People get around, don't they? I've heard that you have traveled a great deal."

"You have?" Helena looked surprised. "Where did you hear that? Do you know someone else in the family? Robin, perhaps?" A shadow crossed her face. "Are you a friend of Robin's?" The friendliness had disappeared from her voice.

Fitz took that in swiftly. He smiled. "I am in fact here to speak with Mr. Fenroy," he explained. "However, I wouldn't call us 'friends.'"

Helena sighed. "Then it must be something about the theater, I suppose? And here I'd hoped it would be a social call. Someone I'd met in passing who was just now paying a visit. That used to happen often, you know? People used to just come by, we'd chat . . ."

"I'd be delighted to chat with you, Miss Lacrosse," Fitz assured her. "May I hold your basket?" Helena continued to clip blossoms, while Fitz carried the basket along behind her. "I can't imagine anyone who wouldn't be happy to chat with you. But you seem upset. Has something happened? Do you not receive callers anymore?"

Helena shrugged. "There was an ugly press campaign against the Lacrosse family," she told him. "At least, that's how it started. People withdrew for a while. By now we should have been able to return to the way our lives were before. But then Robin came up with this idea of the theater!"

Fitz raised his eyebrows. "You don't like the theater?" he asked. "That confounds me! Here, in this garden, I see the most beautiful setting, the very picture of a living sprite, a creature that one would wish to paint . . ."

Helena tensed. "The dignified portrait of a society lady is something quite different from posing in costume in front of an audience," she said sharply. "People from our social class—and I hope that includes you, Mr. Fitz—attend the theater and perhaps spend an evening with reputable, serious, and well-known actors. But they don't mix with mere players!"

"So people are avoiding you, Miss Lacrosse, because your relative is acting in the theater?" asked Fitz, genuinely puzzled.

Helena shook her head. "It's more Robin that's doing the avoiding. He's gone quite mad and only cares about his theater! Everything you see here, Mr. Fitz—the house, the garden, my roses—won't exist anymore. Mr. Fenroy plans to sell it all, to live more 'modestly.'"

"He's taking away your home," Fitz said. "He's cutting you off, the way one might cut a rose." He gestured toward the basket. "They are gorgeous, these blossoms. But without the garden, the bush, the earth, and the gardener's care, they will perish."

Helena nodded, surprised. "Yes! The way you put it—that's exactly how I feel! What—what was it you wanted from Robin again?" She seemed to be seized by a last trace of mistrust.

Fitz put on a serious face. Perhaps he was spoiling his prospects for a job in the theater, but he might manage to find out something about Vera Carrigan's death. After all, Helena Lacrosse had been in Rotorua at the time, and she clearly wanted to tell the truth.

"I . . . came here to ask him something. It's about a death. In Rotorua, almost three years ago. Robin Fenroy was in Rotorua then, wasn't he?"

Helena nodded bitterly. "Oh, yes. That's where it all started. I can't believe how foolish I was then! How naive! I was happy to have a new relative, and I thought he would fit into my life without a snag." She sighed. "To tell you the truth, I thought he would save me. I was as good as married. A few more chances to travel, and then I'd be stuck here, married to a man who lived for his factories—my factories! I was supposed to inherit everything, not Robin."

"And you were entitled to it," Fitz said, cautiously encouraging her.

Now she would tell him her life's story. People opened themselves up to him without reservation. Sometimes it took patience to listen, but what they revealed could prove useful. Helena now admitted what she had hoped for when she met Robin: that he would distract Walter Lacrosse. Her grandfather, who had long rued the absence of a male heir, would give him a management position in the company and eventually pass the directorship to him. If that had happened, Harold Wentworth would have left her alone and Helena would have been able to marry whomever she wanted.

"But it all went much more quickly than I'd thought it would. And at first it all seemed fine. Robin wasn't interested in the business." A smile played over Helena's face. "He turned everything over to March, and he was there for me alone. It was wonderful! He was so attentive, he went everywhere with me, was always polite, always patient. We had so many guests, and it was clear to everyone that we belonged together. I thought he would marry me."

Fitz expected to see tears in her blue eyes, but they remained dry. Helena was over her grief. Instead, her face shone with sheer anger.

"And then all of a sudden, this! A theater! A perfect stranger—an old actor—and a half-grown child with angel's curls that Robin can't take his eyes off of. The two of them have positively bewitched him! He said to my face that he didn't care for me. In front of everyone! He's going to sell the house out from under me, my accounts at the shops are closed . . . What do I need a new autumn wardrobe for, anyway? I don't go out anymore. Oh, invitations come for Robin and me, but he doesn't even read them. What am I supposed to do? Go alone? A lady attending balls and receptions without an escort? What kind of impression would that make?"

Helena had worked herself into a perfect rage as she paced around the garden. Fitz followed her with the flower basket.

"That doesn't sound like the behavior of a gentleman," Fitz said. "Least of all like a man who owes everything to you. You discovered him, you generously did without your inheritance . . ."

Helena nodded emphatically. "All of this actually belongs to me," she said bitterly.

"But getting back to Rotorua," Fitz said. "Robin Fenroy was a member of a theater company there, wasn't he?"

"If you want to call it that." Helena scowled. "A normal person would be ashamed to put on such plays. Supposedly Robin wanted to get away from it, but he didn't have any money. And he claimed there was some kind of blackmail going on too."

"So you saved him," Fitz said soothingly. Helena nodded in agreement. "But you see, that's just what I wanted to speak to him about," he improvised. "You say that he accused the owner of the company of blackmail. And then he was involved in her death. That raises questions."

"Really?" Now Helena was listening attentively. "Is Robin under investigation? By the authorities? Are you a detective or something?"

Fitz shook his head. "No. This is a matter of personal interest only. Miss Carrigan . . . she had a lot of bad luck in life. She wasn't happy with the kind of

theater she was producing either. But there was nothing left for her to do. Many people had a false impression of her."

"You mean she wasn't blackmailing Robin?" Helena asked.

"No." Fitz's tone was emphatic. "She wanted to keep him in the company. She . . . well, in a manner of speaking, she loved him."

Helena gasped. "You mean there was something between her and Robin?"

Her eyes blazed, and in them, Fitz read what she was thinking: Robin had been involved with Vera, and now he was trying to start a relationship with the half-grown child she'd mentioned. She, Helena, was the only one he had never loved.

"In any case, I'm concerned about the circumstances of her death," Fitz said, avoiding her question. "A man and a woman go out for a walk together, and only the man comes back . . . that's always a scenario that raises questions. Questions that no one in Rotorua wants to answer."

"You were in Rotorua?" Helena asked.

Fitz nodded. "The situation is very important to me," he emphasized. "What do you know about it? After all, you were there at the time. You must have heard something."

Helena nodded again, but her expression darkened. "Yes, I did. There were rumors going around, although the hotel wanted to hush it up. It was . . . an extremely ugly story. If Miss Carrigan was close to you, perhaps you'd rather not hear it." Fitz waited, confident that Helena wouldn't keep the story to herself. "She was . . . scalded to death!" the girl said, the truth bursting out of her. "Boiled alive! It must have been dreadful. She was in a hot spring, and all of a sudden a geyser shot out that must have heated the water to at least boiling. She couldn't get out in time."

Fitz swallowed hard. The thought alone made him sick. "How did she get into it in the first place?" he asked then. "Weren't they just going for a walk, she and Robin? How did she fall into a pool?"

"Supposedly, she got in of her own accord," Helena said. "We tried the springs too; the water was wonderfully warm. But after the eruption, it was forbidden. And for good reason, as Miss Carrigan's tragic death shows."

"So they blamed her for her own death?" Fitz snarled through clenched teeth.

Helena shrugged. "That's what I heard."

"And the only witness was Robin Fenroy? Who made no attempt to rescue her? And who might even have pushed her in?" His eyes now blazed as angrily as Helena's had before.

"Why would he want to do that?" Helena asked, confused.

Many motives had occurred to Fitz. It might very well have been that Vera had tormented Robin mercilessly until he snapped. Or Robin had planned it as a way to escape her clutches. Vera had likely threatened him to keep him in the company.

"That I don't know," he said more calmly. "Of course at that time, he didn't know that he'd inherit a fortune. Maybe he wanted to take over her company— he and Lockhart. Miss Carrigan's property has completely vanished. There is no clothing of hers, no jewelry, no money. Someone must have taken it. Someone profited from her death."

Helena looked up at Fitz fearfully. "I never looked at it that way," she murmured. "Will you talk to him? Will you find out the truth? I mean, if Robin actually did have something to do with her death, then—then he's dangerous . . ." Suddenly the concern vanished from Helena's eyes. "Are you thinking of avenging your friend's death?" she asked warily.

The two had circled the garden and were standing in front of the tall doors into the house. Fitz handed the basket back to Helena.

"I think," he said slowly, "that we should keep our little talk to ourselves. Perhaps we have common interests."

Helena held the door for him. "I must be sure that no innocent people are compromised," she said, without looking at him.

"I'll get back to you on that," Fitz said. "And I can only emphasize it once again. It was very stimulating speaking with you. You deserve to have your place in society restored. If there's any way I can help you . . ."

"I'll get back to you on that," Helena said with a cool smile.

Helena Lacrosse wasn't of Vera Carrigan's caliber. Still, Linda Lange would have known that it was time to worry.

# Part 7

## A MIDSUMMER NIGHT'S DREAM

### DUNEDIN (SOUTH ISLAND)

#### MAY–JUNE 1889

# Chapter 65

"I'm supposed to play a fairy? Little Peaseblossom? But Father, that's a tiny role!" It was rare that Lucille Lockhart got upset, but when Bertram announced the parts for *A Midsummer Night's Dream*, she spoke up, sounding hurt.

"What did you think? That I'd let you play Titania?" Lockhart laughed. "Child, you've never even been on a stage before!"

"I didn't mean Titania," Lucille conceded. "But why not Hermia or Helena! A few more lines than just 'Here I am!' and 'Hail, mortal!'"

"We're combining the roles of the fairies in the first scene of the second act," Robin said. "We don't have enough actors to give Titania such a large fairy court as Shakespeare envisioned."

"That way, you'll have a scene with Robin too," Bertram remarked. "It was his idea to combine the roles."

The fifteen other members of the cast laughed as both Robin and Lucille blushed. But it was kind laughter. So far, the atmosphere in the Globe Theatre's provisory rehearsal room had been relaxed. Bertram and Robin had hired young actors almost exclusively; only one had more than a few years of stage experience: Martha Grey. Like Bertram, she was very good, but too old to play the young heroines.

"I don't want to cast thirty-five-year-olds as Juliet," Bertram had said at his first meeting with Robin about the future theater. "Or fifty-year-olds as Hamlet. It's always said that one needs a certain amount of maturity to embody these roles, and if it's done right, the audience won't even notice the actor's age. But I think that's nonsense. According to Shakespeare, Juliet is fourteen. In the original, she was played by a boy before his voice broke. He can't have been very mature. And Hamlet . . . maybe he's eighteen, twenty at the most. Tragic, yes, but mature? In any case, I prefer young actors. You will play the biggest roles, Robin, after you've had time to build up to them. We'll organize the season to begin with plays like *Macbeth* in which the main roles can be older, and we'll start you and Lucille and the other young actors with supporting roles."

Robin had agreed enthusiastically, and he had requested *A Midsummer Night's Dream* for the grand opening. Bertram would play Oberon, Martha Grey would play Titania, and Robin would be Puck. It was one of his greatest dreams come true, and the younger actors were also satisfied with their roles. Only Lucille was disappointed. The part of the fairy Peaseblossom was hardly worth mentioning, even if she now had a few additional lines.

"It's also because I can't favor you above the others," Bertram told her later when they were sitting with Robin in March's improvised office. "Neither the critics nor other cast members should be able to say you only get the good roles because you're the director's daughter. You also shouldn't get parts because you're 'cute.'" He cast a sharp glance sideward at March, who was sitting at her desk engrossed in work. She had also suggested thrusting Lucille into a big role. *Romeo and Juliet* with Robin and Lucille would have made the theater famous right away. March didn't care whether the critics huffed about favoritism—audiences would have flocked to the performances. "The only reason anyone gets a part here is because they are right for it," Bertram continued, "and because they are ready. You will make a charming fairy, my dear."

"Besides, you'll get to fly," Robin added. "That will surely be fun."

The flight of the fairies in Titania's court would be a triumph of stagecraft, and it was an innovation that March had insisted on including. As before, the young woman thought Shakespeare was boring, especially if the actors spoke their lines in front of simple, immobile sets. A few fireworks, booms, and sizzles when a ship capsized in a storm, flexible sets among which the actors could move as though in real life, and a turntable that allowed for quick position changes made a play much more exciting for the audience. Clever lighting could help as well. For the first time in Dunedin, the audience would be in complete darkness as soon as the play began, while the stage glowed in the light of a complicated construction of gas spotlights. There was even an orchestra pit.

Bertram Lockhart thought all of that was unnecessary. In his opinion, the talent of the actors should be enough to captivate the audience. But Robin, after some initial doubts, was thrilled by the possibilities that the theater offered.

March had also found the ideal man to realize her visions, a young carpenter named Josh Haydon. Just like Robin, Josh had fallen in love with the theater when he'd attended his first performance. But instead of being attracted by the spotlight, his interest was backstage. He had a thousand ideas about how to enchant the audience. Hoists and pulleys were now being installed in the drawing loft at his behest, and there were new lighting bridges and winches. With the help of these installations, the four fairies—Peaseblossom, Cobweb, Moth, and Mustardseed—would be able to float in spectacularly when Titania called them.

"Whatever you do, don't let the girls fall," Bertram said. "What about the other stagehands? Has anyone applied for the job? We have enough people to build the sets, now we need some who are prepared to push them around."

It was easy for Fitz to get a job at the theater. March and Josh Haydon, who were doing the job interviews, were actually quite impressed by his skill and experience. He told them that he'd worked in a theater in Auckland years ago, and supported his claims by tossing around theater terms. Haydon let him begin right away. The renovation work in the building was practically finished, and now all that was left to do was the decoration and installing the seating and stage equipment.

"If we do it together, you'll know just as well as I do how everything works, and you'll be able to step in if I'm ever unavailable," Haydon said. He was impressed by how quickly Fitz comprehended the technical aspects of the equipment. Haydon showed him the main cables that were used to move the sets with the manual counterhoists, as well as how to install them. He also explained the purpose of the counterweights.

"For the below-stage area, I came up with something special," Haydon continued. "You can lower parts of the stage into the floor. It's very easy. We're going to have spectacular shows here!"

As Fitz was introduced to the stage technology, he got to know Robin, who was more interested in it than the other actors were.

"After all, it's my theater," he said cheerfully. "I want to know how everything works."

Fitz discovered that he didn't share Vera's opinion of the young man. In her letters, Vera had described Robin as weak willed, shy, and indecisive, and she had sometimes made fun of his contemplative ways. If that had been the truth—and actually, Fitz didn't doubt Vera's judgment—then Robin must have changed. Was it because of his sudden wealth? Or had something happened to him even before Vera died? Had he discovered his courage and freed himself from his chains in a drastic manner? Of course, that applied to Bertram Lockhart as well, who, according to Vera's letters, had been a drunkard and a wreck, whereas now he ordered around young actors with self-assurance.

During the next few weeks, Fitz had plenty of time to think about it as the first sets arrived and the rows of seats had to be installed. He helped energetically with everything, and observed Robin as well as Bertram and his daughter during their rehearsals. He was impressed with all three, but that couldn't make him forgive them. To the contrary. Hadn't their perfect collaboration only been made possible through Vera's death? Now Fitz felt a stab of jealousy. Robin, Bertram, and Lucille would enjoy success and admiration, while he himself slaved away in a subordinate job and Vera burned in hell. He still didn't know if Robin had anything to do with her death, but he knew exactly what Vera would have advised him to do in the current situation. Helena Lacrosse regretted having helped Robin claim his inheritance. If Fitz helped her to get things back to the way they had been before, she would be grateful. If Robin were to have an accident, for example . . . Fitz was convinced that he could get a few thousand pounds out of it, if he played Helena right. Vera, ever unscrupulous, wouldn't have hesitated for a second.

For himself, he could justify revenge. Revenge for Vera's murder would fill him with pride and make him a little more able to accept her death. The deed would finally ease the anger that had been simmering inside him since he'd lost Vera. Murder itself, however, was something else entirely. Fitz had never taken the law very seriously, but to kill an innocent man in cold blood for someone's financial benefit? At first, Fitz couldn't convince himself to make serious plans, which was why he hadn't sought out Helena again. Instead, he was watching and waiting—a strategy that wore him out because it inflamed his anger. However, his patience would soon pay off.

Fitz was painting the decorative molding on the wall of the auditorium with red and gold paint when a young woman entered the theater. She was very slender, and wore a simple but elegant blue dress with a darker blue jacket over it. Her smoothly pinned-up blonde hair was adorned with a small matching blue hat, decorated with a bit of tulle. The young woman gave the impression of being a well-off servant or a teacher, harmless and boring. Her face was quite pretty, and her calm, violet-blue eyes glowed as she watched the actors rehearsing on the stage. She slowly made her way down the center aisle to the front row, and Fitz was about to say something when Robin Fenroy noticed her. He waved cheerfully, but finished speaking his lines before he interrupted the rehearsal and jumped down from the stage to greet her.

"Leah!" Robin reached out both hands to his visitor. "How wonderful that you stopped by! Why didn't you come sooner?"

"I didn't want to scare you," the young woman said with a mischievous smile. "Otherwise you might have thought that I was trying to get a part."

The two of them were still holding hands and smiling at each other. They weren't in love—at least not anymore. Fitz sensed that, at least on Robin's side, there had once been a little interest—but now the two were very familiar, almost conspiratorial.

All at once, Fitz remembered: Leah! The third member of the Carrigan Company. Fitz edged nearer to listen.

"Even if you had, that hardly would have terrified me," Robin said. "Though our esteemed director might not have granted you one." They both smiled.

"Bertram knows I don't have any talent," Leah said. "And being onstage was never any fun for me either. I'm much happier in the day nursery. I wanted to thank you for the job, too, Robin. It's so wonderful to see how the children are blossoming! Also, the mothers are so much happier now that they know their little ones are well taken care of and they can see them during every break."

"Oh, right, you're in charge of the nursery in the dressmakers' workshop!" Robin said, remembering. "Don't thank me, thank March. She recommended you for the job, didn't she?"

Leah nodded happily. "It's all so wonderful! Mr. Mint, the new plant manager, is very pleasant. He's strict, he has to be, but he's good-hearted, and he consults the reverend if something is wrong. And Peta . . ." She broke into a wide grin. "He asked me to marry him."

Robin beamed right back. "I'm so happy for you. Come now, I'll show you the theater. Of course, I sent you tickets for the grand opening, but it's nicer like this. You can take off your coat, by the way. The entire house is heated. It wouldn't work any other way. Otherwise the fairies would freeze, and the women in the audience wouldn't be able to wear silk evening gowns."

He helped Leah out of her mantilla, and Fitz seized his chance.

"May I bring this to the cloakroom for you, madam?"

He had barely finished speaking when he noticed something. A silver brooch was gleaming on Leah's dress, in the shape of a flying swallow.

Fitz gritted his teeth. He remembered the day he'd bought that brooch. After the episode with the military settlers, he and Vera had gone to Auckland together. He'd gotten a job in the theater, and Vera had ensnared actor John Hollander. After a while, she'd moved into the apartment that Hollander bought for her, and Fitz had made his way to the South Island. He had intended to return to Rata Station, the farm that belonged to his wife, Linda. Fitz had planned to find some kind of advantage for himself, perhaps to make up with Linda or acquire part of the farm in a divorce. In the end, it hadn't worked. But in any case, when he'd bought the brooch, he had assumed that he would be separated from Vera for at least a few years. "I'll fly away, but I'll be back," he'd said, and of course she had made fun of his sentimentality. "I don't need any bauble to remember you by," she'd replied. "You are unforgettable, Fitz." Fitz didn't know if Vera had ever worn it, but it was enough for him that she'd kept it. And now it was on that little trollop's dress!

Robin noticed the brooch at almost the same moment as Fitz.

"Did you . . . keep everything?" he asked, pointing to the piece of jewelry. "All of her things?"

Leah shook her head. "No, only this brooch. I sold everything else. This isn't worth very much, but it's pretty. The other pieces were much too flashy for me."

Robin smiled crookedly. "Miss Carrigan didn't have the most refined taste," he remarked.

He accompanied Leah to the stage. Fitz dropped Leah's jacket on one of the seats and followed them. He didn't want to miss a word.

"Do you ever think about her?" Leah asked softly.

Robin nodded. "She haunts my dreams. Her death . . . I keep hearing her screams."

Robin opened a door for her that led into the stairwell and finally out to the stage. Fitz couldn't follow; it would have been too obvious. He waited impatiently until they reached the backstage area and found a place where he could eavesdrop again.

"At first, I was mad at you," Leah was saying as Fitz ducked behind a girder. She was sitting on a stool that had been made to look like a tree stump, and Robin was leaning against a "tree." "Even though of course I knew that you couldn't do anything . . . I know how she was . . . she could make anyone furious. In the meantime, I think that, as terrible as her death was, it was basically a good thing. She got what she deserved. Don't torture yourself for it, Robin."

Robin shook his head. "I don't. I don't regret anything either. It's just not easy to forget. There are just certain images that don't go out of one's head so easily."

Joe Fitzpatrick clenched his fists. So, Robin Fenroy had had something to do with Vera's death. And before Fitz obliterated all of the boy's memories once and for all, he would force him to admit exactly what he had done. For now, this was enough. All of them, Robin, Bertram, and Leah, had profited from Vera's death. And they would all pay for it! Robin Fenroy would be the first to go to hell.

As soon as he was sure that all members of the company were in the theater, Fitz went to find Helena.

"We have to meet very soon, somewhere discreet," he said once the butler had stepped away. "I don't want to be seen here, and above all not in front of Fenroy, Lockhart, or Jensch. But there are things we have to talk about. It won't have any effect on the innocent."

"It will look like an accident," Fitz assured her, when he saw her early in the evening of the next day. "With a little luck, it might even *be* an accident. I'll sabotage the rigging system that Robin's little girlfriend is using to fly like a fairy. He must have told you about that, right? It's a spectacular entrance. The fairies float in over the audience and land in front of Titania. It all works with ropes and cables. One day, Lucille Lockhart's flight will stop over the orchestra pit, and part of her harness will break. Then she'll be hanging about fifty feet up, and won't be able to go forward or back. Robin will climb down the cable and attempt to free her. Perhaps he'll fall himself and break his neck. If not, the cable will break and both he and the girl will fall into the orchestra pit."

Helena considered this for a moment. "But what if he falls and doesn't die?" she asked matter-of-factly.

Fitz was impressed by her callousness. He had pegged her as being much more fearful. And she had chosen an excellent location for their meeting—a coffeehouse in the Devil's Half Acre—as well as excellent camouflage. Helena was wearing a simple dress that she could easily have been mistaken for a factory worker in. She told him that she'd bought it for her brief stint volunteering with the day-care center at St. Andrew's. Her fine blonde hair was hidden by a scarf. No one would recognize Fitz either. He lived in a furnished room near the theater, quite far from St. Andrew's. No one in the Devil's Half Acre had ever seen him before.

"Then unfortunately, there will be another accident," Fitz said. "The cable will tear down one of the big gas lamps, and there will be a fire."

"But the others would put it out," Helena said. "Aren't there four fairies that fly in? And why would Robin be above the stage instead of on it?"

Fitz smiled condescendingly. "Robin and Lucille will be alone in the theater that afternoon or evening. With me, of course, but they'll only realize that when it's too late. And of course I'll make preparations. The equipment will be a little out of kilter the day before, so it will make plenty of sense to try it out again before the show. But it's not a sure thing. If they don't test the rigging system, then I'll put everything back the way it was and come up with a new plan."

Helena frowned. "I'm going to Australia soon, and the others will be moving into a house near the theater," she said. "We found a buyer for the house in Mornington. Time is pressing, Mr. Fitz."

Fitz shrugged. "I can't do much about that. This is a game, Miss Helena. And believe me, I know how to play it very well!"

# Chapter 66

Robin gazed down from the lighting bridge and enjoyed the view of his theater. The next day, it would awaken to life. The premiere had been widely announced, in style, and over ninety percent of the tickets had been sold. The new theater with its modern equipment had been the talk of the town since March had given Mr. Spragg, the intrepid reporter from the *Otago Daily Times*, a tour. Robin could hardly wait for the performance. Most of the members of his family would be sitting in the first row! His parents and Carol, Jane and Te Haitara, and even Mara and Eru were expected to arrive the following morning. Aroha and Linda were surely already in Dunedin; they'd been coming by ship from the North Island. Franz and Bao weren't with them. So soon before the winter vacation, there was much to do in the school in Otaki, and the hotel in Rotorua was surprisingly well booked for the time of year. Someone had to be on duty. Robin thought with amusement that Aroha would have probably preferred to have it the other way around—Bao was much fonder of Shakespeare than she. But Aroha couldn't miss Robin's first performance in his own theater, nor a chance to see her mother and grandmother again. Robin had planned to pick her up at the harbor, but then he'd found a message from Lucille in his room that worried him. The girl had never written to him before.

*Dear Robin,* it said in her girlish handwriting.

> *I'm a little bit scared about the flight of the fairies tomorrow during the premiere. The rigging didn't work at all well today. It kept catching in a strange way. Mr. Haydon is going to check it, but I'd be much happier if I could rehearse the flight one last time. Will you meet me in the theater at six? Please? Lucille.*

Her letter had set a flood of emotions through him. Lucille wanted to see him. At the theater. Alone! Of course he would meet her, but he found the problems with the rigging hard to believe. No, she must have been using it as an excuse, at least partly. Lucille was longing to be alone with him just as much as he wanted to be with her. Robin's heart pounded as he thought about her stepping onto the stage, looking around for him, and smiling when he spoke to her. He imagined her delicate form in front of him, her sea of fine brunette curls, and her gentle, gold-flecked eyes.

And now, as Lucille appeared on the stage below him, he pointed a spotlight at her and laughed when she started in surprise. But she composed herself immediately, and like the born actress she was, began to enjoy herself right away. She spun around, smiled, and played with the effects of light and shadow. She had left her coat in the dressing room and was wearing a reform dress, as most of the actresses preferred to do during rehearsals. She had tied up her hair in a ponytail and looked like a fairy in the magical forest set up on the stage. The shadows of trees and flowers danced around her.

"Lucille!" Robin called.

The girl gazed up at him with a gleam of mischief in her eye. *"What's in a name?"* she recited. *"That which we call a rose, by any other name would smell as sweet. Romeo, doff thy name, and for that name which is no part of thee, take all myself."*

Robin smiled. *"I take thee at thy word. Call me but love, and I'll be new baptized. Henceforth I never will be Romeo."*

"That would be a pity!" Lucille said. "I'd so love to play it with you someday."

"Then you'll have to be up here on the balcony, and I below in the garden," Robin replied. "Now, come up. You wanted to practice flying again."

Lucille disappeared into the stairwell and then climbed up the ladder that led from the rigging loft to the light bridge.

"Did I?" She sounded just as enchanted as Robin had felt before she'd arrived on the magical-looking set. "What gave you that idea?"

Robin's brow creased. "You wrote to me." He handed her the precious letter.

Lucille read it with a puzzled expression, and then pulled a letter out of her pocket. *My dearest Lucille,* it said in clearly masculine handwriting, although not Robin's own.

*I know it sounds foolish, but in certain ways, Puck is also a fool, and perhaps I'm feeling the role a little too strongly. Perhaps I'm already enchanted, like the forest where I will meet the most beautiful of Titania's fairies. Lucille, I fear words will fail me when I greet you on the stage tomorrow. The sight of you will paralyze me, the way it has done since I saw you for the first time. Then everyone will laugh at me, and your father will chastise me, and I will be the laughingstock of the theater. You don't want that to happen, Lucille. So if you have pity on me, if you wish to show me mercy, then please meet me alone in the theater. Let me see you without the distraction of the others for once, let me hear Shakespeare's words from your lips again, so I can gather the courage to speak my own. I realize my request is presumptuous. Would you consider it, nonetheless? At the theater, at six o'clock? Robin.*

Robin blushed as he read the words.

"A beautiful letter," Lucille said devoutly. "As though it was written by the poet himself."

"Except it's not from me," Robin admitted. "And it's also a little . . . pompous."

Lucille frowned and looked back to the letter. "So you would have preferred it if I hadn't come?"

"No!" Robin yelped. "I—I'm happy . . . I mean . . . I just wonder . . . who wrote these letters, Lucille?"

Lucille shrugged. "Well, I'd guess Frederic and Marian. They're both pranksters."

Frederic and Marian were both younger members of the company, and they were playing Lysander and Hermia.

"A prank? You mean they wanted to make fun of us?" Robin glanced around suspiciously, as though he were afraid that the rest of the ensemble were about to leap out from behind the set, howling with laughter.

Lucille smiled indulgently. "What else? Maybe someone wanted to . . . bring us together."

Robin smiled back. "Whoever it was, they managed it. We're both here."

Lucille nodded seriously, although her eyes flashed. "And now? Would you really like to go through your lines again?"

"If I didn't want to, but would prefer . . . to kiss you, would you want to fly away?" Robin asked.

Lucille raised her face to his, her lips parted slightly. "Of course not," she whispered.

Fitz watched impatiently as Robin gently took her in his arms and kissed her. This could take some time, especially if it escalated. Fortunately, he thought Lucille was too innocent, and Robin too much of a prude. The delay was annoying, but it couldn't be changed. He had considered formulating Robin's letter to Lucille a little less explicitly, but he couldn't think of any other halfway believable reason for him to ask the girl to come to the theater. Well, at least he'd made them happy one last time. They should be grateful to him and Helena. Helena had written Lucille's letter.

So far, everything had gone smoothly, aside from one small thing. Fitz had seen Linda Lange at the harbor when he left his boardinghouse to go to the theater. His ex-wife had stared at him in disbelief, and then gotten into a hackney cab. Now he didn't know if she'd actually recognized him, and that bothered him. He would have preferred to get all this over with quickly.

Linda Lange wasn't sure if the man she'd seen on the pier was really Fitz. After all, she hadn't seen him for over twenty years. During the crossing to the South Island, however, she had talked to Aroha about him constantly. For that reason, she thought it was more likely that she'd mistaken someone else for him than that he was actually there, and she didn't say anything about the encounter to her daughter, who was already sitting in the cab. The young woman had felt ill during the crossing, and seemed exhausted even now. Linda thought it made more sense not to burden her, and felt justified when Aroha immediately excused herself upon arrival at the house in Mornington.

"Mama, do you mind if I go rest a little?" she asked with a weak smile. The butler had assured her that she could use the same room she'd shared with Bao several months before. She was surprised that Mr. Simmons was still working there. March had suggested that in the future, he should take over the management of the catering, coat check, and cleaning services at the theater, and he had seemed to feel quite honored by the offer. But he had respectfully told Aroha that, before the house in Mornington was sold, he didn't want to change jobs. He couldn't leave the house before its owners did.

"I'll show you around later," Aroha told her mother, who was gazing with just as much surprise at the inside of the Lacrosse house as she had at its façade.

At that moment, March walked into the entrance hall, ready to go out. She greeted Aroha cheerfully, and Linda politely. She hadn't seen Linda for years, and had to laugh when Linda actually remarked how big March had gotten. The older woman's eyes crinkled with amusement.

"Would you please show my mother the house?" Aroha asked as Linda was remarking on the luxurious atmosphere. "I'm not feeling very well, I'd like to lie down for a while."

March glanced at the huge ornamented wall clock.

"If it doesn't take too long. I have to go to the vintner. Simmons says the owner still hasn't delivered the champagne. He already bothered him about it once, but it would be best if I checked up on it myself. A premiere without champagne would be a catastrophe, after all." She smiled at Aroha and made a gesture of welcome to Linda. "Come with me, madam," she said, imitating the voice of a bored travel guide. "We will begin our little tour with the salons, where family gatherings take place, although at least fifteen children with their in-laws and grandchildren must be present in order to make it worthwhile to heat such large rooms."

As Aroha withdrew with a sigh of relief, Linda followed March through the salons, the ladies' and gentlemen's rooms, the library, and the garden. Like Robin, Cat, Aroha, and Bao, she was amazed at the scale of the rooms, the elaborate chandeliers, the thick carpets, and the heavy furniture. She was especially interested in the weapons cabinet. She peered curiously through the glass at the guns laid out on shelves.

"Such elegant hunting weapons," she said. "Did they belong to old Lacrosse? Or does Robin shoot clay pigeons?"

March laughed. "Robin buries himself like a kiwi as soon as he hears a shot," she said impertinently. "He's a vegetarian, you know, and he cries even when a sheep is shorn. They were Lacrosse's, but no one uses them. Helena can't shoot either, and even if she could, I wouldn't know what for. So far, I've never even seen a rabbit around here."

"Perhaps Mr. Lacrosse went hunting somewhere else," Linda said.

March shrugged. "Either that, or he just liked the way they looked. But they work perfectly. If you'd like one, take your pick. They're going to be sold anyway, and Robin will hardly be getting any poorer if one fewer goes up for auction."

Linda was very interested. "I'd like to trade my ancient fowling piece for one of these nicer models. But not without asking Robin," she said. "Are all the things here actually going to be auctioned off? The furniture and the silver?"

March nodded. "Some of the furniture has already been moved. Robin furnished his new home with a few of the simpler pieces, and generously allowed the Lockharts to help themselves so they can set up the pretty house in George Street they're moving into next week. And of course, Helena is allowed to keep her favorite pieces. It won't be difficult to organize their transportation to Australia. But she hasn't shown any interest in making choices."

"Where is Helena, anyway?" Linda asked, paging through an elegant tome from the library. "I was looking forward to finally getting to know my cousin."

March frowned. "I don't think she's thrilled about getting to know any more relatives," she said. "Not to say that she wishes that the ones she already knows would die of the plague. When the house was successfully sold, she threw a tantrum, and now she's sulking. She hardly ever leaves her room. When she does, it's only to complain that there aren't enough servants here anymore to serve her around the clock. But she's going to have to get used to that. We're keeping almost all of the house staff busy at the theater. No one was fired, and I need their help to prepare for the premiere. Of course, Helena doesn't understand that. We'll all be happy when she's on her way to Australia, but actually, she doesn't even want to go there. She just can't think of any alternative, even though Robin is prepared to be generous with her. If she wanted to start a business or something like that, he would finance it, even if it wasn't profitable. But she doesn't want that. If you ask me, she simply doesn't know what she wants."

"That's sad," Linda said.

"She just gets on my nerves," March admitted. "So, any other questions, or shall I take care of the champagne now?" The two of them had just reached the grand entrance hall again.

"Where is the famous portrait hanging?" Linda asked. "The picture of Suzanne, who apparently looks so much like Robin. Did Robin take it already?"

March laughed. "Robin? He only looked at it once. And Cat didn't have it sent to Rata Station, even though she inherited it. It's hanging over there; I thought you'd seen it," she said, pointing.

Linda stepped closer to examine the painting. "So it is. I missed it somehow. But I have the feeling I haven't been seeing straight all day. Before, at the harbor, I thought I saw Fitz."

"How do you know Fitz?" March asked. "Were you already at the theater?"

Linda spun around in alarm. "I was married to Joe Fitzpatrick! The question is, rather, how do you know him?"

March, who was already on her way out, stopped short. Her brow creased. "Fitz . . . Patrick Fitz. He's our stagehand. Very useful fellow. We're happy to have found him." She had a quizzical expression on her face. "The similarity of the name is rather strange, however."

"More than strange! This can't be a coincidence." Linda shook her head. "What does he look like? Rather short, dark hair, bright-blue eyes?"

March nodded, now looking concerned. "Eyes like Aroha's. You're right, that's why he always seemed a little familiar to me! We have to talk about this, and with Bertram and Robin too. But I really have to go see about the champagne. I'll be as quick as I can, and we'll see each other this evening."

Linda bit her lip. She couldn't wait until evening before she spoke to someone about Joe Fitzpatrick.

"Where is Aroha's room?" she asked.

Linda didn't take the time to admire Aroha's elegant suite and the canopy bed where her daughter was stretched out in her shift.

"Are you feeling better?" she asked.

Aroha nodded, smiling. "It's nothing serious. It's just that I can't take all that rocking on the ship right now," she said, stroking her belly.

"You're pregnant? And you're only telling me this now?" A look of delighted wonder crossed Linda's features. "That's marvelous, my dear! I'm truly happy!" she said. But Linda's joy quickly gave way to worry. "Aroha, I saw your father in the harbor before. I didn't say anything, because I thought I'd been mistaken, but March just told me that she hired a 'Patrick Fitz' as a stagehand. The description matches. Can you make sense of any of this?"

Linda was very uneasy, but she hadn't expected Aroha's dramatic reaction.

"I'm afraid so, yes!" she said, jumping to her feet and reaching for her clothes. "I didn't want to upset you or make Fitz look bad, so I let you believe that he came to Rotorua to look for me. But actually, he was looking for Vera Carrigan. When he heard that she was dead, he asked questions that no one wanted to answer. After all, it was a horrible story and not exactly an advertisement for our hot springs. Fitz did find out that Robin was a witness to the accident—and I think he was trying to figure out if Robin had something to do with her death. But then he gave up—"

"Because he found you, and because he got distracted by the job at the hotel," Linda said. "But then he remembered again, and showed up here using a false name."

Aroha nodded fearfully and turned her back so Linda could help button the dress. "We have to warn Robin, and have a word with Fitz. Perhaps he really just wanted a job as a stagehand, but I don't know."

"No," Linda said. "There are too many coincidences. Where is Robin now?"


Robin and Lucille were lying next to each other on the lighting bridge, but were much too busy to find their position uncomfortable. Robin had pulled Lucille's dress off her shoulders and was delicately kissing the tops of her breasts. In whispers, he told her how soft her skin was and how sweet she smelled. Lucille stroked his hair and his neck, and whispered compliments back to him. She was excited, and her breath was coming faster. Before Robin could bare her breasts completely, she carefully pushed him away.

"Slowly," she said. "I—I don't want to yet . . . I mean, not everything. I need a little time."

Robin nodded, kissed her shoulders, and then tidied her dress.

"We have endless time," he said, and pulled her head against his shoulder, burying his face in the fullness of her silky hair. "I will never do anything you don't want me to. Everything that happens should be perfect. I love you, Lucille Lockhart. Like Romeo loved Juliet. Only now do I understand that completely. I would die for you . . ."

*Then get on with it!* Fitz thought. He was on pins and needles. Robin and Lucille had been at it for over an hour, and it wasn't at all clear that they'd have the theater to themselves for much longer. Sure, Bertram had given the actors the afternoon off, but it was entirely possible that Josh Haydon might get the idea to come test the stage equipment one more time, or the overzealous March would inspect the kitchen again. By this time, Fitz had wanted to be long since headed back to the inn. Or even better, already safe in his room. He hadn't been seen leaving. The landlady had only noticed that he'd gone to his room at noon. If he could slip back in just as secretively, he would have a decent alibi.

"Don't be so dismal," Lucille said with a laugh. "I'd much rather live with you! And act with you. It will be wonderful. We'll bring all the greatest plays to the stage. We'll be famous."

"Everyone will say how beautiful you are," Robin said.

"And how well you act!" Lucille replied. "We'll go on tour sometime, won't we? I want to see the world. You and I with the Robin Fenroy Company."

"The Lucille Lockhart Company!" Robin countered.

"The Lucille Fenroy Company?" Lucille asked coquettishly.

"Is that a marriage proposal?" Robin inquired.

"*Thou know'st the mask of night is on my face, else would a maiden blush bepaint my cheek,*" Lucille recited. "*In truth, fair Montague, I am too fond, and therefore thou mayst think my 'havior light . . .*"

Robin laughed. "*Lady, by yonder blessed moon I vow, that tips with silver all these fruit-tree tops—*"

"*O, swear not by the moon, th' inconstant moon, that monthly changes in her circle orb . . .*"

Fitz rolled his eyes. It was going to take time. The two of them doubtlessly knew the entire play by heart. He was close to abandoning his efforts when Robin sat up.

"Lucille, I've never been so happy," he told the girl. "But we have to get moving. Aroha and Linda must have arrived at the house already; they'll be waiting for us. And your father will wonder where you are. We could announce our engagement . . ."

"I'd rather not," Lucille said, startled. "Not—not before Helena has left. Lately she's been glaring at me as though . . . Well, she surely suspects something between us. And she hates me."

"No one could hate you," Robin said, and kissed her again. "I just mean we should go home now. Or do you want to practice the flying scene one more time? Josh told me that he'd checked the pulleys again because something was jamming them yesterday, but maybe we should really run through it one last time. Just so Titania's fairies don't get stuck in midair."

Lucille giggled. "The reporters would love that! I can just see the headline: 'A Midsummer Nightmare.' Fine, let me fly. Though, honestly, I don't need the wires. I've been flying the entire time!" She gazed at Robin with her eyes aglow, and kissed him again.

Fitz trembled with excitement. He would finally get his revenge. They were going to do it.

Robin carefully placed the harness around Lucille's slender body and pains-takingly fastened the buckles. Then he fastened the harness to an inconspicuous cable, which was connected by a pulley to another over the orchestra pit and stage. He went to the winch so he could lower Lucille slowly after she'd com-pleted the circuit over the orchestra pit. It was supposed to look as though the fairies were gliding smoothly back to the ground. The cable was a little loose, but its tension was adjustable with a pulley tackle. Robin checked to make sure it was properly connected, and then waved to Lucille. She floated briefly over the auditorium in a gentle arc, and then arrived at the orchestra pit. There, she was quite far above the floor. Lucille smiled down toward the stage, as though Titania was already expecting her. All at once, her flight came to a halt.

"I'm stuck, Robin." Her voice didn't sound nervous, and she wasn't kicking in the air either as Fitz peered out from his hiding place. The girl seemed to have complete faith in the mechanics, and apparently no fear of heights.

"Wiggle around a little," Robin advised. "Perhaps the rollers are jammed, or the cable has a rough spot. If you can get over it, you'll probably start moving again. Damn it! We'll have to fix that."

Lucille began to swing back and forth, and then she shook her cable.

Fitz watched her nervously. Her harness would have to come apart soon, or his plan wouldn't work. If the situation didn't get more dramatic, Robin wouldn't try to climb down to her. Fitz began to have doubts about his plan again. But then, after another powerful shake, Lucille cried out. The harness around her hips came loose. She was hanging only by the shoulder straps. She clung to them fearfully.

"That's enough, I'll lower you now," Robin said. "Don't be scared, I'll have you down in a minute." He began to work the winch again, but that too turned out to be blocked. A skilled craftsman like Josh Haydon would have worked out very quickly how to release it, but Robin panicked. "Wait, hold on tight, I'm coming!" he cried, looking around hectically and finally reaching for a rope that was hanging in a coil on the wall. Apparently, he was planning to take it with him. "I'll come to you, and then we can slide down on the rope."

"Just be careful," Lucille shouted. "Can't you just toss the rope to me?"

Fitz clenched his teeth. That was a weakness in his plan. If Robin did that, Lucille would get down by herself. But Robin shook his head.

"You might not be able to catch it. No, just hold on, I'm coming."

"Does anyone know where Robin is?"

Linda and Aroha rushed through all the rooms of the house. Finally, they found Mr. Simmons and two of the maids. They were packing valuable crystal glasses in carefully cushioned crates.

"Mr. Robin is at the theater," the butler replied, allowing himself a smile. "With young Lucille. She requested an extra rehearsal. Something about the performance was unclear."

"Oh, really?" Jean, one of the maids, paused in surprise. "Well, she told me that *he'd* asked *her* to meet him. She was terribly excited. Such a sweet thing, I can absolutely understand Mr. Robin—"

"Watch your tongue," Mr. Simmons scolded. "Please, a little more discretion for your employer, Joan."

Joan blushed, looking chastised, but Linda shook her head.

"No, please keep talking, Joan," Linda said. "What do you mean, you can understand Robin, and why was Lucille so excited that he wanted an extra rehearsal?"

Joan's blush deepened. "Well, because it wasn't a rehearsal. He expressed himself rather romantically, and pretended they had to go over the lines again."

"Were you spying on them?" Mr. Simmons asked indignantly.

Joan shook her head quickly. "No! She gave me the letter to read. I—well, I help her dress, so I'm fairly close to Miss Lucille. Please forgive me, Mr. Simmons, I—"

"It doesn't matter, it's all right. Now, stop apologizing," Linda said, interrupting her. "So Robin wrote Lucille a love letter?"

Joan nodded shyly.

"As far as I know, it was Mr. Robin who received a letter," Simmons remarked stiffly. "A note. He found it in his room, and then told me that he was off to the theater. He asked me to please excuse him, Miss Aroha, Mrs. Lange. He will be back in time for dinner."

Mother and daughter exchanged urgent glances.

"Is anyone else at the theater right now?" Aroha asked.

Mr. Simmons shrugged. "Perhaps, depending what rehearsals have been planned—"

"Of course not," Joan said, risking another scolding for interrupting Mr. Simmons. "That's why Miss Lucille was so excited. Mr. Robin wanted to be alone with her."

Aroha rubbed her temples. "Please have the carriage prepared for us, Mr. Simmons. Or no, stop a hansom cab, it will be faster. We must get to the theater as quickly as possible!"

Linda was already headed toward the study. She walked directly to the weapons cabinet. "Unlock it," she said curtly to Mr. Simmons. The butler gave her a look of confusion. When he didn't react immediately, she raised a chair and smashed the glass with it. Then she reached for one of the guns and handed another to Aroha. "Hurry! I just hope we aren't too late!"


Fitz adjusted the position of the gas lamp a little and stepped into the light. Robin and Lucille were also surrounded by the glow. Robin blinked in the brightness and called for help.

"Who's there?" Robin had to twist his neck to look up. Then he saw Fitz, and the relief in his voice was clear. "Come, quickly, you must help us!"

"I must?" Fitz asked, leaning over the rail of the lighting bridge. "Like you helped *her*?" His voice was a threat.

"Helped who?" Robin asked.

"Now, don't act like that. You admitted it to little Leah. And now I really want to know. What happened between you and Vera? What did you do to her?"

Fitz went to the anchor of the cable, and began to work the pulley tackle that would tighten or loosen it.

"Vera Carrigan?" Robin asked, bewildered.

"Exactly." Fitz released the cable from its mount, only holding it in position with the winch. "You were there when she died. You killed her."

"You're mad!" Robin cried. "I didn't touch her. Vera got in the spring because she wanted to. I warned her, but she wouldn't listen. She was trying to provoke the spirits, and then the geyser erupted—"

"I don't believe a single word," Fitz said coldly. "You wanted to leave the company, but you were too weak, so you killed her instead." He stared down contemptuously as Robin desperately continued to work his way along the cable toward Lucille. "And I'll get the others too! The ones who profited from her death; the ones who wear her jewelry and stole her theater."

"You're mad!" Robin repeated.

Fitz let go of the winch, and the two young actors rushed toward the floor. Fitz hoped Robin would lose his grip and fall backward into the orchestra pit. But he clung to the cable with courage and strength born of desperation when Lucille began to scream. He didn't let go when the cable jerked to a halt either. He didn't hit the floor of the orchestra pit, but remained hanging a good five yards above it. Lucille's fall was stopped only about a yard above the floor. The girl clung to the safety harness and sobbed hysterically. In her distress, she didn't immediately think about loosening the shoulder straps and just letting herself fall.

Robin, however, kept his cool. Fitz watched in disgust as he continued along the cable toward Lucille. If he could reach the line she was hanging from, he could slide down it and get her to safety.

Fitz didn't think for long. The gas lantern was the only solution before Robin had his feet on the ground again. The fire would spread quickly in the orchestra pit full of velvet-upholstered chairs and wooden music stands. A cellist and a harpist had left their instruments there as well. Fitz was hoping for an explosion when the huge lamp hit the floor.

In a desperate rush, he began to pry it from its mount, only to reel in shock as a shot rang through the theater.

"Hands off!"

Fitz turned in surprise, looking directly into the eyes of his ex-wife. She had a hunting rifle trained on him.

"Don't you dare move," Linda said. "You know that I'll shoot you!"

Fitz grinned. "You might shoot at a Hauhau warrior," he said, "but not at me, Lindy. I saw you before at the harbor. You've hardly changed at all." As he had expected, her tense expression wavered when she heard the old nickname. "Your dress is a little frumpy, perhaps. Just right for a reverend's wife. But you're still as pretty as ever. And still quick on the draw." Fitz glanced sideward at the lantern. It was still hanging by one screw. If he could manage to push it over somehow, its own weight would make it fall. When all hell broke loose down below, he might be able to get away. He began to reach toward the lamp, pretending he was gesticulating as he spoke. "I got to know our daughter, Lindy," he went on. "She's a beautiful girl."

Linda lowered her weapon a little. But then Fitz was looking directly into the barrel of his daughter's gun.

"Get away from the railing, and the lamp!" Aroha shouted. "Farther," she ordered, as Fitz slowly obeyed.

"My God, Fitz!" Linda cried. "Are you out of your mind?"

"More likely possessed by a demon," Aroha declared. "Fitz, Robin had nothing to do with Vera Carrigan's death. There was an investigation that confirmed his version of events. Her dress was found at the edge of the spring. She certainly wasn't pushed in, as you seem to believe. The only reason it's being kept a secret is so the spa guests won't panic. It has nothing to do with covering up a murder."

"And even if it did, the conviction of a murderer is up to the police." Linda now placed herself between Fitz and the gas lamp. "Taking the law into your own hands based on a crazy suspicion . . . My God, Fitz, what has become of you? What did Vera Carrigan do to you?"

Fitz glared at her. "What if she didn't do anything to me? What if I've always been what I am?"

Linda sighed. "Omaka was right. She said you and Vera were two of a kind. That's why you loved her, wasn't it, Fitz? You didn't have to hide with her."

"Where is that bastard?" Robin tore open the door to the drawing loft. His face was twisted in rage, his clothes ripped and smeared with blood. His hands were flayed from climbing along the steel cable. Surprised by his sudden appearance, Aroha and Linda lost their focus on Fitz for a moment and he took his chance. He dove over the railing, grabbed another cable, and slid down to the stage below.

"Shoot him!" Robin shouted to Linda, who was closest to the rail. "Don't let him get away!"

Robin turned on his heel and ran down the stairs, so he could head Fitz off at the bottom.

Linda aimed her weapon at Fitz, but found she couldn't pull the trigger. She couldn't kill her daughter's father in front of her. Aroha didn't share her mother's scruples or her marksmanship. She fired in Fitz's direction, hoping she could frighten him into surrendering, but of course it didn't work.

The women watched as Fitz reached the floor and ran behind the stage.

"Do you think Robin will catch him?" Aroha asked her mother as she carefully climbed off the lighting bridge.

"I don't know if I should wish it on either of them," Linda murmured.

Fitz considered briefly if he should take the back exit for the actors or the front doors. The back was safer, because it didn't lead into broad, crowded Rattrey Street, but into a side alley instead. From there, it would be easy to disappear. Fitz just didn't know if it was unlocked. He had come through the front entrance himself, and Linda and Aroha had certainly done so too. Robin and Lucille might have also come through the backstage door and could have left it open, but if they'd locked it, he would be trapped. He chose the front door.

Fitz rushed down the corridor to the foyer, and spied Robin just as he was coming out of the stairwell. He continued toward the exit, and almost ran into Lucille. She was standing in the middle of the foyer, completely disoriented in her bloodstained dress, her hair flying in every direction. Robin must have left her alone in the orchestra pit so he could chase Fitz, and now she had come to find out what was going on.

Fitz saw his chance. He quickly stepped behind the girl, grabbed her shoulders, and placed the point of the knife he always carried at her throat. Lucille let out a suffocated cry.

Robin froze in midstride. "Don't you dare hurt her!" he shouted.

Fitz laughed. "You aren't exactly in a position to threaten me," he said. "To the contrary, I have the better cards. Just wait and see how I play them. Perhaps I'll just go outside with her, we'll walk a few blocks and then I'll let her go. But only if you don't follow me, that is. But perhaps I'll do the same thing to your beloved that you did to mine. Of course, I wouldn't be as brutal as you were.

Your cousin Helena told me that Vera was scalded to death. Actually, she said it more dramatically. She was boiled alive! I'd hardly be able to top that."

He caressed Lucille's throat with the knife until blood trickled out. Lucille whimpered.

"I didn't touch Vera Carrigan," Robin said desperately. "I didn't kill her!"

"And what if it's enough for me that you wanted her dead?" Fitz asked.

He backed slowly toward the exit, dragging Lucille with him. He would have liked to provoke Robin a little longer, but he was afraid that Linda and Aroha would arrive.

"When did you talk to Helena?" Robin asked, confused.

Fitz laughed. "Oh, dear Helena and I get along splendidly," he said. "She also has a certain interest in getting you out of the way, Robin Fenroy. Who do you think left the love letter on your bed, and on little Lucille's?"

Robin didn't want to believe it, but he had no strength left to think clearly.

Fitz kept edging toward the doors. "So, my sweet, walk now," he whispered to Lucille. "I can't appear in the street with you like this, but you can be sure that my knife will find its way to you if you do anything stupid. I have nothing to lose. Do you understand?"

Lucille nodded, horrified.

Fitz dragged her past the box office and through the fancy glass doors, outside and down the three steps in front of the building. He was completely focused on the girl he was pulling by the hand, and the man he was escaping from. He didn't notice the people on Rattrey Street who scolded as he barged into them, nor did he hear the shrill ringing that announced the approach of the trolley.

"No!" Lucille stopped just short of the tracks and braced her feet firmly on the ground.

Fitz whirled furiously and began to shout. "Didn't I tell you—"

His voice was interrupted by an earsplitting squeal. The cable car driver had pulled the emergency brake, and the wheels threw sparks on the tracks. Lucille began to scream. She freed her hand with a desperate yank, and felt herself being pulled backward at the same moment. An onlooker had rushed to help her. He skidded and fell with her on the cobblestones.

"Don't look," the man said as he sat up. "It won't be a pretty sight." He placed himself between Lucille and the trolley, which had finally come to a halt. Then he helped her up. "Are you hurt?"

She shook her head.

"Lucille! Oh Lucille . . ." Robin rushed toward her and took her in his arms. He was laughing and crying with the relief of having her back, alive and uninjured. He gratefully stammered his thanks to her rescuer, who was just brushing the dust off his suit. "If there's anything I can do for you . . . My name is Robin Fenroy."

"Dr. Paul Finn," the man said with a bow, and picked up a black doctor's bag. "It was an honor. If the young lady isn't hurt, then I will see to the . . . other victim. It's best you remain here until the police arrive. They will need your statement."

The physician turned to the small crowd that had gathered around Joe Fitzpatrick's lifeless body. The trolley driver also stood there, deathly pale. The passengers had gotten out and were speaking animatedly with one another. There was blood on the tracks.

Robin led the trembling Lucille back to the theater.

"There's nothing we can do here," he said softly. "If the police want to talk to us, they'll find us. Linda and Aroha are here, and they're surely worried. Let's take the back entrance and then go home. You should rest, and I need to have a word with Helena."

# Chapter 67

The visitors from Rata Station arrived around noon the next day, and March proudly showed them the theater. Carol, Mara, Cat and Chris, Jane and Te Haitara admired the huge auditorium with red velvet-upholstered seats for the audience and tall windows that could be blacked out by midnight-blue velvet curtains. The foyer and stairwell were fitted with thick carpets. A few of the heavier pieces of furniture from the house in Mornington, as well as vases and paintings, added to the theater's atmosphere.

"A temple to the spirits of money," Jane whispered to Te Haitara, who was struck dumb by the sheer grandiosity of it. During the course of their marriage, the Maori chieftain had seen various *pakeha* buildings and large hotels, but the Dunedin Globe Theatre took his breath away.

"More like a temple to the spirits of art," Mara said with a smile, and then checked the acoustics of the huge room by playing her flute on the stage. Eru hadn't joined her. He was uncomfortable in large crowds, and wanted to avoid the *pakeha*'s fearful looks when they saw his tattooed face. "Not that the spirits need all this luxury, but I can feel them here."

As usual, Jane didn't feel anything, and felt justified when she exchanged glances with March. Her granddaughter, too, rolled her eyes. This theater hadn't been built for the spirits, but for Dunedin's elite.

"The actors' dressing rooms are less ornate," March explained. "But they're also spacious and bright. It will be possible to expand them later if the company grows, or if other productions are done here. Robin and Bertram only think about Shakespeare. But if our theater is actually supposed to make money, then we'll need to host a musical or ballet every now and then, or a modern comedy."

The young woman's eyes flashed in anticipation of making the theater into an economic success.

While Mara chatted with the musicians tuning up in the orchestra pit, and Cat and Carol admired the paintings in the foyer as Jane appraised their value, March led the men up to the drawing loft. She showed them the pulley system that Josh Haydon was still working on.

"Were you able to repair everything after yesterday?" Chris asked worriedly.

Josh nodded. "Completely, sir. Actually, nothing was really broken. Fitz had been working here for weeks, and he knew his way around the equipment. Fortunately, he didn't know that the cables were especially well secured," Josh said with a smile. "I arranged that because Mr. Robin also wanted to operate the system himself. And you know how actors always have their heads in the clouds."

March shot him a conspiratorial smile.

"The only question was whether Lucille was ready to take the risk again," March said to Mara after she had returned to the other women. "Robin was so worried about her tender soul that he wanted to cancel the flight of the fairies. But Bertram insisted. The show must go on, and all that." She nodded approvingly.

"The whole thing must be terribly upsetting for the girl," Mara remarked. "Didn't anyone consider postponing the premiere?"

"Postponing?" March looked at her mother as though she were out of her mind. "After all the preparations and the announcements in the paper? After the ticket sales? Absolutely impossible. Robin wouldn't have even considered it, and neither would Lucille. The theater is more important to them than anything else." She laughed. "Robin was less furious about Fitz's attempt to kill him than the fact that he'd been planning to set the place on fire. He just couldn't get over that last night. Someone wanted to burn down his theater! Our little Robin had murder in his eyes. I think he would have done worse to Fitz than the train did, if he'd caught him."

"Still, it's a terrible thing," Cat said. "But we should go back to Mornington now and get dressed for the evening. I'm also eager to see Linda and Aroha. In her last letter, Aroha said she had a surprise for us."

A few hours later, they were all standing around a table in the foyer of the theater, sipping champagne and watching the audience stream in. Te Haitara looked a little uncomfortable in his tuxedo. Jane had insisted on it, even though March would have enjoyed the newspapers' reaction to his chieftain's garb. The Maori tradition was represented only by Mara, who was wearing a traditional skirt and top, as she did for her flute concerts, combined with a cape decorated with kiwi feathers. Her hip-length hair was loose. Mara got just as many admiring glances as her beautiful daughter; March wore a tight, champagne-colored evening gown with a low neckline.

Chris also felt uncomfortable in his tuxedo, just as Cat did in gowns that required a corset. But a glance in the large mirrors in the foyer pleased her. For this evening, she had ordered a gown of dark-green silk that cascaded in flounces over a hoop skirt. It was decorated with accents of pounamu jade. Her pale hair was crowned with a jade-embellished tiara that Chris had given her for their twentieth anniversary. She also wore a tiny jade *hei tiki*, a carved god figurine that had belonged to her Maori foster mother, Te Ronga.

Jane was wearing pearl jewelry with a dark-blue silk gown. She preferred a bustle to a crinoline and hoop skirt. Her seamstress was accustomed to reassuring her that it would make her figure look less full. Jane herself didn't really believe it, but comforted herself with the fact that Te Haitara particularly admired her Rubenesque curves.

Linda and Carol were wearing the simplest dresses. Neither had had anything new made for the premiere. Carol wore the evening gown that she'd worn the first time she'd ever been in a theater in Dunedin, when the Bandmann-Beaudet Shakespeare Company had performed there. Linda wore the black-velvet dress that she wore at school for special occasions, together with her gold medallion. Cat smiled when she recognized the necklace. It was an heirloom from Cat's first foster mother, Linda Hempleman, after whom her daughter had been named. Looking at it, Cat felt the same warmth inside as she did when she touched Te Ronga's *hei tiki*. But back in Mornington, when she'd looked again at the portrait of her biological mother, she felt nothing. At that moment, she decided not to take Suzanne's portrait back to Rata Station. It would be better if Robin hung it in the theater. At least he had reason to be grateful to his grandmother.

To Aroha's delight, she still fit into the reform dress that she'd bought with Helena at Lady's Gold Mine. It was easy to move in it, and she was therefore the most relaxed of all the women. That afternoon, she'd distributed invitations to her family. The next party would be her wedding to Bao.

"What are you going to do with Helena now?" Aroha asked March, who joined her after greeting several important guests.

Helena Lacrosse was just entering the foyer. Dressed in the latest fashion, a diamond necklace and matching tiara set in her intricately styled hair, she walked arm in arm with a tall man whose muscles seemed to be about to burst through his tuxedo. Helena's face was pale, but she tried to act normal, and greeted everyone she encountered in a friendly way. But Robin's family didn't waste a glance on her. Only Peta, who was just entering with Leah, regarded her skeptically.

"We aren't going to let her out of our sight until she's on the ship bound for Australia, and it disappears below the horizon," March told Aroha. "Robin is paying that young man to accompany her. He's part of a security service known for its discretion."

"You aren't holding her accountable?" Chris asked. "After all, she was involved in plotting a murder, and might even have instigated the crime."

"Barely involved, I think. She hardly would have come up with the idea by herself," March speculated. "Regardless, we couldn't prove anything, and just imagine what would happen if the press got wind of it! I thank all the gods and spirits that Fitz's death wasn't connected to the Lacrosse family, even though Robin foolishly introduced himself to the doctor. Fortunately, Dr. Finn seems to be understanding and discreet. I spoke to him this morning. He's over there, by the way, with his wife." March smiled and waved at a slender man who was just coming out of the cloakroom. He was accompanied by a young woman with dark hair and a fancy evening gown. The two of them approached Reverend Burton and his wife. They were probably part of his congregation.

"Lucille was adamant about sending him tickets for the premiere," March said. "I delivered them personally and told him a bit about what had happened. He understood that we didn't want to make it public, especially since it didn't have any further consequences. Fitz didn't manage to do any real damage, and he won't be able to in the future either."

"I suppose I should be mourning him," Aroha said quietly. "After all, he was my father."

Linda squeezed her arm. "You hardly knew him," she said. "None of us really did. And he didn't care about either of us. The only person who was ever important to him was Vera. Perhaps he's reunited with her now."

"That's a reason to fear death," March remarked. "Or perhaps a reason to change for the better. I'd much rather deal with the endless boredom of heaven than meet the two of them in hell."

Then the ringing of a melodious bell summoned the audience into the theater. March listened with pleasure to the cries of delight as the visitors entered the opulent space. The huge chandelier, a masterpiece of crystal, bathed the room in warm light. Ushers in red-and-blue gowns—formerly maids from the Lacrosse estate—led the ladies and gentlemen to their seats. The musicians entertained the expectant audience with an overture until finally the lights were dimmed and the curtain rose. Theseus's palace glowed in bright colors. The dimming of the auditorium made everything onstage look much more intense, just as Robin had hoped. Even Aroha was captivated when Theseus appeared.

But the audience was truly entranced in the second act, when Robin and Lucille came onstage as Puck and Peaseblossom. The young man with the wreath of flowers in his blond hair and the exquisite girl in her flowing robes danced around each other, teased each other, unable to disguise how much in love they were. Shakespeare hadn't planned a romance between the two fairies, but he would have enjoyed their performance. Later, Lucille flew in with the other fairies, graceful, fearless, and too joyful to be nervous. Robin played Puck with delightful ease. He was charming with Bertram as Oberon, and Martha Grey as Titania.

During the intermission, March was already receiving compliments for the actors' skills, and of course for the special effects. Her mind spun, thinking about what kinds of effects they could use in *Macbeth* and *Richard III*. Then the curtain went up for the last time, and the twists and turns of the plot untangled themselves. Finally, Bertram and Martha spoke their blessings as Oberon and Titania, before the closing monologue was left to Puck.

Robin took the stage with the sinuous movements of an animal. His Puck was an enchanting spirit, a child of nature, a laughing, joyful fairy.

*"If we shadows have offended, think but this and all is mended: That you have but slumbered here, while these visions did appear."*

Robin beamed as he recited Shakespeare's words, becoming briefly serious as he spoke of the hissing serpent whose wickedness he and the others had just barely escaped. A shadow seemed to cross his flower-crowned brow. For all his lightness, this Puck also understood the pitfalls in life. Robin knew very well the power he held over his audience, and he enchanted everyone who shared his dream with him.

*"So good night unto you all. Give me your hands, if we be friends, and Robin shall restore amends."*

Robin bowed, and as the people began to applaud, the other actors came onto the stage behind him. The enthusiastic audience demanded one curtain call after another, and Robin bowed along with Bertram and Martha. The actors strode triumphantly to the edge of the stage, and finally Robin reached for Lucille's hand. She had been standing at the back with the other fairies. He brought her to the front of the stage, and for the first time, received his applause with the woman who would one day be his Juliet, his Katherine, his Viola, and his Miranda. He sought the gaze of his family, and saw approval and admiration in his father's eyes, tears of joy in his mother's and half sisters', and finally the shining faces of March and Jane. He'd put even *them* under his spell. No one could resist the magic of his art.

Robin suddenly didn't care what would be written in the newspapers the following morning. He pulled Lucille close and kissed her.

# Afterword

*Haere mai, e tai, kei te wera te ao!*
Come and see, the world is on fire!

*—Hori Taiawhio*

I originally wanted to introduce the book with the traditional words of Sophia Hinerangi's husband during the eruption of Mount Tarawera, but then it seemed too depressing. The eruption was followed by the catastrophe in the Tarawera region, which destroyed several Maori villages, doubtlessly the center of this story. I made an effort to portray these events as authentically as possible, based on eyewitness reports and photographs of the damage. I hope I was able to create a concrete image. In addition to my fictional characters (Koro Hinerangi among them), Sophia was a real person who worked as a tourist guide, and was supposed to have been the mother of seventeen children. All the people whose fate I described in the story were real. Nor did I make up the omens, including the ghost canoe and the sacrilege of offering honey from Mount Tarawera to tourists. I find the latter particularly bizarre: the ghost canoe was actually seen by a group of tourists, the Maori oarsmen who were rowing their boat, and Sophia Hinerangi. And apparently, all the people who ate the forbidden honey died. It is remarkable that only seven *pakeha* were among approximately 120 victims of the eruption.

Even without the natural catastrophe of Mount Tarawera, I find the development of the New Zealand tourist industry in the nineteenth century fascinating. The boom was started in 1870 by a visit from Prince Albert, who enthusiastically reported his impressions. The popular destinations were Milford

Sound, the Whanganui River, and of course the Pink and White Terraces, as well as the nearby hot springs in Rotorua. The Terraces were considered the eighth wonder of the world at the time. In the region surrounding Mount Tarawera in particular, the Maori played a large role in marketing the attractions. As I described in my story, they were able to do this more or less to the satisfaction of their guests. All of my descriptions are based on travel reports from newspapers of the time. Begging and inflated prices were just as much a part of it as well-organized tours, and the Maori danced and sang for their visitors.

The Rotorua region is still a center of Maori tourism today. Nowhere else in New Zealand can such diverse offerings of Maori cultural experiences be found, or at least the chance to see a few dances, enjoy *hangi* firepit cooking, or buy local crafts. A small part of the Pink and White Terraces that were lost in the eruption of Mount Tarawera were rediscovered several years ago. However, they are underwater, and can only be viewed by divers.

Since the volcanic eruption, tourism business in the Rotorua region has been largely taken over by the *pakeha*. The most important sights are now the thermal fields with their hot springs and geysers. They, too, are described authentically in the book. And yes, the government actually considered piping the geysers in the area so they would spray more spectacularly than the competition—for example, in Iceland.

The other catastrophe that determined the fate of my heroine, Aroha, the train accident in the Wairarapa district, is also based on reality. On September 11, 1880, under exactly the conditions that I described, three train cars derailed on the Rimutaka Incline. There were many people seriously injured, and four children died. However, they were *pakeha* children.

Another important subject in New Zealand that had a great effect on my protagonists was industrialization and the beginning of the labor movement. Reverend Waddell made history with his stirring sermon. Here, too, I stuck to the historical facts as closely as possible. There was a woolen mill in Kaiapoi and an industry magnate called Mosgiel who ran factories in Dunedin. I changed his name slightly because I mixed factual and fictitious elements into his story. Martin Porter and Harold Wentworth are purely fictional characters, and fortunately, there weren't any spectacular factory fires in New Zealand during the period in question either. But the daily lives of the factory workers were portrayed accurately.

Silas Spragg's newspaper article, which was published after Waddell's sermon and described the daily lives of the seamstresses, has been translated into modern English, but is factually true to the original. Anyone who wishes can read the article on the internet. Based on all my German and English sources, I made a great effort to describe the lives of the factory workers without exaggerating. The conditions were catastrophic, although they were questioned earlier in New Zealand than they were in other countries. Child labor was frowned upon there from the very beginning. Voices such as Reverend Waddell's in his famous sermon of October 1888, the Sin of Cheapness, were never paid much attention in the mother country of England, for example.

The consequences of the sermon and the following newspaper reports for New Zealand were also impressive. In 1890, the government established a commission of inquiry, to which Waddell belonged, and passed more extensive laws regulating working hours and conditions. At the same time, New Zealand's first women's union, the Dunedin Tailoresses' Union, was founded. Reverend Waddell was its chairman, but the women very soon took matters into their own hands. The Tailoresses' Union, with their active representative Harriet Morrison, contributed significantly to the fact that women in New Zealand were granted the right to vote as early as 1893. That strong historical personality has also made an appearance in my book *The Tears of the Maori Goddess*.

Unfortunately, the exact words of Reverend Waddell's sermon don't seem to have been passed down; at least I wasn't able to find them. I reconstructed his words with the aid of newspaper articles and various reports.

Riots and attacks against Chinese immigrants also took place on Dunedin's streets in 1888, although not in such close temporal proximity to Waddell's sermon as in my story. The attacks were the direct result of the assembly of "honorable Dunedin citizens" that I described. Bao describes the problems of his compatriots in New Zealand several times very vividly, so I don't have to repeat myself here. The important thing is that I stayed as true to reality as I possibly could. Bao is of course a fictional character, but the reality I described for him is not very far from the truth. Empress Cixi was a historical figure, and the political and social conditions in China are authentically described. The empress actually supported a program for sending young Chinese men abroad for commercial and educational purposes, and to study languages and culture for diplomatic ends.

Unfortunately, I couldn't prove the existence of the Berlitz School in New Zealand during that time period. However, the Berlitz method of learning a new language was already known. Berlitz started his famous school in Philadelphia in 1878, and his book *The Logic of Language* was published in 1877.

The history of theater in New Zealand, however, was easy to research, as it is very well documented. Here, too, I allowed the protagonists of my novel to convey much of it in their own voices. At the time of the gold rush, there was a boom in the theater business, and many traveling companies were founded. Later, when my character Robin was looking for work, interest in theater was at a low point. Of course, a successful company would still have been able to get by, such as the Bandmann-Beaudet Shakespeare Company, which Robin worked with in Dunedin. They were actually working in that city during the time in question. The same goes for Louise Pomeroy's troupe. She, too, was working in Christchurch at the time. It's very likely that Elliot also gave lessons between his acting appearances. He had done so earlier when he lived in Australia.

Robin's own theater, the Lacrosse family, and their story are purely products of my imagination. Recently an amateur theater group has appeared in Dunedin with the same name, the Globe Theatre, but this similarity is a coincidence and has nothing to do with my novel. I also thoroughly researched the lives of the upper class, including the rather bizarre Victorian burial traditions.

# Acknowledgments

THANK YOU!

> Finish writing your book. We'll take care of all the other stuff!

When I was finishing this book, I received an email with that message from my Spanish editor. And now that the book is done, I would like to warmly thank everyone who takes care of "all the other stuff" while I'm writing. Without the people who help me with all the work surrounding my books and marketing them, and especially Joan Puzcas and Kosa Ana, who conquer life's daily challenges with me, I would never be able to devote myself with such relaxation and focus to my writing. After all, at the same time we are also taking care of eighteen horses, a mule, a llama, eight dogs, and eight cats. Most of them are charity cases: animals that no one wanted and that wouldn't be able to lie happily in the sun anymore without us. Thank you, Nelu and Anna, for taking as good care of them as I do, and therefore making it possible for me to travel to book presentations in distant lands!

My editors, Melanie Blank-Schroeder and Margit von Cossart, played the biggest role in the creation of my books. They always approach the revision of hundreds of pages with joy and verve, offering helpful suggestions, and keeping the timeline consistent. Otherwise I would get completely confused about the age of my main characters and various dates and measurements. I can write well, but I am not very good at math!

I would also like to thank Bastian Schlueck of the Garbsen Agency for the fact that I don't have to worry anymore because there is enough money for all the horses and children! One could simply not have a better agent. Even though he denies again and again that he can walk on water, he really can!

Also many thanks to Christian Stuewe, who helps to spread my books all over the world. I am extremely happy when a volume in an exotic language appears in the mail! Thanks to all the editors, translators, and employees of publishing houses between China and Chile who make that possible. I would especially like to mention Edicones B, my Spanish publisher, which I no longer see as a license publisher, but rather as a second literary home. They are always there for me, whether at book fairs or award ceremonies. I would also like to thank Juan Bolea and the Zaragoza City Council for awarding me the Premio Internacional de Novela Histórica in 2014. I enjoyed the time with you very much, and I appreciate the fact that there is always a publisher at my side. Special thanks to Marta, Olga, Mercedes, all the Carmens, and of course, Ernest Folch.

My friend Susana Salamanca Amoros helps me navigate the challenges that the Spanish language presents to me. Many thanks that I can always email her if I don't understand an interview question, for her brilliant support of my Facebook page, and for the fact that she is almost always present at my book presentations, readings, and presentations!

*Sarah Lark*

# About the Author

*Photo © 2011 Gonzalo Perez*

Sarah Lark, born in Germany and now a resident of Spain, is a bestselling author of historical fiction, including the Fire Blossom Saga, the Sea of Freedom Trilogy, and the In the Land of the Long White Cloud Saga. She is a horse aficionado and former travel guide who has experienced many of the world's most beautiful landscapes on horseback. Through her adventures, she has developed an enduring relationship with the places she's visited and the people who live there. In her writing, Lark introduces readers to a New Zealand full of magic, beauty, and charm. Her ability to weave romance with history and to explore all the dark and triumphal corners of the human condition has resonated with readers worldwide.

# About the Translator

*Photo © 2011 Alex Maechler*

Kate Northrop is a translator and lyricist who grew up in Connecticut and studied music and English literature in the United States and the United Kingdom. Her travels led her to the German-speaking region of Switzerland, where she's lived with her Swiss husband and their two bilingual children since 1994. Her professional translation credits include Sarah Lark's Fire Blossom Saga and Ines Thorn's Island of Sylt trilogy. As a lyricist, Kate has been signed to major music labels and publishers. With more than eighteen years of experience, Kate now runs her own literary translation business, Art of Translation. Visit her at www.art-of-translation.com.